THE FOUR FAMILIES

COUNTS OF EIGHT | DANCE WITH DEATH | PAS DE TROIS

BRYNN FORD

More from the Author
www.brynnford.com
brynnfordauthor@gmail.com

CONTENT WARNING

This dark romance series involves many triggering elements which may be upsetting for some readers. A complete list of tropes and triggers can be found on the author's website.
at brynnford.com/triggers.

SERIES NOTE

The Four Families is a complete dark romance trilogy following Anya & Ezra's forbidden romance in captivity. The books are not standalones, and they must be read in order. This omnibus contains all three books in the trilogy!

BOOKS BY BRYNN FORD

THE FOUR FAMILIES
Counts of Eight
Dance with Death
Pas de Trois

THE FOUR FAMILIES SPIN-OFF
King of Masters

EMBER GLEN
Spark of Madness
Blaze of Misery
Embers of Mercy

STANDALONES
Sugar Wood
Jagged Line Paradise

LAWLESS
Coming Soon!
The Darkness We Hide

COUNTS OF EIGHT

BRYNN FORD

For dark romance readers everywhere, you are my people.

Thank you for being unapologetically daring.

Anya

"COME WITH ME and do exactly as I say," Nikolai hisses into my ear.

My arm is already hooked through his at the four families' talent reception as he drags me away from the crowd and down an empty hallway. I always go with him and do exactly as he says because I have no choice in the matter.

We're following Vigo of the Vittori family down one of the many halls in the O'Shea family's ostentatious estate in Ireland. Nikolai steals surreptitious glances behind him to see if we're being followed. Everything about this screams *danger*, but as his slave, so does everything else in my life.

I'm practically jogging to keep up with him. His strides are too long and sharp for my petite height to match. My high heels click with every step along the hardwood floor as he drags me along, echoing in the empty hallway. Nikolai huffs out a low grunt of agitation and stops abruptly. I nearly topple as he whips around to face me. He bends, shoving his shoulder into my gut and wraps his arms around the backs of my knees. He stands, lifting me, hoisting me up over his shoulder with ease.

"Must you always draw so much fucking attention to yourself?" he growls.

Being swept up over his shoulder catches me off guard and I feel lightheaded for a moment as the top half of my body is flipped upside-down and dangles over his back.

He strides off faster than before, presumably still chasing after the Head of House for the Vittori family. We turn into a room and I hear the door click and lock shut behind us. Nikolai tosses me off his shoulder carelessly, as always, and I fall onto a plush chair.

The room we're in reeks of cigar smoke and my vision seems clouded. A fireplace burns bright orange in front of me and the air is warm. Nikolai doesn't sit and neither does Vigo. Both men square off with each other in front of the crackling flames. I look back and forth between them as they stand seething.

"So," Nikolai finally says, "what information do you have?"

"Information isn't free, Nikolai," Vigo Vittori replies in his heavy Italian accent with a sinful looking smirk.

Nikolai holds his hand out toward me. "You can take whatever payment you like from her as long as you return her alive and able to dance."

My heart sinks low in my gut, rolling a wave of anxious nausea through my entire body. My neck muscles tense up immediately with the knowledge that I'm about to be used.

I'm in shock.

I belong to Nikolai.

He's never shared me.

Vigo looks me up and down and nods his approval as Nikolai casually adjusts his cufflinks. "Deal. I'll take her for the night."

Nikolai laughs. "The night? I don't even know if I can trust your sources, Vigo. Particularly since all signs point to your family as the ones who brought down that plane and my entire family along with it."

"My sources? The information I have comes straight from the horse's mouth. I have the recorded phone conversations to prove it."

"Give me the recordings," Nikolai demands.

Vigo laughs. A humorless smile twists his features into something that looks purely demonic. His deep, honey-brown eyes glow inhumanly with the reflection of firelight. Thick, jet-black hair frames his devious expression.

Black—a color that seems so fitting on him.

Dark and all-consuming.

"You think I'm just going to hand them over?"

"I've offered you payment. I'm no fool, Vigo. You've been pining over Anya for years. You should be grateful for five minutes with her," he sighs, pauses, then lets desperation lead him into concession, "but I'll grant you two hours."

Two hours with *me*.

I think my heart stops beating. I no longer feel the thrum of my pulse. My breath has been stolen from me. Nikolai is fiercely possessive and territorial. I could have never guessed he would offer me up for another man to use, especially not this one.

I wonder if rape from one man feels different than rape from another. I know it can't possibly be better. My instinct tells me that with Vigo, it will be worse.

My eyes burn a hole in Nikolai's black tuxedo jacket, seething with the wish that he had been killed along with his family last year in that plane crash. He made it crystal-clear that he would cut off my head and serve it on a platter if it ensured he got what he wanted—information on why that plane went down.

Vigo's aura suggests that decapitation might be preferred to letting him use me. At least then it would all end. At least then it would be quick, maybe even painless.

Considering the option, Vigo looks me over appraisingly. "I'll take her for two, but I'm not giving you the recordings. I'll let you listen to them under my supervision once I'm satisfied with the payment I've received."

"If you're not handing over the recordings, then I'm not giving her up for two hours. *One* hour and you let me hear the recordings. And I supervise your use of my slave or no deal."

"Are you serious?"

"Do I look like I am anything other than serious?" Nikolai snarls.

I can only see the side of his face where his lip twitches upward in the corner. I can picture the look in his gray eyes without having to think about it. I know it all too well. I know how his skin wrinkles into crow's feet when he narrows his eyes. I know how his cheeks twitch as his nostrils flair in frustration.

My breath and my heartbeat kick-start in a rush as Nikolai's hand twitches at his side. My spine straightens instinctually, sitting up straighter, preparing for the inevitable urge to flee before his temper ticks.

Surely a demon must recognize the Devil—just as Vigo recognizes my master.

"Fine, fine," Vigo holds up his palms, "I don't care if you watch. Maybe she'll enjoy that."

Nikolai makes an amused sound. "She won't. But I don't care. I just want my information. Anya…" He holds out his hand as he says my name and I stand.

I reach out my trembling hand as my nerves run cold and make me shiver from head to toe. He pulls me to stand next to him, snaking his arm around my waist and holding me tightly to his side. His fingers dig into the side of my stomach and my muscles twitch beneath his rough touch.

"Before I hand her over, tell me which of the four families were responsible for the death of mine? Tell me, and then I'll give you the hour before we listen to the recordings."

Vigo waits a dramatic beat, though none of this matters to me at all. "The Campbells."

Nikolai's lip twitches as it twists into a sneer. "The fucking Americans. I knew it."

His hand slips from my side to my back and shoves me forward. I stumble on my heels, but Vigo's arms reach out and snatch me. I feel sick, nauseous, not just in my stomach, but throughout my entire body.

"Don't worry, beautiful, I've got you," he croons in his overbearing accent.

I shove at his chest, managing to push him away one step, but he rushes me. I wouldn't stand a chance getting away as Nikolai remains a brick wall behind me. Trying to back away, I bounce off his chest and fall right into Vigo's arms again.

Nikolai steps up behind me and pulls the zipper on the back of my black evening gown. He tugs at the straps and they fall down my arms, the entire sweeping, sequined dress slipping off in one swift motion. I tug and pull backward, trying to break free from Vigo's hold, but Nikolai stops me. He grabs my long brown hair, twists it around his fist, and yanks hard. I gasp with the sharp sting of it.

His breath is warm against my ear. "If you fight him again, I will hurt you, *rabynya*."

I swallow hard, pressing my eyes shut to center myself. I reach deep down within my soul to find the blizzard that's always lying in wait. I let the storm blow in around my heart and freeze it, making me cold and hard against the oncoming assault.

Nikolai's hand skims up from the back of my thigh to my ass and squeezes tight, bruising me with his fingertips. "You may use her ass and her mouth, Vigo, but her cunt is off limits. That belongs to me and me alone. You may give her pain, but you will not harm her in such a way that will prevent her from dancing. No broken bones, no sprains. She is a talent slave, after all, not one of your broken dolls to toss around. I need her strong enough for her new dance partner who is arriving next week. Do you understand?"

I have a new partner arriving next week?

Another stolen boy to help me entertain *moy khozyain. My master.*

My heart races, thumping painfully behind my ribs and tears rush to glass over my eyes. I blink them away, refusing to let them fall, letting them freeze inside my internal snowstorm instead.

"Oh, yes, I understand," Vigo says. "Now hand her over and start your clock, Mr. Mikhailov. I'm eager to take my payment for your information."

Nikolai releases me with a hard shove forward and I let Vigo drag me away to the bed in the far corner of the room. With the blizzard snow falling over my soul, my emotions are hidden behind a layer of ice. The ice protects me from the pain of being present in this moment that reminds me that I am a slave to the Mikhailov family.

I am Nikolai's belonging.

CHAPTER 1
Ezra

Present

ONE HEAVY BLOW to the side of my head knocks me sideways. I drop to my knees from the force of it, which is exactly what they want from me. An aura of pain whips around my head, pulsing an ache inside my skull. If I was able to see, I imagine there would be flashes in my vision—dark spots of pain as it throbs. The black hood they put over my head hours ago prevents me from seeing anything at all.

I grunt, planting my right boot firmly on the hard ground beneath me, straining against the pain in a vain attempt to push to my feet. I stumble, unbalanced with my wrists zip-tied behind my back.

Someone grabs me at the elbow and I act on impulse, pushing myself full force against the touch. I use my weight to barrel into them, but it's no use. Three other hands are on me in an instant—grasping me, pushing me, forcing me down to the ground. There are voices all around me, some shouting, some ordering, all in a language I don't understand.

When they get me to my knees for a second time, they keep me there. Powerful hands press down on my shoulders as I try to shake them off.

"Get off me!" I shout, though I don't know who I'm shouting at.

"Stop fighting them. It will only delay the inevitable."

I freeze at the unexpected croon of a strong female voice. I had heard only men since I was captured, and the change surprises me, though the sound is muffled through the fabric hood.

"Good," the woman says once I stop struggling.

"I suppose you wish to know why you're here," she says.

She speaks in English, but there's a hint of an accent there. She speaks fluently, but it's clear English isn't her native language. The clipped syllables and rushed flow of her words hint at something Slavic.

Am I still in the Ukraine?

I know that can't be right. I was in Kyiv for a performance yesterday when I was taken. I woke up on a plane and had to have spent hours there. After we landed we traveled by car for another two, maybe three hours before I landed on my knees here.

My breaths are heavy, agitated from the fighting. It's hot behind the hood, each exhale adding fresh heat. It feels like a slow suffocation. I want this damn thing off my head, not just so I can take a clean breath, but so I can see the fuckers who are holding me down.

"Where is *here*?" I demand.

"*Here* is home," the woman tells me. "That's all you need to know for now."

I laugh humorlessly. "Home?"

"Take that thing off his head. Let me see him."

There's a whoosh of air as my face is freed from the obstructive barrier. I squint as bright, fluorescent lights overwhelm my vision. I blink rapidly, determined to get my eyes to adjust quickly so I can assess my surroundings. I was under that hood for so long that it's nearly painful to open my eyes.

I flinch as fingers wrap around my chin. They're delicate and soft as they tilt my head to the side. The odd touch ignites a brief, electric spark that puts me off my game enough to hate it. I jerk my head to the side, forcing the hand that touches me to fall away.

I force myself to look up, though the light burns behind my irises, and take in the sight of the woman standing before me. She's petite, her dark brown hair tightly pulled back into a low bun, and thick, matching eyebrows spread broad across her wide eyes.

Blue.

Clear, crystal blue eyes.

Cold as ice blue eyes that cut into mine like a spiked icicle falling from a rooftop gutter above my head.

She looks young and old at the same time, and she doesn't smile. Subtle frown lines along the sides of her mouth indicate a prolonged season of displeasure.

She appraises me sourly, then lifts her head to look beyond me and speak to someone somewhere behind me in the room.

"*Moy khozyain.*" The foreign words are forced from between her plump lips in what I finally work out to be a Russian accent. "Another hip-hop dancer? Is this the best you could give me?"

I study her face as she speaks. She looks disappointed, humbled, frustrated, and terrified all in one expression. Her eyes blink and she flinches at the same time I do. A forceful voice booms from somewhere behind my head with an accent that matches hers.

"How dare you ask me that? Remember your place, *rabynya*." His tone is gruff, insistent. "I will expect your apology for questioning me later this evening."

The woman's eyes drop to the floor, darting quickly away at the command. "*Da, khozyain.*"

I turn my head, craning my neck to see the man with the forceful voice, but I only catch a glimpse of him exiting the room before cold skin lands on mine again. The woman's hand comes down hard across my cheek, slapping me to get my attention. I sneer, lifting my head to look at her.

"Who the fuck are you?" I demand.

"I am your master. You are my slave. The sooner you accept this, the easier it will be for you."

Her insinuation that I should just accept whatever fucked up situation I've been forced into pisses me off, fueling the flame of my instinct to fight. I find myself faltering as I feel the surge of adrenaline to attack this small, likely fragile woman in front of me. But I need to take her down to distract the men on either side of me, each holding one of my shoulders, just long enough so I can take them out and get the fuck out of this place.

It's a place that looks so safe and comforting and familiar with its pristinely kept hardwood floors, mirrored walls, and bright lighting.

It's a dance studio large enough for thirty world-class dancers to practice in. It doesn't matter if the space feels comfortable to me, there's danger here. I shove down all the warm feelings it threatens to bring to the surface and let the rage take over.

One and then the other, I plant each foot firmly onto the floor as I lift to my feet without warning. I rush the girl, lunging after her with a guttural groan of determination. She expects my attack, shifting and side-stepping in an attempt to get out of the way. All she manages to do is lessen the force of my blow as I duck to ram my shoulder into her gut. It knocks her to the floor, and she lands with a thud as I fall on top of her.

For a beat, a mere nanosecond of time, our eyes connect. Hers soften for the briefest moment of vulnerability before they immediately freeze over again into glacial blue.

She's stronger than I had anticipated for such a tiny thing. Before I can get off her and back onto my feet, her hands grip my shoulders with deadly intensity and her fingertips curl, digging in deep as she pushes back.

She rolls me onto my back and climbs on top of me, settling her weight against my hips, which press my hands painfully into the hardwood floors beneath my ass. They're still zip-tied, crossed at the wrists which are sore and raw from the way the plastic cuts in, deeper and deeper every time I struggle to break free.

Though her weight is minimal, it's still existent, still forces my knuckles to grind against the cold floor, causing them to bruise and ache.

It's not long before the two other men who had been holding me on my knees reappear, coming up on either side of me to help her hold me down.

Are these really the best henchman they could find?

Each man places a hand on either shoulder, grinding me down to the ground as the woman lets anger cloud her features.

The man with the real muscle looks down at me with his teeth bared as he pushes down on my shoulder, his white snarl adding a little brightness to his five o'clock shadow. His dark brown eyes flicker with determination. I can sense he's annoyed with the way this has ruined the careful, modern styling he's done to his ashen-hued, thick, light-brown hair.

Satisfied that I'm properly subdued, the woman nods to the men and slowly stands. "This is the last time you will behave like this, *mal'chik*."

"Fuck off."

She steps up to my side and lifts her right foot. This is the first time I notice she's wearing pointe shoes.

It's a goddamn ballerina holding me hostage.

I laugh at how ridiculous this whole situation has become.

She lowers the point of her slipper to the hollow of my throat and I swallow as she presses down. I can't help but notice the graceful curve of her foot as she points it with the ease of a natural-born dancer.

"I'm capable of balancing on nearly anything, *mal'chik*. I could rise here against your throat, shift my weight onto your windpipe, and crush it underneath the pressure. I suggest you choose to behave if you wish to live. Death in this place has little meaning. That's a lesson I intend to teach you quickly."

I fight the urge to cough as she shifts, her knee bending as she moves more of her weight onto the foot that slowly suffocates me.

Death by ballerina.

There's a pathetic way to die, though it makes for a killer headline.

With my hands pinned painfully beneath me to the hardwood floor, my shoulders forced down, and this fucking ballerina's hard-tipped pointe slipper on the vulnerable hollow of my throat, I feel completely powerless.

Pathetically, embarrassingly powerless.

I try to speak, to use my voice to get her to stop, but it just comes out as a croak as she presses harder. The side of her lip curls up and it makes me want to wrap my hand around her throat and choke the look out of her myself. I stop my struggle, conceding with stillness and gradually, she lessens the pressure on my neck. When she lifts her foot away, I cough and clear my throat and cough again.

She tilts her head to the side as she looks down at me. "Would you like a drink of water, *mal'chik?*"

"My name…" I huff out a sharp breath, "my name is Ezra. I don't know who the fuck this *mal'chik* is, but you've got the wrong guy."

She shakes her head and clicks her tongue. "No. You are *mal'chik*. It means *boy* and that's all you are to me."

I cough again. "I'm no boy."

"You're wrong. You're a boy and a slave and that's all. You will call me master and you will do as told."

"Like fuck I will."

"Get him up," she tells the men holding me down as she walks to the center of the room. "String him up in the corner and leave us."

Together, they lift me, hoisting me up from beneath the elbows as I get my feet beneath me. Exhaustion from my ordeal over the last twenty-four hours is starting to sneak in as my most recent burst of adrenaline rapidly recedes.

The recent blow to my head teams up with the brief deprivation of oxygen to gang up on me, forcing my body to truly feel the effects of it all for the first time.

The fight in me drains as moments pass. I try to tap into my reserves, but they're practically depleted. I'm unable to stop them as the men drag me to a far corner of the room. They cut the zip-ties from my wrists and trade it for rope, wrapping it around and around my wrists, now in front of me. I try to hide my intent as I lift my hands to swipe across my face, something I've been itching to do since my nose started to bleed from a hit an hour or so ago. There's still some fresh blood resting inside my nostril.

I try to catch them off guard, taking a swing at the man to my right, but I'm weak. Instead of getting the upper hand, I get hit once, twice, three times in the side of my stomach, aching pain shooting up my side with each strike. My body folds around the area of attack as I grunt in yielding.

They attach the free end of the rope around my wrists to a pulley system suspended from the high ceiling. I look up as my arms are dragged high above my head to see several of these suspension systems peppered across the ceiling.

By the time my arms are settled in place, stretched far above my head, I know I'm trapped. I yank down, twisting my arms against the binding, but it's useless.

Satisfied with their work, the men casually saunter out of the room, walking away as if what they'd just done was perfectly normal.

Just another Tuesday at the office.

Music jolts me back into defensive mode as it rings out over a speaker system in the studio. My head whips around, searching for the source of the classical piano music that starts to play. I catch a glimpse of myself in the mirrored wall to my right.

I look like hell.

My dirty blond hair looks particularly dirty, falling in grungy pieces around the crown of my head. There are dark circles under my normally bright and well-rested green eyes and my sandy skin is brushed with smudges of dirt.

My jeans look like they've been drug through the mud, the pre-manufactured tear near the knee of the right leg is ripped open into a gaping hole. The collar of my T-shirt is stretched out and uneven from someone hoisting me up by the fabric. There's dried blood on my face and hands from wiping at my bloody nose.

My whole body aches from hours of fighting.

My eyes catch her movement in the reflection from the mirror first, a graceful line of a woman sweeping her arms and stretching her legs. I turn my head to watch her as she begins to dance.

As much as I already hate this bitch, I still can't tear my eyes away from her. Her movements are precise perfection. She's a frozen heart that melts to music and dissolves to dance.

Fuck her.

As she lifts to the tips of her toes and stretches her arms high above her head in a way that mirrors my own captive position, I can make out the full shape of her. She's slender, like every other ballerina I've ever met, yet has a touch more curve in places that draw curiosity to see what's beneath the stretched-out fabric of her black leotard.

This woman wishes to own me, to do me harm, for what reason, I still don't know. But the sight of her talent in motion gives me goosebumps, makes my heart thump and my thigh muscles twitch to be in motion with her on the dance floor.

A dancer always dances.

The song comes to an end and so does her movement. Her eyes immediately lock onto mine and again comes the glacier from the icy blue, scraping slowly but steadily across the space between us.

She strides across the floor toward me with all the poise of a dancer exiting the stage after a performance.

She sighs. "I wasn't expecting you today. You've interrupted my rehearsal."

"I hate to break it to you, princess, but this has interrupted my whole life. So why don't we just cut ties now and get out of each other's hair?"

"No one leaves once they're brought here." Her eyes shift away, then back to pierce mine again.

I let my tired head fall over onto my arm. "Please spare me the cryptic bullshit. What am I doing here?"

"You're here to dance."

"To dance?"

"I require a partner for our annual performance. My last didn't live up to my master's expectations…" She steps closer, invading my personal space. "That partner is gone now, and you are here to replace him."

"Gone?"

"Yes, that's what I said. Why do you keep repeating me? My English is excellent, can you not understand me through my accent? I lived in New York since I was eleven. Perhaps I've developed another accent that you have trouble understanding." She tilts her head as her words drip with sarcasm.

The side of my mouth curls up. I might have found her interesting if it weren't for the circumstances.

"I understand your words, but it doesn't help me understand why I'm here."

Her eyebrows knit together. "I told you, *mal'chik*, you're here to dance. All you need to do is accept that and obey me and we will get along fine. Continue to fight and there will be consequences," she turns her head toward the door, "for the both of us."

"What consequences?"

She circles and disappears behind me. I turn my head as far as I can, feeling the need to keep my eyes on her every move. I can only see the shadow of her movement in my peripheral vision, but I hear the clunk of something hard thud against the floor.

Thud, thud, thud, with every other step she takes, moving to stand beside me. I crane my neck to look around the back of my arm and see her there at my side, a black cane in hand. I watch her eyes as they rake across my body, surveying me with an appraising look.

"You look strong, though you're nearly too tall for me." The end of her cane taps against the heel of my boot. "Yellow boots, jeans, T-shirt. Has my master brought me another beat-boy? A hip-hop dancer? If that's the case, I may as well sign both of our death certificates now." I feel the heat of her breath as she sighs against my side.

"Looks can be deceiving," I reply.

She makes a sound of agreement. "True. So, which is it? What style do you dance?"

I swallow as she steps closer. "Contemporary."

She laughs, though it's without humor. "Of course. You'll have the worst habits of all."

I jump as her hand falls upon my shoulder and my head turns instinctively to look at the source of the touch. Her hand is small, like her, with delicate, slender fingers. Her nails are bitten to the quick and unpolished, the skin around them torn and red in places.

When she speaks again, her voice is smaller, quieter than before, and holds a secret plea that I don't think she wanted me to hear. "I think you're the last, *mal'chik*. I need you to submit to me. I need you to learn the rules quickly, and I need you to follow my instructions carefully."

Her fingers drag across my upper back, tracing an invisible line between my shoulder blades. My muscles jerk at the tickle of her soft touch along my spine as her fingers travel down, her hand stopping at the small of my back.

My chest tightens.

My breaths quicken.

This woman is powerful, there is no doubt about that with the way her touch electrifies me. It pisses me off to react that way to someone who holds me hostage, someone who thinks she has the upper hand, someone who wants me to follow the rules.

"I don't follow the fucking rules."

She lifts the cane and holds it perpendicular to the floor. She swings it to land with a light thwack, flat against my abs, and my muscles jerk as I suck in my gut, flinching away from the black rod. She moves to stand behind me, pressing in closer, reaching around me to grab the other end of the cane with her free hand, pulling both ends back hard. It digs into my torso, creating a line of pressure right across my belly button. I curl around the ache with a low grunt.

"That may have been true before, but it's not true now. You can give me your submission freely or it can be forced from you."

Her body molds to mine along my back as she yanks, tightening her grip with the cane, using her strong body against mine for leverage to dig into me.

"You'll have to force it," I growl.

"That's fine," she breathes, releasing the cane in an instant, and moves away. "I always get what I want."

I open my mouth to bite back, but clamp it shut again when pain shoots through my backside. She strikes me with the cane, right across my ass. I groan. The pain is sharp and ebbs quickly, striking up my agitation.

"That one doesn't count," she says.

I could see her now, standing by my side. My breath hisses through my teeth as I blow out the literal pain in my ass.

"What's your name?" I ask.

"It doesn't matter."

"What's your name?" I demand more forcefully the second time. I'm punished for my insistence with another strike that forces a groan.

"I'll tell you my name when you've earned it with your submission. When I can trust you to obey me, when I can trust you to dance with me, then you'll know my name."

"I'd prefer to know now so I can personalize my hatred of you."

I can see her head dip. "The others hated me at first, too. It won't stop me from breaking you. I have to break you, *mal'chik*. It's a simple matter of life-and-death."

"You won't break me."

"I will." Her head lifts and her arm pulls back. "It's time for you to learn your first count of eight."

I chuckle and hear how tired my voice sounds with the low rumble of it. "Do you really think I'm going to dance for you right now? The moment you untie me, I'm knocking you on your ass and getting the hell out of here."

"You misunderstand me," she says. "I don't mean for you to dance. You're not ready to be unshackled, to be free with me just yet. I don't trust you, and you don't have respect for the situation you've been forced into. The first count of eight you will learn is pain. Pain is what you get when you refuse, when you deny, when you disobey. You'll count as I strike, *mal'chik*. If you refuse or miscount, I'll start again."

She swings hard and the cane collides with my flesh, slicing an even sharper pain than the last through my cheeks, rippling down the backs of my thighs. I try to hide that it hurts, but hell, it stings.

"Count, *mal'chik*. That was *one*."

I purse my lips in refusal.

She sighs. "Fine, we'll start again."

She swings and strikes again, landing with precision over the thickest part of my ass. My thighs clench against the shooting pain that runs right down the back of my legs. It's clear she's practiced at this. She must be, given how much it hurts for such a petite young woman to be swinging that thing at me.

Without warning and without giving me time to choose, she hits me again, but this swing lands across the back of my thighs. I cry out involuntarily and my knees buckle, forcing me to sway in my suspension. She hits me in the same spot, one, two, three more times, each sting more painful than the last.

"Fuck, stop!" I yell at her.

She tries to flatten her tone, but I hear the hint of trepidation. "Now count, *mal'chik*."

As the cane lands against my ass again, I weaken.

Like a fucking coward, I weaken.

"One," I force myself to say.

Her hand softly touches the middle of my back but drops away almost immediately. "Good. Again."

She strikes.

"Two," I say.

I'm rewarded again by the softness of her fingers drawing low on my back, stopping just above my belt buckle before falling away again.

She strikes.

I groan, "Three."

"Very good."

This time, a gentle grazing along my side that makes me flinch.

She strikes.

"Four."

Again.

"Five."

Another.

"Six."

"Good, *mal'chik*. Only two more."

If her goal is to convince me that she gives a shit about the pain I'm feeling right now, she's doing a damn good job. She could make me believe she didn't really want to do it, but I know that would be naïve of me to think.

The woman is beating me, holding me against my will. She would be stupid to think I won't fight her again when my hands are freed and my energy is restored.

"Seven," I manage to say as she hits me, and I hardly have time to blink before the final strikes falls. "Eight."

The cane clatters as she drops it to the floor and circles around in front of me. She stands still, watching me, her chest rising and falling as harshly as mine. She looks the same as she did before, but her face droops with contradiction.

Her blue eyes slice into mine and it shoots through me, just the way the pain shot through me when she struck me with the cane.

"I don't enjoy punishing my partners," she says quietly. "It's simply what I must do to survive. You'll understand that soon enough."

I lift my head to meet her eyes. "Tell me your name."

Her chin rises with dignity, her eyes narrow, her lips purse together. I see a flicker of warmth pass across the cold blue of her eyes like a lightning strike. As quickly as it appears, it's gone.

"You will call me master."

CHAPTER 2
Ezra

THE GIRL WHO thinks she's my master walks in front of me as I'm half-dragged behind her by the same men who first brought me to her.

I can walk, but I'm tired and sore.

My wrists burn from the cable ties and the rope.

My throat aches from the pressure of her pointe shoe.

My gut throbs from punches thrown.

My ass stings from being beaten by her cane.

Apparently, my pace isn't good enough to keep up with Her Majesty, so the men pull me along by the elbows. My hands are tied in front of me with the rope that suspended me in the dance studio.

She glides ahead of us with a dangerous kind of swagger. Her steps are commanding and intentional, yet lack a certain sense of conviction.

I take in my surroundings as I'm led through an audacious mansion estate. The dance studio is on the ground level and leaving that space is like crossing into another world entirely. While the studio had been modern, sleek, and simple, the manor it's attached to is traditional, dark, and cold.

From the west wing, we move toward the center of the home. The hallway we follow surrounds me with burgundy-colored walls decorated with ostentatious gold portraits of people who were more than likely dead. It opens onto a grand entrance, a vast space which allows the ceiling to stretch high above me, two stories high.

To the right is what I assume is the main entrance of the home. The tall, wooden doors have intricate designs carved into long, etched-out rectangles that stretch from nearly the bottom to the top. To my left is a grand staircase, the ends of which curl out at the bottom landing, opening wide across the marbled floors, beckoning us forward to climb the steps.

She takes us toward it and as we ascend, the image of it makes me think we're crossing the tongue of some ancient monster. We scrape its taste buds as we walk up each step and tempt it to swallow us whole.

God, I'm fucking tired.

We turn right at the top of the staircase and follow another long hallway, this one just as dark and looming as the one downstairs. I'm taken all the way to the end, to the very last room in the dead end hallway.

The blue-eyed girl unlocks the door with two different keys in two different keyholes. It's a simple barrier, but an extra step to delay my escape when I attempt it at the first reasonable opportunity. I watch as closely as I can manage from several strides behind but my eyelids droop from sheer exhaustion.

She steps inside, holding the door open for us, pressing her back against it and holding out an arm as if I'm a guest in her medieval castle turned gothic tourist destination hotel.

"This is your room," she says.

The guards give me a good shove and I land on the floor with a thud. I grunt and wince, feeling all of my various pains roar to life at the same time. I swiftly roll onto my back and rise to a sitting position, grimacing from the burn across my backside where the cane struck me the hardest. It's the best I can do to put myself in any form of defensive position when my body and brain are screaming at me to rest.

"Is there room service?" I do my best to play it cool. "I'd love a steak right now."

The side of her mouth twitches and I nearly think she's going to smile. It turns into a sneer instead.

"Your confident charm will be gone within days. If I had any feelings left, I might think I'll mourn the loss. But I don't. And I won't." She blinks, and her eyes stay closed a beat too long as she sucks in a deep breath.

"If you think beating me on the ass with a cane is going to break me, then you're going to be disappointed," I tell her.

"I know that won't break you. What will break you is yet to come."

She looks down at her hands, which are now raised in front of her stomach. Her fingers clutch together and she wrings her hands around the keys she holds. My eyes narrow, zeroing in on the anxiety that she seems to be washing her hands with.

She's still looking down at them when she speaks again, "I think my master will come to see you tonight. I expect you to be on your best behavior," her head lifts, turns toward me, "for both our sakes."

I glance down at my own bound hands before looking back up at her. She's moving toward the exit.

My tone is gruff with irritation, but I try to sound patient because, for some reason, I feel compelled to be. "Are you ever going to tell me your name?"

She halts and turns back to face me. Her eyes rake over me, scraping across my form from my tied wrists up to my face and I shiver.

"Yes, *mal'chik*. When it's been earned. I've already told you that, so quit asking."

My eyes manage to catch hers just before she slams the door shut between us. I hear her turning the two locks on the door before she leaves.

I let my head fall back, though there's nothing behind me to catch it like I wish there were. Instead, I tilt it side to side, stretching my aching muscles before deciding I need to get on my feet. I shuffle them beneath me and steady myself with my fastened hands, pushing my fists down into the cushioned seat of a cream-colored armchair. Dust and flecks of dried blood from my knuckles smear the sheen of the embossed fabric.

I spin and take stock of my room.

Ugly forest-green walls with the same over-the-top gold picture frames and crown molding as the rest of the mansion make the oversized room feel like close quarters. There's a king-sized bed next to the door with a headboard carved as intricately as the front doors in the grand entrance. The pristine white comforter looks untouched, as if it was just freshly laundered, or perhaps, brand-new. I swallow, remembering what the blue-eyed girl told me—that I wasn't her first partner here.

There are no windows.

It's just a cleaner, more comfortable prison cell.

Wandering around the space, I find a small bathroom on the opposite side of the bed and I'm thankful for that, at least. It's bright white inside and it smells of bleach.

I swallow, feeling an odd pang in my gut at the smell.

I walk back into the bedroom and pull open the drawers of the old, sturdy furniture that probably costs more than a year's worth of my New York studio apartment rent. The first four I pull from the bottom of the double dresser are empty. Only the top two drawers have something inside, but the contents are of no use to me for defense or escape. The drawer on the left contains an extra set of clean, white bedsheets. The drawer on the right surprises me.

I find neatly folded T-shirts which, on first glance, wouldn't have made me bat an eye, except that a closer inspection reveals that they're *my* T-shirts. They're T-shirts from the luggage I had packed when I traveled from New York to Kyiv five days ago.

"Shit," I mutter to no one.

I turn, frantically scanning the space for the simple black suitcase and I spot it, sitting in the far corner behind the armchair I'd smudged when I got to my feet.

I rush to it, tossing it down and tearing into it as quickly as I can with my hands tied together. I pull at the zippers, dig into pockets, hoping foolishly that I'll find my pocketknife. I search the whole damn suitcase as if some magical pocket will appear and give me what I need to escape, to defend myself, to help me in any way at all.

But the luggage is completely emptied.

Why did they even bring it here if they've already emptied it?

To taunt me, of course.

I sit back on my heels, letting out a frustrated breath and wishing I could at least run my hands through my grungy hair. I wonder how long I'll have to wait in this room with my hands tied together. The more I think about it, the more I realize how uncomfortable it is for my wrists to be forced so tightly together and it makes me squirm.

I grab the side of my suitcase and shove it hard into the corner wall with a grunt, "Fuck!" I shout. "Fuck, fuck, fuck!"

I jolt, whipping around to look behind me at the door when I hear the locks unlatching. At first, I think the blue-eyed girl who won't tell me her name has returned, but then I wonder if it's someone else. She told me that her master would be visiting me tonight, and I wonder if her master is the same man I caught a glimpse of in the dance studio.

I know I'll find out soon enough as the door creeps open. It's pushed just hard enough to swing wide without bouncing against the wall and swinging back to closed. Instead, it's more like a curtain being drawn, revealing the villain to the captive audience for the first time.

The man stands in the doorway, legs planted strongly, about shoulder-width apart. His eyes are narrowed on me, as if he's agitated by my very presence.

"My name is Nikolai Mikhailov. I'm your new owner." He shares the same accent as the blue-eyed girl.

I push off the floor and get to my feet, trying to do it as steadily as I can so I don't come off as weak. "As I told the girl, nobody owns me."

He steps across the threshold into the bedroom. I feel the force of him moving toward me and I take an automatic step back. I immediately realize what I've done, giving him some semblance of power over me by my instinct to move away. I step forward again, twice, making up for the lost distance.

He stops once he reaches the end of the bed, tilting his head toward it. "Sit. Let's talk."

Without waiting to watch for my compliance, he reaches for the door, pushing it shut. I haven't moved yet when he turns back around to face me. He doesn't speak, just lifts a thick eyebrow, and the corner of my mouth lifts the same way in challenge.

He crosses his arms over his broad chest and cocks his head, and I literally feel the violent vibration of his soul slice through the space between us like a dagger. If the blue-eyed girl is winter, then this man is the fucking arctic circle. I strain every muscle in my body against the eerie feeling his presence imposes. My pride begs me to hold, to stay, to passively resist by remaining in place. But my instinct tells me to obey for now to spare my skin.

I leave the defiant smirk on my face while I slowly move toward the edge of the bed. I don't let my eyes leave him for a second as I lower to sit, perched at the very end. Nikolai shifts to stand in front of me.

He reaches into his pocket and I shift backward as he flicks open a switchblade and moves toward me.

"Hold out your hands," he says with no expression on his face.

"I don't trust you with that thing," I say honestly.

"Hold out your hands, *mal'chik*. I won't ask you again."

I believe him.

I slowly push my hands forward and he reaches out to snatch me, gripping the ropes that bind me where they wrap around my wrists and yanking my arms toward him. I flinch as he starts to saw away at the rope, but I don't dare pull my hands away for fear his blade may slip and injure me.

"If you fight me, you will lose," he tells me with a flick of his gray eyes from his blade to mine. "I'd hate to have to purchase a new comforter for your bed again. Anya's last partner bled all over the last one before his time with us ended."

My heart hesitates a little longer between beats before thumping painfully back into order.

Anya.

Is that her name?

The blue-eyed girl?

I dare to ask the question, "What happened to him?"

The rope separates and falls free and I rub my sore, chaffed skin.

Nikolai folds the blade and pockets it in his tan trousers, taking a slight step backward. "It's of no matter to you. He's gone and you're here to replace him."

With my hands freed, my fight reflex jumpstarts a new rush of adrenaline that forces my instincts to kick in. My head jerks back to look in the direction of the door. I immediately realize that I could slide off the side of the bed, throw the unlocked door open, and make a run for it. But some smarter, saner part of me wonders what the fuck I would do then.

I don't know where I am.

I don't know what or who might be in the hallway.

I haven't assessed this man's physical capabilities, though it's obvious his intentions are nefarious and it's unlikely he possesses an ounce of empathy.

I'm itching to jump and run, the urge to do it literally burns under my skin. My knees jerk up, ready to run and I clamp my palms down over them to hide my intentions. It's too late, though, because this guy already knows what I'm thinking. In a flash, he's got his switchblade out and open again, at the same moment my muscles flex to pull me upright off the bed. I've hardly moved toward the door before he comes after me.

He grabs me by the back of my shirt, tossing me backward and throwing me onto the floor with strength and ease. I'm strong, I have endurance, but the way he flings me with such a simple flick of his wrist puts me in check immediately.

I jump back up off the floor, ready to fight. But looking at his cold face, the same heartless expression he held from the moment he walked through the door, I hesitate. There's no passionate fury, no violent rage, just cool, collected indifference and somehow, that's more frightening.

"I told you," he says, flipping the blade in his hand. "Fight me and you'll lose."

I'm taking in heavy breaths as my adrenaline crests over the peak and starts to fall. "Just tell me what the fuck you want from me. Why am I here?"

"Sit and we'll discuss. Your incivility is unbecoming. It makes me want to shove this blade in the side of your neck and I just might if you don't sit, *mal'chik*."

I lock my fingers behind my head, stretching back before letting them drop with a thud against my sides. "Fuck, fine."

Once again, I'm moving toward the bed, forcing myself to relax enough to sit, though I'm agitated, twitchy, fidgety. It's not easy with him standing there between me and my freedom, threatening to stab me.

I'm not gonna die in this place.

As I lower to sit, he hovers above me. He smells like cigar smoke and whiskey. His prominent brow line shadows his gray eyes, emphasizing his permanently narrowed eyes.

"You are here for one reason and one reason only. I've brought you here to serve Anya, to perform with her."

"Perform for who?"

"Mostly for me. You'll learn more in time. Right now, all I want from you is to understand your place. You are in my home. It's belonged to my family for four generations. You will respect me here as the Head of House. You know my name, but you will call me master. Anya calls me the same as you are both my belongings. But she will also be your master, and you'll refer to her in whatever manner she deems respectable. You will obey her. You will follow her rules. You will not question or fight her. When she asks you to dance, you will dance and you will get it right. If you don't, she may punish you and I will support it. If she can't control you, I will punish her, so know that your actions will impact the entire household. Now, kindly remove your socks and shoes."

"What?" I stare up at him like he's just grown a second head.

He sucks in a breath and his lips flatten into a straight line. "Don't make me ask you again." His wrist ticks and light bounces off the blade, reminding me it's still in his hand.

I shake my head in frustration, but bend all the same, untying the laces of my boots. I kick them off and pull off my socks. I sit back up and plant my hands on my knees, looking up at him with a sneer.

Nikolai side-steps and bends to one knee near the bedpost to my left. My brow furrows with concern as he reaches beneath the bed and I'm twitching to run again. He grabs something that clanks, the sound of metal against metal and I can't sit still. I pounce to my feet and step away, but he's quick.

His hand clamps around my ankle, pulling hard and I nearly lose my balance. I naturally try to kick him off, but he's quick, latching a metal cuff around my right ankle.

"What the fuck?" I shout at him, but it's already locked in place.

I look down to see the cuff attached to a length of metal chain and I don't know how I missed seeing it there before, attached to the bottom of the bedpost beneath the frame. It's cold and oppressive against my skin and immediately, I bend to claw at it.

Nikolai stands and places his switchblade back in his pocket, satisfied with his safety now. I crouch and shove at the bedframe, trying to move the post, but it's solid as a rock, bolted down to the fucking floor.

"I would have given you freedom in your own room with just a locked door, but you've proven you're impulsive and can't be trusted. You're lucky I've seen your talent firsthand, otherwise, I'd end you now and find another to replace you. Anya will struggle with you. I can already sense it. But it will be all that much more satisfying to watch you break, comply, and still fail to satisfy me in the end. Your chains will reach as far as the toilet, but you'll be confined here until I decide to release you. I'll send her for you when I'm satisfied you've had enough time to know your place."

"Fuck you. Both of you."

The corners of his lips curve up ever so slightly and somehow, it makes his look even harsher, his nose more pointed, his jaw more angled and sharper. With his nearly chin-length, ash-brown hair slicked back and deliberately styled, the overall appearance of him screams wolf, predator.

"Get some rest, Mr. Bell. You have some trying times ahead of you."

He slices out of the room, sharp and severe like the blade he carries, and the door falls shuts behind him. I chase forward after him, but my chains stop me before I can even reach the door to bang on it and beg to be let out. I hear the locks turn and I still.

I look up to the ceiling, lacing my fingers behind my neck, and huff out a heavy breath full of anguish, the angsty groan of a caged animal. Rabid vexation rips through me with the jolt of pain that reminds me of my injuries. I shout out my distress to the ugly forest-green walls when the realization finally hits that I am well and truly fucked.

CHAPTER 3
Anya

MY NEW PARTNER'S name is Ezra, though of course I call him *mal'chik*. Not because I want to, but because I know it's what Nikolai will call him and he will insist I do the same—just as he insisted with the other men who came before him.

I despise my native language for no reason other than the fact that it has been used to degrade me for the past three years. I was born in Russia, raised there by my single mother until I was eleven years old before I was shipped off to New York and immersed in training to become a ballerina.

I was happy in that life, but I was stolen away from it three years ago, just after my twenty-first birthday.

I force thoughts of that life away, back into the dark corner of my mind, seal it, and wrap it shut in a black box that reads *do not open* on the side. My eyes narrow at the thought that I had opened it at all today. It was dangerous to remember life when I was free because I knew I would never have that life back.

The lid of the box had cracked open when my eyes fell upon Ezra in the dance studio for the first time. I think it was the emerald-green of his captivating eyes that did it. It reminded me of the fresh and bright green plants I kept in the two-bedroom apartment I shared with a roommate in New York. I had always surrounded myself with shrubs and greenery. I took pride in tending to them as they brought me a sense of brightness, of happiness, of life.

I haven't seen such bright green life in years. Though a vast forest surrounds the estate, it's full of dead trees in the cold of winter that never seems to come to an end. Life is shrouded forever now in cold, lifeless gray.

But Ezra's green eyes brought back the reminder of vibrant life against this cold, ongoing death march. It was as if he reached inside me and pulled out the dusty box of remembrance and hope that I had kept safely tucked away.

Nikolai had given me three dance partners before Ezra. Three men who hadn't met his expectations in performance for the Mikhailov family's turn to host the quarterly meeting for the four families.

Thus, the men before Ezra had disappeared. I presume they are dead. I can't afford myself the luxury of hoping they made it out alive because that would give me hope that I might someday do the same.

Hope is a dangerous thing and Ezra's spirit still thrums with that electric spark of lightness. I could feel it when I touched him. I could sense it pulsing from his soul. But because I'm forced to dance, I have to force Ezra to dance with me. That means I need to control him, and not just because Nikolai expects it.

I have to control him to protect myself. If he can't dance to my master's expectations, then this may be it for me. I've felt Nikolai's patience with me waning, his frustrations growing, and he takes it out on me.

I will remain in control.

I will make Ezra submit.

I will train Ezra to perform with me in the perfection that Master requires.

I will do this by being the woman to strip his hope from him piece by tiny piece until he has none left. Only then can I control him, use him. Only then could I even consider the possibility of a predictable, complacent survival in this nightmare life. I don't even consider the possibility of escape anymore. I don't believe it's possible outside of death.

I swallow and pinch my eyes shut, steeling myself as I approach Nikolai's master suite. The door is open because he's waiting for me.

It's been hours since I brought Ezra to his new room and I know Nikolai has been there as well. I've since showered, styled my long, dark chocolate colored hair so that it tumbles in wavy tresses, reaching down to the middle of my back. My master prefers it down when we're alone.

I wear a simple, black silk chemise for him under the long oriental-style robe that covers me. I've tied the robe shut tightly around my waist, double knotting the bow. I know it will prove to be no barrier for Nikolai because he takes what he wants but it makes me feel better all the same.

The silky floral fabric feels soft against my arms and I make a useless wish that it will remain on my body tonight. The softness of it is a comforting embrace that, once removed, will expose me to be used.

I cross my arms over my body, stepping over the threshold into his suite, shielding myself from what is to come.

Nikolai is sitting on one of the two oversized armchairs in front of the fireplace, his back to the door. The fire burns orange and bright, and I can feel the heat of it from where I'm standing. I can see he's still dressed in his usual attire—a button-down rolled up at the sleeves and open at the collar, covered by a tweed vest, tan slacks, and sleek dress shoes. There's a glass of whiskey in his hand and one ankle is crossed over his knee.

With a soft voice, I announce my arrival, "*Moy khozyain.*"

My master, in Russian.

I hate the words and it feels so much worse to say it in his language than in mine. I'm fluent in both, but I was building an American life when I was taken and forced to live in his world.

He allows me to speak with him in English, a small grace he granted me after my first year of obedience. It's something so simple, but it gives me a small amount of power. I refuse to let go of it and choose to speak English whenever I can. Still, I am required to address Nikolai in his native tongue, though he's fluent in both languages as well.

"Close the door and sit beside me, *moya rabynya.*"

Moya rabynya.

My slave girl.

"*Da, khozyain,*" I say, pressing the door shut behind me and crossing the room.

I walk around the armchair beside him. It angles toward him, facing the fire, and I slowly lower to sit.

He takes a sip of whiskey from his glass and speaks without looking at me, "Ezra Bell is impulsive and reckless. He's overly confident and sarcastic. But I've watched him perform, and I know he is more talented than the other partners I've given you."

His head turns slowly, and I lower my gaze toward the floor before he can make eye contact. I haven't yet determined his mood tonight and know it's better safe than sorry.

He prefers my submission.

Perhaps that's why I'm so insistent on maintaining control over my dance partners. One of the many reasons among simple survival.

He continues and I can feel his eyes take me in. "If you can break him, he will be a good partner for you. If you train him well, you may win back my favor this year."

I knew his enchantment with me was fading, but the way he reminds me makes me feel cold inside.

"*Da, khozyain.*"

"Look at me, Anya."

I lift my chin and meet his gray eyes. The side of his mouth twitches, attempting to form a small smile.

Happiness isn't a feeling he's accustomed to.

"Come here and let me look at you," he says.

He has trained me not to hesitate, so I don't. I come to stand in front of him and he nods his head toward the floor, so I fall to my knees as he uncrosses his leg and sets his whiskey on the side table. He spreads his legs apart and leans forward, reaching out with both hands to hold my face, his fingers landing softly against my cheeks.

"You look beautiful, Anya."

"Thank you."

Nikolai sighs on a low growl as he shifts closer in his seat. "What do you think of Ezra?"

I try to breathe deeply, but the air catches in my throat. I swallow and harden my exterior shell before responding, "If you've selected him for me, I'm sure he'll make a fine partner."

"That's not what I'm asking you." His grip tightens against my jawline. "Do you find him attractive?"

With a flip of a switch my shields are up, armor on. This little game of entrapment is a favorite of his when he's feeling particularly brutal, when he's feeling particularly weak.

"I'm not concerned with his appearance, only in his ability to perform."

His right hand slides back along my jawline and his fingers dig into my hair. "Answer me truthfully. Do you find him more attractive than the others?" His jaw clenches and his eyes narrow in on mine, digging deep.

He'll know if I'm lying so I have no choice but to answer truthfully, "*Da, khozyain.* But I belong to you."

He bends, leaning in close. His lips are a mere inch from mine, his breath hot against my face. When he exhales, I smell his whiskey.

"Prove it to me."

I close my eyes, but only for a moment. "Tell me how and I will."

His fingers curl into a fist around my hair at the side of my head. Nikolai bares his teeth at me as he yanks my head sideways, growling out a command, "Take off your robe."

I inhale a breath of courage and reach down to loosen the knot. It slips apart, removing the barrier of my armor.

It already feels like defeat.

It *always* feels like defeat.

I remain strong, though, because I won't give him the satisfaction of knowing that.

I let the silk glide down my arms and it falls to the floor, encircling me as though it knows it's my only protection. One of the thin straps of the barely-there chemise has fallen, and Nikolai's eyes are drawn to it. His head dips and he presses his lips to my bare shoulder before sinking his teeth in.

He is the predator and I am his prey.

Always.

The bite makes me flinch and groan, and he mistakes the noise for wanting. Nikolai hears what he wants to. He wants me to want him, so I let him believe it if it keeps the peace.

I have the scars to remind me why that peace must be kept.

He pulls back and moves his hands to grip my shoulders and starts to push me sideways. "Get on your hands and knees, *rabynya*."

I turn and fall on my hands as he's forcing me to the ground. I'm on all fours beside the crackling fire with only the small sheath of silky fabric to hide me. He drops to his knees and climbs up behind me. He grips my hips with both hands, fingers digging into my sides as he slides up behind me. His knees are inside my legs, nudging my thighs, encouraging them to spread wider for him.

I let my head fall forward in defeat as one of his hands trails up the back of my thigh, creeping over my rounded backside to lift the hem of the short nightgown. Internally, I whimper at the touch, knowing the pain that's to come from this position, knowing which part of me will be violated tonight in front of the fire.

He reaches out to fist my hair behind my neck and pull my head upright. His hips thrust against my bottom and I feel the bulge of his erection through his trousers.

"I wanted to give you pleasure tonight, but you were disrespectful to me when I brought you a new partner, questioning my choice. So, instead, I'll take my pleasure from you and fuck you until you bleed for me. I want your tears tonight, Anya. Give them to me and I'll spare you the pain of being burned."

He holds my hair so tightly that I can't turn my head, but my eyes flicker over to the flames burning beside me. My eyes burn just as hot, and though the determined woman inside wishes to deny him those tears in favor of flames, I can't, and he knows it.

This has happened a thousand times before and it will happen a thousand more before I'm given the gift of freedom or death and it damages me still.

When he fucks me in that forbidden entrance from behind, it always hurts and it always brings me tears and it always gives him power.

"Tell me who you are," he growls.

I struggle to keep my voice steady. "I am slave to the Mikhailov family. I am your belonging."

He suddenly lets go of my hair and my head jerks forward. I don't look over my shoulder when I feel his hands move between me and him, his buckle coming undone, his zipper being pulled. I retreat inward and try not to think too much. I try to listen only enough to follow his commands and move on from this vile moment as he's sliding my underwear down to expose me.

Nikolai reaches around me and his fingers graze over my lower belly. "I need you wet for me if you want to lessen the pain."

My stomach rolls in nausea.

His hand moves lower and his fingers glide across my sex, finding the spot that he knows will trigger my arousal.

My body always betrays my mind and my heart in these moments. Nikolai is talented in touch, an experienced, older man—fifteen years my senior. Though his soul is filthy with violence and coldness and brutality, he is still a physically attractive man. I hate him almost as much for being beautiful on the outside as I do for being so disgusting on the inside.

Though it sickens me that my body reacts to him at all, it's a good thing that I do because it lessens the pain of his intrusion.

There was a time once when I felt something more for him, early in my captivity when I felt starved by loneliness and was desperate for human connection beyond his violence and hatred and the torment he caused me. It was a day when I was emotionally vulnerable and pathetically needy.

That day, I had come to him, sought him out in hope of comfort from my master. I came into his room as he was taking a shower. In my naïve despair, I went to him in the bathroom and stood waiting in the doorway. He saw me standing there through his glass shower door and watched me as he finished bathing. The room had filled with steam by the time he got out. I saw something different in his beauty that day, and I haven't seen it since. I saw something raw, exposed, as broken as I felt.

He came to me, glistening with droplets of water. His damp hair, which he normally straightens and slicks back, was wavy around the edges in the steam, softening the severe lines of his predatorial features. He stood in front of me that day, his presence quiet and unassuming for the first and last time. He watched me and waited for me, and it was only moments before I bared myself to him.

I pulled off my clothes, piece by piece, revealing my body to him willingly, bit by bit ceding control in foolish wanting. I'd let down my guard, weakened my defenses, and opened myself to him. He kissed me sweetly, touched me softly.

He backed me up against the countertop and fell to his knees for me. That day, he made me come with his fingers. He studied me with attentive eyes, watching as I became aroused for him, watching my wetness shine as it slicked his fingers, exploring all my most private places. It was the first and only time I felt so connected to Nikolai that I felt like I wanted him.

I held onto that time he made me feel so good because it was the only recent memory I had of feeling worthy and worshipped. I pretended that's all it was during moments like the one I'm experiencing with him now. I have to remember the way he touched me then, the way he made me feel, I have to think of it to become aroused for him now.

His touch is the same now as it had been then, but it doesn't make me feel the same. This touch is different because it's a lie, a manipulation of the truths he discovered that day when he made me come so completely undone for him. That day for me was a connection, but for him, it was a mere study and he uses his knowledge against me now.

I let him touch me, forcing my body to react, obliging him with the physical reaction he wants as he spreads my wetness all across me, dragging it along my crack, to the place he wishes to defile me.

He's already pressing his erection against me, eager to force his way inside. I scream when he finally does, showing me no gentleness, no time for adjustment, no mercy. He buries himself to the hilt and I feel like I'm being ripped in two. Nikolai folds his body over mine and pushes me down to my elbows, forcing my ass higher into the air.

I'm enveloped by him, consumed by him, oppressed by him.

"Tell me how much I hurt you, *rabynya*. Give me your tears and tell me of your pain."

"You hurt me more than anyone ever could, *moy khozyain*," I say truthfully as tears slip from my eyes.

He will never understand how true that is. I might have found a way to love him if he hadn't abandoned his humanity.

I could have loved a monster.

But I could never love the Devil.

CHAPTER 4
Ezra

THE SKIN AROUND my fingertips is raw and peeling from my useless attempts to pry the metal cuff from my ankle. I'm weak, starving, lost inside the dark spaces of my mind.

"Nikolai Mikhailov," I say into the desolate space of my room.

I won't forget the name of the man who chained me to this bed and left me here alone. I've been without food, without sunlight, without company for a long damn time. I picture myself as a wilting leaf on a flower that is slowly wasting away and dying in a cold, dark space.

I'm losing my fucking mind.

There's no clock and I don't wear a watch, so I have to guess at how long I've been locked in this room. It feels like it's been a week, but in reality, it's probably been a little over two days.

For the first time in my life, my fight has drained out of me. I'm slumped on the floor with my back against the bed, my head dropped onto my arms that rest on my knees. My anger has been replaced by need, basic need.

All I want right now is food, a proper shower, a full fucking glass of water. All I can do right now is drink from the bathroom faucet and it runs slow with low pressure. I can reach the toilet, but I can't even get to the shower with the chain shackling me in place.

I slept the first night, though the fight in me still existed, jerking me awake every now and then. I'm more tired than I've ever been, and I've had nothing but time to sit and wait. It's an agitated rest to be shackled, locked in a room with nothing to do but stare at the ugly walls and talk to myself.

And I've decided that I'm not that great of company.

Surprisingly, I've been thinking about the blue-eyed girl. She seems familiar to me, but I've been struggling to place her. For a while, I wonder if she just seems familiar because she's the only person besides Nikolai Mikhailov that I've had any contact with in days.

The more I try to connect my memory of her in my brain, the more I wish I could see her face. I think if I could look at her again after all this time spent trying to place her, that I'd know.

It was something about her presence, the way she holds herself, the way she dances. Maybe I've seen her perform somewhere. More likely, she just reminds me of any number of dancers I've seen before.

I know it's more than that, though.

It's something in those sapphire eyes.

Fuck.

I'm grasping at straws, trying to remember things, to make connections that aren't really there. It must be my brain's way of staying active and keeping me sane.

I laugh out loud at the thought of sanity. I feel like it's right on the brink because at this point, I don't know whether anyone is coming back for me.

When will I eat?

Will I starve to death in here?

Is Nikolai Mikhailov's the last face I'll ever see?

Fuck, I hope not.

I don't think it would bother me so much if the blue-eyed girl's face is the last I see.

He called her Anya.

I suppose I should stop thinking of her as the gorgeous blue-eyed girl with the grace of an angel, but at least the thought of a beautiful face somewhere out there helps me feel a little less alone.

I hear the locks on the bedroom door turn, but I don't turn to look. I know I'm just hearing things because I thought I heard them before. A couple of times, actually, but no one was there.

"*Mal'chik.*" The voice slices into the room and I spin to see her at the door, the blue-eyed girl.

She comes into the room and sets a tray on the side table next to the armchair. I've stilled and I blink at her, unmoving because I don't believe she's actually there.

Her hair is down and I can see how long it is, tumbling in perfect, coffee-colored waves down her back. Her eyes seem even bluer than I remember and her features softer. Perhaps I'm just happy to see another human because I recall hating her so fervently when I arrived, but at this moment, she's truly stunning to look at.

A sight to behold.

An angel swooping down into my hell.

I'm losing. My fucking. Mind.

"Is your name Anya?" I ask.

Her eyes narrow. She steps back and reaches up to tuck a strand of hair behind her ear.

"It's *master* to you, and I command you to eat."

The muscles in her neck move as she swallows, and I think I see hesitation before she leaves the room. As the door shuts behind her, I finally come back to life. I spring to my feet, but my chain prevents me from reaching the door before she turns the first lock, then the second.

For a moment I'm pissed at myself for being so slow to act. But I forget quickly about the fact that I'm alone again when the smell of fresh, warm stew fills my nostrils. I go and lift the tray that Master left for me and sit on the edge of the bed.

I flinch before I pick up the silver spoon with the intricately carved swirling design on the handle.

I called her Master in my own damn mind.

"She's not my master," I say out loud to remind myself that these people don't own me, but it doesn't come out very convincingly, so I say it again, "She's *not* my *master*."

I have a fleeting moment where I think I should refuse the food and go on a hunger strike. After all, they want me to dance with her. I won't be able to if I'm starved and malnourished.

My mouth curls up sideways in the corner as I say to nobody, "That will show them."

But the smell of the soup is nearly intoxicating after being denied nourishment for so long. Steam curls as it rises from the dark broth. I dip my spoon into it and stir, noting the colors of the vegetables.

Fresh orange carrots.

Precisely green peas.

Flawless white chunks of potato.

Perfectly tender chunks of beef.

It all looks freshly made and my mouth is watering.

I scoop and lift the spoon to my lips and eagerly take a bite, hunger strike and scalding broth be damned. I devour the entire bowl before I even notice the warm bread and scoop of butter beside it, and I scarf that down, too.

Now that I've eaten, I feel refreshed, renewed, hopeful I can survive this ordeal long enough to escape. I stand and set the tray back on the side table by the armchair and hesitate.

I've already scoured the parts of the room I can reach. All the drawers and built-in cabinets are empty. Anything I could potentially use as a weapon or tool has been removed from the room.

I'm still cuffed.

I'm still locked in.

I'm still captive.

I look down at the empty soup bowl and suddenly feel deceived by the brief jolt of energy it's nourishment gave me.

I feel fucking betrayed by it.

I reach down and snatch the bowl from the tray and hurl it across the room. It slams with a thud and bounces off the far wall, entirely intact.

It doesn't even give me the satisfaction of shattering for me.

I think another day has gone by when the door finally opens again. This time, I jump up the moment I hear it, eager more than before to eat with the tease of food I was given yesterday. I spin to face the door and the blue-eyed girl enters the room.

Her hands are empty and my stomach grumbles in disappointment. She's hard and cold again, not the way she looked when she brought me the soup.

"On your knees," she commands, closing the door behind her.

I waver.

Her eyes pierce into mine and though no part of my psyche wants to bend for my captor, my knees fold all the same. I lower to the floor, but I keep my eyes on hers, my expression dark with the anger I feel at myself for obeying so quickly. I don't even know why I did.

"Good," she says with narrowed eyes as she moves closer. "Eyes on the floor."

"I'm not taking my eyes off you," I growl.

"I'm flattered, really, but you will obey if you want to eat."

Her challenge ignites my stubbornness. "Then I guess I won't eat."

Her eyebrows slant down toward her tiny, round nose and she tilts her head as she regards me. A curious look spreads across her rosy cheeks. Boldly, she walks to stand right in front of me. I could reach out and grab her, tackle her to the floor, hold her hostage until Nikolai Mikhailov returns.

If he ever returns.

And what the hell would I do when he does?

My heartbeat surges with the urge to do it—to toss her to the ground and pin her beneath me and force her into this captivity along with me. It burns heat inside my chest that coils and festers.

She hovers above me and her chest rises and falls sharply with a quick breath. I can nearly feel the air rush out of her on the exhale, and I breathe it in. The cool, wintry breeze of her breath melts over the fire burning in my chest. It drips like a waterfall into my stomach, tugging unnecessary need into my belly. The feeling persists when her icy fingers touch my chin, grip me firmly, and pull my head up higher to look at her.

Her voice is a low whisper. "Remember this while you sleep tonight, *mal'chik*. You made the choice not to eat."

I open my mouth to clap back at her with a snarky reply, but I don't even get the chance. With a graceful spin, she releases me and turns, striding with sure steps to the door.

She's gone before I can even blink.

It's fuck all o'clock on the forty-second day of December in the grand old year of two thousand thirty-seven or some bullshit.

I don't know whether it's night or day anymore.

I've been fed three times since they brought me here and my interactions have been limited to brief exchanges with the blue-eyed girl. Each meeting ends with me frustrated in my stubbornness and inexplicably more desperate to obey her, though I fight it.

    I don't think I'm going to fight it when she comes back.

    If she comes back.

    God, I hope she fucking comes back.

CHAPTER 5

Anya

KEEPING MY INTERACTIONS with Ezra brief and cold has been more challenging than it was with any of the others. He was broody and sullen with me—understandably so—and it should have put me off.

It *does* put me off, but in a fiery sort of way that makes me *want* him to keep fighting me for control.

Of course, I don't want that—my survival depends on his submission. I need his submission to be able to train him, but he hasn't given it to me yet.

He's been locked in his room for five days, has earned meals only three times, and I'm concerned because I need him to be strong enough for the way I manage my rehearsals. Time is wasting away while I wait for him to cave and concede control, and I've finally come to my wits' end. He's not pliable and easily manipulated like the others had been.

In my life before, I might have enjoyed that quality about him, but now, I find it infuriating. As I approach his room, I place a hand over my belly and take in a deep, steadying breath. The way he regards me whenever I enter his room is unsettling in a way that makes my pulse race. He's not aware of his effect on me, or at least, I don't think he is, but I have to be careful with my reactions.

I meet his snarky tone with a snarky tone of my own.

I meet the intensity of his eyes with my own piercing gaze.

I meet his fire with my inferno.

I know I must be careful not to fan the flame too high, though.

Everything must be carefully controlled with him.

I unlock the door and open it carefully, stepping inside and shutting it behind me. Ezra has just risen to his feet from sitting on the edge of the bed and whips around to face me. His shirt is off, though his jeans remain intact. I catch a glimpse of his defined torso at the moment his eyes narrow on mine and my fingers twitch at my side.

I think with certainty he's going to be difficult today, but then his face droops in defeat. He circles to the stand in front of the end of the bed as I walk across the floor to meet him and, without my directive, he lowers to his knees.

I take in a sharp breath of surprise as he sits back on his heels and places his palms on his thighs, lowering his eyes to the floor. He is the chiseled statue of a man kneeling in worship and I am the object of his adoration.

The part of me desperate for some semblance of control in this tortured life aches for him to be mine completely, hopeful that this submission is given beyond his desperation for food and comfort and connection. I know that kind of submission as I give it daily in exchange for the things I need for survival. For the first time, I want more than that from this partner. I just don't know exactly why.

I stand in front of him, close enough for him to reach out and touch. I stand there waiting, wondering if he is trying to trick me into complacency so he can attack, but he doesn't move. I decide to test his obedience.

I walk backward a few steps and stop. "Crawl to me."

His shoulders slump as he sighs, but he drops down and crawls to me all the same. My stomach clenches at the vision of his shoulder muscles flexing with the slow, crawling movement. My attention is drawn to his ankle when the metal chain clanks its insistence that he does not go any farther.

I shudder, remembering the ache and irritation of the hard metal cuff. Mine was on for two weeks when I first arrived here years ago. It always bothered me to see my partners wearing it when they first arrived. But the reminder of it now, on this partner, triggers something more visceral within me. I can feel it on my ankle as though I am wearing it myself.

"If I remove the chain, what will you do?" I ask him.

He lifts his head, but he's too close to me on his hands and knees and our eyes don't meet. He doesn't reply.

"Will you obey me if I remove the chain? I'm not interested in being attacked. If Master finds me here injured or dead or held as your hostage, he will slice you open and mercilessly rip out your organs. So, if I remove the chain as a reward for your submission, what will you do?"

He shifts to sit back on his heels. "I'll obey."

"Look at me and tell me again."

Ezra tilts his chin upward, meeting my eyes with that sparkling green that reminds me of life and sunlight. "I'll obey. Please, just take it off."

I sigh. "Go sit on the bed and wait. I'm going to leave to get you food. If I come back and you've moved from that spot, the chain will stay and you'll remain is this room for another night. Do you understand?"

His eyes narrow with a flicker of hope, immediately replaced with fear. The fear is what I want, what I need to keep him under my thumb.

I should be happy to have seen it cross the vibrant green, but it makes my stomach roil with nausea instead. I don't understand the feeling because he's just given me the obedience I need to control him.

Watching me, he rises to his feet in front of me, and as he comes to his full height—probably a good six inches above me—I feel an urge to step back. I won't step back, but regardless, the urge is there. The way he holds me with his eyes, the way his presence pushes heavy against my chest, my heart…it frightens me.

I'm thankful when Ezra nods slowly and steps backward, watching me for two steps before he turns and lowers to the bed. I let out a breath of relief when he finally lets go of my gaze, letting his head drop as he rubs his palms nervously against his jeans.

"Good, *mal'chik*," I tell him, then clear my throat. "I'll return within the hour."

His head snaps up to look at me again and I'm caught up in the fear his features hold. I feel a need to reassure him like I've never felt before.

"I'll return, Ezra. My word is good. I don't have any reason to lie to you. I promise." I leave the room and lock the door before he can respond.

Why did I make a promise?

I know better than to make promises here. Though it's a promise I intend to keep, I know Nikolai could call for me and force me to break it by no fault of my own. I've never promised anything to any of my partners before and my forehead wrinkles at the thought that I've just done it now.

I walk briskly to the kitchen on the ground floor, all the time wondering how I could do such a stupid thing. But more importantly, I wonder *why*.

I make a quick lunch for Ezra.

Mal'chik, I remind myself.

I hurry because suddenly I'm terrified that Nikolai will show up and demand my time. It's been years since I've made a promise to anyone and the thought of breaking it makes me want to cry. I have no right to make promises to anyone when my life is not my own. I feel tears well behind my eyes as I put his food on a tray and lift it from the butcher block island.

I turn and a fresh kind of panic I haven't felt since my first weeks here at Mikhailov Manor rushes inside me. I expect to see Nikolai standing there, but he isn't. Still, the panic that he could have been ignites my anxiety all the same.

It was always terrifying to turn and find him waiting for me when I didn't expect it, but now I've gone and made a promise.

A promise to be somewhere.

To be there for someone else.

And I can't stomach the thought of breaking it.

My chest tightens as all the air rushes out of my lungs. I take two steps forward but then halt because painful sobs stop me dead in my tracks.

I spin back toward the counter, setting the tray down with a clatter, but at least I manage not to drop it to the floor. I grip the counter's edge, lean forward, and sob over Ezra's meal.

It's been so long since I've felt so much that I don't even know how to handle my own outburst. I have no choice but to let it overcome me. I let go and let it grip me and it's painful to relinquish control. My body trembles with the purge of emotions that I don't understand.

When I finally decide I've had enough of this bullshit, I stop.

I stop crying.

I stop wallowing.

I stop fearing.

I take back control, harden my heart, let ice freeze over the bits of my soul that just thought they could melt. I grab the tray and march back toward Ezra's room before emotion can stop me again.

I stop at Kostya's door in the same hallway first. Kostya is one of the men Nikolai pays to protect me, or so he says. Really, Kostya is an escort, following me and my partner during the day, ensuring we don't attempt escape or suicide or murder. He's a distant cousin of the Mikhailovs, but that means nothing. At the end of the day, he's just one of the hired help.

Kostya is younger than Nikolai, but older than me. He told me he was twenty-eight when I was first brought here three years ago, when I was twenty-one. He opens the door after I knock, dressed for the day in a plain black suit and tie, as always. He's starting to grow out his ash-colored facial hair, and it's just a hint longer than his usual five o'clock shadow. His hair is styled nicely, thick strands that wave to one side from where they are parted.

The cut on his cheek from wrestling with Ezra when he was first brought in seems to be healing nicely, but I don't tell him that.

I don't talk to Kostya.

I don't think I can trust him.

He comes with me and opens Ezra's door. I don't have to give him my keys because he has a set of his own.

I walk in and my heart thumps hard once, twice, to find that Ezra has obeyed. He remains motionless as I bring the tray into the room and set it on the table beside the armchair.

"Eat first," I tell him, "and I'll remove your chain before I go."

"Before you go?"

"No talking," I snap. "Eat and listen."

He stands to grab the tray and sits back down on the bed, digging in without hesitation.

I speak slowly and cautiously, aware that my emotions just got the best of me and I will *not* let that happen again. "After you eat, *mal'chik*, I want you to take a shower and get dressed. I'd like to take you to the dance studio today."

His head snaps up. "You mean, leave the room?"

"Only so long as you are obedient. There is a man who serves Master to protect me. You've met him. That's Kostya by the door." I nod toward him in the doorway. "He brought you here."

He scoffs, "Like I could forget."

"He will hurt you if you try to hurt me. And then I will hurt you."

"And then your master will hurt you for failing to break me?" he says it so plainly that it gives me pause.

I don't respond to his question. I don't want him to think I'm weak or that I'm afraid of my master.

I can't show that I am.

"If you behave, you might get to dance for me today."

He drops the spoon he was holding onto the tray, some of his fire returning as he stares up at me with narrowed eyes. "And if I don't?"

I step forward into his space, looking down at him where he sits on the bed. "Then you'll remain here, shackled and alone, wondering when your next meal will come. Does that seem like the more appealing option to you, Ezra?"

Ezra.

Shit.

I shouldn't have said his name.

He tilts his head at me, and I know he knows I've slipped up. "No, it doesn't."

I straighten, lifting my chin. "Then you'll obey."

It's a command, not a question.

He lifts an eyebrow and begins to eat slowly, so I step back. Several quiet moments pass in awkward silence before he speaks to me.

"Am I allowed to talk to you?"

I tilt my head, noticing the loneliness in his features. It's a look that's hard to recognize unless you've experienced it yourself.

And I have, in spades.

I tuck a strand of hair behind my ear, thinking I should have pulled it back in a bun before coming in here. I look older, more serious with my hair pulled back tight.

"Yes, you're allowed."

"I know I'm supposed to call you master, but can you just tell me…is your name Anya?"

"Yes."

"Nikolai is your master?"

"And yours."

"Why? Why are we here? And why am I bound and mistreated while you have free range to go wherever you want?"

I chuckle, crossing my arms over my chest. "You haven't even begun to understand mistreatment. I've earned certain freedoms and it's taken me years of trust-building with my master. You should start by giving me your full submission and perhaps you'll get lucky with similar freedoms."

"I don't believe in luck."

"Neither do I."

There was a pulse, a beat of connection and immediately, I knew I shouldn't have allowed a concession in the form of agreement. All the same, I didn't regret it. Especially when the corner of his lip ticked upward in an almost grin.

I need to get out of here.

"Do as you're told, *mal'chik*. I'll leave you to eat and shower."

I reach into my pocket to pull out the small key that releases the latch of the metal cuff. I bend at the knees, lowering in front of him. I have to lift the hem of his jeans, sliding them up his leg to reveal the hidden latch of the cuff. My fingers graze his skin in the process and he jumps at my touch.

"Hold still," I warn with a cold look. "If Kostya thinks you're about to harm me, he may come after you and the result would be less than ideal."

"Sorry, it was just…" he hesitates. "Your fingers are cold."

I insert the key and twist it, relieving Ezra of the burden of being shackled. "Cold like my heart." I stand. "Don't mistake my conversation for connection, *mal'chik*. I'll rip your heart in two if you make the mistake of thinking you and I are anything more than master and slave."

"I wouldn't dream of it, *Master*." Sarcasm seeps from his pores like sweat, a natural response for him.

He angers me.

He lights a fire in my chest and it burns in my belly.

The almost welcome heat overwhelms me, and I reach out and slap him just to put out the fire. His head falls to the side, but before he can reach up to touch the spot where I hit him, I grab his chin and yank his head back to me. I sense Kostya moving in closer, on the defensive.

I bend and put my face close to Ezra's, giving him all the coldness I can muster from deep within my wintery soul. "This is not a joke, *mal'chik*. If you had any idea what Nikolai is capable of, then you would cut the bullshit right now. I suggest you forget connection and conversation and get used to loneliness. It may save you in the end."

Before I can read into the look of softness and sympathy behind his lively green eyes, I turn on my heel and storm out of the room. Kostya exits behind me and I lock the door as swiftly as I can manage. I dismiss Kostya, asking him to bring Ezra to me in the studio in an hour.

Emotion is welling again, and it threatens to break me entirely. As I rush off down the hallway, crossing the estate to the far end of the west wing to my room, I repeat my own words in my head, giving myself the same advice I've given to Ezra.

Embrace loneliness, Anya.
It will save you in the end.

CHAPTER 6

Anya

I'M ROTATING THROUGH a turn when I catch a glimpse of someone entering the studio. At first, I think it's Kostya and Ezra, and I feel content with that, but as I land coming out of a second and third rotation, posing my arms gracefully, I see that's its Nikolai.

He claps for me, the sound of it echoing in the expansive, open space of my dance studio. I take a bow in curtsy out of politeness—because he won't tolerate otherwise—and he shoves his hands in his pockets, leaning his shoulder against the door frame.

I cross the room to stand in front of him and bow my head, waiting for him to speak or command.

"Is he ready to dance?" Nikolai asks.

"*Da, khozyain.* He kneeled for me today and obeyed my command. Kostya should be bringing him to me soon."

"Good, I'll stay and watch."

My head whips up and I catch his gray eyes. "Why?"

I regret speaking almost as immediately as his cruel demeanor returns. Nikolai reaches out, grabs me by the back of my neck, and spins me. He whips me around with ease and slams me face-first into the mirrored wall beside the door. My hands come up to catch myself, palms flattening against the cold surface and I turn my head to the side just in time to avoid my nose crashing into it. It didn't heal right the last time he broke it, and I don't want to risk going through that again.

His body pins me to the mirror from behind as he curls around me, fingers digging into the side of my neck.

"Are you questioning me again, *rabynya?* I thought you learned your lesson the other night. Or are you just begging for a repeat?"

I keep my voice and my breath steady. "I'm sorry."

"For?"

"For questioning you."

I'm not allowed to ask questions.

I'm not allowed to misunderstand directions and ask for clarification.

I'm expected to know and obey.

Nikolai steps back but doesn't let me go. Instead, he spins me around to face him before pressing his body into mine. His breath is on my face. It's warm and smells of cigar smoke. He strokes the back of his hand gently down my cheek and I fight the urge to recoil, leaning into it to placate him instead of following my instinct to slap it away and run.

"Beautiful girl," he croons, "I nearly miss the fight in you."

He contradicts himself constantly.

Why should he miss the fight in me when he wants my constant and consistent obedience?

"Maybe one day I will set you free in the forest…" He bends to whisper against my ear, "Chase after you, see which hunter finds you first this time, hmm? Will it be me or the wolves that prowl the tree line?"

I'm tempted to sneer at him and ask him what the difference would be, but I don't. I know better than that. I swallow, considering that Ezra might've responded the way I wanted to given the manner in which I've witnessed him communicate with a sardonic temper.

I don't like that Ezra has popped into my head again. It's dangerous to think of the boy when Nikolai has a hold of me.

He'll sense it.

Finally, I respond, "I'm certain it would be you."

He presses a soft kiss to my lips then pauses as he pulls back to look at me. "Yes, I imagine it would. Just as it was when you tried to escape the first time. And aren't you lucky I found you first?"

No.

"*Da, moy khozyain.*"

A throat is cleared nearby and we both look to see Kostya standing in the doorway. Nikolai lets me go and walks away to the far corner of the studio.

There's a black, grand piano there, though I'm never granted the privilege of a live player. I think its presence speaks to Nikolai's self-aggrandization. He fills his home with the appearance of culture and refinement, though he possesses none naturally.

He sits on the bench and waits for me to welcome Ezra to the studio, to direct him, to command him. He's never come in this early to view me with another partner and the thought of it makes my nerves pulse with anxiety. I clench my hands into fists to hide the way they tremble.

Why is he here?

Nikolai could easily just watch from the security camera. There are only two inside Mikhailov Manor and one of them is here, inside the dance studio. The other is just outside the boardroom, near Nikolai's home office. The rest are on the exterior grounds to monitor for escapees or unwanted guests—as if anyone could find the manor if they didn't know exactly where it was.

It was curious to me early in my captivity that there weren't more cameras inside the manor to monitor my behavior, but I quickly learned that secret-keeping is taken rather seriously by the four families.

There are secrets no family wants on camera.

Kostya grabs Ezra by the shoulder, nudging him into the room before pressing his hand between his shoulder blades and shoving. Ezra stumbles but recovers, shooting daggers at Kostya as he looks back at him over his shoulder.

I move to the center of the room and turn to face Ezra. "Come. Kneel."

His forehead wrinkles as he surveys the space, noting Nikolai in the corner. Ezra's eyes linger on Nikolai as he slowly makes his way toward me. When Ezra decides to give me his attention, our eyes connect, blue meeting green, and I feel a pause.

I don't know how else to think of it.

It's a pause in existence.

Briefer than a moment, a quick beat of calmness, nothingness.

It's pleasant.

He lowers to his knees in front of me and I gasp because I truly expected his fight to return the moment Kostya brought him out of his room. His eyes are still locked on mine and when I go to look for it, I see it there, the fight in him. It hasn't gone completely, he's just hiding it away, biding his time.

That should scare me to know he's still got that hope that the fight is worthwhile because it means I'll struggle to control him. Instead, I find that I'm glad it's still there, that *he's* still there.

I'm thinking about him as if I know him.

We don't know each other.

"Eyes on the floor, *mal'chik*," I command and I'm grateful that he obeys. "I want to see you dance today. I want you to show me your best solo, let me get a sense of what you can do."

"Okay," he says slowly, and I can see his brow wrinkling in consideration.

"Can you dance in what you're wearing?"

I rake my eyes over the outfit he's chosen, unsurprisingly similar to what he wore when I first saw him a week ago. Ripped, faded, well-worn jeans and a simple black T-shirt with a logo for a band or something that I don't recognize. I want to ask him about it, though I'm not sure why. I have no idea what bands or movies or books are popular now. Three years is a long time, and I'm sure much of the outside world has changed, gone on without me.

He nods and mutters, "Yes."

"What kind of music do you need?"

He shrugs. "Anything is fine. I'll freestyle."

I scoff, "I want to see your best, not some random contemporary bullshit."

His head whips up to look at me. "It's not random bullshit, I know what the fuck I'm—"

I slap him.

Not because I want to.

Not because I would if we were alone together, though I certainly would have given him a verbal lashing all the same.

I hit him because Nikolai is watching, and he expects it.

Ezra's hand touches his cheek and his eyes burn green fire to ignite the air between us. My breath catches at the look, but I maintain my composure.

"If you're so sure of yourself, then I expect you to blow me away. Stand up and get ready. You dance when the music starts."

I steal a quick glance at Nikolai—a quick look for reassurance that he is pleased with my outburst to discipline. He tilts his head down, a subtle nod of approval, and I exhale.

I catch Ezra glaring at Nikolai when I look back down at him. But then he looks up at me. A shimmer of understanding dances between us and I feel it stir a long-forgotten feeling of connection, of attachment.

Though I wish I could explore this look a little longer, I know I can't.

I whip around Ezra and march across the dance floor, hoping my face isn't as visibly flushed as it feels. I cross to where Nikolai is perched on the piano bench. The stereo system is behind him, nestled into the wall.

I scroll through the selection of songs on the touchscreen to find something slow, dramatic, emotional. Something that will be fitting for him as a contemporary dancer.

Though I never cared to showcase my other partners in their own style, I feel a misplaced need to ensure I give Ezra the best shot to impress Nikolai.

I shouldn't care.

He'll be dancing in my style anyway. Ballet is what I've trained to dance since childhood and it's what Nikolai stole me away to do—to be his own personal ballerina. It's my job to train my partners to be the perfect complement for me in *my* style.

I don't understand the anxiety that overcomes me in hopes that Ezra isn't too weak to perform spectacularly, especially when I don't even know whether he is a spectacular dancer.

I find the song I'm looking for and turn back to see if Ezra is ready. He's standing, though he bends to remove his socks and shoes and moves to place them against the back wall of the room, beneath the barre. He blows out a shaky breath with his lips formed in an "O" shape.

He tilts his head from side to side, stretching his neck, and shakes out his hands and legs. A piece of dirty blonde hair from the longer strands on top of his head falls across his forehead. He brushes it out of his eyes with a flick of his wrist as he lifts his head, searching the room to find me.

I could never miss that green fervor from his eyes shining across the room at me. He gives me a small nod to indicate that he is ready for the music. It's such a normal look, a simple nonverbal communication, the most basic thing…yet it feels so profound.

I nod and he stills. Without looking away, I tap the screen where my finger hovers over the play button and the music gradually rolls in.

He's still looking at me.

He grasps the hem of his shirt and lifts, peeling it up and over his torso, exposing his chest.

And he's still looking at me.

He sways, a soft movement, a gentle rocking from side to side as he stands in the center of the dance floor, bare-chested, bare-footed, wearing only the jeans that are torn and frayed over one knee.

And he's still looking at me.

I shudder when he takes a step and glides right into a coupé turn, spinning three, four, five times with the toe of his left foot resting against his right ankle to form a triangle through his rotations. His balance is impeccable as he leaps out from the turn with impressive strength and height.

I'm already speechless with the first count of eight, and I can't tear my eyes away.

I've never enjoyed contemporary dance. It doesn't follow the strict rules of classical ballet that I thrive on. It takes liberties, breaks contracts, defies conventions.

But Ezra.

Ezra is…a word I can't think of.

Perhaps there isn't a single word for the way he dances.

Perhaps there are too many.

Powerful, graceful, dangerous, beautiful, reckless.

His use of the floor is brilliant. He alternates through turns and remarkable leaps, drawing a large oval around the room with the trail of his movement.

His leaps are the most impressive thing of all. I've seen dancers who can leap gracefully, and I've seen dancers who can leap powerfully. I've never seen one who could do both so exquisitely as this.

The way he twists and turns his lean muscle, dipping to the floor, tumbling over his shoulder, rising again only to spin and push out into another extraordinary leap.

I can't speak.

The song ends long before I think it should, though it still takes me too long to realize it. Ezra has ended his improvised performance like a warrior, kneeling on one knee, fist to the floor, chest heaving as he catches his breath, looking like Superman himself has fallen to the Earth. Every muscle in his chiseled frame is rigid in the picturesque pose.

He tosses his hair out of his face as he lifts his head and looks up. Sweat gives his skin a glossy sheen which emphasizes the enormity of the work he's just accomplished.

I'm stilled, astounded by his talent, and I feel something I haven't in a very long time.

Pure and simple attraction.

Nikolai pulls me from my daze as he rises to his feet from the bench in front of me. "Ezra Bell," his tone is light, unusually jovial, "you are truly incredible." He turns back to look at me. "Isn't he incredible, Anya?"

I swallow and clear my throat. "Yes. Yes, he is."

Ezra stands and he is fury wrapped in grace.

Nikolai claps twice as he walks to meet him on the dance floor. He stands beside Ezra, reaching one arm across his back to hold his shoulders in both hands as he guides him to walk over to where I stand.

I cross my arms over my chest as Nikolai moves him to stand directly in front of me. Ezra looks near hyperventilating with the way his chest heaves, but I can sense it's not from exhaustion from the dance. It's anger, it's defense, it's the spike of adrenaline that I've felt so many times myself when Nikolai comes too close.

"Your new partner is more talented than you," Nikolai says to me with a smile.

A sinful, horrid smile that stabs me in the heart.

My head tilts and my eyes narrow, but I immediately soften my expression, hoping Nikolai didn't see it falter.

"I think you will learn his style, Anya."

I swallow the line of questioning that claws its way up my throat, remembering being slammed into the mirror when I questioned him earlier.

I try to rephrase my questions in a manner of acceptance, but it comes out as utterances and stuttering. "I'm not…I'm not sure I understand…"

It's cold between us in a flash as Nikolai releases Ezra and takes a step toward me. Instinctively, I step back.

"Hey," Ezra shouts as Nikolai closes in on me.

"What don't you understand?" Nikolai asks as he steps in close, looming above me.

"It's always been ballet," I state boldly.

He reaches out to snatch me by the throat, yanking me toward him, and I whimper. "And your ballet performances have always failed to please me."

I can't look at Nikolai and it's not because it's terrifying to watch the evil wash over his face before he hurts me. I'm used to that. It's because I can see Ezra behind him, his eyes wide, nostrils flaring. His fingers flex and bend into tight fists at his sides and he sways in agitation. I try to command him with my eyes to back down. I shake my head to tell him no, but he can't see me through the flash of lightning that ignites his outrage.

I quickly make the leap from nonverbal signals to outright shouting as Ezra lunges for Nikolai.

"No!" I scream.

Ezra grabs Nikolai by his shoulders and pulls back hard. Thankfully, Nikolai releases me before Ezra whips him around and tosses him onto the floor. I jump away, moving my back against the wall, pressing against it as Ezra goes after him swinging. Nikolai turns his head just in time to avoid being punched. Ezra's fist lands hard on the floor beside Nikolai's head and he roars out a groan of frustration.

Nikolai rolls to the side, but Ezra manages to get on top of him and lands a punch to his gut before strong arms lift him away. Kostya is there, yanking Ezra back, who is still kicking and swinging. Seconds later, Ezra's body goes rigid, twitching and trembling from the electric shock of Kostya's stun gun that he's jammed into his side.

As Ezra falls to the ground, Nikolai rolls and jumps to his feet, walking in quick, long strides across the dance floor, his dress shoes clacking and reverberating off the walls, mixing with the sound of Ezra's groans.

He gathers a length of rope that we use with the pulley system on the ceiling, twisting one end around his open hand before grasping it tightly within his fist, a devilish sneer spread across his cheeks.

He comes up behind where Ezra has fallen and crouches down to his haunches above his head, leaning over him and placing the rope across his throat. Ezra coughs as Nikolai pulls the ends around behind his neck, twisting them together.

I squeak as I try to clamp down the scream rising through my chest, knowing that no matter what, I can't let Nikolai know that this affects me.

Nikolai cannot know that my insides are coiling and burning with the fear I feel, knowing that punishment is to come for Ezra.

I've never feared like this before, and I don't even fear for me.

Ezra's hands fly to his neck, clawing at the rope with wide eyes as

Nikolai tugs, heaving him backward, dragging him across the dance floor and toward the door.

I freeze, watching Ezra kick, listening to his strangled screams as he fights to get free. They disappear through the doorway and my heart kickstarts a new rhythm with the need to chase after him.

Not to chase after Nikolai.

To chase after Ezra.

I follow them out of the studio, watching as Nikolai wrenches Ezra by the rope around his throat in starts and stops, one long drag after the other. He does this all the way down the hall to the grand staircase.

I think that's when he'll stop, but he doesn't.

Nikolai steps backward onto the first step, then the second, and lifts on the coiled rope.

Ezra's eyes dart desperately around the room, but he knows he's helpless. He's already overexerted himself with the dance, given how little he's eaten over the past week, and that he's only just been removed from his room for the first time.

Nikolai makes it to the fifth step before he realizes he doesn't care to exert the effort it takes to drag him all the way up. He lets up on the rope enough to allow some slack.

"Roll over and crawl," he commands Ezra.

Ezra rolls to his side, flipping onto his hands and knees and crawls up the steps slowly, panting and breathless. Nikolai still holds the rope around his neck but pulls it from the side as if he was taking his dog for a walk on a leash. Ezra's chest heaves as he struggles to catch his breath.

My eyes burn hot as I follow behind Kostya, who follows behind Ezra with his stun gun out and ready.

It feels like it takes hours to ascend, watching the pain and struggle that Ezra faces in this maddening journey.

I don't know why it bothers me so.

Nikolai has treated all my partners this way. He's treated *me* this way for even longer. I've endured untold pain and punishment at his hand for years.

And still, this bothers me in a whole new way.

He forces Ezra to crawl all the way back to his room like this as he hisses and jeers at him. When we've all crossed the threshold into the bedroom,

Nikolai clamps the metal cuff to Ezra's ankle once again, solidly securing him.

As Ezra sits on the floor, leaning his back against the bedside, huffing and puffing and fighting to catch his breath, Nikolai lets loose.

CHAPTER 7
Anya

NIKOLAI WHIPS THE back of his hand and it lands with a solid thwack to Ezra's cheek. "You clearly don't know your place yet, *mal'chik*. Is this Anya's fault? Has she not done well enough to train you in your submission?"

Truthfully, I hadn't done anything to train him to submit to me. I had hoped leaving him locked up and alone, deprived of light and company and sustenance would be enough to gain his submission. It had worked well enough with the other boys.

Though I had been crueler to them, I suppose.

I didn't want to be as cruel to Ezra.

Mal'chik.

He's the boy.

Just the boy.

"No, no, no," Ezra holds up a palm to Nikolai. "She trained me," he lies. "She trained me well, it's not—"

Nikolai's body freezes in contempt. "Are you lying for her? For *her?*"

"I'm not, it's not her—" Ezra stammers

"Anya," Nikolai points to a spot on the floor beside where he stands, hovering over Ezra, "come."

I lengthen my neck and lift my chin, putting on an air of confidence that I don't feel an ounce of internally. I move to stand where he wants me.

A line slowly creeps along Nikolai's face as his lips stretch at one corner, tilting at the side to form a smirk that makes tingles crawl like spiders along my soul. I shudder from head to toe because I know the look. It's a look that only the Devil himself could make.

"Kostya, you may go," Nikolai commands and Kostya leaves us, shutting the door behind.

Oh, no.

No, no, no, no, no.

"*Moya rabynya*, look what you've done." Nikolai stands beside me and slides his hand up my spine until he catches the back of my neck, gripping me firmly.

"I've done only what is expected of me, *khozyain*. I promise you."

I dare a glance down at Ezra and immediately wish I hadn't. The look he gives me with fearful, wide eyes chisels away at the ice around my heart.

Nikolai is boiling in his hateful violence and its evaporating into rage-fueled lust. He is deviant in his desires, and I can see it happening now in the way it hazes over his features.

"You've made this man want to protect you. And he's only been here a week. How did you do this, Anya?" He laughs. "I know it's not your charm and gentle smile."

You made me charmless and joyless.

I don't respond as he presses his nose into my hair, dragging it upward along my cheek as he inhales me.

"You're foolish if you think making him fall for you will do you a service. He can't win with me. No one can. You know that better than anyone," he whispers against my cheek, his voice low and husky.

"I do know that," I assure him. "I'm not foolish."

"Perhaps not. Perhaps you've found a more effective and entertaining way to get him to obey you."

Entertaining?

"I don't mind his concern for you," he goes on. "It will make him more obedient, a more trustworthy partner, and it will make you a stronger dancer. Because of that, I will finally have the most talented slave."

Nikolai shifts to stand behind me, one large hand flattening against my belly. "I'm going to reward you for this, Anya. And I'm going to do it here so he understands that you are *mine*."

I press my eyes shut and breathe deeply. "I don't require a reward for doing my work."

"Don't be so humble. Besides, the reward isn't entirely for you. It's for him. To show him who you belong to. Now, tell him who you are."

"I am slave to the Mikhailov family. I am your belonging."

His hand slips upward and captures my breast, digging in with his fingers over my black leotard, making me whimper. Ezra jolts and manages to get to his knees but stops abruptly when Nikolai slaps my breast in response.

I flinch and lean back, away from his hand, but I can't move because he's right behind me, holding me in place. He grabs my nipple through the fabric and pinches me violently. My face scrunches against the ache and I hold back the groan that threatens to escape.

"Stop, *mal'chik*," I tell Ezra with as much level insistence as I can muster. "You will obey, you will *not* interfere. He is my master and he may do as he pleases with me."

I don't want Ezra to see this, I don't want to dampen his urge to fight, but I do want him to obey for my sake. I know better than to think that what Nikolai is about to do is a reward.

It's manipulation.

It's abuse.

I have to endure it and I will, but Ezra must obey and stay still. All he has to do is watch my torture, feign his submission to my will, and all will be well.

"Good," Nikolai encourages my mastery over Ezra and runs his free hand down the side of my hair, petting me, stroking down my side, down my belly, lower and lower. "Move the fabric aside for me."

The air shakes its way out of my lungs as I reach between my legs, catching the strip of fabric of my leotard that covers my sex and tugging it to the side beneath my wraparound skirt.

He widens his stance behind me to sink down as he dips his fingers between my legs. He curls around my back, a hot breath of filthy lust rushing out against my neck as he buries his face in the crook.

"Don't—" Ezra begins.

"Shut up, *mal'chik*. Be quiet and be still," I tell him.

My voice is sharp, but my eyes are soft as I silently plead with him not to say another word, not to move unless asked to, to obey without question or hesitation.

Because it will only hurt me more if he doesn't.

"You're going to come for me, *rabynya*," Nikolai demands and there's no air left in the room. "I'm not going to stop until you do, so make it happen if you don't want to be left raw and aching."

"*Da, khozyain.*"

I don't dare steal a glance at Ezra now. It's not the first time my master has violated me in the presence of a partner. But it's the first time I've felt so ashamed by it.

He toys with me, his fingers doing a dance along my entrance to find me dry as the desert. I close my eyes and try to remember the time in the bathroom, the time I came to Nikolai willingly, when he gave me pleasure without pain. I always cling to that memory when he wants me wet and ready for him. But it's not working, and I don't know why. My forehead pinches, straining against the new kind of shame I feel standing here like this in a way I've never felt before.

I can't fail now.

I can't fail at this.

I force myself to recall the way Nikolai kissed me in that memory, the way he held my face with need and devoured me with passion and humility. I tried to remember the way I felt after being lonely and finally connecting with him in a way that wasn't pain or torture, just pure pleasure.

Still, nothing.

"Get wet for me," he hisses against my ear and I hear the hint of frustration building.

The memory dissipates as panic rises up to erase it, hitting me hard over my heart. I put my hand there to feel it beating wildly with anxiety. My fingers brush Nikolai's still on my breast and when this happens, he mistakes it for wanting. His erection presses against my lower back and he hisses before forcing his fingers past the opening.

I whimper at the harshness of his calloused fingers forcing their way inside me dry, and I buck backward against him.

"Come on, Anya," he kisses along my neck, "get wet for me. Show this boy how you respond to me, show this boy what it takes a man to do."

My eyes flutter open in frustration as I try to rationalize my way through my sudden lack of response. I want this to be over, but it won't end until I come. I don't want to look, I try not to look at Ezra, but I know he's looking at me. I can feel his eyes on me, though I had hoped he would look away. I had hoped he would be too horrified or disgusted to look at me.

But I feel his stare.

My gaze slips and his eyes catch mine and I'm locked in beyond choice or reason. There's fear behind the green—and hatred, and shock, and even something more.

I think it's need.

I'm sure it's need when his bottom lip falls open and his breath catches.

"Oh," I breathe out.

I've found my desire in Ezra's green gaze.

Nikolai pulls his fingers back at my reaction, swirling around my clit, completely unaware that I'm watching Ezra watching me. As Ezra shifts uncomfortably, something stirs inside me, swirling with the touch of confident fingers, and somehow manages to turn me on.

I allow a small smile to touch the corners of my lips, so slight I imagine it's hardly perceptible as Nikolai draws arousal from me.

No, it's not Nikolai who draws it from me.

It's Ezra.

But it can't be Ezra.

He's my slave and my partner and nothing more.

I know nothing about this cocky, sarcastic, reckless boy who holds me in his stare.

But if that's true, then why does my body swell as he leans forward while he watches me?

Nikolai toys with me with his expert hands, circling around and around, and actually makes me feel…good.

The scene and the circumstance is lewd, my devilish master with his arms wrapped around me from behind, tugging down on the top of my leotard to expose my breast. He touches me until I'm sinking at the core, folding around his fingers as my body desperately urges me to seek release— whether I want it or not.

Inconceivably, I want it.

Nikolai leans me forward, bending me down to the bed beside Ezra's head and I put my hands down on the comforter to hold myself up. He holds my hip in one hand while the other continues its assault.

It's the same contradiction of feelings I always have with him. I want his fingers inside me, but I don't. I want to let go, for just that moment to feel like I don't have to be in complete control, but I don't. I want the pleasure, but I don't.

My arm blocks my face, breaking my eye contact with Ezra, but it doesn't feel broken, not entirely. I can still feel his stare burning into my skin, threatening to melt my icy core.

Nikolai hooks his fingers inside me, stroking against the spot that's sure to make me lose control. I'm overcome by the urge to fall into Ezra's lap, to unbutton his jeans, expose him, impale myself on him, and rock until I come undone.

Why Ezra?

Why is he in my mind?

The fantasy of him beneath me, still, quiet, letting me use him to get myself off swirls in my belly, clenching through my core, threatening to send me leaping off the edge. I'm panting and writhing against Nikolai's hand, feeling shameful, yet somehow powerful that he doesn't know I'm thinking of the boy beside me and not him.

Pleasure swells and I'm ready for it in a way I didn't even know was possible.

I want it.

I need it.

I'm just about to crest as I hear Ezra exhale beside me.

I whimper out a sound in my heated need.

But I don't peak.

Nikolai rips his fingers out, lets me go, slaps my ass, and sends me wobbling forward. I bend at the knees, falling to kneel beside Ezra on the floor as I whip my head to look at Nikolai over my shoulder.

"I didn't—"

"I know you didn't come. And you're not going to. Learn to control him without gaining his sympathy. You don't deserve any."

CHAPTER 8
Anya

MY HEART SINKS.

My breath catches in my throat.

A sob overcomes me, but I pull it back inside, swallowing it down.

Nikolai leaves us alone in Ezra's room and it takes me moments to catch my breath and regain control of myself.

Silent, sickening moments pass before I lift my forehead from the bed and sit back on my heels. I look down at the floor between my knees and the bed and place my palms flat against my thighs. I breathe in deeply through my nose, pushing air out through my mouth, over and over as I try to shake off the aching need between my legs.

If I were cruel, I could become a master like Nikolai. I could use the slave boy beside me and make him finish what Nikolai had started. But even the thought of such a thing makes me sick to my stomach. It puts perspective back into focus. Nikolai hadn't just brought me to the brink of pleasure, he used and abused me to make a point.

"Hey," Ezra says softly at my side.

I turn my head to look at him. "Don't," I say. "Don't speak. There's nothing you can say right now that will make things any better."

I get up off the floor and reach between my legs to adjust the fabric of my leotard to cover me again. I look over at Ezra and catch his eyes, looking where I'm exposed, then darting away quickly as I cover myself.

"Don't worry," I tell him. "I won't use you in that way."

He looks taken aback. "I wasn't thinking that."

I look at the bulge that's straining against his jeans and he shifts, trying to hide it. He pushes off the floor and moves to sit on the edge of the bed. It's curious that he's aroused, though I suppose it's not all that surprising. Perhaps all men are the same in their violent tastes.

I'm slowly shielding myself with each breath I draw, steeling myself to protect against further emotional pain. "I trust you understand your place now."

I untie, adjust, and rewrap the black chiffon dance skirt around my waist, taking a step back as Ezra climbs to his feet.

I don't fear him, but my eyes narrow, considering that Nikolai left me alone with an impulsive slave who hasn't been properly broken in enough to behave. He attacked Nikolai, after all, and I'm perplexed that Nikolai hasn't taken more care with my safety, at least in sending Kostya back to the room. Once my skirt is straight, I shake my head slowly and straighten to my full height.

"I remember who you are," Ezra says.

"Excuse me?"

"I remember you now. I've been trying to figure out where I know you from and I think I remember. You're Anya Antonov, the soloist from the New York City Ballet that went missing a few years ago."

I lift an eyebrow. "And what difference does it make?"

He shrugs. "It doesn't. It's just interesting."

"Interesting? Well, I'm glad my disappearance serves as entertainment for you."

"You were slated to be a principal dancer before you were twenty-five."

"I was, though that's not my life anymore."

"They called you a legendary talent in the news when you went missing." He pauses. "He kidnapped you?"

"Do you think I came here of my own free will?"

I feel like a liar when I say that. I didn't choose to come here, to be his slave, but I did get on that plane with him all the same when he offered an opportunity to excel in my craft.

How could I have known his intentions then?

"Jesus." He puts his hands behind his neck and the stretch of it emphasizes the broadness of his chest. "How long have you been here?"

"Three years," I tell him and wonder why I'm still here, rooted to the spot, having any sort of conversation with him.

I cross my arms over my chest when I should simply leave the room.

"Have you tried to escape?"

My head falls to the side and incredulity mars my tone. "Is that a serious question?"

A small smile tugs at his lips, though he's trying to hide it. I wonder what it is about me that amuses him so much.

"Where the hell are we?"

I sigh, thinking again that I should leave. Instead, I move backward and lower slowly to perch on the edge of the armchair. I need a moment to come down from this spoiled high anyway.

"I don't know exactly," I tell him honestly. "Somewhere in Russia, but nowhere near civilization."

"Russia." His brow wrinkles as he sits on the edge of the bed. "How have you survived here this long? With him?"

I look at him squarely. "All of my choices have been stripped from me except for one. Dance or die. I choose to dance. That's how I survive."

"He's impatient with you."

"He demands perfection and obedience. When he doesn't get it, it's my fault."

His head snaps sideways to look at me with narrowed eyes. "It's not your fault."

"Of course, it's not my fault. I'm not delusional, *mal'chik*. He hasn't brainwashed me." I narrow my eyes at him as I push to my feet. "I'm a slave. And so are you. Master is right, you need to learn your place."

"Do I?"

I march over and slap him without any conviction at all. "Get on your knees."

He places his hand on his cheek and looks up at me. "What will you do if I don't, Anya? Will you call him back in here? Tell him you can't train your slave? The slave who, in his own words, is more talented than you?"

I latch my small hand around the side of his neck and dig my fingers in before tugging him forward. He could easily pull out of my grip if he wanted to. My hands are tiny in comparison to his neck and broad shoulders. I consider it a win when he lets me drag him forward off the bed and he falls to his knees.

"You're in over your head here," I tell him. "You haven't even begun to comprehend how deep in shit you are."

His eyes are hard and soft all at once as he pleads, "Then *tell* me."

I don't want to tell him everything. It's too much and I don't trust him yet. I need to trust in his submission before I can tell him everything, before we can really begin to rehearse for our performance at the quarterly event. And we need to do that soon.

My shoulders slump and I try to breathe out some of the tension that's straining between us in favor of earning his understanding.

"I will tell you everything. Not now, not yet. First, I need to know that I have your submission, I need to see it."

"I'm literally on my knees in front of you. What the fuck else do you need to see?"

I lift an eyebrow. "I need to see that sarcastic attitude roll off your fucking shoulders. That would be a start."

He gives a gruff sigh. "Okay, *Master.*"

Now he's just being an asshole.

I step away from him and stride toward the door.

He calls after me, "Wait, don't leave me in here, please."

That simple plea tells me what I need to continue to do to break him into submission.

Isolation.

He wants to talk, to interact, to connect, so I'll put an end to that and go right back to the beginning.

"Enjoy your time alone, Ezra," I say.

I walk out, shut the door behind me, and lock it.

A few more days in isolation with minimal sustenance ought to do it.

I hope.

CHAPTER 9

Ezra

IT'S ONLY WHEN I feel like I'm starting to get used to the isolation that I start to fear I'm going insane. It feels like a century has gone by in this fucking awful green room, but I know it's only been a week. I know this because Anya brings me one meal each day and each tray has had a small torn piece of parchment with a number scribbled on it.

The first day there was a one, the second day a two, and so on.

The last meal was day seven.

Seven days with nothing more than a girl walking into my room, setting down a tray, and leaving me alone again.

The only connection I got from her was the scribbled numbers and some small gesture that reminded me of her humanity. Sometimes it was a look or the demure tuck of a strand of hair behind her ear. I think I even got a small smile of reassurance once, but I know I must have been dreaming it.

I actually *had* dreamt it one night, the first night she left me here alone. I felt shame at the dream because it was sexual in nature. My fucked-up brain had memorized the look on her face when she granted the smallest smile the day Nikolai fingered her right in front of me.

What Nikolai had done to her was a violation that made my shoulders tense and my muscles flex with the urge to hurt him. But whatever reaction her body was having to it was undeniably beautiful. And I felt sick for thinking that for even a moment. I felt even worse for dreaming about her pleasure. At least it was consensual in the dream. And it was with me.

I hear the locks turn the day after note number seven.

I climb off the bed where I'd been lying, looking up at the ceiling, and drop to my knees at the foot of the bed. I do this because it seems to please her. I do this because she wants my submission and my trust. I do this because I can't stand the isolation anymore, and I'm nearly willing to do anything for her just so she'll grant me the kindness of taking me out of this fucking room.

Maybe, just maybe, some part of me just wants to please her because I crave her approval in some fucked up way.

She enters and sees me there and though my head is bowed for her, I can see from my peripheral that she's pleased. Warmth spreads across my chest at the thought. As usual, she brings in the tray and sets it on the side table next to the armchair. I expect her to leave immediately, as she has been doing, but she surprises me this time.

Crossing the room, she comes to stand in front of me, then bends and lowers to her knees, mirroring my position. She puts soft fingertips under my chin and lifts my head so that we're nearly eye to eye. I'm taller than her so she's looking up at me.

I think I could deep dive in her blue eyes, get swept away in the hurricane. Her plump, pink lips curve into a smile and I can't help but smile back.

"Your submission pleases me, Ezra," she says.

I feel like I've just reincarnated from the life of a dog back to humanity.

She slowly leans forward. Her cheek grazes my cheek as she seeks my ear to share a whisper, a secret. I want to throw my arms around her and hold on for dear life when her touch ignites my need for connection, for affection.

"Just be sure the cuff goes back on before Nikolai comes into the room."

She stands as swiftly and as gracefully as she kneeled and walks to the door. She pulls it open but hesitates before she leaves. She turns her head over her shoulder and gives me a look. I don't really understand her expression, but her eyes meet mine and I feel relief for the brief moment of interaction in our gaze.

Goddamn, she's a beautiful powerhouse.

She leaves without another word and I'm held in place by that look.

After a minute, I remember how fucking hungry I am and go to the tray she left me. I sit on the floor with it and immediately look for the paper I expect to have the number eight on it, but it's not there.

Disappointment sinks my insides.

I pick up my spoon—she never gives me a fork or knife, regardless of the meal—and it hovers over the plate as frustration sets in.

How can I be so frustrated over a piece of paper with a number?

I know it's because that piece of paper with the number was the only real form of communication I've had over the past week. Its absence rips a weird sort of panic through my chest.

What if seven was the last note?

How will I track how long I've been here?

I search the tray again, frantic to know if perhaps I just missed it. I pick up the plate to look beneath it and my hands freeze mid-air, holding it above the tray. I blink and pause with what I find.

Beneath the plate is a small key.

'Just be sure the cuff goes back on,' she had said to me.

"Fuck," I mutter as I set the plate on the ground beside me and pick up the key.

I don't even take a second to think as I shift my cuffed leg out in front of me. I know right where the keyhole is. I've clawed at the damn thing often enough, trying to find a way to get it off me. I insert the key and twist it. It takes me a few tries, but eventually, it clicks and the cuff falls open.

"Holy shit," I say, jumping up off the floor.

My blood spikes with adrenaline as I run both my hands through the hair on top of my head. I spin with the energy it gives me and try to make sense of this.

She gave me a key.

A fucking key.

'Just be sure the cuff goes back on before Nikolai comes into the room.'

I bend down and pick up the key where I dropped it on the beige carpet. I look at it in my hand, then look at the door, wondering if it's the same key.

I rush to the door and insert the key in the bottom lock, turning it in a hurry. I nearly collapse when I turn it and it clicks. I quickly slide it into the next keyhole just above the first but when I try to turn it, my heart sinks.

It won't turn.

"Shit," I say into the void that is my room.

I try again, but it won't turn.

I try again.

Again.

Again.

And I'm gonna lose my shit if this fucking door won't open.

What is this?

Part of me thinks she's trying to give me hope just so she can yank the rug from beneath my feet. Perhaps the key really was just meant to free me from the bed chain and nothing more. She had told me to put it back on before Nikolai comes, though I have no idea when he's coming.

But why would she do that?

I'm so agitated from the adrenaline and the hope I had that I decide I'm getting this fucking door open. Without thinking, I grasp the doorknob and turn, ready to pull with all my might. I yank back hard and tumble backward onto my ass.

It opened.

The door opened.

The second lock wasn't latched in the first place.

I'm so shocked that I immediately jump up and push it closed again. Then I realize what I've done, worried it will somehow lock automatically, and I quickly yank it open again.

Sweet baby Jesus.

The door is open and I'm not chained. I can leave this stupid room.

I lean my head around the doorframe to peek out into the hallway and find that it's empty. I reluctantly pull myself back inside the room and take a deep breath, knowing that I should take a beat to think this through. My muscles are twitching and jumping, pulsing with each heartbeat with the message to run, run, *run.*

I don't think about an escape plan, I just move.

I creep out into the hallway, tiptoeing past the rows of closed doors. When I come to the end of the hallway, I stop. I can see outward toward the edge of the grand staircase and clearly see all the way across its vast opening to the opposite side of the manor and to a hallway beyond it. I prepare myself with a deep breath and then stealthily move toward the staircase.

I stay alert, looking everywhere, all around me, watching for movement and ready to pounce on the defensive if anyone comes after me.

I have to get the fuck out of here.

No matter what I have to do.

I reach the top of the staircase and I'm about to take off down it, intent for the exit. But when my foot lands on the first step, I'm halted as the memory of soft fingers lifting my chin and sapphire eyes meeting mine floods my sensibility.

I can't leave her here.

She's as much a victim as I am.

She's more of a victim really.

I need to rescue her.

But where the fuck do I find her?

This estate is huge and I've only been in two rooms. Mine and the dance studio.

I step backward, back onto the landing, thinking her room must be somewhere on this level, perhaps on the opposite side. Bravely—or perhaps, stupidly—I head toward the far hallway, opposite the way I came.

I creep down the hall, walking softly, staying close to one side of the wall. I have no idea what the fuck I'm doing or why I'm going to find this girl instead of getting the fuck out of here.

I just know I can't leave without her.

CHAPTER 10
Ezra

"MAL'CHIK," ANYA'S VOICE comes from behind me in a sharp whisper.

I'm startled, nearly jumping out of my skin. I unintentionally take a swing at her as I spin to face her, but thankfully, she ducks just in time.

"Jesus," I say quickly. "Come on, come with me, let's get the fuck out of here."

Her forehead is wrinkled, her blue eyes piercing. She looks down and reaches forward to grasp my hand. Her touch is ice melting my fire.

"Come with me," she demands, spinning me back around and pulling me after her down the hallway.

We pass two doors and come upon a third. She pushes it open, pulling me inside. She releases me just beyond the threshold and slams the door shut behind us.

"What the fuck are you doing?" she demands. "How did you get out of the room?"

"How did I get out of the…" I'm confused. "I found the key you left me. I came to find you so I can get us the hell out of here."

Her expression is taut and she bites her lip in agitation. "The key was for the cuff and I told you to put it back on before Nikolai comes to your room. How the hell did you get out of the room?"

I tilt my head. "I used the key. How the fuck do you think I got out?"

"But it only unlocks the…" Her eyebrows lift suddenly, widening her eyes, and her hand slaps over her mouth. "Oh, my God. I didn't lock it." She spins away and paces a few steps before whipping back around to look at me pointedly. "I forgot to lock the door."

Anya's hand drops to her chest and she swallows hard.

"You forgot?"

"I forgot. Oh, God. Ezra, I'm—"

Her voice catches and I see her chest rise and fall rapidly. In my adrenaline-spiked state, I'm tuned in and aware, and I can practically hear the air going in and out of her mouth as she slumps backward against the closed door.

She didn't mean for me to escape.

She was just trying to give me the comfort of removing my ankle cuff.

I should be angry at the realization but seeing her panic over a mistake that could be costly to her softens me. It slows my rushing pulse. It makes me step back from the ledge. It makes me feel overcome with the need to comfort her.

"Hey," I say, taking a slow step toward her.

She slides down the door gradually until she's slumped on the floor.

"Anya, it's okay. Listen. I'm out now and I can get you out of here, okay?" I try to reassure her. "I wasn't going to leave without you."

She looks up at me with a furrowed brow. "You came for me?"

There's so much confusion and misunderstanding behind her blue eyes and all I want to do is make sure she knows I'm telling the truth. I should be getting her ass up and dragging her out of here before someone realizes I'm gone, but the privilege of staring into the haunting clarity of her eyes is challenging all my instincts.

I nod. "Of course I came for you. We've got a better chance together than we do alone."

That's when she blinks and turns her head away, hiding behind her icy shell. She pushes to her feet.

"I need to take you back to your room. Before Nikolai knows what happened. And you can't tell him about this. Do you understand? You can't ever tell him."

I snap, "Anya. Are you out of your fucking mind? I'm not going back in there. We're getting the fuck out of here. *Now*." I grab her hand and then the doorknob.

She leaps in front of me, slamming her back against the door between us to keep it shut. I let go of the doorknob, but her hand is still in mine.

"*No*," she insists. "There is no getting the fuck out of here."

I step toward her. "What the hell do you mean? Let's *go*."

We're chest to chest against the door and she's not budging. "Ezra, listen to me. There is no escape. You can walk out the front door right now if you want, but you won't make it a mile past the tree line."

I huff, looking down at her.

"There are wolves in the forest. He feeds them, draws them closer to the manor. Even if that wasn't a concern, the forest stretches for God knows how far, and it's dense. Overwhelming and disorienting. I know because I escaped once. I was lucky that Nikolai came after me. I wouldn't have survived another hour lost in that freezing forest if he hadn't found me. There is *no escape*."

That's enough to give me pause and the pause makes me realize how close we're standing to one another. I take a small step back as the realization makes my ab muscles clench in a way that I don't want them to clench for her. I drop her hand and turn, pacing away from her a few steps.

"So, you've escaped before and didn't make it."

"It was a hopeless, useless attempt. I just didn't know better. I don't want you to make the same mistake of thinking there's any hope at all of making it out of here alive."

I whip around to look at her. "That's bullshit. There's always hope."

"You're wrong. Here, there's only survival and you have to follow the rules if you want that. I spent a lot of time and energy trying to believe something different."

She pushes away from the door and steps forward, brushing past me to cross to an ornate dresser against the far wall, on the opposite side of her meticulously made bed. She bends to pull open a drawer at the bottom. She takes out a small cardboard box, about the size of a shoebox, though it's covered in a pink and green floral print. Soft pink roses, I notice, and think it seems so perfectly fitting for her.

Soft and pretty and blooming, protected by unyielding thorns.

She turns to face me, holding it in her arms as though it's a puppy or a child that needs to be tended to with care. We both walk toward one another and meet at the end of her queen-sized bed. She lifts the lid, flipping it over onto the mattress.

"Photos?"

She nods, carefully pulling the photo at the very end of the neatly lined row out of the box. She holds it up to me, showing me a picture of a young girl, probably in her early teens. She's sitting on a city stoop, looking down at a cell phone in her hands. I realize her features are similar to Anya's as I look up at her face then back down at the photo. The girl's hair is brown, but a little more golden than Anya's, and shorter.

"Is she family?" I ask and she nods.

"My sister. Lidia. She was fourteen here. Turn it over."

I flip the photo over and find scribbling on the back.

Two numbers.

Fourteen and thirty-five.

"This is the first picture Nikolai brought me when I arrived here at Mikhailov Manor. Lidia was fourteen years old at the time. I had only just turned twenty-one."

"What's thirty-five?"

"Thirty-five yards," she says.

She takes the picture from me and puts it back inside the box. She plucks the photo from the front end of the row and shows it to me.

"This is from last week. She's seventeen now. Her eighteenth birthday will be in a few months."

I look over at Anya and see the small curve of a smile on her lips. But then she frowns as she flips it over.

Again, two numbers.

Seventeen and fifty.

"Fifty yards. It's the scope measurement from a rifle trained on her when they took the photograph. I get one picture a week. Every year for the past three years."

I'm speechless.

She hands me the photograph and paces away, crossing her arms over her chest. I briefly thumb through some of the other photographs in the large stack, careful not to disturb her carefully ordered row.

"Nikolai's reach is vast, Ezra." She lowers to sit on a cream-colored ottoman near the corner window and I'm momentarily distracted by the sunlight behind her. "If I could somehow even manage to survive the wilderness and find a way back to the real world, it wouldn't matter. She'd be dead within the week. Or worse."

"What's worse than death?"

She lifts her head and meets my eyes. "This."

An eerie prickle creeps along my spine in understanding. What I've endured over the past couple of weeks pales in comparison to the hell she's been put through. I saw first-hand what Nikolai has done to her, the violation of his fingers twisting inside her. There's no telling what he had to do before that to break her, to break a woman like Anya, who is obviously so strong.

The thought of it nauseates me and provokes some weird caveman compulsion that makes me feel fiercely protective of her. I set down the photo and go to her, crouching on my haunches in front of her. Her eyes widen at my bold presence and she sits a bit straighter to pull away from me, though I don't budge.

"We have to work together, okay? If we work together, we can figure a way out of this."

"You're not hearing me. There is no way out of this. It's not just Nikolai. It's an entire empire that reaches across the globe."

"What kind of empire?"

She sighs. "The Mikhailovs are in the business of stealing and selling."

"What, like drugs? Weapons?"

She shakes her head. "No. People."

"You're telling me they're selling people?"

"Yes." She nods. "He knows what he's doing. He knows how to keep us here. He knows how to control us."

I give her a small, tilted smile. "Well, the joke's on him. I don't have any family he can hold me hostage with."

She sighs and her shoulders slump, the movement swaying her toward me. I swear I can feel her soul push against mine.

"It doesn't matter. You can't leave. Neither can I. All we can do is survive."

"And how do we do that? Play by his stupid fucking rules?"

"Yes."

I shake my head. "I don't think I can do that."

She leans all the way forward and grabs my face in both hands. "You have to, Ezra. You *have* to."

I know just how fucked I am when she touches me, when I see the tears of desperation glass over her eyes as she pleads with me. She's the kind of girl a guy like me has a hard time saying no to. I don't want to say no to her. I have the fleeting thought that I wish I knew what she was like in the real world, and I feel my heart tug tight against my chest.

"Okay," I say. "Okay, I get it. But if I put my trust in you that this is what we need to do, I want you to know that puts you on the line. That makes you responsible for my well-being."

A flicker of acknowledgement then acceptance crosses her eyes, and I know she understands me with the way it twists in my gut.

"I know. I just need you to follow the rules. It's less painful for me when you do." She lets her hands fall away from my face and they briefly land on my knees before falling away entirely. "I have to take you back to your room. I have to lock you in before he finds you. You're not allowed to be here, especially without Kostya."

I shake my head. "I can't. I can't go back there."

"You have to. There's no other choice. But I swear, I won't leave you there, okay? We just need to convince Nikolai that I've broken you. That you kneel for me now. If we can convince him of that, then you'll have more freedom in the house."

I put my hands on my knees and push up to stand, lacing my fingers together on the top of my head as I spin and pace. I feel her coming up behind me and I drop my hands to my sides, spinning to face her. Her fingers graze mine as she reaches to hold my hand and I snatch both of hers in mine, desperately craving the small moment of affection.

"I know it's hard," she says softly, "I know. He kept me in isolation for months when he brought me here."

She survived this for months?

If she could get through it for months, I could certainly manage a little while longer.

I sigh and before I even understand why I'm doing it, I step forward and wrap my arms around her petite frame, pulling her into a hug. She doesn't recoil and I'm thankful for that, though I can sense she doesn't know how to respond.

I'm immediately aware of the fact that I haven't showered in a week, other than to splash some water on the most important parts of my body from the faucet in my bathroom. I wish I smelled better for her, and that seems like a petty fucking thought in all this.

I inhale the scent at the top of her head. It's floral and fragrant and bursting with life. It's the scent of fresh cut roses and I can't stop myself from kissing the top of her head. That chaste kiss is what melts her and she presses into me, slipping her arms through mine to wrap around my waist. She lets her head rest against my chest and all I can think of is standing here and holding her.

I really, honestly don't want to let her go.

But the startling sound of the door clicking open kickstarts my heart to get ready to fight for my life, to fight for her life, to fight for *our* lives.

CHAPTER 11

Anya

ONE MOMENT WARM arms encapsulate me, and the next, they're shoving me away. The click of the door startles us both. Just when I think things are going to be okay, that I've gotten through to Ezra, that he understands why we have to play by the rules and submit to survive, it all comes crashing heavy upon our heads.

I fully expect that Ezra will jump into action and rush the door, but I hadn't expected him to do this. He pushes me out of his embrace, farther back into the room, then spins lightning fast and steps forward toward the door, standing protectively between me and the oncoming threat.

I have a moment of hope, dangerous flashing hope, that it's only Kostya coming into my room. But Kostya always knocks and he only comes to collect me when Nikolai calls for me. I know it's Nikolai before I even see him.

"Ezra," I warn, fully expecting to see him launch himself at Nikolai on the attack.

Instead, Ezra steps backward, holding a hand behind him, as if the palm of his outstretched arm could form a protective shield around me. No one, not one of the three men before him, would have done that for me.

My heart skips across an unwilling beat.

Nikolai is seething at the door, though he has yet to cross the threshold. His fingers roll methodically into fists at his sides.

What do I do?

What the hell do I do?

There's only one thing I can think of.

"On your knees, *mal'chik*," I say to Ezra, hoping he'll know, praying he'll understand.

He glances back at me, but it's quick, and then he's watching Nikolai again, bouncing with feral energy.

"*Mal'chik*," I snap at him through gnashed teeth.

He looks at me and I think he sees the meaning in my stare. I think he

81

understands that we have to pretend this is nothing more than me training my slave.

I'll be punished for this regardless.

Nikolai has found me alone in my room with the boy.

But I may be able to lessen the severity of the consequence—at the very least, for Ezra's sake—if we can convince him that this is nothing but bad judgment on my part.

Gradually, thankfully, Ezra comes into understanding. There's a slight bob to his head and he nods to me, lowering to his knees. It's slow movement, his body is rigid with tension and ready to jump back up on a dime if this turns into a fight.

I need him to see that it can't always be a fight.

It only makes things worse.

It only gives Nikolai a reason to punish us.

I slip deep within the borders of my soul to guard myself as I find my shield and step forward courageously, moving in between Ezra and Nikolai. Ezra's agitation is so visceral, it's as if I can feel his pulse through my own, and that connection is unnerving, unsteadying.

I lower to kneel in front of Nikolai, bowing my head in contrition.

"I'm sorry. I know I'm not supposed to bring him to my room. I wanted to show him the photographs of Lidia. I wanted to make him understand."

"Quiet, *rabynya*," he snaps, "Come with me, both of you."

He's growling, practically salivating in territorial possession, reminiscent of the night I once tried to escape and found myself face to face with a snarling gray wolf.

There are wolves outside but an equally dangerous one within, and I'm currently his prey.

I rise to my feet. "*Da, khozyain*," I turn my head toward Ezra. "Come, *mal'chik.*"

His brow furrows, but somehow, he manages to get control of his questioning expression. With a shake of his head, he gets to his feet with a clenched jaw.

Nikolai leads us both out of the room, down the hall toward the grand staircase. My heart thumps wildly against my ribs as I open my stride to keep up with his long steps.

I don't know what he's thinking.

He's silent as we walk, and that's more terrifying to me than if he were to yell and scream and throw me against the wall and hurt me.

There's feral, male energy all around me, one pulsing with ill-intent, the other with ferocious goodness. It's overwhelming the way that it ropes its way around and tugs at me from both sides.

Nikolai nearly runs down the grand staircase and I quickly follow behind, not looking back, simply hoping that Ezra is keeping up and following as he's supposed to. Any step out of line from Ezra right now will only make whatever the hell we're heading toward worse, likely for me.

Nikolai reaches the bottom of the staircase several steps ahead and stops beside Kostya, who is already standing there in wait. He spins around to face us as we chase toward him.

When my foot falls onto the landing, Nikolai snaps, grabbing me by the scruff of my neck. I shriek and my shoulders instantly tense as his heavy hand pushes down on the back of my neck. I know immediately he wants me on the ground, but my body still pushes back against the force.

He bends down as he pushes harder, hissing against my ear, "Crawl, *rabynya*."

I respond to his command and slump to my knees on the hard marble, catching myself on my hands as he releases me with a flick of his wrist that tosses my weight forward. Nikolai walks again, striding forward with the confident steps of a shrewd businessman on his way to roll heads. The click of his sleek dress shoes across the marble reverberates in my bones as I follow him on my hands and knees.

I feel Ezra moving faster toward me and I see him coming up along my side.

"Behind me," I insist. "Don't make this worse."

"Fuck!" The tremble in his voice ripples over my skin.

His voice is tinged with agitation and fear. Thankfully, he falls back in line, though I can see him twitch with frantic, nervous energy.

I know Ezra isn't accustomed to this sort of behavior, but I wish he would come to terms with our circumstances faster. His concern makes this feel so much worse, in a truly unique and thoroughly revolting manner.

Nikolai has already traversed the small hallway that leads to the dance studio and stands in the doorway, glaring at me. I move across the floor as swiftly as I can, flinching at the way the unforgiving marble slams into my kneecaps with every motion.

All I'm wearing are cotton shorts and a well-worn, off the shoulder sweatshirt. Because my legs are bare, the coldness and the hardness of the floor is jarring as my bones knock against it, one knee, then the other, over and over.

Nikolai has moved well inside the studio by the time I make it to the threshold. I keep going, wondering if Ezra might actually explode from the pent-up rage he's barely keeping under wraps. He's practically dancing with the constant movement, with the jolts and twitches that scream so loudly that he wants to fight.

Once I reach the center of the dance floor where Nikolai stands waiting, his foot comes down on the small of my back and slams me down flat to the floor. I turn my head just in time for my cheek to press into the cold floor, my arms and legs sprawling, as the air is forced out of me in a rushed groan.

"You fucker!" Ezra screams. "Get off me!" And I know Kostya is holding him back.

"*Mal'chik.* Please," I barely whisper, filled with sadness, a quiet plea into the empty space and I don't even know if he can hear me.

"You're failing, Anya," Nikolai says to me. "I don't believe for a second you brought him to your room just to show him photographs. You like him. You want him. You're trying to use him for yourself and neglecting your task of training him to perform for *me.*"

"No, I swear...I promise you, I was just trying to show him why...why he can't keep fighting me, trying to escape."

His foot abruptly lifts. "Get up."

I jump to my feet in a hurry and turn to face him.

"Get rope. Tie his hands together."

"*Khozyain*, please, it's not his—"

I stop myself from finishing that sentence.

Why am I defending Ezra?

It's his fault we're in this mess in the first place.

Except...I forgot to lock the door.

It's my fault.

Nikolai's head cocks to the side. "Are you trying to prove my point? You never hesitated to bind a partner in the past."

I shake my head quickly and take a step back. "No, I'm sorry."

I turn and rush off to the corner to gather a length of rope. I take it to where Ezra stands, now with Kostya forming a human barrier between him and Nikolai. His legs are wide, his hands clenching and unclenching, chest pumping with rapid breaths. I slip between Ezra and Kostya and stand in front of him.

"Put your hands in front of you, *mal'chik*," I tell him.

He huffs, overwhelming me with the runoff stream of his adrenaline sweeping all around me. He does as he's told, but his arms twitch and his hands shake. As I start to wind the length of coarse rope around his wrists, I intentionally let my fingers graze his knuckles, praying he can feel my regret for stamping down his hope so effectively.

I twist and turn and coil and bind with practiced mastery. Nikolai is an expert in the art of binding, and he's passed all his knowledge on to me. It's knowledge I wish I didn't possess. When I'm convinced that Ezra is bound to Nikolai's satisfaction, that he's bound in a way that he won't be able to escape without assistance, I step back, bow my head, and wait.

The *click, click, click* of Nikolai's shoes across the dance floor is like a slow ticking clock, counting down the seconds of the oncoming punishment. When I finally feel Nikolai's presence at my back, like a whoosh of arctic air through a door being thrown open during a winter storm, I shiver from head to toe.

"Put your arms behind your back," he says.

No.

No.

No, no, no.

"Please, no, please," I beg unashamedly because I know what he's going to do.

He fists my hair and yanks my head back harshly, forcing me to stare up at the ceiling.

"I'm not asking, *rabynya*, I'm telling."

I swallow and breathe, in and out, closing my eyes to try to find my center. It's shifting and wobbling off course. I bring my shaking hands behind me and try to convince myself that everything is going to be okay.

Nothing is okay, but I have to pretend in order to survive.

Nikolai releases my hair and my head drops forward. I'm caught by green before me. Green eyes that remind me of thriving, vibrant life. Green eyes that throb with radiant energy.

As Nikolai secures my wrists behind my back, I let myself live there in the green because it's the only color that I have to cling to in this overcast, gray, shadow-filled, onrushing punishment.

Nikolai moves to our sides and looks back and forth between the two of us.

"You are both heading for a world of pain if you continue to misbehave like this. You have one job and one job only and that is to fucking dance."

"I think there's a problem then, boss. I haven't gotten paid for this job yet," Ezra says, his voice is flowing magma, hot and wild.

He turns his head, disrupting his eye contact with me in favor of squaring off with Nikolai. "And your benefits plan really fucking sucks."

I sigh and the exhale is filled with a mixture of exasperation, dread, pride, and perhaps, a bit of humor.

Nikolai takes a step toward him, his chest nearly pressed into Ezra's shoulder at his side. "I'm curious..." he begins with a smirk. "How is it possible that Anya has yet to wipe you clean of your arrogance? Her own should have outmatched yours by now."

"I'm not arrogant," Ezra insists, and I wish he would just shut the fuck up.

Every word he utters will add time to the punishment to come.

"Oh, yes, you are. I'm just surprised she hasn't crushed your spirit yet. She did so well with the others."

I see Ezra's face tick at this remark, as if considering something he hadn't before.

"I'm unbreakable," Ezra replies.

Oh, God.

I wish he hadn't said that.

I wish, I wish, I wish he hadn't said that.

Nikolai speaks low and harshly, "Perhaps you are. But I know she is not. Come."

He turns on the spot and walks briskly out of the room. I shake my head at Ezra and his face drops, probably at the recognition of surging fear in my expression. He doesn't know what is to come, but I do. I know and I wish I didn't because knowing makes it that much worse.

I don't wait to make sure Ezra follows behind me as I trail after Nikolai. Kostya will drag him along with the threat of his stun gun if he doesn't cooperate.

Two-and-a-half years ago was the second time I received this punishment. I remember freezing in fear the moment he tied my hands behind my back just like this. I was unwilling and unable to move when he told me to follow after him because I'd experienced this punishment for the first time just weeks before.

I had known the horror that was coming and the fear of it rooted me to the spot. My stubbornness and fear had ultimately only made the second punishment worse—he kept me in longer and it took longer to bring me back. So now, I follow him immediately, hoping my acceptance will make it easier.

If only Ezra will keep his mouth shut, then maybe it won't be so bad.

I look down at the floor as we walk, crossing the estate to the east wing, still on the first level. Walking past the grand staircase, we enter the garden corridor. We're still indoors, but tall, rectangular windows are carved into the dark stone walls every few feet, reaching high above us, the stone curving above to form an archway overhead.

If there was sunlight and life at Mikhailov Manor, it would shine through here, it would bring light into this dark, dark residence. But its perpetual winter, perpetual gray, perpetual cold, perpetual darkness.

We pass through the corridor and veer left, walking down two steps that fall onto a cracked stone-paved landing. This area of the home is a more recent addition, more modern than some of the other parts of the manor which still held their historical décor.

We're standing in an alcove that feels more like a cave, intentionally designed that way. The light from the garden corridor fades back into darkness here, save for the recessed lighting in the stone overhead. The walls are rough, made to look like the rocky interior of a grand cavern, and it's humid, surrounding us with an overwhelming dampness. To me, it's a stony secret passage, a hidden gate that leads to the depths of the underworld.

This alcove serves as the gateway to a steam room that no one uses anymore toward our right. But we'll be going left, in through the single glass door cut into the cave-like wall that leads to the indoor pool.

This is where reality strikes.

This is where my body reacts.

This is where I step backward, lose control, and tell him no.

"No, no, please, *moy khozyain*, I can't…"

"Anya." Ezra sounds as though fear has washed away his reckless energy.

Nikolai comes after me. "Yes, *rabynya*, yes." He snatches me by the elbow, dragging me forward.

I don't fight him, but I resist. I know it's going to happen whether I want it to or not, and though I wish I could be more dignified, more graceful about accepting my fate, my human instinct refuses to let me.

A stirring panic swirls in my chest, pulling into a dense ball that rolls around my ribcage as it lights on fire. It's like a dense star burning bright in a flash of light, then dying, collapsing, becoming a black hole that pulls my entire life force into that single dark space.

Nikolai pulls the glass door open with one hand, dragging me from the elbow with the other as I try to pull away from him.

"No! No, no, no. *Moy khozyain…*" I beg. "*Moy khozyain*, please. I'm sorry, I'll do better. I'll be better, I promise."

I hear how pathetic I sound, yet I'm powerless to stop it—that black hole in my chest is pulling and changing me, taking away my control, altering the way I react.

He shoves me past the door, then Kostya forces Ezra behind me before letting it drift shut. I back away until I hit the side wall and can't go any farther. I keep my eyes locked on Nikolai, suddenly instinctive and defensive like the prey he's made me become.

I can feel Ezra's eyes on me.

I can hear him yelling.

I can sense him struggling.

I can see Kostya tying Ezra's bound hands to a towel bar that's bolted into the sturdy wall.

I know all these things are happening, but my conscious is shutting down in my panic. My lungs are working double time, my breaths quickening, and tears singe my eyes, knowing that soon I won't be able to breathe at all.

Nikolai is coming after me now.

I'll be under the water soon.

I'll be entirely breathless soon.

I'll be dead soon.

CHAPTER 12
Anya

NIKOLAI'S HAND FIRMLY wraps around my upper arm and I scream. I scream so loudly and so sharply that everything else in the room stills.

Nikolai stills.

Kostya stills.

Ezra stills.

The smell of the chlorine wafting in the air even feels exceptionally stagnant for an extra beat.

But when that beat passes, everything shifts back into focus. It's a new tilted perspective, but a true one. I can see all too clearly what's happening to me.

Nikolai walks, pulling me along, moving us both toward the rectangular pool. He stops us at the steps, using his toes to kick off his shoes but doesn't dare let go of me.

If he let go of me, I would crumble.

Everything in my body is telling me to fall, to crumple to the floor, curl up into a tiny ball, a tiny, nonexistent ball that evades all attention. I wish to be as small and unremarkable as a stone on a walkway, something Nikolai could walk right past and forget about.

Instead, I feel like a boulder he's stubbed his toe on, the boulder he's now kicking back at in useless frustration, as if kicking me will ease his annoyance.

Kicking me isn't enough to satisfy him, though. He wants to roll me off the cliff's edge, drop me into the ocean, and watch me sink heavily to the bottom.

He drags me to the stairs that descend into the shallow end of the pool and we both step down. My sneakers soak up the water, making my feet instantly feel heavier. He fists the railing with his free hand, using it to pull himself. His other hand pulls me, while I pull back.

I'm facing away from him, jerking in the opposite direction with all my might. His hand slips purposefully down my arm, falling to the rope that binds my wrists at my back and grasps it tightly, using it to keep a firm grip on me. I'm still fighting him on the second step down as he drops onto the pool floor. With one sharp tug, he heaves me backward and I slip into the water, nearly drifting onto my back as it catches my fall from the steps.

I right myself quickly, springing up to press my feet against the blue, mosaic-tiled floor. My hair is heavy at my back, dipped wet at the ends.

Every scream and shout I make in protest echoes off the walls, bouncing back in a haunting chant as if a dozen of me were yelling out their torment all at once.

Nikolai pulls me in front of him and our eyes catch. I beg him with mine, but his are unyielding. He's intent on punishing me. I hardly even remember what for now.

It doesn't matter.

He wants to hurt me and so he will.

My soggy clothes hang heavy on my body. The off-shoulder gray sweatshirt pulls me, drags me, encourages me to succumb to the water and sink to relieve the weight of it.

My whole body is trembling uncontrollably now. My bones feel like they've been wrapped in winter air and every part of me shakes.

Nikolai grips both of my shoulders painfully, his fingers bruising. His head snaps up to look behind me just before he spins me around, forcing me to face Ezra. He stands poolside above us with his arms secured to a towel bar on the wall that's level with his chest.

I make a mistake.

I look at Ezra.

I see his horrified expression and I *feel* it inside my chest.

I feel his fear, his pain, his terror swirling with mine, and it's more painful than any feeling of horror Nikolai has ever managed to pluck out of me himself.

"This is what you need to understand, Mr. Bell," Nikolai's voice bellows, echoing in the wide, open space. "Anya is mine. If you try to win her heart, play on her sympathies, you both will lose. This is what you will get."

I feel the curl of his fingertips around my shoulders, the grip of his hands as he tightens his hold. My pulse quickens, knowing it's happening before I can react to it consciously, logically. All reason slips my mind in fear as Nikolai's weight shifts over my shoulders. I open my mouth to scream instead of taking a breath like I should have and then he's pushing me down.

Ezra strangles out a horrified scream and then his sound fades into a whoosh, a rumbling void that soaks up our shouting and washes them away. Tepid water rushes into my nostrils and I snap my mouth shut to create a barrier the only way I can.

I'm buried beneath the surface now, only its water that holds me in my grave instead of soil.

I don't immediately fight. Although I knew it was coming, it still takes me by surprise. The shift from air to water is entirely bewildering. It takes me a few seconds after the initial shock to remember what's happening, where I am, who's holding me down.

My knees are on the tile floor. All I want is to break free from Nikolai and get to the surface. I lean forward and drop my body down to the pool floor, using the way he pushes down on me as leverage to go deeper. I flatten my body and roll, facing the surface above me. Nikolai's hands have lost their grip and fallen away.

I thrash and kick and rise above the break as Nikolai rushes for me. I manage to stand, but it's only just long enough to take in a deep breath, only just long enough to hear the echoes of Ezra's distress for me bouncing off the walls.

Nikolai wraps his arms around my midsection and my soaked, heavy hair whips around my face, strands covering my mouth and nose. He spins me fast in his hold, this time grabbing the ropes around my wrists with one hand and grasping the back of my neck painfully tight with the other.

He bends me forward at the waist, forcing my face into the water, pushing me down beneath the surface, drowning me again. I squirm, throwing every ounce of energy I have into fighting him.

But I'm failing.

He's got a hold on me and no matter what I do, there is no getting away from him now.

The adrenaline in my body fights with my experience. It tells my brain to fight, though experience knows there is no point. Experience knows that Nikolai won't let up. Experience knows that I've drowned in this pool before.

Experience knows I'm going to die here again.

Going against every physical instinct, I force myself to still. I let him hold me under the water and I start to count.

One. Two. Three. Four. Five. Six. Seven. Eight.

One. Two. Three. Four. Five. Six. Seven. Eight

One. Two. Three. Four. Five. Six. Seven. Eight.

I know—because I've been here before—that I can make it to twelve counts of eight.

Nikolai's grip on me hasn't lessened, though I've essentially stopped fighting him. My body still ticks and thrashes every few moments, a natural physical reflex to get me out of harm's way, but I'm aware that's not possible.

I open my eyes as I continue to count. My hair floats and drifts around me in waves that look nearly black in their saturated state. As the water stills around me, I can almost make out the words being spoken and shouted above the surface, though not quite. I hear shouting, yelling. I think I hear a clanging sound, and I wonder if Ezra is strong enough to rip the towel bar out of the wall.

He probably is.

It won't be long now though.

My chest aches. My lungs are strained and desperate for air. Against my will, I inhale, and water rushes into my nose. It burns as it fills my airways and naturally, I attempt to cough it out. But opening my mouth only fills me with more chlorinated water.

I pinch my eyes shut.

One. Two. Three. Four. Five. Six. Seven. Eight.

One. Two. Three. Four. Five. Six. Seven. Eight.

I try to remember it's almost done, it's almost over. Consciousness will soon fade and turn into peaceful darkness. The counting gives me something other than the ache and fear of drowning to focus on.

One. Two. Three. Four. Five. Six. Seven. Eight.

I'm tiring, though my body tries to gasp in air. The time between my unintentional twitches and muscle jerks lengthens and everything slows.

Everything slows.

Except for Ezra. There's the muffled rumble of Ezra's screaming and the echoing, muted *thump, thump* that I can only assume is the sound of him pulling against his bindings.

I think the vibration of his last scream sounds like my name, as if he's yelling my name, yelling for me.

Part of me wishes this is truly the end, not just a false end as Nikola intends it to be. He intends to kill me but bring me back to life. He's done it twice, and this will be the third time. Part of me prays this is it, that he won't be able to revive me this time because I'm tired of the fight.

So, so tired.

I hardly think fighting is worth it anymore.

There is *nothing* for me in this life.

There's no happiness, only pain and torture. There's no end to it in sight, nothing to look forward to.

As blackness creeps around my vision, as I'm starting to slip into unconsciousness, there's a bewildering flash of something bright. An image of green, vibrant emerald green eyes looking at me as if I'm worth something more than this life. As I begin to drift into that unwilling sleep, I see him as a vision, a dream, but it's clear as day who I'm imagining.

It's Ezra Bell and his crooked, sarcastic, entirely charming smile.

I've never had a vision drift into unconsciousness before, and this one is so pleasant, so calming, that I actually wish I could wrap my arms around it and bring it with me into the underworld.

No. Not it, but him.

If this is the end for me, I selfishly want to drag this man down with me, not to hurt him, but to comfort me. Some part of me already knows that if I asked Ezra to chase me into death, just so that I wouldn't be alone, he would.

What a ridiculous thing to think.

That's the last thought I have before the sweet slumber of death engulfs me in darkness and takes me away.

CHAPTER 13

Ezra

ANYA'S DEAD.

She's dead.

He killed her.

That motherfucking piece of shit just drowned her in the pool.

I'm not even aware of what I'm doing, I just know that I'm thrashing and pulling against this bar I'm bound to and I'm shouting. I don't even know what I'm shouting, but words of desperation and anger and fear are spewing out of me like lava from an erupting volcano.

Anya has gone still in the water, yet he continues to hold her there. Her hair floats all around her head, dark brown waves stretch out in strands all around her face. Nikolai has the audacity to breathe heavily with shallow, rapid breaths, as if killing her is an unwelcome exertion of his energy.

"Get her out!" I scream. "Get her out, get her out! Please, you're fucking killing her!"

She's already dead.

I know she is because I felt it the moment it happened. It was a snap inside my chest, an abnormal beat in my heart rhythm that happened the moment her body stopped jerking.

Finally, Nikolai rolls her body over in the water. She's completely limp, lifeless. For a moment, I think he's going to leave her there, but then I see him look down at her. His eyes are satisfied with what he's done, but there's also some sense of urgency behind his movements as he drags her to the edge of the pool.

He walks backward up the pool steps, pulling her with him, and when he gets out, he carefully lifts her and places her on the pool's edge, half on her side because her arms are still tied behind her back.

Nikolai kneels behind her, pulling his switchblade from his pocket, and saws at the ropes that bind her until they break free. Kostya snatches a red bag from inside a small, white box that I hadn't noticed hanging on the wall and ambles back to where Anya lays.

Nikolai rolls her onto her back and leans to place his ear over her heart. Everything is still.

I'm still and I'm never fucking still.

I don't dare make a sound as Nikolai listens for the beating of her heart. He looks up after a minute and nods to Kostya, then they both stand and back away. Kostya returns the red bag to the wall and I realize then it's a defibrillator.

Oh, fuck.

Oh, fuck, oh, fuck, oh, fuck.

I had hope.

For a brief, shining moment, I had hope and now, it's slipping away from me. They're both just standing there, staring down at her.

Waiting.

"What the fuck are you waiting for? Fucking *save* her!" I scream and Nikolai looks at me sharply.

He cocks his head to the side. "Wait."

I can't wait, I need to get to her. I start pulling harder than before, as hard as I fucking can, and it doesn't matter to me that I already know this bar is not budging from the goddamn wall.

"Untie him."

Nikolai hands his blade to Kostya and I take the first breath of relief since the moment Nikolai caught me and Anya in her room.

I'm impatient as Kostya cuts me free and I run to her the instant the ropes fall away. I don't wait for anyone to give me permission, I slam to my knees next to her and lean down over her, looking for signs of life.

I don't know what's come over me. I don't know why the thought of losing her is too painful for me to bear. I hardly know this woman, and I'm only drawn to her for the simple fact that she's the only person I have in this captivity.

That's all it is.

She's my only potential companion and it's nothing more than that.

Yet somehow, I still feel my heart thudding hard against my ribcage as I watch and wait, hoping she's going to cough that water out of her lungs and start breathing again. Regardless of the reason I'm drawn to her, I know

I cannot survive this without her.

Without Anya, I've got nothing to fight for, no reason to fight to survive this bullshit captivity. I just want to see her open her eyes.

"Open your eyes, Anya...Come on...open your eyes."

I've got to see that sapphire sparkle again.

There's a twitch.

Another.

Then she coughs and coughs and water spills from the corners of her lips. She's naturally rolling to the side, so I lift under her shoulder, helping her roll as she continues to cough the water from her lungs. Then she's gasping and shaking and reaching, trying to find something solid to hold onto to. I reach over her and grab both of her small hands in one of mine, squeezing tightly.

"Ez...Ezra," she calls out before her eyes have even opened.

My heart stops.

I immediately feel the icy burn of Nikolai's eyes on my back, but I ignore it.

"Hey, it's me. I'm here." I sigh in relief. "You're okay. You're okay. It's fine now."

She blinks a couple of times before her eyes fully open and they dart around the room. She hasn't realized where she is or what's happened. But she called out my name and my pulse quickens impossibly faster than before.

In this moment of relief after such terror, I realize that she's under my skin. I don't know how or why, but she is.

There's something that connects us.

It's not just the captivity, though I want to believe that's all it is. If it were just the captivity and our circumstance, this wouldn't affect me so profoundly. It wouldn't make my heart beat frantically enough to set off warning bells that I'm at risk of stressing myself into a heart attack, into a tragic and unexpected death of my own.

I know there's something more to our connection when I feel it snap again in my chest, the same snap I felt when she died in the water.

"I expect you are capable of carrying her, hmm?" Nikolai says from behind me.

My eyes are on Anya, watching the pain of her gasping, shaking breaths, looking over every inch of her body as if scanning her with my eyes can somehow heal her.

"*Mal'chik*," he bites.

I growl, "Give her a fucking minute, you sick piece of shit."

Anya's voice is a hoarse whisper, but it still possesses the strength to move a mountain, "No, Ezra. No. Do as you're told."

Her head turns toward me and she blinks. I'm so inexplicably relieved and elated to see that perfect shade of blue again that I immediately comply. My attitude isn't going to help her. I just want to get her out of this echoing, chlorine-saturated torture chamber.

"Yeah," I finally say to Nikolai, "I can carry her."

"Let's go then. Move."

"I can walk," she says, attempting to push to a sitting position with her trembling hands.

I shake my head in disbelief. Before she can move an inch farther, I scoop my hands beneath her body and lift her from the slick ground, cradling her in my arms as her soaked hair spills water on the floor beneath us.

I don't know if it's the sudden movement, but as I sweep her up, she loses consciousness again. Her right arm flops down freely, reaching for the floor in a swaying motion, and her left arm falls limply across her chest. Her head drops back with a jerk, her hair swinging.

"Shit," I grunt, hoisting her up higher in my arms, twisting her body toward me to cradle into my chest.

Nikolai and Kostya are already at the door, waiting impatiently like the pieces of shit they are. I walk, carrying her close against my body as she starts to wake again.

I turn sideways to get through the door that leads us back to the cave-like alcove. As we walk back through the arched hallway with its high windows, Anya finds enough strength to open her eyes again. I make sure mine are right there to meet hers as she looks up at me.

"I've got you," I tell her, and she looks like she believes me.

I hope she believes me.

She shuts her eyes.

"Anya?" I say, worried she's passed out again.

She hasn't.

I know she hasn't because her right-hand reaches up, slipping across the top of my chest and around to grip the side of my neck. Her head turns and she presses her face to my shoulder. The simple action shows me that, on some level, she trusts me. If she knew me at all, she'd know how important that is to me.

I think she must know me because I think I know her.

I know it's a dangerous concession for her to give away her trust.

Normally, it wouldn't be so hard to carry her as far as we have to walk, but I'm weak from malnourishment and tired from the adrenaline repeatedly ebbing and flowing. I hesitate at the bottom of the grand staircase, just for moment to readjust and make sure I don't drop her.

A good partner doesn't drop and as long as she's my partner, I'm not letting her hit that floor.

I'm careful carrying her back up the steps. We turn left at the top of the stairs, the opposite direction of my room. I follow Nikolai as he strides to sweep around the banister, past the hallway where I'd found Anya's room before, and continue going straight. A few more steps leads us to another hallway to our right and we follow it to the end.

Nikolai flings open a door and stands beside it, arms crossed, impatience all over his wicked face.

Reluctantly, I pass him and enter the room with Anya in my arms, making sure to hold her away from him when I turn sideways to get her through the door.

As soon as I'm inside, Nikolai comes in after us and slams the door shut, leaving Kostya in the hallway.

"Is she awake?" he asks.

Anya rolls her head slowly away from my shoulder, turning her face toward the ceiling. "*Da, khozyain,*" she answers, though she hasn't opened her eyes.

I can feel how her body tenses in response to him. It makes me want to hurt him in a hateful way I've never felt before.

"Set her on her feet," Nikolai demands as he brushes past us, walking around the four-post bed to what I assume is an en suite bathroom.

This must be his bedroom.

I lower her feet gradually to the floor and her hands find their way to my shoulders. She holds onto me for stability, but she doesn't have to. It's not like I'm going to take my hands off her while she's so unsteady.

"Take off her wet clothes," I hear Nikolai call from the bathroom.

Her drooping head lifts and she looks up at me, though I can see how the small movement makes her dizzy. She needs to rest. She needs a fucking doctor, but I don't suppose Nikolai is going to get her one.

"Go ahead," she tells me softly, giving me permission to strip her.

I suck in a breath and lift the heavy hem of her wet sweatshirt, pulling up from her waist and working to pull it up over her body. It wants to cling to her, and I have to tug as I peel it up over her head. She lifts her arms to help me and the movement nearly knocks her backward. I quickly snake one arm around her waist and lasso her against my chest. I hold her like that as I tug the sweatshirt, attempting to untangle it from her sopping wet hair which coils through the collar. Somehow, I manage to pull it off the rest of the way and toss it onto the floor.

"I've got you," I tell her.

"You keep saying that," she says sleepily.

"It's true."

Nikolai comes out of the bathroom and I step back from her, just enough to make this embrace look more innocent. And only because I wish to spare her more harm from this abusive son of a bitch who owns us.

He fucking owns us.

He comes over to where we're standing, holding out a bleached white towel to me. I take it and he steals Anya from my hold.

My jaw clenches.

But what the fuck am I supposed to do about it?

There's nothing I can fucking do that won't hurt her more in the end.

Without waiting for her okay, he peels the black sports bra from her body, tossing it aside, then shoves at her cotton shorts. He pushes them and her underwear down to the floor, helping her step out of her clothes.

Just like that, like nothing at all, she's been stripped bare.

Nikolai Mikhailov has stripped every barrier from this blue-eyed girl and exposed her naked and vulnerable to the world. What's worse is that it doesn't even seem to faze her. He's held every part of her hostage for so long that she no longer has any insecurity about being bare so long as he is happy with her behavior.

"Take her." He shoves Anya back into my grip and she curls against my chest as I grip her by both arms. "Dry her off while I get her something to wear."

I nearly slip.

I nearly say, "*How kind of you,*" in my normal, sarcastic way.

But with this girl in my arms—barely alive, weak, and vulnerable—I find some strength I didn't know I had to keep my smart mouth shut despite the way my lips twitch to speak.

She leans into me and I shake out the towel with one hand, wrapping it around her shoulders. I can feel her tremble against my torso and I reach around her back, rubbing over the towel with both my hands, hoping to create some friction to help warm her up.

"I'm freezing," she mutters.

"I know."

I take a breath and pull back a bit so I can move the towel to dry her. I have no choice but to look at her. She seems to sense my hesitation.

"It's okay, Ezra."

I nod, though she can't see it. She can't see it because her head is drooping from fatigue. I slide the towel down her backside and crouch to dry her legs. I work fast, coming back up her front and quickly draping the towel across her breasts before I can look for a moment longer than necessary.

I'm a gentleman, but I'm not blind.

I looked.

Of course, I did.

She's slender and toned and gorgeous beneath her clothes, but she also looks like she's been used as a goddamn whipping post.

Black and blue and yellow bruises mar the otherwise flawless honey color of her skin.

"Come here," Nikolai says, returning to slip a plain, white T-shirt over her naked body. "Bedtime, *moya rabynya.*"

She nods and shuffles as he takes her from me and guides her to the bed, *his* bed. He's actually careful with her now, pulling back the covers and tucking her in. It's messing with my head to see him act as if he gives a shit about her comfort or care.

He starts taking off his clothes. "You can go now, Mr. Bell. Frankly, I don't give a shit if you go back to your room, roam the manor, try to escape in the forest…It's not as if you're going to succeed in getting off the grounds anyway."

I scoff, "So all that time I've spent shackled to a bedpost, locked in a room with two different keys. That was just a fun experiment for you?"

He's down to his boxer briefs and I'm beyond fucking uncomfortable.

"Fun is a subjective term," he says as he walks around the bed.

He climbs under the covers and slides in behind Anya where she lays facing me. She's already asleep. Or she's passed out again.

"Get out, *mal'chik*," he says.

It feels wrong that he's using that word. I know it's meant to be a dig at me when it's used, to put me in my place, but it somehow feels okay when Anya says it.

It feels like something else he's taken from her.

"I hope you've learned your lesson," he adds, just as I reluctantly turn to walk toward the door.

I stop and swing back around to face him. "Lesson?"

"Anya is mine. You are hers, but she will never be *yours*. It's undeniable she has a soft spot for you. She's impressed by your talent and that's all it is. You'll be disappointed if you read further into it than that. You are her dance partner and nothing else. Make sure that remains so, *mal'chik*. It doesn't faze me to hurt her in order to control you. I would sooner kill her before letting her fall for a boy like you. Now you've seen the proof."

"Why the fuck am I here?" I turn my palms up. "Why do you even need me?"

An evil smile spreads wide across his face as he latches an arm around Anya's waist. I know she's passed out again because her body is limp as he pulls her back against him.

"You're here for entertainment."

"You want me to dance," I express with annoyance, "I get it. But she's a perfect soloist, why give her a partner?"

"Why? You assume there's a meaningful motivation for my actions."

"Isn't there?"

"Ezra," he says, "Anya is mine. She's belonged to me longer than she's been held in this manor. I claimed her a very long time ago. But even I grow weary with boredom. The drama a partner brings excites me. It's as simple as that."

As simple as that.

Our captivity is as simple as boredom.

CHAPTER 14
Anya

I WAS REQUIRED to spend two full days in Nikolai's room after he killed me—though he hadn't actually killed me this time. He told me my heart never fully stopped beating like it had the two times before, but we both know it would have given another handful of moments under the water.

There's a strange cycle I've come to expect now with Nikolai. His rage and violence slowly build over time. His frustration begins to grow when he brings me a new partner, and I think that must be the triggering event for his circular pattern of behavior.

His frustration grows into anger, anger grows into rage, rage grows into violence. All of it culminates in my punishment—whether I deserve it or not.

Once the punishment has been dealt, once his violent urges have been satiated, he finds a way to mold himself back into something that almost resembles a human being.

This is why it doesn't surprise me that Nikolai cares for me delicately in the aftermath of such a brutal punishment. I recall him doing the same before and for the life I me, I don't understand why. Part of me likes to believe its remorse that makes him behave that way, but I know it's not.

He doesn't regret hurting me.

He just knows how badly he's hurt me. He knows if he doesn't give my body the rest, care, and nourishment it needs to recover, then I won't be able to dance. That's why he insists that I stay in his room.

It hasn't been entirely awful to be held here for two days. There's a television I can watch, books to read, a small space behind the armchairs where I can do some barre work. He doesn't hurt me, he doesn't rape me, he brings me three meals a day and even sits to eat two of them with me.

It's nothing like the beginning of my captivity with Nikolai. I'm not chained to the bed. I'm not left alone and starving for days at a time. I have things to entertain me. Belonging to him is normal now, and there's a strange kind of comfort to be found in that complacency.

I hate that I think this way now.

Captivity has altered my frame of mind and being aware of that makes no difference.

By the third morning, I'm itching to get out of here, to move, to stretch my legs, to *dance*. I'm pacing the small space behind the armchairs when the door clicks open and Nikolai enters.

I spin to face him, stopping in my tracks.

Coming toward me, he asks, "How are you feeling?"

"I'm well."

He reaches for me and I step forward into his embrace as he wraps his arms around me. He strokes my hair with one hand.

Almost as if he cares about me.

"Do you wish to dance today, Anya?"

"Yes," my tone is eager, but not urgent, "please, *khozyain*."

"If I let you dance today, I expect you to keep a firm hand with Ezra. He's agitated with his concern for your condition. He's worried."

My chest thumps unusually hard at the mention of him.

"I will, *khozyain*. I promise."

He kisses the top of my head. The foolish half of me mistakes the gesture as affection, though my wiser, hardened half knows it's nothing more than possessive posturing.

I'm his possession.

"He's in the studio. Kostya's with him. He's been practicing while you rested." He pulls back and holds me by the shoulders at arm's length. "I'm afraid to tell you that you have quite a bit of catching up to do."

I meet his gray eyes, wanting to ask a question but knowing to phrase it as a statement to keep from upsetting him. "We'll be dancing his style now. Contemporary, not ballet."

"Yes. I expect you to let him teach you, but you must not let him have control. I know this will be a challenge for you, Anya," he strokes my hair again, "but your skill will improve if you can find that balance with him. Perhaps you'll have a partner for more than one performance if you can pull this off together."

All the air leaves my body in a rush.

It's relief, but also fear.

Relief that Ezra might not be taken from me like my partners before. Fear that I won't be able to balance controlling him and learning from him… we both might see the consequences of that. Maybe it won't just be Ezra who disappears forever. Maybe I'll disappear right along with him.

But even in that way of thinking, there's an odd beat of relief.

Nikolai dismisses me and I return to my room, changing into my favorite black, spaghetti strap leotard that crisscrosses over my back and gray, cotton shorts. I throw a pink wrap sweater on, tying it at the side against my waist, and I pull my hair back into a quick, low bun.

I quickly walk to the dance studio, eager to stretch my legs and simply fall away from the world. Dance is all I have here at Mikhailov Manor. It's all I've ever had. Two days without it may as well have been a lifetime.

But there's another reason I'm eager, too.

A reason I don't want to admit.

A reason I *can't* admit.

When I reach the doorway to the studio, where Kostya gives me a nod of acknowledgement, I'm stunned into stillness by that very reason.

Ezra is spinning, flipping, turning, truly and honestly floating through the air as if gravity itself were a chain he was bursting free from with ease. I've seen so many incredible dancers in my time, but I'm simply captivated by the way he moves so effortlessly, so gracefully, so *emotionally*. I swear I can feel what he's feeling just being in the presence of his movement.

He's an artist and right now, he's painting me a picture of fear and rage and desperation.

I don't want him to stop, I want to see the rest of this routine, so instead of walking into the studio, I lean against the doorframe. The floor creaks beneath my feet as I move, and that subtle movement is enough to draw his attention. I can actually see the green of his eyes catch mine mid-leap and there's a shift.

Everything shifts.

Even I shift, as if the doorframe pushed me away from it.

He lands hard on the floor and I know it wasn't an intentional landing. I distracted him. I hate it so much when someone disturbs me in the middle of a dance, so I step inside, ready to apologize.

"I'm sorry, I didn't mean to—"

He rushes toward me, long strides bringing him swiftly into my space. He doesn't hesitate to wrap his arms around my waist and pull me into his embrace, lifting me slightly off the floor.

I'm frozen.

His touch kickstarts my heart and my pulse quickens.

My arms hang limply from my sides as he lowers me back to my feet, then holds me by the shoulders at arm's length.

"I've been so worried about you," he says frantically. "Nikolai wouldn't let me see you, he wouldn't tell he how you were, if you were okay. The last time I saw you was after you drowned and passed out in his bed. I didn't know if something had happened, if you…"

"I'm fine. I'm well. No need to worry."

"No need my *ass*. My middle name is worry these days."

My smile betrays me, slipping out though I try to hold it back. A dimple appears on his cheek as one side of his mouth curls into a half-smile.

"That's a good look on you," he says, letting me go. "The smile, I mean. I don't think I've ever seen you smile."

I swallow and purse my lips, trying to pull the happiness from my face. I'm supposed to be in control here. I can't let him charm me into taking control for himself. There will be consequences for both of us if I can't teach him what it means to be a slave of one of the four families.

But then he smiles at me full-on. It's a smile that takes over his entire face, his entire being, and it ticks inside my abdomen, coiling and tightening low in my belly.

I put my hand on my stomach and breathe out slowly to steady myself against the bizarre and unexpected attraction I have to his natural charm.

My face feels hot.

I turn and walk away from him, hoping I haven't already begun blushing. I stride toward the stereo controls in the corner behind the grand piano to turn off his music.

"Are you really okay?" His voice is tinged with concern and now tiny wings are fluttering in my stomach.

I don't know why I'm having this reaction to him.

I don't like it.

Really, I *do* like it and that's *why* I don't like it.

I'd felt something like this toward my first partner, Jamal. It was just a simple attraction, a small spark of natural chemistry. But it had never evolved past that and I'm so glad it hadn't. If I'd allowed myself to have felt something stronger for Jamal, it would've destroyed me when he disappeared.

I try to shake off the thought of him, but it swiftly morphs into fear about Ezra's future.

No.

I can't think about this.

I shake out my arms and the feeling along with them.

"I'm really okay," I finally respond to him, though I don't turn to look. "I just need a minute, Ezra."

I'm angry at myself for using his name instead of *mal'chik*. But heaven help me, there is nothing boy-like about that man and referring to him as such just feels wrong.

I need to get out of my head.

I need to feel in control again.

I need to dance.

I spin around to face him. He's standing in the center of the dance floor, his fingers locked together, pulling down from where they're laced on the top of his head. His expression is narrowed as he studies me with concerned eyes.

This stance he's in puts his strength on display. He's not wearing a shirt and with his hands up on the top of his head this way, his torso is lengthened and lean. The lines of his dance-sculpted abs are defined and glistening from the sweat of his craft and he looks strong.

Impenetrable.

Unmovable.

Undeniably, irrefutably sexy.

Oh, shit.

He drops his hands and they land with a thud against his sides. That's when I realize I'm just standing here, staring at him, not speaking, not moving. His eyes are narrowed as they regard me with worry, but there's a hint of humor dancing behind the green of his eyes.

"Well, fuck," he says. "See? I really am gonna have to change my middle name to worry."

I lick my lips as they suddenly feel dry. "Why do you do that?"

"Do what?"

"Make everything into a joke."

"Does it bother you? I really am worried about you."

"Why?" I feel my forehead crease in curiosity.

Ezra tilts his head, looking confused. "Why wouldn't I be? Why would I feel anything but worried about you in this shit show we're living in?"

"Never mind." I shake my head. "It really doesn't matter. We should get to work. We need to learn a new routine and prepare for the performance. It's only a couple of months away."

He starts walking toward me and my shoulders tense as he nears the piano bench, stopping just on the other side of it.

"Anya, I need you to tell me what all of this is about it."

I cross my arms over my chest. "What do you want to know?"

"What's with this performance? Why are we doing it? Why does he care? It's a pretty ridiculous reason to have slaves, don't you think? Just to dance for him."

"It's not just for him. I told you, this is so much bigger than Nikolai."

He nods. "Okay, so tell me everything. I have a right to know what this is all about."

I lower my arms. "You'll be disappointed to find out why our lives were stolen from us."

He huffs out an amused sound. He steps forward, straddling the piano bench before he sits down. My mouth falls open watching him and I inhale sharply, exhale slowly.

"I have no doubt you're right. I can't imagine *any* reason being something other than disappointing. Though that's probably not a strong enough word."

"Frustrating," I offer.

He shakes his head. "Nah. Discouraging?" he counters.

"Aggravating?"

"Infuriating."

"Provocative," I say.

He smiles. "Now that's an interesting word choice."

"I don't mean in a sexual context, I—"

What am I saying?

Thankfully, he cuts me off, "Hey, I knew what you meant."

"Right," I say. "Right, I know."

I know I sound moronic and it's really unbecoming for a woman who is supposed to be in charge here.

Ezra pats the bench in front of him. "Can we just sit for a minute? Just talk to me. Tell me what's up here."

I tilt my head, looking at the bench. I'm physically drawn to him. My body wants to be close to him and he's asking me to sit and talk. I know I should remain standing, using the leverage of my height as he sits to re-establish my authority and certify my position of power over him.

But I don't.

I straddle the bench facing him. "There are four families that run a multi-billion-dollar enterprise across the globe. The O'Sheas, The Campbells, The Vittoris, and The Mikhailovs."

"Selling slaves."

"Human trafficking. Yes. It's quite the lucrative business for those involved."

"Christ," he says, shaking his head.

"You and I belong to the Mikhailovs, obviously. But the slaves belonging to any the four families are more symbolic than anything else. Our role is entertainment. Some talent slaves will belong to their family for years, decades, but when the family is no longer entertained, they might sell their slave or..."

"Or they kill them?" he finishes the thought for me.

I've been looking at my hands resting in front of me on the bench, but I lift my eyes now. I connect with his gaze and his interested stare holds me.

I nod. "I think so, yes."

"You had partners before me." He shifts, his eyes darting away then back to meet mine. "Do you know what happened to them?"

"I don't," I hesitate. "I can't think about that."

His gaze is soft and comforting as he reaches out to tap my hand between us. "I'm sorry, Anya."

I've stilled at the touch of his fingertips on the back of my hand. There's just something entirely inexplicable about the way my skin reacts to his touch. It's soothing but at the same time, stirring, fire-starting.

Provocative.

My fingers twitch and before I can stop myself, I turn my hand and open it, inviting him to take hold. I feel relief when he grips it without hesitation, holding my hand without reserve or question or expectation. He holds it confidently, in such a way that it makes my whole body tingle in light-heartedness to be so courageously touched. He's not tentative or wary or afraid that Kostya or Nikolai will see. His touch is just there, it exists for what it is, and my soul feels the vibration of it.

I feel like I've found my steadiness when I start talking again, "The four families meet quarterly to discuss business. I don't know the details. But they rotate their meeting location for each quarter, each taking a turn to host. The family who is hosting is responsible for providing entertainment before business. Once a year, it's Nikolai's turn to host, our turn to perform. The last meeting was hosted by the O'Shea family."

My eyes pinch shut for a moment as I remember being Nikolai's payment to Vigo Vittori for information at that very meeting, just after the O'Shea family talent slave performed.

"So, Nikolai owns us just so we can perform for him and his depraved colleagues once a year?"

"Yes, though it's not that simple…" I look down at our hands because I feel his thumb brush over my skin, "Or perhaps, it really is that simple and that's what makes it so demented."

"It's fucked-up. This whole thing is fucked-up."

I press my lips together. "I know."

"Tell me why I'm here. Tell me why he gives you partners to dance with just to throw them away. Does he do it to torture you?"

"I think that's part of it." I swallow and then lower my voice so Kostya can't overhear from the hallway. "Nikolai chose me a long time ago, Ezra. It's what all the families do. I first met him when I was nearly eleven years old in Moscow. He was observing a ballet class I was taking. He came every day for weeks just to watch. I don't remember much about our meeting, but I remember that he spoke to my mother. He gave her a business card and he gave me a pink rose."

Ezra reaches out and takes my other hand in his and for whatever stupid reason, I let him. The gentle contact feels nice. It feels good.

"A month later, we were moving to New York at the expense of a benefactor. That's all my mother ever told me—that there was a benefactor who funded our move. I never questioned it. I went to public school but spent all my free hours training, practicing. All my dance activities were determined by this benefactor who I knew nothing about.

"Then three years ago, just after I turned twenty-one, he came for me. It all seemed very innocent. He found me one day coming out of the studio after a long rehearsal and introduced himself as my benefactor. His face did seem familiar when I first saw him, and once he explained who he was, I was certain it was the man I had seen observing my dance classes all those years ago. He offered me an opportunity to come back to Moscow with him—a unique training opportunity which would ensure my promotion to Principal at the New York City Ballet. That was everything I'd been working toward, so I didn't even stop to think about how strange it all seemed. I went with him *willingly*.

"He took me on a private jet, won me over with his wealth and power, and I thought I was safe. It was seduction and I fell for it. He brought me here and I haven't left since, except for the quarterly meetings. I've attended all of those with Nikolai. He chose me when I was a child, Ezra. He controlled my life from the age of eleven. He trained me, groomed me. And my family never knew. He paid my mother under a false name in a secret account. There's no way anyone could track him in connection with my disappearance, though even if they could, it wouldn't matter. The four families are more powerful than any political party, than any government. I've never had a life of my own, not really."

He doesn't reply. He just watches me as if waiting for me to say more.

"I think you may be my last partner, Ezra. My last chance."

"What do you mean?"

"You said it yourself, he's impatient with me. He's always been cruel. He's always been controlling and hateful, and he's always hurt me. But he's never been so impatient with me as he has been since you arrived."

"Why is it different now?"

I sigh. "I worry…I think I'll be the next to disappear. I think that if you and I don't do well in our performance that he might get rid of me this time."

"You think he'd get rid of you and keep me instead?"

I nod and let go of one of his hands to draw circles on the bench, looking down at my fingers as if they're interesting to watch.

"I think," I begin, but hesitate, knowing I shouldn't be telling him so much of my speculation, "I think he's ashamed by his preferences. There was pressure on him to choose a beneficiary when he found me as a child. I think finding a female talent was just easier. And a female beneficiary is far and above the standard among the four families." I tilt my head. "I think my dance partners have been the only male talent slaves. I think the Vittoris have some male slaves, but they serve the lady of the house. I don't think there have ever been any other male beneficiaries."

His jaw ticks and he nods. "I get it. He doesn't just want to watch a beautiful woman dance…"

"He wants to watch a beautiful man, too," I complete the thought for him. "You're more beautiful than the others. He's been kinder to you."

He laughs. "This shit is his version of kindness?"

"Yes. This, what you've seen from him, is kindness. You have no idea what he's put me through."

His brow wrinkles. "I have a little bit of an idea. Are you telling me it's been worse than him drowning you?"

I meet his eyes and I know mine have glazed over with ice, the way they always do when thoughts of my various traumatic incidents with Nikolai jump back into my brain.

"Much worse." I sigh. "Things have been changing since his parents and his brother died a year ago. He's become arrogant, bold, self-righteous. Downright vindictive. And he takes his anger out on me."

He pauses in consideration. "I won't let him do that anymore."

"I'm afraid he will come after you, too. There will come a point when he wants you as much as he wants me. You're the first partner since his immediate family died. There's no one here to judge him, and I'm terrified of how he will use us. And when he decides he's done with one or both of us, then he's done. You see the control he has over us now? We can't escape this place. Like it or not, we are his slaves. We belong to him. Our lives are in his hands. But there is one thing we can control."

He says it so I don't have to, "Our performance."

"Yes. And it's the only thing, the only *singular* thing that makes me feel like I can wake up in the morning and go on."

My palms dampen with sweat and I immediately pull my hand away from his. I untie, adjust, and retie my wrap sweater, just to give my hands something to do.

"I shouldn't be telling you all of this. Not now. Nikolai expects us to rehearse," I stand and move to the stereo controls, "so we need to rehearse."

"Okay," he concedes with a sigh, though the tone of it is dripping with sarcasm. "Then let's rehearse. But he wants my style, right?"

Ezra comes up behind me and reaches around me to scroll through the music options. He's looking over my shoulder to do this, his chest pressed against my back and I hold my breath. He lands on a song, starts it, then steps away, moving into the open space.

"Yes," I finally confirm once I can breathe again, "your absolutely reckless, untamed contemporary style." I roll my eyes.

I turn to face him, expecting to see him as depressed and angst-ridden as I feel, and though I can feel those emotions vibrating from him through the air, he's somehow managed to shove them down low enough for me to step over.

He gives me a charming wink. "Reckless and untamed are absolutely my style, babe."

My heart stops.

Reckless and untamed are the exact opposite of what I need for survival. I know that.

And still, the promise lights a fire around my cold, dead heart.

CHAPTER 15
Ezra

"OH, SHIT...SHIT, I'VE got you," I grunt.

Anya reaches her arms out, ready to brace against the hardwood dance floor as she tumbles headfirst out of the lift above my head.

My arm latches around her waist and I grip her side with one hand. Her weight shifts both of us forward and I'm falling with her, though I'm determined to keep her from hitting the ground. I promised her I wouldn't let her hit the floor and I won't, but I'm going down, too.

I'm bringing her down to the floor sideways and I twist to grab her waist with both hands, rolling forward over her, and taking the fall for her. I land on my back as I twist her and bring her down on top of me, chest to chest. Thankfully, I slowed our momentum enough that it's a light landing.

She keeps rolling until she's off me and lays on her back by my side. We're both huffing and puffing because that was a fucking rush.

I turn my head to look over at her and smile. "My bad."

She turns her head to look at me, too. "You swore you wouldn't let me hit the floor," she says with all the seriousness in the world, but she can't hide the amusement that tugs at the side of her mouth.

"You didn't technically hit the floor, *I* did." I grin.

She shakes her head and looks back up at the ceiling, but I see the smile she was trying to hide, though I don't have to see it to know it's there. Every time she smiles, I feel it creep down my spine and threaten arousal that I just can't deal with in this shit storm of a situation.

We've been rehearsing a new routine for three weeks now. We've danced together nearly every day since Nikolai—in all his medical wisdom—determined Anya was recovered enough from the drowning. The more time I spent dancing with her, the more time I *wanted* to spend with her.

Something about Anya twists something inside me with every interaction.

It's a good twist.

A spine-tingling twist.

But it's a deep down, knife-in-the-gut twist, too…because we aren't living in the real world.

It's not like I can date her or something. I can build a friendship, flirt, dance with her, but that's where it all ends. Anytime I so much as think of the possibility of being anything more to her than the man who will help her survive another year in captivity, the reality of our life or death circumstance comes crashing down on my head.

It's the heaviest fucking weight in the world to carry, because honestly, I could fall for this blue-eyed girl. And it's not just that she's literally the only person around.

It's *her.*

She sits up abruptly and looks down at me. "Should we try a different lift? We've been working on this one for a week. If we can't nail it every single time in rehearsal, we can't bank on nailing it in the performance. And we have to nail our performance. You know how important this is."

I reach over and touch her arm. "Hey, I know. But we also have to push the limit a bit. You told me he wants mind-blowing talent. Well, he's not gonna get it from us wussing out for an easier lift."

Her nose wrinkles as her face scrunches. "It's not wussing out…" She tilts her head. "What does that even mean?"

I laugh. "It means giving up because of fear."

"Oh. I'm not fearful, Ezra. I just want a perfect routine."

"Perfection is boring. Besides, I really don't think Nikolai or any of these other assholes would know dance perfection if it bit them in the ass." I squeeze her wrist before letting go and I sit up, leaning back on my palms.

She sighs. "That's what I *hate* about this contemporary shit. Classical ballet has structure, form, technique that I understand. I don't understand the flexed feet and the hard mixed with the soft, and the constant shift between grace and…and…"

"And?"

Her expression ticks then falters into self-amusement, with the smallest hint of a smile. "I don't know. Don't look at me like that."

"Like what?" I'm just smiling at her.

She swallows. "Like that. Like you know something I don't. Like you know more than I do."

My eyes widen. "Well, whoa. That's definitely not true. You know way more than I do about the technique, the form, the grace."

"That's true," she agrees, and I laugh.

I hop to my feet and hold out my hand to her. "Come on."

She takes it without hesitation and shoots icy daggers of longing straight through to my heart as I pull her to stand. The song we've chosen to perform to is playing on a loop and is about mid-way through playing for the fifth time in a row.

I hold up my palms in front of her. "Okay," I tell her, "forget the routine for a minute. I wanna get you out of your head and help you understand what you're missing."

"What I'm missing?" she feigns a disheartened shock, but I know better by now.

I tilt my head at her with a grin and she mimics me to jab right back.

"Hands on mine," I tell her, smiling.

She places her palms against mine and automatically adjusts her feet to stand shoulder width apart, naturally mirroring my position.

I blow out a breath to push out the playfulness I'm feeling and take in another to center myself. "Close your eyes."

"Okay," she says easily, pressing her eyes shut, trusting me immediately.

My chest puffs out proudly at the fact that I've earned that trust from her. She doesn't give it easily and I take it seriously.

"My eyes are closed, too," I tell her and wait a beat.

She opens one eye, to see me staring and smiling at her. We both laugh and she slaps my palms.

I shut my eyes. "Okay, okay, I'm serious now. Shut your eyes."

I wait until I hear her exhale slowly, calmly, steadily.

"What you're missing is the feeling. The emotion," I tell her. "When you do the steps like you're supposed to, it's beautiful and graceful because…well, you're just naturally beautiful and graceful. But you can get so caught up in the perfection of movement that you forget about the imperfection of soul. The rawness of feeling."

I hear her sigh, but I feel it more. I feel it where my palms touch hers.

"Listen to the music. Really listen to it. And when you start to have a real, emotional reaction to it, I want you to move, but stay connected with me. I want you to move me with you so I can feel what you're feeling."

"Okay…" I can hear the skepticism in her tone.

"Hey, just do this for me."

"I'm doing it, I'm doing it," she says.

I sneak a peek because I can hear her smiling and I can't help myself but to look. I only mean to look for a moment, but I end up lingering, watching her as she shifts into focus. I swallow, watching her breath slowly, watching her listen.

Her face holds tension as she concentrates way too hard. She's trying to think her way into feeling and it makes me want to laugh. She's not naturally stone cold, she's been hardened over time. I want nothing more than to see her crack that shell and watch it crumble beneath our feet, but I don't hold out hope that it will actually happen.

She's not safe here.

She'd need to feel safe to shed her armor.

But then I feel a twitch.

Her palms curve into mine just a little bit harder. I hold steady, giving her something strong and stable to push against. Her fingertips curl and my fingers are itching to curl right back.

I squeeze, bringing my fingers down through the spaces between hers. Her eyes snap open to meet mine and all I can see is sapphire blue. Her fingers drop slowly and now our hands are locked together.

Something inside her stirs.

I can feel it.

She can feel it.

She starts to move and soon, I'm moving with her. It's not our routine, but it's as though we've rehearsed it a thousand times.

Every movement is slow, drifting from one into the other. We're apart at first, but gradually, she's dancing closer and closer to me. Her dancing is soft at the beginning, just fading into emotion, but it's changing, growing.

Every move she makes is sensual and my fucking heart is racing.

I need her.

The intensity I feel dancing with Anya—even just being near her—is indescribable. The way I hated her in the beginning, that powerful feeling, it's morphed and changed as we've gotten to know each other into an all new kind of intensity, a desire-fueled intensity. It's the kind of intensity I want to feel all the time.

It's the splash of cool water on a hot summer day.

It's the rush of performing for a crowd of hundreds.

It's dirty sex on a public fucking beach.

I'm just about to drag her into my arms, but the chance is taken from me. Just like everything else has been taken from me.

Nikolai gives three slow, sharp claps as he enters the dance studio. Anya jumps out of her skin with a gasp, yanking her hands free from mine and spinning to face him immediately.

He's been gone for three days on business, so his sudden appearance startles us both. I lace my fingers behind my neck and stretch as I blow out a heavy breath, watching her walk away from me to go to his side.

"I'm sorry, I didn't realize you were watching," she tells him with a bowed head.

Nikolai taps two fingers under her chin, and she lifts to meet his eyes. "I'm always watching, *moya rabynya*."

I shudder.

"You two dance quite beautifully together," Nikolai says slowly, looking over at me. "You have chemistry."

You can't fake chemistry and he's right that we have buckets of it. It kills me how much chemistry we have. I drop my hands to my sides, worried what he thinks he saw and what he's reading into it right now.

"It's part of the performance," I lie.

"I have something for you, Ezra. Come. Both of you," he says and exits the studio.

Anya and I share a look before we follow him. My look says, *"Well, fuck,"* and hers says, *"Just do as your told, keep your smart mouth shut, and don't make things worse."*

Yes, her eyes speak volumes.

Nikolai leads us upstairs to his bedroom and asks me to shut the door behind us. My shoulders immediately tense because this is unusual. It's unusual for us both to be invited into his room, and even more unusual for the door to be shut. If this were going to be a quick exchange, there would be no reason to shut the door. The sneer on his face tells me to be ready for an attack.

"Both of you, sit," he orders.

He gestures to the two armchairs that are angled toward each other, facing the fireplace. Anya moves immediately to do as she's told, but I'm wary, hesitant. She turns her head back to look at me after she sits.

"*Mal'chik,*" she insists.

I move to sit, but not because he wants me to. I do it because she *needs* me to. She needs to maintain the image that she's in control of me. In reality, she is. I'd do just about anything for this girl, especially if it ensures her well-being.

Nikolai is somewhere behind us and it sounds like he's pulling open a drawer, then shuts it. He comes back around in front of us and walks over to me, handing me a plain, manila envelope.

"I do apologize we haven't been able to provide these to you sooner. You've proven to be so detached from friends and family that it was challenging to find a suitable person for leverage. This is just the first. There will be more now that we've found her."

I look up at him. "Found who?"

His head tilts toward the envelope in my hand. "Open it."

It isn't sealed, so I lift the flap and reach inside. My fingers touch the corner of a small rectangle and I know what it is before I pull it out. Still, when I see the photograph for the first time, it's jarring.

"How the fuck did you—" I stop mid-sentence, flipping the photograph over to look at the back.

Twenty-two.

Thirty-seven.

Two numbers.

My ex-girlfriend is twenty-two years old.

Just like the numbers on Anya's photos of her sister, Lidia, I know the second number is the measurement from the rifle scope.

Thirty-seven yards.

They were thirty-seven yards away from her when they took this photo.

Every muscle in my body tightens, my pulse thumping rage through my veins.

"If you hurt her, I swear I will kill you, Nikolai."

His forehead tilts down toward me with narrowed eyes. "If you hurt me, she will die. I expect you have a good enough reason now to comply and behave."

I *have* been complying.

I *have* been behaving.

Anya's well-being is enough to keep me in line.

But this…

This is next level shit.

I finally feel the fear Anya must have been feeling all these years with her photos of Lidia. I feel Anya's eyes on me, and I turn my head to catch her curious gaze. With shaking hands, I reach over to hand her the photo.

"Who is she?" Anya asks as she pulls it from my fingers.

"My girl—" I correct myself, "My ex-girlfriend. She, uh…she left me a few days before I was taken. In Kyiv."

I really don't want to tell her this right now, but I can see the apprehension on her face. For whatever stupid reason in my illogical brain, I'm more concerned with allaying Anya's potential jealousy over a relationship that no longer exists in any sense of the word. I care about Emma a great deal. The thought of something happening to her because of my actions here threatens to unravel me entirely, and I am truly scared shitless about this photograph.

"You'll receive a new one weekly now that we know who she is and where she is."

"You're a goddamn monster," I tell him.

He shrugs. "It's business. Anya, go take a shower. Don't wash your hair, but clean thoroughly."

Jesus fucking shit.

A thick wall of tension whips up around her as she slowly rises to her feet, ready to comply. "*Da, khozyain.*"

She looks at me and I see her swallow hard, worry dulling the sparkle of her eyes. If I could beat Nikolai to death right now without consequence, I would. For a million reasons, I would, but I would rip out his heart for taking away her spark.

If he even has one.

"Go," Nikolai snaps, sensing her hesitation.

She rushes off to his bathroom and a few moments later, I hear the shower water running. Nikolai moves to the bar cart next to the fireplace, pouring three glasses of what I think is whiskey. He picks up two and brings one to me, taking a seat in the armchair that Anya has vacated.

I look down at the golden-brown liquid in my glass, unsure whether I should drink it or not. I was only just barely legal to drink in the States—just a few months past my twenty-first birthday. I'd gotten drunk a few times before, just like most of the raging, rowdy teenagers I went to high school with, but this was a new drink for me.

Part of me wants to throw it back and ask for a second, just to dull the pain of knowing they're watching Emma, of being held hostage, of all this shit. The other part of me wonders if he's drugged my drink, though I watched him pour it cleanly myself.

"You make a good partner for her. I'm pleased with the progress you both are making with your routine." He sips from his glass, leaning back casually and crossing an ankle over his knee.

I scoff, "Thanks. I'm so fucking glad that our partnership entertains you, *Master.*"

He smiles sideways. "I'm not as put off by your sarcasm as you think I am, Ezra. I'm actually somewhat intrigued by it."

I don't respond, instead deciding I need to partake in drink. I lift my glass to my lips and tilt it back, taking several long gulps until its emptied.

"I'd like to see you and Anya take your performance to the next level. I've been watching your lifts. The way you read each other so clearly without words. You're very in tune with each other, very in sync. I've had her try this once before, but she had no connection with her partner and it failed spectacularly. I think it will work quite well with the two of you."

"Okay," I say, setting my empty glass on the small side table between our chairs. "What is it?"

"I'm sure Anya has made you aware by now…I have a bit of a fetish for the art of bondage. I'd like you to use rope in your routine."

My jaw clenches and my shoulders tense. "I think I'd remember her telling me something like that."

He lifts an eyebrow. "Well, I'm telling you now."

I stretch my neck, tilting my head from side to side. "Okay, so what is it you want us to do?"

"I'll leave the artistic incorporation up to the two of you. But there are certain things you need to know about using rope safely, so I'm going to give you a demonstration tonight."

I laugh. I can't hold it back.

Does he really expect me to believe he gives a fuck about using rope safely?

"Why does it feel like you have more than a demonstration planned?"

He hides his secretive smile behind his glass as he takes another sip. "As I said, Ezra, it's a fetish of mine."

Fuck.

Anya's in his shower right now, *cleaning thoroughly*, as he asked her to. I feel nausea roll through my gut and a punch of adrenaline through my veins. I squeeze my eyes shut and take a deep breath. There's no sense to my sudden agitation because there's not a goddamn fucking thing I can do about this situation.

Nikolai is going to do what Nikolai is going to do, and God help the person who thought they could stop him.

Though I want to jump out of my chair, snatch him by the neck and throw him into the fucking fireplace, I know I can't. I can't if I want to keep her safe.

Anya.

And I guess Emma now, too.

The shower water clicks off and Nikolai rises from his chair. He sets his drink on the bar cart again, then heads for the bathroom door. He doesn't knock or even pause, just barges right in. I expect to hear Anya shriek in surprise, but that's real-world me. Slave-world me knows better. She's no longer surprised by Nikolai's behavior, by the way he treats her. I, on the other hand, don't think I will ever get used to it.

Anya's strength and poise through suffering are absolutely astounding, though suffering is putting it mildly. She's superhuman in her courage, a goddess of resilience. I just wish I knew those admirable traits under different circumstances.

A minute passes with them both in the bathroom and I have no idea what's going on. I stay in my seat, though I'm squirming to jump and run and fight. I'm fighting every instinct I have because I have to. I have to keep my cool to keep her safe. Not that she's ever really safe here, but I have to think in terms of relativity now. And relatively, she's better off if I do as I'm told. Nikolai is going to hurt her either way and the least I can do is not make it worse.

She exits the bathroom first and I immediately look away because she's naked.

I want to look at her.

Fuck, do I want to look at her.

But she's not walking toward me naked by choice. She's doing it because he's instructed her to. She hasn't consented to me seeing her without her clothes on, and fuck if I'm going to be a piece of shit like Nikolai.

She's still walking toward me—I can see her in my peripheral as my legs bounce in anxiety. I'm forced to shut my eyes as she gets close enough to touch. I've become so in sync with her over the last few weeks, just as Nikolai observed, and I can feel her presence all around me.

"Ezra," her voice is quiet, yet strong and insistent, "you need to shower and come back out in your underwear."

My eyes snap open and lift right up to meet hers. She looks scared, nervous, but at the same time, I see that superhuman resilience telling me that she's determined to be okay through whatever the hell is happening here.

I have to admit how glad I am to see that determination in her because I don't have it for myself. She's so much stronger than I could ever be, and I have to rely on her—I have to trust in her to get through this.

Whatever this nightmare is going to be.

My eyes linger on hers, probably longer than Nikolai is happy with, and I nearly want to smile at her when her look tells me to keep my stupid, sarcastic mouth shut and do as I'm told.

I will do as I'm told, as much as it goes against everything I am. I will do as I'm told because I know the consequence of breaking the rules here.

The least I can do is lessen Anya's suffering and I will take on mountains of my own for the blue-eyed girl I might just be falling for.

CHAPTER 16
Anya

EZRA DISAPPEARS BEHIND the bathroom door as Nikolai rounds on me. I feel a thousand different emotions right now and I'm not clear on a single one of them.

"Come here," he tells me, and I go to him without pause.

I'm standing naked in front of him and he takes every advantage, raking his eyes over my body, leering with lust and devious intent. I'm used to this with Nikolai, used to him seeing me bare. He's seen every part of me, violated every part of me. Though it never really gets better, it does become easier to accept, to become complacent.

His hands cup my cheeks and he bends, bringing his lips close to mine. "I've missed you. Kiss me, Anya."

I close my eyes first to retreat inward before he presses his mouth to mine. His lips part immediately, tongue pressing, insistent that I do the same. I open my mouth and he doesn't hesitate to taste me.

I always have a difficult time when he first starts to kiss me this way. He wants me responsive, but my initial response is always forceful rejection, though I've learned to hide it. I used to show it with pushes and shoves, kicks and shouts of protest.

I know better now.

I force my tongue to swirl back around his. It's not that Nikolai is bad at kissing—he's quite good at it. He's quite good at all of this. That's what makes it so much more disgusting, because he knows how to make me give in and want what he's doing to me.

It makes me feel disgusting for wanting anything from him, but he knows my buttons and triggers, he knows everything about me and how to make me needy for his touch in a truly shameful way.

I hear the bathroom door click open as I'm still kissing Nikolai and feel a new kind of shame…a worse kind of shame…a guilty kind of shame. It's one thing to have to endure such atrocious violations of will from Nikolai, but an entirely different matter to have a witness to it.

I had a witness once before, with Jamal, my first dance partner here at Mikhailov Manor. Jamal and I had grown close during his time here. I liked him. He liked me. Nikolai knew it and took advantage of it.

Things were far more violent in those early days, before I understood my place and my inability to escape captivity. When Nikolai raped me back then, I fought. I resisted. I screamed. I can only imagine how difficult it was for Jamal to watch.

He's been gone for a long time, and I don't want to think about him anymore.

Ezra is here to witness my shame on a whole new level, to witness my complacency to Nikolai's abusive will. I just pray that Nikolai has no intention of making me orgasm. I don't want to imagine what Ezra would think of me then.

Would he think I enjoy Nikolai and his touch just because he's capable of manipulating my senses so effectively?

Nikolai pulls away from my kiss, turning his head to look at Ezra. I don't miss the way his eyes run down over Ezra's body. I keep my eyes on Nikolai because Ezra is an unwilling participant, too, and I refuse to take advantage in that way.

Though it's hard not to look.

I see him shirtless nearly every day, as that's usually how he dances. I admire his physique nearly every day. I want him nearly every day.

But that doesn't give me a right to join in Nikola's blatant ogling in a scenario where his choices and rights are as invalid and unwanted as mine.

Still, my greedy eyes dart a glance down to Ezra's black boxer briefs before rising quickly to his face. I can't avoid meeting his eyes because his are locked on mine. It pains me to share his gaze because he's looking at me so intensely. There's fear and concern there, but I don't think it's for himself...I think it's for me.

"Stand at the foot of the bed," Nikolai says to me, turning and walking away to retrieve something from one of his dresser drawers.

I do as instructed, facing outward toward the room. Ezra is still standing just in front of the bathroom, which is around the side of the bed. From where he's standing, he has a clear view of my entire backside and I immediately feel self-conscious. I don't sense his eyes on me. Ezra is respectful, kind, a gentleman, so it doesn't surprise me to feel the absence of his gaze.

Nikolai returns with a length of coarse, beige rope and stands in front of me. "Hold still."

He begins to wrap me with rope, coiling and tying expert knots as he's done for years. The rope is rough, scratching across my skin, and I know it will burn when he pulls it tight.

He knots it behind my back in the center and wraps it around to my front, crisscrossing at my sternum. He twists the rope to form an "X" between my breasts and drapes the long ends over my shoulders. It's heavy to wear and it's already irritating my bare skin. Every movement, no matter how subtle, feels like he's trying to strike a match against my flesh.

He pulls the ends back through the knot at my back and keeps going, eventually securing my arms so they are pinned to my sides, my palms pressed firmly against my thighs. My bottom half is free and mobile, but my top half is entirely bound in the coils which are rubbing me raw.

"I'm thinking you will dance like this," Nikolai says. "Except your arms will need to be free, for safety, of course."

Ezra scoffs behind me, "Safety."

Nikolai's eyes snap over my shoulder to glare at him. "I will teach you how to bind her. In your dance, you will control her, move her with the ends of the rope. You are the puppet master and she is the puppet."

"That doesn't work with our music." Ezra's sharp tone tells me he's losing his temper.

I'm afraid for him more than I am for me, so I chance it and speak up. "Shut up, *mal'chik*," I snap at him. "We'll make it work."

Thankfully, he's quiet again and it only takes a few moments for Nikolai to turn his attention back to me. A wicked smirk tilts the side of his mouth.

"You're doing well with controlling him," Nikolai tells me. "I wonder what else you can command him to do for you."

I swallow. "There's nothing I want him to do for me."

"Nothing?" Nikolai questions. "Nothing at all?"

He snatches my chin between his fingers and thumb and pinches, lifting to tilt upward. He bends, touching the tip of his nose to mine.

"I don't believe you," he says. "I think there are things you both want to do to each other."

"I want nothing from him," I lie. "You provide me with everything I need."

Nikolai chuckles. "You're a terrible liar, Anya. Do you think I don't know you better than that by now?" He doesn't move, but his eyes leave me for a moment, glancing toward where Ezra stands, then back to me. "He wants you. And I'm nearly inclined to let him have you, only because I'm curious to watch, to see what happens. To see if he can destroy you all over again in the ways I destroyed you when I first stole you away."

That's simply not possible. No one could destroy me in all the ways Nikolai had, especially not Ezra. He couldn't and he wouldn't. Still, if anyone is able to orchestrate such destruction, it would be Nikolai.

I shiver.

Nikolai releases my chin and pushes on my shoulders with both of his large hands. "Sit."

I lower to perch on the edge of the plush, burgundy comforter. I'm forced to sit up arrow straight with the way my arms are bound tightly against my sides. I wriggle my hands, clenching and releasing my fingers. They already tingle from the restriction, and I think he's tied the ropes too tightly.

Nikolai kneels in front of me and pushes my knees apart, opening me wide for him. My thighs clench against the exposure he forces, but he's still able to spread me apart all the same. He isn't angered by the way my body reacts, and I'm thankful for that at least. I almost wonder if he mistakes the strain in my thighs as desire for him, if he thinks I clench with need rather than protest.

Surely, Nikolai can't be that delusional. Though he's had me fooled before...

"Ezra," he says, "pull the chair around, sit behind me. I'd like to give you a front row seat for Anya's performance."

"No, thanks. I'm good," Ezra replies flippantly, and I hear the edge to his tone, the crack, the pain.

I flinch as Nikolai reaches into his pocket and pulls out his switchblade, flipping it open easily with a flick of his wrist. I whimper. Every muscle in my body tenses as he presses the tip of his knife against the inside of my thigh.

"Move the chair and *sit*," Nikolai insists, "or...if you prefer to watch her bleed, I can give her yet another scar."

Ezra moves without hesitation. I'm relieved for his compliance, though the fear of pain washes over my sensibility all the same. I watch, feeling like I can't catch my breath, as Ezra drags one of the armchairs from in front of the fireplace and positions it just behind Nikolai's back. I look into his eyes as he lowers to sit. He's shaking his head with a tense jaw. He looks hopeless and I don't like the way it shadows his green eyes. I need them bright for me.

My breathing turns shallow as I feel the tip of Nikolai's blade dig into my skin. I yelp when I feel the sharp pinch of it puncturing my skin, and I look down to see a drop of blood pool and rise to force its way out. My breath catches on a gasp as I realize he's still pushing. It's not the first time he's cut me here and it won't be the last. But it hurts like new every single time he does it.

I don't dare protest. If I tell him no or stop, it will only be ignored. I know that because I'd earned harsher punishment in the past for fighting it. I know it's better to just take it, hold in my protests and tears for later, and purge them alone on my pillow. Still, fear floods through me and makes my body react. My muscles twitch, I breathe too fast, hot tears prickle at the corner of my eyes.

He's marking me with another scar. There's over twenty of them on my left thigh and his blade cuts between two of the white lines. He's looking up at me, smiling, taking such pleasure in my torment. It burns like fucking fire the way he slices into my skin, but my body remembers the feel of it. As much as it hurts, I find I can retreat from the sharp sting. I can hide from the physical pain, focus on something else, sneak my way around it. But I can't hide from the eyes that are searing hatred into Nikolai's back.

Ezra is glaring. If looks could kill, Nikolai would be sliced into pieces and scattered all around the room. Ezra looks as though he's going to pounce, and though I wish he could drag Nikolai away and save me, I know it's simply not possible.

I lock in on Ezra, staring him down until I can capture his attention. After what seems like forever, he finally tears his deadly stare from Nikolai's back and looks up at me. His eyes widen briefly before softening.

I need to hold him here, keep his attention on me. I can't risk what will happen if I lose control of him now.

In an unexpected move, Nikolai pulls his knife away and wipes the flat end of it across his slacks. He smears my blood into his clothing like it's nothing, as if painting the expensive fabric with my life force is merely a convenient way to clean off his weapon. He folds it and puts it away in his pocket. A rush of air escapes me as the tension of immediate danger lessens it hold on me. He's still dangerous, of course, but at least the blade is gone.

Nikolai bends to land a soft kiss on the top of my leg, brushing across my old scars there. He slowly works his way up to the freshly smarting wound, which is far too close to the apex of my thighs. He licks his tongue flatly across the cut, lapping up the blood as if it were some rare delicacy.

I shudder.

I shudder because it's demented.

I shudder because he's sick and twisted.

I shudder because no matter how hard I try to fight it, the heat of an attractive man so close to my sex, sensually licking the inside of my thigh, still triggers my body into reacting pleasurably.

And it makes me hate myself.

My mind and body are out of sync.

Ezra's eyes narrow on mine as he watches. I think he can see inside my soul right now. I think he knows everything I'm feeling and exactly why I'm feeling it. I expect to see judgment reflected there in the emerald green, but instead I see acceptance, perhaps even understanding. It makes me sigh from the relief of his empathy.

Nikolai is taking his liberties with me as his lips and tongue move closer and closer to my opening. My heart beats fast, both for the sensual, languid way Nikolai drifts across my skin and for the way Ezra holds me with his gaze.

I won't look away from him as long as I can help it. His stare is everything that's holding me together. It's everything that's maintaining my sanity. It gives my mind something steady to anchor to, even when my body reacts outside of my control.

My body jolts and I sigh when Nikolai licks across my folds, all the way up and over my clit. He wraps his lips around it, lightly sucking before sticking his tongue inside me.

I fight my eyelids when they threaten to close. Normally, that would be the thing that saves me—that ability to stop looking at the Devil before me and pretend that it's anyone else. But all I want is to stay locked in on Ezra's green eyes. I want to watch him watch me.

As Nikolai begins to draw unwanted pleasure from me with his skilled tongue, there's a moment. A brief, fleeting moment where I lose myself just a little, just enough that I nearly forget it's him between my legs. That moment belongs to Ezra and the way he watches me. My eyes roam over his face to see his whole expression has changed. Everything is still carved from rage, but the rage has lessened with the rise of something else.

Interest.

His curiosity is piqued, and I can't fault him for that. I won't. We're only human after all, and I'm not a complete fool to pretend he hasn't shown interest in me before. What surprises me is how it changes my emotional response.

Nikolai is raping me, for the thousandth time, touching me and trying to pleasure me without seeking or considering my consent. It's vile and filthy, and I fully expect this man to go to hell. I would send him there myself if I could.

But Ezra…

Ezra is right there and his presence changes everything. It shouldn't, but it does. And because it does, I slip.

I moan.

Unsurprisingly, Nikolai thinks I'm enjoying *him*.

"Anya," he growls against my clit as he brings two fingers in beneath his tongue.

I'm struggling to stay upright as pleasure builds within my core, intense and unwanted. Nikolai reaches up with his free hand, shoves between my breasts, and I fall backward onto the bed.

"No." I slip again, protesting the absence of Ezra's comforting face and everything stops.

Ezra pushes to his feet and I lift my head off the bed to look up at him. He takes a step forward, but Nikolai is already whirling around to stop him.

"Go and sit behind her, *mal'chik*, on the bed."

I don't want him to sit behind me.

I *do* want him to sit behind me.

I want him here, but I also want him nowhere near this sexual nightmare.

I'm more conflicted than I've ever been, and Nikolai knows it. He's done this intentionally to torture me and he's successful.

It's all so much worse that I can't move. I'm literally helpless laying on the bed right now. I could kick if I wanted to, perhaps break Nikolai's nose, if I get him just right.

But what good would that do?

Ezra sighs as he moves around to the side of the bed and I turn my head to look at him, trying to tell him I'm sorry without a word. He shakes his head and climbs onto the bed behind me.

"Pull her all the way back and sit her upright between your legs."

"No," Ezra spits out the word harshly. "No, I'm not helping you rape her."

"You will or I will make her bleed. Would you prefer that?"

"Why are you doing this? What the fuck is wrong with you?"

I'm caught between two towering infernos, blazing high and hot and completely overwhelming.

"The same thing that's wrong with you and all other men. Don't pretend you aren't hard right now. I can see it. Lay her down against you and she'll feel it," Nikolai sneers. "We're all fucking monsters. Some of us just found a way to get paid feeding the other monsters. Some of us have learned to enjoy the rewards of being a monster. Anya is my right and my reward, and I will do whatever the fuck I want to do to her. I'll do the same with you. Don't let her make you think for a second that she doesn't want this, that she doesn't enjoy this. I have the taste of her on my tongue that proves how much she wants it. In fact, why don't we let her tell you what she wants you to do? Anya..." he stands to hover above me and I'm already shaking my head, "would you prefer that I cut you, make you bleed again? Or would you rather I fuck you?"

"What the *fuck* kind of choice is that?" Ezra shouts and I flinch at the unexpected force of his voice above my head.

It's no choice at all.

"Quiet," Nikolai broods. "Let her choose."

I press my eyes shut and shake my head, feeling the rope over my shoulders rub uncomfortably against the sides of my neck. Obviously, I want neither choice. He's a sick fuck who has given me an impossible choice to make.

He leans down over me with a sinful smile, leaning on his hands which press into the mattress on either side of my hips. "Use your words, Anya. Would you rather I cut you or fuck you?"

Both will hurt me. I'm partially tempted to tell him to cut me, but I fear he'll take it too far, that he might stab his blade into my gut to spite me and I would die right here on his bed. That doesn't sound like a half bad idea to my fucked-up sanity, but Ezra changes everything. I wouldn't want to make that choice to leave him alone here. At least with me here, I'm the buffer between them—I'm the object of Nikolai's abuses.

When did I become so willing to put myself on the line for someone else?

I suck in a quick breath, blow it out hard, swallow, and bravely dare him, "Fuck me."

"Louder, please, Anya. Convince me you'd rather be fucked."

I spit the words out with hateful passion, "I'd rather you *fuck* me, *khozyain.*"

"Tell Ezra." Nikolai's voice is smooth and even and filled with amusement. "Tell him you want him to help me fuck you."

My eyes feel hot around the edges. "Ezra, I want you to…" I stutter as a tear slips down the side of my face, catching me off guard, "to help him fuck me."

Nikolai bends and kisses my belly button. "Good girl." He looks up at Ezra. "Pull her back and settle her between your legs."

Nikolai steps back and works his belt buckle and I hear Ezra's breath catch and stutter.

"I can't," he whispers, filled with heartache. "I can't. I can't. I *won't.*"

I tilt my chin up toward the ceiling, lifting my eyes to look at Ezra as best I can from where I lay in front of him on the bed. His hands are on top of his head, fingers laced together, and his body trembles. As horrifying as this is for me, it's not a first.

But for Ezra, it is.

"*Mal'chik,*" I say, "do as you're told."

I hope my calm command can ease him enough to do what has to be done.

"I can't do this," he protests.

"You can do this, and you will. Pull me back between your legs. Do it now."

There's a long pause and I hold my breath.

Ezra has to do this.

I have to do this.

Finally, he gives up, gives in, and I sigh a breath of relief that he understands.

"I'm sorry. I'm sorry, Anya. I don't know what the fuck else I'm supposed to do."

He sounds so…broken.

Oh, God.

He slides his hands beneath my back, grasping at the rope and yanking me backward along the bed.

This.

This moment.

This is my undoing.

CHAPTER 17

Anya

NEVER HAVE I ever felt so completely ripped apart. I'm struggling against every fiber in my being not to cry, not to scream, not to fight and beg Nikolai to stop.

My hands are untied. All the ropes have been pulled free from my body, though I still feel them there as a phantom scratch, the threat of dragging burns striking up again every time I move.

Nikolai has chosen to drag out our torture, taking his time fucking me every which way while Ezra is forced to hold me or move me or watch.

He has Ezra sitting in the armchair, wearing his underwear, thankfully for him. I'm on the floor in front of him, on my knees, bent forward over his lap.

I've lost all inhibition. I grip the top of Ezra's thighs at the crease where they meet his hips, unsure of whether I'm hurting him with the way I dig in my fingertips. I have to hold onto something because it hurts so much. I lean into him, letting my cheek rest against his stomach.

Nikolai thrusts into me brutally from behind, taking the part of me where his dick absolutely does *not* belong. It doesn't belong inside me in any way, but especially not there. I'm raw, dry, probably bleeding and damaged, and I just want it to stop.

I want it to stop.

I want it to stop.

I just fucking want it to stop.

The only comfort I have is Ezra. How I hate, hate, *hate* what this is doing to him. He's forced to sit there and hold me while this torture takes place in front of him.

He held me on his lap, squirming and writhing as Nikolai made me come on the bed, a real-life pornography, as twisted and fucked up as it all was. I didn't blame Ezra for being aroused by it, not one bit. But Nikolai made it all the worse knowing that what he was doing to me was affecting

Ezra all the same. He used that knowledge to torture us both, by hurting me and making Ezra watch in his aroused state.

I felt horrible for the way my body shifted against Ezra's erection with every one of Nikolai's savage thrusts. Nikolai knew it was happening. He wanted to hurt Ezra in his own way, keeping him in a state of awareness and arousal throughout my torture.

"I'm sorry," I whisper into Ezra's side as I grip him tighter. "I'm sorry, I'm sorry, I'm sorry."

Ezra lifts a hand to stroke my hair, only once before it stills. His breaths are sharp and ragged. I know what he's struggling against, what he's fighting. I do everything in my power to lift my body from his lap, to limit how much I rub against him, but I can't.

I just can't.

The pain rips through me and it's all I can do to endure it.

Nikolai moves faster, with sharper thrusts, over and over. I feel his heat invade me, his sweat sliding over my backside. He gives one final razor-like thrust and grunts low and long. I feel him spill hot liquid inside me. I let myself have the satisfaction of a single, biting scream as he finally pulls out of me.

And then I start to cry.

He's hurt me like this before, but this is true hell. He's taken me to a deeper level of torment for how he's involved Ezra. Ezra was being raped as much as I was and as soon as the invasion of Nikolai's physical presence is gone, it's all I can think of.

I collapse to the floor as Nikolai puts his clothes back on, literally falling into a naked heap at Ezra's feet. He shifts forward in his seat as I sob, clinging to his ankle as I fold my body around his leg.

He clears his throat and his voice is strained. "Please, let me take her now. She needs to rest."

Nikolai laughs. "Fine. Take her and go, I've had enough of you both for one night."

I'm rising into the air a second later as Ezra scoops me from the floor and I curl into him, wrapping my arms around his neck. He's a tidal wave of calmness crashing in, washing away the debris of this hurricane.

"Oh, Ezra," Nikolai calls out as he carries me away, "don't you want your photograph of Emma?"

I'd nearly forgotten about the photograph of his ex-girlfriend.

Ezra's chest puffs higher as he sucks in a breath. "Keep it," he barks out. "I'm sure you'll be bringing me more."

"Yes, I will."

I know it the instant we're in the hallway because I feel the demon presence of Nikolai fade away. The air is immediately lighter. The smell of whiskey and cigar smoke and blood and sex fades with every step Ezra takes.

I fear someday Nikolai might try to do to Ezra what he's just done to me and the thought of it makes me ill. I know Ezra must feel ill for me now.

Ezra carries me to my room and kicks the door shut behind us. He takes me straight to the bathroom and carefully lowers me to the floor. I squeeze his arms tight, just above the elbows, as he ducks his head down to catch my eyes.

"Hey," he says softly, "I'm gonna put you in the shower, okay? Can you stand?"

I nodded slowly. Of course, I could stand. I'd had to carry myself from Nikolai's room so many times before. I'd had to clean and care for myself in the aftermath so many times before.

But then, why is it so hard to let go of him now?

Why do I feel like I simply can't survive this without him?

Have I grown weak, dependent, needy?

He reaches behind me to open the glass shower door, gripping my shoulder with one hand as if he just can't let go of me now. He turns on the water and holds his hand beneath it as my sobs slow to occasional hiccups of emotion. Then he steps inside and pulls me in with him. He puts me under the spray and closes the door behind us.

I look up at him from beneath the waterfall that runs down my hair and though the water is warm, I shiver.

There it is, finally, thankfully.

A pause.

An offbeat count in the dance of torment that has become my life… *our* lives.

It's a sigh, a breath, a brief reprieve from the pain of this night and the uncertainty of our future.

It's Ezra I share it with.

And then it's gone.

My pain comes rushing back like the volume being quickly turned up to full blast and I flinch.

"Tell me what you need me to do. How do I fix you? How do I make the pain stop?"

I shake my head. "You can't make the pain stop."

He looks down between us and my eyes follow, drawn immediately to the red streak flowing down between my legs, swirling crimson around the drain.

"You're bleeding," he says. "I'm—"

I reach out for his fingertips with mine. "Don't you dare apologize to me for what he's done."

"Anya," he says.

I tug at his fingertips, encouraging him forward and I step into his arms, wrapping mine around his middle. He's hesitant at first, but then he does the same, squeezing and holding me tight. I'm aware of his erection still present between us, but it doesn't scare me the way it should after all I've been through. I know he doesn't want it. The fact that he still has it is a testament to the way he's been violated by Nikolai, too.

Somehow he must know I'm thinking about it. "I'm sorry. About that…" he says.

"That's not your fault," I tell him.

He kisses the top of my head, then pulls back. "If you're okay, I'll leave you alone to shower."

"No, don't go."

His green eyes flicker with gratitude. I think it seems strange at first, but really, I know he needs comfort just as much as I do. He's grateful that I've asked him to stay with me because he needs me, too. We need each other right now.

He nods. "Okay. I won't go."

I close my eyes. "Can you help me? I want to feel clean and it hurts too much to…"

"Just tell me what you need, Anya. I'll do whatever you need."

As risky as it is for my fragile sanity in the moment, I ask Ezra to clean me, I ask him to use the bath sponge to cleanse between my legs. I could do it myself, but I can feel in my gut how much he wants to help me, how much he needs to feel like he's done something to make it better.

We both need cleansing from Nikolai's assault.

He bends to one knee on the tile and starts to tentatively scrub across the tops of my thighs where Nikolai has made four small cuts—four new scars to join all the others. The soap stings, but nothing like the feeling of them being carved into my skin.

He hesitates and looks up at me. "Do you want me to…"

He doesn't finish the question because he knows that I know what he's asking.

"I just want to feel clean, Ezra. I want every trace of him wiped away."

"And you're sure you want me to?"

I nod.

Tenderly, Ezra cleans between my legs. He's soft with me, gentle. He works quickly, doing just enough to make me feel cleansed without lingering. It doesn't feel awkward and for once, I don't feel weak for asking for help. Perhaps it's just because I'm so tired and he's being so attentive, so compassionate. He stands and lightly grips my shoulders, turning me to face the spray of water.

A beat of fear tenses my shoulders. The way he grabbed me and put me under the water without warning takes my mind back to the pool. I have to remind myself that it's just a shower. I can pull my head out from under the waterfall whenever I want. Ezra's touch is light, not harsh like Nikolai's, and I know if I tell him to let me go, he will.

I breathe in courage and tilt my head toward the water, letting it run down my face. It's warm and it surprises me just how refreshing and wholly cleansing it feels. Ezra's still here with me, his hands delicate on my shoulders. He stands a step back from me and I know he's trying to give me space.

Normally it's exactly what I would need.

Nothing is the same with Ezra, though.

It never has been.

Just like I relied on his warmth, his nearness, to get through Nikolai's torment, I need him now more than I ever did. I need to be held and cared for. In truth, I always needed it. I just pretended I didn't for the last three years. I'd become so good at lying to myself that I'd convinced myself it was true.

Ezra came into my life with warmth and light and truth. Truth, even when I didn't know I was living in lies.

I cross my arms over my chest and place my hands on top of his. His fingers twitch beneath my palms and I clutch them in my grip to keep him from pulling away from me. I need him right now and I don't want him to pull away. I pull down, bringing his hands with mine until he gets the hint. He steps closer with my encouraging tug and lets his hands fall to hold my waist. He's still so tentative, so respectful, though I know it's strained. It makes me want to cry all over again.

At the same moment that I lean backward, he leans forward, giving me his chest to rest my head against. His arms finally give in, wrapping entirely around my waist to hold me, and I feel him sigh.

The coldness I've hardened my heart with over time threatens, but Ezra's warmth melts it before it can encapsulate me in ice.

"Are you okay, Ezra?"

He bends his head forward and his cheek brushes against mine. "Am I okay? Are *you*? I don't think either of us are."

"I'll survive. I've done it for three years."

"And how many years more?"

"I don't know."

"I don't want you to just survive. I want you to live, Anya. You deserve a real life. You deserve heaven and he's giving you hell."

"It doesn't help to wish for a different kind of life. This is the life he's given us, and no one is going to rescue us from it. No one."

His chest rises as he takes in a heavy breath, and I know he's nearly ready to spew a mountain of anger and frustration about our situation. But he must know that won't help me now, in this moment. He must know that will only make this hurt more for me.

Instead, he's quiet.

Instead, he's still.

Instead, he gives me peace in the chaos.

When we get out of the shower, Ezra dries me with a towel and helps me put on underwear, some looser fitting pajama pants, and a camisole tank top.

I have nothing in my room that will fit him, so he changes from his soaking wet boxer briefs and wraps a towel around his waist. I can't stand the thought of him leaving me to go to his room just for clothes, though I know it's risky that Ezra and I are alone together at all. Nikolai had drowned me before for this very reason.

His unpredictability truly is jarring.

Still, I convince myself it's okay that we're in my room together because he told Ezra to take me and go. He knew Kostya wasn't nearby. Really, I know this is a stupid thing to convince myself of, but I just need Ezra here with me. I don't understand why I feel this way and I hate that I do.

In any case, I don't want Ezra to leave me and he chooses to stay. He kneels in front of me where I'm perched on the edge of my bed. His skin shines fresh from the shower and I find that I ache with the desire to touch it, to feel the smoothness of it. I imagine it would feel soft beneath my fingertips.

"How do you go on?" he asks with curious eyes. "How do you fall asleep at night and wake up the next morning and *go on?* I think I'm going to have nightmares about this every time I close my eyes and it wasn't even me being hurt."

I speak slowly, softly, "It was every bit as much an injury to you as it was to me."

He shakes his head. "No. That's not true."

"He made you an unwilling participant, didn't he? Did you not feel violated for the way he manipulated your arousal and used it in such a way to shame you?" I sigh. "Rape is rape, Ezra…emotional or physical."

He hesitates and blinks, his brow creasing as he shakes his head. "He abuses us both. You're not wrong about that," he says. "I just don't understand how you…How many times has he done this to you?"

"Alone? More times than I care to count. With a partner? Tonight was the second time. The first wasn't nearly as awful."

I expect him to respond, but he doesn't. He just waits. He gives me the pause I need to find my words and speak them into the shared space between us. It's strange the way he brings my feelings to the surface with nothing more than a patient pause and a look.

A look that makes me feel safe, even when I'm not.

"This was the worst I've ever had it here. Not because of the vile things he did to me. He's done all of those things before…" I swallow. "It was worse because of you."

His face falls and he slumps back to sit on his heels, looking as though he's just seen a ghost. He rubs his hands on the towel straining around his strong thighs, looks down, then back up at me.

Still, he says nothing.

"I had a hard time hiding with you there in the room. I've always been able to retreat to a dark space in my mind, a corner I hide away in when he's hurting me. I've tried to hide in that dark space ever since you arrived, Ezra. I can do it when you're not near me, but when you are…" I pause. "There's just so much light in you that even if I go to that dark corner, it's not dark enough to hide in. I don't think I was ever able to hide from you, not entirely. Having you there while Nikolai hurt me, seeing how he hurt you, nearly broke me." My voice cracks and unexpected tears spill down my cheeks. "I don't know if I'm making any sense. I just…I can't let myself get attached. I can't. I know it only makes it worse, but the thought of losing you…"

I let the tears take over. He lets me cry for a few moments and then lifts back up onto his knees. He reaches for my hands, pulling them from my lap. He moves with slow intention as he puts one of my hands on his chest, over his heart, and holds the other sweetly in his palm. He licks his lips and blinks a little too long, inhaling a deep breath through his nose.

"My heart beats out of control every time I'm with you," he confesses with a gentle voice.

I force an ill-placed chuckle through my sadness, though it's entirely without feeling. "That's because torture and torment follow me like a shadow. This," I tap my hand over his heart where he placed it, "this is because of fear. Because of loneliness. Because of desperation to feel something, anything but the hopelessness for our future."

He narrows his eyes at me and shuffles closer on his knees. I feel the rough texture of the overly bleached towel rub against my shins. His nearness and touch make *my* heart beat faster, but I'm too much of a realist to think anything of it. I won't *let* myself feel anything about it, though I'm starting to wonder if maybe I should.

I want to.

"Don't do that," he says. "Don't patronize me. I know you think you know everything about me, Anya, but you don't. I know the difference between fearing and wanting. I know the difference between desperation and need. My heart beats faster for *you*."

I try to take a breath and it catches in my throat. "Why are you telling me this?"

"I know you fear getting attached, you fear losing me. What you don't know is that I'm already attached. I'm *yours*. And I won't fucking lose you."

He squeezes both my hands tighter, holding the one over his heart and the other on my lap. He looks down and shakes his head, yet again giving me a quiet pause before looking up at me. His green eyes steal mine with life and truth and vibrancy.

Just like that, with a snap that cracks all reason, I'm stolen.

Not by a cruel master, but instead, by a brilliant man who could make me want to hope again.

This is dangerous.

But still, I want it.

I pull on our entwined hands, yanking him toward me as I lean forward and crash my lips against his. He squeezes my fingers and I can feel his restrained desperation when his pillow soft lips twitch against mine.

I feel what he's feeling.

He's aching to part them, to taste and explore me. I hesitate, but its brief. If he'd taken that liberty on his own, pressing me too hard, too fast to open for him, it would've ended right then.

But he didn't do that.

He waited.

He breathes heavy through his nose, patient in the chaste kiss, though I can feel every inch of tension in his body.

I want it because he waits.

I want it more and more with each passing second of complete respect and patience. For the first time in nearly three years, I *want* physical affection.

He is the sunshine to my wilting petals. His light gives me nourishment. Like a rose, I blossom for him, parting my lips with permission to explore this sensation with me.

Ezra's tongue slips inside and though the invasion threatens to shut me down, it's only for a moment. Then the moment passes and inexplicably, I feel free.

He makes me feel free.

I sigh into his mouth, shaking his hands from mine so I can grab his face and pull him closer. I bend over him to deepen the kiss, but he pushes back, lifting higher on his knees to meet me.

His hands fall heavy on the bed on either side of my hips. I feel it dip as he presses down and I know he's holding himself back. He's leaning into me, his tongue sweeping in and around, tasting every bit of me in a silent, desperate plea to have more of me.

I can't give him more of me, not now, and he knows it. Knowing he knows it and yet still doesn't push me sends a flurry of feeling through my stomach, tiny wings that flutter and buzz with the most pleasant sensation.

It makes me want to give him more of me.

And I know I will someday.

Because this man makes my heart beat faster in the best way I've ever known.

CHAPTER 18
Ezra

ANYA KISSED ME two nights ago, and I can't stop thinking about it.

I'm pacing inside my ugly green room after dark, too full of energy to sleep. I still get locked in at night, though I'm no longer required to wear the ankle cuff. I get to move freely—mostly—throughout the manor during the day.

Kostya follows me around more often than he follows Anya. She's proven her submission and trustworthiness over years. All I've managed to prove over months is my impatience and bad fucking attitude.

I'm wishing I could get out of here—go dance in the studio for a while or do something, *anything*, to get rid of this excess energy pulsing through my muscles—when I hear the locks turning on the door.

I wrinkle my forehead, confused because this is unusual.

It's not morning. Dinner was only a few hours ago.

Kostya always lets me out in the morning, never at night.

I move toward the door, instantly feeling defensive, because I don't know who is on the other side of it. Then someone knocks.

They *knock*.

Who the fuck is knocking on a door I don't control?

I throw my arms out, shaking my head, and they fall with a thud against my sides. "Uh, come in?"

The door swings open to reveal my blue-eyed girl standing there, holding the key.

She smiles and it hits me right in the center of my chest. "Hi."

I grin right back at her like an idiot. "What the hell did you knock for?"

She cocks her head. "To be polite. Do you wanna get out of here?"

I almost laugh. "Do you really need me to answer that?"

She rolls her eyes. "Come with me but be quiet. I want to show you something."

"A little rebellion, huh? I like it. Let's go." My heart is thudding against

145

my ribs when I step toward her, then I stop. "Wait, where's Nikolai?"

"He just left. He'll be gone overnight."

"Kostya?"

"That's why you need to be quiet."

She's sneaking me out.

Nikolai's gone and she's sneaking me out for the night.

I feel a rush of excitement jumpstart my senses in a way I haven't felt since I was a teenager sneaking out of my foster parents' house on a school night.

My feet are moving without another thought. I meet her in the hallway, and she shuts and locks the door behind us. She wraps her fingers around my hand and squeezes, pulling me forward as she strides down the hallway.

I get this cold tingle running through my veins the moment her skin touches mine. It makes my spine prickle and rush all the good feelings I have about her low in my gut.

She stops at the end of the hallway and looks over her shoulder at me, holding up a finger to her lips, telling me to keep my mouth shut without even saying a word.

I zip my fingers across my lips and her eyes brighten, lingering on my mouth for an extra beat. I want to grab her and kiss her hard.

We move forward together, quietly rushing down the grand staircase. We turn left at the bottom and move toward the east wing. She pauses as we're about to pass the kitchen doorway and peeks her head in, pulling it right back out and jumping backward. Her backside runs right into the front of my body when she does this and I grab her just above the elbows. She turns her head to the side, and I see the blue of her eyes peeking out from the corners as she tries to look at me.

"On my cue," she whispers.

"On *my* cue," I joke, and she jabs her elbow backward into my gut.

She peeks her head back into the kitchen and gives a quick nod. We walk quickly and quietly past. As soon as we reach the garden corridor, she gives me a quick look—an almost playful look I've never seen on her before—and takes off running.

That one little lightning bolt of happiness she shows me takes on a life of its own, lassoing around me and tugging me along with her.

I run after her.

She leads us down past the pool and comes to a stop at a door to our right, opposite the cave-like alcove that leads to the pool entrance where Nikolai drowned her. She stops to unlock the door with one of the same keys she used to unlock my door.

It opens onto a hallway. I step past the entry and she joins me, shutting and locking the door behind her. It wouldn't stop Kostya or Nikolai from coming after us, but it would slow them down. I'm surprised I'm hardly thinking about what they'll do if they find us sneaking around.

I almost don't care.

We're captives whether we behave or not, so fuck the rules. Especially if this tiny little rebellion can make her look this fucking happy.

She takes my hand again and we walk side by side down the short hallway. It opens onto a foyer, reminiscent of the grand entrance, but much smaller. Same marbled floors, same ornate gold frames and crown molding, same stupid burgundy-colored walls.

Two sets of double doors sit to our left. They're dark wood, carved with intricate patterns like the doors in the grand entrance, only smaller. Anya walks us to the doors and pulls on the handle, opening it wide.

"This is Nobility Hall," she says, gesturing for me to go inside.

I grin as I walk past her and enter the large open space. It's dark, but I see what it is. This is our dance hall. It's where we'll be performing. The two aisleways that lead down to the stage are covered with plush, red carpeting, lined with rows of seats on both sides. I'd guess you could fit about a hundred people in this theater, which seems excessive given that Mikhailov Manor is so vast and empty.

I move forward as the lights come on, first in the audience, then on the stage. The stage is low, nearer to the audience than I would've expected. It's dark black wood and dark black curtains make it all perfectly, poetically haunting. It should be, given that it's tainted by the blood of slaves.

Anya's arm brushes mine as she comes up beside me and I snatch her hand in mine. I hear her take in a sharp breath and I turn my head to look at her, wanting to see the expression on her face. She tucks a strand of hair behind her ear, so demurely, so innocently, and swallows as she shifts her eyes away from my stare.

I want to hold more than her hand and she wants that, too.

I know it.

But I'm not going to push her.

She starts walking down the aisleway and I walk beside her. "This is a fairly recent addition to Mikhailov Manor."

"Oh?"

"Nikolai had it added on when I was fifteen or so, I suppose. Of course, I wouldn't have known then that he'd already had my adult years mapped out for me."

My gut rolls at the thought. "I'll never get over how sick this whole thing is."

She watches her steps, the corners of her lips tugging upward, though it's not a smile. "Neither will I."

"So, tell me what we're doing here."

We stop as we reach the stage. "I just thought we could dance."

She says it so plainly, so sweetly. It takes me back to freedom, when I could just go and do something because I wanted to, when *she* could just go and do something because *she* wanted to. It hits me then what's happening here as I watch the nervous way she shifts from one foot to the other, the way she keeps tucking that same strand of hair back behind her ear.

She just needs some normalcy and for some reason, she feels safe enough to try for it with me. Truthfully, she's risking life and limb to bring me here, and all she wants is to dance with me.

It's not all she wants, but that's all she needs.

I grin at her, nodding. "Yeah, let's do it. Let's dance."

She smiles up at me and fuck, it shoots right to my groin. I almost feel bad about that, as if I don't have a right to crave her.

But damn, do I crave her.

Her smile softens as she looks at me, fading into something even sweeter. She bites her bottom lip and lets out a heavy breath. She's giving me every signal that she'd let me kiss her if I tried.

If we were back in New York, free, just living our lives the way we wanted to, I'd already have my arms around her. I'd already be pulling her close. I'd already be kissing her the way she deserves to be kissed, with complete, reckless abandon.

But I can't do things the normal way, not with Anya. I refuse to scare or hurt her. I'll only give her what she asks me for, and I'll take nothing more.

It looks like she's about to move closer and I hold my breath. But then she slips past me, walking away from me toward the steps at the side of the stage. She jogs up them and across the hardwood floor to center stage, smiling down at me.

"Are you coming up?" she asks expectantly.

I tilt my head to the side, watching her. "Will you dance for me?"

She nods. "Only if you come up on stage with me."

"You got it," I tell her easily and jog up the five steps to meet her.

I move to sit downstage, facing where she stands in the center. I sit down on the hard wood, leaning back on my palms and crossing my legs casually at the ankles in front of me.

"All right, I'm ready," I say. "Wait. Do we have any music?"

"We can't play music. Kostya will hear it and come looking for us." She suddenly looks apprehensive at her own reminder that we're breaking the rules.

My lips curl in a smirk. "I can sing."

She raises an eyebrow. "Can you though?"

"Nah, not really." I laugh.

She shrugs with a smile. "I have music in my mind."

And in her heart and soul.

"I know you do."

With an encouraging smile, Anya dances for me.

For the past half hour, Anya's been dancing around on stage, twirling and leaping and flowing through some of the most graceful movement I've ever had the pleasure of watching.

My cheeks hurt from smiling, and I'm so fucking grateful for that ache. I don't think I've had such a long stretch of happiness since I arrived here. Anya is poised perfection and though I'm aching to touch her, I'd be plenty happy to sit and watch her dance as long as she'll let me.

She comes out of a turn, but strangely, let's it fade to a slow, unusual stop. She doesn't really finish the movement in an elegant pose the way she normally does, always the professional.

She just stops it.

Turning to face me, she touches her lips with her fingers and she lets her teeth nip at her chewed off thumbnail as her eyes shift.

She's nervous, but not in the way I've come to expect.

"What is it?" I ask her with concern.

She lets out a heavy breath and takes three quick steps toward me, stopping abruptly, just at my feet. I almost feel pushed back by the way she rushes me, but it doesn't move me away. I'm frozen to the spot by the way she looks down at me. I push up off my palms, sitting up straighter and lifting my head, making sure she knows she has my full attention.

"The night we kissed, you said you were mine," she finally says.

I somehow feel lighter to have her remember that as *the night we kissed* and not the night Nikolai cut her and raped her while forcing me to watch.

I nod once. "I said I was yours. And I meant it."

She steps over me and drops down to her knees so quickly, I hardly have time to react. In an instant, she's straddling my outstretched legs, settling her ass on my thighs, grabbing my face in her hands.

"Anya," is all I manage to say before her lips fall heavily onto mine.

I can't contain the groan of sheer relief I feel from having her body against mine, her lips on my lips. Her tongue is already fighting to get to mine and the taste of her is something other-fucking-worldly when I let her in.

She lets me taste her and enjoy her delicious mouth for several satisfying moments before she pulls her head back with a snap. Her hands slide down from my face, but drift softly to the sides of my neck. She presses her forehead to mine.

"I don't know what's wrong with me," she says softly.

I hold myself upright with one palm back on the floor, sliding the other around her waist and rubbing over the small of her back. "What do you mean?"

"There are things I want that I shouldn't want."

I lick my lips and tilt my head forward, touching my nose to hers. "And what do you want?"

Her voice is low, her hands slipping around to the back of my neck to hold me to her. "I want things from you."

I press my palm flat against her back and drag her body closer, forcing her to press in and mold against me, and she sighs. She lets me arch her back and flatten her breasts against my chest. Her curves are soft and supple against my body and I want to touch her everywhere.

I want to flip her over, lay her down, climb on top of her and make her feel everything I feel for her. I want to make her feel how desired she is, how needed she is, how loved she is.

"What do you want?" I repeat, tilting my hips to buck up into her, just for a beat, just to feel her.

Her eyes fall shut and she moans.

Like an angel chorus from the heavens, she moans.

Its pleasure filled, not fearing, and knowing that sends a rush of blood to my cock. I lick my lips and press a soft kiss to hers.

Just one.

"Please, Anya, tell me what you want."

She opens her eyes and I'm held captive by her sultry stare. She doesn't speak, but I don't think she needs to. She lets her body speak for her, just as she does with dance.

Her hips shift forward, a slow, long, experimental motion. She slides across my half-hard, denim-covered cock, pressing down and grinding into me.

"Shit," I manage, my breaths picking up their pace.

She holds steady for a few beats before rocking back, then forward again. I know what her body is telling me. She's telling me how much she wants this, how much she wants to enjoy me in the physical sense, but she doesn't know if she can, if she's ready.

I won't show it, but it actually breaks my heart. Not because I know she isn't ready for me, but because of the reason *why* she's not ready.

Nikolai.

He's abused her sexually for so long that she's probably forgotten what good, healthy sex feels like. A thought crosses my mind and now I'm wondering if she ever knew. For all I know, she was a virgin before he took her.

This train of thought alone is enough to keep my urge to whip her around and pin her beneath me in check. I'll let her decide the pace. I'll let her take whatever it is she needs from me—no matter how small—because I am beyond happy to give it.

She leans into me and her weight pushes my back down to the floor. All that worry about my urge to throw her down and she's doing it to me. My heart races and my pulse thrums a heavy beat, ticking through every muscle, as I lower to my back on the stage floor.

I toss her long hair back over her shoulder with a flick of my wrist just before she brings her lips down on mine and kisses me again. I hold her with my hand on her cheek as she moans into my mouth. The sound vibrates on my lips and makes them tingle, and I moan right back so she can feel the same.

She speaks to me between kisses, "Do you want me?"

"Yes, I want you." I lift my hips to meet hers. "Fuck, I want you."

"Would you still want me if we weren't here?"

I grab her face with both hands, her dangling hair tickling over my knuckles. "I would want you anywhere, Anya."

"How can you know that?"

"Because I know you."

She searches my eyes and I'm caught up in the blue of hers as they flicker. I know the moment she finds whatever it is she's looking for because she smiles in a way I've never seen from her before.

It's bright, happy, *free*.

It shines through her eyes and sends a shockwave of need through me, clenching low in my gut.

She knows exactly what her smile does to me because her legs are wrapped around me and I'm rock-hard beneath her. Her hips move again and it feels like heaven. It makes me want to know what it would feel like to be inside her, but I have no expectation that she'll let me find out.

Still, she's pressing and grinding against me hard and heavy now. Her cotton short-shorts leave little barrier between her and my jeans, and I crudely wonder if she'll leave a wet spot there.

Fuck, I hope she does.

"I don't think I can fuck you," she tells me, though she's grinding against my crotch.

"I don't expect you to."

"But you want me to."

"Yes, I want you to. Fuck, Anya…" I pull her down and kiss her, sloppy and wet.

She kisses my cheek, my neck, along my jawline, and my hands are all over her, touching her everywhere. I slide my heel back along the floor to lift my knee because she's pushing down on me so hard, I want to give her something to push back against.

I don't know if she can come like this with all our clothes on, but fuck, I want her to. I want that from her. I want to see her take what she needs, what she deserves, and have that fleeting moment of freedom. If all I can give her is that moment, I'll give it.

My hands slide over her back and slip down over her ass. My movements are slow because I don't know exactly how she'll react. She doesn't stop me, so gradually, I squeeze. She flips her head, tossing her silky brown hair back over her shoulder again and bites her lip, picking up her pace.

We're all but fucking with our clothes on, but somehow this all seems far more intimate.

I've already seen her naked, I've already seen her orgasm, though it was unwillingly. It actually makes me feel a little emotional to think about it because the sounds she's making now, when I *know* she wants this, are entirely different. The sounds she's making are fuel for the fire within my gut. Her sounds are fucking *magic* and before long, I'm urgently eager for relief. She's changing her angle, shifting against my jeans, rolling her hips and rocking hard.

Her long wavy hair keeps falling back down over her face and the ends tickle against my skin as she molds her hips to mine. I grip her ass and hold her against me.

"Ezra," she whispers into my neck and I shiver at the sound of my name from her sweet lips, "are you mine?"

I sigh, my answer doesn't even require a thought. "I'm yours."

She's jerking against me now, jerking and fucking and making me so hard it hurts. I lift to kiss her neck, licking across the hollow of her throat and earning a pleasure-filled gasp from her.

"I want you to come like this," I tell her, nipping my teeth across the side of her neck. "Please, Anya."

Her eyes are drifting shut, but she smiles as she bites her bottom lip. "Yes…yes…just hold still."

"Holding still, not moving." I grin at her, but she doesn't see it because her eyes are squeezed shut with tension.

It's only a few moments longer when her movements become frantic, desperate. The speed and pressure of her rubbing over my cock makes me swell. If she keeps going at that angle, right there, she's gonna make me come in my jeans.

"Jesus. Anya," I groan.

She puts her hands on my shoulders and pushes down hard, lifting her body off me just enough for her to be able to push her hips down harder, grind deeper. She's tensing and panting out these sweet little "*oh*" sounds and I know she's going to make me come.

The "*oh*" sounds hit harder and faster. She's fucking me harder and faster until suddenly, she explodes with the most incredible body trembling orgasm I've ever witnessed. The look of her letting go—of being so free with me, taking what *she* needs instead of giving under force—is so fucking hot that it pushes me right over the edge with her.

"Yes, fuck, yes," I groan as I buck up against her.

I move my hands to her back and pull her against my chest, holding her close. I can feel her heart beating fast, as if it were my own. She scoots down so she can lay her head and hand on my chest and I feel completely wrapped up in her.

We're quiet and still for minutes, just holding each other and breathing together. The hardwood floor beneath my back is starting to become uncomfortable, but the softness above me makes up for it in spades.

I'm determined to savor this moment of rare peace, holding this woman I know I'm falling hard for, but as the peaceful sound of our breathing is drowned by the open echo of the theater, I'm forced out of the moment. The echo of nothingness that surrounds us reminds me that we'll be dancing for our lives on this very stage in just a few short weeks.

I don't know what will happen then.

I don't know if I'll be killed, sold, or kept.

I don't know what fate Anya faces.

It's a thought that's too overwhelming to bear alone. I hold Anya tighter, rolling us over until I'm on top of her. I look down at my blue-eyed girl and kiss her softly, slowly.

I imagine her home with me in New York, laying comfortably in my bed with sunlight bathing her from open windows. I imagine her free and unburdened by captivity. I imagine her happy, truly, always happy.

I make a promise to myself in that moment to find a way to make that life a reality for her.

I'll find a way, even if it kills me.

CHAPTER 19

Anya

I MOAN AGAINST Ezra's lips as he kisses me for the hundredth time on the stage in Nobility Hall. He cradles me and holds me so gently in his arms, and I never want to leave this moment.

But all moments are fleeting and this one is no exception.

"We should talk about the performance," I tell him.

"Now?"

I sit up and my bones ache from lying with him on the hardwood floor. "Yes, now."

I turn to face him, crossing my legs, and he sits up to mirror my position.

"Okay, then let's talk about it." He adjusts his cock as he settles. "Christ, I still can't believe you made me come in my jeans."

I press my lips together to suppress a smile. I'm sure I'm blushing, but he just grins at me without judgment. He looks almost proud of the way he's affected me.

He should be proud.

I've never felt so…powerful.

"So, what do I need to know?" he asks.

I put my hands on my knees and straighten my spine, arching my lower back to stretch out my sore muscles.

"The four families will send representatives to stay here at Mikhailov Manor for the night of our performance. Our performance is really just an opener, entertainment for them. It's a requirement. A tradition, really. The real purpose for their presence is the quarterly meeting, as I told you before, but each family has to provide entertainment and a reception to welcome their guests when they host. That's what we exist for as talent slaves—to provide entertainment for our family once every year."

He rolls his eyes. "Right. We don't get to live our lives because we have talent. We live as slaves so Nikolai can entertain his stupid fucking guests once a year."

I sigh. "I keep forgetting how new this all is to you."

"And I hate that this seems normal to you."

"I don't think it's normal. It's just what is. This has been my life for a while. The reality is that we're not the only slaves. I can't even attempt to fathom how many people the four families have trafficked. And the other families, they have talent slaves like us, too."

"Are they all dancers? The other talent slaves?"

"No. But they're all artists, performers. The O'Sheas just acquired new talent, a singer, I think. The Campbells have a painter. The Vittoris…well, they have several."

"So, the O'Sheas and the Campbells only have one talent slave?"

"Yes. The Mikhailovs only ever had one, as I understand it, until Nikolai became the new Head of House. But the families are only allowed to be the benefactors for one talent slave at a time."

"Why be benefactors at all? Why waste the time and money?"

"It's all a grooming technique, Ezra. The four families want their talent to be…sophisticated, well-developed. The challenge lies in taking a talented person, breaking them into slavery, and seeing who can maintain their talent through turmoil."

"It's fucking sick."

I nod. "There's a bit of an unspoken competition, I think. There's a lot of pressure on the Heads of House to host an entertaining performance before they get into business."

"Nikolai is Head of House for the Mikhailovs."

"Yes, he was the oldest son, so it would have fallen to him regardless, but especially now that his family is all gone."

"What actually happened to them?"

"I think I told you, but they died in a plane crash."

"All of them?"

"His parents and his younger brother. That was over a year ago. It wasn't an accident, though."

"What do you mean?"

"The American family, the Campbells, they tampered with the plane. It's their fault it crashed."

"How do you know that?"

"Because I…I heard the phone recordings that proved it. The Head of House for the Vittori family, Vigo, he came into possession of these recordings and he made a trade with Nikolai, giving him the information at the last quarterly meeting."

I pinch my eyes shut at the memory of being shared and used by Vigo Vittori. I shudder from head to toe. Ezra sees the change in me, and of course, he asks.

"What did Nikolai trade?"

I hesitate. "He traded me. It was only for an hour. But Vigo was… he's…" I don't have the right words to describe that experience.

"What happened, Anya?" Ezra's words are so soft, tinged with care and concern.

"I don't want to tell you about it." Truly, I don't want to relive it in my mind. "I hate Vigo Vittori. I hate him as much as I hate Nikolai. I fear him, perhaps even more." I suck in a sharp breath. "I don't want to talk about it. That hour he used me nearly broke me. Please don't ask me about it again."

He watches me carefully, eyes narrowed in consideration. He swipes a hand over his mouth and swallows hard, as if physical forcing himself to digest all this new and terrible information. There's a minute of silence, of cautious understanding, and then we move forward, and I'm grateful that Ezra doesn't push me to tell him more about Vigo.

"So, Nikolai's family…" he starts carefully. "You knew them before they died?"

"Yes," I tuck a fallen strand of hair behind my ear, "I was Nikolai's responsibility, though, so we didn't interact much. They didn't interfere. His parents were as cold and callous as he is. His brother was kinder. Not *kind*, but kinder."

He nods. "So, we perform. Entertain the sick bastards. Then what happens?"

I look down. "I can only tell you what's happened here in the past." I take a deep breath. "In the past, my partner and I performed and then—"

Suddenly, I'm sucked back in time.

I look to my left, toward the center of the stage and I remember it as clearly as though it was happening right in front of me. It hasn't even been a full year since my third partner was taken from me.

Jonathan.

I'd developed a friendship with him. Of course, I had. He was kind, caring, a good person. He didn't deserve what happened to him.

After we'd performed that night, at Nikolai's quarterly meeting, Nikolai had come up on the stage as we waited to know our fate. I held Jonathan's hand because I was afraid. Jamal and Erik had been stolen from me. I didn't know if they were dead or alive.

Nikolai didn't hesitate after the performance with Jonathan. He strode across the stage with fierce, intentional steps, a look of disappointment and rage brushing the wrinkled lines across his forehead. He ripped Jonathan from my hold. I screamed at him, begged him not to take Jonathan away, to spare him from whatever fate Nikolai had decided upon.

But it didn't matter what I wanted.

It never does.

Nikolai decided Jonathan hadn't met his excessive standards.

I couldn't help but feel it was my fault. I didn't understand, *couldn't* understand, what we'd done wrong. The performance was technically flawless. We'd worked our asses off to prepare and did everything we could.

But still, he took away my only companion.

I'd chased after them as he dragged Jonathan away, through the throng of guests waiting in the grand entrance for the reception, up the grand staircase, down the hallway, and back into Jonathan's bedroom.

Ezra's bedroom.

The door slammed shut before I could cross the threshold. I suppose I should be glad he put the door between us. I heard Jonathan scream, but after that came the silence.

The silence was so much worse than the screaming.

Kostya took me back to my room, ordered me to get ready for the reception, because I still had to greet Nikolai's guests, the four families.

I don't know what happened to Jonathan.

He might have been murdered.

He might have been injured and taken away.

All I know is that I saw Kostya bring the white comforter and bed sheets out of the room the next morning.

Except they weren't all white.

There were splashes of red.

"Anya?" Ezra says softly and I turn my head to look at him.

I don't want to see his blood on his sheets.

I launch forward, reaching for him as I climb into his lap, sitting sideways. I wrap my hands around his neck and nuzzle in close.

"He's taken all of my partners from me," I whisper, pressing a kiss to his cheek. "I don't know whether he's…whether he's killed them or sold them. But he always takes them after the performance."

He nods, pulling me closer, squeezing me tightly. "I don't know what to say."

"Don't say anything." I press my lips to his and he's ready to meet mine with a sweet, slow, passion-heated kiss.

After a minute, he pulls back slowly, just barely, his lips still brush over mine as he speaks.

"Look, I don't know what to tell you except that I'm fucking amazing. I've rocked your world and I'm gonna rock his. My dancing skills are gonna blow his fucking mind. There's no way he's getting rid of me."

Ezra smiles broadly, happily, and I see how his eyes sparkle with humor and hope.

That hope kills me.

But it also makes my heart beat faster.

CHAPTER 20
Anya

I WORK TO catch my breath after the final beat. The air is somber and still as our performance song ends. Ezra and I have just finished our final rehearsal and the knowledge that tomorrow night is our performance for the four families weighs heavy on us both.

Even so, I feel good about our routine. We've practiced and practiced and come as near to perfect as we possibly could. I know Nikolai will be pleased with this performance, and that small sliver of hope clings to me uncomfortably.

I don't know what will happen after the performance. I don't know if he will keep Ezra or take him from me. I don't know that if he does take him from me, whether he will survive or perhaps be sold as a slave commodity, a human asset.

Thinking about it is physically painful, so I try not to.

I'd rather soak in his rays of light before everything changes.

Ezra strides across the stage to me as I rise to my feet from my final position on the floor. He grabs hold of the long, dangling end of the rope that hangs free from my body, walking his hands along it as he approaches me. The rest of it is wrapped and tied around my body. We use the rope as part of our routine because Nikolai demanded it. Somehow, we'd actually managed to create a beautiful dance with it.

I shouldn't say *we*.

It was Ezra who put it all together. His talent for choreography is only outmatched by his talent for dancing.

He unties me and frees me from the binding rope. His brow is furrowed and I wonder what he's thinking.

"I think we're ready," I tell him, hoping he'll share openly with me.

I get a flicker of a smile from him, but it fades immediately.

"What is it?"

He shakes his head as the last of the rope falls free. "I'm just afraid.

That's all."

I want to wrap my arms around him and hold him tight, but not here. Not in the middle of the stage. This is where we will perform tomorrow, in the dance hall named Nobility Hall.

When Nikolai had chosen me as a child, he had this dance hall built just for me to perform in. It's a beautiful performance space, but it's haunting all the same.

"Come with me," I say, taking his hand and dragging him backstage.

Nikolai is wrapped up in preparing the manor for his guests who will be arriving throughout the night and tomorrow morning. Kostya is with us, sitting out in the audience, but pays little attention, always staring down at the cell phone screen in his hands.

Ezra and I have done what we need to do to prove we pose no threat of attempting escape or harm, to ourselves or to anyone else here. We've been granted the small amount of trust to do what we need to in order to prepare for our performance, so I know Kostya thinks nothing of it when we disappear behind the curtains.

The moment we are out of sight, cloaked in shadow between two curtains that hang in the wings of the stage, I reach up to put my hands on his cheeks and pull him down to me. I kiss him softly, kindly.

His arms come around me, sweeping me tightly into his embrace. I release his face to snuggle in close to him as he holds me, pressing my cheek to his strong chest.

"I'm afraid, too," I whisper.

"It's not me I'm afraid for, you know. I'm afraid for you. If he takes me away from you. What will happen to you? What will he do to you, Anya?"

I sigh. "I don't know. I don't care. I feel like I just..."

"Just what?"

"Like we just found each other." I lift my head to look up at him. His hands lift to my cheeks and he holds my face as I hold him tight around the waist.

"I want you to know..." he starts. "I *need* you to know, it's not just our circumstances that draw me to you."

I lick my bottom lip. "I know."

"It's not just our circumstances that make me *want* you."

"I know."

"I'm yours, Anya."

"Mine?"

"Yours."

He bends, lowering his face to mine. His tongue peeks out to lick his lips before he kisses me. His pillow soft mouth smothers mine with tenderness and it makes my entire body thaw to his warmth. I melt into him as he deepens the kiss. With a silent sweep of the tip of his tongue across my lips, he asks me to open for him and I do.

He tastes me with the ferocity of a man in desperate need, but holds restraint enough to do so without taking anything I'm not willing to give. It's so strange that I don't feel like there is anything at all I'm not willing to give with him.

It's dangerous how vulnerable I am with him, how vulnerable I *want* to be.

But knowing our time may be limited, I don't want to hold anything back. I want him to know what he means to me, that I feel for him what I think he feels for me.

A part of me has feared that our captivity is the only reason we feel the way we do for each other because there is no one else. But I know that's not true by the way he's kissing me. Everything in his kiss tells me it's me he wants, and I want to tell him the same.

I let my hands drift from around his waist, roam slowly up his strong chest, fingertips graze over his neck as I wrap them around the back and hold him to me. The pull makes him groan into my mouth and the vibration of it trembles in my core.

I should be fearful of a man in lust.

But I'm not fearful of Ezra, of this.

This is not lust.

Its *more*.

His cautious need tells me he wants me, but only if I want him.

And God, how I want him.

Our kiss strengthens and grows in confidence, becoming more passionate, more urgent, more fervent in need. Deep in the pit of my stomach, I feel him. It's a soul crushing absence that insists to be filled by him.

His lips break free from mine, but move across my jawline instead, nipping and sucking delightfully, all the way back to my ear. He trails down my neck and nuzzles into the crook. We're both panting and breathless and all I can feel is *him*.

"I want everything with you," he says between kisses that are hot against my skin. "I want time with you. I want a real life with you. I want to take care of you and make you laugh. I want to make love to you."

I whimper in both pleasure and despair. "I told you not to hope, not to plan, not to fall for me, Ezra. I told you."

His fingers skim my arms, leaving a trail of prickling flesh. His hands find mine and he lifts them away from his neck to hold them, lacing our fingers together. He brings our interlocked hands down to our sides.

"And I told you that was bullshit." He pulls back to look at me and I find him plastering a snarky smile to his face.

It's not the smile that melts that last layer of ice from around my heart. It's the tears forming a glassy sheen over his eyes.

"If there's a way…" he says to me. "If there's a way to free us from whatever fate Nikolai has planned for us, I promise you, I will find it. I will do whatever it takes. I promise you, Anya."

I let a small, sad smile tug at the corner of my mouth. "Don't make me promises you can't keep."

He presses his forehead to mine. "I wouldn't dare break a promise to you. If there's a way, I'll find it."

I wasn't afraid that he would break his promise.

I was afraid of what would become of him when he found out it was a promise he never had a chance of keeping.

CHAPTER 21
Anya

MY DRESSING ROOM door beneath the stage in Nobility Hall swings open wide. Nikolai enters as I'm sweeping an extra dust of shimmery gold eyeshadow across my lid.

I'm dressed and ready for tonight's performance, though my costume this year is rather plain as opposed to the elaborate, ornately beaded leotards and frilly tutus I'd normally wear to perform ballet. This year, I wear a nude leotard and matching boy shorts. From the audience, it mimics nudity without the crudeness of actually being naked. The rope Nikolai asked us to incorporate is the true costume, masking me in intricate binding.

Simplicity aside, theatrics are ingrained in my performer's heart. Though my hair is pulled back in a simple low bun, I've overdone it with the makeup, using gold, shimmering shadow, dark eye liner and mascara, a deep burgundy lip color, and bronzed blush which highlights my cheekbones.

"Anya," Nikolai croons as he enters the small space, "stand, let me look at you."

I set down my eye brush and turn to stand in front of him. He holds a single pink rose in his hands. It reminds me of the first day I saw him in Russia, at my childhood dance studio when I was eleven. He brings me a pink rose before every annual performance just to bring that reminder to the surface that I am his, that I have been since I was a child. I force a smile because I know he expects it.

"Beautiful as ever," he says, leaning forward to kiss my cheek. "Are you ready?"

"Almost."

"Good." He holds out the rose. "For you."

I take it with another fake smile. "Thank you, *khozyain*."

He steps forward, snaking his arms around my waist and pulls me against him. I don't hug back. I hold my arms out to my sides. He's warm—too warm—with a hint of whiskey already on his breath.

His lips move softly against my ear. "I just want to remind you that the four families will be watching tonight. I expect nothing less than brilliance… for Ezra's sake, and for yours."

He pulls away and it's not soon enough. His smile makes him look like a wolf with a rabbit trapped beneath its paw. My captivity pleases him. My internal battle with coerced compliance is a game to him. He likes to bat me between his paws sometimes, just to watch me squirm.

My gut rolls, churning a warning for me to run far and fast from the enemy who wishes to turn playful batting into painful clawing and tearing.

But the warnings are a waste of energy.

I can't run.

"I won't ruin your makeup with a kiss. You look quite stunning as you are."

I nod. I have nothing to say to him. I'd really like him to leave so that I can focus and prepare to dance for my life.

For Ezra's life.

Ezra.

"Break a leg," he says, and though it's a common colloquialism among performers, the way he says it always sends an ice-cold breeze across my arms.

What would happen to me if I broke a leg?

Would he take me outside and shoot me?

Put the poor, useless animal out of her misery because she can no longer dance?

I've been lucky to have remained relatively uninjured in Nikolai's captivity thus far. I hate that he's just brought me such sharp awareness of the fact that I might only be one serious injury away from being completely useless to him. Another thing added to the millions I worry myself sick over, and all of that brought on by a simple phrase meant to wish performers good luck.

I'm thankful when he's gone, when I'm finally able to exhale.

Though I still have a healthy dose of fear running through my veins, the truth is that the thrill of dancing for an audience excites me. It's an excitement I've been grateful to have even in my captivity. It's something I can hold onto, some small feeling of normalcy in this nightmare.

And I don't want it ruined by Nikolai.

In this dressing room, I can fall away into my mind. I can pretend that I'm preparing to dance on stage as a soloist ballerina in New York. I can make myself believe that everyone in the audience has come here to watch me perform tonight, not because it's a tradition of sadistic slave owners, but because they yearn for the emotion of sheer artistry.

I sit at the vanity and watch myself in the mirror, keeping my eyes focused on my reflection as I turn my head slowly to the left and right. I inspect my makeup and hair for imperfections from every angle. When I'm satisfied that I look the best that I possibly can, I sigh and meet my own shrewd blue eyes in the mirror.

I wonder what Ezra sees when he looks at me.

The thought comes from nowhere, yet it seems like such an important question to ask. He looks at me differently than any other boy…

No.

Man.

He looks at me differently than any other man ever has. The thought of it sends my heart into a flurry, racing fast and fluttering. I put my hand over my chest and I can feel the *thump, thump, thump* against my palm.

If he's taken from me tonight, I don't know what I'll—

Stop.

Just stop.

I can't think about it. I narrow my eyes at my reflection, watching the ice freeze over my blue irises with a glassy sheen.

I'm hard as ice.

A glacier as thickly layered as a mountain.

Impenetrable.

At least, that's what I try to convince myself. No one has chiseled away at my icy shell so effectively as Ezra.

I close my eyes and breathe deeply, in and out, slowly, over and over. I have to focus and center myself. I have to allow myself one brief shining moment of anticipation for the thrill of performing for an audience again. I need all my attention on the dance.

Ultimately, the dance is what will decide Ezra's fate for reasons I'll never comprehend. For the sake of tradition, I suppose. For him, I will forget the rest and put everything I am and all that I have into this performance. With my eyes still shut, I review the steps in my mind, going through each count of eight in my imagination with precision.

One. Two. Three. Four. Five. Six. Seven. Eight.

One. Two. Three. Four. Five. Six. Seven. Eight.

When I finish outlining the routine in my mind, prepared for the steps that serve as the skeleton for the performance, I open my eyes. I remember how Ezra taught me what I was missing in my steps, the flesh that fattens the skeleton and makes it into something real and powerful.

Heart.

Emotion.

I need to bring that reckless abandon to the surface, but I'm afraid of losing control. I know Ezra would tell me that losing control is exactly what I need to do, but I'm afraid to do that alone. I'm not sure I can let go on my own. Perhaps it's something I can only do with Ezra.

I need him.

I need to see him, touch him, find the missing piece in him.

I stand and open the door to exit my dressing room. As if I've summoned him with my mind, he's there on the other side of the door, ready in his tan slacks that fit him like skinny jeans, barefoot, his perfect upper body exposed, shirtless.

Ezra.

He's standing, waiting there for me.

The whole world stills for a beat as I try to decide whether to crumble in sudden panic or let my heart take flight on the wings of the butterflies in my stomach.

I don't decide.

I just let the butterflies take control.

He alone is my missing piece.

He opens his arms and I step forward to hug him close.

"You look incredible," he tells me softly against my ear.

He pulls back, holding me by both shoulders and looks me square in the eye. "You ready?"

I can't help but to smile at him. His presence gives me peace. I'm suddenly so overcome with the pleasant anticipation of performing for an audience again, that I've all but forgotten about the onrushing imminent doom.

How does he do that?

How does he make me feel this way?

I let myself forget the fear for the moment because I'll be forcefully reminded of it again too soon.

Ezra and I walk hand in hand from the dressing room beneath the dance hall, up the black staircase, and to the wings of the stage. Ezra gathers the coarse brown rope that's already coiled in a heap on the floor, waiting and ready to be used. He lifts it from the floor, shaking out the twists and turns, and begins to wrap me with it in the same way we've rehearsed over and over.

Every brush of his fingers over my barely-there leotard is electric, a static spark with every movement. He feels it, too. I know he does. I know the way he twitches with the anticipation, the way he responds to the adrenaline that spiked for the both of us the moment our feet touch the stage.

He's a performer, just as I am.

This is our happiness, however brief.

I spin around to face him as soon as the rope is tied, and bounce through my feet, hopping up and down, warming my muscles and shaking out some of the excess energy.

He smiles at me, brightly and beautifully. Ezra holds up his hands, palms facing me, and I put my hands against his.

I still.

So does he.

He captures me with the intensity of his eyes and my heart stops.

"I've got you," he says and I sigh.

"I know you do."

"We've got this."

"We've got this," I repeat.

He bends, laying his forehead against mine. We both take a deep breath in perfect sync. His touch centers me, realigns the shifting pieces of my broken soul, and with a final deep look into his emerald eyes, I'm ready to dance.

The curtain is drawn shut. The long end of the rope that binds me is draped over the pulley at center stage. Kostya raises its slowly from the wings, up, up, up above our heads. Ezra holds steady at the free end of the rope that dangles from the pulley. The other end comes out from the knot at the middle of my lower back.

Ezra pulls and I rise from the floor.

I pose in my starting position, one arm reaching behind me to grip the length of rope that suspends me as if I'm trying to pull it down, my limbs posed in a way that suggests a fight, a struggle for freedom is about to take place.

In so many ways, it is.

I nod at Ezra, who then nods at Kostya who takes the signal to pull the curtain, revealing us to the audience. As it slowly rises, Ezra pulls hard, ensuring the rope is taut, creating a striking visual angle with he and I at the ends and the pulley at the vertex, far above us, out of sight.

My pulse thrums with the exhilaration of an audience, even if it is filled with such vile creatures as the four families. I've never done a routine like this before, one that is so raw and reckless.

As the haunting melody plays, we begin with theatrics. Ezra has taught me some aerial basics, nothing that would have me starring in any circus shows, but enough to work with the concept of our dance. I struggle, I twist and turn, I climb the rope and spin to a dramatic fall, never for a second doubting that Ezra will hold steady and strong.

The more I struggle and fight against the binds that hold me, the weaker my suppressor becomes. The closer I come to reaching the floor, the weaker he becomes. It's a slow, dramatic fight until finally, my toes touch the stage.

That's when he drops the rope.

I grab it from the floor, dragging it toward me with swiftness, hand over hand, as he reaches and chases after it. When it's all bunched between my hands, he reaches me and stops. There's a beat where his solid frame looms above me, threatening to take back control. This is the beat where I finally break a sweat, though it's not because of the athletic movement—it's from the commitment in his eyes. The rawness that resembles a captor fighting his captive for ultimate power. It's so real, I can feel it in my bones. It fuels me, inspires me for our performance.

This is how we dance.

Push and pull.

Run and chase.

Fight and struggle.

Win and lose.

Ezra and I argued a lot in choreographing and practicing this dance, but there was one thing we both agreed upon without question.

I win.

Ezra's hands are on me for most of the routine. We've made it look as though I'm fighting to break free from his hold, though really his hands hold me steady, keep me balanced as I spin and twirl around him.

When I finally break free from his grip, I run to the corner of the stage, pausing through a dramatic beat to prepare for the next sequence of intricate lifts and turns. I'm about to run after him, on the attack, leap into his arms.

It's a true leap of faith.

If he doesn't do his part, I'll fall.

But I know that he *will* do his part. I trust in that.

I trust in *him*.

I stealthily ensure that the long, dangling end of the rope falls down between my legs and then I run for him. If I don't curl around the rope just right, his arms could tangle in it and restrict him from finishing the lifts. Either one of us could get injured, though worse than that would be the failure of our performance.

His arms spread wide, open to catch me as I run and when I hit my mark, I leap, forward and up, spinning through two quick, vertical rotations in mid-air before his arms close around me. He snatches me into the safety of his embrace just as gravity tugs me back down. The rope has curled perfectly around my leg.

Two counts later, I'm spinning, my head dropping toward the floor as he turns me like the hands of a clock. The moment I'm upside-down, I reach for the floor and roll my body down to meet it, chest, to stomach, to hips, then legs slithering down to the stage. I flip to my back and Ezra reaches underneath me, locking the bend of his elbows beneath my armpits. He drags me backward several steps as I let the pull lift my body from the stage, his steps picking up speed enough to raise me from the floor and he spins both of us.

I arch my back, tightening my torso to position myself properly and as one of his large hands shifts to grip the flesh of my ass, he pushes me upward. I flip as he guides me, throwing my legs backward over my head, rotating my body until I'm perched on his shoulder. I pose there, held gracefully with my hips against his shoulder, arms raised above me before twisting and rolling my body down the front of him, falling perpendicular to the floor.

He catches me just before the stage rises up to meet me, exactly the way we rehearsed. Now that we've nailed the lift, I feel the rush of emotion overwhelm me that we've done it.

There's more to our dance, and we continue spectacularly, but with that one sequence complete, I know we've just defied gravity together.

Even though the routine ends with me on the floor and Ezra reaching one last time for the dangling end of the rope, I'm crawling away, clawing my way out, fighting until the very last, ending how we began, with theatrics.

The music fades into silence.

Deafening silence.

It's just heat and sweat and the sound of our heavy breathing.

What happens now?

My mind swirls with the question, my heavy heartbeat pounding it into my brain with a steady rhythm.

What happens now?

Out of the terror of silence erupts applause. A short breath of relief and I'm brought to life again.

Not only has the familiar, beautiful sound of applause burst from the audience, but I turn my head and see that there's a standing ovation, too.

The four families are giving us a standing ovation.

The four families.

I forget how to breathe.

The four families are here.

The elation of a perfect performance doesn't fade, it falls, drops off a cliff into deep, dark depths.

Ezra is bending, holding out a hand to me to help me rise. I take it and stand slowly. As he leads me toward front and center stage, the applause echoes in my ears until it's completely overwhelming my senses.

I feel like I'm falling.

I squeeze Ezra's hand tighter as my free hand lifts to press over my erratic heart, feeling the *thump, thump, thump* through my fingertips.

We bow together and stand in waiting.

I feel Ezra look at me. I turn to look at him and that's when I feel it crack inside me, the glacier that protects my heart and soul.

It's breaking.

It's melting.

It's falling into a sea of emotions and it threatens to wash me away in a tidal wave of fear.

I rush for Ezra, crashing into him, wrapping my arms around his waist, holding him with all my might. I'm so aware that I'm still being watched. The curtain won't fall. Nikolai will remain seated, in the same spot he always sits, until every last person leaves the theater. He'll come up on stage and he'll take Ezra away from me.

Oh, God.

He can't take him.

Not Ezra.

I press my cheek to Ezra's chest as I squeeze him tighter. "I can't let him take you, I can't. Ezra, I can't. I can't. Don't let him take you."

I hear how frantic I sound, and I don't know where it's coming from. I've always been so strong, I've always been able to keep my dignity, but Ezra's changing me.

He *has* changed me.

His arms cradle me closely. He kisses my hair, then I feel his chin rest on the top of my head.

"It's okay," he says. "It's okay. I've got you."

He always says that and I know, if it were up to him, it would be true. He would have me.

I turn my head to look out into the audience. Our guests, dressed in their finest black-tie worthy attire, are exiting the theater, making their way back to the grand entrance for the reception. The side conversations and quiet chatter appears so normal from the outside.

Nothing about them is normal.

They are the wealthy elite.

Powerful.

Influential.

Buyers and sellers of human lives.

Kings and queens of the underworld.

The forty or so guests drift out from the half-full theater, but, as always, Nikolai remains in his seat, almost as if he's guarding the place where he sits. A dog marking his territory. It's not even the best seat in the house and I've never understood it.

There he sits, regarding the both of us with a look of consideration, a look that says he hasn't made up his mind yet. I tense as I get caught in Nikolai's stare and now we are connected, though I don't want to be. I feel like I have no choice but to keep my eyes steadily on his as everything and everyone else moves around us, but we three remain still.

Finally, the theater clears, and Nikolai rises to his feet. He buttons his jacket and tugs at his sleeves, adjusting his cufflinks. He looks severe in his sharp black suit. I'm sure any normal woman would find his appearance attractive tonight.

They say the Devil can charm, after all.

Nikolai runs a hand down his front to smooth out the lapels and steps out into the aisleway. Then he walks, step by careful step, over the red carpet. Coming to the end of the aisle, he turns and walks the curve along the front of the stage. My heart is ready to burst out of my chest.

It hurts.

He walks up the five steps on the side of the stage and I spin around to face him, putting my back to Ezra, putting myself between the man I'm falling for and the man who might take him from me.

Every one of Nikolai's steps resonate within me, vibrating through my muscles, aching in my bones. When Nikolai comes to a stop just in front of us, looking like the Devil himself and playing God with our lives and freedom, I hold my breath.

He exhales, tilts his head, regards us again with consideration.

Then, a nod. A simple nod.

"That performance was nothing like I expected it to be."

What does that mean?

"It was *so* much more." He claps once and grins. "Brilliant! Both of you."

Both of my hands come up to cover my mouth from the shock of his words.

I don't know what this means.

I didn't expect this reaction from him. The unexpected is nearly more panic inducing than the expected horrors I've grown accustomed to.

I don't know what this means.

That fresh panic rips through me, tearing apart my rehearsed calm and lighting a fire to an unhinged part of me I thought had died three years ago.

I throw my arms down to my sides and step forward. "You will *not* take him from me, Nikolai Mikhailov. You've taken my life, my freedom, all the best parts of me. But I won't let you take him."

He cocks his head and smiles at me, licking his lips before he says, "Come here, *rabynya.*"

My breaths quicken, but I inhale slowly to try to steady them. I can't let him see my fear, though it's there.

It's there in spades.

I step forward, one, two, three steps and I'm less than a foot in front of him. Though I would normally bow my head this close to him, I lift my chin instead.

Yes, Ezra has changed me, and I'll be damned if I'm going to lose him now. I'll go with him if Nikolai wishes to take him from me, make us both slaves to a crueler master or give us death.

"I'm going to let that outburst slide, for one reason and one reason only..." Nikolai's hands reach for my neck, sliding up either side to hold my face firmly at the jawline, "you were stunning tonight. You danced more beautifully tonight than you ever have."

He bends, pressing a soft, chaste kiss to my lips. I'm frozen in stunned silence, confused beyond belief. When Nikolai speaks again, he keeps his lips close to mine and holds my attention with his gray eyes.

"I'm going to let you keep your pet, Anya. I like that he's brought your light back, your fire. You've been so cold with me and I much prefer your warmth. So, I'll let him stay, allow him to spark that fire in you so long as he keeps it burning. But you know that if you cross a line with him, I will know. If you fuck him, I will know. You are *my* belonging and I choose what you do with your body," he lifts his head, his eyes leaving mine and he looks beyond me, over my shoulder, "and yours, *mal'chik*. Do you both understand me?"

I swallow hard and somehow manage a quick nod. "Yes. *Da, khozyain*."

"And you?" he says to Ezra over my shoulder.

I press my eyes shut, so fearful that a sarcastic comment will shoot from between Ezra's lips

He clears his throat. "Yes. I understand."

Nikolai bares his teeth, tilting his head, squeezing my jaw too tightly. "I understand…what, *mal'chik?*"

I hold my breath for Ezra's response.

"I understand. *Master.*"

My eyes flutter shut and my shoulders relax, so thankful Ezra understands, so thankful he's behaved, so thankful that Nikolai hasn't torn him from me.

"Come, *mal'chik*. Kneel beside Anya. Show us your obedience."

Please, Ezra, please.

I feel him approach almost immediately and his heat is comforting. I see him beside me as I turn my eyes to look and Nikolai does the same. I hear him huff out a rough, agitated breath, but he lowers to his knees all the same.

"Good, *mal'chik*," Nikolai says.

His tongue runs across his bottom lip and his eyes narrow in a look I've only come to know as wanting. Only Nikolai isn't directing that look at me… he's looking at Ezra.

For today we are safe. But now I fear that the interactions to come will be more brutal, more terrifying than ever before.

Because they're going to involve Ezra more and more.

My mind is spinning, wondering if everything I thought I knew was wrong. Maybe stealing my partners from me was never about punishing me at all. Maybe it was about finding the right fit to satisfy all his needs.

I shake my head against Nikolai's grip on me, but he squeezes me, forcing me to still, forcing me to give him my complete attention.

"You have twenty minutes," Nikolai says. "Get cleaned up, get dressed, and come find me. Both of you. I expect you to remain at my side throughout the reception. After, you will have the evening to yourselves to celebrate your successful performance while I discuss business with my colleagues." He steps closer, invading my space. "Remember who you belong to. Don't make me regret giving you that freedom. If you do, I assure that both of you will have regrets of your own."

Finally, he releases me and strides away.

I burst into tears.

I'm still half-panicked, yet half-relieved.

I'm happy yet horrified.

I have no idea what just happened or why. I know I should count my blessings and be thankful that Ezra is still here beside me. Yet I can't fight the nagging feeling that something so much worse than losing Ezra is to come.

CHAPTER 22

Anya

STANDING IN FRONT of my wardrobe, I struggle to select my dress for the reception—a black-tie affair. Nikolai placed two gowns in my wardrobe to choose from for this evening.

One black.

One bright fuchsia.

He always does this. He always gives me two gowns to choose from. One was always black as night, the other bright as day.

I always chose black before.

Everything around me was black when Nikolai tormented me by stealing away my partners. Men I had grown to trust, men I had developed friendships and connections with, only to have them ripped away for no good reason other than Nikolai's incessant dissatisfaction.

There's an itch of confusion in my mind that I can't quite seem to scratch.

What was different about this performance?

Is it Ezra?

What will Nikolai do with us now that he has us both?

Will he hurt Ezra in all the ways he's hurt me?

I cross my wrists over my chest, rubbing my hands on my upper arms, adding friction to ease the chill from the foreboding shiver that refuses to let me feel okay about anything.

It all feels so wrong.

It still feels like Nikolai is going to tear Ezra from me at any moment. I know he could if he wanted to. That's all it takes with him, a simple choice and the Earth shifts beneath my feet.

I'm still standing here, staring at the two gowns as I hear a knock at the door. I know it's not Nikolai because he doesn't knock. I know it's Ezra and not Kostya alone when I hear the knock continue unnecessarily, tapping out a jaunty rhythm against the wood. It makes me smile and for that moment,

I'm able to let relief wash over me that he's still alive, he's still here, and he's still mine.

I go to the door and pull it open. Ezra stands in front of me, slick and smooth in his black tuxedo, vest, and tie. The sandy blond hair that's longer on the top of his head is slicked back, styled impeccably, and his grin threatens to split his beautiful face in half.

He looks down at me and his eyes widen. "Something's missing."

My dress is missing.

I've just opened the door in my underwear and strapless bra. Not that I have any shame for being exposed in this nightmare manor. Ezra has had the misfortune of seeing me every which way from Sunday by force rather than by choice. I just hate that it's become so normal that I hardly notice it anymore when I'm bare and exposed.

"I don't know which dress to wear," I say, taking a step back.

He steps inside the room and I push the door closed behind him. Kostya is in the hallway, lurking as always, and though I used to care enough to leave the door open, *always* open, I've lost my will to try to appease Nikolai. He won't care tonight, anyway. The four families are here for the quarterly business report, so aside from the reception, he'll be otherwise occupied.

In the past, I'd spend that time crying alone in my room, grieving the loss of another partner, wallowing in my misery, pleading desperately with gods, angels, with the universe itself to take me into death along with them. With Ezra still here, the first of my partners to survive past the performance, I don't know what we will do with our time tonight.

My breath catches in my throat when it hits me that Ezra and I have time together.

Uninterrupted time.

Tonight.

"Show me what you've got," he says after I've closed the door.

My head snaps up to look at him after being so lost in thought. "What?"

"Show me the dresses. I'll help you choose."

He swallows and his eyes drift, skating over the curves of my body. That hungry look of a man in lust should set off warning bells inside me, but it doesn't with him. It clenches low and deep, and I find that I don't mind it all that much.

I might even like it.

I might even crave more of it.

I walk over to the wardrobe and grab the bottom of each gown, pulling on them so they swing out by the hanger.

"I've always worn black."

"So, wear black."

"It doesn't feel right."

"So, wear pink."

"It doesn't feel right, either."

He holds out his hands. "Okay, I'm at a loss here."

"Why are you in such a good mood?" I narrow my eyes at him, unintentionally short with him.

His forehead wrinkles as if he's confused by my question. "Because I'm not dead, Anya."

Because he's not dead.

He's not dead and he's not gone.

I exhale, slowly releasing the pettiness of such an insignificant decision as the color of my dress.

It doesn't matter.

All that matters is that we've performed, we've completed our task, I'm alive, he's alive, and we're both here, together in my room with the door shut.

We look at each other.

We breathe in at the same time.

We move at the same time.

He opens his arms for me, and I give him my body to fill them. I think he expects me to wrap my arms around his waist and hold him, but I need something more, a greater connection.

I grab his cheeks in both my hands and pull his face down to meet my lips. I rise onto my toes to press my mouth harder to his, but then he bends, pressing back, pushing me down to my flat feet. He steps forward and I step backward with him until I collide with the open door of the wardrobe, slamming it shut as he kisses me with force.

His body arches forward into mine, molding with me, as if he could move right through me. When a groan escapes through his lips—a guttural sound of need from deep within him—I feel it rattle inside me, shaking my core.

My hands slip around to the back of his neck, my fingers lacing together and holding him too tightly. I sigh into his mouth, a whisper of a plea to give me more of everything. His tongue licks mine, swirling deeper inside my mouth, tasting me with ferocity that makes dampness pool between my legs.

His hands slam against the wardrobe on either side of my head with a thud that makes my heart leap. I feel his body tremble along mine as he uses the leverage to force himself to stop.

As quickly as the kiss began, it ends. Ezra pulls his head back, though his body still pins mine to the wardrobe door.

"I'm sorry, I don't mean to be so...insistent."

"Don't apologize," I pant, putting a hand on his chest. "You don't have to stop."

He smiles, but it almost looks sad. He lets his forehead fall to rest against mine.

"When we took our final bow, I looked at you and I thought...I thought, what if this is the last time I ever get to look at her?"

"Ezra." I sigh and my body rolls forward, curling into him.

"I know I should be fearful," he goes on, "I know we're still in a shit situation, we're still slaves, I *know* all that. But fuck, Anya, I'm so grateful to be alive, to have even just one more day with you."

I feel his sincerity in my gut, and it warms me from the inside. He melts me in ways no one else ever could. Ezra is my sunshine after the snowstorm in my soul, a springtime thaw that makes the ice inside me a heavy puddle rushing desire through my veins.

My words rush out of me and I don't regret them. "I love you."

He answers me with a happy sigh. "I love you," he whispers as he places a soft kiss to my lips.

"Mine?"

"Yours."

My hands fall to his hips and now all I can think about is touching him and being touched by him. I want to feel him, keep him close, live in the reality that Ezra is still here with me.

Alive and mine.

Mine.

His hips rock forward. There's a brief flash of fear through the logical part of my brain, the part of me that fears the motivations of sexual touch. But that fear dissipates swiftly as my heart kick-starts, pulsing fire throughout my entire body, effectively shutting off the rational thought that tells me to be careful.

I pant, grinding my hips forward to meet his as I realize just how much I want him.

I need him.

I need him so much it makes me feel desperate and that scares me.

I'm almost thankful when Kostya raps loudly on the closed door to my bedroom and yells, "Five minutes."

Ezra jumps back, shaken from the reverie of being mine, and blows out a heavy breath, linking his fingers together on the top of his head.

He grins at me still standing there in my underwear and my knees go weak.

"Pink," he says with a playful look in his eyes. "Wear the pink dress. It'll go with your cheeks."

I touch my fingertips to my cheek and it's warm, surely flushed as warm as the deep fuchsia of the gown inside my wardrobe. I smile back at him and probably turn magenta for the way the heat inside me prickles like fire sparking beneath my skin.

His hands drop as I open the wardrobe to pull out the dress. I unzip it and push my arms through the bottom of it, shimmying it down my body. The style hugs my curves almost precisely. I shake it into place and turn my head over my shoulder.

"Zip me?" I say to Ezra.

He steps up behind me and I feel his heat. His fingertips tickle my skin as he pulls the zipper up slowly.

The mermaid style dress is tight over my body until it hits my knees. There, it fans out around me, fading into a chiffon sort of fabric that layers to create the mermaid effect.

The thick straps hang intentionally off the shoulders, sweeping an elegant line across my chest, dipping into a sweetheart neckline between my breasts. I wouldn't normally have much in the way of cleavage, except for the way this dress presses everything together so tightly.

I spin to face Ezra and he gives me a once over.

"Perfect," he says, and I feel like the most wanted woman in the world for the way he stares at me with those emerald eyes.

I hurry into my shoes and take a quick look in the mirror, making sure I look perfect per Nikolai's scrutinizing standards. I place one hand over my stomach and take a deep breath, knowing that Ezra is about to see just how deep into the underworld he's been taken.

CHAPTER 23

Ezra

EYES ARE ON us as soon as we begin our descent down the grand staircase. We walk hand in hand down the marble steps, following Kostya, who leads us to the reception. There's no applause or appreciative welcome.

Just eyes.

Eerie, watching eyes amidst the quiet chatter.

It makes me feel agitated, uneasy, but I try not to care too much. I'm fucking alive and I'm still with Anya and happy for that much. I expected to be dead by now, or at the very least, on my way to a new owner without her.

I don't know how I would survive separation from my blue-eyed girl. I love her. And now that I know she loves me, too, I've vowed to myself to find a way to save us both, come hell or high water.

I lean over to her, "Did you go to your high school prom?"

She turns her head to glance at me with confusion before looking back down at the steps she treads carefully in her high-heeled shoes.

"What?" she asks.

"Prom. Did you go?"

"No," I see a hint of a smile tugging at her lips, "I had a dress rehearsal that night. Why?"

I grin. "Figures. You were probably too cool for prom, weren't you?"

There's her smile. "And I would've been too cool for you."

I put my free hand over my heart, feigning ache. "Ouch. I'll try not to take that personally. Though it's probably true."

"Mm-hmm." She's still smiling.

"If we'd gone to school together, taking you to prom would've been a highlight for me. I'd consider myself a damn lucky man to be the arm candy for a girl that looks so hot all dressed up like this."

She looks over at me as we reach the landing. "You should consider yourself a damn lucky man to be my arm candy for this."

She meant it to be light-hearted, but she looks sad immediately after she says it.

I let go of her hand and place mine on the small of her back, leaning over to whisper close to her ear in reassurance, "I do."

She looks up at me and our eyes meet and it's soul-searing. I don't want to look away. What I want to do is kiss her. But I feel the oppressive cold of a deep winter freeze swirl around us both as Nikolai approaches. I straighten but keep my hand on the small of her back, stepping a little closer because I'm feeling fiercely protective.

"Come with me, you'll greet my colleagues with grace or suffer the consequences later," Nikolai says, looking at me when he says it.

He holds out his arm, expecting Anya to take it and fuck, if that doesn't make my blood boil. I don't want to take my hands off her. I want to keep her close. I don't know anything about these people other than the fact that they are a part of some sick slave trafficking empire. That alone makes them beyond dangerous. Because we are slaves to them, I don't know what to expect here. I don't know how we'll be treated. I don't know whether Nikolai will let them touch Anya or hurt her.

I know he shared her once with a Vittori.

Will he do it again?

The thought of it sends tension right through my shoulders and threatens to spark an adrenaline rush. But then Anya looks at me, granting me a small smile and a nod—a look that tells me we're okay right now—and I trust her. Against all reason, I trust her instinctively and it calms me. She steps forward, away from me, and slips her arm in Nikolai's.

Anya is so graceful and confident and so fucking strong I could nearly cry just watching her walk the way she does with her head held high through her pain and suffering.

I follow behind as Nikolai takes us to stand at a high table without chairs, draped in an elegant gold tablecloth that reaches all the way to the floor. A cocktail waitress walks past, as if this were some ordinary rich people party, and I wonder who she is and whether she's a slave, too.

Nikolai grabs two glasses of champagne from her tray as she walks by and she flinches as he moves, her face twitching with telltale signs of fear as she tries to remain calm and composed. Nikolai doesn't seem to notice or care and brings us the glasses as the poor girl walks away.

He sets one down in front of me and the other in front of Anya.

"Drink," he says. "Enjoy yourselves. You've done well. Tonight, you may celebrate that."

Anya lifts her glass and throws it back without hesitation. I see the tension written all over her face and I don't blame her a bit for taking the alcohol for what it is, a way to escape the reality of our situation.

I smile at her as she finishes her glass and sets it down on the table, then I drink from my own. But I'm taking it slow.

I want to be alert.

I want to be aware.

I want to be able to fight for her if some weird slave empire shit goes down.

What the fuck is this life?

Anya's eyes go wide as she looks beyond my back. At first, she looks as though she's going to retreat and hide somewhere inside her mind, but then she pulls her shoulders back, lifts her chin, brings coldness to the surface in the way she does to protect herself.

I glance over my shoulder to see what she's seeing. There's a man and a woman approaching us. They share bronzed complexions, though the woman is fairer toned with dark, jet-black hair, and dark eyes. They both have an aura that pulses severe and dangerous, like monarchs of an evil empire.

Nikolai steps out to greet the man with a handshake, the woman with a kiss to her knuckles. I want to gag over the formalities and forced politeness between slave traders.

These people are fucking sick.

Nikolai holds his arm out toward Anya, beckoning her to come to his side. I freeze watching them. She's stiffened and my hackles are up. I'm ready to pounce at the way she regards the man with fear and contempt.

"You remember Anya," Nikolai says to them as she steps into his side, his arm wrapping around her waist.

"Of course," the woman says, stepping forward to kiss Anya on the cheek. "You were lovely tonight."

Anya forces a cold smile. "Thank you."

The man rakes his eyes over Anya appraisingly.

That man is bad news.

I know it immediately.

The woman looks at me and steps closer as she speaks to Nikolai, "You've decided to keep the partner this time, I see." She smiles at me. "Wise choice, Nikolai. He is quite stunning."

I narrow my eyes at her.

"Renata Vittori," the woman introduces herself to me and I hear the accent more clearly now in her name.

Spanish? No, Italian.

She looks to be about Nikolai's age, though she's as stunningly fit as a twenty-something. She stands out from the crowd in her ivory-colored romper where all the other women wear gowns. The wide pant legs give the appearance of a gown, though, with the way they sweep together, and the V-neck cuts all the way down between her breasts. Her long, black hair tumbles in waves over her shoulders and she's tall, taller than me with her stilettos on. She's an attractive woman, oozing power, though the vileness of her intentions pulses evil.

She holds out her hand, but not for me to shake. Her fingers are curled down, knuckles presented, as if she expects me to kiss her hand the way Nikolai did.

Should I bow at your feet, dear queen of the underworld?

I swear, these fuckers.

I do what I have to do to keep the peace and keep Anya safe. I don't want to get kicked out of the party and leave her alone with these jackals. I take Renata's hand and bend to kiss her knuckles.

Wait.

Vittori.

Is that the man who…

Just as I lift my head, I see Nikolai pushing Anya toward the man. He snatches her by the wrist and drags her toward him, pulling her into a hug that's anything but friendly. Her arms dangle behind her back as she tries to avoid giving any sense that this is welcome. I see the goosebumps forming on her arms, the tremble of her hanging limbs. He kisses her cheek then releases her and she steps back immediately.

"Ezra," I'm thankful that Nikolai says my name to pull me out of my onrushing murderous rage, "this is Vigo. Head of House for the Vittori family."

I lift my head in acknowledgment but give him no more. I know now that this is the man Nikolai used Anya for as payment. This is the sick fuck he shared her with, nearly ruined her with. My hands shake with rage that threatens to explode through my fingertips.

It takes everything I've got to reign myself in, to pretend I'm an obedient and civilized slave, to stop myself from launching at him and ripping the crooked smile from his face with my bare hands.

"I don't know why you keep pretending, Nikolai. We all know about your tendencies. You should sell this one off." Vigo nods toward my blue-eyed girl and I want to strangle him. "Keep the boy for yourself. We all know that's what you really want."

Nikolai swallows and I've never seen such perfectly controlled rage. Whenever I've seen that pointed look of anger wash over his features in the past, he's taken it out full force on Anya without restraint. The same look is there now, but he controls it. Which tells me he *can*, yet he chooses not to with my girl. He *chooses* to hurt her.

"With all due respect, Vigo, I tire of your commentary on my slave choices. Perhaps you should be more concerned with your own." Nikolai looks pointedly toward a young woman I hadn't noticed before standing behind Vigo. "She looks as though she's about to faint from malnourishment. Do you care for her at all?"

He's not wrong. The young woman standing behind him with the long, blond hair wobbles, though she stands still, as though she's near fainting from exhaustion or hunger or ailment. She has dark circles under her eyes that she's tried to hide with makeup, but it only emphasizes how swollen they are from tiredness.

She's thin, too thin in her red, satin gown. A dress like that should cling to a woman's curves, but the poor girl has been flattened out, as if all the fat in her body has been sucked out with a vacuum. The girl is not well.

Vigo laughs. "I take care of myself, Nikolai. She is present to take care of me and my needs. Or have you forgotten what a slave is for?"

"I prefer my slaves to be strong enough to care for my needs. It just goes to show some people don't know how to properly break them in. Besides, she's talentless, Vigo. Her skills as a pianist are mediocre at best. You may as well have brought along one of your broken dolls in her stead. She's worth no more than any of them. You choose poorly and you train poorly."

"And I suppose you believe your Anya is worth more? A slave is a slave, Nikolai. They all become broken dolls in the end."

"As I recall it, *Vigo*," Nikolai practically spits out his name, "you rather enjoyed your time with my Anya at the third quarter meeting. We both know she's worth far more than you're willing to admit."

Anya steps sideways and bumps into the table. It lets out a sharp screech as the metal pedestal scrapes along the marble floor. I grab the edge of it as it moves toward me and settle it. She looks over at me and I catch her eyes, giving her a small smile and a nod of encouragement that says *I've got you.*

She swallows, her blue eyes telling me how fearful she is, though I doubt anyone else can see it. She knows how to hide her fear behind the icy blue glaciers that keep her soul concealed.

"I did enjoy her," Vigo admits with a tilt of his head. "I suppose she does have a certain quality about her, doesn't she? Behaves as though she's broken, though it's clear she's not. I can imagine paying a rather large sum to be the man to watch that last bit of light fade from her eyes. It will happen one day. All little dolls break in the end."

Nikolai looks far away, far beyond Vigo. "Anya can't be broken."

"Perhaps I should purchase her from you. Prove you wrong."

"To what end, Vigo?"

Nikolai looks bored with this conversation, though the expression seems forced. He snakes his arm around my girl's tiny waist, lassoing her tight to his side.

A hand suddenly lands on my back and makes me jump. I look over to see it belongs to Renata. I shrug my shoulder to shake her off, but Anya catches my eye and subtly shakes her head.

"Oh, come now, Nikolai. I'm sure you've grown bored of Anya by now. Especially now that you've found the perfect boy for your secret fantasies, hmm?"

Anya's head bows and I see how quickly her chest rises and falls. She's upset, of course she is, this entire exchange is the stuff of nightmares.

Nikolai looks down at my blue-eyed girl. "Bored isn't the appropriate term." He regards her with some sort of twisted longing that I've never understood.

"Then what is?" Vigo asks.

Nikolai looks pointedly at him. "Exasperated."

"Well," Vigo begins with a crooked smile, "when exasperation turns to boredom, give me a call."

"You try too hard."

"What will you do with her when she can no longer dance?"

"I will have no use for her then," he says it so coldly, so plainly, that I believe him.

"Consider that. I'll happily take your scrap now that you have a new model." Vigo glances at me.

"Boys, enough of this," Renata finally speaks. "Nikolai has finally given us the performance he's been wanting for so long. Let's celebrate that before we speak about business. This is highly undignified."

As she finishes her sentence, a young man approaches, handing her a glass of red wine. She gives him a smile of gratitude, flipping her long hair over her shoulder, and he leans in to kiss the side of her neck before moving to stand behind her.

He bows his head in servitude, but can only bow so far because a black leather collar is latched around his throat. His thick, dark hair is shaggy, unkempt in an intentional sort of way that makes him look younger than he probably is. He stands complacent, looking practically content. It's clear he's a slave, though he doesn't seem extraordinarily bothered by his circumstance.

"My apologies, Renata," Nikolai says. "As I've always said, you'd make a far more dignified Head of House than your tiresome brother."

Vigo laughs humorlessly, clapping Nikolai on the shoulder. "Let's be glad she isn't. She'd outsell your family in no time at all. She's far more ruthless than I am in her asset accrual. Then again, it's not all that difficult to outsell your family. Hardly a family anymore, is it? Quite the burden to carry it all alone."

Nikolai looks suddenly haunted, almost…human.

"Vigo," Renata chastises him, "let's not bring that up." She tilts her head with a sympathetic look at Nikolai. "I'm so sorry."

Coldness settles over him again. "It's no concern of yours, Renata. I've made a settlement with the Americans to rectify their error in judgment. I'm grateful to your brother for providing me with the evidence needed to seek justice. There is a rather large sum to be paid in reparations."

"I hope it's not purely monetary."

"Money could never be justice enough for what was done to my family."

Renata smiles, almost hopeful. The two gracefully bow out, the small, malnourished blond and the collared boy following behind them. The girl glances back at Anya and me with a look that almost resembles jealousy.

As if anyone could be jealous of our circumstances.

Unless…her circumstances are that much worse than ours.

And the man who *makes* them worse has his sight set on my blue-eyed girl.

CHAPTER 24

Anya

THE FOUR FAMILIES and their slaves traverse the steps of the grand staircase at the end of the reception. The slaves will all be shackled in the guest rooms with the same style of chain Nikolai used to chain me in my early months with him, the same chain we shackled Ezra with and all my partners before him. Then, they'll be heading to the boardroom on the third floor of the manor. It's a room that's off-limits to slaves. It's reserved only for the four families to use annually when it's Nikolai's turn to host the quarterly meeting.

Ezra and I remain with Nikolai at the bottom of the grand staircase as the guests file out. I count my heartbeats like dance steps as it thuds against my ribcage, wondering what will happen now, hoping against hope that Nikolai will be kind and grant us a reprieve tonight like he promised he would.

"You've both pleased me this evening," Nikolai says, tension clear in his voice and the way he holds his shoulders. "My colleagues are impressed by both your talent and your obedience." He looks at Ezra. "You've done especially well in dulling your impulsivity. I'll give credit to Anya for her training with you."

I exchange a glance with Ezra. He smiles through his eyes, and though Nikolai can't see it, I can. It makes the corner of my mouth tug upward, threatening a smile I shouldn't wear in front of my master.

"I require Kostya's assistance in the boardroom tonight. This meeting is of special importance to me, and I need to focus my attention on that." He sighs. "This is probably against my better judgment, but the both of you are free for the evening. You will remain indoors. You may go wherever you like within the manor."

He takes a step toward us. "Stay *off* the third floor of the west wing where the guests and their slaves are staying. If I so much as smell the scent of you up there when I walk through later," he reaches forward and snatches my wrist with one hand, holding it up between us as he taps the top of my pinky finger with his other hand, "I will cut off your little fingers myself. Both of you. You will be quiet. You will be civilized if you run into any of our guests. Do you think you can handle yourselves?"

"*Da, khozyain,*" I say.

"Yes, Master," Ezra follows suit, though I can hear the eye roll in his tone.

I think Nikolai hears it, too. He tugs me forward by the wrist and jerks me roughly against his chest. He bends to kiss me, forcing me to open my lips to let his impatient tongue slip inside. Against my wishes, I kiss him back. Not because I want to, but because I know he demands it.

But it's strange.

The kiss is weak where it's usually strong and demanding. He releases me, looks me over with a quick flick of his eyes, a cursory glance, and then he's gone.

Nikolai strides up the grand staircase, lonely master of the manor. I almost feel sorry for him, but I don't know why because I've never felt that before. Maybe it was something in the way he kissed me, with intention but without expectation.

The fleeting moment of empathy slips from my mind swiftly. Ezra and I are left alone, watching him walk away, knowing he'll be occupied, Kostya will be with him, and we will be free together for the evening.

As free as we can be inside the home of our master with no way to escape.

Ezra looks at me and grins the widest, whitest, most perfect grin I've ever seen, and it draws some long-lost need for joy from deep within me. My heart skips a beat as Nikolai rounds the corner at the top of the staircase, the last person in the manor to disappear from our sight.

I remain still as the chatter from above fades and dissolves. I don't know what to do with myself now, but I don't have to wonder for long.

Ezra grabs my hand and we lock our fingers together as he drags me away toward the dance studio. He walks so fast and his strides are so long that I nearly have to jog to keep up with him, which is next to impossible in these heels.

"Wait," I tell him.

I pull back on his hand to free mine from his grip and stop dead in my tracks. I bend, rustling up the chiffon layers of the fanned out bottom portion of my mermaid-style gown, and wrestle with the straps of my shoes. I struggle to reach around and beneath the layers, but Ezra has already anticipated my need.

He kneels on one knee in front of me and reaches out to free me from my shoes. I put one hand on his strong shoulder to steady myself as he pulls off the first shoe, admiring the natural golden tones of his sandy blonde hair.

"I think Prince Charming is supposed to be putting the shoe *on* Cinderella's foot, not taking it off," he says with a smile, "but this is cool, too."

I bite the corner of my lip to hold back a bursting grin. "Are you comparing me to Cinderella or you to Prince Charming?"

"Both," he lifts his head to look up at me after he pulls off the other shoe and dazzles me with a pure white, sparkling smile, "obviously."

"Obviously."

He gets to his feet and holds out my shoes, which I take in my left hand as he grabs my right. We're off again, fast walking, smiling, nearly giggling like teenagers as we make our way to the dance studio.

It's as if I'm young again, home alone for the first time, my mother having decided I'm finally responsible enough to be left on my own in a big empty house.

Only I've snuck in a boy.

Ezra pulls me into the dance studio, and closes the door behind us, only he forgets to turn on the lights at first. It's dark, save for the moonlight that shines in from the high windows near the ceiling. The light reflects off the shine of the hardwood floor, flickering in a soft dance as the edge of a cloud obscures the rays.

"Turn on the lights," I whisper to him.

Alone in my favorite room at the edge of night, it feels sacred in the dark.

"Come dance with me in the moonlight," he whispers back.

I whip around because his voice is behind me. I see the outline of him moving toward the center of the room.

Wings flutter senselessly in my belly and I sigh, letting my eyes fall shut for a few blissful moments of peace, relishing the sheer joy of anticipating something good, something wanted.

I open my eyes and move toward his dark figure in the center of the room. His hand is there to meet mine as I reach out to him and he pulls me into his embrace. I throw my hands around the back of his neck, assuming the standard slow dance position of all awkward young teens falling in love at a school dance.

I don't need the lights on in this space at all. Not when I have Ezra. He is my eternal sunshine, my life force, my renewal. He refreshes my soul and makes me believe things I shouldn't. He gives me hope I don't deserve to have. He makes me want to fight again.

We sway together without music. After minutes of silence, Ezra's hands on the small of my back pull me closer until we're simply hugging one another.

"Let's say, for theory's sake, that tonight is our last chance to be free, to be together like this…" His voice is quiet, almost sad, and that alone threatens to break me. "How would you want to spend it?"

I swallow, tilting my chin up to look at him, though his face is awash with shadow. "I don't know how to answer that," I tell him honestly.

He smirks. "Oh, come on. I'm sure you've dreamed of what you would want to do if you ever got me alone."

He's being his usual charming self, flirting with me. But my response to that isn't light and teasing. It's hard hitting honesty that has to come out.

"I dream of it all the time, Ezra."

The sway stills as his emerald eyes shift along the lines of my face. The moonlight paints a bright strip right across them, as even the light is drawn to his bewitching green gaze.

"This is all I have ever wanted," I tell him in a hushed tone, "to love and be loved. To be cherished for my soul, not for my talent or my monetary worth. I think you see me."

His eyes hood, a wrinkle creasing his brow. "I do see you." He bends to press his forehead against mine. "If giving up my freedom is the price I have to pay to be yours, then I will pay it. I don't regret a thing if it means I'm yours."

My face tenses against the beautiful soul ache, unaccustomed to these feelings of joy and wanting.

Boundless wanting.

"You're mine," I remind him—remind myself.

"I'm yours," he says, and our lips collide.

I drift against his body as his arms tighten around me. We breathe heavy through our noses, saving our mouths for the only thing they were meant for.

I feel it now.

Our mouths were made for kissing, and only for kissing each other.

My hands creep up the sides of his neck as he tilts his head, deepening our kiss. I want him against something, the wall, the floor, the piano, I don't care. I just want to press into him as closely as I possibly can and savor the sweet, sweet flavor of temporary freedom we've been granted.

Ezra must be able to read my thoughts through my moans. He moves, walking me backward until I press against the mirror that lines the wall and I know we're out of range from the security camera now. The freedom in knowing that strips away the last layer of reservation. There's no caution in this kiss now, no hesitation or fear for whether we will be found. As that realization washes over me, it bathes me in heat that melts my core.

His lips fall to my neck and he kisses me everywhere, down the sides, along my collarbone, across my jaw line. I'm breathing heavily and my hips thrust forward of their own will as my back arches, succumbing to the gravity of him.

"I'm sorry," he huffs out between hot kisses, "if I'm too rough."

I chuckle and the sound of it is hoarse, wanting. "Too rough?"

With my body molded to his, I push back and spin us both, shoving him against the mirror instead. I reach between us to unbutton his jacket and pull out his tucked in dress shirt. I slip my hands beneath the hem and feel him, really feel him for the first time.

I trace the outline of his firm stomach with my fingers. His skin is warm to touch, soft but tautly stretched over his carefully developed abdominal muscles. I can feel him flex and jolt at my touch.

"Jesus," he mutters, "I want you, Anya."

His tone is lustfully deep, sinful and sweet. The sound of it pulls at my heart but also sends a sharp bolt of desire straight through to my core, clenching low in my belly.

I pause, looking up at him. "I want you, too."

Removing my hands from beneath his shirt, I lift to my toes, holding my hands against his strong jawline and pressing the softest, most delicate, most meaningful kiss I've ever given to his soft, full lips.

My mouth brushes his as I speak in a hushed tone, "Make love to me tonight."

His eyes narrow as his head nods. "Just tell me where, tell me how you want me, and I'm yours."

I take his hand and pull him out of the dance studio, intent on taking him to any one of the random bedrooms in the manor that's not currently occupied by a guest or their slave. We leave the dance studio and practically dance down the hallway, through the grand entrance, up the stairwell, then we stop on the landing.

"I want to be in your bed." He steps closer. "I want to give you a good memory to hold onto in your room at night in case he doesn't…"

In case he doesn't keep us both here, together.

In case one of us doesn't survive.

As morbid as the train of thought is, it's reasonable. I don't have to think about it. As soon as the words come out of his mouth, I know I want that, too. I want to take him to my room, be with him in my bed. No matter what happens to us after tonight, I can always close my eyes at night and think about something good that happened there.

I can have the smell of him on my pillow.

A pleasant shudder rolls down my spine.

I nod. "Okay."

"Okay." He takes my hand and we walk together toward my bedroom.

We make the trip in silence, entering my room quietly, shutting the door behind us. The space between us is still heated, still full of need, but there's a twinge of awkwardness now that we're here, standing in the truth that something delicate and precious and meaningful is about to happen.

My heart beats for this moment, awkwardness included. It all feels so normal, so natural. The anticipation of being with someone for the first time, the curiosity over what it will be like, the subtle worry that it might not be everything you expect it to be, but knowing it could be so much greater than you ever imagined.

I've ached for this kind of normalcy for years and Ezra has given it to me. I'll be forever grateful to him for that.

Eager to have his hands on me again, I turn my back to him and glance over my shoulder. "Unzip me?"

I feel his heat swirl around me as he moves closer, sweeping me up in a summer storm. His fingers tickle my skin as he pulls the zipper down slowly. He steps in closer as I nudge the dress to fall off me to the floor, his hands falling against my sides, his lips pressing to my neck.

I moan from the softness of him, the gentle coaxing. Though I suppose he's no more or less gentle with me than Nikolai. Nikolai knew how to touch softly, how to intrigue me, how to tease my body into wanting things my heart didn't want.

But Ezra is my choice.

He could lay rough hands on me and it would still feel good because I chose it.

He's my choice.

This is my choice.

"This is my choice," I whisper, not meaning to say it out loud.

I nearly want to cry for how good that feels.

Ezra's hands still, his kissing stops. "Do you want me to stop?"

I feel the tension he holds pulse through the palms of his hands, yet he controls it.

He controls it because he's not Nikolai.

He cares about me.

He cares about what I want.

Still, I have to ask, "If I told you I didn't want to do this tonight..."

"We don't have to do anything you don't want to. I just want to be with you."

His voice sounds so sad, I can hardly bear it.

I spin to face him and his hands fall away. I reach behind me and unhook my strapless bra. I let it fall to the floor and stand in front of him, topless, exposed, waiting.

My breath catches in my chest and my heart skips a beat to see the way he looks at me. He desires me, there is no doubt about that, but it's so much more. There's a certain curiosity in his expression, the face of an explorer coming upon new land.

"I don't want you to stop, Ezra. And I don't want you to ask me again." I step toward him. "I don't need you to be careful or gentle or whatever kind of man it is you think I need you to be. I just want *you*. I want your passion, not your restraint."

I reach for his shoulders, shoving off his jacket, then I yank on his tie, dragging him down to me. He bends and kisses me, stepping forward against me and forcing me backward with his steps until the backs of my knees hit the bed behind me.

I bend to sit, looking up at him with wonder in my eyes at the way he took my permission and ran with it. I let out a sigh of relief. I don't want to be treated like a broken girl, least of all by him.

He drops to his knees in front of me and presses my thighs apart with his hands. He kisses me with passion I've never felt before and it hits me like a tidal wave. His fervor crashes into me and washes over me. It strikes in my core and my stomach clenches in pleasant need. I can feel the fabric of my underwear dampen with the evidence of how strongly I want Ezra.

I loosen the knot of his tie and he pulls it free, tossing it aside as I get started on the buttons of his vest and shirt. He stops kissing, pulls back, looks down to watch my hands work at the buttons.

My face flushes at the way he pants there on his knees. He looks at my hands as though they held the answers to all the questions in the universe. His eyes catch mine from beneath his lashes and I smile. The way he looks at me makes me feel powerful.

He makes me feel strong.

He makes me feel wanted.

When his shirt is finally on the floor where it belongs, I reach for him, pulling him in close until my breasts brush against his bare chest. His hands are still on my thighs, gliding upward, grazing the rough scars Nikolai has left there.

Ezra looks down as he rubs his thumb over the freshest one, one he witnessed being made in Nikolai's cruelness. It's still raised, still red, still healing. Then his lips replace his thumb and I gasp at the feel of it. I run my fingers through his hair as he kisses my scars, each and every jagged line that crisscrosses my skin.

I hate them.

I think they're ugly.

But his sensuous attention almost makes me glad to have them there.

I dig into his sandy blond hair as he leaves a trail of heartfelt sensation up the inside of my thigh. I moan when he kisses over my panties, surely feeling the wet spot forming there. Before I know it, he's slipping the fabric down from my hips. I put my knees together so he can drag them from my body, and I scoot back on the bed, lowering slowly to lay in wait for him as he unbuckles his pants and kicks off his shoes.

"This feels stupid to ask given our circumstances but…" he pauses as his pants come off, leaving him standing in front of me in gray boxer briefs, "do I need to wear a condom or something?"

I smirk, shaking my head as I prop up on my elbows to look at his perfectly sculpted dancer's body. He's already hard for me, straining beneath his briefs, and I just wish he would take them off already.

"No," I tell him, "there's a private doctor that he brings in, gives me a birth control shot every three months. Nikolai doesn't have sex with anyone else and he's…he's only shared me once."

My shoulders stiffen at the unwanted memory of being used by Vigo Vittori as payment for information. The one and only time Nikolai shared me with another. Even then, my pussy was off-limits to him. Nikolai tested me for disease anyway, and I was cleared.

I hate that Nikolai is present in my mind at this moment. I want to forget about him, about Vigo, about everything that has to do with the four families.

I just need Ezra to fill me up, overwhelm my senses, take control of my mind, and make me feel something other than constant fear and terror and hopelessness.

"I don't want to talk about that," I say quickly. "I'm clean. Nothing to worry about."

I bend one knee, sliding my heel backward along the mattress and spread my legs apart, just a little farther, in invitation.

He lets out a sigh of relief at the opening I give him. "Thank God." He grins.

The underwear comes off and he practically pounces on me, climbing over my body and covering me like a warm blanket on the winter of my soul.

He kisses behind my ear. "I want to feel everything with you, Anya."

He slides down my body, lips dancing across my skin, until he finds my hardened nipple and swirls his tongue around it.

I moan when he flicks his tongue over it, teasing me into pleasure. He rubs his thumb over the other and the feeling of it is so perfect that I find myself already panting desperately in my need for him.

I've never wanted anything more than I want Ezra.

He reaches down, lower and lower until his fingers find my wetness. He slides two fingers inside me and I gasp. He stills, a look of concern mixing with the lust in his green eyes, and I worry he's going to stop.

It angers me.

If he stops, we'll regret it forever.

I narrow my eyes at him. "Don't you dare stop. Don't you *dare.*"

I don't know if it's what I say or how I say it that ignites him, but his eyes become green fire burning a hole through me. I want it to burn me hotter, brighter, faster. I want his flames to consume me entirely.

With the spark, he shoves his fingers deep inside, his fist pressing against my pussy as he stretches me roughly, reaching deep, deep within me as if he could touch my very soul that way. It's as if he needs to be buried inside me as much as I need him to be.

His mouth lands heavy on mine, devouring me with a wet, sloppy, passionate kiss. He curls his fingers over my G-spot, stroking and pressing so hotly it makes me sweat. He rests his forehead against mine and watches me as he digs into my core. With urgent need, I rock against his hand, fucking his fingers just as much as they fuck me.

Ezra has brilliantly taken a hot moment and made it hotter with the way he groans, the way his eyes sear mine with dirty intent, the way he grinds his cock against the side of my hip with every thrust of his fingers.

We rock and grind as we pant and moan together.

His voice is a deep, dirty, husky tone that threatens to undo me, to turn me into a wanton woman who actually needs sex to survive. I've wanted to *want* for so long, and Ezra has made me want everything raw and dirty he can think to do to me.

"I want you to explode," he says. "I want you to come on my hand, let my fingers feel what my cock has to look forward to."

I hiss out a breath through my teeth. "You have to work for it." Its half-dirty talk, half-truth.

He grins. "Oh, I'll work for it. Then I'll for work it again and again. I'll work all night until you tell me to stop, Anya. I don't want this to end."

"Never." I dig my fingers into his hair at the back of his head and pull him down to me, kissing him fiercely.

His thumb slips over my clit as he curls his fingers and I gasp into his mouth. There's no rhythm to our kiss, it's just clumsy, urgent wanting.

It's reckless, just like Ezra.

He doesn't stop working me for minutes. He's as desperate as I am to get me there. I feel everything he's doing to me from the inside out. I feel raw, exposed, vulnerable, yet it's so, so, so good.

My climax claws its way out of nowhere. My body stiffens, tense against the building pleasure in my core, but Ezra keeps moving inside me, over me, all around me.

He's everywhere and everything.

But I have to stop him.

Before I tip over the edge, I have to stop him because I want to take him with me. I *need* to take him with me. I think I'll die if I don't take him with me.

I slide backward, forcing his fingers to slip out of me. "Stop, stop," I tell him. "I'm not ready yet."

He looks crestfallen, hurt, concerned. "What did I do?" He thinks it's his fault.

"Lay down," I demand, pushing at the center of his chest. "I want to make you feel what you make me feel."

He lowers to lay back on his elbows and I climb over him, straddling his hips. My hair falls around my face as I grip his jawline with both hands and bend to kiss him.

I glide slowly along the length of his cock, making him slippery with how wet he's made me.

"I want you," he breathes against my lips.

I reach between us to grasp him, guiding his tip where I need him most. He slips inside me with ease when I lower and we both groan at the feel of it.

I barely remembered what this was like—the feeling of mutual, shared pleasure.

The feeling of *wanted* pleasure.

He's buried to the hilt inside me as he kisses the side of my neck and I breathe heavily against his ear.

"Mine?" I ask.

He nips at my skin with his teeth and a shiver runs down my spine.

"Yours," he promises. "Yours, yours, yours."

I rock back and forth with him all the way inside me and he lifts his head to look at me again. I look past the green of his eyes and see his heart, his soul. Everything that he is and everything that I want is right there beneath the emerald surface.

I let my forehead rest against his as pleasure builds quickly with the slow swaying motion. I can feel tears crowding behind my eyelids when I blink.

As Ezra slips an arm around my waist to hold me close, I feel entirely overcome with emotion.

All at once, it's desire, need, longing, hoping, hating, grieving pain. The pain slices across my chest and pushes out a single gasping sob that I didn't expect. But the pain only fans the flame of the heat grinding between my legs.

I'm afraid Ezra will see my pain and try to stop this, but he surprises me. He sees my pain and feels it with me and loves me through it.

He tucks a strand of hair behind my ear and brushes a tear from my cheek. He looks as sorrowful as I feel, knowing that tomorrow we will go back to being slaves. It won't be possible to do this again because privacy will be gone. Kostya will go back to following our every move. Nikolai will go back to tormenting us with his violence.

It makes me angry.

Rage-filled lust rushes and my pussy pulses with the building need. I grind my hips harder, feeling Ezra's thick cock swelling with his quickly oncoming relief. The pulse of him against my G-spot and the stimulation of my clit as I push down hard, rubbing it frantically on the skin of his lower stomach, pushes me closer to the edge.

Where the pain fans the flame, the anger I feel pours fuel all around us.

It ignites without warning, exploding into the most all-consuming orgasm I've ever felt. Just as I start to come down from the most perfect wave, Ezra thrusts up, pumping into me hard and fast, and comes with a groan, my name slipping out from between his lips in the sweetest sound.

I hate myself for doing it, but I start to cry.

I cry from relief, from anger, from overwhelming pleasure. I cry for the knowledge of what we are, what I want us to be, for where we are trapped and for the tragic hopelessness of the unknowns yet to come.

Ezra wraps both arms around me and lays back on the bed, holding me, stroking my hair, petting me, as I cry into his chest.

"I won't ever forget this," I tell him when the worst of it has passed.

"It won't be the last time," he replies with a quiet, desperate determination in his voice.

He is the strength I never knew I needed.

I know how dangerous it is to have hope.

But knowing the danger doesn't keep me from hoping when it comes to Ezra.

<h1 style="text-align:center">CHAPTER 25</h1>
<h1 style="text-align:center">NIKOLAI</h1>

"THE EVIDENCE AGAINST the Campbells is overwhelming and I demand reparations. They plotted to kill off my entire bloodline. It's only by luck I'm still standing here in front of you today. You all would have seen significant losses the last three quarters had they been successful in their plot," I speak candidly to the four families in the boardroom.

"I agree," Vigo Vittori chimes in.

He's twirling a pen in his hand as he leans back in his black leather executive chair at the boardroom table.

"Blood taken requires blood given," he says.

"I understand recourse has already been settled upon, is that correct, Nikolai?" Cordelia O'Shea, the oldest of our generation in the O'Shea family line, asks.

She isn't the Head of House because she's female, her cousin Murphy has that power. But she's allowed a seat on the board for her position as the eldest. The same is true of Vigo's older sister, Renata.

"Let us hear this settlement for a vote," Renata says.

She sits regally in her chair, pushed back from the table as if she's too good for it. Her legs are crossed, her arms intentionally placed on the arm rests, and her spine is arrow straight.

She's always had the appearance of a queen with her skin that's nearly too fair-colored to belong to a Vittori and her jet-black hair that's always perfectly styled in long waves over her shoulders. Her high heels are far too tall for practicality and she wears a perfectly tailored romper rather than an evening gown like the rest of the women.

She thinks she's above them.

It's true, she is.

"I'm curious to know what you've deemed to be a fair settlement for such a heinous act," she says with a tilt of her head.

I grin. "As your brother so shrewdly stated, blood taken requires blood given."

I've been waiting for this delicious moment for over a year, since the day my parents and my younger brother died on one of our planes that went down on its way out of Italy.

Everyone thought the Vittoris had done it.

It was their homeland.

But I knew better.

The Vittoris and the Mikhailovs haven't traditionally had the best of relationships, but that was only because both of our families fought so hard to be the best of the four. It had always been neck and neck between our two families.

But as the Campbells in the States started to increase their sales figures, they became tiresomely cutthroat. Instead of behaving like businessmen and improving their practices, they came after my family, hoping their exclusive trade line that ran through Pakistan would give them the edge on arguing for a takeover when no one was left in my family.

But I hadn't gotten on the plane that day.

I smile to myself, knowing how differently things might have gone for them had I gone down the way they wanted me to. They hadn't accounted for my obsessive and meticulous nature when it came to completing my work on travel. I needed two more days to wrap up loose ends, and I finished my work as expected before flying home to arrange the funeral for my family.

It's what my parents would have expected.

I launched my own investigation, paying vast sums to get the information I needed. The largest sum was paid to Vigo for the recorded phone conversations he'd come into possession of. I paid him by sharing Anya, something I had sworn I would never do.

But when it came down to finding out what really happened to my family and seeking vengeance on the transgressors, even she was a price I was willing to pay. She'd proven by then that she would never love me anyway, and I was drowning in my grief. The combination had been enough for me to justify handing her over to Vigo for an hour.

He'd been fucking brutal with her.

More than I'd ever been.

I'd hoped it would make her grateful for what she had with me, but instead, it made her indignant. My resentment grew daily, exponentially since that day. It compounded each time I saw her dance with Ezra.

That fucking beautiful American boy who thought he could make her love him.

None of it matters now. This is the time I've been waiting for. I'd gotten my proof that the Americans tampered with the mechanical integrity of our aircraft with the intention of bringing it down.

I've presented my evidence to the board.

I've struck a deal with the Campbells for retribution.

Now it's time for the fucking Campbells to pay.

Charles Campbell stands slowly, straightening his lapels and smoothing his jacket. His graying hair and slow movements show his age. His ever-growing gut shows his lack of care for his rapidly declining life expectancy.

He takes in a deep breath and speaks humbly to the room, "When Nikolai came to me with this news of what my son had done, I was devastated." He sniffs, his eyes glassy, but it doesn't bother me. "Blood taken requires blood given. I'm making a…a fair trade in reparations—" His voice cracks as he begins to cry like a fool and lowers back to his seat.

I take over for him. "Three of my family died. My father, my mother, and my brother. I'm taking the same from the Campbell family. He's agreed to hand over the Leblancs—his sister Fleur, her husband Gerard, and their son Leo."

Vigo slams his hand down on the table. "I object to this. What you've presented makes it clear that Chandler Campbell," Charles' son, "is directly responsible for the orchestration of your family's death. Why is he getting away without paying his debt?"

"I assure you," Charles says, "Chandler is repaying this debt to our family. He's been stripped of his place as Head of House."

"And who is taking his place, old man?" Vigo asks.

Clearing his throat, Charles replies, "I am."

Renata floats her hand up from the arm rest as if to silence them. "And who will become the Head of House when you die, Charles, hmm? I understand that Chandler is the only direct Campbell descendant remaining who carries the family name."

"My granddaughter Callista still carries the name," Charles says.

"A woman cannot be the Head of House. Do you plan to produce another heir?" Renata continues.

"Well, no…"

"Well," Renata tilts her head and speaks as calmly as a river flows, smoothly but with the power to chisel mountainsides, "I would suggest Leo Leblanc be given the title of Head of House and Chandler be handed over for execution. It seems only fair given that Chandler has masterminded the slaying of the Mikhailov family."

"Let's put it to a vote," Vigo agrees.

"But, no…you can't—" Charles attempts to interrupt and I cut him off, leaning forward and slamming my hands down on the boardroom table.

"Enough from you! You and I have come to our agreement, Charles. Three from your house for the three taken from mine. I gave you the option of selecting the three and we both knew full well the final decision would rest with the board. Now, shut your mouth and let the board vote."

Charles breaks into pathetic, sniveling sobs that I roll my eyes against.

Vigo rises from his seat, coming to stand beside me at the head of the table. "Official vote. All in favor of reparations to the Mikhailov family by the blood of Fleur and Gerard Leblanc and Charles Campbell, say aye."

A resounding agreement.

A beautifully vengeful, resounding agreement.

I straighten and smile, crossing my arms over my chest.

"All opposed," Vigo says, "say nay."

Charles shoots to his feet, his oversized gut nearly lifting the table on his way up. "Nay! We had an agreement, Nikolai."

"And the agreement is being honored by the wishes of the board," I sneer at him with a tilted head.

"It's done," Murphy O'Shea adds, "Leo Leblanc will become the Head of House for the now former Campbells. The family bloodline will continue with the Leblancs for future generations and we will no longer recognize the power of the Campbells. Reparations should be paid immediately."

"Egan is watching over the Leblancs now. I'll go and ask him to bring them here." Cordelia stands and leaves the room.

I nod at Kostya. "Lay down the tarps."

When I say this, it sends Charles into another tailspin of useless sobbing.

If I still had a heart, I might give a shit that he's about to lose his son.

But I lost my humanity two decades ago, the first time I acquired a human asset and sold her to the highest bidder when I was just nineteen years old. I signed a contract with the Devil seven years after that when I chose Anya to become my talent slave. I was twenty-six and she was just a child. The Devil came to collect on my soul the very day I collected Anya three years ago.

The empty space where my soul used to reside is now filled only with anger, mistrust, resentment, and vengeance.

There's no room for anything else.

Cordelia O'Shea returns with the Leblancs, black hoods over their heads, their arms secured behind their backs with cable ties. Their grunts and wails beneath the black hoods bring a smile to my face.

Finally.

Finally, I will get to avenge my family.

Egan O'Shea and Kostya force them down to their knees on the blue tarp that's been laid out at the front of the boardroom. I expect the blood to splatter everywhere, but at least the tarps will mostly protect my carpets from the stains. There's a reason my family chose to install red carpet here, after all.

The hoods are lifted from their faces to reveal them each gagged with black fabric they bite between their teeth. Their eyes are wide and curious as they look around the room to see that they are here with the four families. I can see the flicker of thought run across their eyes that perhaps they are safe here, they see their family member Charles, after all.

Then Cordelia ushers Chandler Campbell into the room and my face alights with sinister glee. He walks in behind her, adjusting his navy-blue suit jacket, thinking he's being called in for business.

I can't wait to blow the cocky smirk right off this bastard's face.

"I suppose you've decided to reinstate me as Head of House, then," Chandler says with an arrogant grin and a tilt of his head.

"No, dear." Cordelia taps his shoulder and gives him a crooked smile before she returns to her seat.

I pull my switchblade from my pocket and circle around to Leo Leblanc. His parents groan and attempt to shout through their gags as I approach him from behind. I bend and slice the zip ties that bind him and step back.

Leo leaps to his feet, a frightened baby bird in the eagle's nest. He pulls his fabric gag from his mouth and presses his back to the far wall, his parents crying on their knees.

I look to Chandler, who stands stoically like the callous bastard he is. I point to the spot on the tarp next to Leo's parents with the tip of my knife. It crinkles beneath my shoes as I shift my weight.

"Come. Kneel," I command.

Chandler looks dumbstruck. "Excuse me?"

"I'm sorry, son," Charles sobs like a fool, pushing his fingers beneath his glasses to pinch the bridge of his nose.

"I don't understand…"

"You laid the plans that killed my family, yes?" I say. "Blood taken requires blood given. The board has ruled. Yours is to be given as reparations along with Mr. and Mrs. Leblanc. Leo," I turn to the young man trembling against the wall, "take a breath. You've been spared. In fact, welcome. You've been voted as the new Head of House for the Campbell family. Excuse me, now the Leblanc family."

The four families applaud in chorus.

"You may have Charles' seat. Move, Charles."

Charles rises slowly and turns away from the scene at the front of the room. Like a coward, he abandons his son in favor of cowering in the far corner. He's too weak to face his child, to tell him goodbye, to watch him die.

Leo looks to his mother and father on their knees and only begins to move as his mother nods at him eagerly, tilting her head toward the seat. At least she has the presence of mind to understand how lucky her son is to be spared, let alone to be given such a prestigious role within the four families.

Chandler still hasn't moved.

"Accept your fate, Chandler," I growl at him.

He shakes his head, backing away toward the door. "No, no, you can't do this."

Renata snaps to her feet. "Enough with the theatrics. So dramatic. Kostya, grab him and *make* him kneel. Let's get on with this. We have other business matters to attend to."

Kostya wrestles Chandler to the ground in front of me on the tarp. I haven't seen a sight so beautiful as the back of his head as he fights and screams for his life. Vigo hands me his gun—the same one he always carries in his chest holster beneath his jacket.

"Full magazine," he tells me. "One round for each of them and plenty to spare."

I cock the gun and press it to Chandler's dirty blond hair. His American arrogance and sand-colored locks flash across my vision as familiar.

Ezra Bell.

Ezra *fucking* Bell.

Ezra and that perfect golden hair and those goddamn green eyes that only look at her.

At Anya.

My Anya.

I exhale and squeeze the trigger, unloading three rounds into the back of Chandler Campbell's head. Blood sprays across my carefully tailored suit and feels warm against my cheek. I feel the liquid where it splashed onto my bottom lip and I swipe my tongue across to taste it. It's metallic, the taste of pure fucking justice.

The room is silent in waiting, only broken by the pathetic sob from Charles in the far corner of the room and a sharp cry from Mrs. Leblanc through her gag. Her sound interrupts the reverie of this satisfying moment, so I swing my arm and take her out next. Her body topples sideways onto her husband and he groans loudly as he falls to the floor. I take a step to make sure my aim is true and unload one last round into the side of his head.

Three crimson pools spill slowly out onto the tarp, puddling from beneath the three heads.

Blood taken requires blood given.

Vengeance served so sweetly.

My chest heaves with the immediate relief I feel from finally avenging my family. I reach up to swipe the blood from my cheek and swirl it between my fingers, watching the way it coats my skin in the most brilliant shade of crimson imaginable. I let out a heavy breath, letting my arms fall to my sides and tilt my head toward the ceiling. I take in a deep cleansing breath, trying to savor the moment.

But the relief is fleeting.

Now I have blood, but I still don't have my family.

I still don't have Anya's love.

I still don't have Ezra's desire.

I am still without.

And I am angrier than ever.

I hold the gun out toward Vigo, but he waves it away.

"There are plenty of rounds left for you to injure a certain dancer if you don't want a reason to torture yourself with her presence any longer."

My eyebrows slant inward as I narrow my eyes. My gut reaction is to tell him to fuck off, but there's some small part of me that hears him, a small part that feels understood in my torment over her.

That same part thinks she deserves to be one of his broken dolls.

I turn my head to glare at him. "I'm not selling you Anya." Though, for the first time, I'm not entirely sure I mean it.

I wonder if she's the reason why my relief for this moment was stolen away so swiftly. Because she torments me daily, giving her attention to Ezra, but even worse, receiving his attention in return.

I fucking hate them both for that.

The vengeance in my heart is returning anew. I don't feel satisfied that I've caused enough hurt to those who've hurt me.

For the first time, I sincerely wonder if offloading Anya to a crueler master would satisfy my obsession with hurting her and finally give my mind the reprieve it deserves.

I give Vigo another glance, a nod, then lift the back of my jacket and tuck the gun into my belt.

CHAPTER 26

Anya

MY EYES BLINK open from what was perhaps the most serene sleep I've experienced in years. I'm curled around Ezra's back where he sleeps on his side next to me.

I don't know what time it is, but I normally wake up several times during the night.

Never content.

Never feeling fully safe.

I suffer nightmares that wake me often.

But as I awaken now from a peacefully dreamless sleep, I feel refreshed in a way I've never felt before.

It's because of Ezra.

I nuzzle my nose across his spine and breathe in. I inhale the heady scent of him and kiss the center of his back tenderly.

I'm certain it must still be the middle of the night and that we probably have a few more hours of peace before I need to wake Ezra and make him leave. I don't know how Nikolai would react if he knew Ezra had been here and shared my bed. I'm risking a lot as it is not to wake him now and send him away to his room.

I roll onto my back with a yawn, my eyes drifting shut again, and I stretch my arms above my head. My bare breasts lift out from beneath the sheet and the cool air in the room brushes over my nipples, making me shiver. It's such a stark contrast to the heat of pressing them against Ezra's warm body.

I smile to myself, recalling the way he touched me last night, the way he sucked and licked and teased and made my entire body explode from pure nirvanic, *wanted* pleasure. He helped me find heaven in his arms, even if it was only for a few hours.

But then I realize those hours are done.

There's a prickle of awareness creeping over my skin.

Untangled from Ezra's overwhelming, calming aura, my heart claws its way up my throat with the swift drop-off of my sudden descent back into hell.

I can sense *him* in the room.

I hold my breath and open my eyes slowly.

Daylight peeks in from behind the closed curtains.

It's morning.

We slept all night.

And Nikolai stands beside the bed.

I swallow hard.

Inhale, exhale, inhale.

I sit up slowly, trying my best to limit my movements on the mattress. I don't want to wake Ezra. If I can just get Nikolai out of the room, let him punish me for this in whatever way he chooses, maybe I can spare Ezra the pain of having to witness it.

My pulse is pounding and I will my heart to stop beating, just until I can leave. I'm afraid Ezra knows my heart too well, that he'll feel my fear in his sleep and wake from dreamland into a nightmare.

I stand slowly. Nikolai doesn't step back, so my bare chest bumps his as I get to my feet.

"You've become an ungrateful bitch, *rabynya,*" he spits the words at me, his nostrils flaring.

I whisper, "Just punish me and get it over with."

He reaches around and grabs a fistful of my hair, yanking back hard. I nearly yelp, though I try to remain quiet, as he forces my head to angle far to the side. My hands reach for his in a vain attempt to pull him off, but he holds me in place.

"Please…" I beg. "Please, please don't wake him."

I'm done for, but part of me hopes that Ezra might be spared the pain of witnessing my torment.

"Don't wake him?" he repeats with a growl. "Don't wake him?!"

"Shh, please, please…"

But it's too late.

Ezra startles. It takes a moment, but he realizes what's happening quickly enough, though Nikolai is already dragging me across the room by my hair. Ezra leaps after us, both of us clad in only our underwear.

As Nikolai pauses to pull the door open so he can drag me out into the hallway, Ezra runs for him.

"No!" I shout at Ezra because there's no point in fighting.

Ezra never touches Nikolai, never even comes close. He stops dead in his tracks, then holds his hands up in surrender before taking a slow step backward.

I glance over to see that Nikolai holds a gun in his free hand. He holds a gun and he's pulling me out to punish me. An arctic wind whips around me, a frozen brush across my skin, and my spine tingles with a rush of fear.

I scream, "No! Nikolai, please."

"I told you that you were on thin ice. I fucking *warned* you." He's come completely unhinged with the rapid way he speaks, a piece of his disheveled, ashen hair falling across his eye. "I knew you would do this, I *knew* you would. You never gave me a chance, Anya, from the moment I brought you home."

Brought me home?

"Home? You're pathetic, Nikolai. This was never my home."

"It was *always* your home. Since you were eleven years old this was your *fucking* home. You were lucky to have me as your benefactor. I paid for your talent! I own it, it belongs to *me!*"

"And I've paid my debt for it with blood, sweat, and tears."

"You've paid nothing. *Nothing.* Not so much as your gratitude. And perhaps that's why you are so ungrateful. You owe me."

"She owes you shit," Ezra interjects bravely.

Nikolai cocks the gun that's still aimed at Ezra. The sound is enough to shake my tears loose, rattling my bones into jumping at the simple yet foreboding *click.*

"No, no, Nikolai, please. I'm sorry. I'm so sorry. Just tell me what you want me to do and I'll do it. Don't hurt him, *please,* don't hurt him."

He tilts his head looking down at me and I dare to stare back. Something flashes across the gray, something desperate, something primal, something I might almost mistake as heartache if I didn't know better.

"What is it?" he snarls. "Did you fall in love with this one? You let him fuck you and now you're in love?" He laughs and it's one of the most terrifying things I've ever heard.

He swings the gun around and presses it to my temple. I whimper and flinch. Ezra is saying something frantically, but I can't make out the words.

My brain roars. It's been lit on fire by fear and it screams to escape the cage of my skull. I can't think of anything other than dousing these flames, dampening the terror.

Nikolai still holds me firmly in his grip with his fist around my hair. I sob, the cold metal reminding me of death and how close it is to becoming my reality. For the first time in so, so long, I don't secretly wish for death to take me.

I don't want to die.

I want to be with Ezra, wherever he is.

Nikolai releases my hair and I immediately step back. He moves toward me, aiming the gun at the center of my forehead with his outstretched arm.

"Walk," he says to me, holding the door open.

The fire in my head roars again, telling me to do what he says, to obey the man with the tool that could end me in less than a second.

I don't glance at Ezra.

I can't.

My eyes refuse to look away from the gun.

I don't dare turn my back to Nikolai, so I back myself out of the room, taking slow, careful steps. I creep backward down the hallway until Nikolai gets fed up with my pace.

"Turn the *fuck* around and walk, Anya," he shouts.

I jump, my bare breasts jostling, reminding me of how exposed I am. It takes all my thought and all my strength to force my body to turn, to take my eyes off the instrument of death that's threatening my very existence.

I move slowly toward the grand staircase, topless, with nothing but my panties on to cover me, knowing full well the four families are still here to watch my punishment, or perhaps even my death, in full glory.

I cross my arms over my chest, then drop them to my sides, deciding that I'd rather keep my dignity with my head held high rather than try in vain to cover myself in shame.

The only shame I feel is thinking that hope and I could reconcile our differences.

"Down," Nikolai tells me when I reach the top of the grand staircase.

I descend slowly. I felt nearly on top of the world walking down this very staircase last night in my pink gown, walking hand in hand with the boy I fell in love with. Now I descend with an ache in my chest and fear pulsing through my veins.

I'm not walking down to an empty entryway as would normally be the case. The four families mill about, crossing the space, talking to one another, some of them have their slaves with them.

Everyone turns to look as I make my way down the stairs and step down onto the marble floor.

"Kneel," Nikolai says, and the gun is against the side of my head again.

I flinch then quickly lower to my knees on the floor.

He's going to kill me here.

Everything stops.

The four families still and quieten.

I can feel every eye in Mikhailov Manor upon me.

It's a show for them, a dramatic event to entertain them. It's no different than the performances given by the talent slaves.

I feel lightheaded, sick to my stomach, and my hands are shaking with one question bouncing around inside my skull.

Am I going to die today?

Sound comes back to me in a rush as I suddenly think of Ezra, remembering he's here, he's watching this and powerless to stop it. I snap my head to look at him, just feet away, as my fire-engulfed brain explodes in pain with an all new kind of terror.

What will become of Ezra if Nikolai blows my brains out in front of him? If he's forced to see me lifeless on the floor, blood pooling around my head and staining his feet?

God, no.

I can't bear to think of it. Tears that wipe away any dignity I might have had left drip down my cheeks against my will. I sniff and tilt my chin, lifting my head a little higher, hoping it masks my fear.

It's not for me or for Nikolai.

It's for the man I fell in love with.

That man is losing his mind with worry right now. It's evident to everyone around us with the way he shouts and swears and tries to fight against Kostya. But the gun that Nikolai holds puts us both in our places.

Though I still feel Ezra's rage vibrating in my soul, Nikolai startles my attention away as he shouts to no one and everyone who will listen.

"Let this be a lesson to all of you ungrateful whores. You belong to your master. Your *body* belongs to your master. You do not get to choose who you give it to. Vicious, conniving *sluts*, the whole lot of you."

No one bats an eye at Nikolai's behavior. No one intervenes to stop him. I am nothing more than a talent slave and Nikolai can end my life right here and now if he wishes to.

He steps forward and my body jolts.

I press my eyes shut tight.

I breathe slowly.

I count.

One. Two. Three. Four. Five. Six. Seven. Eight.

One. Two. Three. Four. Five. Six—

END OF BOOK ONE

COUNTS OF EIGHT
PLAYLIST

STREAM ON SPOTIFY
bit.ly/spotify-brynnford

ANYA AND EZRA'S PERFORMANCE SONG
Hallelujah by Jeff Buckley

Heart Killer by Gossling
bury a friend by Billie Eilish
Trampoline by SHAED & ZAYN
Dance Monkey by Tones And I
River by Bishop Briggs
Six Feet Under by Billie Eilish
Black Hole Sun by Nouela
Wicked Game by Chris Isaak
Iris by Kina Grannis
Unsteady by X Ambassadors
If the World Was Ending by JP Saxe & Julia Michaels
Love Me Now by John Legend
Sweet Dreams (Are Made of This) by Marilyn Manson
I Will Survive by J2 featuring Blu Holliday

ACKNOWLEDGMENTS

I've been dreaming of writing and publishing a dark romance for years—though I honestly hadn't expected this story to be the first. Anya and Ezra just kept on nudging me to tell their story and so, here we are. I'm so thankful that you decided to come along on their journey!

My beta readers—Rachel, Danielle, Carrie, and Kaylan—are nothing short of amazing! Thank you all for the helpful comments and feedback that helped me make this book the best it can be! A special thank you to Rachel for helping me catalog and keep track of all the details.

To my editor, Silvia, a huge thank you for helping me clean up my manuscript. You gave me much needed confidence in Anya and Ezra's story and I can't wait to work with you on the rest!

I'm so grateful for the amazing people at Najla Qamber Designs for making such a beautiful book cover and putting on the finishing touches with the interior formatting. You are all amazing to work with and I'm so thankful for the beauty you brought to this story!

Thank you to my husband. You've always believed in me and supported me in this crazy writing journey. I know you don't always "get it" but you're still understanding of my need to do this thing. You're the best!

To friends and family who've supported me along the way, thank you for being there for me!

Finally, a huge thank you to all you daring readers! Dark romance readers are definitely my people and I'm so happy my book made its way into your hands (and hopefully into your heart, too). I hope you enjoyed reading "Counts of Eight" as much as I enjoyed writing it—sorry for the brutal cliffhanger, but at least you've got something to look forward to, right?

DANCE WITH DEATH

BRYNN FORD

For dark romance writers everywhere, your boldness inspires mine.

Thank you for being unapologetically daring.

PROLOGUE
NIKOLAI

2 ½ Years Ago

CRIMSON CIRCLES THE drain beneath my feet. With my head bowed beneath the flow of water, I scrub the dried blood from my matted hair. I hadn't planned to get my hands dirty on this latest business trip, but it had proven necessary.

I had to disband an entire factory after one of our commodities escaped. The local authorities had zeroed in on our site in Budapest after the young blonde money-maker somehow got away from the men I paid to steal her, keep her, and train her.

She went to a local hospital and the police were called in to take her statement on what she had told them was a kidnapping.

It was.

But if she'd known better, she would've kept her mouth shut. Needless to say, the girl has…disappeared, as has the police report she filed.

All of my Budapest commodities are gone.

Decommissioned, so to speak.

I've potentially lost hundreds of thousands that could've been made from these female assets. They were the reason I had blood on my hands. But they weren't all a loss. I was able to recirculate half the girls through my family's other factories in Prague and Minsk.

My stress is at an all-time high. This is not how I expected my trip to turn out. I'm not exactly looking forward to explaining to the board why the Mikhailovs no longer have a factory in Budapest. Furthermore, it will give my father a reason to blame me for any losses we incur next quarter, regardless of the fact that his needless interferences were the reason our sales tanked last quarter. All of this on top of the fact that I've returned home to deal with a surly talent slave who continues to deny me her submission.

I toss my hair back as I lift my head from beneath the flow of the waterfall showerhead. I blink the water away from my eyes and movement from within my private en suite bathroom catches my attention. I turn my head and stare through the steam-fogged glass enclosure.

I can see that it's my *rabynya*, and I can feel her there as well. Her fear of me is still palpable and it makes me hard, but it also frustrates me. She's a fighter, and though she's become reluctantly obedient, I haven't yet earned her full submission.

But then, why is she here?

I watch her standing there in the doorway that links my bedroom and bathroom, and she watches me, too. I finish cleansing myself, scrubbing away the blood that dried on my skin during my long journey back from Budapest. Blood she'll never know had been present at all.

As I rinse the last of the soap from my skin, she takes a step, moving from where she wavered in the doorway to firmly plant herself in my bathroom.

I dip my head beneath the water to hide my smirk. I turn off the water a few moments later and pop open the shower door, reaching out to pull a white towel from the bar on the wall. I scrub it over my hair briefly before wrapping it around my waist. I step out, dampness coating my skin, knowing the shine will highlight the lines of my muscles to aid in luring her in.

I walk to her, stopping just in front of where she stands. I look down at her bowed head, wondering if this is the moment she's chosen to show her submission, to give me her loyalty.

I wait.

She lets out a sigh and then takes off her shirt. She's bare beneath. I fight the urge to smack her perky little mound and twist her nipple until she screams for me to stop, but I force myself to stay still.

She takes off her cotton shorts next, the ones that mold to her beautiful, rounded ass and creep upward when she dances in them. I should be surprised when her panties come down, when I suddenly find her naked in front of me, but I'm not.

I knew this day would come.

I let her linger this way, in her own purgatory where she came to me needy and waits for me—bare and vulnerable—to give her what she wants.

"Tell me what you want, *rabynya*."

I already know what she wants.

Attention.

Affection.

Comfort.

Touch that brings her pleasure instead of pain.

She's sad that I took her dance partner from her. But Jamal just wasn't quite right for her—or for me—so I'd had to take him away. She's lonely, completely unaware that a new partner will be given to her in just a couple of months. I'm happy to let her think that I am the only place she will ever be able to turn for comfort.

She *should* turn to her master to fulfill that need.

I have every intent to take advantage of her fragile state.

Boldly, she lifts her head and slowly meets my eyes. There's fear there behind the sapphire blue—fear and desperation and longing.

"I want you, *moy khozyain*."

I grip her waist with both hands and turn her, backing her up to the marble countertop. She swallows, her eyes locked on mine as I stare and press myself against her. I loom above her, my breath steady but heavy, exhaling my internal flames over her, reminding her that I was born from hellfire.

A reminder that she's come to the devil asking to be burned.

Her features have softened from her normal cold as ice stare. Her eyelids seem heavier as they droop to hang a sultry frame over her blue irises. Her eyebrows are relaxed from the way they usually slant toward her nose, wrinkling her forehead sternly. Her lips are parted and rosy in color, and I feel her shallow breaths puffing against my throat.

"You want me," I say slowly, pressing my half-hard cock against her. "You want me…to do what?"

This question is her test.

Will she back down, afraid to speak her truth?

Will she prove herself to be a rebellious slave and demand rather than ask?

Or will she tell me what she thinks she needs and sweetly ask her master to oblige her?

I tilt my head, watching her carefully as she decides how to respond. I run my finger through a single strand of her dark brown hair, dragging it all the way down to the end. She presses her eyes shut as her breath catches in her throat.

"I want you to…to make me feel like I'm not alone. To share pleasure with me. Will you please, *moy khozyain?*"

She opens her eyes and I capture her chin in my hand. I gently tilt her head upward so she's forced to look at me. I'm happy with her response because she's acknowledged her subservience. She must ask without expectation, knowing that her master will decide the answer. Eventually, I will have her trained to know better than to ask me for anything, but I'm feeling generous.

Perhaps because my violent rage has so recently been released upon the now decommissioned commodities from the Budapest factory.

I bend over her slowly, seductively, inch by inch, lowering my lips until they touch hers. It's hardly a brush of my lips on hers, but it melts her. She slinks and I let go of her chin, letting my hands drift down her chest. As my fingertips drag over the peaks of her nipples, they harden instantly. She whimpers and I smile.

"Do you feel lonely, Anya?"

She swallows. "*Da, khozyain.*"

"Do you want to feel cared for?"

"*Da, khozyain.*"

My hand falls between her legs and I cup my hand over her cunt. "Do you want me to make you come?"

Her whole body sinks against my grip. "*Da, khozyain.*"

I take off the towel, letting it drift to the floor as I bare my hard cock. She gasps, surely expecting me to bend her over and fuck her hard, as I normally do. But instead, I lower to my knees, seeing the opportunity in this.

I drag my fingers along her folds, teasing and testing as I watch her face. She's dripping wet with need for me. While I intend to enjoy watching my slave finally submit her will to me, I also intend to learn. I study as I touch her, cataloging every twitch of her features, every gasp, every whimper, every moan.

But something interesting happens in my study—I lose myself in her pleasure. As time ticks on, as my fingers work faster, harder, testing the pressure and speed she needs to make her come, I find myself in awe of the look on her beautiful face.

Could she be more?

She comes on my fingers, hard and sated, with a drawn out "*oh*" falling from between parted lips.

She *is* more.

She always was.

But I'm the devil and she's not ready to reign in hell with me—she may not ever be. But this…this is promising.

She came to me.

She gave herself to me.

She took a grave risk in coming to me this way. Her experiences with me would have told her that I might beat her, burn her, drown her, fuck her, hurt her in any manner of my choosing. That gamble may have been just enough reason for me to provide her with an insurance policy. If she can give herself to me now, perhaps she will be worthy of me in the future.

Only time will tell.

CHAPTER 1

Anya

ONE. TWO. THREE. Four. Five. Six. Seven. Eight.

One. Two. Three. Four. Five. Six—

Nikolai's gun slams against my temple, knocking me sideways onto the floor. A ringing sound explodes behind my ears and my vision blackens at the edges before clearing.

I start to push off the floor with my palms, but the hard heel of Nikolai's dress shoe slams down heavy on the outside of my left ankle, holding me in place.

He twists his foot, grinding into my flesh. I'm dumbstruck and silent in the moments before my brain registers pain. I'm confused at first, but as he lifts his foot and slams it back down again on the same spot, jamming the hard ridge of my ankle bone painfully into the marble floor, I know exactly what he's doing.

Over and over, he stomps.

Each stomp is more forceful and intentional than the last. He grunts with each slam, his teeth bared and anger flashing blackness in his eyes. His slicked back hair becomes undone—along with his self-control—and ash-brown strands fall across his forehead with each movement. The darkest rage I've ever seen contorts his face, and I see him as none other than the devil before me. It's as if my pain has sent me straight down to the depths of hell to be punished as he pleases in his kingdom of nightmares.

Each hit jolts pain through my entire body like I've never felt before.

His foot slams.

My ankle bruises.

The pain shoots sharp and fast up through my leg, into my hip, screaming warnings at my mind to get away.

But I can't.

My muscles stiffen, guarding against the attack, but there's nothing I can do to avoid the electric current of crippling ache that shoots through my leg with each hit.

Over and over again.

And then there's a crack.

I open my mouth to scream, but no sound comes out. Everything is dulled by the consuming pain, even the sound of my own torment.

My ears ring for what feels like an eternity of silent aching and then, without any warning, the volume of reality is suddenly unmuted and cranked up as high as it will go.

I scream.

I break into sobs.

Something's torn or broken or completely fucking shattered inside me. All I can think about is the pain for long, searing moments.

Nikolai stops.

He stills.

He crouches on his haunches beside me, reaching out to wipe tears from my face.

"Don't touch me!" I shake my head, jerking away from his touch.

He pinches my chin sharply between his fingers and thumb. "Perhaps now you understand the pain I felt finding you naked with him in the bed *I* gave you," he seethes.

My face responds with a twisted grimace of disgust as I meet his eyes. If I didn't know him as well as I do, I might say his gray eyes look glassy, covered in a sheen of angry tears. I look a little longer, stare a little deeper, hoping to see something there, *anything*—something more than the washed-out gray that masks who he truly is.

"Rotten whore," he spits before pushing to stand and my gaze falls away from his toward the floor. "You can have what's left of her, Ezra. I don't suppose she will dance anytime soon. She's useless to me now."

Ezra suddenly appears at my side, and I realize only then that Kostya was there, holding him back. As Nikolai walks away, Ezra kneels beside me and I roll onto my back in heaving sobs.

He reaches beneath my shoulder blades, lifting me gently, curling me toward him and hiding my naked breasts from the world around me. A true gentleman even amidst the horror; I love him all the more that he provides me whatever little comfort and protection he can when so much power has been stripped from us both.

A swift motion catches my eye and I turn my head to look just as Vigo Vittori rushes toward us. My breath charges wildly in and out of my lungs, nearly forcing me into hyperventilation.

Vigo is coming closer, walking fast. When he comes upon me, his leg sweeps back and I hardly have a moment to figure out what he's doing.

"No!" Ezra shouts, and tries to shift me away, but it's too late.

Vigo kicks, driving his toe into the side of my injured ankle. A whole new lightning bolt of pain shoots up through my leg and my head rolls sideways on Ezra's lap as I try to curl away.

"Whoops," Vigo says flippantly as I grunt and whimper through another explosion of pain.

He steps over my writhing body to get to Nikolai. I watch over Ezra's shoulder as I pant out breaths filled with pain. Vigo claps Nikolai on the back as he runs a trembling hand through his disheveled hair.

What right does Nikolai think he has to be shaking over this when I'm the one writhing in pain?

"Come, let's discuss business," Vigo says, glancing back at me with vicious intent. "I think I can make you a fair offer for your talentless slave. I could use another broken doll. Tell me how much your broken Russian doll is worth to you."

Ezra once asked me what could be worse than death.

I thought it was this life, but I think I'm about to discover an even more terrifying existence.

I'm about to be sold to the Vittoris.

CHAPTER 2
Ezra

ANGUISH IS A word I didn't know the meaning of until this very moment.

Torment.

Suffering.

Those words meant nothing to me before now.

The tears of my blue-eyed girl spill onto my bare thigh as I cradle her, curling her against my body. I'm shaking, truthfully trembling from head to toe.

And I feel completely useless.

"Fuck you, Nikolai!" I scream at his back. "You're a coward, a weak excuse for a man."

I regret opening my mouth before the words come out, but my mind is on a different plane of existence and I'm not thinking clearly.

He whips around to face me and there's a beat that pauses us both in a rage-fueled stare. His eyes are glistening with smoky gray fire and his features are clouded with violence.

I've never been afraid of this man.

Not until now.

I keep my eyes on him as he rushes forward, his hair falling in ruffled pieces across his creased forehead. I flinch as he pulls his arm back, fist raised, his lips snarling and baring his teeth.

He's coming after me *now.*

I roll Anya onto her back on the cold marble floor to get her out of the way as I rise up to my knees, ready to defend myself. But I'm so jarred by what's just happened, so off-centered by it, that my reaction is slow and pointless.

His fist collides with my cheek, his knuckles bumping into the side of my nose as he follows the throw of his punch all the way through. He hits me so hard that my head throws to the side, catching me off-balance. I put my hands out to catch my fall to the floor and my palms land with a smack against the marble.

I shake my head, throwing off the reverberation of the hit, and I push up to my knees again.

Nikolai doesn't say a word to me.

He doesn't spare another glance.

He doesn't grant another opportunity for insult.

He walks away with Vigo Vittori, heading up the grand staircase with sharp, quick strides. I take a steadying breath, watching, waiting, until he turns and disappears from our sight at the top of the stairs. Silence gives way to noise and stillness returns to movement.

As I turn to help Anya, I find she's already pushing up to a sitting position, powerfully using adrenaline to fuel her independence. Black streaks from her tears stain her face, remnants of the make-up she wore last night.

I reach for her face, holding her head still so I can search her eyes, but she's already sheathed her blues in ice. As I brush the tears on her cheeks with my thumbs, I practically jump out of my skin at the unexpected touch of gentle fingertips on my shoulder.

A woman crouches beside me. I notice Anya's eyes widen as I turn to look at the person who appeared suddenly at my side. Renata Vittori balances gracefully on her haunches in her high heels, wearing a perfectly tailored pant suit.

The side of her mouth curls up and her tongue clicks. "Heartbreaking how quickly he's destroyed you both. A shame really, your performance was stunning. I was looking forward to next year's entertainment. I suppose all things come to an end, though, don't they?"

"Leave us alone," Anya growls.

I'm surprised by her demeanor, though I understand it. She speaks through clenched teeth, jaw tight, rage and hurt painting a dark shadow over her beautiful features.

My hands fall from her face as Renata forces her way in, lifting Anya's chin with two fingers. "If my brother purchases you, you won't feel quite so confident in your tone with our family. If you thought Nikolai had a firm hand with you…" she trails off, jerking her hand away, causing Anya's head to bob.

Renata uses my shoulder to push herself back to her feet and she strolls away, heels clicking on the marble. She glances over her shoulder at me and the corner of her mouth curls up, giving me a look I can't decipher. But it's a look that makes my stomach hurt.

Anya starts to shift onto all fours and I rush to her on my knees, putting my hands on either side of her waist, whether to stop her or to steady her, I don't even know.

"Get me out of here," she huffs through a heavy breath. "Get me out of here, Ezra."

I nod though she isn't looking at me. "Where?"

"To my room, take me back to my room."

"Okay," I agree, and rise to my feet.

Anya doesn't wait for me to help her; she's slowly crawling forward, wincing as her injured ankle slides over hard, cold ground. She's as stubborn as ever in her independence.

"Stop," I tell her as I bend down to grip her sides. "Come here."

I pluck her from the floor with ease. Her tiny frame, my strength, and the fury inside me make it considerably easy to lift her. I turn her against me as I hold her and she latches her hands around my neck. She's huffing out breaths of pain, as though she's laboring through it. I don't even want to try to imagine the hurt she feels right now. One glance at her quickly bruising and swollen ankle tells me it's not right. I can't say for sure whether it's broken, but it's definitely not fucking right.

Kostya follows as I step onto the staircase. "She goes to her room, you go to yours," he says.

I ignore him and keep moving, shaking my head in disbelief that he thinks I'm just gonna drop her off and leave her. He's gonna have to fight me if he wants to separate me from her.

I take Anya up the grand staircase, feeling the eyes of guests upon us.

Is someone going to stop us?

Try to hurt us more?

Take her away from me?

I don't know anything about the four families except for the fact that they are all monumental pieces of shit.

I don't tear my eyes from my girl as I take her upstairs and the knife in my heart twists to see her this way. It's not the first time, but fuck, I'm so sick of seeing her like this that it's making me fucking insane.

"I've got you," I tell her, but I don't know if I really do this time or if I ever really did before.

She can't respond, and I'm not even sure she hears me. She's just trying to get from one second of pain to the next. I move faster as fresh liquid pools in the corners of her eyes. I make it down the hallway and rush her into her bedroom, moving toward the bed.

"No," she stops me, "put me on the chair."

I take her to the armchair in front of the window, lowering her slowly to sit. She keeps her injured leg outstretched in front of her and props it on the ottoman, placing her uninjured right leg down on the floor. Her hands fall naturally toward her wound, landing just above her ankle.

"There's tape and…and adhesive wrap," she says, pointing to her dresser, "in the top right drawer."

I pull it open and find what I need right away. Her drawers are meticulously organized. Her underwear is folded neatly beside her well-worn ballet pointe shoes and the supplies she uses to care for her dance-battered feet. I bring her what she asked for and Kostya's hand lands on my shoulder.

I shrug it back, shaking him off. "No. I will fucking break your nose if you try to take me from her right now."

His eyes narrow on me, then dart to her. "Five minutes," he concedes and steps back.

I'm shocked by the concession, grateful for it, but I don't have the time or concern to mull it over. I drop to my knees beside Anya. She's picked up the roll of half-inch-wide white tape and is picking at the edge, trying to free the end of it from the roll. Her agitation grows as she *picks* and *picks* with trembling fingers.

Pick.

Pick.

Pick.

"Fuck!" She throws the tape onto the ottoman. It bounces off, tumbling to the floor and rolling away. Her fingers dig into her hair and she yells again, "Fuck!"

My shoulders tense, my entire body gone rigid at the way she unravels.

It's wrong.

This is all wrong.

I force myself to keep my cool, but I feel like I might unravel with her. I lean and grab the roll of tape, forcing my hands to stay steady, not to tremble and mirror her actions, but to be strong and give her the steadiness she so desperately needs.

It's all I can give her.

I pull the end of the tape free and keep my voice calm. "Where do you want this?"

She exhales long and slow. "I need to immobilize. I don't know if it's broken."

She pants as if getting those words out were an exhausting feat. Looking down at her rapidly swelling foot, I understand why.

"Okay," I tell her. "It's okay, Anya, I've got you. Just tell me what to do and I'll do it."

With every second that passes, an invisible syringe of uncertainty injects an ounce more fear into my veins, rushing through me painfully, bringing fiery rage into my chest.

I push down the anger and fear.

I have to.

I can't lose it when she needs me the most.

She points to a spot on her leg, a couple of inches above her ankle bone. "Wrap it all the way around my leg here, tight, but not too tight."

I nod and unwind the tape, ripping off a piece that's large enough to wrap around her slender leg. I stick the end on the side of her leg and put my thumb over it, holding it in place as I give a tug to make it taut. I wrap it around—the piece is long enough to go around almost twice—and rub my fingers over it to make sure it's secure.

"Take another piece," she says, then pauses, blowing out a shaky breath through her lips. "Put the end here." She points to the piece I've just wrapped around her. "Straight down, over the ankle bone, under my foot, back up the other side. *Tight*, Ezra."

I do as she tells me, but before I wrap beneath her foot, she sucks in a deep breath and pulls her toes backward. Her face contorts as her foot trembles and she releases it, letting it fall forward again to a relaxed position. Fresh tears push their way from her eyes and she grits her teeth.

"Oh, God," she sobs. "Fuck. You have to push my foot back, Ezra. Hold it while you tape it."

Shit.

Seeing her this way, knowing the pain she's feeling, literally rips me in half. I can honestly feel it tearing down the middle of my stomach. My own tears threaten to spill, but as hard as it is, I pull everything back inside me and hold it in.

I've gotta keep my shit together for her.

I wrap my hand slowly and tenderly around the side of her foot, barely touching, watching her eyes for change with each millimeter of movement as my skin brushes along hers.

"Just do it," she grunts out her insistence to get this done and over with. Her voice is a growl, primal and animalistic.

I don't warn her, I just do it. I pull her foot back until her toes are pointing at the ceiling, forming a right angle with her leg. She lets out a shriek and groans, panting through the agony again.

Loving instinct nags in my gut to let go of her foot, to step away, to stop causing her this torture. But I fight it and pull the tape around her foot tight, securing it like a stirrup all the way around to the other side.

"Quick," she huffs. "Two more pieces around to hold it up. Cover it all tight with the wrap."

I work fast, adding more tape just as before to stirrup her foot in place. I take the athletic bandage wrap and cover the tape, coiling it around her ankle and over her foot.

We both huff out a breath when it's done.

"Do you think it's broken?" I ask.

"I don't know. I can move it. It hurts. It just hurts so much, Ezra."

I bend, pressing a kiss to the edge of the bandage on her leg. "What can we do for that? Will he send a doctor? Does he have medication here?"

She falls back in her chair, her head tilting to the ceiling as she rests it on the back. "He's the one who did this to me. Do you honestly think he would send me a doctor? He didn't when he broke my nose."

"He broke your—" I stop myself, hearing the tone of my voice rising in tension.

Stay calm for her.

I shouldn't be surprised to know he's broken other parts of her body before. I've seen how effectively he's destroyed her.

"We need to get you in bed, get your foot propped up to help with the swelling."

Her chest heaves in slow, concentrated, heavy breaths.

She's still for moments.

But then her breathing suddenly skips and stutters as sobs fight their way out of her lungs. She lifts her head and falls forward, reaching for me, and I'm right there to meet her. Her hands grab my shoulders and she's trying to pull me into her arms, but I'm wary, right next to her ankle, and I don't want to hurt her or have her hurt herself.

I shift as I get to my feet and scoop my arms beneath her legs, lifting her from the chair, moving her toward the bed. When she practically screams her panic into my skin, right over my heart, it vibrates inside me from head to toe. It shocks my very being and jolts me into tears right along with her.

I lay her down softly on the bed and reach over to grab extra pillows. I start to pile them beneath her foot—one, then another—trying to get as much lift as possible to help reduce the swelling.

I bend over her to kiss her cheek, her forehead, her lips. I don't give a shit about what Kostya sees, though I suppose I should. He might tell Nikolai I had my lips on hers again. But when she's hurting, when she needs me the way she does, I can't bring myself to give a fuck. He's already hurt her. He's already—

Fuck.

He's talking to Vigo about my blue-eyed girl.

A fresh wave of nauseous unease washes over me as I press another kiss to her shoulder. I straighten, intent on getting a shirt or something for her to wear so she's not lying there topless, but apparently, my time has expired.

Kostya's hands land on my shoulders and yank me backward. I stumble away from the bed before rolling my shoulders and throwing my right arm with a fist intent on decking him as I spin. He ducks the punch and comes after me. The fucker is quick, grabbing my wrist and twisting my arm behind my back. He wrestles my other arm around behind me and holds my wrists together with both his hands, grinding my bones together.

"Your room. Now," Kostya demands, spinning me and pushing me toward the door.

"At least let me get her some clothes—" I whip my head around to look at Anya, but he wrenches me again.

"Just go!" she shouts before her voice is swallowed by a sob. "Just go, Ezra. Don't make it worse."

I want to be with my girl.

I *need* to be with my girl.

But I can't.

I'm being forcefully taken from her when she needs me the most.

I plant my feet, trying one last time to resist and get back to her, but our eyes meet and her voice is quiet and steady, though it's forced. "Please. Don't make it worse."

If our love had a theme song.

Don't Make it Worse.

CHAPTER 3

Anya

ONE. TWO. THREE. *Four. Five. Six. Seven. Eight.*

One. Two. Three—

"Fuck!" I scream out at my ceiling for the millionth time over the course of the day.

The swelling is getting worse. The exposed part of my foot where my toes peek out bulges painfully against the tape and wrap Ezra had applied for me hours ago. I can see it's changing colors. A dull shade of gray-blue peeks out from beneath the edge of the bandage.

I huff out breath after breath, hoping that some of the pain will subside with each exhale, but it doesn't—it only gets worse. I try to let my mind drift to something else, *anything* else, but I can't. It just hurts so much and I can't even count my way through it.

I'm going to get up, I tell myself. *I need to get up and move.*

With a grunt, I swing my legs over the side of the bed. I yelp as I slowly lower my left ankle to the floor. I dare to let my toes touch, just a tap to the carpet to test how it feels.

Even the simple softness of the carpet shoots a bolt of lightning through my foot. But I know I need to try. I have to try to stand and find out whether it's broken. I inhale deeply and push through my good foot to stand, settling all my weight on my right side. Carefully, I roll my injured foot flat to the floor.

Toes first.

Then the ball of my foot.

The arch.

The heel.

I'm tensing every other muscle in my body in fearful anticipation of pain until my foot rests on the carpet. I suck in another breath and gradually shift my weight from right to left.

Inch by inch.

Pound by pound.

Before I can stand fully with my weight balanced equally on both sides, I'm cursing and lifting my foot back off the floor. It hurts too much and I just can't bear it.

Will this heal?

Will I ever dance again, or has he ruined me for good?

Tears burn as they form a layer over my eyes and threaten to spill down my cheeks. But then I steel myself, straighten my spine, tap into my last reserve of strength, and force myself to take one single, goddamn step.

"Shit…" I tremble, trying to hold back an oncoming sob. "I can do this. I can do this."

I hobble once, but I'm forced to step through the ball of my injured foot. I can't flatten it on the floor and put weight on it at the same time. But I can do this. I can limp on my toes. I can get to my dresser. I can finally put on some clothes.

But then what?

I stagger, uneven step after uneven step, until I reach my dresser. I opt for a black, silk chemise nightgown—pants are far too complicated for me at the moment—and put it on quickly.

My stomach growls, hungry for the lunch I missed, but there's no way I can make it down the grand staircase to the kitchen. Even if I could, I have to consider how Nikolai might react if he sees me.

The image of Vigo swinging his foot back and ramming it into my ankle pops back into my head. It's an image that punches painfully in my gut. It makes me want to fall to the floor and crumble in fear. He wants to buy me and Nikolai walked away with him.

Would Nikolai really sell me?

He'd always told me that I would be useless to him without my talent, and he'd just taken my talent away.

Oh, God.

What if I never dance again?

The most unsettling thing of all is the fact that he hasn't come to check on me yet. He hasn't come to kick me while I'm down. He hasn't come to soothe me while gaslighting me into believing this was all my fault. He hasn't come and I've never been more terrified.

Everything is happening so fast. Last night, I thought I had at least another year with Ezra. Though it would have been another year of captivity under Nikolai's control, it would have been another year of survival, nonetheless. I could have loved and been loved for the first time in years.

I gasp as I realize that being loved was what led to this. Ezra had made a mistake falling for me. It was a tragedy that I'd fallen for him, too. Now we are both going to pay the price, though I don't know how high that price will be yet.

I make a slow trip to the bathroom and somehow manage to wash my face and brush my teeth. I force myself into utter denial of the reality of being sold to another and how that might change my life. My mind only presents me with a detached concern that Vigo may not grant me time to care for my personal needs in the way I'd grown accustomed to.

If I'm sold to him, will I have my own bathroom?

Will I have my own room?

Will I be stuffed into a box and shoved beneath his bed, only to be let out for his entertainment and abuse?

A cold prickle runs up my spine, causing me to shudder in fear of that possible reality. Then I let that prickle ripple away from my body and put that energy into caring for myself while I still can.

I just can't face the idea of being sold. Denial may save my sanity. I allow my thoughts to separate from my reality and float through a pretend existence where my pain is only felt if I think about it; where the coming events of my day are going to be normal, business as usual. But every few seconds, my foot moves or my weight shifts, and the pain shoots through me all over again. As each jolt of pain ebbs, it pushes me down, the gravity of my emotion warning that I might soon be a sobbing mess, flat on the ground beneath me.

I use the toilet, but as I hop and turn to wash my hands, I hear the door to my bedroom fling open and it startles me.

Is it Nikolai?

Vigo?

I'm frozen as I hear movement just outside the bathroom door. It's cracked open, but all I can see from where I'm standing is the shadowed outline of a man. They move forward and the shadow grows larger.

I jump as the bathroom door swings wide without warning and I nearly topple, swaying off-balance. I grip the edge of the countertop to steady myself and realize quickly that it's Kostya.

He doesn't move. He just stands there, still and brooding in the doorway.

Has he come to take me to Nikolai?

I wait.

But he doesn't command me. He doesn't grab my arm and pull me away. He doesn't do anything at all.

A few breathless moments pass before he reaches into his pocket. He steps toward me, and though I want to step back, I can't. I'll fall if I try.

He slams his palm down on the corner of the countertop and leans forward. "Hide them. Only one a day."

He tilts his head down in a nod and as quickly as he appeared, he's gone. It takes me moments to relax enough to let out the breath I'd been holding. I look down at the countertop to see three small, round, white pills in the spot where his hand landed.

My heart leaps. I reach for them immediately, plucking them from the marbled surface, and hold them in my palm. I turn my hand over to look at them and I hesitate. I don't know what these are. My first thought is that they must be for pain, but I can't fathom why Kostya would give me something for that on his own.

Nikolai was so furious with me. He *wanted* to cause me pain. I can't imagine him asking Kostya to give them to me.

What if this is a trick?

What if these little white pills are meant to drug me, hurt me, drive me into the depths of insanity?

But…what if they'll make the pain go away?

My body forcefully rejects any thoughts of denying myself the possibility of relief. Though the rational and stoic part of me tells me I should flush them down the toilet and muscle through the pain, I know I just don't have it in me to endure this any longer—no matter the risk of taking an unknown drug.

Without allowing myself another moment to think, I toss one of the white pills into my mouth and turn on the faucet. I cup my hand under the flow to catch some water and tip it into my mouth.

I swallow.

I close my eyes.

I pray for relief.

Where am I supposed to hide these?

I start my slow, strained hobble back into my room, crossing to the bed. I bend to open the drawer on the nightstand. I open the forever closed copy of Vladimir Nabokov's "*Lolita,*" a book that has sat in that nightstand in all of its mockery since the day Nikolai first brought me to Mikhailov Manor. I place the pills on the pages within and close the book. I shut the drawer and let myself fall backward on the bed, scooting carefully and lifting my ankle to rest on the stack of pillows Ezra had arranged for me before.

As my eyes fall shut, my memory flashes with a lightning bolt of green, the brilliant color of Ezra's eyes. I put my hand over my heart, feeling the *thump, thump, thump,* as I wonder what he's thinking about and if he's okay.

What will Nikolai do with him when I'm gone?

When, not if.

I start to cry, my emotions finally catching up to the physical pain, bringing about a whole new kind of ache.

Heartbreak.

Heartbreak for me, for Ezra, for us and what we had, what we could have been, what our lives would be if we'd never been stolen but had found each other all the same.

I gave him my heart and he gave me his, but it was all for nothing. We weren't allowed our own possessions when *we* were the possessions. We had both let down our guard, gave into love, and in that love, we lost control.

But God, it had felt so good to lose control with him.

I turn my head, looking toward the center of my bed, and my mind tugs at memories of our love making last night. It was stupid and reckless to do it here, and now we're paying that debt. Though I should regret it with every jolt of pain in my ankle, I find that I don't regret it at all. Ezra had given me the best night of my life and my bedsheets still hold the smell of him. It's a sweet peaches and cream sort of scent mixed with the raw masculinity of his natural musk—like summer and sunshine.

I close my eyes and breathe in the scent of him on my pillow, forcing my mind to wander through those memories of our night together. It isn't long before I start to feel the effects of a foreign chemical running through my system, making the memories twist, shift, and morph into strange waking dreams.

I guess another thirty minutes or so pass before the pills truly start to take over. I spend that time internally screaming, hating myself, hating Nikolai, even at times hating Ezra for his very existence and the fact that he wasn't here with me to ease this pain with pleasure.

Then, the pain begins to fade, not disappearing entirely, but dulling into the background. An invisible ring of calmness swirls around my brain, looping around my senses and corralling them together into a faraway cage inside my mind. Feeling is there—pain and emotion, love and anger—it's all there, but it's distant, secluded.

I feel something resembling peace.

I shut my eyes again and begin to count until I finally fade away into a dreamless, painless sleep.

One. Two. Three. Four. Five. Six. Seven. Eight.

One. Two. Three. Four. Five—

CHAPTER 4
Ezra

"OPEN YOUR EYES, *mal'chik.*"

Something *thwacks* against my cheek and my head rolls on my shoulders. Another *thwack* and my eyes snap open.

I lift my head with a gradual wobble, coming out of an awkward sleep where I'm sitting upright. As my head rises, memory creeps in from the corners of my mind. I recall that I was in my room before, pacing and panicking about Anya being left alone. I remember Nikolai coming in with Kostya. I remember yelling, throwing a few punches, then going down hard after a blow to my head and a stun gun into my side.

Now I'm in a room I don't recognize.

The space is large and open—it's probably about half the size of our dance studio—with a high ceiling. There's a picture window across the room from me that spans the entire width of the space. The crisscrossing muntin divide it into smaller square panes, slicing across the sunlight which shines in from low on the horizon. Sheer, ivory-colored curtains hang open on either side of the vast window, framing the light in the way they stretch from floor-to-ceiling.

The room is neat, its openness broken only by a few pieces of furniture. Off to my left is an oversized, wooden desk—there's a stack of papers resting on top and an expensive-looking executive chair behind it. There's a seating arrangement in front of me with a couple of cushioned armchairs, angled toward each other, across from a brown leather couch. In the far corner of the room, near the window, sits another matching armchair.

And then there's me.

I attempt to lift my hand to run through my hair, but it's trapped. I look down to see that my arms are tied behind a tan, cushioned chair and I've been positioned with my back to the corner of the room, in line with the door. I'm situated in such a way that I can see everything happening in the room. There's something unsettling about that and it rolls nausea through my stomach.

I pull on my arms, but they're tied tightly at the wrists behind me. Coarse rope is coiled and wrapped around them, irritating my skin. My shoulders ache from this position with my arms wrenched behind me. I try to move my legs, but my ankles are bound to the chair legs. I tug against my restraints, but they don't budge. I only earn myself more rope burn in the process.

My muscles feel tired when I move and my head aches. The way they knocked me out succeeded in wearing me down enough that I hardly have it in me to fight to get free.

Nikolai moves in front of me, looming above, looking down upon me with his arms dangling at his sides and his fists clenched in annoyance. I tilt my chin to look up at him and his gray eyes catch mine.

"I've brought you here for one reason and one reason only," he says. "You deserve to be punished for your indiscretion with Anya. Now you're going to witness the consequence of her actions."

"Where are we? Where's Anya?"

"We're in my home office."

"*Where's Anya?*" I nearly shout at him.

"You'll see her in a moment," he tells me.

A shadow of movement behind Nikolai catches my attention. I blink, making sure I'm seeing clearly as Vigo Vittori dissolves from a grayed-out blur into clarity. He moves to sit on the armchair in the far corner. He crosses his ankle over his knee and leans back, laying his arms casually on the rests— calm and cocky as fuck—as if he's here to enjoy the festivities.

My neck muscles tug instinctively, bunching with tension as I drag my eyes away to look up at Nikolai.

The way Nikolai's face contorts in a strange mixture of rage, hurt, and heartache, I know something's not right.

When has anything ever been right here?

My heart skips a beat, then begins to pound roughly, bringing me from still resignation to caged-animal status with only a few pumps. I jerk, throwing my entire body forward against my binds, but it's useless.

Nikolai doesn't flinch.

My binds don't loosen.

All I've managed to do is force the coarse fibers of rope to rub into my raw skin just a little bit deeper. The door clicks open and my head whips toward it.

I hope it's Anya.

God, I hope it's not Anya.

Kostya appears first, holding the door open as he grips Anya's elbow, supporting my injured, limping, blue-eyed girl as she hobbles forward into the room. She flinches with every other step. She limps on the ball of her foot across the traditional ivory and green rug that covers the hardwood floor. There's a dull *thud* on the carpet each time she sets down the cane she uses to support her weight—the very cane she beat my ass with the first night I was brought to Mikhailov Manor.

The roaring thump of my racing heart stops. The tender organ falls into my gut with a crash that makes me sick. Anya does her best to stand straight, to keep her shoulders back and her chin held high in her usual powerful way, but the internal struggle is written all over her beautiful face.

My stomach rolls and heaves.

I feel sick seeing her this way, her ankle battered and her soul power-squeezed in a vice.

Kostya shuts the door behind her, and she moves on her own to the center of the room. She turns her head to look at me and she tells me a thousand words with her brilliant cobalt eyes.

I'm sorry.

I love you.

I have no regrets.

But…move on from me.

Stay strong and move on from me.

Her eyes say it so profoundly, it's impossible to ignore.

Forget about me and move on.

It makes me gasp. She's given up hope. It's as clear as the spotless windowpanes in front of us that she's given up hope.

My chest heaves with heavy breaths as she looks away from me. She stares straight ahead, facing the center of the wooden desk as Nikolai moves to sit behind it. Settling into the oversized chair, he resembles a king sitting on his throne, the master and ruler of everyone in this room.

"I do not know where to begin with you, *rabynya*," he says with an edge to his tone. "I do not know which words are best to describe what your actions have made me feel."

Bravely, my girl responds out of turn, "I'm never at a loss of words to describe the way *your* actions make me feel, *khozyain.*"

Perhaps I've rubbed off on her a bit. It makes me proud, though it also scares the shit out of me.

Nikolai slams his fist down on the desk and we all jump, startled by the sound and force of it.

Except for Vigo.

He doesn't startle; no, instead he *laughs*, and my spine runs cold.

"I should have listened to my father," Nikolai says through gritted teeth, spitting heat and fury at Anya. "He told me you would turn out like this. He warned me what would happen if I let a slave have as much freedom as I've granted you."

Anya tilts her head. "Freedom?"

Nikolai stands, whipping around the desk, and he strikes like lightning. He wraps one large hand around her throat and lifts. I half-hope she'll raise her cane and beat the shit out of him, but in her surprise, she drops it, her hands coming up to cover his.

"Get your hands off her!" I scream and writhe.

He lifts with force until she rises to her toes on her one good foot while the other foot hardly touches the floor at all. She's nursing it carefully, even when she's being attacked.

"I gave you a home," he scolds as she claws at his hand. "I gave you food, shelter. I bought you clothing that other women would be jealous to have in their closets. I gave you space. I gave you a place to dance. I cared for you, and all I got in return was a slap in my face for letting you spend time alone with your *pet.*"

Anya's eyes widen as she swallows, fighting against his chokehold. But then, she forces her lids to droop, narrowing her gaze at him pointedly. Somehow, she's found her strength to finally fight back against him, but for the life of me, I can't understand why she's fighting him now of all times.

Because she's given up hope for a future.

She chokes out the words, "Ezra is my lover, not my pet."

I sigh, letting out a harsh breath. For the first time I feel the irritation she always had with me. All the times I fought back with my words, all the times I just couldn't keep my mouth shut, and she'd give me that look. I feel her side of it now.

But I also feel impressed.

Proud.

Happy that even when she's facing an uncertain and violent future, she would use that word and call me her lover. But then I feel sick, sad, on the verge of heaving in shallow sobs of heartache for what's happening to her… to us.

Nothing good can come from this situation.

Nikolai releases her with a snarl and she falls heavy to her feet. She loses balance, tilting awkwardly toward her injury, and crumples to the floor, catching herself sideways on her palms.

"I no longer wish to look at you," he says, turning his back on her and circling around the desk to sit regally in his chair. He opens a drawer and pulls out a pen. "I gave you everything you needed to be happy, and you've done nothing but disappoint me. I know now that you were never worthy of being mine. You have been a lesson for me, *rabynya*. An expensive and time-consuming lesson. Women are best left to being whores and sluts, a hole to fuck and nothing more."

He flips a page from the stack on his desk and scribbles on one of the papers. He flips a few more and scribbles again. "You're no different. You're just another slut who will spread her legs the first opportunity she's given. I'm selling you to Vigo. Consider it your lifelong punishment for betraying me so brutally."

He's fucking selling her to Vigo Vittori.

Instead of thrashing and screaming, I'm stunned into silence. I'm so disturbed by this news that I can't move.

I can't breathe.

I can't think.

I blink, once taking me to darkness and again bringing me back to reality. I blink back into existence and my gaze falls on Anya. Her sapphire blues are right there to meet me.

She's still on the floor.

She hasn't risen.

Her face hasn't changed.

If anything, she looks accepting, as though she expected this news all along. I think we both had, but the reality feels as though a chisel has been slammed into a long crevice in my soul, finally splitting me, forcing me to break apart and rip right down the middle.

She holds me in her eyes as tears form in hers, making shimmering pools of blue. That's the moment it hits me—I might never see my blue-eyed girl again. Adrenaline rockets through my veins, jolting me back to my livid, violent, fully aware self.

"Don't you fucking *dare!*" I flail, throwing myself viciously against my bindings. "Don't you *dare* fucking sell her to that monster! I swear to God, I'll kill you! I'll kill all of you, you fucking monsters!"

Nikolai pushes to his feet, laying the pen down on top of the stack of paper. He tilts his head toward Vigo and side-steps out from behind the desk. Vigo stands from the armchair in the corner, taking his time to button his black suit jacket, brushing his hands down to smooth the fabric before crossing to the desk. He takes Nikolai's place behind it and lifts the pen.

"No!" I scream. "Don't you fucking sign that, you piece of shit! Sign that, and you sign your own goddamn death certificate. I'll murder you and your entire fucking family!"

"There's a long line of people who would like to end my family," Vigo says casually, not even bothering to look up at me. "You'll have to get in line."

He scribbles on one page.

Then another.

He lays the pen down and reaches out to shake Nikolai's hand. Their palms meet with a clap that bursts like lightning in my mind.

The deal is done.

"I think I've taken up enough of your time, Nikolai. I'll be taking my new belonging home now."

Home.

Fuck, where is he taking her?

How will I find her?

What the fuck do I do?

"Don't do this." I stare Nikolai down, begging unashamedly. "Don't do this to her. You know what will happen to her if you let him take her. Don't do this. I know you don't hate her as much as you say you do."

"Shut your mouth, *mal'chik*, or I'll shut it for you," he growls, but he can't maintain eye contact with me.

He knows what he's doing, what he's done.

Fuck, it's done.

Anya has shifted to all fours on the floor and her head hangs in defeat. Vigo crosses to her, crouches down to his haunches in front of her, and lifts her chin with his fingers.

"Tell me who you are now, *schiava*."

I don't know any Italian, but it doesn't take a genius to figure out what he's calling her.

Slave.

Just the same as Nikolai.

Anya's voice is a whisper, but it doesn't waver. "I am slave to the Vittori family. I am your belonging."

Nikolai slams the drawer shut on his desk after returning the pen, a reverberation of wood smashing against wood. For a moment, his eyes are hazy, conflicted, and his shoulders slump, unnaturally heavy. Then he straightens, lifting his chin with a snap, and storms to the door.

"You may go," he tells Kostya as he passes. "Leave Ezra here. I'll return for him when I feel like it. Anya is Vigo's concern now."

He flings the door open and breezes past. Kostya follows him out and the door slams shut behind them.

"No need to be sad, my Russian doll." Vigo tilts his head as he strokes Anya's hair. "We will have fun together. Just you wait and see. Go and say goodbye to your pet before we leave. I'm afraid you won't be seeing him again for quite some time."

Her back rises with a sharp inhale but otherwise, she remains still.

"Go on, my doll." He pushes to his feet and circles around behind her, a predator eyeing his prey. "Crawl to him...unless you want to learn what happens when you make me wait."

Anya moves forward, carefully dragging her injured foot as she crawls to me across the carpet. When she reaches me, there's a pause, an eerie stillness of uncertainty. Then, Vigo puts his shoe on the back of her swollen ankle. I don't know how she managed to squeeze her unusually wide foot into her sneaker or pull on the tight jeans she's wearing. Her eyes widen as she registers a fresh round of pain.

He presses down slowly and I'm chomping at the bit. "Get your fucking foot off her," I growl.

He grins. "Your infatuation with each other is quite perfect, you know." He removes his foot and crouches beside the both of us. "I will always have leverage with you because you both went and fell in love. Give me your sadness, hmm? Have one last moment together, a treasured, tragic goodbye that will torture both your minds late into the night." His smirk is devious and he stands suddenly. "Up, *schiava*. Climb onto his lap and don't keep me fucking waiting."

Anya's head drops for a beat, but she lifts it again just as quickly. She slowly places her hands on my knees, one and then the other. Sliding her slender fingers forward for purchase, she pushes hard through my thighs to carefully bring herself to stand.

Somehow, she manages to spread her legs and straddle me, settling on my thighs. She always did have impeccable balance, but it seems so much more impressive when she's forced to do this with only one walkable foot.

Air rushes in and out of my lungs. My brain is overloaded with the sensory stimulation of Anya on my lap and with Vigo by my side. It's a swirl of good feelings and awful feelings and eerie, creepy vibes from the pervert demanding to witness our final goodbye.

"Very good," Vigo says beside us, stepping closer, nearly touching my side. "Now, have your tragic goodbye."

Anya shakes. She tries so bravely to hide it, and though Vigo might not see it, I can feel it. She swallows hard as her eyes meet mine. The blue softens as her icy armor melts away and my heart finally fails. It can't find a steady rhythm. It speeds up and slows down and stops and starts.

It's erratic for her.

I don't give a shit about giving Vigo his tragic moment to hold over us. I don't care what he witnesses. I just need her to know before she's gone. I know she feels the same when she drops her forehead to mine, drawing my energy and attention to focus solely on her. She cups my cheeks in her delicate hands.

"I love you," I tell her. "I love you more than my freedom. I'm not giving up, Anya, I won't."

She sighs. "I love you, Ezra. That's why I need you to let me go. Just focus on yourself, okay? Survive."

She tilts her head to press a soft, precious kiss to my lips. Her gentleness is still and chaste. But after a few moments, I part my lips, begging her for more. She gives, letting us fall into a sultry kiss.

Is this the last kiss?

I hold nothing back, pouring all my love, my heart, my soul into my kiss, taking the time to taste every inch of her mouth. I memorize the way she tastes, the way her body feels molded to mine, the glorious heat between her legs in the way her desire is inexplicably linked to mine. I sob once into her mouth as I feel her tears slip along both of our cheeks. I taste the salt of them as they slip down over our lips, bleeding into our kiss.

It's one of those perfect moments.

Tragic, yes.

But perfect, all the same.

Until Vigo insists on reminding us how our lives have been destroyed beyond reason.

He grabs Anya's hand and lifts it away from me. The motion breaks our kiss and we both turn to look as he places her small hand on his tented trousers.

Sick motherfucker.

My passion for her explodes in a supernova of rage against him. I lose control of myself and thrash again, but I only end up hurting Anya in that uncontrollable surge. She slips backward down my legs and clamps one hand down hard on my shoulder to hold herself up. It was an instinctual clench of her grip to grab hold of something rather than falling backward to the floor—only her other hand had already been removed from me and had instinctually grasped Vigo's groin.

Her hand grips his erection momentarily and then she rips it away, tilting her body away from him with a gasp.

He only smiles.

"Patience," he says, snatching a fistful of her hair and yanking her off me without any effort. "You will have plenty of time to interact with that, my pretty little girl."

He drags her toward the center of the room by her hair. She scrambles to stay on her feet, only she's forced to use her injured ankle to do that given the swiftness with which he pulls.

The pain on her face screams loudly in my soul.

Vigo releases her in front of the leather couch. She's lost her balance entirely with the way he tosses her around and she immediately falls to sit.

I've seen her scared before. I've seen the look on her face when she thought she was going to die by Nikolai's hand. But this fear that grips her is something else entirely. It's the uncertainty of what's next that scares her, and fuck, it terrifies me, too.

Vigo bends, reaching down to grab the cane she walked in with earlier. He holds it out for her and she takes it from him slowly, eyeing him warily as she does.

"Use it now to walk if you must. Come," he commands, walking to the door.

"Anya," I call after her as she rises, fighting through pain with tears pouring from her eyes.

The look she gives me is something indescribable.

She looks…lost.

Broken.

Hopeless.

Yet still *devoted*.

Taking in a long, steadying breath, she asks, "Mine?"

"Yours," I reply.

It was never a question that I would always belong to my blue-eyed girl.

CHAPTER 5

Anya

WHEN I FIRST came to Mikhailov Manor over three years ago, I brought with me a single suitcase. I'd left New York with Nikolai willingly, not knowing that I was meant to be his slave. He revealed himself as the benefactor who had funded my talent development over the years, and he offered me a training opportunity in Moscow that I simply couldn't pass up.

He told me to pack everything I would need for a two-week excursion into a single suitcase and leave with him right away. I should have known better when he told me I couldn't contact my family, couldn't tell my roommate or my friends.

He made it all seem so urgent. I was barely twenty-one at the time. I was naïve. I thought I was invincible. I convinced myself that this man—with his handsome face and charming smile—couldn't possibly mean to do me harm. He'd been my secret benefactor after all—an attractive older man who wanted to give me his attention.

So, I did what he asked, packed my suitcase, and left.

Sitting in the backseat of the black sedan in front of Mikhailov Manor, I watch as Kostya brings that same silver hard-shell suitcase to the car. The trunk pops open and I spin in my seat to look, though all I can see is the raised trunk lid blocking my view. I hear a thud, as I assume the suitcase is tossed inside, and then the trunk is slammed shut.

I meet Kostya's eyes for a quick beat and he tilts his head toward me in farewell. I pat unconsciously over the pocket of the jeans I had somehow managed to pull on. I have two more of the white pills Kostya had given me tucked away there.

My gut tells me to save them, to hide them somewhere safe as soon as I arrive at the Vittoris' home. My gut tells me more pain is to come, which will be harder to endure than the pain swimming around my ankle.

I didn't see Nikolai again after he stormed out of his office. He hadn't even said goodbye to me. It shouldn't matter, but in some twisted, warped way, it hurts my heart. The things he said to me when he signed the papers and sold me to Vigo had hurt.

Acknowledging that hurt reels nausea through my belly. His words shouldn't matter to me. He hates me now, just as he always had.

At least, I thought he always had.

Somehow, what he said to me in his office makes me question everything I thought I knew about him. He called me a slut and a whore, but he had also said that he cared for me. He thought he gave me everything I needed to be happy.

Happy?

But it doesn't matter anymore.

My life with Nikolai is over.

My life with *Ezra* is over.

No. Stop.

Don't think about it.

I gulp down my heartache as I straighten my spine, sitting up taller in my seat. I turn my head to look out the tinted window to my left, away from the manor, watching as the wide, white flakes of snow steadily fall to the ground.

Ezra melted the ice of my soul. His love warmed me, thawed me from winter to spring. He gave me hope where there was none, and I'm grateful for that. It was nice to live in that lie for what we had, but I know it's over now.

If we're lucky, the best we could hope for is a brief sighting of one another at the next quarterly meeting in three months. But I don't know that either of us will survive that long.

Tears climb from deep within me, threatening to crash onto a shore of pain from the tidal wave of grief that swells. If I let these tears fall, if I let myself think about my love with even an ounce of hope, I will drown in this heartache. Falling in love dropped me into this sea of hurt and *I will drown in it.*

I can't let that happen.

I have worse trials to face as Vigo's new slave.

I let the slow snowfall inspire me, freezing a thin layer of ice over this grief-filled sea. It's cold and the ice hurts me in other ways, but it provides a surface to stand upon, allowing me to walk above my grief as it churns and waves in a torrent of despair-ridden water below. Walking on this thin ice is a torturous way to survive, but it keeps me from drowning. The ice will thicken over time. The more Vigo hurts me, the more layers of protection I will add.

I have to.

It's the only way to protect myself.

The car door to my right opens and I turn my head to watch as Vigo slides into the backseat beside me, slamming the door shut behind him.

I turn away and wipe the welling tears from my eyes with the back of my hand. I do it quickly, hoping he won't notice, but I know he probably will. I can feel his attention on me, hot and oppressive.

The last of the guests from the four families—aside from Vigo—and their slaves and drivers left yesterday. Kostya slides into the driver's seat and takes us to the helipad to meet the pilot.

Vigo's eyes are on me as Kostya pulls away, starting down the long drive from the manor steps toward the gate in the distance. I spin in my seat to look behind me as we drive away and my heart stops.

Ezra's been set free from his bindings and I see him at the entrance, screaming at Nikolai. He sees our car and he rushes down the steps and out onto the driveway, running toward us.

No.

Go back inside. I shake my head, wishing he could hear my internal thoughts.

His rash actions always make everything worse.

Yet, in the same way, they make everything better.

I watch the man I love chase after me, though we both know he'll never reach me. It's one final moment, one final *I love you* to wrap around my heart before the ice freezes it solidly in place.

I watch as Ezra drops to his knees in defeat, knowing the impossibility of the situation. Then I force myself to turn around, press my eyes shut to harden myself, and turn back into the cold, hard bitch I was before Ezra appeared in my life as a slave.

Within that cold hardness lies contempt, returning quickly and rising a ball of indignation in my chest. I look over at Vigo to show him my disdain. Our eyes connect, but all I see is a dangerous sort of humor where my heartache, to him, is entertainment.

He lifts his arm and stretches it to lay across the back of the seat behind me, leaning in close. "Tell me, what was it about Ezra that made you fall so hard?"

I cross my arms over my chest and turn to look out the window, watching as we pass through the gate at the end of the drive and turn onto a dirt road that cuts through the thick forest.

"I don't want to talk about him."

He chuckles. "Of course not. It breaks your sad, fragile heart, doesn't it?"

I glare at him, but he seems disinterested in my reaction.

He pulls his arm back and reaches behind him to grab his cell phone from his back pocket. I look away when disinterest falls naturally into total disregard, and I hope he's done talking to me. Thankfully, he seems to be, tapping away on his phone screen.

Vigo reminds me of Nikolai in many ways. Both of them are handsome, quite unfortunately disarming in their good looks. Vigo is only a year younger than Nikolai, though he looks nearly a decade more youthful. Nikolai has always let his anger age him, but I know Vigo doesn't carry the stress of his vileness the same way.

Vigo finds humor in his torment.

His eyes hide his madness, which is all the more unfortunate for the victims who capture his attention. They could bewitch prey into believing they were safe with him. The soft, honey-brown color of his irises are unique in the way they give him a light, warm, youthful appearance. His thick, black hair falls in precisely styled, imperfect curls, framing his face in ebony waves. He's lean and tall—taller than both Nikolai and Ezra. There's a certain kind of power he holds in his height alone, being able to look down upon every monster and master he comes into contact with.

He's smooth, sophisticated, handsome, depraved, and dangerous. But all my time spent with Nikolai has prepared me for whatever is to come from this horrendous beast.

I can survive this.

I can survive *him.*

But do I want to?

We follow a winding, dirty path for thirty minutes through the swiftly darkening forest. I know this because there's a digital clock on the dashboard that allows me to count the minutes as time passes in tense, horrible silence.

From the narrow, dusty car path, surrounded by dense foliage, the forest opens without warning onto a clearing. The car crawls forward into the large circle of open space, angling off to the left as it moves forward toward the black tarmac at its core. A helipad exists in the center and resting upon it is a helicopter. This is the only way to escape the Mikhailovs' land. The helicopter doesn't stay here—it only comes when Nikolai calls for it.

The car creeps to a stop, and as the engine cuts off, the propellers of the helicopter whir into life, beginning a slow spiral above the craft. Vigo and Kostya slip out of the car without a word to me. I scoot across the seats to the other side of the car and peer out the window, letting my eyes transfix on the propeller blades as they move.

My one and only method of escape is coming to life in front of me. But instead of taking me away to safety, it will take me into a captivity that's likely worse than I dare to imagine.

The trunk is slammed shut before I even realize it was opened, the sound of it startles me. Kostya drags my suitcase toward the helicopter as Vigo approaches the sedan, flinging the door open beside me. I flinch as he thrusts his hand inside, beckoning me.

"Come," he orders.

I shrink away from his outstretched hand. There's an independent woman in me that I suppose Ezra brought back to the surface—she scoffs at the gentlemanly offer to assist me from the vehicle. I want to balk at the offer, but then I realize that I do actually require assistance. I nearly start crying, realizing how Nikolai has disabled me, hopefully only temporarily.

I sigh, taking his hand in resignation, and I carefully shuffle out of the car. I'm thankful for my dancer's balance as I'm forced to stand on one foot, the gravel surface proving to be an uneven and uncomfortably lumpy landing. He doesn't offer me the cane he'd taken from Nikolai's office before we left.

Did Kostya put it in the helicopter with my suitcase?

I'm forced to hop a couple of steps toward the back of the car so Vigo can slam the door shut behind me. Then he drops my hand and regards me with a lift of his thick, black brow. The corner of his mouth twists upward and there's humor in his eyes as he turns and walks off toward the helicopter.

He comes to stand beside it after fifteen or so paces, his strides long and quick. He turns toward me, still balancing precariously beside the car.

"Come," he shouts to me, summoning me forward with a wave of his hand.

My eyes follow the path his feet traveled. Fifteen paces for his long legs would be twenty for me under normal circumstances. But I was trading strides for uneven limps and hops, half of them along bumpy gravel before shifting to black asphalt. My eyes trace the path I need to walk and find Vigo at the end. He's smiling gleefully at the torment he's about to witness. He wants to watch me struggle; he wants to view my pain, my disgrace.

I won't let him have the satisfaction of watching the pain brush across the features of my face. I steel myself, inhale deeply, and force myself to take a normal step, with both feet on the ground. My ankle screams, aggressive agony tearing through my limb. It takes everything that I have to hide the fact that I'm screaming on the inside. I'm determined to walk to him without the humiliating limp, determined to hide my weakness, but my internal scream slips out to an audible whimper with only the second step.

I lift my injured foot from the ground as I huff out a few breaths, blowing out the urge to cry and sucking in strength to get there.

Just get there.

There's no other way for me to do it but to limp on the ball of my foot.

I see the satisfied smirk adorning Vigo's face as I concede to my injury. It pleases him to see me succumb to my shame, the ballerina broken so effectively that she can't even walk.

Oh, God.

Will I heal? Will I be able to dance again?

Kostya walks past me as I move forward, and he catches my eyes before tapping the backs of his fingers twice beneath his chin.

Chin up.

I'm surprised for that brief connection with him, and I'm thankful for it. I never really trusted Kostya, but I recognize the kindness in that gesture—not to mention the pills he gave me. Perhaps I misjudged him from the beginning.

His gesture reminds me that I'm strong, proud, and determined. I lift my chin to show Vigo that truth as I continue onward. I force a subtle smile to my face, a look of determination meant only to anger him, because I want to wipe that look of amusement off his face myself.

The blades of the aircraft pick up speed as I come within reaching distance of Vigo. They whip the wind and dirt from the ground beneath me. He turns away and climbs on board, offering me no assistance, but I wouldn't take it anyway.

I reach deep within to pluck out my stubbornly independent streak, giving myself the fortitude required to finish this part of my journey. I force myself to move, to push, to ignore my pain for the moments it takes me to step up and drag myself inside the fuselage.

Panting, I fall into the seat beside him, and he smiles at me, perfectly pleased with himself for being such an arrogant prick.

I feel some relief once I'm finally sitting, thankful that I have the weight off my foot. At least the seat is comfortable. The interior of this helicopter is extravagant, practically screaming that it belongs to one of the four families with its leather seats, elegant overhead lighting, hardwood-inspired flooring, and extra leg room.

I push down on the arm rests to straighten myself in the seat. Vigo reaches across me, his hand darting across my legs. I jerk backward at the brush of his fingers along my thighs, scooting my bottom back as far as I can. He shoves his hand down between my hip and the armrest, rooting around until he finds the latch for the seat buckle. He pulls it out, drawing the strap across from the other side of me, and secures me in my seat.

His hand drops and lingers on my thigh and I don't take my eyes off it. I can feel his breath, hot and sticky, against my neck as he leans in close. His fingers slip up the inside of my thigh and I act on instinct, even though I should know better. I smack his hand and push it away, throwing his unwanted touch from my body with a snap—something I *never* would've done with Nikolai.

And then, I flinch because I realize what I've done.

I brace for his anger, for new pain to come raining down on me.

But it doesn't come.

Not as the fuselage door is shut behind me.

Not as the co-pilot climbs aboard.

Not as the helicopter lifts from the ground.

Instead, I'm met with the same sinister, knowing smile that's haunted me since I was used by Vigo before, when Nikolai gave me to him as payment for the information he wanted about his family's death.

I shudder at the look.

He reaches for me again, but this time he drags his knuckles down the side of my cheek. Again, I act on instinct, ignoring everything I've learned about being a proper slave. My gut tells me to fight Vigo, not to submit, and it goes against everything Nikolai has groomed me to become. I flip my arm around to toss him off, but he snatches my wrist in his hand, again with a smile.

He pries my fisted fingers open with his other hand and sucks my index finger deep into his mouth. I swallow as my body sinks away from him, my face scrunching in disgust. He pulls my finger out slowly, his teeth grazing across my skin. His silent, unwavering eye contact is unsettling.

He releases my wrist and turns away, settling back in his seat. He ignores me again in favor of his phone. When I'm certain his attention is locked on his screen, I rub my hand on my jeans, urgently wiping his saliva from my finger as I finally release the breath I'd been holding.

Soon after, we lift into the sky and I look out the window at the grounds below. The dense forest stretches on for miles around Mikhailov Manor.

The first time Nikolai took me off the grounds by helicopter was to attend my first quarterly meeting. That was several weeks after my one and only escape attempt where I'd gotten myself lost in the woods and came face to face with a gray wolf. Nikolai had come after me and found me just in time.

That one attempt had been all I needed to know that escaping wasn't possible. But when he flew me away that first time weeks later and I looked down at the forest below—just as I am now—I fell into a crippling panic. It took the view from above to cement the fact that I was completely and utterly at his will—at the will of the four families.

It reminds me that I never stood a chance of breaking free.

Ezra doesn't stand a chance of breaking free.

I press my palm to the window as we pass over the shadowed outline of Mikhailov Manor, trading it for dark and desolate wilderness.

I'm forced to watch as we leave my love behind.

My possibility, my hope, every good thing Ezra brought to my life is gone.

Done.

Over.

And I don't know if my heart will ever beat the same way again.

CHAPTER 6

Anya

WE SPEND THIRTY minutes on-board the helicopter before we land on a private airstrip. It belongs to the four families—owned and operated, just the same as the airstrips in Italy, Ireland, and Louisiana—and I can make an educated guess that it's off-grid from the authorities. We transfer from the helicopter to a private plane owned by the Vittoris and in no time at all, we're taking off into the night.

This next part of the journey will be long. I recall from my previous trips with Nikolai to the quarterly meetings hosted by the Vittoris that the plane ride was four or five hours nonstop.

Those hours with Nikolai in close quarters had always been trying. Thankfully, he'd spent most of that time on his laptop or phone, preparing his sales facts and figures for the meeting ahead. When he wasn't doing that, of course, he was enjoying the free use of my body for his pleasure.

As the plane levels out at its cruising altitude, Vigo pockets his phone and turns on me with that twisted smile. My heart hammers for the uncertainty of how this time will be spent alone with Vigo, remembering how Nikolai could so brutally use and abuse me, and wondering how much worse it will be with this monster.

My hands tremble as my mind flashes back to when Vigo used me once before.

Suddenly, I'm very aware of the pills in my pocket and even more aware of how my ankle throbs and burns. Travel hasn't been kind to the swelling, and I feel the pain of it more and more as minutes pass. But that pang in my gut that tells me to wait to take another pill, to bide my time, to get through for now because I'll need them more later, returns with unsettling force.

"Get up," Vigo commands. "Come to me."

I should behave as I've always done for Nikolai.

I should get up and go to him without question, and I should do it immediately.

But he was right before. Ezra has brought my fight back to life and I can't seem to let myself do as I'm told. Ezra had nearly managed to bring me back to the woman I was before captivity, and I knew how dangerous that was now.

Yet, in a visceral way, it somehow feels like a betrayal to do as I'm told now. If I were a better slave, I would say it feels like a betrayal to the master I've known for over three years, but that's not true.

Obeying feels like a betrayal to Ezra and to the light and fight he brought back into my life.

Stupidly, I ignore the command and tightly press my eyes shut. I send a private message to Ezra in my mind that he is *mine* and I can nearly hear him echo back his own promise.

Yours.

Vigo speaks with an eerily calm tone and I open my eyes to see a sickening smirk on his face. "I think you underestimate my disregard for your well-being, *schiava*. I will happily jump up and down upon your broken foot." He repeats his command, "Get up. Come to me."

I stare at him. "No."

Oh, my God.

Why did I just say that?

Why am I being so stupid?

My love for Ezra has made me so fucking stupid.

His smirk ticks but doesn't falter as he unbuckles his seat belt and rises to stand. We're alone in the cabin, sitting across from one another in an arrangement of four, oversized, cream-colored leather seats. He could do anything he wanted without interruption from another. The awareness of that prickles beneath my skin as he steps toward me.

"Get. *Up.*"

I lift my chin to look up at him and instantly, I feel small…small and insignificant as he towers above me. The way he looks at me shakes me to my core. Without even making a conscious decision, my hands fall to my belt and unbuckle it, and I rise to stand.

He opens his arms. "Come here."

I take one wobbly step toward him and the distance is closed. Chest to chest, I'm forced to let him wrap his arms around me. His feet shuffle him closer, pressing up against my body.

"Arms," he says, his chin resting on the top of my head.

With great shame, I snake my arms around his waist.

"There's a good girl. *La mia piccola bambola Russa.*"

I grit my teeth in frustration and fear as he speaks to me in Italian with a quick tongue. It terrifies me not to know what he's saying.

"I don't understand Italian," I tell him, trying to soften the hard edge that keeps finding its way to my voice.

"You will learn some," he says. "You are *my little Russian doll. La mia piccola bambola Russa.*"

Oh, God.

I don't want to end up like one of his dolls. I've heard Nikolai speak of Vigo's habits before, his tendency to collect and keep women caged and at his mercy. I've seen first-hand how uncared for they are—malnourished, tired, unhealthy, fearful. Of course, I knew I would become one the moment I was sold, but the understanding of what that would truly mean hadn't registered until now.

"Good girls do as they are told. *Sì?*"

I press my eyes shut and force out the reply he wants from me. "Yes."

"*Sì, Papà,*" he corrects me.

My gut clenches as nausea rolls through my belly.

I don't need him to translate that.

I'd always known Vigo preferred younger girls. I knew he was depraved. But if this captivity was going to be a "*yes, Daddy*" situation, then I was fully unprepared for the sickness that might be waiting for me in his keep.

Somehow, I manage to repeat the words out of necessity, though my voice cracks, along with any defiant resolve I thought I had against obeying him like a good little slave.

"*Sì, Papà.*"

His hands crawl up my back and his fingers spread my hair apart into two thick sections from the back of my neck. He brings the long ends over both of my shoulders, half on one side and half on the other, until it dangles in front of each of my breasts. As he steps back to look at me, his hands come forward over my shoulders. He grips each section of hair in his hands, fisting the parted lengths in his grip next to my ears. His hands form makeshift ponytail holders, clutching my long hair in two pigtails.

He grins that demonic grin of his. "You are older than my other dolls, but you still look young like this. You'll be perfect."

"Perfect for what?" I ask quietly as I stand still in front of him.

He clicks his tongue, tilting his head. "*Papà* did not give you permission to ask questions, *bambola Russa*. Get down on your knees and apologize."

Vigo turns and moves away. A few short steps take him to a couch, situated sideways along the outer wall of the cabin, just behind the cluster of four seats we sat in before. He lowers to sit on the matching cream-colored couch and leans back. Vigo spreads his arms wide and lays them dominantly across the backrest. He spreads his legs apart and beckons me with a tilt of his head.

"On your knees. Crawl to *Papà*."

Papà.

If he says that word one more time, I might vomit all over his leather seats.

I obey because I have no other choice, though that feeling of betrayal still haunts me. I bend carefully, shifting all my weight to my right foot as I lower to the floor. I attempt to be graceful about it, but really, I'm only letting myself fall, catching myself on hands and knees.

There is nothing graceful about me with this horrid injury, and I feel tears spring to my eyes at the thought of it. I was once one of the most graceful ballerinas in the world—it kills me to think that this injury won't be treated, it won't heal correctly, and as a result, I may never dance again.

It's a possibility I can't fathom so I force that thought away, back to the dark corner in my mind.

Even with my weight off it, I feel a whole new kind of hurt as the floor pushes against the top of my ankle, forcing extension of my tendons and stretching them painfully. Thankfully, it's not far to travel, crawling to him as he asked. It's a few short drags of my swollen ankle across the floor before my head is in-between his knees.

I look up at him and wait.

"You know what I want you to do." He reaches down and unlatches the buckle of his belt, but he returns his arms to the back rest before finishing. "Do the rest. Take care of your *papà*."

I swallow the bile that threatens to force its way up my throat. I shuffle forward on my knees and I have to put my hands on his legs to steady my wobbling, queasy body.

I reach forward to finish what he started—to unbuckle his belt, unhook his button, pull down his zipper. Vigo bites his lip as he regards me with his head cocked to the side and a satisfied smirk.

"Show me how well Nikolai has trained you. Take out my cock and suck."

My eyes remain open though it feels like they're closing as my mind drifts inward. It's incredible how easily I can slip back into servitude for survival's sake, doing what's commanded of me in order to endure for another day.

Nikolai *had* trained me well, truthfully, and so I knew how to get through this. It's nothing more than a job, a task I have to complete.

I'm sorry, Ezra.

I have to obey to survive.

Still, Vigo's aura manages to make it all the more repulsive. There's something wrong with him, something unnatural about him that screams madness. Somehow, I think giving him a blowjob on his private jet will only register as a one on his sickness scale to ten.

I do what I have to do.

I pull down the elastic band of his underwear and free his gradually hardening cock. His girth doesn't outmatch Nikolai, but his length does, enough that he could easily choke me with his erection.

But comparing two monsters is pointless. Neither of them are Ezra. Neither of them could ever compare to the way Ezra could fulfill all my wants and needs. I gave him my heart and soul completely, and he gave me his. Regardless of the fact that this sexual act is forced beyond my control, it feels like infidelity, disloyalty.

The shame of that is heavy on my mind, though I try to drift away like I'd always done with Nikolai. I inhale courage and freeze my soul with an icy barrier to grant myself fortitude. I lean forward and suck the tip of him into my mouth.

Vigo groans and his large hand lands on the back of my head. "*Sì*, that's a good girl." He presses down. "All the way."

He gives me no time to adjust to his intrusion as he pushes my head down hard. I cough and gag around his length, my stomach heaving as he sinks into the back of my throat. My eyes widen and I feel them begin to water. He holds me in place though I try to lift my head away. I huff in breaths through my nose and he simply won't let up.

His hips lift from the seat to pulse his cock inside my mouth, impossibly deeper, as his fingers dig into my scalp, burrowing in painfully hard. I force my eyes to close, trying not to vomit, focusing on the shallow breaths through my nose.

But then he takes that away from me, too.

His fingers come down to tightly pinch my nostrils shut.

My eyes snap back open as I gag and splutter and truthfully fight for air. "*Si, la mia piccola bambola Russa,*" he moans. "Take it."

My heart races as adrenaline kicks in, panicking me into fighting him. But it's no use, his grip on my scalp is tight and his cock in my mouth is oppressive. He's not letting me get away. The sooner I accept that, the better.

I *know* that.

And I could have just given in and gotten through it before now.

But now, *now*, Ezra's green eyes flash across my spotty vision and suddenly, I'm angry.

I'm angry and frustrated and furious because I let myself lose control. I let myself fall in love with him. I let myself hope again and that was the most dangerous thing of all.

No.

Having hope wasn't the most dangerous thing.

It's the aftermath of hoping, the loss of it, that endangers what is left of me now.

Still, the lightning flash of Ezra through my mind inspires the bit of fight he'd somehow managed to conjure up in me before I was sold. I unsheathe my teeth and clamp down on Vigo's cock. This startles him, and he thrusts upward hard, stabbing at the back of my throat. I haven't bit him hard, just a nip to catch him off guard.

He digs his nails into my scalp, gripping my hair and pulling me back forcefully. I gasp for a breath as my lips slide free from his invasion. Saliva drips sloppily from my mouth as he separates me from his cock. He pulls his hand back and slaps me, his knuckles punching into my skin as he strikes me with the back of his hand.

I tumble to the side, landing on the floor as I yelp from the unexpected hit and the new burst of pain. My vision blinks out, then fades back in with dots of light around the edges.

I scramble to get up, managing to get on my hands and knees, facing away from him, but he's already standing, ready to come after me. His foot lands hard on the back of my swollen ankle and I scream.

The pain shoots a crippling ache through my leg, making me freeze, my body going rigid to tense against the hurt.

He's on me like a lion leaps for a running gazelle. His arms latch around my waist and he flips me over in a flash, slamming me to the floor. I land heavy on my back and the little air I've managed to catch escapes with a whoosh.

Vigo's hands find my knees and spreads them wide as he scoots up between them, kneeling. He reaches for the button on my jeans, pulls the zipper, and tugs my pants down with a hard jerk. My body drags toward him as he wiggles and peels the denim away, taking no care for the way my ankle flops as he gives a final tug and I scream from another jolt of pain.

He pushes his pants down, and without so much as a beat for me to cope with what's about to happen, he grabs my hips and drags me toward him, my legs open around him. He slaps my sex with the back of his hand, forcing me to whimper in disgust with the painful slam of his hard knuckles.

No.

No.

No!

I pick up my legs, preparing to kick, but he places his hands on my hips and digs his thumbs into the hollow spots between bones on either side.

As I start to cry, I shout, "No!"

I'm unable to fight as he tilts my hips, lifting my bottom from the floor. I can't fight as he pulls me closer. I can't fight as he angles his tip.

Then he slams into my pussy, hard, raw, dry.

I don't even try to hold back the tears now. They pour from me freely as Vigo painfully fucks me.

"Good girls don't hurt their *papà*. Good girls take cock with gratitude.

Thank me."

Fuck you.

I fucking hate you.

I hope you die and suffer an eternity in hell.

I don't want to prolong my agony.

I turn my head to the side and say, "Thank you," between sobs and feel like a coward for doing it.

Vigo fucks me until he's done with me and leaves me a crying mess on the floor. He covers himself, straightens his suit, returns to his seat, and pulls out his phone as if nothing had happened.

He's done with me.

For now.

I stare blankly at the cabin's bathroom door beside me.

I feel hopeless, helpless, already dead.

My tears only come harder and faster when I think of Ezra. I can't help but think of him. My life with Nikolai had been a complacent wreck of servitude, but it had been predictable.

My heart feels shame now because I'm angry with Ezra. The raw ache of being fucked dry was something I'd been able to endure before. But then Ezra showed me love, showed me pleasure, showed me wanted touch and affection, and in doing that, he ruined me.

He loved me and he ruined me.

All at once, I feel as though I love him and hate him. I love him for everything he gave me, and I hate him for giving me anything.

Ezra gave me love.

Ezra gave me hope.

Ezra lifted me higher than I knew I could go.

And because he did, I have farther to fall in disgrace.

CHAPTER 7
Anya

WE'VE ARRIVED IN Palermo, but this is not our final destination. We've landed on another private airstrip where we transfer from the jet to one of the Vittoris' helicopters. Now that we've arrived in Italy, we'll be trading land for water, flying across the Tyrrhenian Sea. The Vittoris have their own island, somewhere off the coast of the mainland, though I doubt it could be found on any map.

The four families work together to keep their secrets, using their wealth, their reach, their political power, and social influence to protect them.

Our helicopter charges ahead into the darkness, crossing over the deep black sea which looks still, almost peaceful in the night.

But it doesn't fool me.

That black ocean below is ready to swallow a person whole if they should fall into its serene trap. It was much the same as Vigo. He always seemed so…unaffected, so calm, appearing still and quiet. He was, by all accounts, a subtle man…until his internal storm broke the surface into crashing waves and twirling violence.

Another twenty minutes have passed by the time our helicopter lands and I'm exhausted.

I watch out my window as we close in on the Vittoris' private island. It's a tragically beautiful place. There isn't a sandy beach around the edges, but rather mountainous drop-offs where the seawater has rubbed away at the edges of land over time, creating steep cliffs.

As panic begins to spread across my mind, I imagine the rocky edges eroding away with great speed, the brutal ocean splashing across and scrubbing away the filth of the four families, reclaiming the island and swallowing it whole.

But truthfully, the sight of their rocky shores is magnificent—magnificent and overwhelmingly disturbing. Escape from their shores is impossible without an aircraft, but it doesn't matter.

I'd given up on escaping a long time ago.

Our helicopter lands at the edge of one of the cliffs—we can hear the waves violently crashing against the mountainous side, even above the roar of the helicopter rotor whipping the propeller blades overhead. The breeze they create is chilling in the winter air.

It's not far to the car and I manage to hobble to it mostly without issue. As I settle into my seat and look out through the window over the cliff's edge, I briefly wonder if I should have hurled myself over it. I shiver, not just from the cold, but from the thought and how easily it had come to my mind.

Am I capable of doing such a thing?

Am I capable of ending my own life?

A driver takes us away from the helipad at the cliff's edge, following a gravel road that curves around and down toward a hidden path. The dirt-covered road is obscured from above by some of the most fascinating pine trees I've ever seen. Nikolai told me once they were maritime pines. Their trunks reach tall toward the sky, no branches hung low, only splitting off at the very top where they sprout into plush, green pine needle clusters that look like soft grass overhead.

I watch the trees pass by on our silent drive to our final destination. The car stops ten minutes after we've left the helipad, and my mind circles around panic-inducing thoughts.

Where will he keep me?

How will he hurt me?

Who will I be when he's broken me completely?

Ahead, illuminated by the headlights, is a grand, metal gate. It's framed by two large, stone columns on either side. A letter V is engraved on a circular plate at its center. Moments later, the gate slowly reels open, the V splitting right down the middle.

As we drive through, I turn in my seat to watch it close behind us, noting that a black metal fence extends out beyond the two stone columns on either side. The fencing goes as far as I can see before disappearing into the darkness.

We travel the dirt path, which continues beyond the gate for another thirty seconds or so. Then, the rumbling of the wheels over gravel switches to a smooth and pleasant silence as we shift onto a concrete paved driveway.

Turning to face forward, I watch the headlights lead as we follow the path.

Gradually, the Vittoris' massive home is revealed. We trade concrete for cobblestone as the car turns and passes between two more large stone columns. There are lantern-style lights affixed to the tops, signaling the entrance to their piece of the underworld.

Beyond the lantern-lit columns, the grounds open onto a vast cobblestone square. In the center rests an ornate fountain with three-tiered bowls which rise from the middle. There is no water running through it now, perhaps because it's the middle of the night, but the stillness of it seems somehow disquieting.

The driver circles the car around the fountain and parks just in front of the main entrance to the mansion. He practically leaps from his seat, exiting the vehicle swiftly to open the door for Vigo. Vigo gets out without a word and I remain still. I have no desire to move.

I'm not ready for this.

I'm not ready for whatever is to come.

Vigo doesn't care what I am or am not ready for.

The driver arrives at my door and pulls it open. I get out slowly, carefully, begrudgingly, taking care to keep the weight off my injured ankle as I rise to my feet. As I settle my balance, the driver pops open the trunk. He pulls out my silver hard-shell suitcase and places it on the beige and brown cobblestone as Vigo stands beside him, typing furiously on his cell phone. He stops then, putting the phone inside his pocket.

He looks up at me, then to his driver, taking in a breath as if he's just come back to reality after being lost in cyberspace. I would be perfectly happy to have him ignore me in favor of his phone—anything that keeps his attention off me.

He tilts his head toward my suitcase with a furrowed brow. "You can toss that," he tells his driver. "She's a slave. She doesn't have any belongings."

Does his driver speak English? He must.

Vigo wants me to understand that I am nothing, that I *have* nothing here. Otherwise, I imagine he would have given that command in his native tongue.

My chest sinks as a heartbroken sigh rushes out of me. I don't know what's in that suitcase or if there is actually anything in it at all. But it's *my* suitcase and *my* belongings. More than anything, this makes me feel worthless.

My pictures of Lidia…Are they in there?

My ballet shoes?

My clothes?

My goddamn pillowcase that smells like Ezra?

Goddammit!

At least with Nikolai I still had pieces of myself. Vigo has taken away my humanity before we've even crossed the threshold of his garish home.

I open my mouth to let words of objection tumble out, but I clamp it shut immediately. It's pointless to argue with a master who cares nothing for me—the heartache and pain it would cause is avoidable and so, I choose to avoid it.

"*Si, signore,*" the driver says and tosses what's left of my possessions back into the trunk.

Vigo moves around him, coming in close to me. I manage to avoid stepping back as he invades my space. He straightens, bringing himself to his full towering height, and looks down upon me.

"A few things you need to know before we go inside. Members of my family are addressed with respect. You don't cross their path or mine. When you're not in your cage, I expect you to stop and bow your head when you see a Vittori, and wait for them to pass or direct you further." He tilts his head, reaching out to pluck a strand of hair from my shoulder, and twists it playfully around his finger. "Not that you'll be out of your cage when you're not with me. But what you're doing right now is disrespectful. Bow your head to me."

I shut my eyes as I lower my head in defeat.

"Good. Now try to keep up. I'm tired and I need to get you settled in your new accommodations before I can rest. Come. Follow me."

He turns and stalks off with long strides, and dammit, he's quick. I limp along after him with no hope of catching up. He enters his home through a wooden door set back in an alcove. It's two steps up onto the landing; two steps that I struggle to hop over beneath the brick-layered archway that beckons us to the front door.

Somehow, I manage my way inside to see Vigo impatiently waiting to close the door behind us. The moment I enter, I'm met with an unsettling feeling, a feeling that nags in my stomach that I don't belong here, and that I need to leave immediately.

Only, I have no choice.

I have no option to leave.

The uneasy feeling is going to be a permanent part of my life now.

Part of that feeling is the sound.

There *is* sound here—voices, faraway music, the noise of multiple people living together under the same dwelling. Mikhailov Manor had been filled with such overwhelming silence that I'd nearly forgotten the noise of living. And that's all the more disturbing because this is sound made from the lives of monsters.

I look around as Vigo yells out something in Italian, and a female voice responds somewhere in the distance. It looks different without the members of the four families gathered here for the talent reception and quarterly meeting—I'm able to see the details of my new prison.

The entrance is wide open. The receptions I've attended in the past have been held right here over the square-tiled flooring. Entryway tables beside me stand tall and narrow, accentuated by ornately framed mirrors above them. The russet-colored frames match tiny square tiles on the floor, which punctuate the corners of the larger taupe tiles, making a pattern of large and small squares.

A few steps past the entryway door is an alcove that opens to the left, a transition into rich, hardwood floors designating where the piano room begins. A black, grand piano sits on the far side near a large window with a small seating area in front. I can recall listening to one of the Vittori talent slaves play piano here before.

There's a staircase to the right which curves around the wide, rounded entry space, leading up to a balcony landing at the top. Past that single balcony is an archway, though I can't see beyond it from the ground floor. There's an ostentatious gold and crystal chandelier that hangs from the center of the space, blocking my view.

I stare at the steps and their curved, metal railing, wary, wondering if I'll have to find a way to drag myself up to the second floor.

God, I'm just so exhausted.

"Come," Vigo says and walks straight ahead.

I follow him as he strides across the wide, circular space. Straight ahead is an open archway that leads into the kitchen. There's a gigantic island immediately in front of us, the long edge spreading out to my right, easily spanning eight or nine feet. This kitchen is stark white and sterile, in direct contrast to the warm, mahogany and cinnamon tones in the entry.

It's far too clean and it reeks of bleach.

The smell triggers me, reminds me of the smell in Ezra's room after Jonathan was taken, after I'd seen Kostya bring out his old bedsheets with their splashes of red. My pulse accelerates and I gasp in a shaky breath.

Vigo turns right before reaching the island and walks along the side of it closest to us, moving straight toward a dead end beside the refrigerator.

Except, it's not a dead end.

He presses on the drywall and it pops open, swinging on a hinge—a hidden doorway. I nearly stumble backward in surprise, but I catch the edge of the island to steady myself.

Behind the camouflaged entry is a metal door with a keypad. Vigo pauses so he can cast a smug glance at me over his shoulder.

"Your new home is behind this door. Would you like to see?"

No.

Fuck no.

Though I'm shaking my head with wide, frightened eyes, I know the only acceptable answer a slave should give, so I quietly say, "Yes."

"Try again."

I swallow and force my pride down my throat, my voice coming out as a horrified whisper. "*Si, Papà.*"

"Good little doll."

He enters a code onto the keypad and the metal door clicks open.

I can hear my pulse pounding in my ears.

A stab of instinct punches in my gut, telling me that my new existence will be unimaginably worse than I feared.

CHAPTER 8
Anya

THERE'S A PART of me that wants to fall to my knees, grovel, and beg for Vigo not to take me behind that metal door. I want to plead with him, tell him I've been trained well, that I've been a good slave for Nikolai, and that I'll be compliant, obedient—I'll be better than I was on the plane.

God, what has my life become?

Nikolai has been slowly sucking the life out of me for years, edging me into submission until I gave in completely. Yes, I had fucked up falling for Ezra, bringing him into my bed, betraying Nikolai's trust, but I'd been a model captive before my indiscretion. I had paid my dues. I'd earned graces in his home, been trusted to do what I was told, was given freedom to go about my business when Nikolai was working.

Some sort of righteous indignation rises suddenly in my chest, an oddly placed feeling of superiority that I was a slave who should be treated better than Vigo's usual standards.

But it's stupid to feel this way.

A slave is a slave. I belong to Vigo now—he's the master of my fate. Still, it's hard to shake that feeling and it upsets me more when I realize where it comes from.

Ezra.

He had built me up, made me feel proud, cherished, loved, *worthy.* Ezra has efficiently and viciously ruined me with his love.

I *hate* how he's ruined me.

But fuck, how I miss him, want him, love him with every ounce of pain his turbulent presence has brought into my otherwise predictable slavery.

Mine?

Could he still be mine if he no longer exists in my world?

Vigo holds out his arm, drawing me from my chaotic swirl of emotions, and beckons me forward. I move slowly, knowing there's no use in fighting it, though I still wish I could.

I reach Vigo and peer beyond him. There's a dark staircase beyond the door and looking down it makes my heart stop beating.

"Down," he commands. "Go."

I'm terrified to find out what's at the bottom of that staircase. The walls against either side of the steps are painted solid black. I can see a light shining from the landing at the bottom, but all that's visible is a light-gray concrete floor. My heart starts beating again with a jumpstart that makes my pulse thrum, pounding behind my ears, beating out the message that there is danger here.

Run.

Run far and fast.

I will my beating heart to slow because I can't run from this. I press a hand over my chest and close my eyes, inhaling a steadying breath so I can focus on one step at a time in this nightmare.

But then Vigo kicks at the heel of my uninjured foot and I snap my eyes open, quickly reaching out to grasp the doorframe with both hands. With most of my weight on my good foot, his incessant tapping at my heel threatens my balance.

"Time is tick, tick, ticking away. Go now," he says, timing the way his toes tap against my heel with his *ticks.*

I make myself do what I have to do.

Slowly, I descend, leaning all my weight against the rail as I hop down the steps. It's embarrassing to be so inelegant in my movement. My pride is in my grace, and I've lost all of it with this one dreadful injury.

Hop after hop, step after step, I arrive in the basement. I no longer need to put all my intent and focus on making it down the stairs and so, it shifts to taking in my surroundings.

I see, but I wish I could unsee.

"I'll be right down. Forgot something," Vigo calls from the top of the steps.

No.

No, no, no.

I want to go back.

Take me back to Nikolai!

This cold room at the bottom of the stairs is no larger than the bedroom

I was given at Mikhailov Manor. To my left is a concrete wall that matches the concrete floor.

But to my right…To my right…

I hear Vigo's footfalls on the steps behind me and I whirl around, crashing into his chest as he lands on the bottom step.

"I'm a good slave. You know I am. You don't have to lock me in down here. I won't attempt an escape. I promise you. I *promise*."

He smiles down at me sinfully with his hands behind his back. "Oh, I know you are a good slave. But this is where I keep my dolls. This is your new home, *la mia bambola Russa*."

I swallow hard as he steps forward, forcing me to step back, his chest pressing against me heavy and insistent. He moves steadily and I move with him, though I don't want to.

Beside me is a floor-to-ceiling wall of plexiglass, divided into three separate compartments, each only just wide enough to fit a twin-sized mattress.

And in each of the three boxes are women.

One in each box.

They look starved, tired, lonely, seething. I'm sure there are a plethora of other terms which could be used to describe them, but I simply can't name them all. They each sit slumped in their corners, shaking, fearful, eyes trained on Vigo as they cast surreptitious glances beneath their lashes with their bowed heads.

A bright light shines overhead in each of the transparent cubicles, illuminating their crude living quarters. A blanket and pillow, stained and dirty, on top of a thin mattress on the floor. A small metal toilet in the corner. Holes drilled into the plexiglass at head height for air and to speak through. Metal dog bowls sit on the cold, hard concrete flooring.

Vigo moves until my back slams into the far wall, the last of the three boxes beside me. I jump at the pressure of Vigo's aura as it pulses blood lust after me.

"Please," I beg, bowing my head, ashamed, contrite, desperate.

"I think you've been spoiled," he says to me. "I think you have a bit of a chip on your shoulder. You think you're cold and dead inside and that nothing can hurt you. Well, I will be glad to be the one to educate you. I can always find a way to hurt you more. There is a bit of a problem with your accommodation, though."

"P-problem...?" I stutter.

What's happening to me?

I don't stutter.

I'm confident.

I'm concise.

I *was*, but perhaps here, I am not.

He tilts his head toward the third cage. "The problem is there's already a doll living in your house."

The girl inside senses her presence has been noted. She slowly stands from where she sat in the corner but she doesn't step forward.

"Each of my dolls gets their own private space. But I suppose my math was a bit off when I purchased you. You see, I now have four dolls, you included, but only three doll houses. Of course, there is only one reasonable way to fix this problem..."

My inhale is shaky.

He presses against me, pinning me to the wall with his body, though his hands remain behind his back.

What's behind his back?

"Well? Aren't you going to ask about my brilliant solution?"

Unwillingly, I ask, "W-what's your solution?"

His face brightens with a demented sort of smile and it twists nausea through my stomach. He steps back and moves toward the third cage. The woman inside moves away, pressing her back against the far wall. Her hair is pulled into two, long, tangled pigtails, as though it's been some time since it's been brushed. She wears a simple cotton dress—reminiscent of child's clothing—with a plain A-line shape that ends at the knees.

She's visibly trembling as Vigo approaches. I watch as he enters a number into another keypad. The door pops and opens just a crack. Vigo is careful not to show me what he's hiding, keeping his back turned away from me. I expect to see the girl attempt an escape as Vigo steps back, making a clear exit for her.

But she doesn't.

She shakes her head viciously, eyes wide and wild, shivering in fear of him.

What has he done to her?

My God.

What will he do to me?

"Get in," Vigo commands me.

"Please…*please*…" I beg him.

"Begging is disrespectful. It's weak and pathetic. Are you weak and pathetic, my little Russian doll?"

I take in a quick breath and pause before speaking, making sure my voice comes out steady and calm. "No."

"Then, get in."

My mind screams at me to run, to fight, to cower, but I manage to move my body forward despite the screaming sirens in my brain. My eyes well up with fearful tears as I step across the threshold from the open space into the transparent box.

The other woman and I both jump at the sound of metal clanging against the concrete floor. Vigo has tossed in a kitchen knife. My eyebrows bend in confusion, but then the hinged plexiglass shuts and I whirl around, slamming my palms against it.

"Anya, pick up the knife and kill her." Vigo grins. "Do it quick…before she decides to kill you with it first."

He steps back and crosses his arms over his chest. His head tilts to the side. His honey-brown eyes burn into something resembling hellfire.

When I hear the blade slide against concrete, I whip around to see the woman holding the knife. She backs into the corner again like a feral animal, though she holds it at her side, pointing the tip outward toward me.

Oh, God.

My breath catches and stutters in my chest. My heart races at lightning speed. My sudden distress signals my body to pump adrenaline, hard and fast, through my veins.

My life is in immediate danger and I have to protect myself. I don't even feel the pain in my ankle as I rush backward, stepping onto the thin mattress so that I can press my back to the opposite corner.

Why didn't I pick up the knife?

Oh, God.

She's going to kill me!

My mind prepares for a fight, but then the woman starts to cry. Streams of tears fall like waterfalls down her pale, sunken cheeks.

I don't know what she's thinking, if she's about to attack me or crumble into a sobbing mess. Her anguish tempts my own, and though it nearly makes me want to give up, give in, let her rush me with her blade and end what's left of my life, I know that I can't. That fight that Ezra brought back to life within me rears back and roars through my heart.

Yours. I can hear his voice inside my mind and it refuses to be ignored.

I stand defensively, ready to fight her for the knife and kill her if it's what I have to do.

But I will wait for her to make the first move.

And she *does* make the first move.

Only it's not the move I expect.

She looks at me, her dark eyes catching mine. She speaks in perfect English and her accent is undeniably American which, of course, reminds me of Ezra.

"If you're smart, you'll do the same," she says to me, then turns her eyes to Vigo. "I'll finally be free of you."

A certain and oddly peaceful grin spreads across her cheeks. It's a look that will haunt my dreams for years to come.

She lifts the knife, sets the edge of the blade against her throat, and slices herself open with composed determination.

I scream.

I scream as blood rushes from her gaping throat.

I scream as she falls to her knees.

And as the light leaves her eyes and she tumbles sideways to the ground, I sob.

I see red.

Red, red, red.

Everywhere.

It's splashed across my clothes.

It coats my skin.

It pools over my sneakers as it continues to *pulse, pulse, pulse* from her body, as her heart persists to beat it out of her severed veins.

I scream again.

As the pulsing spurts of blood slow, as my mind drifts back into my body, I turn my head to look at Vigo, who remains on the other side of the see-through cage.

And he's smiling.

Vigo is smiling the grin of a satisfied man, a blood-lusting man who knew this would be the outcome and has just been granted a most gratifying release.

My voice comes out as a shaky whisper as my body trembles and shakes out of control. "You're sick. You're sick, you're sick, you're sick."

He sucks in a long, slow, deep breath. "No, *schiava*. I am well. I am very, *very* well."

My new home is a transparent box, spattered and stained with blood, and decorated with a body.

Vigo left after the girl killed herself.

I haven't been able to move and I don't know how much time has passed. My back is still pressed against the plexiglass corner, as far away from the dead girl as I can get. I'm not sure whether I'm still breathing. I must be, but the only thing my mind is actively aware of is the sliced and bloody body on the floor, the stench of copper, the drying blood caked on my sneakers.

I don't know what's happening around me, if the other women in the other boxes are crying, screaming, or silent. I have no awareness other than blood and death before me.

Time must be passing as my legs grow weak and tired, and I slowly slip down to the mattress beneath my feet.

The blood of a dead slave coats the floor around my perch, an ocean of red surrounding my island mattress.

I close my eyes and try to force myself to think of something else, of anything other than this living nightmare, but my mind can't track a conscious thought.

My heart, though…My heart knows what I need.

It pumps an emerald green blaze through my veins, which ignites a flash fire vision beneath closed lids. Behind the fire blazing over my eyes is the man I fell desperately, tragically in love with; the man who both loved me and ruined me. The memory of his smile, of his snarky tone, and his warm embrace, holds me safely inside my mind.

My brow furrows as I squeeze my eyes shut tighter, imprisoning myself with Ezra inside the faraway pocket of my awareness. If I can stay here, I can stay safe. If I can keep the memory of him bright and vibrant in my thoughts, maybe I can survive here.

A twinge of pain in my ankle tries to pull me from my internal world to my external reality. My brain had shut down my pain receptors with the adrenaline rush in what I thought was going to be a fight for survival. But now that the immediate threat is gone, the physical agony returns full force.

Then I remember the pills from Kostya.

I had two left when we departed Mikhailov Manor.

I shift and dip my hand into my pocket. I don't have to dive far as my fingers find one twisted in the fabric near the opening.

Only one.

I move that pill to my other hand and dive back in, searching for the second, but it's gone. It must have fallen out in Vigo's haste to rip my jeans from me on the private jet.

Damnit.

I should save this one.

I should hang onto it until I urgently, frantically need it.

But I urgently, frantically need it now.

It's not so much the pain I need it for as it is the escape the strong drug brings for my mind. I *need* the escape.

Without another thought, I pop the white pill into my mouth and swallow it dry.

I close my eyes and breathe deeply, willing the medicine to shut me down, to take me from this nightmare and into a beautiful dreamworld with Ezra.

CHAPTER 9
Ezra

I RUSH TO my door in a heartbeat the moment I hear the metal key push into the lock from the outside.

I'm gonna pummel his ass the second he walks in here.

The night Anya was sold, Nikolai had set me free with just enough time to chase after the dust kicked up by the quickly retreating car. The piece of shit wanted it that way. He wanted to torment me by making me watch her leave. But the real kicker was that it was tormenting him to watch, too—whether he'd admit it or not. I'd seen the flash of regret in his eyes as the car turned off the manor grounds and drove out of sight.

I'd gone after him then, sought out a fight, but I was so blinded by my grief that he took me down with hardly an ounce of effort.

I wanted to kill him.

But there was something about the heartache of losing the person I love most in the world that took the fight right out of me.

My chest had ached, my heart had raced, my lungs had burned from the gasping breaths of shock that shut down my system. I had crumpled to my knees in front of Nikolai, feeling as if all the best parts of me had been scooped out, leaving me a hollow, empty shell of the man Anya loved.

Frankly, I'm surprised Nikolai hadn't killed me, with the way I sniveled on my knees. I was a pathetic, sad, broken man who had nothing else to lose. Perhaps he'd known there was nothing else he could do at that moment that would hurt me, there was no way to punish me further. But why he let me survive, why he kept *me* and sold *her*, was still a mystery to me.

I'd sat beside the front doors of the manor until Kostya returned from taking Anya away from me. Together, he and Nikolai herded my sad ass back to my room. I was a lump, a heavy brick to carry. They locked me in without shackling me to the bed, and I've been here for a day, maybe two, left to my own devices.

My grief caught fire in that time, burning in the pit of my stomach.

290

It spread from limb to limb in a massive wildfire until my entire body succumbed to the relentless flames of rage.

I burned.

I seethed.

Fire licked over my soul, taking me straight to hell, showing me the lust that demons have for violence and depravity.

And the hellfire demon burns bright inside me now, ready to knock the devil off his fucking throne.

I have one palm pressed heavy against the wall beside the doorframe, the other on the knob, ready to pull and swing it wide the second the key turns. My chest heaves, sucking in a shaky breath as I prepare to wrestle the man who broke me to the ground.

But the second lock never turns.

Instead, something slides past my foot and I immediately look down to see something slip under the door. Just then, Nikolai's muffled voice comes through the closed door. "Just a reminder for you, *mal'chik*. If anything happens to me, she dies within a day. If you insist on fighting me, fine, fight me. But it will do you no good."

"*Mother*fucker." I grip my hand into a fist and slam it where it rests against the wall.

I bend and pick up what he's slid under the door. It's another picture of Emma, my ex-girlfriend, one of the few people who has been in my life for more than a season and would always have a piece of my heart. Though things didn't work out between us, she was one of the only people who knew the real me, someone who stuck by me when shit got tough, someone who would always be like family to me.

And he was holding me hostage by one of the only people I actually gave a shit about.

He's just adding fuel to my fire.

"I guess you should tell me what the fuck you want then before you open the door. 'Cause I'll tell you what, fucker, I'm ready to break your fucking nose the second this door opens. *Fuck*, would that feel good to my desperate fucking knuckles," I shout.

I can hear his amused chuckle, though it's faint through the door. "Could you fit anymore profanity into one sentence? At least you've found a way to make your anger entertaining."

"Open the *goddamn* door, you colossal *ass*hat, and say that to my face like a *fucking* man."

Breaths pass as we both wait for his response.

Adrenaline kicks up in my veins and whooshes through with speed and fury.

I hear the key turn in the second lock and I am *ready*. Grasping the knob again, I tug and tug until the lock clicks. I throw the door open, flinging it wide.

My brain can't even process what's happening as my body takes over. Nikolai is standing there, arms stretched out to his sides with a sinister *I-don't-give-a-shit* smile plastered to his face. I think Kostya is standing there, too, but my eyes are blinded and intent on Nikolai.

I charge forward, pull my elbow back, curl my fingers into a tight fist, and swing at his face. He ducks just in the nick of time like a goddamn ninja.

As he bends away from my right arm, I uppercut him with my left. Though he's quick, he's not quick enough to miss two in a row. The punch lands hard. He wobbles, taking a step back, and I take advantage to sucker punch him in the gut once, twice...

I collapse under his weight as he bends over my head, clawing at my back to find purchase as they scramble over the fabric of my black T-shirt. Somehow, he grips my waist and spins me with a grunt. Grabbing the collar of my shirt at the back of my neck, he forces me upright.

My head whips back as I try to assess my next best move. He pushes me toward the wall and my head flies forward. My forehead crashes into drywall and bounces off, throwing me back a step. I put my hands up in time to ease the next blow as he throws me against the wall again—luckily, I catch myself with my hands.

His hand clamps around the back of my neck and he pins me face-first to the wall with his body.

"Are you done now?" he asks.

"Not a chance," I spit.

I fling myself backward, my head tossing back and a bruising pain shoots through the back of my skull as I jam against his nose. He groans and steps back, and I whip around to see him doubled over. His fingers come up to touch his nose, then he looks down at them to see the blood I drew.

I huff to catch my breath after the frenzy and a smug smile creeps across my cheeks. In that moment, I'm blissfully aware that I caused him an injury that made him *bleed*. It makes me pause in my fury to relish the moment. That brings me back to reality enough to notice that there are two other people in the hallway.

It's not just Kostya standing beside us, but a girl who looks scared shitless. Her hair is dark and long, like Anya's. She struggles against Kostya, who tries to lift her from the floor. She seems to have fallen to her knees in fear, curling around herself like a scared child, though she's at least as old as I am. My face drops at the look on hers.

This is a stolen girl.

An unwilling slave, just like me and Anya.

This sad young thing was stolen from her life. The newness of her circumstance is etched into her cheeks by the trails of her tears.

I bare my teeth at Nikolai, ready to knock him to the ground, but he holds up a palm to stop me as he straightens to his full height. "Touch me again and I'll hurt her," he threatens.

My agitation screams in my gut, shouting at me to hit and kick and hurt until he can't feel hurt anymore, until he's lying on the ground lifeless.

But a twinge of softness in my heart settles me.

I feel Anya grip my heart, like a ghost who haunts me. It's as though I can see her bright blue eyes in my mind, that look she would give me that told me to keep my mouth shut and follow the rules. She wanted me to keep the peace, not just for my benefit, but for hers, too. She needed me to do what I was supposed to do because it wasn't me he hurt.

It was *her*.

And now it's the unknown girl losing herself to sobs beside me.

I close my eyes and breathe, slowly, steadily, willing the violence that burns so bright beneath my skin to fade, willing the adrenaline in my veins to stop pulsing. The only thing that could ever calm me in this hell was Anya's sapphire blaze and the determination and strength in the husky tone of her sweet voice.

Yours, I say into my mind, and somehow, I find the peace to care about the well-being of this girl having a meltdown on her knees.

I lift my hands, palms facing Nikolai in a gesture of surrender.

"Your inability to control your impulses will someday destroy you," he tells me as if he's an older, wiser mentor.

He's certainly older.

Maybe wiser with experience.

Never anyone's fucking mentor, least of all mine.

"Maybe. But I've got nothing left to lose."

"Well, then. If you no longer care about Emma Mayfield's wellbeing, I'll put in the call now to end her. Of course," he cocks his head, "she is young… in good shape. Perhaps we can take her and sell her instead," he muses.

I bare my teeth. "Don't you fucking *dare*."

"What does it matter to you, *mal'chik*?" he asks with mock innocence. "You just informed me that you have nothing to lose." He waves a hand at Kostya. "Make the call."

Kostya reaches into his pocket with one hand while the other clings to the girl. He slips out his cell phone.

"No!" I reach out a hand as if I could halt him with some magical power through my palm. "Don't make any fucking calls. I'm done, okay?" I hold up my palms in surrender and lower slowly, begrudgingly, to my knees. "See? I'm done."

Nikolai tips his head at Kostya and he puts his phone back in his pocket. I sigh in relief, and in defeat.

"Good. I wanted to introduce you to your new dance partner."

"What?"

"Her name is Sasha. She's fresh to captivity, as you can see by her pathetic state." He casts a sideways glance in her direction with a look of disapproval. "I'm afraid we need to evict you from your room."

"Evict me?" My eyebrows knit together, then come apart again as I understand. "You're going to lock her in there."

"Yes. She needs to be situated close to Kostya and so, she needs your room."

The girl starts to speak in rapid succession, her words stuttering and starting between her cries. I don't understand a word she's saying, but it sounds like Russian. Nikolai affirms that it must be when he bites back at her, shouting something in his native tongue that makes Sasha flinch and sink back on her heels.

"She doesn't speak English," Nikolai tells me. "I imagine that will make dancing together a challenge, but you have a year before the next performance. Plenty of time for you both to learn enough about each other to dance together."

My head is shaking before he even finishes his sentence. "No. *No.* I'm not dancing with anyone else. Anya was my partner…*is* my partner. Always will be. I refuse to dance with anyone else."

"Don't be *fucking* stupid, Ezra. Anya is gone. She's not coming back. You will never dance with her again. The sooner you accept that, the better your days will be."

"Here? As if my days could be anything but shit living here with you."

He wraps his hand around my throat, sliding his grip up beneath my chin. He lifts with enough force that I'm made to stand, planting one foot, then the other, rising to my feet. I stumble backward as he pushes and slams my back into the wall behind me. He brings his face too fucking close to mine, close enough that I can smell the whiskey on his breath.

"Don't bite the hand that feeds you, *mal'chik*. I won't bother to threaten you with violence because it only drives you. But I will use your empathy against you. I will do terrible things to that girl to punish you. You know that I will."

He leans in closer to whisper to me and his stubble brushes against my cheek. The scratch of it triggers every violent molecule within me to attack the creep who is far too close to me.

I shove against his chest, but he doesn't budge. He shifts his hand, pressing his thumb over my windpipe and I freeze, knowing that if I fight him, if he presses too hard in the right spot, he could crush it and kill me.

"Show me respect or I will hurt you in all the ways I hurt Anya."

The way he hovers there, wavering deep in my personal space for more than an awkward beat, chills me, freezing my spine straight. He pulls his head back and gives me a secret grin, an expression that I'm sure will haunt my dreams.

And then he lets me go.

"Come," he says, turning and walking away. "You'll stay in Anya's room. Kostya will retrieve your belongings after he shackles Sasha for the night."

"Anya's room?"

He stops and looks down at the floor, hesitating before glancing back over his shoulder at me. "The room that *was* hers. She won't be coming back to claim it."

The hesitation was too obvious for him to hide.

Does some part of him miss her, too?

Does he regret making the worst mistake of his life?

Does he regret washing away the only color in this gray world?

Anya was that color.

She was bright sapphire eyes, rosy pink lips, burgundy and bronze cheeks. She was hickory and mocha hair, and honey skin. She was sparkling white and glacial blue, frozen beneath her protective layer of ice.

Anya.

Where are you?

What are they doing to you?

The reminder that my blue-eyed girl is gone slices across my heart, stopping it for several beats and suddenly, overwhelmingly weakening me. It makes me tired, too tired to fight anymore tonight. The ache of it lifts from my chest, rising to a lump in my throat, swirling around my mind and squeezing my brain in an aching vice.

My body takes over for my mind, my feet moving me forward to follow Nikolai down the hallway.

I hear Sasha scream, hear her fight Kostya, and then there's the slamming of the door that makes me jump.

I feel sad for the girl, I truly do. But I'm doing all I can for her by complying.

We reach Anya's room.

Not her room. Not anymore.

Nikolai unlocks it with a key. It had never been locked before, not as far as I knew. Anya had been with Nikolai for so many years that she'd earned his trust and the freedom to move about the manor as long as she obeyed.

But now he uses a key.

It's smart.

He shouldn't trust me.

He opens the door and lets me pass and I halt three steps past the threshold. The room looks the same as the night we left it. The bed sheets are still rustled and twisted from the night of passion we shared. My tuxedo and her bright pink dress from the reception are still haphazardly discarded on the floor. The pillows I'd propped beneath her injured ankle are still piled on the bed.

Nikolai hasn't touched a damn thing since she left.

But why?

"She's gone." His voice behind me is far too soft. "She's not coming back. And it's because of you."

I whip around to face him but remain silent, brooding.

"I left the room alone. All of her possessions remain except for a few items that were sent with her to the Vittoris."

The fucking Vittoris.

"Why?" I asked.

"To remind you. To *punish* you. I want you to smell her on your pillow at night. I want you to see the last thing she wore. I want you to be reminded in every possible fucking way that she was here, you had the pleasure of her company, and now she's gone. Because you broke her. You stripped her of her obedience, willed her to misbehave, and tempted her to fall in love with you. I want you to live in that shame, that guilt. She's gone from both our lives now and it is all because of *you.*"

I open my mouth to speak, but he steps back and slams the door shut. I don't even react. I don't lunge for the door. I let him shut it and lock me in.

He wasn't wrong, but he wasn't right, either.

I had broken her…not her soul, but her armor.

I had tempted her…not to fall in love, but to hope.

I step forward, moving into the room and everything I see is Anya.

Unease strikes hard and fast in the center of my chest, causing my body to shake. I put my hands on top of my head, lacing my fingers together as I pace through my anxiety beside the wardrobe.

"Goddammit," I mutter under my breath, but I'm not satisfied with the intensity of my cursing. "*Fuck!*"

My fist comes down and slams against the closed wardrobe door. I pull my arm back immediately, shaking out my hand against the pain of instantly bruised knuckles. I instinctively wrap my hand around my aching fist and blink against a vision, a memory…Anya pinned to the wardrobe door with my body as I kissed her.

This is my fault.

This is all my own goddamn fault.

I was the one who suggested we come to her room to have sex that night. I wanted her to have a memory of me to hold onto in case Nikolai ended me.

That was so *fucking* stupid of me, and now Anya is paying the price for it.

"Fuck!"

I need her. I need her so desperately that I would offer up my own goddamn life if it meant I could spend one more minute with her. The universe is playing a sick joke on us—allowing us to find each other, giving each of us our soul mate under the worst of conditions, only to rip us apart again.

I feel empty.

Hollow.

My feet have me moving toward the dresser, wondering if he's left something of hers behind, some token or memento I can cling to. I open the top drawer and find that it's full. Everything is still here—her precisely folded panties, her tattered and worn pointe shoes.

I reach for the pale pink shoes, dingy and scuffed from endless practice. The ribbons that would tie them to her ankles are wrapped around the slippers, holding them together. I draw the pair closer, clutching them in tight hands, pressing them to my chest.

Shit.

It hurts.

I pause.

There's a full drawer of underwear here.

I set the ballet shoes on the top of the dresser and start pulling open drawers. Nearly all her belongings are still here. I go for the bottom right drawer and my heart falls into my stomach to see the same green and pink floral-patterned box that she'd shown to me in my early days here at Mikhailov Manor.

The pictures of her sister, Lidia, are all still here. Everything that held worth to her is still here.

He didn't even have the basic human decency to send her with her own goddamn underwear.

My heart leaps and rushes.

I move toward the bed of twisted sheets, eyeing the pile of pillows I had set for her to ease the swelling from her injury. I lower to sit on the edge and the fuchsia gown on the carpet calls for my attention.

I bend to pick up the dress from the floor, clutching it in both hands. I bring it close to my face, press it to my nose, and inhale deeply, slowly.

The scent of her remains.

Roses.

Sweet but strong.

Soft but heady.

My lungs stutter, forcing a burst of air that rushes out of me as a sob. The sob shakes me and forces unwanted tears to spill and I feel weak…so fucking weak without her.

I drag the dress along with me as I roll to lay on the bed. Hugging it close in my arms, I cry out my ache, breathe in her scent, and lose myself in the precious wreckage our love has left behind.

Anya

I LAY AWAKE in my cage, looking up at the ugly gray ceiling. You could hardly call the thing I lie on a mattress. It's worn and thin, and I swear I'd probably be just as comfortable lying on the concrete floor.

I rest my arms behind my head as I stretch, flex, and rotate my foot. I kick my leg into the air, trying to work through the healing sprains and regain something resembling flexibility.

I've been nursing my injured ankle for the past week, forcing myself to rest it as much as I force myself to move it, knowing I need to engage the muscles and tendons to get them healing properly. It's getting better slowly. The swelling has gone down and the pain has decreased, though my mobility is still quite limited. I still wonder whether it might be fractured, though there isn't anything I can do if it is.

I'm not walking normally yet—not that I've had much opportunity to walk—but I practice as often as I can, pacing the three steps it takes me to get from one side of the box to the other.

Vigo has only taken me out of my box once since we arrived. He had left me inside with the dead slave while he slept comfortably in his room my first night here. He returned the next day to remove the dead body with the help of his younger cousin, Lorenzo, and the driver who brought us here from the helipad.

While they worked to dispose of the remains, Vigo had taken me to a walk-in shower behind the staircase, something I hadn't noticed—couldn't have noticed—when I'd first come down the stairs.

He'd stood and watched as I scrubbed myself clean of the blood that coated my skin. He took my clothes from me but never brought them back. Instead, he dressed me in a plain, baby-blue cotton dress. It has an empire waistline and flares out softly from beneath my breasts, which stops just above my knees. It has cap sleeves that draw tight around my bicep with elastic through the hems, causing the sleeves to pleat and puff over my shoulders in a youthful way.

I wasn't given a bra or underwear, just the blue dress that was a better fit for a child than a woman. And I've been wearing that same blue dress ever since.

There's another household slave who brings us food and water once a day. The uniform of his slavery is clear and consistent. It's always blue jeans, bare feet, naked chest, and a black leather dog collar.

Things here had been otherwise uneventful. Though every part of me still ached and seared with the burning need for space to walk and leap and dance, I found myself wondering why the girl had killed herself rather than use the knife to stab me, to attempt to survive.

She'd thought death was a better alternative.

As for me, I suppose I had already endured slavery and uncertainty for so long that I struggled to wrap my mind around why that girl so quickly chose death. It's not that the thought of taking my own life hadn't crossed my mind in the past.

It had—of *course*, it had. Especially on the worst days with Nikolai. But I couldn't imagine making a split-second decision to slit my throat.

What had Vigo done to her?

How much longer before he does it to me?

I have to force my mind away from the thought whenever it pops into my head. The vision of her body on the floor, blood spurting in pulses as her heart beat it out through the gash in her throat…it threatens to break my sanity.

As much as my mind wants to know, wants to be aware of what is to come to protect me when it finally does, I refuse to ask the other girls. I don't ask and they don't offer. Mostly, they cry or scream or try to talk with each other and with me about plotting an escape.

I have no interest in deluding myself into that false hope. I want *nothing* to do with an escape plan because I already know it's impossible. Escape will only lead to punishment and torture when they're inevitably caught.

Hoping is dangerous and these women are dangerous thinkers.

I'd learned that the blond in the first box next to the staircase had been here a month before I arrived. The brunette in the middle had been here for nearly three months. The girl who committed suicide before my very eyes had been here for a year.

That's all I know and all I care to know.

I'd belonged to Nikolai for three goddamn years. I'd left my childish misbeliefs about personal liberty behind long before these young women could even dream of the vileness of slavery.

I'm sure both women think I'm a cynical bitch for the way I scoff at their discussions of escape, for the way I balk at their sobbing fear and hopeful camaraderie. But I can't afford to lose myself again in caring for another slave's well-being, and I *refuse* to form any sort of attachment to these women.

Perhaps I've too easily accepted my fate, too easily given into the idea that I will be a slave for the remainder of my life.

Except…I know that I'm right.

The dark men are everywhere, and they own us—it's an epitaph written on the gravestones of women everywhere before they are even born into this world. The four families have a vast, worldwide reach, but they aren't the only ones who do this.

I wish it weren't true, but I know that it is. I have to survive it on my own.

"Anya?" the brunette in the middle box whispers to me.

Her palm is pressed to the plexiglass that connects our boxes as she sits on the floor.

I know her name is Bianca, but I don't let myself think of her as anything other than the brunette girl in the middle box. Connecting with another human being is what got me into this mess in the first place.

"What?" I reply, trying all at once to sound calm, but also as if I don't care that much to respond.

"If the three of us work together, I really think we can come up with a plan to—"

"*No*," I interrupt her with a forceful and determined answer.

"Why? Why won't you help us?"

"I promise you, escape from this is not possible. There's only survival or death. The sooner you accept that fate, the better off you'll be for it."

The girl shakes her head at me before turning to face the other direction, but I have one last thing to say to her.

"Hope is dangerous."

"It's *not*," she snaps back at me. "Hope is all we have. And if we just work together—"

I turn my head sharply to the side to look at her. "And if we just work together, then what? Do you know how to get out of this box? Even if you did, what would you have us do then? The metal door at the top of the stairs is locked from the outside."

Bianca opens her mouth to interject, but I keep going, pushing up from my prone position to lean back on my elbows, "Let's say, by some miracle, you get through it. Do you think you're just going to run off into the night?" I scoff. "Where will you go? How will you get off this island? You do know the only way on or off is by helicopter, right? What, do you plan to fling yourself off one of the massive cliffs and hope you don't bounce off a rock on the way down? Even if you didn't die from the fall alone, do you honestly think you could swim to safety?"

"I don't know, but—"

My eyes narrow on her. I know my building frustration is entirely misplaced, but it doesn't stop me. "Right. You don't know. It's not something we're going to figure out. Not on our own and not together. If you keep hoping there's a way out, it's only going to hurt more when you realize there isn't. This is *it* for us."

She mumbles something that sounds like, "Selfish bitch," before she turns her body away from me.

I internally flinch at the name calling, but I don't let it show. I just look away from her and lay back down, getting right back to my kicks and stretches. It's not the first time another girl has called me a bitch. I wasn't exactly the warmest or friendliest of people before my captivity and I've only grown colder over the years.

Ezra thawed me. It was tropical paradise when I was with him, but I've become arctic cold again. It's the way I have to be to protect myself. I have to shove any understanding or sympathy for these girls aside so I can focus on myself.

I *have* to.

It's the only way to survive.

I didn't have the means to pay the price of hoping for something better.

Entrechat. Pirouette.

Entrechat. Pirouette.

Entrechat—

"Would you fucking stop already? Christ!" Bianca shouts at me through our shared box wall.

I stop mid-jump, landing hard on my feet in exasperation. Pain shoots through my ankle with the rough landing—my healing tendons require control and precision. She paces in the cage beside me, her fingers digging into her hair and pulling.

"All day with the goddamn *dancing*. All fucking day!"

I glare at her, doing two more pirouettes on my good foot out of spite. I do feel bad for her frustration, but I would've lost my mind by now had I not been able to do what little dancing I can do inside my cage. We're all falling to pieces in this strange sort of isolation. We're only taken from our boxes twice a week to shower behind the staircase.

Vigo has taken the other two girls upstairs on some type of rotation system, once every couple of days. He hasn't taken me upstairs yet, but I've learned my place after only a month here.

We're Vigo's broken dolls.

You're not fucking broken, Anya, Ezra's voice shouts in my head.

It's jarring, making my muscles jerk. The shock of its clarity lowers me to the floor, and I sit on the cold concrete with my legs stretched out in front of me.

My fingers touch my lips and I nibble on my thumbnail, feeling a jolt of lightning flash through my body at the sound of Ezra in my mind.

It's stirring the way he comes back to me so unexpectedly, so powerfully. If I close my eyes and inhale slowly, I can nearly smell the way his dance-induced sweat mingled with the soft peaches and cream scent of his soap. It was always the most intoxicating mixture of sweetness and masculinity.

I'm lost in that thought when Vigo comes down the stairs and I lift my head to look at him blankly. It takes me moments to blink back from memories of Ezra to reality, but as he walks past the first box, his eyes catch mine and lock me in.

He stalks past the middle box and my breath catches in my throat. He stops in front of my box—the third and final box—and cold sweat forms at the back of my neck.

I push slowly to my feet, tugging my stupid blue dress down to ensure it covers my bare bottom. He steps closer to the box and I step back on instinct. He enters a pin on the keypad entry, and I step back again, then again.

As the door pops open, he tugs on it, swinging it wide. "Come with me," he grins.

Oh, God.

Be strong, just be strong.

I pause for a beat, then lift my chin and move slowly toward him. I won't fight it like the other girls do with him every time he comes for them. I'd rather save my energy for when it's needed most.

And I have a feeling I'm going to need it once we're alone.

I can nearly sense Ezra's disappointment in my resignation, knowing he would've attacked, tried to fight, and run. But I quickly let go of that disappointment as I exhale. I know better than to fight the inevitable.

Still, my heart pumps wildly against my ribcage.

He holds his arm out toward the staircase. "Up you go. Stop and wait for me when you reach the kitchen."

No.

Don't go.

Don't go, don't go, don't go.

It's the first time I've been asked to go upstairs and my pulse beats steadily with the warning, *don't go, don't go.*

But I have no choice.

CHAPTER 11
Anya

I MOVE PAST Vigo to the staircase. Though I'm moving better now—I am even able to do some jumps and turns in my tiny cell—my foot is still stiff and a bit inflexible as I walk.

It feels immeasurably better to point my toes, to let the muscles and tendons extend and stretch—it's somehow easier to jump and turn. Walking, though, I feel pain where my ankle bends with each step. This staircase may as well have been a mountain for my aching, underused muscles, but I hide my pain and reach the top all the same.

The metal door is open and I step past it into the kitchen. There's a brief gut reaction that tells me to run, but I'm frozen in place as I come upon Renata Vittori. She's standing on the opposite side of the bright-white kitchen island. I keep my head lowered, but I look up at her from beneath my lashes.

The woman is wealth's goddess. She sips a sepia-colored liquid from a short, crystal glass, her free hand pressed to the countertop as she leans upon it. She wears a stunning, cream-colored dressing robe, all silk and long, with deep red outlining the hems of the sleeves. Intricately designed florals of burgundy and deep purple cover the creamy fabric. All she wears beneath is a matching silk red nightgown. Her jet-black hair, which matches her brother's, falls in pin straight pieces over one shoulder, shiny and clean and perfectly styled.

From her manner of dress, I gather that it's either late at night or early in the morning. There are no windows in the basement, so time is evasive. Given that she's drinking liquor rather than coffee, I'm guessing it's nighttime.

Vigo appears beside me and shuts the metal door, hiding it behind the hinged drywall as Renata greets me.

"Anya. I suppose I should say *welcome*. Are you behaving better these days? How long have you been with us now?"

I cast my shadowed eyes sideways toward where Vigo stands, my heart racing, wondering if I should respond, if I'm *supposed* to respond. It's the first time I've been upstairs since my arrival and I don't know the rules.

That makes me unsettled more than anything else.

"You may speak when spoken to," Vigo tells me as he shifts, pressing up against my backside.

His lips brush my shoulder casually as if we know each other, as if we are a couple.

Carefully, I respond to Renata, "Yes. I've been here several weeks, I think."

"Four weeks," Vigo clarifies.

His hand lands on my hip and he leans into me. I lurch forward with a gasp, my back arching to get away from him, but he harshly grabs both hips and yanks me back.

Taking a sip of her drink, Renata asks with a smug look on her face, "And how is your ankle healing?"

"Better," I say tersely. "Thank you."

Renata looks sharply down beside her. "Stop eating, Luca, that's enough. Up."

I jerk back in surprise as a young man rises from the floor behind the island next to Renata. I recognize him immediately. It's the same shirtless, bronze-skinned, black-haired man who brings us our food and drink each day. She called him Luca. He always wears the black collar around his neck, but now there's a long, black leash attached to the C-ring at his throat. My eyes follow the leash to its end, finding that it's held in Renata's hand resting on the countertop. The young man wipes his mouth with the back of his hand as he stands, and Renata reaches out to scruff her hand through his hair.

I swallow hard, trying to take in all that I'm seeing, but I'm struggling to process. They behave as if everything that's happening is normal, just another day with the Vittoris. The collared boy seems almost content with the way he reacts, leaning into Renata's touch, dipping to press his lips to the curve of her neck.

Renata's smug grin widens as she returns her attention to me. "Do you think you will ever dance again? Pity what happened to you. The blond boy that Nikolai selected to dance with you so brilliantly showcased your talents.

I thought he was quite appealing."

I don't speak at the reminder of Ezra, I just nod. I wish I could tell her that I *can* dance, that I *have* been dancing in my box, that I *will* dance for real again someday. But it would only come out of me with an Ezra-style snarky retort which most likely will get me in trouble so, I bite my tongue.

She turns to face her leashed slave as his lips dip down toward her collarbone. "I hope you two have a lovely evening," she says as she digs her fingers in his hair, lifting his head and letting him kiss her.

Is the Vittori island on another planet entirely?

Standing here in my child-like blue dress, watching a collared slave boy kiss his female master…It hurts my head to think about how bizarre and awful these people are.

And what bizarre thing does Vigo have planned for me?

Vigo puts his hands on my shoulders and pushes me forward, guiding me toward the arched opening up ahead on our left, leading out of the kitchen. Just as well, I feel like I'm in shock trying to understand what kind of rabbit hole of depravity I've fallen into.

Vigo shuffles me toward the staircase in the entryway. "Up you go."

I climb slowly, cautiously holding onto the metal railing that curves with the staircase, up and up to the balcony landing above.

Another mountain I've climbed and survived.

He guides me through the arched opening and leads me down a hallway to our right. We pass several doors, some open, some closed, some that are silent, some that carry voices speaking in Italian, a language I don't understand. Finally, we come to a stop.

Another keypad to gain entry. He unlocks and opens the door.

I start to suck in a deep breath to steel myself against whatever is about to happen to me in this room, but I only suck it in halfway before his hands slam against my back and shove me forward. I falter, stumbling past the threshold, but somehow manage to stay on my feet.

I whip back around to face him. I don't want to have my back turned to him anymore.

I back away as I watch him shut the door and he engages another lock from the inside with another pin. This one is meant to lock me *in* with him. I can't just turn the knob and run.

My heart is racing far too fast to process anything other than the fear for the unknown. Vigo stares at me, honey-brown eyes pulsing lasers that burn across my skin.

He licks his bottom lip and my body clenches unpleasantly, wanting to curl in around itself, wrap into a ball, and hide away from him in a dark corner.

He points to a spot behind me. "Sit. Brush out your hair."

What?

I look where he's pointing. Beside two windows covered with thick, brown curtains, I see a small vanity against the wall. It has a cream- and tan-marbled tabletop and it sits beneath a rectangular mirror on the wall.

On the marble tabletop there's a wooden jewelry box beside what is perhaps the most elegant-looking hairbrush I've ever seen—silver-plated and carved with some sort of raised design that I can't see from where I'm standing. A small cushioned stool rests in front of the vanity, inviting me to sit.

I move cautiously, casting my eyes back and forth to watch his movements until I reach the seat. I lower onto the stool and catch his eyes through the mirror as he approaches from behind.

His command was clear. I know what he expects me to do, so I don't bother questioning the odd request to brush out my hair.

I hear Nikolai's voice in my mind. *Good slaves don't ask questions, they just do.*

In a strange way, his voice is a comfort, only because it reminds me of a time when I knew the rules and the consequences for breaking them, a time when I understood.

I don't understand this newness with Vigo and his odd family.

I pick up the handle of the silver-plated brush and examine the backside of it. I draw my fingers over the elegant swirled floral design within the chrome. The bristles are soft, the color of wheat.

"Brush," he barks, and I jump from the unexpected harshness of his tone.

"*Si, Papà,*" I nearly gag on the words.

The words he wants in response to his commands make me sick, but I'm thankful for the clarity, a rule I'm capable of following.

I shake out my long, tangled hair, letting it fall over my shoulders, and I begin to brush. There are knots and I have to pull the soft bristles through with some force.

I brush and brush until my hair is soft and sleek and smooth, until he tells me to stop. He approaches my side and reaches out to open the wooden jewelry box, pulling out a pair of elastic hair ties and two lengths of white, silky ribbon.

"Part your hair," he begins, and I lift my eyes to meet his in the mirror. "Tie each side just below your ears."

Pigtails.

Oh, God.

He really does want me to look like a child.

My chest heaves with a heavy breath and I swallow hard. I reach to pick up one of the elastic ties. I gather half of my hair together over one shoulder and tie it off with the elastic just beneath my ear, exactly as Vigo had instructed. I do the same with the other side.

"Tie on the ribbons," he says, and my hands shake as I reach for one.

With trembling fingers, I wrap the ribbon over the elastic, looping and tying it into as neat of a bow as I can manage, then I repeat it on the other side.

Looking at my reflection kickstarts my pulse.

The pigtails.

The innocent white bows.

The childish blue dress.

The cap sleeves that puff out in a juvenile way.

He's dressing me up to look like a goddamn child.

A doll.

The words that I said to him my first night here, before he left me to sleep with a dead body, bounce from dark corner to dark corner in my mind.

You're sick.

You're sick.

You're sick.

His eyes watch me in the mirror as I take in my reflection.

Can he hear how loudly my mind screams those words at him?

You're sick!

He's proud to have me think of him as a sick bastard. It's written all over his face with an arrogant smirk. He turns and walks to an ornate dresser on the other side of the room, near the door.

I swivel on my seat to look out at the space, taking in my surroundings with a rapidly beating heart. There's a king-sized bed to my right, neatly made with a comforter that looks more like a golden weaved tapestry. A short, tufted bench sits at the foot of the bed, resting on top of the massive, Oriental-style rug that's plush beneath my bare feet. Everything in the room is shades of gold and tan, an otherwise expected looking bedroom in a mansion of this size.

Vigo comes back to me carrying a pair of white socks. "Put these on."

I reluctantly take the socks from him, holding his gaze with my wary eyes.

"You know I've wanted you for years, Anya."

The statement freezes me, but I don't respond. I just bend and slip one sock on over my toes, rolling it up over my calf until it stops just below the knee.

He groans and I gag.

"When Nikolai let me use you as payment for my information about who killed his family, I knew I had to have you in my collection. Such a beautiful little doll. *La mia bambola Russa.* I've fantasized about you since that night."

I slip on the second sock and slowly lift, sitting up straight with a bowed head.

"Stop being such a good little girl," he snaps.

What?

"You're not a good little girl at all, are you?"

"I don't—"

"Don't talk back to me."

"I'm not—"

"Get up."

I stand, my forehead wrinkling in confusion. I don't understand the game he's playing.

What are the rules?

How do I follow them?

I don't know this dance, these steps, this performance.

How do I survive this?

He steps forward, suave and sleek in his pressed black slacks, crisp white button-up, and silk black tie. He grabs me by both shoulders, yanking me up to stand and whirling me around so he can sit on the stool instead. He lets go of me and begins to roll up his sleeves.

His eyes burn a hole through me. "Turn around. Lift your skirt."

I hesitate.

Suddenly, I feel more vulnerable and exposed than I've ever been. I've felt my fair share of exposure and vulnerability at Nikolai's hands, but fuck, everything here feels so wrong.

Wrong.

Wrong!

You're sick!

I spin around slowly, putting my back to him as he switches from one sleeve to the other. My fingertips brush my skin as I grasp the hem of my dress, lifting it slowly. Inch by inch, I expose my bare ass to him.

He lets out a low moan behind me and my gut rolls.

"Bend over."

Just do as you're told.

I bend.

His hands land on my hips, his thumbs rubbing circles on my cheeks.

"Tell *Papà* how naughty you've been."

"I don't understand what you want from me."

I yelp, wobbling in his hold as teeth sink into my ass, not playfully, but hard and bruising.

Nikolai's done that before. If this is all this will be, if all I have to do is serve as the unwilling subject for Vigo to play out his sick sexual fantasies with, then I can do this. I can survive this. I've done it for years before with Nikolai.

Except…

There was something about the way Nikolai wanted me as *me*, rather than a doll without a name, a fantasy, that somehow makes that seem as though it were reasonable.

Reasonable?

Nothing in my life is fucking reasonable.

Vigo's tongue runs over the deep bite and my muscles clench against it. He pulls back and a hand releases my hip to slap me there instead, making me shriek.

"Tell me," he says again. "Tell me you've been a naughty little girl who needs to be punished."

My lips purse, refusing to form the words, but his fingertips dig hard into my hip bones.

"I've been bad, *Papà.*"

He growls, "*Sei una cattiva ragazza.*"

What did he say?

Should I respond?

Is that a command?

A question?

I don't speak fucking Italian!

I say the only thing I can think of that might appease him. "*Si, Papà.*"

He responds with a heated groan and pulls me backward, forcing me to sit on his lap. His erection presses into my ass from beneath his tented trousers.

"I'm going to punish you." He kisses the back of my neck at the base of my spine using lips and tongue. "Does that scare you, little doll?"

My brain is screaming at him, wondering what the hell I'm supposed to say. I don't know what he wants. I don't know if he wants me to be scared or excited or some strange mixture of the two. I don't know if he wants me to fucking crawl like a baby and suck my goddamn thumb.

What do you want from me?

He brings his lips to my ear over one of my pigtails. "You don't need to be scared, little one. *Papà* only punishes you to make you better. Get down on your hands and knees."

I obey, more than happy to separate my ass from his erection. He adjusts my skirt to flip it all the way above my hips, ensuring all my private parts are on full view for him. It's quiet for a few stressful breaths, but then his hand lands with a smack against my cheek. I rock forward on the impact, but quickly readjust, knowing more spanks are to come.

And they do come, one after another after another.

But it's truly nothing for me, given all that I've been through. He hasn't hit me all that hard and he stops rather quickly. I'm beginning to think Vigo might be survivable, but I know getting my hopes up too soon would be stupid.

"Tell me how sorry you are. Beg for forgiveness."

I swallow. "I'm so sorry, *Papà*. Please forgive me."

"Is that how you beg? With your back to me?"

I stifle a sigh, pushing back to sit on my heels. I take a quick moment to brush my skirt back down to cover myself before turning to face him. I scoot toward him on my knees.

"I'm sorry, *Papà*."

He grips my chin and tilts my head up, forcing our eyes to meet. "Beautiful little doll of mine, you know I don't want to hurt you."

I try to play his game to appease him, but I have to force the words out, stagnant and unfeeling. "I know, *Papà*. I'm sorry. I'll be a good girl."

God, how this nauseates me.

Vigo leans forward, pressing a soft kiss to my lips.

He lingers with his mouth on mine.

I watch him warily with open eyes and I'm surprised that his remain open, too; he's watching me just as carefully. There is a certain something in his uniquely honey-colored eyes that could easily set off a spark of attraction, a false feeling of trust with the allure of his good looks. He's a beautiful predator designed by the devil himself to tempt his prey with his charming good looks.

Just as I was tempted away from the world I knew by Nikolai.

Fuck, I hate him!

I hate them both!

I finally realize he's not holding me in place, so I yank my head back with force, angrily breaking the odd kiss that twisted a shameful pinch of lust in my belly.

Maybe I am just a whore like Nikolai says.

I don't deserve Ezra's love.

"Why don't you go and play with your rabbit, sweet girl?"

Vigo tilts his head toward the window beside us and I follow his eyes. I'm surprised I didn't notice it before, though I really didn't notice much of anything when I first walked in. There's an oversized, pink stuffed rabbit resting on the floor between the windows.

"You want me to…play with the rabbit." I'm careful to speak it as a statement, not as a question.

He grins at me and whispers, "Yes, go play. Crawl to your bunny."

I do as he tells me, getting back down on all fours. I crawl the short distance to the rabbit and sit back on my heels, lifting the plush toy from the rug. I look back at him over my shoulder, my eyes searching for some hint that I'm doing what I'm supposed to be doing. He gives me nothing but smoldering, sickening heat.

I look away quickly, glancing down at the bunny the size of a cocker spaniel in my grip. I have no idea what he wants me to do. I'm trying to sort out what this kind of fantasy entails with little direction from him. I think he must want to see me like a child playing with her toys, but I don't know if I can do this.

As sick as it makes me, I know this schoolgirl fantasy isn't all that uncommon. I should be able to do this. As far as the world of sex slavery goes, this is nothing more than a fetish, a kink.

I should be able to do this.

But then, the simplicity of this makes me wonder why the girls in the boxes beside mine fought Vigo so hard when he'd come to take them. They were *desperate* not to go with him. It makes me wonder why the woman who called my box hers before me was so willing to slit her throat and end her life the second the opportunity presented itself.

On the surface, this looks like nothing more than a fantasy, but as Vigo comes up behind me, the pulse of his aura tells me this isn't it—this fantasy isn't the thing the other girls fear.

There's something more coming.

My fingers dig into the velvety fur of the pink rabbit as my spine tingles in fearful anticipation.

"You love that pink bunny so much, don't you?"

My muscles tense. "*Si, Papà.*"

"How much do you love it?"

My brow furrows. "I…love it very much *Papà.*"

"Show your bunny how much you love it."

I hesitate for a moment and then bring the stuffed animal close, hugging it to my chest like a child would.

Is this what he wants?

"Yes, you love that toy so much. Why don't you give it a kiss?"

Odd.

So fucking odd.

I give the bunny a quick kiss on the nose.

He lets out a long, heated breath and out with it comes his sickness, rushing out into the room, swirling all around me, coiling me in its sinister hold.

"Now fuck it."

CHAPTER 12

Anya

"WHAT?" THE QUESTION shoots from my lips.

"Fuck it," he repeats. "Wrap your legs around it and fuck it. Rub your clit on it until you come."

Oh.

No.

No, no, no, no, no.

I know I can't say *no* to him for fear of how he'll hurt me if I do, but I can't do what he's asking me to do.

I won't do it.

I *won't.*

My head shakes back and forth, urgent in my protest, as he comes up behind me. He slips down to his knees, scoots in close, molding his body to my backside. My fingers squeeze around the bunny, drawing into tight fists through my agitation.

Vigo reaches around me, his hands clamping down on my wrists where I grasp the toy in my clenched fists. He pushes down, trying to force my hands and the bunny between my legs.

For the first time in a long time, I refuse. I absolutely, unwaveringly refuse to obey this order.

"No!" I shout, opening my fingers in hopes of dropping it.

But his hands slide quickly over mine, lacing our fingers together, forcing me to grab hold of the stuffed toy as he shoves. I clamp my thighs together so he has nowhere to go but my lap. Vigo is so much stronger than me, though… forceful. He wiggles the toy as he presses, somehow managing to wedge the damn thing between my clamped thighs. He's got just enough of an opening to thrust it down hard between my legs.

I spread my knees apart, hoping he'll let go and it will fall, giving me a chance to toss it away.

But he doesn't let go.

He grips my fingers tighter, digging our hands into the bunny as he takes advantage of my spread knees, forcing it harshly against my naked sex. I lean backward, trying to get away from it, but his body is rigid, unyielding at my back. With my fingers still locked with his, he rubs the toy harshly against me.

"That's it. Fuck it, Anya. Fuck that bunny you love so much. Show Daddy how much you love it."

"Stop!"

My movements are frantic. I push my hands down harder, trying to break from his grip. I lean my body back, pushing against his.

I want this to stop, I want this plush, velvety symbol of innocent childhood far away from my sex. It's such a depraved thing he's forcing me to do, and it's all the more heinous that my stupid body could possibly have any response to any touch that doesn't belong to Ezra.

But it fucking does…and I couldn't be more ashamed.

My ass is held against his crotch as he holds me tighter against him, as I try to slip backward away from the bunny. He uses that to his advantage, and he begins to rock. He rocks our hips together, rolling them slowly forward and back, all the while holding the toy between my legs.

And no matter how much I hate it, no matter how I try to fight this—to keep my body from responding and my mind safe from this nightmare—my body responds traitorously.

Wetness rushes to my core and my clit swells as his forceful rubbing turns to gentle rocking on the toy jammed between my thighs.

"Please, stop," I beg, though my voice loses its strength, it's determination, as he draws unwanted pleasure.

"Stop? Which part do you want me to stop? The way I'm moving you?" His lips fall to the side of my neck, beneath one of my pigtails. "Or the way I'm pleasing you? Tell *Papà* what you want."

"I…I want you to stop. All of it."

Weak.

I'm fucking weak.

My voice, my willpower, my sexual need.

I'm weak with all those things and I've never felt so deeply, brokenly ashamed of myself.

Except, I *have* felt this deeply, brokenly ashamed before. It was when Ezra had first arrived at Mikhailov Manor. When Nikolai fingered me in front of him, told me to come, but stopped before I could, just to humiliate me and leave me wanting. I'd felt shame then for the way my body responded to Nikolai's touch, for the way I tried so hard to get there, to come, to find my release simply because he'd wanted me to.

But Ezra had been turned on by the show of it, too. He'd always been turned on by the way Nikolai used me simply because our bodies are human, and they don't always react in the way we want them to.

I'm fed up with this nightmare, with letting other men control what my body does and doesn't do. I'm tired of responding because they make me respond. But if my body is going to take over anyway, if my body is going to let me feel pleasure from this sickness, then maybe I should just let it. Maybe if I let it, I'll take some of my power back.

I force my mind to jump the hurdle of shame and give the fuck in.

This is my life now.

No more Nikolai.

No more Ezra.

No more Ezra?

That thought fuels an indignant fire in my chest, burning through the barrier of my ribcage and ripping deep down into my belly. I let the blaze take over, my stomach clenching and drawing wanting into my swollen, aching pussy.

"You want me to fuck it?" I hardly recognize the sound of my voice, rising to a pitch of hysteria. "Then let me go and watch me fuck it."

He releases my fingers, though his hands only draw as far back as my wrists, resting there lightly. He stops rocking, but I take over for the both of us. Clamping my thighs around the stupid pink bunny, I roll my hips, holding it in place with my hands so my clit can rub against the soft surface.

"Tell *Papà* how you feel."

"Dirty." It was the sad, sorry truth.

"You feel like a dirty little girl?"

"*Sì, Papà.*"

"Don't stop, dirty girl."

His hands slide backward along my arms, though his body stays in place, his hips moving with me as mine rock. I'm thoroughly disgusted with myself, but I'm taking my fucking power back. He's gonna make me do this, like it or not, so I'll let myself like it because I have nothing else.

He pulls his hands away and I feel him shift behind me. At first, I think he's unbuckling his pants, but that's not what happens. He's shifted his body so that he's leaning a bit toward the left and he holds my hip with his left hand. I don't know where his right hand is.

Probably on his dick.

Though, I know it's not on his dick because I feel his hardness against the small of my back.

"Take a look at this…" I hear him say as I rock and rub. "Daddy's little doll. Sweet and dirty and aching for it. Do you like it, doll?"

"*Si, Papà,*" I hiss with sarcasm on a whisper.

I'm determined, so fucking determined to relieve this ache in my body. It's the ache of everything I've been through, everything that's been done to me, everything that's to come. It's the ache of finding hope, finding love with Ezra and having it ripped away from me so callously. It's the ache of knowing I may not see him again…

"Come on, Anya, get there."

Tears spring to my eyes and I shout at him, though I continue to defile this stupid toy. "Shut up, shut the fuck up!"

He lets me go and leaves me there, stepping back, and I know he's just standing there, watching me as I writhe like a whore, fucking for nothing more than a quick, fleeting release.

It coils in my pussy, throbbing, pulsing, screaming at me to rut and fuck and claim my release. It builds and builds before it crests and I feel the familiar break, the crippling tension just before, then the exploding release of an orgasm.

But it doesn't feel the same.

It doesn't feel good.

There's not an ounce of that pleasurable feeling through my clit. All I feel is a flood of painful emotion rushing through the released tension in my muscles with the absolutely ruined orgasm.

I remain powerless.

There was never any power for me to take back.

"Very nice, Anya, well done."

I whip my head to look at Vigo, tears painting stripes down my cheeks as fresh tears rush behind them to fill my eyes to the brim. But even through the sheen of liquid, I can see what he's doing. He's got his smart phone in his hands and he's holding it up, recording me.

"Anything you want to say to Nikolai? Or perhaps that slave boy you seem to have affection for? Maybe Nikolai will show it to him if you ask nicely."

Vigo laughs and it's filled with the black evil in his heart. My eyes narrow on him, my breaths are hard and shallow, my muscles burn to hit and kick and hurt him.

I jump to my feet and leap after him, knocking the phone from his hands, and it tumbles to the floor. As he bends to reach for it, I bring my knee up, hoping to catch him hard in the gut, but it's barely a nudge.

His hands latch around my wrists and he pushes them wide apart, dragging them down to our sides, bringing them together again in front of us. He puts both of my wrists in one of his large hands and grips the back of my neck with the other. He drags me close, pressing his forehead to mine as he bends down over me.

I'm held firm in his grasp, though I'm not done fighting him yet. I kick at his ankles, but he only chuckles as he burns me with the intensity of his gaze. I keep my eyes locked on his, determined not to give him my submission.

"Now there's that fight. I was wondering what happened to it."

I snarl, suddenly ravenous to hurt him as I try to thrash my wrists from his hold. "I know how to pick my battles."

"You've chosen the wrong battle," he says with a grin.

In one motion, he takes me down to the floor. He falls forward on top of me, causing my knees to buckle. My ass hits the ground first as he comes down on top of me, and the air is knocked free from my lungs as my back and head fall back against the carpet. I thrash my legs, wiggling, squirming, fighting to get out from under him, but he's relentless.

He's nothing like Nikolai.

Nikolai would punish me when I fell out of line. He would hurt me in his anger for my disobedience, but he did it to teach me a lesson. Normally, he took care of me afterward, or at least made sure I had what I needed to care for myself.

But this…Vigo forcing me to fuck a child's toy while he records it is just ruthless, reasonless debasement without any justification.

But Nikolai wasn't justified in hurting me, either.

What is wrong with my twisted mind?

With that same demonic grin, Vigo pins me beneath him, his body heavy on mine, taking my breath away.

"Take out my cock," he tells me, baring his teeth.

I shake my head. "No."

He bends, sucking my bottom lip between his teeth and clamping down *hard* until I scream from the pain of his blood-drawing bite.

"Take it out or I'll do that to your fucking nipple."

I huff, moving my hands between us to unbuckle his belt, part his zipper, and push down his slacks and underwear just enough to expose him. The moment it's out, he plunges inside me. It's as though his intrusion takes up too much space and forces my tears out to make room.

He fucks me hard and fast as I quietly cry beneath him. It's not about the pleasurable feeling of getting off for him, it's about controlling me, having that power over me. That's what he wants.

Any power I thought I could take back from selfishly and filthily seeking my own release has been sufficiently ripped from me.

He comes inside me with a grunt and a groan and that fucking smug grin. The mess of his ejaculation inside my body makes me want to scream and so, I do, like a mad woman.

I scream as he chuckles, gets to his feet, and tucks his cock safely behind his trousers again.

"Come with me." He easily returns to calm and collected, so unlike Nikolai. "You're a filthy, disgusting, slutty little mess. Let *Papà* give you a bath."

I stand naked and shivering in Vigo's en suite bathroom as he lets the clawfoot tub fill with lukewarm water.

The tan tile is chilly beneath my feet and the cold air whips around me like a wintry breeze. My pigtails are still in place with white ribbons, though haphazard pieces have fallen free and the back has matted and tangled from being fucked by Vigo on the floor of his bedroom.

Vigo dips a hand into the water when the tub is nearly full and turns off the faucet.

"It's ready, climb on in."

I glare at him, my arms crossed over my chest, trying to keep the warmth in. I don't want to get in that tub. I know that once I get into that tub, something terrible is going to happen and I don't want to know what it is.

"You can get in on your own or I can put you in. Your choice."

As if that's even a choice.

I step forward with hesitancy. I carefully lift my foot from the floor and sink it beneath the water's surface. Instant panic strikes my chest and I step back out, backing away.

I think Nikolai has done well giving me a healthy fear of water.

Vigo turns to me and plucks me from the floor with ease. He grips me by the waist with his two large hands and I naturally grab hold of his wrists, though I don't know if it's to push him away or to hold myself steady.

He whips me around and carries me to the tub. He's so tall and strong that he easily gets my feet above the tub's edge before I can protest. I kick mid-air, trying to grip the rounded edge with my toes, but he plops me down in the water with a splash before I can find purchase.

The whoosh of the water as it splashes with my landing, the feel of it rapidly rising from feet to knees prompts me into a fearful stillness. I stand, shivering and trembling harder than before, terrified to sit, terrified to put my face any closer to this substance that could drown me.

"Sit," he orders. All I can do is shake my head. "*Sit.*" His tone is sharper and he places his hands on my shoulders.

My fingers jump to fight him off, my eyes widening at the trigger that makes me feel as though he's going to push me beneath the surface—the way Nikolai had done three times before in the pool at Mikhailov Manor.

"Sit or I'll make you sit," he warns with an even tone. He removes his hands from my shoulders in a show of good faith.

Still, all I can do is shake my head and shiver.

He steps back and tilts his head coolly. "*Papà* only wants to give you a bath. You're filthy. Don't you want to feel clean again?"

He's baiting me to sit in the water and the bait he's dangling is inviting. I feel disgusting and want nothing more than to cleanse myself of every trace of him. Though my brain begs me to keep my head as far from the water as possible, my body forces me to bend. I slowly lower, taking sharp and shallow breaths as my body fights with my mind, tripping the wire of anxiety to a point of distress.

Tears are falling again, but somehow, I've managed to do the impossible—I'm sitting in a tub full of water. Though my hands grip the edges of the tub so hard my knuckles are white, my breaths are quick and my heart is racing, I'm sitting in the water.

With his sleeves rolled up, Vigo flips his black tie over his shoulder so it's not dangling in front of him. Dripping soap onto his hands from the bottle of wash beside him where he kneels on the tile, he dips his hands beneath the surface and I flinch. The water pulses, rolling out and back toward me as I move. My breath catches in my throat and I hold back a sob.

"I'm just cleaning you," he says with a smile, as if that should make everything better.

I try to steady my breathing through clenched teeth as his hands slide between my thighs. My eyes are wide, though I wish I could press them closed and find a safe space in my mind.

He gropes under the guise of cleansing me, though I'm feeling anything but clean as his fingers dance in and out of my pussy, circling around in-between my crack.

But then he stands, yanking his hands from the water so swiftly that I let out a scream as it splashes across my face, a droplet landing on my eyelash. I see him turn away, but when my panic sinks in, I can't care about what he's doing. I throw myself backward, away from the spray and start to push to my feet.

But Vigo is back at me in a flash.

He's there before I can shift my hands back along the edges of the tub to push off. I see his sinister smile as he spins around to face me, but I don't see the needle coming toward me until it's too late. Before I can find the strength to climb from the tub, he plunges the syringe that came from nowhere into the side of my neck .

"What did you do?" I demand to know as he tosses the syringe behind him onto the floor haphazardly. "What is that? What *is* it?"

Almost instantly the awareness of my sense of touch begins to fade.

Am I still gripping the edge?

I look at my hands to see that I am, though I can't really feel it. Then I see my fingers loosen, slowly losing their grip. I snap my head to look at him where he kneels beside me, his forearms leaning against the tub's edge, his chin resting on his arms, his head tilted, watching me with curiosity and amusement.

Sick amusement.

He speaks to me as if we're two old chums having a friendly conversation. "It's a paralytic agent. It's a fascinating drug. It freezes you inside yourself. Within a minute or two, you'll lose the ability to control your body. You won't be able to move. Completely paralyzed and at my mercy and it will last for *hours*. But here's the fun part. You'll remain conscious and awake and aware the entire time. Your eyes will stay open, unless I choose to press your lids closed, though I can't think of a reason why I would want to do that, *la mia bambola Russa*."

Panic has taken hold of me entirely. My grip is weakening. My body is slipping. I open my mouth to speak, but I don't know if it opens. I try to scream, but no sound comes out. I'm slipping, slipping, sinking in the water.

"Before he sold you to me, Nikolai disclosed that he used water as a serious punishment for serious offenses and that it was quite effective with you. Disclosure of such things is standard in the paperwork when selling a slave, you understand. So, of course, I thought, *what a fun game that would be to play with you, Anya.* You didn't think I'd only play daddy with you and send you on your merry way, did you? Of course, you didn't. As you so rightly observed your first night here, *I'm sick*. It's true and I fucking love it. In moments, you'll become a real living doll and I will break your mind in ways you never imagined possible."

Slip.

Slip.

Slip.

My body drifts.

I fight to keep my head above water.

I thrash with every ounce of strength I can muster, but the water remains still. It's still and clear as my chin dips in. There's a ripple across the surface as my hands finally fall free from the side and drop into the water. My lips go under.

Somehow I'm able to remember to take a deep breath, inhaling through my nose, as I dig deep to my final reserves. I fight the paralyzing drug for one last moment, one last breath before my nose slips beneath the surface.

Vigo reaches one hand out above the water and waves at me, a demented grin plastered to his face. Then my eyes fall under, welcoming a rush of soapy water that stings.

I'm under.

I'm under and I can't move.

I'm under and I can't breathe.

I'm under and I can't fight, can't save myself.

I can't even close my eyes.

I have to watch above me as the distorted image of Vigo leans over the water, watching me with an amused expression.

Pull me out!

Pull me out!

Pull me out!

I'm helpless.

God.

Please.

Pull me out!

I know I can make it to twelve. Twelve counts of eight before I slip into unconsciousness. It's all I can do—count. I can't fight, I can't scream. All I can do is drive myself mad with panic or force myself to focus and count, give my mind a task to take it from this madness.

One. Two. Three. Four. Five. Six. Seven. Eight.

One. Two. Three. Four. Five. Six. Seven. Eight.

One. Two. Three. Four. Five. Six. Seven. Eight.

I internally scream out in relief as Vigo's hands ripple the surface, slip beneath my head, and scoop me out of the water. My lungs scramble to take in air through my nose—I can't even part my lips to gasp. He lets me go again and I slide under.

One. Two. Three. Four. Five. Six. Seven. Eight.

One. Two. Three. Four. Five. Six. Seven. Eight.

He drops in a washcloth and presses it over my face, covering my eyes, my nose, my mouth.

Now I know why the other girls fought so hard to remain in their boxes in the basement. I know why the girl in my box had chosen her own death so easily. This isn't a punishment for poor behavior. This is nothing more than torture for torture's sake.

And like a hammer to a porcelain doll, he's going to shatter my mind into a million irreparable pieces.

CHAPTER 13
NIKOLAI

I LEAN BACK in my chair, letting my head fall back and my eyes drift shut. I try to relax and enjoy the feel of Sasha's pretty lips around my cock, but her softness simply isn't the same. She may have the same brown hair, dark eyebrows, and feminine frame as Anya, but she doesn't suck like her, doesn't taste like her, fuck like her, feel like her.

I comb my fingers into Sasha's hair at the back of her skull, grip firmly, and yank her head back. Her lips break free of my cock with a pop that's more annoying than satisfying. She looks up at me with puppy dog brown eyes, wanting to please her master and wondering how she's failed.

She's a weak piece of ass that I've already grown bored with. Still, my dick is hard. If I could just find a way to shut up the gnawing voice of my dead father, the voice who tells me that I'm an ambivalent, pansy-ass, pretty boy, then I could do what I really want to do and fuck *his* mouth.

I glance over at Ezra, who is fuming in the armchair beside mine in my bedroom. His knee bounces with his anxiety. He's a ball of furious energy that's constantly on the verge of exploding, especially when I force him to sit and watch as I do terrible things to Sasha.

I haven't involved him in the ways I did when Anya was here. I can't say for sure why. Perhaps it's because of Sasha. She's a weak little girl, eager to please. She fell into servitude so quickly and so easily that it has honestly put me off.

Anya was obedient and submissive, she followed my commands and aimed to please, but it wasn't for some delusion that she could make me fall in love with her. Sasha's eyes told me she was a hollow shell of a young woman with daddy issues; a girl who would crawl on her knees and beg for an ounce of affection.

Anya would crawl and beg, too, but it was for survival, not desire.
Fuck.
Sasha speaks to me in Russian, the only language she knows. She

apologizes to me and offers me her pussy. She fucking *offers* it, just affirming to me that all women are sluts and whores.

Ezra's arms are crossed over his broad chest, a permanent scowl etched to his face, and his eyes are narrowed on the flames blazing in my fireplace. Fuck, I want to wipe that look off his face with my cock shoved in his mouth. But there's a buzz inside me, a painful vibration that ticks up every time I start thinking about how much I want him, and it shakes me right back to reality with my father's voice, the words that have haunted me for years.

Ambivalent.

Pansy-ass.

Pretty boy.

I toss Sasha away by the hair and she catches herself on her palms. She looks up at me with questions in her eyes, wondering what she's done wrong. It's pointless for her to question because she can't fix her failure. Her failure is simple—she's not Anya.

I tell her to get on all fours so I can fuck her from behind without having to look at her face, but my cell phone pings and buzzes in my back pocket, distracting me. Once, twice, three times in a row the texts ping through—I should've turned it off before I started fucking my slave's mouth.

I shift in my seat, reaching behind me to pull my phone from my back pocket. I look at the screen and narrow my eyes in curiosity.

I've got three new messages from Vigo Vittori.

We're not exactly friends, so this is unusual. Given that I sold him my girl a little over a month ago, the prickling on the back of my neck tells me this has something to do with her.

Not 'my girl.'

My slave.

I sold him my slave.

My thumb twitches, hovering over the screen as the thought of her death flashes across my mind. If he's killed her, there's no doubt in my mind he'd tell me about it. If he's killed her then…

Fuck.

I set my phone down on the side table between me and Ezra and shove my erection back into my pants. I stand, pat Sasha on the ass, and tell her to get the fuck out. Then, I pick up my phone and stride across to the far corner of my room beside the window.

The door closes behind Sasha as she leaves. There's no reason for doubt in my mind that she'll do anything but go right back to her room. It's so fucking pathetic the way she's bowed to me so quickly. I don't think I'd care if she offed herself or tried to escape into the wilderness.

I feel Ezra's eyes burning a hole in my back once she's gone. He wants to leave, too, and it's simply for that reason that I make him stay while I open the messages Vigo has sent to me.

`VIGO` Breaking in your girl. Thought you might enjoy this.

Below the text are two videos. The stills that show before I press play already have rage bubbling in my blood.

He knew it wasn't a choice for me.

He knew I'd have to watch.

Whatever vile things he's doing to her, they're no viler than what I've already done to her. There's one thing Vigo and I have always had in common—there's a sickness in our blood passed down through generations. It's a sickness shared by every member of the four families, dating all the way back to the four fathers who established our secret, conglomerate slave trade.

Those four villainous fathers had met by chance two centuries ago, fleeing their homelands against prosecution for the heinous, murderous crimes they had committed. They might have been some of the most prolific serial killers in history had the secret not been kept. But in their chance meeting, they chose to form a coalition, working together to evade charges of their various crime sprees by agreeing to provide alibis for each other in turn.

They were able to return to their homelands, build normal lives, breed children as depraved as they were, and the four families have carried on with the debauchery ever since. The partnership among the four fathers proved to be profitable for everyone. They quickly found themselves in the business of selling and trading human lives, which proved to be their most profitable and satisfying venture.

The descendants of those four fathers never stood a chance.

We were born sick.

I rub my hand over my face, shake my head, and press play for the first video.

It starts and my pulse thrums as Anya comes into the screen. She's on her knees, wearing a stupid blue dress that makes her look like a fucking child, and her hair is split into two ponytails, tied with ribbons. She's fucking—I narrow my eyes at the screen and then they widen in surprise.

She's fucking a goddamn child's toy.

Vigo is pressed up behind her, their bodies molded together, and he holds up his phone, high above their heads, angling it down to show them both rocking and grinding together. I didn't think to turn down the volume on my phone before clicking play so I get to hear their sordid dialogue.

"Take a look at this. Daddy's little doll. Sweet and dirty and aching for it. Do you like it, doll?"
"Si, Papà."

Ezra is leaping from his chair and running after me in a flash, practically stumbling across the room in his haste to get to me.

"That's Anya's voice. What is that?" he asks. "What the *fuck* is that?"

I growl at him, "Get on your knees, *mal'chik*. If I want you to see it, I'll show you."

He begrudgingly drops to his knees beside me, knowing that I'm his master and he'll obey immediately if he wants anything from me.

I'm still the goddamn king of this castle.

His bare chest heaves with the heavy breaths he's taking. Part of me wants to torture him by leaving him wondering. Part of me wants to torture him by showing him this video.

Either way, it will hurt him.

Hurting him makes me feel like I'm in control.

But the video continues.

Vigo is no longer rocking behind her, he's standing back, filming her fuck herself to completion on a toy. Then, she's looking at the camera, tears streaking down her pretty cheeks, and my gut rolls with something resembling nausea. It's an uneasy feeling I'm not accustomed to and don't really care for.

I flinch to see her launch herself at him so unexpectedly. She attacks him and the phone falls to the floor. Though all it manages to capture visually is the ceiling, it still records the sound.

Ezra falters, his shoulders rounding and slumping, one hand landing over his heart as the other presses down into one of his strong thighs, holding himself up lest he should crumble to the floor. He hears what I'm hearing, the sounds of Vigo and Anya struggling and fighting, exchanging words.

"Take out my cock."
"No."
"Take it out or I'll do that to your fucking nipple."

The sound of Vigo fucking her, coming inside her.
The sound of Anya letting out a single, sharp scream.

"Come with me. You're a filthy, disgusting, slutty little mess. Let *Papà* give you a bath."

That's where the first video ends. I run a shaking hand through my hair.
Why am I shaking?
This is what I wanted.
I sold her knowing he'd do this to her.
I click on the second video and stare at it for exactly five seconds before my hand opens inexplicably and my phone tumbles to the floor.
Anya underwater.
Her blue eyes wide and wild.
Motionless.
Drowning.
Ezra scrambles to grab my phone as Vigo says something on the clip about the fucking paralytic drug he's always used with his broken dolls. Anya is one of them now, because of me.

I pace away, not giving a shit that Ezra has picked up my phone, that he screams in pain seeing Anya underwater. I don't care when he clicks back to watch the first video. I don't flinch when he throws my phone at the wall and it crashes to the floor.

It's not necessary for me to punish him for touching my property. What he has seen on my phone is proving to be punishment enough.

He screams, his fingers digging into his hair as he curls forward on his knees, as if the heartache in his chest is a dense, dying star, pulling every other part of him toward its center as what he's seen slowly destroys him.

I should be glad.

It's what I wanted—to offload the bitch who betrayed my trust and fucked her pet when I gave her an inch of freedom for one fucking night. I wanted to hurt them both for hurting me so effectively, for her refusal to give me a spoonful of love for all the years I took care of her, for his refusal to look at me with anything other than hatred and disgust.

I don't need his disgust.

My father gave me enough to last a lifetime.

My throat gathers a lump. My heart pounds. My hands tremble. My eyes burn.

I don't know why, but suddenly I feel like I've made a mistake.

I don't make mistakes.

I have to sit. I go back to my armchair and slowly lower. My elbows fall to my knees and my head falls into my hands.

"You did this." It's a quiet hiss of truth from Ezra after several quiet moments. "You did this to her. You sold her to a fucking sociopath, and he's going to ruin her in ways you never could've dreamed of."

I lift my head slightly from my hands, turning to look toward him. "Is that meant to compliment or insult me?"

"Neither." He chuckles behind a sob. "It's just the fucking truth."

"I know what I did."

"Do you? Do you really? Do you understand that you signed her death certificate when you sold her to that monster?"

"He's no more of a monster than I am," I try to convince the both of us.

"You're right," he concedes, his head bobbing lightly. "You're worse."

He pushes to his feet and my armor locks into place. I stand and square off with him as he steps toward me. I force a sneer, though I'm aching as much as he is.

I don't ache.

Nothing hurts me.

My father's voice echoes around me. *Ambivalent, pansy-ass, pretty boy.*

"You handed her over to him. Whatever happens to her now is your fault." His fists clench at his sides.

"Of course it is," I agree. "I own her, I choose what happens in her life."

"You don't own her anymore. He does!" Ezra shouts. He points a finger behind him through his outstretched hand, aiming toward where he left the phone, as if Vigo were standing there himself. "He chooses if she lives or dies now! He chooses if he hurts her, helps her, treats her like a fucking toy. And it's all because you weren't man enough to face the fact that she doesn't love you, doesn't want you. She knows how weak you really are. Beneath the orders and the threats, you're nothing, and she knew that."

I feel like a cornered wolf and that's how I behave. I bare my teeth at him, practically growling a warning at him before I attack. I rise from my chair and he stands as I swiftly move toward him. I slap both my palms against his chest and slam him hard against the wall behind him.

He flips his wrists between my arms, knocking my hands off, but I come right back, pressing my forearm against his neck. I shift my arm to jab my elbow into the hollow of his throat before he tries to throw me off again. I press in.

My face is an inch from his as I dig into the spot. "I'm not nothing. I am *everything.* Everything you wish you could be, everything she wishes she could come back to now. Maybe with Vigo, the bitch will understand how good she had it with me. I'm happy for her to live with the regret of her choices for the rest of her life."

"I don't even know how to respond to such bullshit. You're a bullshitting, motherfucking, son of a bitch, Nikolai. You're pathetic."

I tilt my head, pressing harder with my elbow. "What the fuck is wrong with you? You're a fucking slave. I can kill you and no one would care. Yet you still push and push and *fucking* push me."

Ezra's eyes narrow to slits and mine do the same as he snarls, "You took away the best thing that ever happened to me. I have nothing left to lose."

I'm rage filled.

Indignant.

My blood boils and hates and loathes.

And it pulses that shameful lust through my veins.

My mouth crashes on Ezra's before I even know what the hell I'm doing. I've taken him off guard and he stills, rigid in my hold as I press my lips to his. I kiss him long enough to inhale and exhale one trembling breath. Then I step back and whirl away from him, stalking across the room as he stands there in a stupor. I bend, pick up my phone from the floor, and type out a text on the newly cracked screen.

`NIKOLAI` Bring her to the next quarterly meeting. I'll bring the boy. Let them torture each other with their pathetic longing. They deserve it.

CHAPTER 14

Anya

I'VE BEEN ONE of Vigo's broken dolls for a total of three months now. I only know this because I'm on my way to the next quarterly meeting of the four families as Vigo's escort.

The Campbells' estate is nestled and hidden away safely in the Louisiana bayou, somewhere near New Orleans. Though I'm told it doesn't belong to the Campbells anymore. The American family is now headed by the Leblancs—still descendants of the founding Campbell family by blood, but no longer by name. They'd given power to the son of a Campbell sister whose name had changed to Leblanc by marriage.

There was a reason females weren't allowed to be the Head of House for their family, and it was because they might marry off and change their names. It would be an upheaval to the family name that held its reputation with the powerful elite—from buyers and sellers, politicians and law enforcement. Of course, any logical person might ask why the women simply choose not to change their names when they marry. The only answer that would be given was that it's because of tradition.

Thus, this change from Campbell to Leblanc strikes me as unexpected. It's unusual—an uncharacteristically dramatic change in leadership. I don't know the details of why it happened or what it means or if it means anything at all.

Honestly, I couldn't care less.

The only thing I care about right now is the fact that I'm clean, fed, out of that godforsaken box with the ability to move and walk and talk. As Vigo's escort, I'm at least given the grace of being cared for enough to look decent for the Leblancs' talent and reception. I'm only ever out of the box when Vigo wants to play with me. That *always* means being drugged.

I suppose I should be grateful that he gives each of his dolls time enough to recover between doses, though recovery only involves wallowing in fear trapped inside a clear, plastic box.

In three months' time, he's stripped all substance from within me, leaving me a broken, hollow shell of a woman who wishes daily for the release of death.

I'm not entirely sure why Vigo is bringing me with him to this quarterly meeting. Having been stripped of my talent, I'm no longer considered a talent slave. Talent slaves travel with their family to the meetings, but I suppose I didn't really know what to expect belonging to the Vittoris. They're the only family who keeps multiple slaves in their home for themselves. I think they enjoy creating their own rules.

It's taken nearly two days to travel from Palermo to New Orleans with the stop off in Lisbon for fuel on the Vittoris' private jet. And with so many people on board, Vigo has managed to keep his cock in his pants.

There's Renata and her slave Luca, their younger cousin Lorenzo, and one of the family's talent slaves, a pianist named Olivia. She's the blond girl I remember seeing with Vigo and Renata at Nikolai's talent reception three months ago. She looks healthier now than she did then. I guess she used to belong to Vigo until Lorenzo took a liking to her.

Vigo's mostly ignored me on the flight, constantly staring down at his phone. I'm glad for that because it keeps his interest off defiling me.

Much to Renata's dismay, we have to travel via airboat to get from the airstrip in Louisiana to the Leblancs' estate. It's hidden away and only accessible through the bayou.

Renata fusses with her long, black hair as the boat whirs forward, whipping it behind her. The boat scurries and splashes through the muddy water, and I take in the swampy air with gratitude. The brush of the wind over my cheeks feels divine. Renata has the privilege of snobbery, fussing over her tangled hair and ruined clothes. I hide a secret smile that the cream-colored Prada suit she was stupid enough to wear is spattered with mud.

She should've known better as she's been to the estate before. Why she would choose such impractical travel wear is beyond me. I didn't have a choice in my travel wear, but Vigo at least had the foresight for practicality, I suppose. He had given me the same skinny jeans and plain shirt I had worn the day he took me from Nikolai, though the jeans feel a little looser now.

We whip through the eerie bayou landscape where water has risen high, making the trees appear as though they were drowning. The dreamlike landscape—where we sail through a hazy, watery forest—almost feels magical, almost like freedom.

Almost.

The Leblancs' estate appears from the parting swamp fog like a haunted daydream. The home is tall, foundation high above the overflow of the water line. White columns run all the way across the square-shaped front profile of the estate. The spaces between the columns on the top floor are fenced with black lattice work, which match the black shutters around its many windows. The left and right sides of the home are set back a bit, framing the center square of the house, making it look proud and ostentatious.

There's a narrow, paved stone walkway leading from the dock where the airboat lets us off. It's another thing for Renata to fuss over when one of her stiletto heels gets caught between two uneven stones. She utters a string of Italian curse words, prompting a petty, almost normal looking argument between her and Vigo.

Vigo points at her feet when he speaks, shaking his head, presumably judging her choice of footwear. She yells back at him and eventually, he pockets his phone with a huff, going back to help her yank her shoe from between the pavers as she leans on Luca for support. I stand and wait for my masters to end their petty squabbling.

Renata, refusing to lose face again, removes both of her shoes and strides ahead of the group—fearlessly barefoot—toward the main entrance of the estate. It's a good fifty yards to walk to the entrance.

As we approach, we're greeted by an anxious looking man. He jogs down the front porch steps, watching his feet, pushing out a nervous breath from between rounded lips as he straightens the lapels of his navy-blue jacket.

His tousled, thick, blond hair reminds me of Ezra's. From a distance, I suffer a beat of hoping. But I quickly set aside any foolish ideas that Ezra might be here. Nikolai always brought me, not my partners, to the quarterly meetings with him. Though, I suppose Ezra must be his only slave now.

Unless he killed him, too.

I stop dead in my tracks at the thought, pressing a hand over my heart, pressing hard until I can feel the beat through my palm.

No one notices that I've halted, not right away, because we're slaves. We walk behind our masters.

The man from the house greets Renata first, holding out an outstretched hand, as she charges ahead. She doesn't take it. Instead, she leans in for him to kiss one cheek, then the other, in greeting.

"Vittoris," the blond man says. "Welcome!"

"Leo." Renata turns on her pleasant business persona. "How are you adjusting to becoming the new Head of House for the Leblancs?"

His brows lift and lower as he huffs out a breath and tilts his head. "About as well as you'd expect, I suppose. I didn't…Well, I didn't know much about the Campbells, er, their legacy, with the four families. The family trade. My mom never shared much and well, I understand now. So, here we are." He holds out his hands.

He looks far too young to be a Head of House.

He behaves far too anxiously to be a Head of House.

The others are Nikolai, Vigo, and Murphy O'Shea, each as ruthless, arrogant, and unambiguously sociopathic as the last. This man, Leo, is going to be eaten alive if he doesn't pull his shit together, and quick.

We're welcomed into the home and shown to our rooms. I'm to stay in a room with Vigo. The dark-gray space we're given feels as oppressive as it looks from the moment we cross the threshold. The four-post bed of the relatively small space is draped with off-white fabric. The hardwood floor beneath our feet creaks with each step, and the dark walls make it feel like a cave. There's a length of chain attached to an ankle cuff resting on the floor. The chain is secured to a metal loop that's been bolted down through the flooring next to the bed.

That chain is for me—to keep me locked up when my master attends the board meeting later.

Vigo asks me to shower and prepare for the talent and reception that will begin in just a few hours. I'm both surprised and thankful that he gives me some time alone in the connected bathroom.

I'm also thankful there's no bathtub here, only a walk-in shower. The thought of him drugging me and tossing me into the swamp water still crosses my mind, making my heart skip a beat. I can only hope the events of this quarterly meeting will keep him occupied enough to spare me his torment. At least until we have to return to the Vittori mansion in Italy.

I sigh, shaking out my long, damp hair. I have a make-up bag full of unfamiliar products and I've been directed to make myself look presentable, though I don't really know what that means to the Vittoris. I knew how to prep when I belonged to a Mikhailov, but everything feels foreign now.

I look over at the dress Vigo has given me to wear this evening for the talent and reception. A floor-length, golden silk gown hangs on the back of the bathroom door. It's a beautiful dress, and a part of me looks forward to putting it on, to play dress-up, to pretend life is as good as the dress looks.

Digging through the make-up bag, I find a palette of eye shadow and decide upon subtlety. I brush on soft brown and shimmery gold eye shadow. I add a bronzing blush over my foundation to highlight my cheeks, and I choose a deep burgundy lipstick.

As I finish up my make-up, Vigo opens the bathroom door without warning and it startles me. He barges in, though I stand nude in front of the sink.

He looks me up and down. "This is a good look for you."

I swipe on another unnecessary layer of lipstick as I ignore him. I look the worst I have ever looked. I've lost weight since I've been in his care, weight I didn't need to lose. My body feels week. I haven't truly danced in months and my muscles have lost their strength such that every movement requires a great deal of effort. I used to move with such ease and now, I'm just a fragile little doll.

Vigo smacks my ass as he moves toward the toilet and undoes his zipper, standing just behind me as he relieves himself. I take my dress from the hook on the door and carry it into the bedroom, just to get away from him.

I put it on and move to the standing, full-length mirror in the corner of the room to look at my reflection. I can't help but see myself as a sickly, thin shell of the girl I used to be. The dress should cling nicely to my curves, but it hangs off me in places it shouldn't. The spaghetti straps keep slipping from my shoulders and I know I'll be fussing with them all night. At least my face looks like my own, though I'm starting to see the lines where my cheeks will hollow out if I lose any more weight.

If I broke this mirror, could I slice my throat open with one of the shards of glass before Vigo stops me?

The thought bursts into my mind with force. My breath catches in my throat and tears fill up my eyes because now I'm thinking about it.

I'm really thinking about it.

If there's no hope for change, for freedom, I wonder how much longer I can survive in this life.

"Tell me what you think," Vigo asks with his hand on the small of my back.

He leads me around the Leblancs' estate ballroom that's been setup as an art exhibit. Four oversized windows line the long outside wall, letting the pink and red hues of the sunset filter the space in an eerie glow.

Two ornate crystalline chandeliers hang overhead, giving the room an austere mood. The golden hue of the light complements the golds and reds and tans in the floral-patterned carpet that spans the space.

At first glance, the event looks normal. A group of wealthy socialites gathering in a grand ballroom to view an artist's work.

The Leblancs' talent slave—a tall, slim brunette who looks utterly exhausted—stands near one of her many paintings decorating the walls of the ballroom.

Vigo slips his hand upward to grasp the ends of my hair and gives them a tug, awaiting my response.

"I think…I think these paintings are sad."

Vigo chuckles softly. "They are rather boring to look at, hmm? I would prefer to watch you dance over looking at these stupid paintings. Perhaps without your clothes on, around a pole. Maybe I'll have one put in your cage so you can practice for me."

"You disgust me," I tell him boldly, stupidly.

His hand slips down my backside, coming to rest over one cheek, as he bends to whisper in my ear, "Mind your manners with me or you'll regret it."

I swallow, backing down, because I believe him.

We move around the outer wall, observing the painting slave's works of art. The paintings are rather beautiful in a tragic sort of way. If I could paint my slavery and everything I've felt over the years, I imagine it would look similar.

Dark colors.

Abstract with menacing strokes.

A mixture of intention and improvisation—just the way Ezra and I had danced.

My intention mixed with his improvisation.

I would give my life just to see him again.

I might give it anyway.

I observe the social niceties and expectations Vigo has for me, keeping the essence of myself firmly inside my mind. I'm lost in my head, staring blankly at one of the paintings as Vigo speaks to someone behind me. They talk about business and other inane things as I drift.

But then a sudden spark, like static electricity, prickles across my skin. I think nothing of it at first, but then there's a gradual awareness, a tingle of response to a familiar aura. It forces me from the dark corner of my mind and drags me back to reality.

"Vigo." Nikolai's voice dances into my ears.

For the first time, I don't fear the sound, I welcome it.

My heart thuds as I whirl around. Nikolai's presence may be oddly welcome, but his isn't the aura that sparked awareness, the aura that crawls over my skin, begging to be noticed.

"Ezra." His name slips unintentionally from my lips.

Their eyes fall upon me for the way I speak out of turn. But I don't care, *can't* care, because Ezra is here and he's caught me in his sparkling green eyes, full of happiness, wonder, and worry all at once. It's as if the Earth has taken a breath at the unexpected sight of him and I feel the land shudder beneath my feet.

Three months.

Three months since I've seen his face.

Three months since I've heard his voice.

Three months since I've felt the rush that comes from being near him.

I had cursed myself for falling in love with him when Vigo became my master. I tried to write him off, tried to think of him as the man I loved for a season, never to be seen again. But all this time has passed, and I still want him, love him, *need* him.

We both step toward each other, moving together like a dying star and its lonely planet, eager to find our orbit together again. But Nikolai slams a hand against Ezra's chest, pushing him back, and Vigo snatches me by the wrist, pulling me swiftly against his side.

How can that spark still exist between us after all this time?

I need to touch him, hold him, kiss him.

My stomach aches for him. A hollow spot I didn't know existed opens wide and begs me to fill it with the love I can only feel in his arms.

"Where's your new girl?" Vigo asks Nikolai, nudging me in the side with his elbow. "Did you hear he's replaced you with another ballerina?"

My jaw sets as I jerk my stomach away from him.

"It's almost as if he had someone lined up to replace you before he even sold you, *schiava*. You're lucky I wanted you, don't you think?"

Vigo bends to kiss my cheek and I try to pull away. He grabs my chin and forces me to look up at him, planting a firm kiss on my lips. I want to spit on him, but I wouldn't dare. He slaps my cheek for my struggle nonetheless, and I wish I *had* spit on him.

Nikolai's arm whips out to slam against Ezra's chest once more, holding him back when he lurches forward. Then he continues the conversation coolly, as if no movement had occurred.

"Sasha is in our room with Kostya," Nikolai replies with civility, though his eyes narrow on Vigo. "She's not quite ready to make an appearance yet."

"Ah, you've found a fighter then?"

"Quite the opposite, actually. She bores me." I can feel Nikolai's eyes on me.

Mine are on Ezra.

"So strange seeing you at a reception without Anya at your side." Vigo baits Nikolai's anger, putting his arm around my waist and tugging me closer into his side. "She's been your faithful companion for years."

Vigo steals my attention, his hand sliding up the side of my waist. He stretches his long fingers across my breast. I still myself in his hold, knowing better than to fight.

Ezra is ready to pounce and part of me wishes he would. He could start a fight and get us both killed, but then at least our shared torment would be over for good.

What's wrong with me?

Nikolai's lips purse into a straight line. "And now she'll be your companion."

Vigo laughs and it's menacing in its coolness. "I doubt that. She's neither faithful nor a companion to me. And my girls don't survive years. You know that, Nikolai." Vigo claps him on the shoulder.

Nikolai shrugs him off. "They might survive years if you took better care of them."

Vigo tilts his head. "Are you so concerned now with Anya's survival? You were rather flippant about her well-being when you sold her to me."

"The contract you signed with me is anything but flippant. Perhaps you need to review the well-being clause you agreed to."

Vigo shrugs and I stare up at him, wondering what the hell Nikolai could be talking about.

Well-being?

Since when has my well-being been of anyone's concern?

I suppose I can't deny that Nikolai did provide far more toward my care than Vigo has ever attempted to do. That didn't mean he cared about my life now. Nikolai was the one who sold me to such a neglectful and despicable master as Vigo. In many ways, that makes him worse—Nikolai chose this for me.

My eyes turn to him, shooting icy cold daggers straight from my soul.

"I urge you to consider the importance of being a man of your word, Vigo. You know how the board will lean on such matters. Lovely catching up with you." Nikolai smiles as charming as the devil himself, then he nods to me, *acknowledges* me. "Anya."

I suck in a sharp breath at the way his eyes cast an appraising glance over my body. He's glanced a million times before, but this glance is filled with disappointment, anguish, perhaps even…regret? He snaps for Ezra to follow as he turns to walk away.

There's a moment, only a brief, tragic moment, where Ezra meets my eyes before he's forced to move. In that moment, we speak silently, hurriedly through looks and electric sparks which only exist between the two of us.

I love you.

I miss you.

I need you.

I'm going to save you.

The last message is from his eyes to mine and it meets me with such ferocity and truth that it almost feels as though he can save me.

I can't control myself and I speak without thinking. "Mine?"

Ezra rushes toward me. It's stupid for me not to, but I can't seem to fight the pull. I drag myself from Vigo's grip as Ezra's hand latches around my wrist, tugging me into the warmth of his embrace.

We wrap our arms around each other for no more than a moment, but it's the most fulfilling moment of my life.

"Yours. Always yours," he whispers just before Vigo and Nikolai rip us apart.

Ezra turns with Nikolai's rough hands on his shoulders, guiding him away. Looking back at me, he grants me a small smile. That small smile lights me on fire. I have to fight every part of my body to remain in place rather than run after him again. We've already tested our luck and it failed us.

When Vigo commands me away, I'm forced to tear my attention from Ezra. It's painful, forceful, like being ripped from orbit. I feel colder with each step he takes, only just realizing how cold I have been for the past three months without him.

Ezra has always been my sunshine. My life may cease to exist without his warmth. It *doesn't* exist without his warmth. I've been brutally reminded of everything I need, and its everything I can never have.

The hollow spot inside me will never be filled.

Another hour or so passes as we wander listlessly about the space. I tail behind Vigo as he engages in small talk with other members of the four families. My eyes are vigilant, constantly searching the room for Ezra, but I don't see him or Nikolai again in the ballroom.

Vigo doesn't seem to care when I lag behind a few paces, giving myself a small reprieve from the overwhelming pulse of his evil aura. Perhaps he does care, perhaps he intends to punish me later for trailing behind, though I can't bring myself to care.

What worse could he possibly do to me?

Give me death?

A reprieve from the pain of existence?

I'm within his periphery. It's not as though I could escape the home unnoticed. Even so, I know from years of experience that the exits are closely guarded for that very reason. Still, it doesn't stop me from contemplating an escape plan.

I could sneak up to the second floor.

Hurl myself over the balcony's edge.

It's a morbid thought, but it comes naturally.

It's a stupid thought, though. I'd probably survive the fall, only to injure myself further and suffer more in Vigo's captivity.

But there are other ways to do it…other ways to end it.

Oh, God.

Ezra can't save me.

No one can.

I want to spare us both further misery.

Fighting for my survival is only prolonging our pain.

I don't know if I can keep fighting.

I'm exhausted, hollow, and just fucking tired of this captive existence.

I want to be done.

I want to end it all.

CHAPTER 15
Anya

I RESENTFULLY PUT a hand on Vigo's shoulder for balance as he bends before me, latching the metal cuff around my ankle and locking the padlock that secures it to my leg. The standing mirror shows our reflection and I see how empty my soul is through my eyes. They used to be a vibrant shade of sapphire and now they are a cool, gray-blue, open wide and vacant.

Did they look that way before I saw Ezra tonight?

Vigo stands, turning to face the mirror and blocking my reflection as he combs his fingers through his wavy hair. Then, he straightens his jacket.

I can't help but to think that mirror would shatter nicely into sharp edges.

"I'll return in a couple of hours. Just keep quiet and don't do anything stupid, hmm?"

Vigo turns to me, slipping an arm around my waist and drawing me close. I turn my head away so I don't have to look at him, but he grabs my chin and forces me to regardless.

"Do not worry, little doll. *Papà* will return to take care of you." His hand slips down over my ass and squeezes. "I might even be generous tonight and let you come on my cock if you behave yourself."

I'm tempted to laugh.

To think that the pleasure of coming on Vigo Vittori's cock should be incentive enough to change my mind about killing myself is absurd.

Kill myself?

Have I decided to kill myself?

I swallow the retort that threatens. I don't really have it in me anymore to spare the energy and I'm just ready to be done.

But am I really ready?

He's disappointed in my lack of response, though he doesn't let on. He enjoys knowing he's tormented me into responding out of anger or fear or frustration, and I've learned that denying him that gratification makes *me* feel better on some level.

He shoves me backward and I stumble, landing roughly on the bed behind me. He gives me a look, almost as if he knows what I've been thinking about, but thankfully, he leaves without another word.

I rise to sit on the edge of the bed where he's left me. I feel a certain sense of satisfaction in that final look he's given me. It was a look of confusion, frustration, morbid curiosity.

He knew death was on my mind.

I breathe deeply and weigh my survival on a scale of truth.

Am I so certain that no one can save me? Yes.

Will ending my life take the pain away? Yes.

How horribly will Ezra mourn my loss when he hears about it? Terribly, but then he can focus on saving himself.

Tears well at the thought of what this will do to him, but I know he'll be better off when I'm no longer a concern. Though the thought of leaving him permanently feels like a dagger to my gut, I know I want this.

I want death.

I want this horror story to end.

The affirmation in my mind brings me a strange sort of calm—the peace of knowing that I've made a decision, right or wrong.

Break the mirror.

Cut your wrists.

Be done before he returns.

If I act now, it can all be over soon. I would no longer feel the pain of loving and losing the only person who made me feel truly alive. Seeing him tonight only reminded me of how dead I already am on the inside—I died three months ago when we were ripped apart.

There is no rescue, no salvation for us. Only crippling heartache and tormenting longing.

My hands grip the bed at my sides as I look into the mirror. My breaths quicken as I envision my macabre plan. In my mind, I can see the glass shattering, breaking into a thousand pieces and spilling to the floor. I envision picking up a piece of my own broken reflection and sliding it across my wrists.

A shiver crawls up my spine and I close my eyes. Immediately I feel like

I'm underwater again, looking up at Vigo through waves and ripples as my temporarily paralyzed body slumps deeper beneath the surface.

I gasp as my eyes snap open.

I can't go through that, not again.

Never again.

I bend and take off my shoes. I leave one where it rests on the floor and pick up the other as I stand. I move in front of the mirror and stare at my reflection.

Am I the same girl I was with Nikolai?

Am I the same girl Ezra fell in love with?

Somewhere inside I think I'm that same girl, but my strength has been stripped from me in Vigo's ownership. I know I would've died a long time ago had I been with Vigo from the beginning…If it had been Vigo who had served as my benefactor since the age of eleven…If Vigo had been the one to steal me away over three years ago.

It was all a cruel joke of fate. It was by chance that Nikolai found me in that dance studio when I was a child. It was by chance that he picked me. It could have been anyone else, but fate had chosen me, and it had been breaking me into smaller and smaller pieces ever since. Ezra had managed to put some of them back together for a while, but seeing him tonight just reminded me of how impossible a task that is. It broke me all over again.

I'm not the same girl I used to be. The girl I am now is so desperate for freedom that she's willing to do whatever it takes to get it the only way she knows how.

I hammer hard against the mirror with the stiletto point of my shoe. It cracks, splintering across the reflective glass. Though no pieces have fallen to the floor yet, it effectively shatters my reflection.

I don't even want to see my reflection anymore.

I slam my shoe again, hitting the same spot I hit before, and a few small pieces above it fall to the floor. I hit again, farther down the mirror, and the entire top half falls with a whoosh to the floor. I jump back as the sharp edges pool on the floor beside my feet.

I lower to my knees slowly, eyes searching the remnants for a suitable sliver. Light reflects off a triangular piece on the floor and I reach for it. I'm careful, shaking off the tiny, dusty shambles that rained down over it like glass snowfall.

I shake my head and laugh to myself.

Why should I be careful given my intentions?

My hands are trembling because of my intentions.

Because I can't believe I'm intent on doing this.

Can I really do this?

Just do it.

Get it over with.

I tap the sharp tip of the glass piece on the side of my left wrist. Without even pressing, I can feel the sharpness of the triangular shard. This is going to hurt—I wonder if I'll be able to push through the pain to cut deep enough. My heart races.

I push down on the spot, just a little, just to test.

A little more.

A little deeper.

My face scrunches in pain as I drag it, slicing hardly a hair's width into my skin. A large drop of blood pools and falls, followed by a trickle that lasts for only a few seconds. I haven't done any damage.

I exhale, pushing out the breath I'd been holding, and out with it, tears begin to flow. I don't think I can push through the pain of this enough to sever the veins, to let blood flow free from my body until there's none left for my heart to pump to my organs.

The *pulse, pulse, pulsing* spurts of blood from the neck of the woman who lived in my box before me suddenly flood my memory. She'd sliced her throat, fast and easy, and was dead in no time at all. Her blood had spurted from her body with each final beat of her heart.

Perhaps that would be easier...

I lift the sharp tip and place it against the side of my neck.

I press in, drag a microscopic amount, and feel the small line of blood trickle down the side of my neck.

With the blood comes the tears.

Tears for everything I've been through.

Tears for the life I'll never have.

Tears for the pain of what I'm about to do.

Tears for the love I've lost forever.

Ezra.

Those emerald green eyes of his flash across my mind, just like they had the last time I'd almost died, when Nikolai held a gun to my head. Just like they had when Nikolai drowned me in the pool.

Here they are again. Emerald gems that sparkle and mesmerize and give me an inexplicable sense of peace, calm, tranquility. It strengthens my resolve to end my suffering now. At least I can chase those green eyes into the bliss of unconsciousness.

I pull the make-shift blade just a little farther, testing the pressure and depth and more blood trickles down my neck. But I know this is only surface bleeding. I need to press in harder—a quick draw across my throat and I'll meet my end.

Do it.

Don't do it.

Just do it.

You shouldn't…

Just do it now!

I dig the tip into my skin.

The door crashes against the wall as it's flung open wide.

I turn my head to look, pulling an unintentional, shallow stripe across my neck with the blade, hardly nicking the surface as Vigo bursts into the room.

"Did you think no one heard you break the fucking mirror?" He points his finger at the wall right beside the mirror. "Renata's on the other side of that wall, you stupid girl."

He marches across the room and hovers over me before I can decide how to react. It's not instinct to kill oneself, so I don't have the impulse to quickly slice my throat open before he reaches me—though I wish I had. Instead, I waver, frozen, waiting stupidly until he decides for me. He bends and frees me from the ankle cuff. He snatches my wrist, twisting and yanking me upright, forcing me to drop the shard as he pulls me to my feet.

"You really should have been quicker about it, baby doll. Now you've given me something to look forward to."

My mind is so muddled, confused by the swift change of events. "What?"

"Your punishment."

Fuck, fuck, fuck.

He's right.

I should've been faster.

I shouldn't have hesitated.

I should've been braver, stronger, more determined in choosing my fate. Because now another fate was going to be chosen for me.

I plant my bare feet as he yanks back on my arms. He manages to drag me out into the hallway. "Just let me *die*, Vigo. Let me do it, let me go!"

His grip slips from my wrist, the blood he's smeared around creating a thin, slippery coating. Free from his grasp, I spin, ready to run back into the room, grab that piece of glass, and finish what I started before he can catch me, but when I turn, I slam hard into a solid brick wall of a man who catches me with both hands on my waist.

Nikolai.

Nikolai?

I look up to meet his cold, gray eyes and they regard me with curiosity, concern, and the same familiar hunger that was always there from the beginning.

His eyes lower, surely observing the blood that's now dripping down my chest, staining the top of the fabric of my gown.

His voice is eerily quiet when he speaks. "What did you do, *rabynya?*

CHAPTER 16
Ezra

MY BLUE-EYED GIRL is fractured, splintered right down the middle from the untold horrors of her servitude to Vigo.

I don't see her at first, but I hear her voice. I hear her yell, "Just let me *die*, Vigo!" and the words rebound painfully around my skull.

Our timing is somehow perfect to run into them and witness this moment. Nikolai was bringing me back to the room to shackle me in for the night before heading off to the boardroom. I was coming down the hall behind him when Vigo tore from his room just in front of us, dragging out a girl in a flash of gold.

The flash of gold was Anya in the gown she'd worn at the reception.

"Just let me die, Vigo!"

My adrenaline spiked, muscles twitching, everything within my veins pounding with the message to grab her, run with her, *save* her.

But I've learned that my adrenaline doesn't have the privilege of conscious thought. It doesn't understand that I can grab her, I can run with her, but I don't have a way to *save* her.

Not yet.

My heart hurts to see the state of her as she crashes into Nikolai. She looks thin, frail, exhausted, but more horrifyingly, she looks determined… determined as she tries to run back into the room after begging for death.

It punches into my gut when my mind clears enough to see the red. The disturbing crimson smears on her left wrist and hand. More smears across her chest as it drips from a short line on her neck.

"What the fuck…" My voice is quiet at first until I make sense of what's happening, of what she tried to do. "What the fuck, Anya?!"

I don't care about my place in this fucked up world. I storm past Nikolai and reach for Anya's bloody wrist, taking it in my hand. Her eyes fall to where I hold her for a beat, then lift to meet mine with a look of resignation mixed with shame. The look shows me a fissure in her existence that threatens to split her soul apart. It has me ready to set off a fucking bomb in this place.

But then she's pulled from my grip as I'm pulled from her. Vigo takes me by the shoulders and spins me before slamming me face-first into the wall.

"Don't touch my slave," he sneers before releasing me.

I spin to face him, but before I can punch the look off his entitled face, Anya's sobs draw me away.

"Let me go," she cries, fighting against Nikolai's hold. "Let me go, let me go, let me *go!*"

"Why would I let you go, *rabynya*? So you can attempt the coward's way out again? Try to kill yourself?" Nikolai pulls his hand back and slaps her. "How *dare* you do something so goddamn selfish."

Nikolai's shoulders shake, his expression an unusual mixture of rage and fear as Anya crumbles before my eyes, devolving into sobs of heartache so deafening that it brings me to my knees.

Vigo grabs Anya away from Nikolai. "She needs to be punished for this. I'm taking her to the board. She's been with the four families far too long to allow this sort of behavior, and I will *not* give her the satisfaction of death. She hasn't earned it because I haven't finished with her yet."

Anya chuckles darkly. "He hasn't finished with me yet, Nikolai. I haven't *earned* death." Her joyless laugh twists her features into a grim scowl.

Nikolai's brow furrows, his eyes narrowing in concentration as he looks at Anya. She's sinking away from Vigo, her body limp and exhausted in her sobbing, like a wilted rose trying to sink back into the Earth from which it sprouted.

Nikolai's eyes flicker, his brow line straightens out, and he looks at me pointedly, though he speaks to Vigo.

"Good. I'll bring the boy, then, too. Lock them together. I guarantee he won't allow her to attempt this again while her punishment is being decided."

Only a man as fucking arrogant as Nikolai Mikhailov would put his slaves alone together, knowing that one would prevent the other from committing suicide.

He wasn't wrong.

Anya cries, "Please, please punish me, but don't hurt him anymore. Don't hurt him. Don't hurt Ezra."

That hurts me.

I hurt so badly because of her, *for* her.

I feel everything she's feeling as if I were feeling it myself, and it's the most fucking painful thing I've ever known.

Vigo's already dragging her away down the hallway. I follow as Nikolai stalks after them. We head back downstairs to the ground level and pass the empty ballroom on our right.

Just past the ballroom, we turn right down a hallway, but it dead ends about five strides ahead. At the end, there's a pair of wooden, double doors propped open—the entrance to the boardroom.

This alcove in front of the doors is brown and bleak and formal. Leo Leblanc appears from behind the doors, sensing the presence of some of his guests.

"Come on in," he says to Nikolai and Vigo, but tilts his head looking at me and Anya. "I'm sorry, was there something wrong with their shackles, or…"

The poor guy wracks his brain trying to figure out why Nikolai and Vigo brought their slaves along with them.

"No," Nikolai says. "We have a matter of punishment to arrange for a slave. Is there a room nearby we can lock them in until the meeting is over? She cannot be left alone."

Leo looks Anya up and down, seeing her bloodied, sobbing form and seems to have trouble sorting out what's going on. I just want to get to her so I can hold her but these giant pieces of shit stand in my way.

"She tried to commit suicide," Nikolai clarifies impatiently.

"Oh. *Oh.* Yes. Actually…" Leo brushes past and gestures for the group to follow where he leads.

Vigo grabs Anya by the elbow, dragging her along beside him roughly, and I seethe as I follow behind Nikolai. Turning right from the alcove, we walk in the opposite direction of the ballroom. We turn left into a room two doors down.

It looks like a home office space, though it's rather small considering the size of the estate.

Leo crosses the room, dodging furniture in close quarters, and moves behind the wooden desk that rests in the center. He bends to reach beneath it and the bookcase beside us suddenly swings open—a hidden door.

"We can put them down there. No need for supervision."

"Show us." Nikolai waves a hand, waiting for Leo to lead the way.

Leo gives a quick nod then rushes around toward us. He pulls the hidden door open wide, crosses the threshold, and we follow.

We're cloaked in darkness just a few steps past the hidden entrance. When we come upon light again, it's from a lantern-style fixture on the wall, lighting a path down a cement spiral staircase.

It's like we've stepped back in time and entered a medieval fucking torture chamber. Coming off the staircase is literally like walking into a dungeon. It's a wide square room with concrete walls and floors all around us.

Leo moves across the room and bends, picking up two large metal cuffs, much larger than the ankle cuffs in the bedrooms.

"These go around the neck safely," Leo explains. "Will that do?"

Vigo puts his hand between Anya's shoulder blades and shoves her forward, stepping after her as she stumbles. "Yes."

"Don't fucking put that on her," I practically growl.

Nikolai pushes me forward after her. "Shut up."

Anya is quiet and still, her tears and her blood slowing to a trickle as Leo positions the metal cuff. He closes it around her neck and secures it with a padlock in the front. A long, heavy chain dangles from the back, attached to a hook in the floor. It's at least as long as she is tall.

Her hands come up to touch the metal collar, her fingers gripping around it, trying to slip in from the top and bottom—it looks like there's at least some give and she won't be strangled by it.

That grants me one small reason for relief, but it's short lived to see how far she's fallen into resignation. She doesn't fight or complain. She just backs up against the wall and slumps, slowly sliding down the wall until she sits on the floor.

She's given up and it fucking kills me.

I won't fucking let her go through this alone.

I don't fight, I don't stall, I don't argue.

I step forward, take the cuff from Leo, and put it around my own damn neck. I let him secure it with the padlock and immediately lower to sit beside my blue-eyed girl.

Fuck everyone.

"In a few hours, after we've taken care of business and decided collectively upon the appropriate measure, we will return to deliver Anya's punishment."

I wave my hand dismissively toward the staircase. "Fine. Fuck. *Go.*"

Vigo turns and stalks up the staircase without another beat. But Nikolai hesitates, looking at the both of us. My hand is twitching, aching to cross the two inches of space between us to touch her, hold her, hug her, kiss her.

But I won't until they're gone.

I won't put her at risk like that.

Nikolai's eyes narrow, flicking back and forth between us. There's a contemplative look there that I don't think he knows he's sharing, but I see it.

He's lost in the stare for a few moments before he finally shakes off the look. He turns away slowly and heads back up the spiral staircase. Leo finally follows after. I wait until I hear the hidden door at the top of the staircase click shut, and when I hear it, the lights lower to a faded dimness. They remain on, just faint, and Anya looks like a shadow beside me.

I reach my hand out to touch her, but she beats me to it. She falls sideways, leaning heavily against my shoulder. I feel heavier and lighter all at once. The air rushes out of my lungs as I angle toward her, wrapping my arms around her and pulling her close.

Even when everything in the world is wrong, it's all made right when she's in my arms.

She cries, her face falling to my chest as her skinny arms sneak around my waist. "I'm sorry," she says. "I'm sorry. I can't do it anymore. I can't live like this. I just want it all to end."

I'm stalled on the tracks and her words are a freight train barreling into me. I don't know what to say to her to make it better, so I just tell her the truth.

"My life means nothing without you in it, Anya. If your life ends, my life ends."

She stills.

She raises her head slowly and I can see the blue of her eyes in the dim light. The shade is dull in this lighting, but it's my blue-eyed girl all the same. Everything that makes her Anya is still right there behind the cloak of color. Seeing her again, after all this time, reminds me how hard I fell for her.

I told her once that my heart beats for her, but I didn't understand the absolute truth in that until this moment. I feel like I've just been resurrected in her arms.

Her fragile, malnourished, too thin for her arms.

"I'm yours," I tell her, picking up her tiny arm to inspect the bloody cut she made on her wrist—it's small and seems to have stopped bleeding. I let go and lift both of my hands to hold her cheeks, to brush the tears from them with my thumbs. "Always yours."

Her eyes flicker as they search mine, the familiar flicker they've always had whenever she's looked at me seeking honesty, rawness, and truth. Truth is exactly what I'll give her.

"If you die, I die," I tell her.

Her head tilts, falling heavy into my palm and her expression softens.

"Ezra, I…I wanted to hate you," she says, and I wait for her to continue, though her silence stretches through several beats. "I wanted to hate you for making me fall for you, for disrupting the predictability of my captivity with Nikolai, for making me fall so hard and so deep that I risked everything to be with you, just for that one night in my bed. But I don't hate you. I could never hate you. My life without you is meaningless pain. And that's all it's been since he sold me." Her voice cracks as fresh tears spill.

I press my forehead to hers. "But…wasn't that one night with me worth everything? I'm really good in bed."

The sound she makes is magic. It's a sob, but there's a laugh behind it that forces her to smile and fuck, I can't help but grin at her. I lick my lips before tilting my chin forward, pressing my lips softly against hers.

I don't know why it surprises me that she kisses me back, that she parts her lips and invites me to kiss her deeper, but it does. It surprises and calms me, and it excites me and scares me.

Anya makes me feel everything more intensely than anyone else ever could.

She tried to kill herself.

My breaths quicken with the deepening kiss, the intimacy with the woman I love who has been gone from my life for months.

She tried to kill herself.

My heartbeat races with the passion I feel for her and the passion beats out a pulse of wanting, but even more so, of anger.

I'm angry.

I'm angry with *her*.

She tried to kill herself.

I pull my head back, though my grip remains firm on her cheeks.

"Why the fuck did you do this, Anya? Did you really try to kill yourself? Why? Why would you do that to me?"

I press my lips to hers again, unable to dampen this fiery mixture of love and rage that's starting to boil in my blood.

"I'm sorry," she says between heated kisses. "I just need it to end, I need it to be over."

"Over? No. No, it's not over. Not like that. I promised you, didn't I?" I kiss the corner of her lips. "I promised you that if there was a way for us to escape this nightmare, I'd find it."

Her eyes narrow and she yanks backward, dragging herself free of my grip. "There's nothing for you to find. There never was. The only escape is death."

I throw my head back against the wall, digging my fingers into my hair from the roots. "Fuck. That's not…it's not—" I stumble over my words. "Death isn't the only escape. I have faith in that. And I need you to have faith in me. Don't you have faith in me?"

She turns toward me, moving to sit on her knees. She reaches out to brush her thumb along my jawline.

"I have faith in you, Ezra. All the faith in the world. But I can't have faith in you finding a way out when I know there isn't one." She sighs, her head falling to the side as she watches my expression shift. "I can't believe how much I…"

"What?"

"How much I need you. All my reasons made so much sense to me when I cut myself. But now, alone with you…the only thing that I *know* is how much I need you."

Everything in me softens.

I reach for her and she reaches for me. She climbs onto my lap, hiking her dress up toward her hips to straddle me. Both her hands grip my cheeks and she bends to kiss me with a fierceness I couldn't have expected in her current state. But I meet her with fierceness of my own, a heated passion for her that's been bottled up deep inside for far too long.

Her tongue seeks mine out, battling to taste me as if she's been starved and is finally being fed. If I thought her fragile body could take it, if these stupid chains weren't so goddamn heavy on our necks, I would flip her, slam her to the floor, and bury myself deep inside her until someone forcefully dragged me away.

I need to be inside her—as shitty as it is to admit in this hell—and I would feel bad for feeling that way if I didn't know how much she needs it, too. Every part of her body hums for it, a tingling, pulsing aura that flows from her and electrifies me with every brush of skin on skin.

She and I are meant to touch.

Our souls demand it.

Our hearts beat for it.

Maybe it's arrogant or cocky even to think it, but I know that our separation did this to her—more than Vigo's torment, whatever it is he did to her, because our separation was worse. And seeing each other before, in the ballroom, knowing we would only be torn apart again…that's what broke her.

My heart can't handle that.

I need to mend her, put her back together, make her whole again.

Her lips break from mine only to land on my face where she presses fevered kisses on every inch of exposed skin.

"Mine?" she whispers, her voice suddenly heavy, powerful with desire and need.

"Yours," I reply, sliding my hands across her back.

I hold her close as I sit up straighter, scooting my ass all the way back against the wall. Her arched back presses her body against mine as I move my hands to run up her thighs, slipping beneath the bunched fabric and reaching for her hips. My fingers skim across skin, nothing but skin, even where the fabric of her panties should be.

If this were the real world, I'd think it was hot, but it's not the real world.

This is all real.

It's just not the real you want to know.

"He doesn't let you wear—"

"Shut up," she snaps, leaning back to look at me. "Don't finish that sentence. Don't say another word about him."

She snatches my wrists in both her small hands and yanks them away from her body. I think she's going to scold me, yell at me, move away and stop touching me.

Instead, she grips my wrists tighter, pushes my hands to the wall on either side of my head, and bends to kiss me, holding me in place.

Fuck.

I won't say another fucking word.

She leans into my hands, letting the wall support her weight. Our kiss becomes a frantic, heated devouring of each other, and I'm losing my mind with how much I need her, every part of her.

Her hands slowly loosen their grip on my wrists. Her palms slip over my palms and our fingers lace together. Her hips move as she inhales deep through her nose and our lips break. She drops her forehead to mine.

"What's wrong with me? How is it that hardly ten minutes ago I wanted to die, and now all I can think about is making love to you?"

I lick my lips. "The same thing that's wrong with me. We fell in love."

Her body rolls, rocking forward and back with all the grace of a dancer. "You're the only thing that makes me feel alive. I want you."

"So have me, Anya. I promise you, whatever you want from me, I want it from you, too."

Anya bites her lip for an adorable microsecond before letting go of my hands. She reaches between us and works at my buckle. Sitting back on my thighs, she unbuttons, unzips, undoes me completely so she can have what's hers.

God, she makes me hard.

In literal hell, she has the power to turn me on.

She lets out a shaky breath as she fists my shaft and shifts her body. The tip has barely brushed across her warmth and wetness before she sinks down, taking me inside her completely. We groan in unison, both feeling the same relief of being two broken pieces that have just been put back together.

I don't give a shit whether she moves or stays still, just the feeling of being inside her is like being home. Nevertheless, it feels fucking amazing when she moves, grinding slowly. She gives me her eyes instead of her lips and somehow, that feels even more amazing.

The brightness of her blue irises is returning. The fight in her is coming back with her desire, with our connection.

Our connection is everything.

Without it, we're nothing.

"I'm better when I'm with you," she says.

"We're better together." I kiss the corner of her lips.

She reaches for my hands again, our fingers braiding together and holding tight. I bring her knuckles to my lips and kiss each finger with sensual softness, earning gentle puffs of breath from her lips as she gives me her soul-deep gaze.

She rolls her hips slowly, an erotic dance that only she could ever perform for me so spectacularly, and it feels so fucking good. She's building me up, so excruciatingly hard, making me desperate, making me want to take and take from her until she's given me every piece of her soul.

I'll keep the pieces within my own soul, protect them, keep them safe.

Her eyes flutter as she fucks, her thick eyelashes fanning over the blue and making her look otherworldly, like a fairy or a forest nymph or a goddamn mermaid.

Fuck.

I don't even know how to describe it.

She's just fucking magical to watch, especially as my name falls from between her plump, burgundy lips.

I drop her hands and grab her face, holding her steady while I kiss her with force. My mouth presses hard to hers, forcing her to open for me, to let me in for a taste. Her hands cover mine as she obliges, giving me her tongue to suck on. She whimpers and her body sinks, conceding to the pleasure I know is coiling in her belly.

I sit up taller, forcing her to lean back while she fucks me. She puts one hand behind her, gripping my thigh just above my knee for support as I kiss her roughly.

If I thought she could take the pressure of a man laying on top of her, if I thought she could mentally handle giving me the control and letting me climb over her, I'd throw her down, fuck her roughly, make her feel so wet and so good that she'd never let me stop.

But she's been hurt too many times and letting her ride me feels just as damn good.

She moans into my mouth and her ass swirls as she changes her angle. Our kiss breaks as she digs her hand down hard, almost painfully on my knee, and she's fucking me in short, quick strokes. Her eyes lock on mine and I'm letting go. That vibrancy is turning up like a dial with every second that passes, her brightness rising and radiating light into the room.

Nothing could be more intimate, more sexy, more ethereal and beautiful as the expression on her face as she uses me for her pleasure.

And thank *God* for the sounds she makes. The same puffed out little "*oh*" sounds I remember from the times before when she came with me.

Not ever when she came for Nikolai.

Only when she came for *me*.

It felt like a goddamn privilege that only I knew what her true pleasure looked like, sounded like, felt like.

It feels so fucking good.

Just like before, the "*oh*" sounds lengthen, lose the harshness in their tone, become more like rushed breaths that have to come out each time she exhales. When she's jerking more than rocking, I feel her pulsing pussy drag my orgasm out of me. She's pulsing and squeezing around me until she lets out one last, long, purely satisfied "*oh*."

I lower my hands from her jawline to her waist. I grip her hard, holding her in place. I bend my knees, plant my feet, lift my hips from the floor, and fuck and fuck and fuck until I explode inside her. I come long, slow, with a final groan as her spasming muscles clench tight around me.

We don't move.

We just breathe and exist together.

The bubble of serenity we were granted the privilege of hiding inside while we made love to each other gradually fades away.

In its place returns the cold concrete beneath my ass, the damp and musty smell of a basement in a house in the bayou, the noisy clank of our chains as we shift into more comfortable positions.

Anya's inner thighs are slippery and soaking wet from the both of us. I don't want her to wear the evidence of our indiscretion, so I pull out my stupid blue pocket square and reach between us as my cock slips out from its place in heaven. I press it against her to soak up the liquid that's dripping from her and it feels almost more intimate to take care of her this way than it did to fuck her.

She sucks on her bottom lip for a beat, watching me as I wipe away the wet evidence of our fucking.

"I love you, Ezra," she says.

I breathe in the words as she climbs off me slowly, adjusting her dress and sitting beside me again. I put my cock away and I shove the pocket square down into my pants pocket as deep as it will go.

"If you love me, then promise you won't try to leave me again. You're strong enough to survive this. You owe yourself that chance."

I turn to look at her as she slips her hand in mine and I lock our fingers together. I look deep into her eyes and see her there; I see her strength coming back, her survival instinct reviving and renewing itself.

I don't kid myself to believe that the thought of ending all of this with her death won't come across her mind again. I know it will. It will be present until I get her the fuck out of here, until I save her. I just need her to keep her strength long enough for me to figure a way out of all this.

"I don't think I can promise you that," she says so bluntly that it twists in my gut.

"Fine. You don't have to promise me that. As long as you promise me that you'll give me enough time to try, that you'll stay alive long enough to give me a chance to save you."

She sighs. "Ezra, I can't—"

"You *can*," I tell her, "and you will. I know you will. Even if you don't think you can right now. Just…tell me you'll give me time, Anya. Please."

She closes her eyes before her head falls to my shoulder. "I'll give you as much time as I can."

I don't feel great about the way she says it, but it's agreement so I'll take it. In truth, I don't know how much time she has. I don't know how long it will take for Vigo to grow bored with her or lose his temper and kill her or sell her to someone else. I don't know how long she can continue to survive the kind of torture he inflicts upon her.

I lean over to kiss the top of her head. "I don't blame you for wanting to end it all. Really, I don't. But you went and made me fall in love with you, so

I feel like you kind of owe me."

There's humor in my tone and I know she hears it. I can feel the joy from her smile even if I can't see it all that well.

"If I owe you, then you owe me, too."

"Hell yes, I owe you. I owe you too much to ever pay back."

She looks up at me, her tone turning serious again. "Debt forgiven. I don't think either of us stood a chance." She smiles softly, but sadly. "We were doomed from the start."

I hesitate before I ask, "Do you regret it?"

Her eyes brighten, shining a light in the dark space. "No. I don't regret anything."

I have a fight ahead of me.

I don't know how I'll do it, but one way or another, I'm gonna save my girl before she loses herself again.

CHAPTER 17
NIKOLAI

"ANYA'S BEEN QUITE the little rebel in recent months, hasn't she?" Renata notes unnecessarily. "First letting Nikolai's boy into her bed and now this. Perhaps she should be sold outside of the families to a client."

"Selling her would only be offloading the problem to a customer," Cordelia O'Shea says. "I would never sell a rebellious commodity to one of our loyals—unless they requested it, of course, which in my experience, is rare. It might be best to decommission her and be done with it. Or let her do it herself if she's so desperate for death."

My head snaps toward Delia sitting on my left. "No. Her transgression doesn't warrant decommissioning."

"Agreed," Vigo adds. "Why should we give her exactly what she wants? Regardless, I'm not done with her yet."

"Then what do you propose?" Renata asks.

Vigo straightens in his seat, spreading a sadistic grin across his face. He opens his mouth to speak, but I don't give him a chance.

"Give her to me tonight," I say.

"Are you serious?" Renata chuckles.

"Yes. She needs to be put in her place. Clearly, Vigo has pushed her too far." I give him an admonishing look. "I can put her right again."

Vigo leans forward, pressing his elbows to the table and steepling his fingers beneath his chin. "And what makes you think that?"

I lean back in my seat, feigning a disinterested sigh. "Because I know her better than you do, Vigo. And let's not fool ourselves. She never once tried to end her life in my care. You've broken her to pieces, and someone needs to put them back together if you intend to keep her."

"What makes you think—"

I lean forward with a snap. "You signed a contract with me, and I expect you to honor the agreement. You've already breached several clauses you agreed to for her welfare, so I suggest you stop pretending that I'm *asking* for

366

a night with her. Your lack of decorum necessitates it."

Renata tilts her head at Vigo, her dark eyes narrowed. "Is that true? Have you neglected to abide by your contract?"

Vigo's lips twist into a slow, wide smile as he leans back from the table. "It depends on how you look at it."

"Bullshit." Murphy, the O'Shea family Head of House, sits back, crossing his tattooed arms across his broad chest.

"Aye," Delia agrees, and her words drip with sarcasm, "I'd be happy to review the contract with you if you're having trouble interpreting it, Vigo. I'm sure Nikolai has laid out clear terms for you in his sale." Vigo's smile fades as Delia speaks. "What are the consequences set forth for breach of contract, or has that not been laid out? I assure you that the board would lay out an appropriate consequence if Nikolai neglected to write one into the contract."

Vigo has always had a bit of a soft spot for Delia. She had successfully seduced him once—more than a decade ago when they were in their twenties—to gain a favorable trade deal through Lisbon. If anyone could shut him up, it would certainly be Cordelia O'Shea. And she seems to have done just that.

Vigo's eyes don't leave her as she tosses her soft, strawberry blonde hair over one shoulder. She plays him like a fiddle with her intentional flirtation. It's a skill the women of the four families develop carefully from the time they begin to blossom in their teens. Our business decisions are made by men and men alone, though that doesn't mean we haven't all suffered the influence of one of the powerful women in our ranks. They're as ruthless as the men, though they have the finesse of womanhood.

"Fine," Vigo finally says to me, though he looks at Delia. "Have her for the night. Straighten her out and set her right."

"And?" Delia tilts her head.

Vigo leans forward, licking his lips before he responds, "I'll sit with you to review the contract. Let you straighten me out and set me right."

She smiles. "My pleasure."

Vigo leans back slowly in his seat, placing his arms on the rests and smoldering at the woman.

I refuse to let relief touch the features of my face that I'll have a night with Anya. I don't need to feel relief for it. Fuck, I don't even know why I suggested it.

You know why.

"Very well," Renata says, jumping in to take the lead like she always does. "Nikolai will have Anya tonight and return her to Vigo in the morning. Leo, why don't you move us along to the next agenda item?"

Leo Leblanc may be the Head of House for his family, but he was never meant to be. Since the four fathers began their cooperation generations ago, the American family has always been the Campbells.

But then they went and killed my family, and I got my retribution at the last quarterly meeting hosted in my home. I killed the previous Head of House, Chandler Campbell, along with Leo Leblanc's parents. Three from their family for the three of mine whose lives were stolen. With no other suitable male Campbell in the line, our board agreed to appoint Leo, making a major change that was unprecedented.

The Leblancs were distant relatives, and though they knew of our world, they weren't living in it. Furthermore, Leo was relatively young to be thrust into this role with no previous knowledge of our criminal dealings—not that he had a choice. At only twenty-seven years old, he became the Head of House for a family he knew little about.

Murphy, Vigo, and I had our whole lives to prepare for our roles, and at thirty-five, thirty-eight, and thirty-nine respectively, our life experience far exceeded Leo's. Nevertheless, he was Head of House for his family and he has to make decisions as such.

Leo swallows and clears his throat, leaning forward on his elbows on the table. "Yes. Next item is the matter of Murphy's..." He looks down at his notes on the table in front of him. "His bride?"

I roll my eyes at Leo's apparent lack of preparation, but more so at his seeming inability to appear confident *despite* his lack of preparation.

Thankfully, Renata has more patience for the young, blond-haired protégé she seems to have taken under her wing. She's managed a rather impressive collection of young boys in her care over the years, so it's unsurprising that she's taken a liking to him. She takes over the agenda item on Leo's behalf.

"Murphy has petitioned for an early bride," Renata says.

My eyebrows raise in surprise. "Really?"

"I'm impatient." Murphy shrugs, speaking in his Irish accent. "What's the point in waiting until I'm forty to find a suitable wife?"

A cold reminder that in five months' time, I will be forty and forced to discuss the selection of my own wife. My argument against which is untenable, though the secret I've been keeping for nearly three years will be forced to come to light. It's not as though the revelation of which would be an outright surprise to anyone here. What I've done is not entirely unheard of within the bounds of the four families, but my recent decisions—decisions I might perhaps be willing to admit I have some regret for—will make the conversation of my future bride difficult to say the least.

Delia sighs. "I've tried to talk him into waiting until it's his time," she sends a chastising look to her cousin, "but he insists he wants a bride now."

"All of the Heads of House must agree for us to move forward with an early petition. What are your votes?" Renata asks.

"Agreed," I reply.

Vigo follows, "Agreed."

All eyes fall to Leo and he straightens in his seat. "You're petitioning to get married?" he asks for clarification.

My impatience grows and I sink back into my seat, crossing my arms over my chest.

"Aye," Murphy replies, exasperation lifting his eyebrows in a manner of mockery.

Leo clears his throat, finally realizing he should fall in step and vote as the other Heads of House. "Agreed."

"Petition granted. Congratulations." Renata's smooth, thick voice pours out like honey. "I'll prepare you a portfolio of suitable women to join the four families."

"Actually…" Murphy uncrosses his arms, leaning forward on his elbows on the table, "I already have someone in mind. A fiery little thing I had the pleasure of meeting by chance last time I visited the States."

"Murphy." Renata folds her hands. "You know your bride must be approved."

"And she will be." He flashes a grin at Renata. "I'll send her details to you for approval and you can pass it along to the Heads of House for the final vote."

Renata watches his features carefully, a stare of truth-seeking. She waits for his grin to falter and fade, but of course, it doesn't. Murphy O'Shea is not one to back down.

"Fine, then. Send me the details and we'll make a decision at the next quarterly meeting. Fair?"

"Fair." His grin broadens and he leans back in his chair.

One thing our women get the first say in is the choice of brides for the Heads of House. Our women need to be vetted carefully before brought to marry into the family. They need to be an appropriate blend of submissive wife and ruthless leader.

Someone like Anya.

It's a combination that, for obvious reasons, isn't easy to come by. I'm actually quite intrigued to learn more about this bride Murphy intends to wed.

The intrigue, however, is fleeting.

My mind drifts as Renata assists Leo in moving forward with the agenda—discussing family sales figures over the last quarter.

It wanders to the sight of Anya, bleeding and begging for death in the hallway. I'd be lying to say it wasn't a shock to my system to see her unraveled. I'd unraveled her myself more times than I can count, but never so completely.

Vigo has ruined her.

My jealousy has reached its peak, aiding my imagination in drawing up all the vile things Vigo must have done to her. It's not that he's done anything to her that bothers me, it's that he has broken her enough to attempt to find death on her own. She was apathetic about life when she was mine, but she hadn't actively sought the escape of death. She still had that fight left in her, even if it had been slowly fading over the years.

Just when I thought it was coming back, that I was about to have everything I wanted with my *rabynya* and her precious pet, they went behind my back and fucked each other. More than that, they fell in love. Not with me, but with each other.

They were both supposed to be mine—my faithful companions…my willing slaves to offer me comfort on the nights when my grief kicked up and switched on my rage. They were meant to be my reprieve, my outlet for the sexually violent release I needed to get my head back in the fucking game. But they'd ruined it before it even began.

I hate Anya for her betrayal, but there is this nagging, shrill voice from somewhere deep inside me that saw her bleeding in the hallway tonight for what I'd wanted her to be from the beginning.

She'd been there for me, however unwillingly. Her presence had always been a constant which dampened my evil spirit and kept it in check. When she finally broke as my slave and gave me her constant submission, she was the willing angel from heaven who let me clip her wings and use her in all the vile ways I wanted to use her. In doing so, she saved countless others that the devil inside me would have destroyed.

Since she's been gone, the blackness has been seeping in, swallowing my soul bit by bit. I no longer have her goodness to balance my evil, and her absence has forced me to recognize it. The recognition requires gratitude, though I'm loathed to grant it.

Still, I have a mission with her tonight. A mission based on a longshot and a lie that I told Vigo when I sold her to him. A lie that's listed in the very contract I used to barter my time with her tonight. Personally, I don't give a shit about any consequences I might earn for fraud or breach of contract. I only care that Vigo does as he promised when he signed it, and I know the lovely Cordelia O'Shea will keep him in line for that.

My hopeful outcome from this evening is highly unlikely from a statistical standpoint and it may make no difference to Anya, or to myself, in the long run.

But my attempt will absolve me of the burden of gratitude I somehow feel is owed to her for the years she granted me her submission so willingly.

I wish to owe no debt.

I wish to make my attempt at granting her an insurance policy from our night together, then wash my hands of her.

Then I wish to take Ezra home, to find a way to make him and Sasha the companions they need to be to satisfy the demonic urges within me.

CHAPTER 18
Anya

BEING WITH EZRA again has both energized and drained me. To think of how determined I was to end my own life only to be brought face to face with him just after my failed attempt…

I'm embarrassed.

I'm ashamed.

I'm guilt-ridden.

Perhaps it was fated for us to be reunited when we were. I don't know, it's difficult for me to believe when fate has made my life so miserable.

Miserable until Ezra.

Every moment I'd shared with him alone, from the day I met him, has been filled with passion. Whether it came out as hatred, anger, lust, or fierce and powerful love, every memory I had of him with me was passionate. Our passion fueled me to keep fighting for another moment with him; though at the same time, it drained me of my last dregs of energy so that I felt hopeless and exhausted in his absence.

I need him to be with me forever.

I need him to feed me that fuel every moment so it doesn't burn out when he's gone.

I'd nearly snuffed it out myself tonight, and I know I'll only try again when it dies down to a flicker, a sparking ember.

I made him a promise, though, a promise to try, to give him time to save me. And while I don't believe it's possible, I'll keep my promise to him. I'll try my best because having his love is the only thing that matters to me.

I'm thankful for the fire he's lit inside me when Vigo and Nikolai come to retrieve us from the dungeon. I hope and pray that neither man will smell the sex on us. I suppose it doesn't matter because I know I'm going to be punished for trying to kill myself regardless…I just don't know how.

Leo is with them and he unlocks the metal choker from around my neck, freeing me. I bring my hands up to rub the sides of my sore neck, relishing the freedom from such an oppressive chain. Ezra stands but Nikolai holds up a palm to stop him.

"You'll remain here tonight, Ezra."

I whip around to look at him and his eyes blaze, narrowing at Nikolai.

"Excuse me?" Ezra says.

"Anya will be with me tonight. She and I will need our time… uninterrupted. But don't worry, I'll have Sasha brought down to keep you company."

Ezra's nostrils flare. "What are you going to do to her?"

Nikolai shakes his head. "That's none of your business. Say goodbye to your pet, *rabynya*, you won't be seeing each other again for quite a long time."

"No," I say and dash toward Ezra at the exact moment Nikolai reaches out to grab my wrist.

I fly into Ezra's reaching arms and he clamps them tight around my body before Nikolai can touch me. The shackle of Ezra's embrace is the only binding I want.

His lips brush across my ear. "Remember you promised me. Give me time. Please."

I press my face into his shoulder, sucking in a long, deep breath to inhale the sweet scent of him one last time. Then I'm violently taken from him with Nikolai's fierce hands gripping my waist and tearing me away.

I nod at Ezra, acknowledging my promise to him.

Nikolai drags me toward the steps by my wrist and I manage to twist back around to steal one more glance. Ezra's brightness shines and threatens to knock me off my feet with the way he grins and winks at me. He could almost have me fooled that everything is okay. I smile in return before I'm pulled out of sight.

Oh, God…the way he makes me feel.

My palm crushes against my bloody chest, over my heart, and I mourn the rush of him fading with each melancholy beat of my hopeless, helpless heart.

I stand beside the locked door in the room Nikolai has been given for the evening. My back is pressed against the wall as I wait for direction on the manner in which I will be punished by my former master.

I was granted the unfortunate privilege of meeting my replacement, Sasha. A girl who looked similar to me, for all intents and purposes, but who was nothing like me at all. She bowed to Nikolai with a needy, desperate sort of submission, not in the way I had learned to submit over time. I learned it was best for my survival, but I had always abhorred my own behavior when I had to bow.

Unlike me, it's clear this girl wants Nikolai's approval, not for her safety, but for her self-esteem. I almost feel sorry for her naivety, but my heart just doesn't have the space to concern myself with her. In any case, she was taken out of the room soon after I arrived and I'm left alone with Nikolai, locked in the room with no way out.

I watch as he pours a drink from a bar cart near an unlit fireplace. A sitting area with a couch and two armchairs separates us across the large space, and a traditional, mahogany four post bed sits threatening on the opposite side of the room.

He turns as he lifts a glass of whiskey to his lips and I'm surprised to find that his eyes aren't immediately filled with lust and violence.

"Come sit, Anya. Let's talk." He tilts his head toward the sofa. "Would you like a drink?"

My eyes are wide as I subtly shake my head. "No."

He stills, watching me, waiting for me to obey. Though I wish to stay right here, with my back pressed firmly to the wall, I know I must submit and do as he wishes. Slowly, I push away from the wall and walk forward. I circle around one of the armchairs with my eyes plastered to his. I reach the couch and lower to sit as he takes a long, slow drink from his glass, then sets it back down on the bar cart.

He moves swiftly, crossing to sit on the couch beside me, and I jolt at his sudden movement. There's still a cushion's length between us, but I'm wary for how long that will last. I'm sitting straight and stiff, my spine rigid and chin lifted, and I have to turn my entire body to face him. He settles into the corner, lifting his arm to rest along the back of the couch and crosses one ankle over his knee. Though I'm tense and terrified, there's also some strange part of me that feels a sense of relief, only for the reason that I've been spared a night with Vigo.

But have I really been spared?

Boldly, I ask the question that begs to be answered, knowing he may punish me worse than ever simply for asking. But I need to know, and this silence is overwhelming.

"What is my punishment and why are you giving it?"

I brace myself for his violent outburst, drawing my body back toward the arm rest behind me, but it never comes.

His head tilts. "Do you wish Vigo were giving it?"

"No," I reply truthfully.

His forehead wrinkles. "Why is that?"

"Because—"

"Have you found that I'm a kinder master than he is?"

I swallow thickly, my eyes turning toward the unlit fireplace. "You're no kinder."

"Don't lie to me, Anya," he hisses. "You attempted to take your own life tonight."

I suck in a sharp breath, turning to face him with the full force of my confidence returning, self-preservation be damned. "He may have driven me to it faster, Nikolai, but you were driving me there all the same."

There.

I've done it.

I've brought the devil out of him.

His crossed leg comes down as his face twists to rage. He throws himself across the couch at me and snatches me around the throat before I can protest.

"You had everything you wanted with me. Everything you needed. I even let you keep your fucking pet."

Incredulity overcomes me and I'm lost to it, neglecting my sensibilities that tell me to succumb, to give in, to submit.

"He's *your* pet, Nikolai. Don't play me for a fool. The dance partners weren't for me, they were for *you.*"

His gray eyes flash with a lightning strike that sets fire to his features, a puff of black smoke sweeping across his irises.

"They were for *both* of us, Anya. I was building a life for us, regardless of how you choose to see it."

He keeps saying my name and I hate it. He acts as though he thinks of me as a person when all I've ever been to him is his talent slave.

His *rabynya.*

His *slave girl.*

I choke against his grip as he drags my body down the couch, pulling me beneath him until I'm flat on my back. He pins me there with his hips settled on mine and I cough when he finally loosens his grip on my throat.

His nose touches mine as he bends over me. "I would've kept you forever."

The edges of his voice soften in a way I've never heard before. I gasp, flinching at the sound of it, his hot breath dancing across my skin. His eyes spark with the truth of his admission and it's as though he's stabbing me in the heart with it.

I take in a deep breath, my chest and belly rising to meet his as I fill my lungs. "But you didn't keep me. You sold me."

His eyes flicker to my lips. "Because you betrayed me."

"You hurt me, tortured me, used me for years, Nikolai. What would you have gotten out of keeping me forever? How long would that forever have been? Every time I looked at you, I hated you more. I hate you now more than ever."

My eyes burn as I speak my truth openly, no longer fearful of his retribution because it doesn't matter. He has me for the night, but no punishment he could serve would compare to the torment to come—the torment of waiting for Ezra to save me before my lust for death returns, too overpowering to deny.

"You disgust me," I tell him, tempted to spit on him, baring my teeth.

His nostrils flare as the corners of his mouth lift into a snarl. I open my mouth to insult him more, but he smothers my words with his open mouth on mine. His kiss crashes down on me so ferociously that it freezes me, still as a statue. His tongue sweeps inside my mouth, seeking mine, and my anger ticks. I slam my hands against his chest and by some miracle, take him off guard. I push hard enough that he topples off the couch and I take the opportunity to rise and flee.

Except, there's nowhere for me to go.

And I've just denied the devil.

I move to the far corner of the room, expecting him to already be upon me before I spin and press my back against it. But he hasn't chased me. He stands, hovering in front of the couch where he fell, fists clenched at his sides, stance wide and domineering.

"Your punishment, *rabynya*," he begins, and I brace myself to hear the worst, "will not involve pain or fear. Your punishment is pleasure."

What?

He stalks toward me as I work to make sense of what he's telling me.

My punishment is…pleasure?

"You betrayed me. You gave your body to someone it didn't belong to with careless regard for your master's wishes. Tonight you tried to take your own life. Your body and your life do not belong to you, they belong to your master." He arrives in front of me and I hold my breath as he presses in close, his body molding to mine. "Your punishment will be your own body's betrayal against your heart and mind."

I turn my head as he leans in close, just to avoid his piercing stare.

"I intend to seduce you, Anya. I'm going to touch you in all the ways you wished I would touch you before. I'm going to make you wet with need. I'm going to bring you to the point of aching for my touch until you willingly drop to your knees and crawl to me."

His fingertips gently trail over the tops of my thighs, slowly gathering the fabric of my gown. "And then I'll remind you of Ezra because then you will know how you have betrayed him. I'll return you to Vigo, sexually satisfied, though your heart will ache with the weight of your disloyalty knowing what you and I have done, knowing how you dripped with need for me as you begged for my cock."

My breathing grows rapid and shallow as he speaks, as his fingers reach beneath the gathered hem at my knees and creep upward. If he were to succeed in the punishment he proposes, the aftermath would truly be the worst punishment I could ever endure.

He knew I'd given my heart entirely to Ezra and he wished to use it against me now. If I'd ever felt anything for Nikolai, one ounce of caring or concern, one hope for his humanity, it no longer—

Oh.

His fingers graze upward across my flesh and his hands turn sensually to grip the crease where my thighs meet my hip bones. He breathes lightly against my neck as he runs his nose along my skin and his thumbs rub gentle circles over my sensitive flesh.

My whimper is involuntary.

I don't want to want this.

At least, my mind and my heart don't.

But my body betrays me as always, especially in the aftermath of my sexual experience with Ezra when we were chained in that secret room. Once with Ezra didn't feel like enough, and my body continues to hum with need for him after coming on his lap so spectacularly.

Ezra had primed me for more sexual touch and now I'm receiving it from Nikolai.

This makes me hate Nikolai so much more as my skin prickles with awareness, my body excited for this touch that isn't harming or hurting. Sensation is deceitful in the way it clouds my mind in the moment, even knowing how it will hurt my heart when it's gone.

Maybe I am just a horrible slut.

I don't deserve Ezra.

"Do you recall the one time you came to me willingly, Anya? It was not so long after your first partnership with Jamal ended…a few months before I brought you Erik to dance with." His lips caress the skin behind my ear. "I was in the shower when you came to find me in my room. Do you remember?"

Did I remember?

Of course, I remembered. He'd taken Jamal after our performance failed to meet his standards. He was my first partner and I was so lost after Nikolai took him away. I'd developed a connection with him—not the same as my soulmate connection with Ezra, nothing could compare to that. But I'd been distraught, heartbroken, struggling to come to terms with the reality of my captivity.

The day he's asking me about held the only halfway decent memory of Nikolai that I had. It was the memory I'd had to conjure up time and time again, each time he forced me into sex that I didn't want. It was the only orgasm I had with him by choice and it was only because I was desperately lonely that day.

I'd been naïve in my loneliness then, just seeking comfort, and his behavior that day might've changed the course of our entire relationship as master and slave. There was a part of me that thought we could be something more.

But I'd been wrong.

He'd only used my willingness that day as a means to study my sexuality so he could use it against me—like he's planning to do now—to force me into pleasure that I don't want and didn't ask for.

"I remember," I tell him plainly, forcing my focus to the unlit fireplace, trying to imagine flames as a distraction to the way he touches me.

"Do you remember how I made you come on my fingers?"

I swallow as his lips skim across my skin to kiss the hollow of my throat. "You used me." My voice is monotone, detached. "You didn't want me the way I wanted you that day. You used my willingness against me."

He pulls his head back to look at me, his gray gaze piercing mine as he grips my chin and turns my face toward his.

"And you're so fucking sure that's all it was for me?"

He smacks his palm against my cheek, not hard, but hard enough that it shoots a sting across my face and startles me.

I narrow my eyes at him. "Yes."

His fingers move until both hands hold my face at my jawline. He holds me there as he leans in to kiss me, bruising my lips with his. He pulls his mouth from mine with a smack of his lips and rests his forehead against mine.

"You're as inobservant as you are beautiful, Anya."

He's such a filthy, goddamn liar.

"You'll have to try harder if you wish to seduce me into thinking you ever wanted more from me than unwavering obedience to bend to your sadistic will."

A smirk tilts his lips. "I missed this version of you...the one that fought me."

"How could you possibly miss it? You literally beat it out of me, Nikolai. I have the scars to show for it."

"You don't remember what happened the day after you came to me, do you?"

"I don't know what you're talking about."

He licks his tongue across the flat line of my mouth, then bites my bottom lip, tugging it hard, causing me to whimper. Both of his hands move to grab me by the waist as he walks backward toward the bed, pulling me with him. He lowers to sit when he reaches the side and spreads his legs wide, dragging me in to stand between them.

My brow furrows as his fingers slip beneath the straps of my dress, sliding them off my shoulders. I wait for him to say more as he tugs on the dress, encouraging it to fall from my figure and tumble to the floor. I wait as his rough palms test the weight of my bare breasts, the tops of which are covered with my dried blood. I wait as his thumbs brush the peak of my nipples, coaxing them to harden, spreading warmth through my stomach. I wait as his eyes latch onto mine, sending me a look that burrows into my soul.

He sighs, uncharacteristically and dangerously calm. "It's just as well you don't remember."

The sexuality he draws over my skin seeps into my pores and lights a flame of physical desire that I don't want. I fan the flame, turning it toward my anger instead.

"Remember *what?* Do you wish to pique my curiosity? You have it. So tell me."

"It doesn't matter anymore. I sold you to Vigo. You're not mine…not anymore."

"Except that I'm here with you now and you're behaving as if you still hold ownership over me."

"You weren't even mine when I had you."

He says it smoothly, calmly, in a way that takes me completely off guard. Nikolai has never been smooth or calm with me; he's been angry and jealous, lust-driven and violent. He's been aggressive and hateful and unpredictably brutal. This is so off-character that the back of my neck prickles with baffled and cautious awareness.

I could almost believe his sincerity with the look of his eyes as they soften, but I've never known a soft side to him. Except for the day he mentioned when I came to him willingly—but that was years ago. It was all a rouse to study me. It might have felt sincere at the time, but I know him better now.

So, what happened the day after and why can't I remember?

I have to know.

I drop to my knees between his wide-open legs and grip each of his muscular thighs. I slide my hands forward until they meet his hips, turning the tables on this seduction.

"Tell me what happened the day after." I bring temptation to my tone. "Please, *moy khozyain.*"

I bring my hands together to meet at his buckle and his hands snap to mine in a flash, snatching them in both his large hands and leaning forward. He brings my hands to his lips to kiss my knuckles and nausea strikes in my belly.

He's not allowed to be gentle with me.

Only Ezra has earned that right.

"If you don't recall then there's no point in telling you. No one else of importance knows. Don't ask me again."

I stare at him with ferocity as my brain works to go backward in time.

What happened the day after?

What the hell happened?

I vaguely remember Nikolai's brother bringing me to his office.

But why was I with Nikolai's brother?

We were drinking.

Yes.

His brother had forced me to partake until I reached a point of total inebriation before taking me to Nikolai's office. They were both there, so was Kostya. And there was another man, too...someone I'd never seen before and haven't seen since.

But why was he there?

"We signed something," I say slowly, testing the words for myself more than to ask him.

Nikolai grabs the back of my head and yanks me toward him in a flash. His lips fall against mine to silence me and he's successful because I'm too lost in searching my memory to fight him off. He moans against my mouth, parting my lips with a sweep of his tongue. I kiss back, an old habit from when I was his obedient little fuck girl.

Nikolai stops kissing for a beat and speaks with his lips brushing against mine. "Sit on my cock, Anya, sink me deep inside you."

My brain stops searching for the memory and snaps me back into the moment. My heart beats faster, pulsing an old, familiar danger signal through my veins. My eyebrows slant toward my nose in determination as I yank my hands away from his grip.

"No," I tell him and my heart races, knowing how stupid it is to refuse him, but feeling compelled to all the same.

I sit back on my heels, turning my face away and brace for his rage, his outburst, his violent attack against my bold disobedience.

But it doesn't come.

Instead, his hands rush to remove his clothes. He stands, his hips only inches from my face as he loosens and removes his tie before working the buttons of his shirt. He tosses them both aside and rushes to his buckle. I'm frozen, shocked, overwhelmed, dangerously curious that he hasn't beaten me, cut me, bent me over and fucked me painfully from behind for my refusal.

In moments, he's naked before me, cock standing proud and thick, heavy with lust. He lowers quickly to sit on the edge of the bed again, grabbing my hair on the way down and dragging me forward. I think he's going to force me to take him inside my mouth and I swallow hard. But he surprises me yet again; instead, he lifts up on my hair, pulling a thick section high above my head and tugging painfully until I'm scrambling to get on my feet to lessen the pressure.

My breaths quicken, my heart thumping hard. I see the Nikolai I once knew return now that he's descended into a feral, sexually desperate state.

He releases my hair once I'm standing and grasps my hips. He pulls me forward, wrapping his arms around my waist and kissing my belly button. His tongue sweeps out, drawing flat across my skin and my body responds. He breathes out harshly through his nose, the rush of air heating my flesh, and I watch his shoulders tremble as he inhales my scent.

He *trembles*.

I've seen him in the throes of passion, but I've never seen him tremble with need. I struggle to make sense of that as his fingers reach down to cup my bottom, squeezing and pulling me closer. His lips graze lower, traveling down until he reaches the curls above my sex, and the heat of his breath drags sensation down with it. I feel the rush of need dampen my core and sadness rushes with it, too.

Nikolai lifts me with his strong arms, slipping his knee between my legs, forcing them apart. He shifts me until I'm straddling him. With one arm wrapped firmly around my back, he reaches between us with the other, grasping his thick erection and positioning me to take it.

I press my eyes shut and feel a tear slip from the corner, gliding slowly down my cheek. He lines me up and pushes me down, making me take his cock all the way, deep inside me. I let him take my weight, let him hold me against him because I've lost the strength to hold myself up.

This is too much.

It was only hours ago that I made love to Ezra, just like this. And Nikolai is taking that moment from me now. It hurts so much more that he's behaving differently than I've ever known him to be.

He pushes my hair over my shoulder so it drapes behind my back before he kisses the nick on my neck where I attempted to cut myself.

"I dare you not to move," he says to me. "I dare you not to fuck me, to hold still while I touch you, kiss you, lick you, drive you to the point of madness."

Bastard.

Anger replaces my sadness and it kickstarts my pulse, racing a fever of rage through my veins that threatens to explode from my pores. I can't stop myself from lashing out, not now, not while he tricks my body into wanting pleasure from him.

I shove my hands against his bare chest, pushing as I arch my back away from him. He doesn't budge and I remain firmly in his grasp with his arms tight around me. I shout out my anger and beat my fists against his chest, but it doesn't faze him. Instead, it only heightens his awareness and feeds his lust.

His mouth clamps over the crook of my neck and he sucks in a gentle, sensual rhythm—not his usual biting fervor; this time it's softer and more sexual. I could cry with the way he worships my skin with his mouth, drawing across my collarbone to the hollow of my throat as I lean away.

I thrash and pull as his head dips for my breast, sucking my nipple into his mouth and rolling his tongue around it.

"Stop," I plead, my palms landing flat on his chest to try to shove him away one last time.

But then he groans as he sucks, sending a shivering vibration like a lightning bolt from my nipple straight through to my clit.

"Stop," I say again, but my voice is softer, weaker.

My hands slip from his chest, my body melting to the good feelings that ripple from my core. I look down at Nikolai and he releases my nipple to look up at me. He's panting in need as he watches me and I realize I'm panting, too. It's from the exertion of fighting him.

No, it's the feeling of his swollen cock shoved inside my throbbing cunt.

I am a slut, a whore—just like Nikolai said.

"I can't…" I say, but it's more for me than for him.

I wish he would just take me and be done with it. I wish he would slam me to the ground, fuck me until he comes, then leave me to pick up my broken pieces on my own. But instead, he watches me, caresses me, heats my skin with his desperate breathing, and fills me with dirty, wanton need.

I need to move.

I need to fuck.

I need to come.

I need, but I don't want. It will tear me apart to hold that burden of guilt, for being the woman who made the choice to fuck another for her own pleasure. I can't do that to Ezra.

I can't.

"I hate you," I whisper.

"You can hate me while you fuck me," he breathes against my throat, turning his head to kiss a line along my jaw all the way back to my ear.

His tongue flicks my earlobe and I jolt, surprised by the feel of it, and the movement rocks me forward. We both groan with the small movement of my hips over his. Only his groan is pure pleasure where mine is tinged with a thousand painful emotions.

I push out a heavy breath, dropping my head to look down between us, forcing myself to see the shame of our physical connection. Somehow I hope to convince my body to stop this madness, this nightmare where I want to rock and grind and fuck Nikolai until I come.

But looking is a mistake because the bastard is so tragically attractive.

I feel torn apart. My mind screams for this to stop, my heart pounds with sadness and shame, my body swells and slickens and begs for a release at any cost.

This is when I realize how little strength I have left—at the moment I rock back then forward with intention.

Goddammit.

Nikolai groans, holding me tighter, burying his face in the side of my neck, and I shudder.

He's not supposed to hold me like this, touch me like this, let me fuck him like this. I hate him more than ever before—yet I need this release so much. I need to fuck, to take all the good feelings he stole from me.

My hips move of their own free will, rocking forward and back, forward and back. I press down, slackening in his hold to ensure he's sunk inside me as deep as he can be because the swell of him feeds my pleasure.

"I hate you," I pant out as I move. "I hate everything about you."

"Show me how much you hate me, Anya. Fuck me with every ounce of hatred you possess."

Why is there a hint of weakness in his voice?

His hand finds its way to my breast and he pinches the hard peak between his fingers, rolling it sensually. The roll sends pleasure tumbling around my insides, falling down, down, down to my throbbing clit, making me clench with desperate need for release.

I grip his shoulders in my palms and I fuck. I fuck hard and dirty like the slutty slave he's reduced me to.

"I want it back," I huff. "Give it back."

Surely, what I'm saying makes no sense to him, but I don't care. It doesn't matter. I want him to give back everything he's stolen from me.

Happiness.

Security.

Freedom.

Ezra.

He took Ezra from me by selling me.

Ezra's green eyes and smile break through the cloud of brokenness in my mind. Though I know it should halt me, should stop me from fucking, instead it sparks an explosion inside me.

I scream out my relief as I come with visions of Ezra swirling through my mind. The release is so strong that it's nearly painful. It clenches every muscle in my body until every part of me bursts with pleasure and relaxes into dopamine-induced bliss.

I'm only barely aware as Nikolai flips me onto the mattress, slamming me down on my back and rutting inside me until he comes, spilling a rush of warm liquid inside me.

My entire body is limp, lax from the overwhelming orgasm, and I feel as though I have nothing left in me to give. Exhausted and defeated, I begin to cry.

Nikolai kisses the tears that stream down my cheeks, licking them away.

"That's a good girl, *rabynya*. Don't worry. I'll be sure to tell Ezra that I didn't hurt you tonight. I'll let him know how you fucked me and came harder than I've ever felt before."

I let my head fall to the side, looking at the wall. "Tell him what you want. He knows me and loves me all the same…" I turn back to look him in the eye. "Not that you would know anything of love."

He stills and a flicker of something passes across his eyes only to disappear into the abyss of his soul. "I know more than you think."

He climbs off me and crosses to the fireplace, lifting the half full glass of whiskey he'd set down before.

"Don't move," he instructs. "I intend to fill you at least three more times tonight."

I press my eyes shut, letting tears pour from beneath my lashes until there aren't any more to spill.

CHAPTER 19

Anya

I'M ORDERED TO put my dress back on and sit quietly in the chair when someone knocks on the door. It's early morning, the sun just beginning to rise and casting an orange and yellow glow from the windows.

Nikolai is still in a state of undress, fresh from our morning shower together. He promised me three, but he fucked me five more times. The final session ended only ten minutes ago in the shower.

He'd bent me over and rammed into me from behind with my hands against the wall. It felt like it went on forever, my pussy sore and overused. He insisted that I come again on his cock and I'd run out of carnal energy to force my body to submit beyond my mind's will. But Nikolai insisted, and he always gets what he wants. As a result, my pussy is swollen, painful, and rubbed raw.

I feel like dying now just as much as I did before.

I perch on an armchair near the fireplace, wearing last night's golden gown. The blood stains remain along the neckline, but the dried blood has been washed clean from my skin. The slices I made in my neck and wrist stopped bleeding, though the fresh marks serve as an immediate reminder of what I've done.

Nikolai pulls the door open, revealing Vigo standing there and panicked nausea coils around my insides like a snake. I pull my legs up to tuck them beneath me and I curl into a tiny ball on the chair.

"I've come to collect my pretty little doll," Vigo says.

Nikolai works to fasten the buttons on his shirt as he tilts his head to beckon him inside, only it's not just Vigo. Kostya and Leo have come along, too, escorting Sasha and…Ezra.

Ezra's eyes search the room. I lift my head and straighten my spine at the tingle of awareness I feel. Our eyes meet and he moves, rushing past the others as though his life depends on touching me.

Maybe it does.

I feel that way about him, too.

I stand, whipping around the chair in a flash. My arms open for him and our bodies crash together with force.

No one protests or stops him, but naturally, he's taking me away from them, pushing me backward as he holds me tight, walking me to the farthest wall in the room. He doesn't stop moving until he has my back to the wall. He holds me tight, refusing to move.

My heart is pounding for no other reason than his body pressed against mine. My current and former master are in this room with no escape. Danger swirls around us like a dark cloud. But being in his arms feels like constant lightning strikes, shocking me with a relentless fire of desperate need.

"I love you," I whisper into the side of his neck. "I love you, I love you."

My hands slip up to catch his cheeks, and I look at him, giving him all the sadness and hurt and love and longing that's twisted and tangled in my soul for him. His green eyes give it all back to me in equal measure and it's how I know he's the only man that ever would've been for me.

"Made for each other," he says to me.

The perfection of his words—reflecting exactly what I'm feeling inside—crushes my heart in all the beautiful, tragic ways love ever possibly could.

Urgency washes across the reverie and he dips his head to kiss me. I hold nothing back, swiftly seeking his tongue to mingle with mine, to speak that language without words that only the two of us know. It takes only seconds to lose myself in him, to forget the world around us and drown in the pure satisfaction of his lips on mine.

But then I open my eyes and I see Vigo.

He stands just behind Ezra's back, hardly a foot away.

It startles me to see him so close and I pull my head back too harshly, breaking our kiss. The back of my head lands with a thud against the wall behind me and my eyes narrow on the demon himself, angry with the way he so cruelly pulled me back to reality.

Ezra registers my unease, his face falling as he sees my expression. He spins around, pinning me between his back and the wall.

"Well, isn't this a precious moment? It really is too bad that no one gives a fuck about a slave who can make love to them sweetly. We might've been able to sell you two as a package deal." Vigo clicks his tongue and Ezra presses harder against me, protective in his stance. "As it were, my clients prefer something a little more extreme. So, I guess it's time for me to take back my sad, broken little doll so I can rent her out for what she's useful for—dark, dirty, heathen fucking."

I gasp as I see Nikolai rush toward Vigo from behind. He reaches him quickly and drags him away by the back of his shirt. I grip Ezra's biceps, willing him not to react and flee when all I need is him right in front of me, keeping me safe. I turn my head and rest my cheek against his back, breathing in his scent.

Nikolai drags Vigo across the room and they stop in the corner farthest from us. They speak in hushed tones, though we can hear them all the same.

"I thought you understood the terms of your contract," Nikolai seethes. "You spent the night reviewing it with Cordelia, didn't you? Or were you too busy fucking each other to handle business?"

"Relax," Vigo tells him with a knowing smile. "I'm only trying to get a rise out of them."

"Anya is *not* to be shared. Have you been renting her out to your clients?"

"No, though she has had a fair number of offers since the video of her fucking that stuffed rabbit in her sweet little pigtails and blue dress. I'm losing money off the bitch by following your terms, Nikolai. You should be grateful she's still alive."

"How much?"

"How much?" Vigo cocks his head to the side. "How much *what?* How much have I lost?"

Nikolai inhales a thick breath and speaks through bared teeth. "How much to buy her back?"

"*What?*" Ezra says and they both snap their heads to look at us.

Their tempers flare, heating their discussion.

"I'm not selling her back to you, Nikolai," Vigo tells him. "I enjoy tormenting her far too much to give that up for money. In fact, the torment it causes *you* makes her priceless to me." I can hear the smile in Vigo's tone.

Cocky bastard.

"You said you're losing money on her," Nikolai asserts. "Sell her back and cut your losses."

Vigo laughs. "You make it easier and easier to deny you every time you open your mouth. Every ounce of passion for her that you show me strengthens my desire to keep her and do awful, *awful* things to her. This conversation is over, Nikolai. Unless you want to go to the board and waste their time asking them to reaffirm what you already know. She is *mine* now. I purchased her fairly and that's that."

I hear the way Nikolai hisses through his teeth. "Then you can go and take her back from my slave."

Ezra straightens to his full height and widens his stance.

"Order him to move aside," Vigo requests.

"I have no interest in doing that. You want to take her back with you, so take her back. Fight him if you must. I don't care."

Kostya barks out harsh words to Nikolai, asking him in Russian if he's lost his damn mind, though not in those exact words. Nikolai only orders Kostya to be quiet.

I think Kostya might be right.

I think Nikolai *has* lost his damn mind.

Vigo whips around and charges across the room toward us, stopping just in front of Ezra.

Ezra presses back into me, protecting me, though I can feel his muscles twitch, ready for a fight.

"Move," Vigo orders him.

My heart skips and stutters, then bursts into a pounding rhythm. My hands squeeze around Ezra's arms. I know my fingers are digging into his flesh, but he lets me dig, thank God.

I don't want to go back with Vigo.

But I also don't want Ezra to get himself into trouble. Vigo grins as he postures, sending out notice with his stance that he's prepared to fight Ezra.

Between the two of them, the air rumbles with the anticipation of combat. Two overwhelming forces, one darkness and one light; their auras sizzle and crackle where they crash together in the space between.

It's overwhelming.

It feels almost inevitable that these two forces should collide and explode to release the searing tension.

Ezra has gone rigid, every muscle in his body tense and braced for attack. The way he covers me, protects me, stands up to fight for me melts my icy heart all over again. He's putting himself at risk of future consequences, yet he does it for me.

Damnit, if that doesn't make me love him so much more.

Ezra reaches back to tap the side of my hip with his hand. I know without words that he's encouraging me to let go of his arms. He wants me to remove my touch so he can focus on fighting for me.

This fight won't end well. One of them will get hurt, probably both, and it won't resolve anything. Whether Ezra fights Vigo or not, Vigo is taking me back to my box. I will still belong to the Vittoris. I will still be tortured and brutalized. I will still be without Ezra.

Let him fight.

In resignation and in love, I force my fingers to loosen their grip and slip away from his arms.

Ezra steps forward, tilting his head from side to side to stretch his neck. He pushes his navy-blue suit jacket to fall off his shoulders and onto the ground. He tosses the dangling end of his necktie over his shoulder and clenches his fists, sending Vigo a clear message.

"You're gonna have to go through me to get to her."

The look of Ezra bristling with rage and readying himself to fight also sends *me* a clear message. It rushes straight past my senses and clenches deep within my core. Pride and wonder and a deep, primal need spiral around my insides and it makes me feel…everything. I feel everything for him.

Vigo lifts his chin, an upward nod of acknowledgment, with a sadistic grin of entertained delight. He pauses, taking his time to remove his precious cufflinks. He casually rolls up his sleeves as Ezra rolls his shoulders, clenching and unclenching his fists, preparing to deliver a beating.

Then there's a silent beat of waiting.

Nikolai remains in the far corner of the room with his arms crossed over his chest, his head tipped to the side with a look of curiosity on his face. He shows no signs of interference.

Is he hoping Ezra will start this fight so Nikolai will have an excuse to punish him later?

Why hasn't Nikolai stopped him yet?

Why haven't I stopped him yet?

Because I don't want to.

I lift my hand to graze down Ezra's spine. Though it should be, it's not a touch meant to soothe him, to calm him, to encourage him to back down. It's not a touch that tells him to keep his cool so he doesn't make things worse. It's a touch of finality, a touch of acceptance, of encouragement, because I've had enough of this shit, too.

That seems to be all the encouragement he needs. I can nearly hear his overused adrenaline pump whirring into action. He steps forward and Vigo lurches.

They collide in fists and fury.

They're both snarling wolves snapping and clawing with brute force.

Ezra swings a side jab that collides with Vigo's skull, just to the side of his left eye. Vigo turns out of the hit, spinning around and charging toward Ezra like a linebacker, catching him in the gut with his shoulder and pushing him back. They're quickly coming toward me. Ezra manages to hold steady for a few beats, but I yelp when he stumbles, jumping and scrambling away after he lands on his ass in front of my feet. Ezra doesn't fall to his back, though. He fights to sit upright, reaching over Vigo's back and punching his sides, over and over.

Vigo climbs, trying to push Ezra down on his back so he can get on top and pummel him, but Ezra is strong. He grabs Vigo's skinny hips and flips him sideways, rolling on top of him as quickly as he can. Straddling him, Ezra squeezes his knees in against Vigo's hips to grip him in place. Ezra grabs Vigo's tie and wraps it around his fist, pulling just enough to lift his head off the floor. Ezra punches and punches and punches at Vigo's face until blood spurts from his broken nose.

I can only see the side of Ezra's face in his manic beating, but it looks like he's smiling down at Vigo as the red spatters his pristine white button-down shirt and stains the carpet beneath them.

Ezra hits.

And hits.

And hits.

I've never felt so many things at once. Watching Ezra defend me makes me feel proud and powerful. It makes me feel love and deep respect for him. It makes me feel horror and fear for the consequences to follow. It makes me feel strangely aroused and desperately needy for this formidable man who gave me his heart.

"I hope you die, motherfucker!" Ezra screams down at Vigo, lost in his violent rage. "I'll fucking kill you!"

"*Mal'chik!*" My head snaps up at the sound of Nikolai's voice, but Ezra doesn't stop, doesn't even acknowledge that he heard it. "That's enough. Stop."

Ezra punches.

He hits.

He pounds.

Nikolai's nostrils flare and he storms forward—I know I have to stop Ezra before Nikolai gets to him. Ezra might start swinging at Nikolai and only God knows what would happen to him then.

"Ezra." I say his name softly but firmly, as a command of my own, because he is mine as much as I am his.

Only a second passes before Ezra stops. He lets go of Vigo's tie and drops his head onto the carpet with a thump. Ezra's chest heaves as he inhales and exhales heavy breaths.

Confident that Ezra is no threat to me, even in his violent fury, I step forward and reach out to touch him. My fingers only brush his shoulder before he snatches my hand in his bloodied ones. He stands in a flash, whirling around to face me and throws his arms around me. This time I'm pulling *him* backward, wanting to protect him from the consequences to come if he'd been given seconds or minutes longer. He might've beaten Vigo to death given more time.

I don't even know what the punishment would be for a slave killing a Head of House.

I wanted Ezra to kill Vigo.

Then Nikolai.

Even Leo Leblanc and Murphy O'Shea.

But killing them probably wouldn't matter to our freedom. Their reach is so vast that I don't even know how we could ever fully escape if we were lucky enough to get away.

Regardless, my love and loyalty to Ezra has strengthened immeasurably over these short moments. He would do anything for me. He would put his life at risk for me. I know I have to keep my promise to him—I just don't know how. There's still a nagging voice in the back of my mind that tells me death would ease all my suffering.

Maybe that voice will never go away.

If that's true, then I have to find a way to silence it.

"I'm sorry," Ezra whispers to me, holding me tight in his vice-like embrace. "I shouldn't have done that. I know." He kisses the crook of my neck, silently telling me of his regret.

"No regrets," I tell him plainly, squeezing him. "I love you. I love you so much."

"God, I love you, Anya." He spreads his legs apart to sink to my height so he can be closer to me. "I love you. I'm yours."

"I know you're mine. Always."

"I'll save you. I promise." He grabs my cheeks and kisses me with an explosive passion in the aftermath of his rage. I want nothing more than this—his lips on mine, his tongue aggressively seeking the taste of me as I open for him. I don't even care about the blood on his hands that smudge my cheeks. It's Vigo's blood and that makes me feel somehow more powerful, more capable of survival.

He pulls back and gives me his gaze. I relish the vibrancy of his eyes, knowing that he'll be taken from me at any moment. His green eyes and my blue mingle. Between the two of us we are green earth and blue ocean—forces formidable on their own, but together entirely unmovable, unshakeable, significant, and mighty.

Ezra is the savior who rescued me, then destroyed me. He is the lover who showed me pleasure that made the pain more profound. He is the soul mate who completed me, then ripped me apart with his absence. He is the end and the beginning and everything in-between.

Then Nikolai rips him away from me and I fear our in-between may be done too soon.

Our end may be coming.

The Vittoris stay an extra day at the Leblancs' estate to allow Vigo time to recover. He'd suffered cuts and scrapes and bruises, though the worst injury he received was a broken nose.

He would be fine.

As a slave, I'd suffered the same injuries, though not necessarily all at once. Still, if a tiny, insignificant woman such as myself could continue vigorous dance rehearsals with a broken nose, surely Vigo could quit whining like a small child and pull himself out of bed.

Who's weak and pathetic now?

Renata sends me to the Leblanc kitchen to get more ice for Vigo's swollen jaw. She sends her slave, Luca, with me to ensure I don't try anything stupid.

Like grab a kitchen knife and finally cut my throat open wide.

She doesn't understand that I don't require suicide watch because I'd made a promise to Ezra to try—to do my best to stay alive while he tried to find a way to save me. No such way existed, but Ezra deserved to hang onto his hope, even if mine had been lost. He *needs* that hope—he needs to hope and dream and believe in something more. It's part of what makes him Ezra, and I love that about him. So I'll pretend I haven't given up on a future for as long as I can… for his sake.

When we reach the kitchen, I'm surprised to run into Kostya. I would have thought Nikolai would have left when the O'Sheas had, and that was hours ago. Kostya catches my eye with a fearful yet determined sort of look that draws my curiosity.

I do my best to be surreptitious, telling Luca to go on through the large kitchen and look in the walk-in pantry for some plastic bags to put the ice in. He's so used to blind obedience with Renata that he immediately walks away.

Kostya takes advantage of Luca's absence and rushes toward me. I take a step back, unnerved by his eagerness. But we both stop and still when he's just in front of me. He looks left and right, checking for anyone who might be watching, and my eyebrows draw together.

He reaches into his pocket and pulls out an object. Reaching for my hand, he places the object on my palm and closes my fingers around it.

Kostya whispers to me in Russian. He tells me to use it when all feels lost, that Ezra will be given one as well. He tells me to hide it, keep it silent, and only use it when it's absolutely necessary. Because when the battery dies, that's it. He has no way to get me another.

I look down at my hand, jaw dropped open at what he's given me.

A cell phone.

A small, cheap texting-and-phone-calls-only kind of phone.

I ask him why.

He tells me he made a promise to Nikolai a long time ago—a promise to keep my heart beating even if Nikolai stopped it himself.

Kostya promised Nikolai he'd keep me alive?

Kostya knows how much I need Ezra to get me through hell with Vigo. He tells me I'll find only one contact listed on the phone when I turn it on, but I should wait until I'm home with the Vittoris and the phone can be hidden.

I'm baffled speechless.

I had distrusted Kostya for all these years.

But he'd given me pills when I was in pain, and now he's giving me a phone to text Ezra.

Only, he looks conflicted about it. I ask him if Nikolai told him to do this and he tells me no, rather emphatically. I know he's telling the truth by the way his eyes dart around the room, watching for anyone who might see or hear us.

Luca returns rather abruptly and Kostya turns on his heel, vanishing down the hallway before I can thank him.

Once again I'm grateful for Luca's blind obedience as I send him back inside the kitchen to fill one of the plastic bags with ice. I take that time to stuff the phone deep inside my jeans pocket, thankful the bottom of my shirt flares out loosely, just enough to hide the bulge until I can secure it safely beneath my mattress in my box at the Vittoris.

Luca and I return to our masters with the ice requested and my heart twitters with a flurry of excitement. There's something to look forward to, though it may be short lived. The phone battery will lose its charge at some point. But sometime soon, when I need him the most, I'll be able to reach out and contact Ezra.

Perhaps all is not lost.

Not yet.

CHAPTER 20
Ezra

SEEING ANYA—ONLY TO be taken from her again—was almost as hard as not seeing her at all. Her rosy scent is starting to fade from the pink evening gown I sleep beside in her room at Mikhailov Manor. Each night it fades a little more, only sinking me further into fear.

Fear of forgetting her scent, her smile, the electric crackle of her touch. Fear of losing her entirely.

It's only been a week since I saw her last at the Leblancs' and every minute that passes without a plan to save her makes me more fearful. Saving her and doing it soon is all I can think about now. My mind has spun its way through thousands of escape plans—a thousand possibilities and all of them are shitty. I know the odds are stacked against us—the probability of me actually finding a way to save her is next to nothing—but it won't stop me from trying.

I run my brain through a new train of thought while I sit on her armchair by the window and flip through the box of pictures of her sister Lidia. I've started keeping my pictures of Emma here as a reminder that any escape plan comes with high stakes for all of us.

Anya had received and placed the last picture of Lidia in the box the week before Nikolai sold her to Vigo. Looking at it now, I can see how they have the same smile. It's bright and true and has the sort of quality that makes you feel like you're special if you get to see it. On the back, as with all the pictures, are two numbers.

Eighteen.

Thirty.

Lidia's eighteen years old now. She looks happy in this picture, bright and cheerful. She looks more like her big sister now than she did in her younger pictures. Though it hurts my heart to see these—to look at Anya's sister, to see Emma, and know they're being stalked just for a weekly photo— it humbles my more outrageous ideas for escape. These pictures remind me that I can't just improvise, I can't be reckless, I can't fuck this up.

The picture I hold is the last one of Lidia. Nikolai hasn't brought anymore of her since Anya was sold months ago, though I continue to get new pictures of Emma.

Is Anya getting pictures of Lidia from Vigo?

Is Lidia alive?

Have they stopped watching her?

Maybe she's safe.

Of course, she's not safe…none of us are safe.

When the door to my room—Anya's room—bursts open wide without warning, I merely glance up from the picture in my hand. Though I was certain I'd see Nikolai standing there, I tilt my head in curiosity to see Kostya instead. Nikolai rather enjoys being unexpected company, so I'm surprised it's not him standing at my door. He's been gone a lot lately, though. He left again on business travel only a day or so after we returned from the quarterly meeting in Louisiana. Here we are, a week later, and I have yet to see him make an appearance.

Kostya steps inside without invitation and shuts the door behind him. My heart starts thumping against my ribcage, though I can't really place the feeling. I'm not exactly fearful of Kostya, not in the way I am for Nikolai and his unpredictable rage. But I am uncomfortable with him since I don't really have him figured out, which makes me nervous.

Kostya hurries across the room toward me and I sit up straighter, confused by what he's doing. But then he stops right in front of me. We pause in a weird kind of stillness as he looks down at me and I look up at him. A look of uncertainty flickers across his face, as if he's not sure why he came in here in the first place, or perhaps he's second guessing himself.

I don't ask the question, I just wait.

After a moment, a decisive expression wipes away his uncertainty and he reaches into his jacket pocket. In one motion, I set the box of pictures down on the ottoman in front of me and stand, curling my fists, ready to fight if he's come here to kill me or—

Why would Kostya kill me?

Why wouldn't he?

He holds out his hand in front of me and I freeze.

There's a cell phone in his palm. One of those small, prepaid things you can grab and pay cash for on your way through the checkout lane.

"I take a big risk for you," Kostya says in his thick Russian accent and broken English.

I realize then that I've never really spoken to this man. He's just kind of existed in the background.

My eyes dart between the phone and his face, trying to figure out what the fuck he's doing and *why*.

"We have many of these. Paid in cash. Business done this way. I stole two."

"Two? You stole two phones? From who?"

"*Khozyain.*"

There's a Russian word I'll never fucking forget.

He stole them from my *master*.

"Why?"

He sighs, setting the phone down on the ottoman. He rubs a hand over the back of his neck and turns his head to look at the door with urgency.

"You do not tell him."

"I won't tell him," I affirm, my heart thumping harder. "Is this a way out?"

He shakes his head. "Not for escape. Do not call the police. They will not come here. Mikhailovs pay for silence."

Well, fuck.

I know he's not bluffing. I'd be surprised if Nikolai *didn't* have the local police in his pocket—though local would probably be a relative term considering how far we are from anything even resembling civilization.

"Then what is this for?"

"I give one to Anya at the Leblancs'. One phone. One battery. I do not think she can charge it. But I give it to her."

"But *why?*"

"I make promise to Nikolai long time ago. Keep her heart beating even if he hurt her. Stop him from killing her when he lose control. I know she will hurt self again if she does not talk to you."

My heart stops.

"I can call her on this?"

"No," he says firmly, stepping closer. "No, you cannot speak. Only text. You cannot risk the phones being found. Keep silent. You understand?"

I nod though I'm stunned into silence. .

"She sent text, ten minutes ago. You should reply soon."

"She texted?"

He nods, taking a backward step.

"Keep it silent. Keep it hidden. He finds it and I will say you stole it."

I reach down, lifting the small, black phone from the ottoman as if it were a precious, fragile jewel. "Understood."

He turns and walks toward the door, but I stop him just as he grips the knob.

"Hey. I don't know if this is some kind of sadistic trick you and Nikolai have masterminded just to fuck with me, but if it's not…thank you."

"It is not trick," he says pulling the door open. "You are welcome."

He leaves and I fall back into my seat as I stare at the small screen. There's one unread text. I sigh, swiping a hand over my face. I know this could be fake. Hell, it's more likely some sick plan for Nikolai to torment me further by making me think I'm texting Anya.

Yeah, this might be a setup…but what if it's not?

It's a simple phone. A few click-throughs show me immediately that there's no internet, no apps, nothing helpful at all. It's not a touch screen and certainly not a smartphone. It's made just for phone calls and texts.

Without giving it another thought, I open the message that's waiting. It's from a phone number that has already been entered as a contact on this phone. In fact, it's the only contact listed.

Plain and simple, the text is from **A.**

Kostya must have set that up before giving us the phones to make sure no one texted from another number that I might mistake as Anya.

A Mine?

I sink back in my chair, lifting my hand to grip my hair as I stare at the screen in disbelief.

Only Anya would send that text.

I know it.

It's that punch in the gut feeling of just *knowing* it's her that makes me unintentionally hold my breath.

She sent her message twelve minutes ago. I have to hurry with my reply. I don't know what her living conditions are like—whether she has privacy to text me without someone catching her, whether her time to do this is limited.

E Yours.

My knee bounces as I hold the phone in front of my face, staring, waiting more anxiously than I ever have been before, just hoping for a reply.

"Come on…please, Anya," I whisper at the phone.

Two full panic-inducing minutes pass before a reply pops up on the screen. The phone is already set to silent and it will have to stay that way, meaning I'm going to drive myself insane waiting and staring at this thing.

A Is it really you?

I laugh, the breath I'd been holding rushes forcefully from my lungs. I feel relief, happiness, sadness, fear, and joy all at once. I know anybody could text that simple message, but I know it's her. I *know* it in the pit of my stomach.

E Who else would it be?

A It's really you.

My legs spread wide and I lean forward, resting my elbows on my knees as I type.

E Are you okay? Are you safe?

Our conversation continues, one reply after the next.

A Safe? Really?

E You know what I mean. Can you do this without getting caught?

A I think so. But I can't charge it. When the battery dies, that's it.

E Then we should make the most of our time.

A What are you suggesting, E?

I reason that Kostya must have entered my number in her contacts, too. He put her in mine as **A**, so naturally, she sees my messages as being sent from **E**.

E Your tone suggests a wandering mind, A.

A You're imagining my tone, E.

E Am I?

A Not entirely…I miss you.

E I miss you. So fucking much.

A couple of minutes pass without a reply. Though my fingers twitch to send another message, I wait. I wait because I don't know her situation or circumstances. I don't know where Vigo keeps her, whether it's safe for her to be texting me right now. I'm not going to risk her being found out by incessantly sending her texts—even though I think I could write her a goddamn novel right now and still not tell her everything I need to.

A I'm really trying, E. I'm trying to keep my promise.

Shit.

There's an implication with this message. She's trying to keep the promise she made me at the Leblancs', her promise to stay alive, to give me time to work out a way to save her. But this message tells me she's struggling because she has to *try* not to kill herself.

Fuck.

She has to *try*.

I shoot to my feet and pace the floor, pent up energy springing my legs into action.

What do I say to her?

What can I possibly say to that?

E I know you are and I love you more for it. Just for trying.

I squeeze my eyes shut after I press send. I think I can nearly feel her sigh from wherever the hell she is tonight.

A I don't want to be morbid. Distract me. Give me some peace.

E Just tell me what you need. You know I've got you.

A I don't even know what I need.

E Dick pic, maybe?

There's a pause.

I almost think that was a stupid thing to say, but I also know Anya. Sometimes she just needs a reminder that she's allowed to smile over something ridiculous, that she's allowed to take a break from being so damn serious. Though I am second-guessing it now because this situation has earned seriousness to the highest degree. And I know my sarcasm tends to get lost in translation, so...

A Send it.

E Seriously?

A NO! I don't think I've ever laughed out loud here. Not until just now.

Snark met with snark. I've met my match with her. My cheeks hurt from the wide fucking grin on my face.

E Damn. I had my pants off and everything for you.

A Did you really?

E I guess you'll never know.

A I wouldn't be offended if you did. Actually, I'd be offended to find out that you didn't.

E Take my pants off for you?

A Yes.

Every message sends excitement rushing through every part of me.
Anya excites me.
Face to face or through secret texts on a prepaid phone. My body tingles just to know it's her on the other end of the line. She's fucking *everything* to me.

I pause halfway through typing out a reply when she sends another message.

A Do you remember the first time we kissed?

Of course, I remembered.
It was the night that Nikolai forced me to help him rape her. I'd carried her back to her room that night, took care of her, cleansed her in the shower. We both admitted that night that we felt something connecting us. I'd told her that my heart raced for her. It was true then and it's true now, and I know that will never change.

E Of course I remember. How could I ever forget?

A I wanted you that night.

A I dreamed about you that night.

A I woke up, soaking wet between my legs and aching for you.

Jesus.

I lick my lips, running a hand across my mouth. Three texts sent from God knows where and this woman already has me half-hard.

E I dreamed about you that night, too. I woke up hard.

A Is that unusual for you? ;)

Did she just send me a fucking winking face?
Jesus Christ.
That's adorable.

E Not unusual since I met you. Did you touch yourself? After dreaming about me?

A I wanted to.

E But you didn't?

A It was the first time in three years I felt like I wanted to be touched. I just wasn't ready that night.

E But two days later in Nobility Hall…

We dry fucked like two horny teenagers, I want to write, but I don't.

A I was ready for it then. I felt safe with you.

E That means everything to me.

A That I felt safe with you?

E Yes.

A I always feel safe with you. I wish you were with me now.

E I'm so sorry. I feel like I've failed you, A.

A He's coming.

"Shit."

I burn a path into the rug with my panicked pacing. My veins pulse with adrenaline I can't resolve. If Vigo's coming for her now, I can't help her. I can't do a goddamn thing. If I thought it was hard before, it's nothing compared to the fear I have now.

He's coming, she wrote.

He's coming.

And I can't help her.

He's coming.

The last text I got from Anya was a haunting message sent a month ago.

He's coming.

I've all but died inside, not knowing what happened to her, where she is, if she's okay. I've devolved into a shell of a man who can hardly get out of bed.

I only eat when Nikolai forces me to, threatening to hurt Sasha if I refuse. I only sleep when I'm so beyond exhaustion—from dance rehearsals and being involved in Nikolai's sadistic torture-fuck sessions with poor Sasha—that my body forces itself to shut down.

I'm not the man Anya fell for right now, and I don't think I have it in me to become that man again until I know she's okay.

He's coming.

He was coming for her a goddamn month ago.

Did he find the phone?

Does he have her tied up somewhere?

Has she been tortured endlessly since the day we last texted?

Is she even fucking alive?

I know she's still alive. I know I would feel it in my soul if she were dead. Maybe that would be preferable to the alternative in my mind—where she's been locked up, tied down, fucked, beaten, and tortured for a goddamn month.

If she's going through half the shit I have nightmares about every time I collapse on her pillow, I wouldn't even blame her for breaking her promise to me and ending it all. I'd even pray she gets the opportunity and the courage to do it. And then I'd do the same thing because there's nothing left for me in this world if she's gone.

Fifty-two days.

Fifty-two days of waiting.

Fifty-two days of incessant, secret phone checking.

Every time I pick up the damn thing, I hope, pray, sacrifice my soul to whatever god in the universe wishes to take it, that I'll see that divine notification that I've got one new message.

That's all I want.

One new message.

I get up from the bed I can't seem to fall asleep in and wander to the dresser. I pull out the pink and green floral box of photographs and sit on the armchair. I sigh, deciding whether it's worth pulling out the phone to check. It'll only depress me further to see there aren't any new messages.

Still, I reach for it.

I'd never forgive myself if she had texted and I didn't see it just because I was too depressed to check. I was grateful that Kostya helped me keep it charged. I knew she couldn't charge hers, but at least my phone was ready to receive a message from her. I brace myself for disappointment.

I lift the basic-as-fuck cell phone from where I keep it hidden in the box of photographs and click the button on the side to illuminate the screen. My spine shoots straight and I fumble with the phone, doing a double take.

One.

New.

Message.

I jump to my feet, the box of photos flipping off my lap and crashing to the floor, the pictures spilling out into a jumbled pile of rectangles. I step over it, pacing forward a few strides from the sheer burst of energy provoked by that little envelope icon on the screen.

I click to open it.

A Mine?

She sent it to me five minutes ago. My fingers type faster than my brain can work.

E Yours.

E Are you okay? Tell me you're okay.

E Wtf happened?

A I'm alive. I wouldn't say I'm okay.

E I've been so fucking worried about you.

It takes her two minutes to reply. Two minutes that threaten to make my head explode and my heart collapse like a dying star.

A Has it really been nearly two months? That's what it says above my text. God, it feels like a year. He came for me unexpectedly when we last texted and I had to hide the phone. Didn't have time to turn it off. By the time I got back to my box, the battery had died. Got lucky. Risked my life to use Vigo's charger today, but only got 30%. Tell me you love me, quick.

E I fucking love you.

A Was the 'fucking' really necessary?

E Yes. Tell me you love me, quick.

A I love you more than my own life. I hope you know how true that is. I'm only alive because I made you a promise.

I run a shaking hand through my hair, trying to figure out how to respond. I read that last line three times in a row. *She's only alive because of her promise.* That means that she's thought about—

E I'm gonna find a way. I'm gonna save you.

I feel like I'm lying to her because I've failed her. I'm not any closer to figuring out how to save her, and I feel my own hope slipping. But selfishly, I keep promising that I'll save her, just to keep her alive, just because I can't stomach the thought of a world without Anya, even when she's suffering a fate worse than hell.

If I were a better man, a *good* man, I would let her go. I would tell her she didn't owe me anything. That she didn't need to keep any promises to me. I don't know what kind of hell she's living in, but I know the feeling I get from Vigo.

What kind of monster am I to ask her to live that hell for me?

I guess I'm not a good man because I can't let her go. I won't let her off the hook. I have to make her keep her promise.

E Just hang on for me. Just a little longer. I'll convince Nikolai to bring me to the next quarterly meeting at the Vittoris. One month. I'll find a way to take you away from this nightmare.

A I just want to be with you. That's all I want.

E Soon, baby. You and me. It's the only thing that matters.

CHAPTER 21
Anya

TIME PASSES BOTH slowly and quickly in this particular level of hell. I can hardly believe it's been two and a half months since I last saw Ezra at the Leblancs' estate; two and a half months since I last tried to end my life.

The few text message exchanges we had are the only thing that keeps me going. It's the only bright spot in the darkness of what my life has become. Even so, day by day, little by little, my strength is waning.

The battery on my phone is dead and I won't get lucky twice. I'd only been able to charge it the last time by risking everything. I had smuggled the phone from my box to his room when he took me one night. I plugged it into Vigo's charger when he left me locked alone in his room—Renata had come to him with an urgent need before he began his playtime with me. He hadn't injected me with his paralytic agent yet, and I was so damn lucky his charger even fit in the cheap, basic phone Kostya had smuggled to me.

My last exchange with Ezra had taken the battery life down to fifteen percent, so it's off and hidden beneath my mattress. It's just enough to have one more text exchange before the next quarterly meeting in a few weeks—when, hopefully, I can see my Ezra again.

I desperately need to see him because I think about ending my life daily. Some days I curse myself for promising Ezra I'd wait, that I would stay alive for him. But because I promised him, I try to keep my word.

It's past sunset and I haven't eaten today, but there's a buffet table in the piano room covered with platters of various finger foods. My mouth waters to see it as Vigo brings me and Bianca, the girl from the middle box, inside the open space. The girl in the first box died.

At least, I think she died.

He took her one night last week and she never came back. He hasn't replaced her, so that just leaves me and Bianca. It's not a comfort to have Bianca living beside me in this torment. She hates me because I won't entertain the idea of working together on an impossible escape plan. She has more hope than I do and sometimes I feel jealous for that. Her disdain for me only adds an additional layer of discomfort and unease to our shared slavery.

The black, grand piano that sits in the room beside the entrance of the Vittori home reminds me of the one in the dance studio at Mikhailov Manor—the piano that was never used, but sat there simply for appearance.

Olivia, the Vittoris' talent slave, stands beside the grand instrument with her hands demurely behind her back. Her eyes focus on a spot on the floor, her head bowed in servitude. She looks much healthier since Lorenzo has started to care for her. Vigo undoubtedly treated her as horribly as he treats me when she was his responsibility.

I think it's lucky for her that Lorenzo has taken an interest. I think he loves her. I can only guess, based on the way he looks at her, and I'm not entirely certain that she loves him back. Though she's healthier now in Lorenzo's care, there's no telling how he behaves with her behind closed doors.

She's still a slave.

Renata stands beside the buffet table, selecting an appetizer and popping it into her mouth. She says something to her collared slave boy, and he opens a bottle of champagne sitting on the tabletop. It pops when he uncorks it and my body jerks at being startled.

Vigo stops, spinning around to face me and Bianca. My eyes beg me to linger upon the sight of nourishment just ahead of us, but I force my head to bow.

"You're here to watch our talent slave rehearse. She needs an audience for practice," Vigo says. "Help yourself to food and drink, then sit on the couch so she can start. Go."

Neither of us wait for a second command. There's food and I've been given permission to eat. Wasting no time, I head over to the table and lift a small plate to fill with appetizers. This might be my only meal for a while, and my appetite has been especially voracious as of late. Normally, I could trick my mind away from focusing on the emptiness of my belly, but that's been harder and harder to do as of late.

I don't bother with a drink—water has been regularly supplied to us, so I'm not concerned with thirst. When my tiny plate is stacked full, I rush to the couch to sit and unceremoniously shovel food into my mouth.

The rest of the group settles on the couch and the armchairs beside it. Vigo plants his ass next to me with his hip touching mine. I wish to recoil, to pull away, but I'm already pressed as close to the armrest as I can be. He reaches to take a bite from my plate, plucking a morsel away and shoving it between his lips before I can protest.

Internally, I seethe.

I turn to glare at him, my eyes cold and hard, but he just smiles at me as he swallows.

I have never loathed someone as much as I loathe Vigo.

Lorenzo appears at Olivia's side and she turns to face him as he touches her arms gently. She tucks a strand of her straight, golden-blond hair behind her ear and her cheeks flush pink as she bows her head toward him.

He taps two fingers under her chin and she lifts. I can't hear what he says to her, but whatever it is elicits a tiny, cautious smile from her. It's so subtle, I can hardly call it a smile, but it's there.

It makes my heart ache for the way one touch from Ezra, one look, one word, could melt the entirety of my icy exterior and turn me into someone even *I* didn't recognize. One moment with him could bring all the best parts of me that I've hidden away for so long to the surface.

He makes me better when I'm with him.

It's painful the way I have to miss him now.

With Lorenzo's encouragement, Olivia moves to sit at the piano bench. He steps away, moving to stand behind the couch as Olivia begins to play. The piece she's selected is somber. The music is melancholy and hauntingly perfect—an eerie soundtrack for the nightmare of my life with the four families.

I only really listen for a few eight counts because my stomach aches, growling at me to focus on shoveling the food inside. I feel as though I could eat and never stop. I suppose it's the forced fasting that makes me feel this way, but God, it feels like I can never get enough to eat.

As the song ends, I follow the lead of my masters and politely applaud. Lorenzo applauds the loudest, his hands smacking together annoyingly just behind my head. Olivia stands and moves beside the piano, taking a simple bow and Lorenzo is beside her within moments. Renata pushes to stand from her chair, but Lorenzo holds up a palm.

"Wait," he begins.

I'm surprised he starts in English, though I assume it's for Olivia's benefit as she's American. Much of my life here is spent listening to other people speak in a language I don't understand, so this is a nice reprieve for my straining mind.

Renata looks surprised—and unsurprisingly annoyed—as she halts mid-rise and lowers back into her chair.

"I need to ask the family for permission," Lorenzo says.

Renata replies in Italian.

"English, please, so Olivia understands."

Renata tilts her head to the side. "Permission to do what?"

"To marry Olivia."

Vigo barks out a single laugh, leaning back on the couch and stretching his arms around me and Bianca on either side of him.

Renata sighs. "You wish to marry our talent slave?"

"Yes. I've fallen in love with her and I want to take care of her."

"Dearest Lorenzo, you're already taking care of her. You don't need to marry her to take care of her." Renata looks at them appraisingly.

"I wish for her to become a part of the family, to be treated as such. I wish for her to be my wife and bear my children."

Oh, God, I think I'm going to be sick.

Poor Olivia.

To think of being forced to marry and bring children into this nightmare. But when I look at her, I see this news doesn't come as a surprise, as if they've discussed this before. Her cheeks blush pink with hope, not fear—I can see it in her eyes.

"It's not unheard of for a family member to marry a talent slave," Vigo states. "Though I think it's only been done with a Head of House. Perhaps *I* should marry her."

I glance surreptitiously at Vigo and see his smart-ass smirk and I have to force myself not to roll my eyes. I actually have to breathe through the nausea that rolls through my insides.

Renata lifts an annoyed eyebrow at her brother. "Do you *wish* to marry her, Vigo?"

"Of course not," he scoffs.

"I don't know why you insist on being so flippant. These are serious discussions, Vigo. In a year, you'll be forty and it will be time for you to select your own bride. I suggest you stop making light of marriage, knowing full-well that your own is on the horizon."

His smirk fades away as she speaks. "I have no desire for a bride."

"It's not a choice, Vigo. You need to continue the family line with the Vittori name."

"And why don't *you* just have the children?" Vigo says to Renata. "You never even had a chance to legally change your name before Giovanni died. You're still a Vittori."

Who is Giovanni, and what does he have to do with Renata's last name?

"I would never besmirch my husband—rest his soul—in such a manner as to marry again. And if I did marry, my name would no longer be Vittori, now would it? How do you propose the name should be passed along then?" she snaps at him.

Vigo shrugs and boredom washes down his features.

"You *will* select a bride next year," she says with a snap of finality before returning her attention to Lorenzo and Olivia. "As for the two of you…" She pauses. "What do you have to say about this, Olivia?"

Olivia swiftly lifts her head from its bowed position, looking first at Lorenzo beside her. He gives her a gentle nod and she looks at Renata.

"If the family wishes to have me, I would be grateful to marry Lorenzo."

"Do you love him?"

Olivia swallows. "Yes."

"Are you willing to give him children?"

"Yes."

"And you understand how your role will change with the family? You will no longer be a slave, but a wife. You will become Mrs. Fiore. Your duty to the Vittori family will come above all else and that may involve dealings which threaten your safety, your well-being, the very core of who you are as a person. Are you prepared to take on such a burden?"

Lorenzo places his hand on the small of her back and she must find strength in that. She lifts her chin a little higher.

No.

Tell them no.

"Yes, I'm prepared," Olivia says and it's clear that she means it.

Renata's eyes narrow as she takes in a deep breath, regarding the two of them with precise consideration. "We would need to find new talent and with only weeks until we host—"

Olivia boldly interrupts Renata, "I would still like to perform."

I turn my head to watch Renata, sure she won't be favorable to such an interruption. But I'm wrong. A slow smile lifts her cheeks.

"She's loyal to the family," Lorenzo says. "Please."

Renata nods as she looks at Vigo.

"Fine," Vigo says. "Of course, we'll have to put it to a vote with the board, but I don't see why any of our colleagues would deny it."

Lorenzo and Olivia let smiles light their faces as they both sigh in relief. Lorenzo hugs Olivia with such force, it nearly knocks her backward.

It breaks my heart.

What has made me so undeserving?

What have I done that's so miserably awful as to give me this lot in life?

To see anyone happy in love right now makes me sick. It makes my chest feel tight, my muscles feel weak, my belly roil with nausea, my head spin with dizziness.

It makes me sick.

Sick.

Actual bile rises in my throat.

Oh, God, I'm going to be sick.

I can't vomit here in the piano room, on Renata's precious carpet. Even when my stomach threatens to purge its contents, I have to consider the consequences of my body's involuntary reactions.

I jump up and run, heading for the bathroom that's just down the hall. The moment my ass lifts from the couch, Vigo yells for me, jumping to his feet and chasing after me. I make it to the bathroom before he catches up, shove the door open, and reach the toilet just in time to purge the only food I've eaten in twenty-four hours.

"Fuck." I hear him at the open door. "Are you sick?"

I want to give him my middle finger, roll my eyes, and tell him, *"Obviously,"* but I bite back the urge. Instead, I just nod, which only adds to the dizziness.

He leaves me.

I don't know if he's coming back to get me.

I don't know if he's just going to leave me here in the bathroom all night.

I don't know if I'm going to vomit again.

I just feel *off.*

All I know is that I'm a sad, sick, pathetically broken little doll, and I'm running out of time for Ezra to save me.

CHAPTER 22
NIKOLAI

I EMPHATICALLY DESPISE the quarterly meetings hosted by the Vittoris. Since it's hosted at their home in Italy, the entirety of their extended family—at least those associated with the work of the four families—are in attendance. It's a noisy, boisterous affair that only serves to remind me that my own family is gone.

The one singular thing I have to look forward to at this particular event is seeing the woman I've so precisely groomed to hate me over the years.

I had planned to bring Sasha as my escort for the evening, but that hadn't worked out. Suffice it to say, I'd lost control of myself, and in a moment of fury over Ezra's pathetic depression, my rage took hold. In my fury, I'd killed her.

I didn't feel badly about it. She wasn't the first person in my life that I'd murdered.

But I'd felt…something.

Not that I felt anything about murdering Sasha—the groveling little whore had it coming. The *something* I'd felt was for the reminder of what I'd given up, the understanding that I'd sold a girl I'd never genuinely wanted to die, and tried to replace her with someone like Sasha.

Anya made me hate her viciously sometimes, but she never bored me. I'd always enjoyed watching her internally struggle through the torment I handed her, especially watching her with her partners and the power struggle she endured. But Sasha never really seemed to have anything going on in her stupid little head.

The something I'd felt when I strangled the life out of Sasha was regret because I'd sent Anya away. I understood that my anger had reached its peak because I missed the bitch who betrayed me.

I missed Anya.

In that feeling came the furious realization that the regret I felt could not be rectified. The woman I regretted discarding could *not* be replaced, and so, the replacement had to go.

That is why I killed Sasha.

Because of Anya.

I brought Ezra with me to this reception for two reasons. The first was that he'd asked…begged, really. His ridiculous sniveling over her appealed to my regret because on some level, somewhere inside my heartless soul, I understood what he missed. He and I weren't so dissimilar after all. We were both reckless, impatient, impulsive—he even had a little violence in him, though he seemed to be able to tamper his. I recognized the innate goodness in him, the light inside of him—a light I'd once thought I might have possessed had I been born outside the world of the four families.

But I couldn't change my fate and the darkness was a part of me. Still, I had a disgusting fondness for Ezra, a soft spot I hadn't had with Anya's other partners, and I knew it was there because I saw so much of myself in him.

The second reason I brought Ezra with me is that I enjoy his companionship. He hates me and I love the spirited rivalry it elicits between us. I want more from him. I desire him. I *will* take from him.

Someday.

When the timing is right.

When my father's voice gets the fuck out of my head and lets me be who I am.

"Where the fuck is she?" Ezra says to me in a hushed tone.

He's surly about the fact that we've already witnessed the Vittori talent—the pianist who seems much brighter than I remembered her being in the past—and have been at the reception for an hour and still haven't seen Anya. I'm also on edge about the fact that she hasn't made an appearance, but I don't let on. This is a business event first and foremost, and I cannot allow that to be overshadowed by a personal interest.

"I don't know," I bite back at him as Delia and Murphy approach. "Be *quiet.*"

I greet my colleagues from the O'Shea family in kind, though I find Ezra's continued agitation only seems to fuel my own. Murphy is telling me about the bride he's chosen for himself that we'll be voting for approval at the meeting later, but my attention is drawn away toward the top of the wide, curving staircase.

Vigo has appeared, dragging along a wisp of a girl at the top of the staircase. I start to turn my attention back to Murphy and Delia, but then I realize that it's no wisp of a girl ambling along behind him.

It's Anya.

So thin that I hardly recognize her.

Ezra lurches forward, brushing past me as he spots her, and I reach out to snatch his elbow, yanking hard to pull him back.

"Where do you think you're going?"

He looks at me with annoyance and nods his head toward Vigo and Anya descending the steps.

"Stand behind me," I snap at him. "Do you think you can just leave my side and stroll over to a Head of House? Mind your place, *mal'chik.*"

He settles into his place behind me, though his presence is anything but stable. His agitation is palpable, and though I normally enjoy putting him on edge, I feel my own instability at the sight of her. I can't focus on controlling him when I'm so bothered trying to control my own volatile reaction.

I manage to smile and nod in polite conversation with Murphy and Delia. I try to behave as though I'm paying attention, but the frailty of the girl I once considered strong enough to be mine continues to steal my attention.

What has he done to her?

"Bloody hell, what has he done to her?" Delia echoes my inner thought.

I follow her eyes to see that she's looking at Anya and Vigo, as well.

"Wanker," Murphy adds. "It's one thing to deny a meal or two when breaking-in your slave, but she looks as if her grave's already been dug."

I breathe in deeply through my nose, anger rising at the confirmation of my colleagues that my former talent slave, my beneficiary since her childhood, has been vastly mistreated. I storm forward, no thought to my steps, just a boiling, festering need within my chest to demand answers as to why *my* slave has been so poorly lacking.

As I push through the throng to meet them at the bottom of the staircase, I hear the rushed clicking of Delia's shoes as she rushes past me. Her hand touches the crease of my arm as she moves in front of me and I have half a mind to whip the back of my palm against her face for her interference.

But then Ezra passes me on the opposite side in a flurry and my attention must go to him. I grab him by the elbow and fling him back behind me as I step forward.

Delia has already closed in on Vigo, stepping swiftly and forcefully into his space as Anya curls in around her center, shrinking away from him, from *us*.

"I thought we had an understanding of the provisions in your contract with Nikolai." Delia's nostrils flare with indignation, her lips pull tight over her teeth as she speaks. "We spent an entire *night* at the last quarterly meeting going through it together."

She's as black-and-white about following the rules as any of us—perhaps more so.

Vigo's eyes graze across her regal form with a flicker of interest. "Perhaps you should spend another night going through it with me, Cordelia."

Delia taps his wrist. "Not here, Vigo." She turns away from the rest of us, taking a few steps and he follows her like a dog—she's the only woman Vigo has ever let lead him. I would say their pairing is unusual, but many pairings within the four families are on the side of unexpected.

I turn back to Anya, hovering there in a shapeless, blue, silk gown. It hangs from her body rather than clings to her curves, and I can't help but mourn the loss of those womanly imperfections.

In fact, I had hoped I'd see something more there at her waistline…

I reach for her, grabbing her right wrist at the exact moment Ezra grabs her left and she's suddenly a frozen deer in the forest having come face to face with two predators. I'm the only true predator here, so I take her by force.

She nearly falls into my arms from how weak she's become. I wrap my arms around her waist and brush the hair across her forehead, studying with narrowed eyes as she sways in my hold, her back arching so she can look up at me with fierce, cold eyes. The blue is particularly glacial tonight, brought out by the matching color of her dress.

"What has he done to you, *rabynya?*"

She may not have the energy to stand, but she somehow finds enough to retort, "*Rabynya?* No. Not, *rabynya. Sono una bambola rotta.*" She gazes up at me with a disquieting sneer. "I am a broken doll now."

There are a million things I could say to that unnecessarily sarcastic comment, but not a single one of them finds its way past my lips. Looking down at her now—compared to all the ways I've looked down upon her before—I feel…guilt.

I should've known better than to think that Vigo would uphold his end of the contract. I'd carefully crafted the contract of sale to provide clauses that should have ensured Anya's well-being while she remained alive, though of course, the length of that time was his to choose.

I thought having it on paper would be enough.

Clearly, it's not.

Even Delia, whom I'd consider a friend under appropriate circumstances, doesn't seem capable of helping him understand. She had spent time with Vigo at the last quarterly meeting reviewing the contract of sale at the recommendation of the board. Undoubtedly, they had squandered their evening hours engaging in more interesting matters between the two of them. It was happening even now. Though Delia had pulled Vigo aside at the sight of Anya, one glance in their direction shows me that she's too easily taken under Vigo's spell.

Regardless, it's not her place or her problem, and I don't wish to make it so. I could let the board select a consequence for Vigo's breach of contract, but that may result in an unfavorable outcome for Anya.

Apparently, I give a shit now.

I'll deal with this myself.

Anya shoves her weak palms against my chest, hardly even registering as a push against my bulk, but I release her and let her step back.

I turn away from her and go to Vigo as Ezra pulls her into his arms. I don't care that he does it, it *almost* seems reasonable at this point—given her state—that someone should hold her up so she doesn't crumple to the floor and break a hip on the way down.

She's fragile now.

She was never fragile in my care.

She was strong. She could take anything I did to her.

Now I fear she may tip over if I exhale too strongly.

I approach Vigo as he's leaning in to whisper something against Delia's ear. "I want to buy her back."

They both freeze, holding their intimate position except for Vigo's head that turns toward me. "Buy her back?"

"You heard me."

Vigo kisses Delia on the cheek before pulling away and turning to face me squarely. "No."

I sigh. "Name your price, Vigo."

"No. I'm not selling her back to you. We've had this discussion before, and it's done."

I step forward, gritting my teeth with frustration. "Name. Your. *Price*."

"Four million," he says with a mocking smile.

I stifle a laugh. "I sold her to you for less than one and her value has depreciated in your care." My upper lip snarls and my nostrils flare as Vigo crosses his arms over his chest, casting a sideways glance. "Fuck. I'll give you two million."

Vigo throws his head back and laughs. "You can't be serious, Nikolai. Who in their right mind would pay that much for a talent slave who has lost her talent? For a woman who looks like *that*…" He nods his head toward her and I glance.

Ezra holds her sweetly, his arms wrapped around her tightly as if he's afraid to let her go.

He should be.

I observe her overly slender form, the brittleness of her body, and though I can't argue with the look of her, I can argue the reason that she looks that way.

"She looks like that because of *you*," I tell Vigo. "In my care, she was healthy. She had curves, desirable flesh. You've dissolved that flesh through starvation until nothing but bone is left."

"And that is my right as her owner."

I swipe a hand over my mouth, feeling the weight of my vengeance to have sold her to him in the first place sit down heavily across my shoulders.

"Three million," I offer.

Vigo laughs. "I wouldn't have sold her back to you for four million. I wouldn't do it for five. The agitation this causes you is worth far more than any sum you could offer me. Consider that my final say on the matter. Anya is mine, and she will remain mine until the day she dies."

My fists clench at my sides and I don't even have to turn and look to know how Ezra catches on fire from this conversation. His adrenaline spike is visceral, and I feel it at my back, fueling my own.

"I'll give you ten," I say and it's my final fucking offer, my final fucking *ridiculous* offer to end this matter.

"You're a real chancer, aren't ya?" Murphy says, coming up beside me and clapping me on the back. "Quite the risk offering up such a large sum for a slave in her condition. Take this to the board, Nikolai."

I shrug his hand off my back. "This is no game of chance. I understand the risks of her remaining in his care. And if I take this to the board, she'll be decommissioned."

"Why does it bother you, Nikolai?" Vigo asks, taunting me with a tilt of his head. "Does she matter to you now?"

I don't have to answer his questions.

"Ten million for Anya." I hear how pathetic and desperate the offer sounds.

Ten million for a slave?

"No," Vigo says, his face dropping swiftly into seriousness as he reaches out a hand toward Anya. "Come with me, my little Russian doll."

Anya looks up at Ezra and it's as if a million words are spoken between them with just a look. It's almost as though she's saying goodbye to him and it feels like someone has driven a knife into my hollow chest. I have no heart, so the knife only grates between my rib bones, slicing around, trying to find purchase on the beating pump that doesn't exist.

It reminds me just how empty I am.

Vigo takes Anya and they go, heading toward the grand staircase. She's hardly arrived at the reception, only to be gone again in a flash.

What was the point of bringing her down here in the first place?

I glance up at them as they climb the staircase, Vigo taking the steps at a near jog as Anya barely drags herself up by the railing. He reaches the balcony landing at the top and turns to watch her frail form amble to follow. Vigo's eyes meet mine and a dreadful smirk appears on his face.

I immediately understand why he left with haste—to punish *her* for *my* offer. Except it's not a punishment if she hasn't done anything to deserve it. It's just torment for torment's sake—for Anya and for me.

My offer has been denied.

I may be empty now, but I remember the promise of Anya's warm body and penetrating eyes and the way that would fill me for the moments we were together. It was the only thing that kept me getting out of bed and continuing on when my family had been wiped out. That promise kept me from eating a bullet on several occasions.

Now I'm faced with a choice.

Accept that I can't buy her back and that I will be forced to live without her or do something about it.

I can do something about it tonight.

I look at Ezra, who looks as though his grief and rage might swallow him whole. The decision I've made is going to require reckless abandon.

I knew no one who was as recklessly impulsive as Ezra.

I have an idea of what I want to do, though I wish I didn't feel so compelled to do it.

It's risky.

Dangerous.

Yet I know it's time for me to play my trump card, take responsibility for what I've done, and ensure Anya's future.

I don't want to feel guilt or shame or responsibility. Those are feelings I'm not accustomed to and feelings I don't intend to have for much longer.

I must rectify my shame by taking back what's mine, the only family I have left. It will cost me my reputation and respect within the four families, but what can they do? There are no other Mikhailov men to replace me…and apparently none on the way.

Consequences with the board be damned.

I'm going to steal Anya back.

I'm taking her tonight.

CHAPTER 23

Anya

I SLUMP TO sit on the cold tile floor the instant Vigo brings me into his bathroom upstairs. I'm exhausted. The last dregs of my energy have been drained. I just want him to leave me for the night so I can rest.

I should be wary about the fact that he's brought me to his room, rather than return me to my translucent box in the basement. My tired brain doesn't have the capability of worry. Even seeing Ezra again, though it electrified me for the moments he held me, wasn't enough to jolt me from this overwhelming exhaustion.

Vigo leans over the sink, peering at his reflection in the mirror. He picks a comb through his hair, adjusting the style to perfection, and turns his head to one side, then the other to inspect his profile. He straightens and runs his hands over his lapels to smooth his jacket. "I'll be gone for several hours."

I nod feebly from my pathetic position on the floor, my back leans against the wall beside the clawfoot tub.

"I thought you might enjoy a change of scenery for your evening, so I'm keeping you here rather than returning you to your box."

Every word I speak in response is dripping with sarcasm, though I find a way to hide the tone in my voice. "That's very kind of you, *Papà*."

He pauses before he slowly spins to look at me. "I've had a lovely little idea rolling around in my head and this seems like the perfect time to try it out."

A quake bursts inside my chest, shooting warning vibrations throughout my entire body. I scoot back, straightening my spine against the wall behind me.

"I will gladly go back to my box tonight and save you the trouble."

I *want* to go back to my box.

He's got that look on his face that tells my heart to beat faster, to get the adrenaline pulsing through my veins so I can run.

He moves in front of me, holding out his hand. "Come here."

Somehow, I manage to lift my trembling hand to meet his and he pulls me to my feet. My body sways toward him, my head light and dizzy because all I've consumed today was some water early this morning. Vigo holds me steady with his hands on my waist.

He tilts his head toward the clawfoot tub and his teeth appear behind his lips as they part into an awful grin. "Get in the tub."

The word burns my lips as it bursts forth. "*No.*"

"Yes." His eyebrows lift with glee. "Look, it's not even filled. I just want you to sit in it, that's all."

That's not fucking all and we both know it.

He's a lying, tormenting, sick son of a bitch, and we both know that, too.

"Get in. Unless you'd like to suck my cock first and *then* get in. That would be fine, too."

The last goddamn thing I want is his dick in my mouth. Though my heart threatens to explode from my chest in panic over the tub, I turn to move toward it.

"Good girl," he tells me, letting go of me.

I take one step forward toward the porcelain bathtub and gradually lower my quivering hands to rest on the edge, gripping it tight. I pinch my eyes shut and search my soul for a bit of strength, just enough to get my leg over the edge. It takes every ounce of emotional strength I have left, but I do it. I lift my leg, swing it over the edge, and drop my foot slowly to the bottom.

I blow out all the air in my lungs as I steel myself against the rising panic, sucking it all back in to give myself the strength to bring my other leg over the edge, too. The stiletto of my shoe slips along the porcelain bottom as I shift my weight, but I right myself quickly. I cross my arms over my chest as I rise, shivering as I stand in the tub he's tortured me in over and over again.

Vigo comes forward, reaching out to touch my arms and rub them in a motion that mimics comfort. His touch is anything but comforting.

"No injection tonight, I promise."

I shake my head in disbelief; I don't trust his word.

"No injection. Just sit. All you have to do is sit."

His eyes implore me to submit, to do as I'm told. I lower because I'm tired, wary, and weak in every sense of the word. Tears well and begin to drip down my cheeks, but I lower. I tremble and cry on my way down, but still, I lower.

The porcelain tub is hard and unforgiving beneath my butt, and it's uncomfortable to sit here in the center of it. I couldn't relax my body enough to lean against the edge if I tried, so I remain upright, my knees bent in front of me.

Vigo's not happy with this though.

He places a hand on my chest and pushes hard. The fabric of the dress I'm wearing glides easily along the smooth surface and he pushes me until my back is resting against the far edge of the tub.

I'm rigid, my head shaking from side to side. Vigo grabs my cheeks and bends deep over the edge, touching his nose to mine. "All you have to do is sit here." He kisses my forehead before he releases me and steps away.

I'm frozen as he walks into his bedroom.

Is he leaving me here? Like this?

I shut my eyes, squeezing them to blink away the remainder of the tears that form pools there. I open them wide again when I hear him return.

My head snaps to look at him and I see he's come back with a cable tie. Instantly, my hands fly out to grip the edges of the tub, but it's no use. In a flash, he grabs both my wrists and squeezes them together.

"No, *no!*" I cry and thrash, trying to wiggle free from his grip.

He's quick, lassoing the tie around my wrists and securing it so tight that it digs into my skin painfully. It's as if I can feel the bones of my wrists touching, grating against each other.

"Don't leave me here." I quickly descend into hysterics, sobbing and shouting, "*Please,* don't leave me like this. *Please!*"

Vigo smiles, touching a finger to his lips as if to hush me, before darting out of the room again.

I'm getting out of this fucking tub.

I turn my body and stretch my fingers, doing my best to grip the edge with my crossed hands. I can't get purchase with my feet as my narrow heels easily slip over the smooth surface.

I stop abruptly when Vigo comes in carrying an oversized standing mirror and something dangling from his fist where he holds the wooden frame.

He doesn't pause, doesn't stop, doesn't even look at me. He just moves forward. He lifts the gigantic mirror, twisting it sideways, and flipping it toward me.

I shout and move back, releasing my grip from the tub's edge just in time to avoid having my fingers smashed. He sets the mirror, glass side down, over the rim of the tub, covering it completely across the shortest length, the frame hanging off the edges. My spine presses to the back of the tub as I scoot away, but he keeps moving.

As he starts to slide it back toward me, I realize what he's doing. He's trying to trap me with it. He's trying to cover the tub with a fucking oversized mirror.

The end of it shoves toward me until I can move no further. The top framed edge of the mirror crowds me, taps against my chin and I straighten to lift above it, but then he shoves it against my throat.

He grins at me above the top of the tomb he wishes to create for me. He yanks the mirror back a couple of inches and tilts his head down. "Duck your head."

Air jumps in and out of my lungs in quick, short bursts, my chest hopping with the panicked intake of oxygen.

"No," I tell him. "No!"

"Yes," he says. "This or the injection, your choice."

My face twists in pain at the impossible choice he's giving me. I don't think I can face the injection again, the inability to move while remaining awake. But I also don't want to be trapped inside this tub. I know that's his intention—I see the coarse rope he's brought in now along with the mirror.

I choose without any choice at all, the words falling from my lips freely. "No injection."

He nods. "Under you go, then."

My entire body shakes, the epicenter of a quake radiating out from the pit of my stomach. Somehow, *somehow*, I let myself slip. I let the smooth porcelain take me as my body slumps down the back edge. Vigo slides the mirror over my head. It's massive, large enough to cover the entire top of the tub, trapping me inside with my own dark reflection.

"Are you comfortable in there, *bambola Russa?*" he asks, then laughs.

The mirror shifts, sliding further over the edge by my head and light appears suddenly at the far end by my feet. He's left a gap there.

He's left a gap where the faucet runs.

He can't.

He won't.

He wouldn't.

Of course, he will.

I put my hands against the glass and push.

I expect the mirror to be heavy, but not to be immovable as it is. Maybe I just really am that weak now.

"Put your hands down, Anya. I haven't finished tying it in place yet."

Tying it in place?

I scream, "Let me out!"

"Hush, *la mia bambola Russa.*"

I scream.

I shout.

I squirm and thrash.

But there's no point. My muscles are weak. My body is exhausted. Vigo can't be persuaded once his mind is made up.

And I feel done.

I'm done.

I let my head fall back to rest against the tub and give myself up to the sobbing mess I've become.

The mirror shifts left and right, and I hear him loop the rope around, over the mirror, wrapping beneath the clawfoot tub to secure it. Over and over again the mirror shifts and he tugs the rope…shifts and tugs, shifts and tugs.

When the shifting finally stops, there's a beat of silence in the room. It's the strangest, most horrifying beat of silence I've ever experienced.

Is he gone?

Will this be it?

Spend a few hours in the tub and that's all?

No, that can't be.

Just as I'm about to take a breath to settle into the silence, he speaks. "I'm curious to know whether you have the strength to keep your head above water, *bambola Russa.* Has your brief encounter with the slave boy given you your fight back? I suppose we'll find out soon enough. I've been wanting to do this since you tried to kill yourself last quarter. Poetic, isn't it? To be trapped with your reflection considering you tried to kill yourself with the broken shards of it before."

I open my mouth to scream at him at the exact moment that I hear the familiar squeak of the faucet handles being turned, at the exact moment water begins to flow heavy and fast from the spout into the small gap he's left. Cold water pours onto my feet and I yank them back with a jerk, only to result in my body slipping farther down in the tub.

The water slowly warms to tepid as my panic overheats to boiling.

I scream.

I shout for help.

I beg for mercy.

The fabric of my dress saturates. A thin layer of water runs under my legs, spilling beneath my back and the pool starts to rise.

Slowly, *slowly*, the water rises.

I stare up at my shadowed reflection in the mirror and see a dead girl staring back at me.

This is it.

This is how I will die.

And the only regret I have is not falling in love with Ezra sooner, faster, from the moment I saw him and felt that immediate spark of awareness that he and I were in some special way connected.

Soul mates.

Meant to be.

Made for each other.

I love him, even though he's failed me.

I hold no blame for the fact that he couldn't save me. It was an ill-fated promise he made, and I'd known it from the start.

And to think he's here tonight, perhaps with a plan, hoping for a chance to reveal itself to him so he can take me away from this place. But I think we both knew the only way I was leaving was by death.

I hope he knows that I tried my best to stay alive for him.

Vigo whistles a tune that would sound cheerful under normal circumstances but is haunting in its joviality now. The roar of the water as it spills into the tub mingles with the eerie tune, wrapping around my fear and choking it into panic.

I scream one last time, loud and long, with all the anger my soul possesses for what the universe has done to me.

But still, the water rises.

This is the end of everything.

Vigo waits until the tub is practically overflowing to turn off the faucet, and as soon as he does, he's gone.

I think I might try to wedge the heel of my stiletto beneath the drain stop, maybe lift it enough to get the water to drain out. But then I realize I can't. The drain is internal, activated by a small metal lever that I can't reach from inside the tub.

"Shit!"

Shifting my body, I unintentionally roll sideways. My muscles are weak, and I struggle to keep my face above the surface. As my cheek dips into the water, my body jerks, thrashing until I'm facing up again. A wave rolls through the tub, pulsing against the side and returning, though some of the water spills out at the gap near my feet.

Maybe I can splash out enough water to give myself some space to breathe without straining every muscle in my body to stay afloat. I thrash some more, trying to get as much water from my porcelain coffin as I can.

It takes less than a minute of battering my body against the water before I'm forced to stop.

My body is weak.

I feel truthfully and completely drained now.

I slip under the surface in my exhaustion, barely able to bring myself back up again. I can't stay afloat. And even when I can hold myself above the surface, the mirror reminds me of what's beneath, showing me a reflection of my watery grave.

Vigo knew my strength was gone.

He'd been preparing me for this particular torture, withholding nourishment, exercise, the basic things a human needs to stay alive, to survive. He knew I might not survive this.

I'm not going to survive this.

Oh, God…I'm not going to survive.

I quickly shift from a slow growing panic into outright madness. I flail in the water, fling my arms and legs, let myself drift beneath the surface to whip the water with my body, hoping to spill as much water over the edge as I can.

The barrier Vigo crafted is rudimentary, so of course, it isn't a watertight seal. Still, it's proving to be effective enough because the water stays with me. The waves I create with my whipping body just hit my reflection in the mirror above me and crash back down to smother me again from above.

The fearful girl I see in my reflection taunts me and my madness shifts focus. Though I don't have the power to even nudge the barrier above me, I lash out at it all the same. I curl my fingers into fists and pound my knuckles against the glass, over and over and over. All I manage to do is splinter the surface, bloodying my hands for my effort.

I can't keep doing this.

I'm done now.

Done with all of it.

The fighting. The torment. The struggle.

I'm done.

I float, using what's left of my adrenaline to keep my face above the surface.

But I know I need to let go.

Giving in is what's best for me now. This was always my fate and fighting it only prolongs the suffering.

I can't do it anymore.

Then why am I still holding on?

I keep fighting because of him, because of Ezra, because of that dangerous fucking hope he brought into my life that somehow we could be together and happy.

I want that life with him.

I want it *so* fucking much.

Wanting something this much sets fire to the frozen shell around my heart and burns me with a blaze of angry fire, fire I can't let out because I'm trapped in this water-filled coffin. It's enough blazing energy to punch out his name in a piercing shout, a last-ditch effort to beg the universe to change my fate, to change *our* fate.

"Ezra!" I scream.

It's a declaration, a shout to no one and nothing that Ezra is the first thing on my mind, the last thing on my mind, the *only* thing on my mind as I prepare to let go of life.

I pound my fists at the splintered glass one last time. It sends a rippling crack in a diagonal line, cutting across the reflection of my face. I blink, the last of my tears falling as I watch how the sapphire color of my eyes deepens into a dark navy-blue in the mirror.

"Please," I mutter sadly at my reflection.

A plea to the girl in the mirror to fight, to find her strength, to hold on just a little longer.

You promised him…

You promised you'd hold on as long as you can.

I press my eyes shut, force my shallow breaths to lengthen in a long steady flow, and focus on floating. All I have to do is float. Float through one count of eight, then another, and another until this careful dance with death is over.

I bring forward the memory of our dance in Nobility Hall and focus on the routine. I run it through my head step by step, beat by beat, as if preparing for the performance—an encore of the dance that changed everything. Each eight count gets me closer to the end of this, closer to peace.

And so, I count.

One. Two. Three. Four. Five. Six. Seven. Eight.

CHAPTER 24
Ezra

I BLINK, STILL frozen in disbelief at the state of my blue-eyed girl as she disappears from sight. My entire being is still in shock from the sight of her, practically dragging herself up the staircase by the railing.

Fuck, she'd been so frail.

Skin and fucking bones.

I think my heart has stopped beating.

My lungs have forgotten how to take in air.

My body has forgotten how to move.

But then, everything explodes back to life all at once. My system is flooded with the incessant need to run to her, to save her, to do fucking anything at any cost to spare her future torment.

I move without thinking, ready to take off at a run. I make it one step before Kostya leaps in front of me and I nearly slam into his chest. Then Nikolai grabs the collar of my jacket, flinging me backward. He grabs my shoulders and physically turns me away from the staircase.

"Go. Move. *Move.*" Nikolai shoves at my back, pushing me through the throng of guests.

He pushes me until we make the clearing and turn down a hallway beneath the staircase.

I need to go after her.

I slam to a halt, spinning around to face Nikolai. He grabs the lapels of my suit jacket, fisting the fabric and shoving me until my back is against a wall.

"Shut up and listen to me, *mal'chik,*" he tells me as Kostya catches up to us, standing at our side. "I'm stealing her back tonight. I need you to focus so you don't fuck it all up, do you understand me?"

Stealing her back?

He wants to steal her back?

My muscles twitch at the thought. I was ready to fight to the death to save her, but I didn't have a plan. The only strategy I had come up with was improvisation. That may work with my dancing, but I have no idea what the fuck I'm doing here on my own.

But I can't wrap my head around working with Nikolai. Helping him steal her back would only mean bringing her back into servitude to Nikolai.

But that's better, isn't it?

At least then she'd be with me—maybe we could plot a real escape together.

"Are you serious about this?" I ask him.

"Am I ever anything but serious?"

I don't even know how the fuck to respond to that.

"I'm listening. Tell me what to do and I'll do it."

His jaw ticks. "I wish all your concessions were given so easily."

I grit my teeth. "When it comes to Anya, you know I'll do anything."

"Be careful with your promises. Someday I might come collecting."

"Are we having a pissing contest or do you want to tell me your plan?"

He pulls me toward him by my jacket and then slams my back to the wall again. I hit with a *thud* and the air rushes from my lungs as the back of my head bounces off. He lets go of me and takes a small step back, glancing at Kostya before looking at me again.

"You're going to do exactly what your instincts tell you to. You're going after her," he says.

"What?" Frustration washes over me and I throw up my arms. "Why the fuck did you stop me then?"

"Because I need us on the same page. You're going to fight me off here and run after her. Back through the party, up the stairs."

"And that's your plan? I'm just supposed to run after her? Then what?"

"Then we take her back."

"Together? Or do you plan to off me once I deliver her back to you? Because I'll tell you what, I'm not letting that happen. She fucking needs me, especially with you."

"This isn't a negotiation," he hisses through his teeth.

"You can't do this without me. She's on the edge, Nikolai. If you kill me once you have her back, she'll find a way to kill herself—you and I both know she will. She'll have nothing left if you do that."

His eyes blink with offense, flickering with something resembling hurt.

"She would have me."

It almost makes me feel sorry for him.

Almost.

I sigh. "I will help you. You know I will because I want her the fuck away from the Vittoris. But I will also protect her from you at the expense of my own goddamn life." I step forward into his space. "I will lay down my life for her and if you make it come to that, then you'll have *nothing* left because she will chase me into death. You *know* that."

He grinds his jaw. "Are you *done*? We're wasting time."

"Tell me that you hear me, Nikolai."

"I hear you." He plants his palm on my chest and shoves me, bouncing my back off the wall again. "Now hear me. I'm still your goddamn master and you will obey me, so listen closely. Anya is *mine.* She has always been *mine.* I made a mistake selling her to Vigo, but I'm ready to rectify that mistake. I'm bringing her home because she belongs to *me.* Help me get her back to Mikhailov Manor and we will discuss your status as her pet. And mine. Now. Do we have an understanding?"

My fist desperately wants to collide with his face, but I fucking hear him. I have to hear him and go with this because I want my girl back. I was going to chase after her anyway…at least this way, I'll have back-up.

I suppose when you're in hell, it's better to go with the devil who rules than the rogue demon. At least the devil can grant my wishes before taking another piece of my soul.

All that matters is Anya.

I feel her fading.

It's a snap that bursts right over my heart, the familiar vibration of her slipping away from life. I'd felt that snap before—when Nikolai had drowned her in the pool.

"Understood," I tell him. "Tell me what to do."

He lets out a breath. "You're going to run and Kostya and I will come after you. Simple. It won't seem suspect to anyone here. You *are* an unruly slave, one who just can't seem to control his goddamn emotions when it comes to that girl. You go after her and we go after you."

I shake my head, trying to make sense of this too-damn-easy-to-actually-work plan. "If I run, everyone will see. They'll just follow you to help you get me under control. We won't be able to help her then."

"No one will follow. There won't be a need with Kostya and I handling it, and we'll tell anyone who tries the same. You wouldn't be the first slave who tried to run impulsively at a meeting. We don't have much time. We need to take her before everyone starts leaving the reception. There will be enough people moving about then to cause a distraction so we can sneak out with her. I've always hated the excessive guest list when the Vittoris host, but I suppose large numbers play in our favor today."

I link my fingers together on top of my head. "But they'll know. They'll know what you did when you don't show up to the meeting, won't they? What happens then? Will she even be safe if you take her back? What will they do?"

"What happens then is my problem, not yours. But we need to take her back to Mikhailov Manor tonight. There's something she needs, something I need to tell her, something I need to give her."

"What?"

His nostrils flare and he grabs my shoulder, shoving me back in the direction of the reception. "We're wasting time. *Run.*"

Fuck.

This is really happening.

Not only is Nikolai letting me go after my girl, he's demanding it. When my heart unexpectedly drops into my gut, I don't give it another thought. That sinking feeling punches me with the instinct I've been waiting for and it's guiding me to do just what he said. *Run.*

So, I run.

I rush back into the reception and barrel my way into the throng of people milling about. My sights are set on getting back to the staircase. My shoulder bumps into someone on my right and as I veer left, I nearly slam into a pair of chatting women. I turn and sidestep between them as they jump back, spilling whatever was in their glasses.

As I reach the bottom step, I hear Nikolai's voice booming after me. "Ezra. Stop!"

I glance at him over my shoulder, seeing him and Kostya rushing after me, but I know he doesn't want me to stop. It's all part of the plan.

I take the steps two at a time, propelling myself up the staircase as quickly as I can. I reach the balcony landing and I hear footfalls on the steps behind me.

"It's fine, we've got him." I hear Nikolai say and hope that's enough to keep everyone else the fuck away.

It just seems too damn simple, though in my time with the four families, I've come to understand that nothing happens with an ounce of reason.

Left is right.

Up is down.

The moon is the goddamn sun.

I move through the open archway, looking left and right, unsure which way to go. But then my pulse starts pounding, adrenaline kicks in full force, and I feel like I just know where to go.

I turn right.

I take off on a run down the hallway. There's a row of doors, and though I feel a sense of urgency now, I don't even know where to start.

But then fate deals me the perfect hand.

A door opens and Vigo steps out. My heart stops but starts again with a fury as he closes the door behind him. He looks up and he sees me, and we lock in on each other with a heated stare. He cocks his head to the side and a slow smile twists his features.

Heat simmers beneath my skin, pulsing through my veins, boiling into desperation to punch and kick and hurt this man. I want to break his nose again. I want to break every bone in his body. I want to watch him bleed.

I take this matter into my own hands just as Nikolai and Kostya arrive behind me. I charge, sprinting down the hallway. Vigo is too cocky for his own damn good, opening his arms and widening his stance tauntingly, daring me to attack.

But I don't need a dare for this.

Something's wrong with Anya, I *feel* it, and I need to take him down fast.

I crash into Vigo at a run, and though he tries to hold his ground, I'm stronger. I charge him backward as I shove my body against his midsection. I don't stop pushing until he loses his footing and stumbles awkwardly to the ground, falling onto his ass.

I nearly roll over him on the impact, but I manage to land on top and stay in control. I punch him in the side, then again on his bony hip before he gets his bearings. With a grunt, he lands a jab to my jaw and the force knocks me off-balance. I topple sideways and he rolls on top of me, hitting me with a fury of fists.

Two to my cheek.

Three to my stomach.

One that lands on my shoulder.

Another on the side of my head.

Vigo disappears as I blink away the black spots across my vision, his weight suddenly lifted from where it sat hard on my middle. I scramble to my feet to see Nikolai slamming him face-first to the wall.

"Where is she?" Nikolai growls.

I go straight for the door Vigo came out of, jiggling the handle, but it doesn't budge.

"She's in here. But it's locked. There's a keypad," I inform Nikolai.

"Tell us the code, Vigo."

Vigo laughs, his cheek pressed flush against the wallpaper. "No. Do you really think it will be that easy to take her from me?"

I watch as Nikolai reaches into his pocket and pulls out his switchblade, flicking it open with his wrist. He shifts to bring the knife around to Vigo's throat and his grip on him loosens. Vigo manages to whip around to face him, but Nikolai shoves his weight against him, jabbing the tip of the blade at the center of his throat. Vigo freezes, but the sinister smile doesn't fade from his face.

"You want to know what's funny?" He chuckles. "She might be dying in there right now and here we all stand, on the wrong side of the door. And I'm the only person who can let you in."

Nikolai presses the blade and a single drop of blood pools, rolling down Vigo's throat. "Tell me the code."

"Nikolai. *Nikolai.*" Vigo clicks his tongue. "I'm so sad for you right now. You've let your slaves slither their way into your mind and rot your senses. What kind of threat is this?" His eyes flick down to the blade. "Are you going to kill me? What do you think the board will have to say about that, hmm?"

Nikolai holds steady in his ruthlessness. "Tell me the code."

"No."

"Tell. Me. The. Code."

A muffled scream comes from beyond the door that we can't open, and I swear to God it sounds like my name. We all turn to look and Vigo takes advantage of our distraction.

Just as I return my attention to Vigo, his hand slips inside his jacket. It all happens in a flash. Nikolai returns his gaze to Vigo, Vigo whips out his gun, cocks it, and presses it to the side of Nikolai's head.

Vigo's smirk turns into a sneer. "Ask me again to tell you the code. I dare you."

The sound of her voice and the adrenaline pumping through me steers me away from reason and into pure, base instinct. I see an opportunity in their stance, in the way Vigo holds the gun at an awkward angle.

I attack.

I barrel into them, knocking them both to the ground sideways, and the gun goes flying. I'm lucky Vigo doesn't accidentally pull the trigger, luckier when it lands a yard away and doesn't go off, but I'm also fucking lucky that it worked. Vigo is disarmed.

Trying to get to it first, I clamber over them, but Vigo rises up, knocking me sideways over Nikolai. Vigo gets onto his knees and crawls toward it, reaches for it. Kostya leaps, snatching away the gun just in the nick of time. Stepping forward, he aims it at Vigo.

"Open the door," Kostya says.

We all look up at him and I'm surprised to see the worry in his eyes.

"What, are you going to kill me?" Vigo says, raising his palms like a trapped prisoner. "What then? If I'm dead, I can't give you the code."

Nikolai twists his body, reaching out. He stabs Vigo with a brutal thrust to the outside of his thigh.

Vigo screams, falling on his side as Nikolai leans over him. His hand is still on the knife that's jammed inside Vigo. He twists the blade and Vigo shouts even louder. Thankfully, there's enough noise from the guests downstairs to drown out the screaming, but Nikolai slaps his hand over Vigo's mouth all the same.

"Tell me the code or I will take your life, consequences be damned." Nikolai bends, leaning in close, their noses nearly touching. "Do you see how serious I am now, Vigo? Your life means *nothing* to me. But hers? I want her life back." He chuckles. "I'm willing to bet ten million sounds like a pretty good offer now, doesn't it?" He rotates the blade inside him again, eliciting another sound from Vigo that resembles a dying animal. "Too bad that's off the table now. But I'll give you this…If she's still alive and you ensure that we make it back to Mikhailov Manor unharmed, I'll refund what you paid for her in full. Good faith."

"The board," Vigo practically spits with fury. "The board will have your head for this."

Nikolai rips out the knife, pulling out a stream of blood that spurts across the hallway, splashing across my clothes. "The board can do whatever the fuck they want *after* I've taken her home."

Nikolai stands, holding the blade at his side, blood coating his hand and jacket sleeve. His hair has fallen from its perfectly styled, slicked back look into pieces, matted in places from blood spatter.

"The code," Nikolai says, and he truly looks like the devil himself.

I'm horrified by the sight of him.

Vigo groans, covering the wound with his hand. Contemplation wavers in his eyes, but then he swallows…a decision made. He proves his cowardice, conceding, showing in fact that he is but a lowly demon under Nikolai's devil reign.

"7-4-2-5."

With lightning quickness, I type in the code and nearly die from relief when it opens. Instantly, I forget about it all.

I forget about Vigo lying bloody in the hallway.

I forget about Nikolai hovering above him with a devilish glare in his eyes.

I forget about Kostya holding the gun.

I push the door open and run inside to save my blue-eyed girl.

CHAPTER 25

Anya

ONE. TWO. THREE. *Four. Five. Six. Seven. Eight*

One. Two. Three. Four—

My eyes snap open. I blink against the clear water. My dark hair forms a floating halo around my head and the reflection in the mirror above is distorted by the soft rippling effect of the water I've sunk beneath. I jolt, startled again as another thump reverberates against the side of the tub, echoing through the water as a dull roar.

Another thump, then another.

The splintered crack in the mirror turns and light peaks in just above me.

The mirror has moved.

I watch, almost peacefully in my breathless delirium, as it shifts, as it jolts with force from one side to the other. Then suddenly, it jerks back and I can see light above me. Though it's not just light there.

It's life.

Pulsing, vivid green life.

I knew the last vision I would see was of Ezra's green eyes before drifting into unconsciousness. I *hoped* for it. But I'm surprised by the overwhelming vibrancy of this oxygen-deprived hallucination.

I'm pulled from my reverie with a whoosh, waves rippling into whirring droplets as my body rushes backward with a jerk. Sound returns full force as my head breaks through the surface and suddenly, I'm alive again. I feel hands grip beneath my arms as I'm dragged toward the back of the tub. Up and over the edge I go before my body falls to the floor.

My mouth drops open wide on instinct, gasping, sucking in as much air as I can gather now that I'm free from my watery prison.

"I've got you," the voice behind me huffs, pulling me backward, nestling me between strong legs.

Is this real?

Am I alive?

I pant for air as I blink rapidly, taking in the sight of the white tiled floors beneath me. I see my silk blue gown clinging to my legs, the silver sparkle of the stilettos strapped to my feet and a man's legs on either side of me. His hands grab the hair that's stuck to my cheeks and pulls it aside as my eyes follow the line of his leg, back and back. I turn my head and lean to the side so I can see my savior, but of course, I already know who it is.

"Ezra," I say. "Ezra?"

I feel the air leave his lungs as his chest sinks, my body slumping back against his. "It's me. It's me, baby. I'm here. I've got you."

We breathe together.

My eyes meet his in utter disbelief.

I watch him as I wait for the dream to end, for the illusion to shatter. But this is real.

It's real and he's saved me.

A whole new sense of urgency washes over me because I can feel it pounding from his chest. He's come to save me and there's no time for the reverie.

"I'm gonna get you out of here, okay?" he tells me.

My brow furrows as I look at him. "Are you really here?"

He grabs my shoulders and turns me, drags me backward, lifts my fragile body and sets me on his lap. My love cradles me in his warm arms and suddenly, everything in the world feels right again.

"You're really here," I admit to myself. "Oh, God, you're really here."

I shiver in his arms but I am, in fact, in his arms and that's all that matters.

He squeezes me tighter and bends to capture my lips as I look up at him. It's a quick, soft kiss to my lips followed by harder, more insistent kisses to my cheeks, forehead, and hair. I realize then that he's trembling, too, though his must be from the rush of chemicals in his veins as he came upon this horrifying scene and worked to save me.

"You saved me." I blink at him in awe.

His chest still heaves with the heavy breaths of exertion from freeing me, from seeing me nearly drown in the tub. But a slow, charismatic, and undeniably characteristic smile spreads across his face, lighting up his eyes, and the world has never looked brighter.

"I don't think you've ever looked so happy to see me."

He makes me smile. I was just knocking on death's door and still, Ezra makes me smile.

Though I want to remain in his arms forever—with his warmth enveloping me and his smile brightening me—I'm quickly coming back to life. With that returns the realization that time is not on our side in this life.

"What now?" I ask.

"Can you stand? Walk?"

I'm still breathless, but I manage a nod. "I can. I can run if you need me to."

His eyebrows knit together. "I might need you to. Hang on, stay right here. Don't move."

I don't question him.

My faith in him is so strong right now that I'll do whatever he says, because he found me, he *saved* me. I nod my understanding as fervently as I can, which is to say, barely at all.

Carefully, he lifts me from his lap and sets me down on the tile. He slips out from beneath me and slowly stands, his hands never leaving my body, not for a second, as he turns and bends to face me. He makes sure I've got enough balance not to topple over as he props my back against the wall. I watch him the entire time, trying to understand when I became so helpless and needy, when I gave over my trust to him so completely.

When he brought you back from the dead.

He gives me a hurried grin and I smile back.

"I love you," I tell him, because the words just have to come out.

"I love you," he says quickly with a bright flicker of flame behind his eyes.

He dashes past the bathroom doorway and rushes into Vigo's bedroom. "She needs dry clothes." I hear Ezra say to someone.

Moments later, there's a response. "Here. This is best we can do. Hurry."

Kostya?

Ezra returns almost immediately, clothing laid over his arm. He crosses the room and sets them on the countertop before he turns toward me. His eyes dart around the room until he sees the towels resting on the bar on the wall across the room. He hurries to grab one and adds it to the pile on the countertop. He comes to me and crouches to his haunches and dear God, I can't stop looking at him.

"We need to get that dress off you and into these dry clothes, okay? We have to hurry."

"We're really leaving? You really found a way for us to escape? Did Kostya help?" I'm so hopeful with the urgent way he speaks, the way his body rushes through the movements.

He puts his arms around me and lifts me from the floor until I'm standing upright before him, drenched and trembling in his hold. I sway a little from the quick transition from sitting to standing, but he keeps me steady.

"It's not…This isn't a real escape, Anya. But I am getting you the fuck away from the Vittoris."

I shake my head as his eyes skim over my dress, trying to figure out the best way to remove it when my arms are still bound in front of me with a cable tie around my wrists. He finally decides upon tearing the straps, slipping his fingers beneath the one on my right shoulder, and giving a sharp tug to break the thin piece of fabric.

"I don't understand."

He reaches for the other strap and rips that one, too. "Nikolai. He sent me for you."

"Nikolai." My face contorts in confusion. "Nikolai Mikhailov? The man who called me a slut and a whore and sold me to Vigo?"

Ezra puts a finger to his lips to hush me, lowering his voice. "He's in the hall. We need to hurry."

Ezra's hands skim my curves as he slips the broken dress down, peeling it from my body. His gentle touch ignites my soul and wakes me up, bringing me back fully from the dead into screaming, urgent life.

But as he quickly dries me with a white towel, I feel…confused.

Ezra has come to save me, but this is no rescue if I'm returned to my former master. Though, the alternative was to have died in the clawfoot tub on my right. I glance over at it as Ezra helps me remove my shoes.

He wraps one of Vigo's plain, white dress shirts around my back, bringing the sides together in front of me. I let my arms fall so he can button the shirt over the top of them. It's not perfect, but it's dry clothing that will cover me until he can cut the cable ties.

"Shoes. Fuck, how do I get you shoes?"

"I don't need shoes. I'll go barefoot."

"We're going outside, Anya."

"I'm a ballerina. My feet are already destroyed from dance. I really don't care, just forget about the shoes and get me out of here."

Get me out of here…and take me back to my former master?

How on Earth has Nikolai become the master I prefer?

What is wrong with me that I feel relief?

He nods. "Then just stay with me, okay?"

"I'm always with you, E."

He freezes, locks in on me.

"Say it again, A."

His strong hands grip my cheeks and he presses in close. I snatch my bottom lip between my teeth as he lowers his face to mine.

"I'm *always* with you," I tell him again.

His tongue sweeps out to lick his lips and then he kisses me, a slow gradual press that turns into a possessive bruising. I part my lips to seek his tongue and he gives it easily.

I could be under the water right now and still be able to breathe with the way he kisses me. His kiss breathes life back into me, and I only wish I could put my arms around him right now. But the kiss ends far sooner than I want it to, because it *has* to, because we need to leave.

He leads me out of the bathroom, out through Vigo's bedroom, but I freeze in the doorway, taking a step back in fear.

Blood.

Everywhere.

It pours from Vigo's leg.

It drips down Nikolai's outstretched arm.

One master holding the other at gunpoint.

"Her hands are bound," Ezra says.

Nikolai dares a single glance back at me. He double-takes as he sees me with my wet, tangled hair, dressed only in an oversized dress shirt, barefoot.

"Bring her here," Nikolai commands.

Ezra grips my elbow, pulling me forward beside him. I follow his lead, glad to have it when I feel so overwhelmed, so exhausted, so weary.

We come up beside Nikolai and he hands the gun to Kostya. Then he turns to me, giving me a once over as I do the same. I feel like cowering in front of him. He's covered in blood, disheveled, his eyes wild and unhinged. I can't believe he's kept his temper so controlled—it's so unbelievable that I'm certain he'll unleash it upon me any second now.

"Give me your hands," he tells me.

Ezra helps pull the hem of the shirt up as I push my hands forward. Nikolai wipes the blood off the flat edge of his switchblade on his slacks and brings it to my wrists. I flinch as he slips the tip between my wrists and the plastic cable tie, remembering the scars he gave me on my thigh with this very knife. He slices the tie free and folds his blade, returning it to his pocket.

I snatch my hands away as Nikolai turns. I wiggle my arms through the sleeves of the buttoned shirt and work to roll them up over my forearms. Ezra takes my hands in his, caressing his thumb gently over the red indentations made by the cable ties digging into my flesh.

I jump when Vigo screams, turning to watch as Nikolai jabs his finger into a wound on his thigh.

"I guess we'll be leaving the party a little early tonight. Give my best to the board. I'm sure they'll be interested in scheduling a follow-up with me soon," Nikolai says.

Wait. What is happening?

Why is Nikolai doing this?

Why does he want me back?

Vigo laughs as Nikolai stands, ushering us past Kostya toward the staircase. "Go on. Take your leave. I'll let you go. But Nikolai…I'm coming after you. I'm coming for all of you. First," he pants through his pain, "I'll kill your slave boy. I'll string him up and gut him like a fish and make her watch. Then I'll do the same to her. And I'll kill you last, Nikolai."

I don't hear anything after he threatens Ezra.

Gut him like a fish?

Over my dead goddamn body.

I don't take Vigo's threats lightly.

He's sick, twisted, and abhorrently vile.

And I've had enough.

He nearly killed me tonight. He's put me through a hell worse than I ever could have imagined, even after belonging to Nikolai for all these years. Now he's lying here on the floor, weak, bleeding, pathetic...

And threatening to gut my man?

Fuck no.

I see red.

I see his blood and I want more of it.

Something twists inside me, a desperate, nagging need that demands to be fulfilled—a need that *must* be filled before another second of my tragic life ticks by.

It's anger.

It's rage.

It's a fury of brutality.

It's an urgent need to prevent his violence with violence of my own.

My feet move me, march me forward, and I'm at Kostya's side in moments. I hear Ezra shout at me as my hand slips down Kostya's arm. Nikolai reaches for me as my fingers cover Kostya's grip, but he doesn't get to me in time. With my index finger over Kostya's on the trigger, I aim and squeeze.

CHAPTER 26
Ezra

BLOOD EXPLODES FROM Vigo, coating my skin in the viscous, crimson life force.

Anya is red.

Red from her forehead all the way to her bare feet.

Her arms slowly fall to her sides and her fingertips slip from their grip over Kostya's. Her sapphire eyes blink, a blue light shining out from the crimson coating that frames them.

Fuck.

She just killed Vigo.

"Anya!" Nikolai snaps, but she just stares. "We have to go. *Now.*"

I take her by the hand and drag her away.

Together, we run.

I grip her elbow as we reach the staircase, worried she might fall in her tortured state. But her adrenaline must be furious inside her because she keeps the pace with ease. The party is still going on downstairs, but people are moving. We're not the only ones on the staircase and there's talk of a gunshot.

They'd heard, but Nikolai's status ensures we aren't questioned by the passing guests who don't serve on the board. He moves in front of Anya as Kostya and I flank her sides. She's the bloodiest of all of us, and only wearing a man's dress shirt, so we all silently agree she needs to be hidden. We slow our pace to descend the steps but people are looking, taking notice.

I focus my rampant burst of energy on protecting Anya, following Nikolai, and getting the fuck out of here. Somehow, we make it to the front door and because we're with Nikolai, the guards let us pass. But as we pick up our pace again outside, we hear the chaos erupt inside.

"Which car?" I ask Nikolai quickly.

We rush along the row of parked black SUVs that all look the same to me. He points at a vehicle, only two car-lengths away now, as we pass the fountain in the center of the paved square.

Kostya jogs ahead, the SUV flashes its lights as he unlocks it with the key fob in his hand. I catch Anya by the elbow as she stumbles with our fast pace, weak and weary. I stop and bend with her as she doubles over, my arm across her back. She cringes and makes a face as she presses her hand to her belly.

"Are you okay?"

"Just a stomach pain, I'm fine," she rushes her words.

The moment before we straighten together, just before we rise to our heights, a gunshot rings out, a bullet whizzing by and striking the car in front of us. I wrap both arms around Anya, pulling her in front of me to cover her from the gunfire as it rings out again and again.

Nikolai turns back, coming after us. He grabs Anya's arm and pulls but I don't want to let go of her. Still, I won't let my pride get in the way of her safety, so I relinquish my hold and I push my hand against the small of her back, shoving her forward as Nikolai pulls.

As we run away, Kostya turns and runs back toward the house, pointing Vigo's gun at the person firing at us. It's one of the guards we passed at the front door—he must have been alerted about the discovery of Vigo's body upstairs.

"Go!" Kostya yells, tossing the car keys in our general direction as he shoots.

"Get the keys!" Nikolai demands.

I let go of Anya and turn back, taking two quick steps and bend to pick them up from where they landed on the ground. As I rise, Kostya falls, his shoulder jerking back, nearly spinning him all the way around before he lands.

He screams out his agony on a single syllable, "Go!"

"Shit!" I chase after Anya, positioning myself behind her to protect her as multiple guns crackle the air with violence.

We have to leave Kostya—he's too far from us now to help him and he's not the one we need for survival. I shove down the twinge of guilt that arises, knowing that he tried to help us. I'll let it grip me later when we're not in immediate danger.

We make it to the car and just as I reach for the handle, Nikolai and

Anya go down—he falls and she's dragged down on top of him. Blood sprays and Anya screams. My pulse pounds, my ears ring, there's a terrified moment where I just stand and look in horror, not sure who's been hit or where.

Then Anya stands, unharmed.

She only fell because Nikolai dragged her down with his grip.

Nikolai gasps, blood spilling from somewhere in his midsection. The part of me that's wanted him dead for so long cheers, but then fear grips me. If he dies, there is no escaping the Vittoris. He's the only person who can get us off these grounds and I *have* to take Anya away from here. If we don't escape now, we'll both die here.

"Get in the car," I tell her as I pull open the back door and grab Nikolai beneath his arms.

I use the strength that only adrenaline could grant me to hoist him from the ground. Anya runs around the car, climbing into the back seat and reaches across. My beautiful, exhausted, malnourished blue-eyed girl finds some strength left to help me do what needs to be done. Our eyes catch for a single moment as I shove and she pulls. We feed each other in our gaze— fortify our collaboration, solidify our connected determination to survive this.

Nikolai falls limp, lying across the bench seat, and Anya catches his head in her hands, guiding him to rest upon her legs. I slam the door shut and run to the driver's side, just in time to avoid another onslaught of gunfire as more people run from the house.

We're off and driving in no time, heading toward the end of the driveway and the gate that locks us in.

The gate.

The fucking gate.

"How the fuck do we get past it?"

"Nikolai," Anya says. "What do we do?"

"My cell phone," he gasps.

I watch impatiently in the rearview mirror as Anya frantically checks his pockets. She finds his phone inside his jacket pocket. She holds it above him with trembling hands and he reaches to unlock it with his fingerprint. He instructs Anya to tap through several screens and he unlocks pages twice more with his fingerprint scan before entering an eight-digit passcode.

Anya's eyes narrow and she quietly says, "That's my birthday."

"Easy to remember," Nikolai replies on a breath.

She taps once more and like a fucking miracle, the gate mechanism whirs. It slowly swings open, too slowly for my preference. I back the car up and come forward again, angling around the gradual opening to drive through as it's still swinging. The tail of the car bumps the iron bars on the way through, but it's just a tap.

"Follow…the drive," Nikolai says. "Then left."

I do as he tells me, going far faster than I probably should on these dark, curving roads. I need to move quickly, but I also need to avoid getting into an accident. If we wreck the car, we're fucked.

We follow the winding gravel through twists and turns, hills and dips. When we reach the end, I nearly sigh in relief to be moving onto a paved road. I turn left at Nikolai's direction and speed off into the darkness.

Silence falls over us.

We travel into the night in tense quiet.

We haven't seen anyone following us, no car lights from behind.

We're all startled when Nikolai's phone begins to ring.

"Who the hell is calling?" I peek at Anya in the rearview mirror.

She meets my eyes before looking down at Nikolai. He must have tapped the screen to answer because next, I hear him mumble the name of the caller.

"Renata."

Her voice is on speakerphone and we all hear her clear as day, her voice is low in a calm sort of fury. It's unsettling.

"Nikolai. What have you done?"

"What I had to," Nikolai replies, though the words come out on a whisper.

Is he dying?

How much time does he have left?

I punch the accelerator. We don't have time to waste because I have no clue how to get off this island. As much as I hate to admit it, we need Nikolai alive.

"You *murdered* my brother. He's dead, Nikolai!" Renata's voice wavers almost imperceptibly.

I glance in the mirror again and expect to hear Nikolai's voice in response, but instead, I see Anya with the phone, pulling it closer to her lips. Her voice comes out raw, strong, indignant, *furious.*

"*I* murdered him," she tells Renata. "I shot him with his own fucking gun, and he deserved it."

Half of me is in awe of her bravery, admitting that it was her, knowing that she needs to take that power back for herself. The other half wants to stop the car, rip the phone from her hand, and scream at her for confessing. I'd rather have Renata believe it was Nikolai, or Kostya…or *me.* I don't know what our future holds, but it terrifies me to think that anyone from the four families might have a reason to seek vengeance against her.

"Anya?" Renata sounds surprised to hear her speak.

"Yes," Anya replies.

"How are you with him?"

Nikolai forces out his words and manages to put some strength behind them. "I took back what's mine."

"Anya doesn't belong to you," Renata bites back.

"She's mine. I'll prove it."

Prove it?

Anya's eyes catch mine in the mirror and she looks as confused as I am.

"We're coming after you." Renata's voice sounds calm and collected, dangerous and deadly.

"Always welcome in my home," Nikolai lets out on a single breath of sarcasm.

He pants and my pulse ticks up a notch, fearful he'll pass out before we get off this island.

Renata chuckles and the sound of it is eerie as fuck. "Good. Because I'm coming after you and I'm bringing the entire board with me. We'll deal with you, Nikolai, and your precious ballerina."

Fuck.

A long, haunting silence settles around us again, only punctuated by the sounds of Nikolai's heavy, labored breaths. I look once more in the mirror to see Anya looking right back at me. Her eyes tell me of a million different thoughts and emotions rushing around inside her mind.

I'm feeling them all, too.

But I force all of them from my supportive gaze except for one.

Love.

I give her every ounce of love I feel for her through that brief, single glance in the mirror, reminding her that she's not alone in this nightmare. We're in this together, all the way, until the very end.

It softens her.

Just a little.

Just for a moment.

Because all the fear and dread comes rushing back to the surface for both of us as Renata lets out a satisfied sigh and says something that chills my bones.

It scares me because Anya has admitted that she was the one who ended Vigo's life. It shakes me with a radiating panic that springs from the center of my stomach and radiates outward through my entire body.

The horrifying thing that Renata says presents with resigned commitment in her tone.

"Blood taken requires blood given."

The phone beeps.

The call ends.

And I drive faster.

END OF BOOK TWO

DANCE WITH DEATH
PLAYLIST

STREAM ON SPOTIFY
bit.ly/spotify-brynnford

Devil Devil by MILCK
Walk Through the Fire by Zayde Wølf ft. Ruelle
Consequences by Camila Cabello
The Night We Met by Lord Huron ft. Phoebe Bridgers
We Must Be Killers by Mikky Ekko
Wolves by Selena Gomez & Marshmello
Falling by Harry Styles
Someone You Loved by Lewis Capaldi
lovely by Billie Eilish w/Khalid
Can You Hold Me by NF ft. Britt Nicole
Secret Love Song by Little Mix
Bruises by Lewis Capaldi
I Wanna Dance with Somebody by Rachel Brown
Hold On by Chord Overstreet
The Ruler and the Killer by Kid Cudi

ACKNOWLEDGMENTS

Writing this book kicked my ass…and I loved it. I couldn't have done it without the help of some truly awesome people.

First, I have to thank my readers, especially since I'm still floored that I have any! I'm so grateful you picked up this series and came along on this dark little journey with me. I appreciate you more than I could ever express!

To my beta readers—Rachel, Danielle, and Ashlee—you are awesome! Your insights and notes were so valuable. You gave me confidence that it wasn't a complete hot mess, and helped me to see a few wacky details I needed to sort out. Rachel, thank you for also creating a Story Bible for my series to help me keep track of all the details. Danielle and Ashlee, you make the best teaser pics and edits—they make me feel like a "real writer" and remind me that (holy crap) my books actually make readers feel some kind of way.

Silvia, your editing work is brilliant. Down to the simplest details, and restructuring my overly-worded sentences, you clean the hell out of my manuscript. You're the best!

To all the folks at Najla Qamber Designs, your team is amazing! Najla, the cover you made is nothing less than spectacularly gorgeous and exactly what I had dreamed of! Nada, I'm floored by your book interior design expertise. You bring that extra something special to the reader's experience (and make my books look gorgeous!).

To my husband for corralling the kids away when I just needed to focus, *thank you*. I don't know what I'd do if I didn't have the time and space to write, and you always make sure that I do.

I'll end this by thanking dark romance authors everywhere. Your stories gave me the courage I needed to boldly write, bravely publish, and fearlessly chase a dream. You inspire me!

PAS DE TROIS

BRYNN FORD

For Sara.

Thank you for inspiring me to be bold and brave.

PAS DE TROIS [*French* pahduh **trwah**]

noun, plural pas de trois. ***Ballet.***
1. a dance for three dancers.

(www.dictionary.com)

PROLOGUE
Ezra

BLOOD TAKEN REQUIRES *blood given.*

That's what Renata had said to Anya as we drove away from the Vittori mansion. My girl had left no room for doubt when she'd admitted that she'd been the one to pull the trigger on Vigo Vittori.

I would have lied for her.

I would have told them that I'd been the one to kill him.

But Anya—either with bravery and pride or resentment and stupidity—had revealed the truth clearly. The wrath of the four families will fall on us and my only hope is keeping Nikolai alive long enough to…I don't even know what.

I just know that we need him.

Nikolai's pilot was on standby because of the quarterly meeting, and with his help, the three of us were able to board a helicopter and take off from the Vittoris' island in record time.

No one followed us.

They didn't need to.

They know who killed Vigo, they know where we'll be, and they will come after us in their own damn time.

That's what has me wondering about whether we might be able to escape everyone's grasp when our helicopter lands on the private airstrip in Palermo. When we'd landed there before—on our way to the quarterly meeting—the airstrip had seemed mostly deserted and hidden away. It's located in a valley beneath a rocky mountain cliffside which conceals it from the populated areas beyond.

"We could run." Anya leans toward me, raising her voice over the whir of the rotors, though I can hear her fine through the headsets we're wearing. "When we land at the airstrip, we could run. We don't have to go back with him to Russia."

Anya's thoughts reflect my own. But having her say it out loud forces the deliberation necessary to ensure the best possible outcome for us. It's the photographs that give me hesitation—the pictures I'd been so carefully studying in the green and pink floral box in Anya's room at Mikhailov Manor.

Her sister, Lidia.

My ex-girlfriend, Emma.

Would they be killed if we ran?

That was what we'd always been promised.

It was what kept us from running in the first place.

I bend over in my seat and tap the back of my fingers against Nikolai's cheek. He's prone on the fuselage floor, lying on his back, his body stretched out sideways in front of our feet. He's bled quite a bit and he fades in and out of consciousness, but he responds to my touch, turning his head toward us.

I point across the cabin. "Give me that headset." Anya reaches for it. I put the headset over Nikolai's ears so I can talk to him. His gray eyes flicker toward mine and I can see the intensity of his stare has lessened considerably. "What happens to Lidia and Emma?" I ask him. "Tell me the truth. Will they die if we run in Palermo?"

I feel Anya eyeing me skeptically. Surely, she's wondering why I would bother to ask because Nikolai can't be trusted. We have no allies in this war we've created, but Nikolai is the closest thing we can get right now. He stole Anya away from Vigo. He gave me the opportunity to save her life. He had shown something resembling concern, even if he only meant to bring us both back into his servitude.

Perhaps this monster is capable of human emotions, after all.

"If I die…" Nikolai struggles with his breaths. "If I die, *they* die."

Anya looks back and forth between us, fear clouding her features. I know she hasn't seen her sister in years—not since she was taken by Nikolai—and I know how much she loves her. I sense the conflict she feels, knowing that if there were ever an opportunity to run, *this* would be it. No one would stop us from leaving the airstrip. We could abandon Nikolai and run.

But how far would we get?

Given the reach of the four families—and the fact that they know where to find Emma and Lidia—means that they can find us. And they *would* find us. It was clear in Renata's voice on that phone call.

Blood taken requires blood given.

Christ.

I run a shaking hand through my hair.

Nikolai lifts a hand at us, only just barely able to move it above the floor. "I can keep them safe. I can keep Anya safe. But she must…" he pants, "Anya must come back with me to Mikhailov Manor."

Anya and I look at each other with strain painting our expressions. We both know our options—and we both know the consequences—but the truth is that there isn't really a choice.

If we flee, they will only hunt us down.

If we go back to Mikhailov Manor, we may never leave again. But maybe Nikolai can keep Anya safe from them. The contradiction of everything I thought I was certain about is a total mind fuck.

Anya sighs, her eyes falling as her chest sinks. She turns her head to look down at Nikolai. "It's not enough to keep me safe. Can you keep us both safe? Can you promise that, Nikolai?"

"No. I can't promise that. But I do promise I can keep *you* safe." Nikolai holds her gaze as he pauses, taking a few haggard breaths. "I have things you'll need to show them. Hidden away. Come back with me and I'll help you. I can't do anything if you run, Anya. Get on the plane back to Russia with me and I'll call off the watch on your sister."

A tear slips down her cheek and I reach out to brush it away. She looks at me and the sadness I see in her eyes physically hurts me. "You can still run. You can run when we land. They won't need to come after you. I'm the one who killed Vigo…I'm the one they want. I can…I'll find a way to keep Emma safe. You can run and be free."

She's giving me permission to run without her.

She wants me to run without her?

Fuck, no.

I grab her face with both hands and lean close. "I'm not leaving you. I'm not running without you. If the only way to keep you safe is to take you back, then we're going back to Russia together. I don't care what they do to me, but I'm not leaving you on your own. It's you and me, okay? I'm gonna make sure Nikolai keeps his promise."

"But you could be free, Ezra. I—"

"Don't argue with me. We're going back together. It's already been decided. I told you before, my life is nothing without you." She's fucking crazy if she thinks I'm gonna leave her.

She presses her eyes shut and with a sigh of acceptance, nods. Her hands come up to grip my wrists, holding my hands in place against her cheeks.

"Mine?" she asks.

"Always fucking yours," I reply.

If we're going back, if the four families are coming after us seeking vengeance and blood, I will make damn fucking sure that the blood they spill isn't my blue-eyed girl's.

CHAPTER 1
Anya

MY HEAD IS swirling with too many emotions, the range and depth of which brings aching confusion.

Nikolai spills a trail of blood along the black pavement as Ezra and the pilot carry him across the airstrip from the helicopter to the private jet. I've never seen so much blood as I have tonight—I'm still covered in the splatter from Vigo.

I drag myself up the airstair steps onto Nikolai's jet, stepping carefully with my legs wide, straddling the red trail up the staircase to avoid stepping in Nikolai's blood with my bare feet. I step onboard the luxury plane just in time to watch Ezra and the pilot lay Nikolai on the couch—he just barely fits on it.

I watch him as he lays on his back, bleeding, with one arm on his chest while the other flops off the side of the couch. I can't help but think how frail and weak he looks—two words I would have never thought to call him before.

He took a bullet for me.

Did he save my life?

The pilot rushes off to the cockpit with Ezra's insistence that we hurry. In mere minutes, the plane takes off, carrying us into the night, away from one master's homeland to another's.

The cabin is silent as the plane reaches its cruising altitude and levels out—silent, except for Nikolai's heavy breaths. He was shot in the stomach nearly an hour ago. He's bled a lot, and I don't know what's going to happen to him. I don't know if he'll live or die. My mind splinters as it tries to grapple with the strange mix of emotions that simple fact inspires.

Nikolai may die.

There's relief in that possibility, but there's fear, too. Nikolai stole me back from Vigo. He was angry for Vigo's treatment of me, which is odd to think about, but clearly, it's true. I don't know how to feel about any of this. And the fact that Nikolai first tried to buy me back at a sum of ten million—I know my worth as a slave and it's nowhere near that sum. If the families dealt in rubles instead of euros, that would've been reasonable. But they all deal in euros, even the Leblancs.

It was an outrageous offer.

Ten million.

Then again, I suppose the worth of anything can only be determined by the amount someone is willing to pay for it. Tonight, Nikolai had determined that I was worth ten million.

I don't know whether to feel good or bad about that.

So, while I could—and probably should—stay in my seat, close my eyes, and rest up for the battles to come, I can't think of doing anything other than getting answers from him.

I unbuckle and rise, stepping around Ezra in the seat beside me to move into the aisleway. I cross the small space to Nikolai where he lays helpless on the couch. His eyes are open, looking above him, but they turn my way as I approach.

I stand still at his side. I'm not entirely sure what I want to ask him, what I want to tell him, what I want to do to him. But I just have to stand still for a moment as it happens—as the power that he always held over me pours from him with each breath, mingling with the air between us.

With each uneven breath I take, some of his power seeps into my lungs, swirling like a storm and punching my heart with lightning bursts that fortify me, strengthen me, embolden me. Our eyes remain locked as I willingly and gratefully take that power from him. "Why?"

"Why...what?"

Why did you choose me when I was eleven?

Why did you bring me partners you hated?

Why did you choose Ezra?

Why did you sell me?

Why did you risk everything to steal me back?

I take a step closer, knowing that he can hardly move, knowing that he can't hurt me right now. "Why me? Why did you choose me to live this life of torment?"

I feel Ezra approach before I see him appear at my side. I hold up my hand to stop him because I *need* this exchange with Nikolai without interference, without the distracting pulse of Ezra's pure goodness.

Nikolai lets a smirk curl up the corner of his lips. "You wouldn't believe me if I told you."

I scoff, "I've become fairly open-minded to nonsense over the years, Nikolai." I feel a rush when I say his name rather than call him *master*. "I'm a talent slave serving the four families with dance. An entirely unbelievable and unnecessary tradition of four slave trafficking families, spread across the globe, who descended from murderers. So, please, indulge me with the truth you think I won't believe."

I feel Ezra take a step back and I see him cross his arms over his chest from the corner of my eye. I don't tear my eyes away from Nikolai, but I sense the look on Ezra's face shows something resembling pride and encouragement.

Nikolai's eyes turn to the ceiling again. "I struggled to select a beneficiary before I found you." He sounds breathless and weary. "I was twenty-six and I knew what I wanted. I wanted to find a boy. But I couldn't bring myself to tell my father. He judged me rather harshly for my…ambivalence. I selected your studio at random, showed up that day on a whim. I took one look into the studio and I saw you dancing." He shifts and flinches and I'm glad for his pain. "Anya," his eyes fall on me again, "I felt something deep for you. I was drawn to you. Instantly obsessed. I thought it felt like falling in love."

Oh, fuck no.

"Don't feed me lies," I hiss. "Tell me the truth."

"That's the truth."

"I was a *child*. You don't fall in love with a child!" I step closer, looming above him in the way he always loomed over me.

"It wasn't like that. Not then. I saw…" his breath stutters, "I saw another little girl who kept bumping into you. You gave her that fierce look of yours and when your teacher wasn't looking, you marched over to her, waved your finger in her face, and told her something that made her cheeks go white. She moved as far away from you as she could, and you took center stage. But you were obedient, too, and you followed your dance teacher's instructions perfectly. There was no one else in that room worth looking at. I fell in love with your spirit. I knew someday you'd make the perfect slave."

I reach down and I slap him. "You're *disgusting*. Lusting after a child."

His face contorts in pain. "Lust came later." He closes his eyes. "But I always cared deeply for you, Anya. If I didn't, you would have died a hundred deaths at my hands by now. I made you stronger."

"You made me a *slave*."

"I gave you *everything*. I gave you the life of a Mikhailov."

Ezra makes a derisive sound but doesn't interrupt.

I drop to my knees, just so I can lean over Nikolai and show him the rage on my face. "I would rather *die* than have the life of a Mikhailov."

He chuckles, but it cuts off abruptly with a stuttering breath. "*Rabynya*, that is the exact choice you must make. And you must make it in a hurry. I think I might be dying."

I glance at Ezra and we share a look of confusion. "What are you saying?"

"How have you been feeling?" Nikolai asks.

"What?"

"Have you seen a doctor? Have any blood tests been done?"

"What are you *talking* about?"

"We make our money stealing and selling human lives...but we control each other with lies and secrets."

Ezra steps closer. "What are you trying to say?"

"I put a lie in Vigo's contract," Nikolai groans, crow's feet wrinkling at the corners of his eyes as he squeezes them shut in pain.

Good.

I want him to feel pain.

"What was the lie?" I demand.

"I'm sure if you think about it enough," Nikolai coughs, "you'll figure it out. Maybe in time the truth will grow on you."

What the hell does that even mean?

I shoot to my feet, enraged, indignant, fucking tired of him and the games he plays with my head. But I'm so tired and weak, so hungry, so thirsty, so out of my mind with suffering that I feel immediately light-headed and I stumble to catch my balance. I veer sideways. Ezra's at my side in an instant, catching me around the waist, and righting me.

I look up at him and a green spark catches fire in his eyes. It lights my skin in flames that refuse to be ignored. In the mad rush from Ezra saving my life to fleeing the Vittoris, I hadn't taken a moment to let it hit me that Ezra is with me.

We're together and alive and safe for the moment.

He swallows as he ignites me with his fire and the heat is almost too much to bear. My mind is already overloaded, and my body can't take much more stress. Nikolai is talking in riddles that only induce further frustration. I want answers, yet I don't. I feel jittery and anxious and completely overwhelmed. The touch of Ezra's hands on the small of my back makes me tremble.

It's too much.

It's too fucking much.

I gently push Ezra's hands from me and scoot around him, storming off to the back of the plane. I slide open the door to the small bedroom, marching past the bed Nikolai has fucked me on more times than I can count, and enter the bathroom just beyond it. I slide the accordion door shut behind me. The bathroom is small, but not tiny like a commercial airline bathroom. There's enough space in here to pace three small steps from one end to the other.

I bend over the sink, gripping the rounded counter's edge as I breathe heavily, trying to get control of my rising panic before it grips me. I slowly lift my head and take in my appearance in the mirror above the small sink. I've never looked so awful. My cheeks are hollow, skin sallow, hair wet and matted from being trapped in Vigo's tub.

But worst of all is the red.

Vigo's blood coats my skin and stains the white shirt.

I look down at the buttons and suddenly remember that this is Vigo's shirt.

I'm wearing Vigo's shirt and it's covered in his blood because I killed him.

I shot him.

I killed him.

Oh, God…

My skin is suddenly crawling for me to get it off, and my fingers fumble, trembling as I reach to unbutton the shirt.

Get it off.

Get. It. Off.

The bathroom door slides open and shuts again, but I don't even look up.

"Anya." I hear Ezra's voice.

"Get it off me." One button comes free and I fumble for the next, trying and trying, but my fingers keep slipping. "Get it *off* me. Get his shirt off me!"

"Anya, stop."

Ezra reaches for the buttons to help me, but I'm out of my mind. It only feels as though he's trying to interfere, and I push his hands away as I keep struggling to unbutton this godforsaken shirt.

Are there a hundred fucking buttons on this shirt?!

"Anya." He snatches my wrists. "Stop. Let me help you."

I don't hear him trying to help me; I only feel him stopping me. I yank free from his grip and slap his hands away, then reach for another button. My whole body shakes as this overwhelming agitation takes over and I can't stop it.

I can't stop it.

I need Ezra to stop it.

"Fuck. *Please,*" I beg, words failing me.

In a rush, he's in my space, hands grasping the hem of the shirt that reaches halfway down my thighs. His fingers brush my skin and the jolt of lightning startles me into stillness. He lifts the oversized shirt, peeling it up my body.

"Arms up," he says to me.

In this sudden stillness that he's sparked with his touch, my mind can listen, and I obey.

I raise my arms and he peels the shirt from my body, tossing it behind him on the floor. I would feel stupid for not thinking to do that myself if it weren't for the fact that I'm so acutely aware of his presence, his heat, his power that poses no threat but only exists to care for me.

He pulls several paper towels from the dispenser beside the sink and wets them in the slow-running faucet. Without being asked, he wipes the blood from my skin. He cleanses me without command because he loves me.

I stand still as he wipes my face clean. His movements are gentle, though the paper is rough against my skin. My panicked breaths begin to slow as I watch him work. His brows slant inward, wrinkling his forehead with a look that's focused and caring and worried.

He's worried about me.

He *should* be worried about me.

I'm worried about me.

I let out a breath as my heartbeat wills itself to steady, to calm, to slow. I sigh as he moves from cleaning my cheeks, drawing the towel down to my neck. He scrubs across the hollow of my throat and I swallow hard. His eyes flick upward and meet mine, and we catch on a beat of nothingness.

It's that beautiful nothingness where no mental or physical anguish exists—it's only the two of us and everything is perfect because there is nothing else.

"I'm sorry," I tell him as he curves around to the side of my neck.

"For what?"

"For…being crazy."

He smiles as he gently tosses my hair back over my shoulder. "You've never been crazy. The four families…? Fucking nuts. You? Never."

The edges of the towel flutter across my earlobe as he scrubs the side of my neck. I find that my head naturally falls to the side, opening the curve of my neck to him. Ezra's lips fall open as he looks at me and his hand stills.

My heart skips a beat.

Though I'm blood-covered down my neck and chest, I'm otherwise standing bare and exposed in front of him. It's been six months since I've been naked with Ezra. Yes, we'd had sex in that dungeon at the Leblancs' the night I tried to kill myself three months ago, but it was quick, and we'd remained in our clothing.

But now my chest heaves with a heavy breath as something deep within me stirs, remembering what it was like to be touched gently, to be loved and given pleasure instead of pain.

His breath hitches as if he responds naturally to the coiling tension in my belly—which, of course, he does because our souls are linked beyond reason. His hand lowers, scrubbing over the dried blood on my chest, though his eyes don't leave mine. The blood streaks across the mound of my right breast and his towel doesn't neglect. I gasp as the rough ends of the paper graze my nipple while he scrubs. He's diligent, finishing his work, cleansing me thoroughly of the stains of this awful night.

His eyes burn into mine and air catches in my lungs.

Before he's done, we're both panting, huffing together in an unsteady but shared rhythm—a shared rhythm we'd lost when we were apart.

Nothing else in the world exists.

It's just Ezra and me and heat.

Heat.

"Ezra..." I whisper on a breath.

The paper towel drops to the floor and his hand clamps around my breast. We both exhale heavily on cue, and then we crash. He bends to meet me, and our lips collide, ramming together with bruising, desperate force.

I need him.

I need him more than water, more than food, more than rest. I need him to love me in the way only Ezra can. I need him to flood my senses and take over my emotions and drown me in his endless hope and possibilities.

He pushes back until I hit the wall and he presses into me so impossibly close that I can hardly breathe. But it doesn't matter because I take in air through his kiss. His tongue swirls with mine as he absolutely devours me. I'm trapped by him and it doesn't scare me, it doesn't lead me to panic or fear—it excites my senses.

And I need more.

My arms latch around his neck, yanking him down to hold his face to mine, silently begging him not to stop. His hands fall to my waist and he squeezes, digging in his fingertips. He starts to lift and I jump in frantic determination, tightly wrapping my legs around him.

He holds me against the wall, kissing me with more urgency than I've ever felt before. He feeds me a growl, a groan of need that vibrates his entire body, and it pulls a tight knot in my stomach that only he can unravel.

"Inside me. Please," I manage against his lips.

He groans again, shaking with need. I know how much he wants to sink inside me—he's trembling for it. But he's trying so hard to restrain himself and it's killing me. Of all the men in the world, Ezra is the only one I'd ever want to take me fiercely, passionately, without restraint. But he's just such a damn good man.

Too damn good for me.

He doesn't want to be like all the rest who take and take from me without care or concern. But he could never be like them. I have no fear with him, no shame, no guilt. I *want* him to have me, to love me, to enjoy my body because he's earned it. Ezra has earned my heart and soul, and with it, my body.

I grip his face in my palms, pulling him away from our kiss by hardly an inch. I give him the full force of my gaze. "I need you inside me."

The feral, masculine part of him roars internally—I see the flash fire of it explode behind his eyes. Inexplicably, it makes my stomach clench and wetness rush between my legs with need. Still, he restrains that beast within him.

"You need rest. I don't want to hurt you."

I'm already rocking and rubbing myself against Ezra's waist because he just does something to me that I can't explain. "I can't rest until you come inside me."

He groans and his hips buck up against me. I feel his erection against my bare skin and I've never needed him as much as I do right now.

"Please, Ezra," I beg. "Make me forget everything but you."

He presses me harder against the wall, his hips working. "Jesus Christ, Anya."

He's holding back and it's killing me. I feel like I have to seduce him, and it's such an odd role reversal for me. It makes me feel powerful to know he won't take advantage of me, to know that he *can't* take advantage of me. He's too determined to protect me, to care for me, to keep me safe. He gives me power over him. In a world where I have been powerless and abused for so long, it's a rush to know that he's mine.

And it's the biggest fucking turn-on.

I lean forward, biting his lower lip and sucking on it. I release it and he shudders. "Lay me down and fuck me, Ezra Bell."

CHAPTER 2

Ezra

LAY ME DOWN *and fuck me.*

Anya demanded it and I was compelled to give it.

I hadn't come after her with the intention to do this. I just wanted to make sure she was okay, maybe hold her, comfort her, put her to bed to rest while I went back to get all the answers we still need from Nikolai before he bleeds out and dies—or before I strangle him myself. But it's impossible to be near Anya and not feel the chemistry—that natural draw to be closer to her—and it's been so fucking long since I've seen her.

It feels like an urgent and necessary *need.*

I don't know if her body can handle this right now. She nearly died tonight and had already seemed in such precarious health before Vigo trapped her in that fucking tub. Sex is probably the worst thing she can do to her body right now.

I know that.

But how can I deny her when she commands me so insistently?

She wouldn't encourage it if she didn't want it, though. I know that much is true. I refuse to be another man in her life who tells her what she can and can't do. So, even though giving her what she wants might actually kill her from exhaustion alone, I'm not gonna deny her. I'm not gonna deny either of us when we both need this so much.

Moving one of my hands up between her shoulder blades, I step backward before turning us around. I fumble to slide open the small accordion-style door behind her back, but once it's open, I rush straight to the almost queen-sized bed just beyond it. My knees hit the mattress and I bend forward, laying her down on her back and moving with her.

I can't let go of her; I can't move away.

Her fingers find my hair and she keeps our faces close as we both pant with need, heating the air between us with unsteady breath. My cheek rests against hers as I reach down between us to unbuckle my pants. I don't get up until they're unlatched, and when I do, I slip them off quickly, eagerly climbing back on top of her.

She doesn't need words to tell me how much she needs me to fill her or how she needs me to make the empty feeling of being apart from each other go away. There's a pause as I grab my cock and angle toward her, brushing the tip against her slick folds that beg me to push in deep. She gasps and moans as I let the pause linger, let it heat and catch on fire. There's just breath between us—breath and the aching need to be lost in our love together.

I press delicate, sensual kisses to her cheek. "I've missed you so much."

Her hips wiggle beneath my weight and it only makes me feel heavier, weighted down, like my body and hers need to fuse entirely for us to feel complete. When I finally push inside her—too desperate to drag out the anticipation any longer, too needy for foreplay—I sink in deep.

We both moan with sounds of pure satisfaction when we're finally connected again. This isn't just sex. And if I was honest, it was never just sex with Anya. It's spiritual. It's prayer. It's fucking worship at the altar of our souls. I slip my arms around behind her back and move my hips slowly, with long, full strokes that reach deep inside her as I hold her close.

She moans through a long exhale as she grips my hair, angling my head to kiss me with parted, gasping lips. "I missed you, Ezra. I missed you." Her lips find my ear. "Tell me you missed me. Tell me you love me. Tell me how much you need this with me."

"Anya…" I kiss her cheek, along her jawline, down her neck, but never stop moving inside her. "I was dying without you."

She stays close to me, nuzzling her cheek against mine. "You're mine."

"I'm yours."

"Say it again." Her spread knees squeeze my hips and I thrust faster, with more force and depth, making sure she feels every inch of me.

"Christ," I groan. "I'm yours."

I drive my cock inside her, pushing deep. Each stroke feels like the strike of a match to my insides, heating me, setting me on fire, and I know the only way to put out the flame is to douse it in the wetness of her desire.

She pants beneath me, gasping for breath. "Please…*please*," she whispers against my ear.

"Come for me, baby. Please. I need to feel it." I angle my thrusts upward, faster, rubbing along her most sensitive spot until she squeezes her eyes shut, grasping my hips firmly between her knees.

"Oh…*oh*," she whimpers and with two more thrusts, she explodes, her pussy pulsing around my cock as her stomach clenches and she coils around her center.

She's still coming as her clenching climax drags me along with her. It takes me by surprise the way her pleasure links with mine, twisting around me and pulling me into orgasm. I spill deep inside her with a satisfied groan, the swell of my cock somehow dragging out her orgasm a few perfect seconds longer.

The tip of her nose brushes along my cheek as breath rushes in and out. I turn my head to kiss her with gentle lips and a languid tongue. She wraps her arms around me, holding me close as our bodies slow to stillness.

She opens her eyes and looks at me, catching me fully with her brightness. "I love you." Her blue eyes are vibrant, sparkling, though I can see the exhaustion behind the luster of her love.

"I love you, too." I kiss her once more, slow and wet and lovingly.

Gradually, I pull out and I hate it because it feels so right to be inside her. I roll slowly onto my side next to her and she turns with me, shrinking and curling against my chest. I wrap my arms around her and cherish the feeling of being able to hold her and keep her safe.

"I know hell is coming," she says quietly, "but right now, I feel safe with you." She sighs. "Why can't we always feel this way?"

I run my hand down her side. "Someday we will."

She kisses the center of my chest and it makes my heart skip a beat. "You are hope incarnate. I don't know how you keep the faith." Anya yawns through the final word.

I brush my hand down her hair before kissing the top of her head. "You need to sleep."

"Shit." She starts to sit up. "I need to talk to Nikolai. I need to know what's going on; what we do when they come after us. I need to know that Lidia will be safe…Emma, too. We need so many answers from him and he's—"

"Let me handle it." I pull her back down beside me. "I want you to sleep. You *need* to sleep, Anya. I'll get all of the answers from him."

"I need to know everything."

"And you will."

She tilts her head up to look at me with those piercing blue eyes. "Ezra. It's important."

"I know it's important. It's critical. And I'll get all the answers to all the questions. But we only have a couple of hours before we arrive, and I need you to sleep before then. I need you to get your strength back. Okay? I'm worried about you." I tuck a strand of hair behind her ear. "I shouldn't have been so rough with you. Probably shouldn't have fucked you at all." I grin. "I just couldn't help myself."

She smiles at me. I see her desire to fight me flash across her eyes. But then she yawns again as she's trying to give me her commanding stare and I can't help but laugh. She does, too. I pull her closer, hugging her and kissing her forehead.

"So, are you gonna rest? Or are you gonna argue with another yawn that you're not tired?" I joke.

She giggles and I feel the vibration of it against my chest, over my heart. *Fuck.*

This woman is everything.

"Okay," she concedes with a sigh. "I trust you."

I lift her chin so she has to look up at me and I grin. "Say that again, baby. Slowly."

"What? I trust you?" She bites her lip through a smile. "I trust you, Ezra."

I groan. "Yes, that. That's so hot."

She makes a sexy face in good humor. "I. Trust. *You.*"

I lift my eyebrows. Though it was said humorously, it actually is kind of turning me on again.

"Shit. I've gotta get out of here before you make me hard again."

She captures my lips, taking me off-guard with the passionate force behind her kiss as she pushes me onto my back and rolls on top of me. She pulls back and smiles, looking down at me, her eyes flickering across my features, taking in every inch of my face. She tilts her head regarding me. "I really do trust you."

It's a somber and precious moment when I catch her eyes. Our souls stare and our hearts beat in time. I know there's hell all around us, but I can't believe how lucky I am to be the man she loves. She kisses me again before I roll her back onto the bed and get up. I lift the covers for her and she crawls beneath. For the first time ever, I see peace in her features as she watches me dress. Anya deserves that peace, even if it's only for a few hours. We're safe here together on this plane…for now.

I put my pants back on and finally remove my shirt, leaving it behind on the bed as something for Anya to wear later. Then I leave her to sleep peacefully as I return to Nikolai in the main cabin.

Blood trickles from his side, soaking the side of the leather couch and pooling on the carpet beneath, staining it crimson. My heart thumps an extra beat when I notice his eyes are closed.

Fuck.

Did we miss our opportunity for answers and assurances because we couldn't keep our hands to ourselves?

My hands land on top of my head, fingers locking together as I force out a steadying breath. I drop my hands against my sides with a slap before crossing to him. His head turns toward me and his eyes open slowly. I never thought I would be relieved to see that Nikolai Mikhailov still lives and breathes.

"I'm still alive, in case you cared," he murmurs. "You might have been quieter fucking my slave," he pauses to draw in a ragged breath, "just in case I live." He chuckles darkly.

"She's no more your slave than I am right now. You're weak, Nikolai. You're dying."

"If you came to ask something of me, you're doing a very poor job of it."

I move beside him, kneeling on the carpet next to the pooling blood. "You said you would keep Lidia and Emma safe. I want you to make that happen."

He sighs. "Give me my cell phone."

My head tilts with surprise. His concession without taunting is jarring, but I won't squander the opportunity. I pull his phone from my back pocket where I stored it for safe-keeping and hold it out for him. He unlocks it with his fingerprint, then drops his hand, too weak and too tired to hold it up. He directs me through his contact list, and I scroll until I find CONTRACTORS,

NY—his hired mercenaries on contract in New York City, where both Emma and Lidia happen to reside.

With a pinch of anxiety, I tap the contact and put it on speakerphone for him. It only rings once before the other line picks up, but no one says hello.

Instead, Nikolai asks, "Is the weather better today?"

I squint my eyes in confusion.

"The weather is better than yesterday. What can I do for you, sir?" Comes the reply from the other end of the line.

Was that some sort of verbal code?

"Remove the trace and threat on Antonov and Mayfield."

"You're certain, sir?"

"Yes."

"Consider it done. They'll be left alone and unharmed."

"Thank you."

That's it? This whole time…It was that fucking easy?

I have a sudden feeling of terror that he's joking, that he's about to say he's kidding and order the contractor to murder Emma and Lidia immediately, just as a final *fuck you* to me and Anya. So, I quickly tap to end the call before he can say anything else and set the phone aside where he can't reach it.

"Now, tell me how you can keep Anya safe from the four families."

"I'll tell you, but I want you to promise me something. "

"You're not in a position to ask for favors."

"Neither are you, *mal'chik*. You can let me die without ever knowing," he takes a shuddering breath, "what I've done for her."

Goddammit.

I need answers.

I swallow my pride and force down the tick of righteousness that swells in my chest. "Fine."

"Promise me you won't tell her anything until we're back at Mikhailov Manor. If I die before then, you can tell her what you want."

"What does it matter if I tell her now or wait?"

"I don't know…it doesn't. I suppose I'm hoping for a final dramatic revelation of how I've changed her life and saved her. And I'd like that to happen in my own home." He gasps another ragged breath. "But I don't know if I'll make it until then." His eyes meet mine dead on and pierce me in his gray stare. "I almost don't care if I die. But if I do, I'd like it to be in my own home, Ezra."

Ezra, not mal'chik.

Shit.

The use of my name in his plea reminds me that he's human—a fucking shitty one, but a human, nonetheless. The words spill out before I can think better of them. "You have a private doctor, don't you?"

Why did I even say that?

I don't want this bastard to get medical treatment.

I want him to die.

Still, the human part of me insists that help be offered, if only for the sake of proving to myself that I'm a better man than he is.

"Don't call him. I don't think I can be saved."

It's like he's already given up. It's possible his wounds could be healed with proper medical treatment, but without…he'll continue to bleed until he dies.

He knows that.

And he doesn't care.

I sigh. "Okay. I promise. I won't say a word to Anya until we get back."

"Good. Thank you."

His stare softens before he presses his eyes shut, sucking in a breath through his nose to steady himself. When he opens them again, he looks somehow…haunted. But there's no more time to delay in decoding his expression.

"Tell me everything."

CHAPTER 3
Anya

I'M THANKFUL EZRA encouraged me to rest on the plane. I'm surprised by the fact that I was able to sleep at all, let alone the remainder of the flight. For the first time in a long time, I felt safe aboard that plane, even when I knew it was only temporary. I knew Ezra would watch over me, and Nikolai was incapacitated, leaving all threats to my life behind on the ground.

We'd transferred to a helicopter after we landed at the Mikhailovs' private airstrip in Russia. Ezra and the pilot dragged a bleeding Nikolai yet again from one aircraft to the other. We took off silently into the night, not a word from any of us as we approached the Mikhailovs' vast landscape.

When we finally landed on the helipad in the middle of the dark forest, the pilot left us after assisting Nikolai once more, helping Ezra place him into the back of the car that had been left there. The three of us were alone to make the solemn, silent drive back to Mikhailov Manor.

We could have found his private doctor's number on his cell phone and arranged for him to come and treat Nikolai at the manor, but we didn't.

Nikolai had told Ezra not to and when I asked Nikolai myself, he insisted that we don't call. He said there was no point, and I can't for the life of me imagine why he seems to have given up. It's as if he *wants* to die.

I think we all know logically that he *is* dying without treatment. He was shot hours ago, and the blood loss has been…overwhelming. I think he's only survived this long to make the trip back to his homeland so he could die on his own terms. If I let myself think about it for too long, tears well behind my eyes, burning liquid that has no reason to exist because I won't mourn his loss.

My captor, my master, my tormentor—he's dying and I'm glad.

But then why does it hurt to think about?

I help as much as I can, but it's Ezra who does the work to get Nikolai from the car across the threshold into Mikhailov Manor.

"Take me to the dance studio," Nikolai manages before huffing out heavy breaths.

His face is pale, and blood continues to leak from his injury as Ezra drags him through the main entrance. Mikhailov Manor is large and empty, just as I remembered it being. But the atmosphere is particularly haunting now. My eyes follow the grand staircase up to the second floor. I feel as though the ghosts of Mikhailovs past watch as we bring the last of their line home to die.

The last Mikhailov is going to die.

My pulse kickstarts.

I follow Nikolai's trail of blood to the dance studio, wrapped only in Ezra's dress shirt since we'd left Vigo's bloodied shirt on the plane. Ezra drags him with his arms hooked beneath Nikolai's armpits, sweat glistening across his bare torso from the exertion of moving a body over and over again. Ezra pulls him across the threshold of the dance studio, finally setting him down in the center of the brightly-lit space.

"Okay." Ezra takes a few deep breaths. "We're here. Now tell her where the box is, or I will."

The box?

"What box?"

Ezra talked to Nikolai on the plane while I rested. But all Ezra told me was that he'd promised Nikolai the opportunity to tell me everything himself when we arrived. I don't know why it mattered to Nikolai or why Ezra agreed to it. I only know that Ezra is a better man than he gives himself credit for. I can imagine his heart wouldn't allow him to deny a dying man's last request—even when that man is vile and undeserving of sympathy.

"In Nobility Hall," Nikolai says on a whisper. "The box is under my seat. You know my seat." He's gasping, struggling for air. "Hurry."

Nikolai's seat.

He always sat in the same spot for my performances in Nobility Hall. He'd chosen a favorite spot, and I'd always wondered why he picked it because I knew it wasn't the best seat in the house. But it makes sense now. If he's hiding something so important there—something that he claims will save me from the four families' fury—then it serves to reason he would always sit there and remain in that very spot until everyone else had left after my performances.

"Keys," I say, suddenly urgent to find this box and learn his secrets. "I need the keys."

Ezra pulls the set of keys that he collected from Nikolai's pocket and hands them to me.

"Stay with him," I tell Ezra.

He gives me a nod and I take off on a jog, thankful for the burst of adrenaline that comes from the urgency of it all.

I jog past the main entrance, dash down the garden corridor, and rush to the locked door in the alcove. I find myself fumbling with the keys, my hands shaking. There may as well be someone behind me holding a gun to my head for the way I tremble.

Once the door is open, I move through the short hallway, quickly finding my way to the lobby of Nobility Hall. I take a breath as I stand before the two sets of double doors and slowly, I step forward. I pull one of the doors open wide and move into the darkness.

I head to the light booth to turn on the house lights and take no more than a moment to revel in the twinge of excitement that being in this space always gives me. The twinge has nothing to do with this theater and everything to do with my love of performing.

I make my way down the aisle on the left. I find Nikolai's seat easily enough, but I don't know what to do now that I'm here. It's an aisle seat, so I stand beside it, looking and waiting for something special to reveal itself to me.

I drop to my knees on the plush red carpeting and examine the area. I lift the hinged seat up and down, looking beneath it, trying to find a latch or a lock—something, *anything* that looks out of the ordinary. With a huff of exasperation, I slap my hands on the veneered wood flooring under the seat.

Did I imagine that hollow sound?

I run my hands across the floor, covering every inch until I feel a gap with the pads of my fingers—a miniscule crevice that cuts across the floor in the wrong direction. I claw at it, digging my fingernails into the edge and pulling, but nothing happens.

If it were truly important, Nikolai wouldn't leave it unlocked.

I practically crawl beneath the seat, inspecting the chair, the legs, the floor…but there's nothing.

Nothing.

But then…Nikolai wouldn't get down on his hands and knees to retrieve a secret box, that would be rather undignified of him.

I climb back out and inspect the back rest. My hands roam along the flat back, finding nothing and moving on to the armrests. My fingers slowly graze down the sides, sliding along the outside of the armrests, then the inside.

That's when I feel it—another unusual ridge on the inside of the aisle armrest. When I dig my fingernails into this one, it clicks. A tiny wooden door carved into the intricately-etched pattern at the end of the armrest pops open.

I bend, moving my head closer to look inside it, and sure enough, there's a keyhole. "What on Earth?" I whisper in the empty room.

I already know which of Nikolai's keys will fit this. It's a small keyhole and there's only one tiny brass key on his keyring that appears as though it will fit. I insert the key, turn it, and jump back when I hear something click beneath the seat. I crouch down to look and see that the floor is now uneven—a piece of it has sprung upward on a hinged spring.

I scramble to pull the piece all the way back and find myself looking into a black hole in the ground, at least a foot deep. Other than the gray box sitting inside it, it looks like a void, a place where perhaps all my hopes and dreams and possible futures went to die.

I don't know what's in this box that Nikolai thinks will save me. But Ezra already knows and that knowledge took away some of his brightness.

I feel nauseous.

Time is wasting. The four families could arrive at any moment, and I need to know what's in this gray box that will spare me from harm. I lift it from the black cavern and carefully set it on the carpet. I close the hinged door in the floor, remove the key, and cover the keyhole on the armrest.

Though my curiosity threatens to kill me, I don't dare look inside the box—not here, not alone. Whatever is in this box is going to change my life. I know it. I can feel it. And I can't find out alone.

I pick up the box and carry it all the way across the manor and back to the dance studio, holding it delicately, as if it were a bomb that would explode should I drop it. I hurry inside the studio only to be welcomed by the sound of Nikolai's gasping breaths. They're heavier and shorter than they were before, and it halts me in the doorway.

Ezra is on his knees beside him, grasping his hand, almost comfortingly. Nikolai deserves no comfort...

Then why do I feel thankful that Ezra gives it?

Something inside me feels torn to see Nikolai this way—weak and helpless. He's finally getting what he's always deserved, yet I feel a prickling confusion from my head down to my toes.

Ezra catches my gaze and I lower to my knees on the opposite side of Nikolai. Ezra's expression is mixed with urgency and concern. "He doesn't have much time."

"I know," I reply.

Nikolai's head falls to the side and he looks at me. "Open the box."

I nod and sit back on my heels, bringing the box onto my lap. I inhale deeply, steeling myself against Nikolai's unpredictability one last time.

One last time?

The last time.

I remove the lid and set it aside.

Nikolai speaks, as quiet as a whisper, his voice weak and strained. "Everything is official. Legal."

Inside, there's a letter-sized envelope and a small black box. I reach for the envelope, lifting it with care, my fingers delicate on the paper that holds untold secrets. I quickly glance up at Ezra and he nods. I swallow down my anxiety and open it.

I pull out the pages.

I unfold them.

My hands tremble as I read the words.

Certificate of Marriage.

My heart stops beating.

Anya Antonov and Nikolai Mikhailov were joined in marriage on the twenty-first of September in the year...

Oh, God.

I remember.

This is what happened that day.

That's what he was trying to remind me of when I was forced to spend the night with him three months ago as my punishment for trying to commit suicide.

Nearly a year into my captivity—when I was tired of fighting him, when I was lonely, lost, and desperate—I'd come to his room willingly for the first and only time and he'd made me come with his fingers. He never showed me compassion or caring after. He used the knowledge he gained that day against me, knowing how to use my body to coax me into compliance. I went back to hating him after that, though I suppose that was the time when I stopped fighting and gave him my submission to avoid pain.

But this, this *Certificate of Marriage*, was from the day after that. I remember Nikolai's brother making me drink beyond intoxication. I remember him bringing me into Nikolai's home office. I remember seeing another man who I didn't recognize.

A clergyman.

And Kostya, whose name is here as a witness on the certificate, along with Nikolai's brother.

Then it's true?

"We're married?" I stare at the certificate in my hands. "We're married. Is this true, Nikolai?"

"Yes," he whispers. "I told you, I fell for you." He gasps. "I was going to tell the board when I turned forty."

Forty?

He would be forty in a couple of months.

I look at Ezra, hoping for some sort of clarification and thankfully, he's able to provide it since Nikolai's breaths are becoming erratic. "Heads of House choose a bride when they're forty…to bear children and carry on the family name," Ezra explains solemnly. "He was going to tell them he'd already married you, but he wasn't supposed to marry anyone without their agreement. That certificate would've forced their approval."

With insistence and no warning at all, a bubble of rage rises into my chest and bursts explosively. "Why would you do this to me?" I shout at Nikolai. "Why did you do this?"

"To keep you," Nikolai says. "To make you worthy of me."

"You bastard," I snarl. "*Worthy* of you? I'm worth more than your sick soul could ever afford."

"I know." He's shaking, pale as a ghost, eyes shadowed with his oncoming death. "I know that now. That's why I tried to buy you back. To save you." His eyes flicker toward the box again. "Look."

I pull out the only other item I see in the gray box—a small, square, black jewelry box.

No.

Please, no.

I flip open the hinged top.

Sparkling bright is a large, square-cut diamond ring and a wedding band to go with it.

Hot tears spring to my eyes.

I don't know whether I'm livid or hurt or heartbroken. Probably all three. He took my future from me. He has well and truly stolen my life and this ring is a symbol of my slavery. He tied me to his family. Forever.

"Am I," my voice cracks, "am I a Mikhailov?"

"Yes. Since our wedding."

There's a page behind the marriage certificate proving that it's true. He had my name legally changed—legal in the sense that he paid off corrupt officials, no doubt.

My name is Anya Mikhailov.

I drop the jewelry box and dig my fingers into my hair at the scalp. "No. No, no, no. I'm not. I can't be. I *won't* be."

"You're the last Mikhailov," Nikolai says and I scream.

I scream and I sob and I don't stop until I hear Ezra softly say my name.

"Anya. There…there might be more."

I turn my head to look at him, my vision blurred by the tears that form a sheen across my eyes. "More? What more could there be?"

"I lied," Nikolai breathes out hard. "On Vigo's contract of sale…I lied."

"You lied?" My eyebrows lift, my hands fall hard onto my lap, and I nearly laugh. "Shocking."

"Tell her," Nikolai says to Ezra, panting, suffering.

Good.

Let the bastard suffer.

Ezra closes his eyes for a beat. He doesn't look at me when he speaks. "Nikolai wrote in the contract that you were infertile. That you couldn't get pregnant."

"He *what?*"

"He lied to Vigo. The last birth control shot Nikolai had the doctor give you was three months before he sold you. You've been…" Ezra hesitates. "You've been off birth control for the past six months. The last shot would've worn off just before Vigo took you."

My nervous systems stutters and every muscle in my body freezes. I'm stuck in place for what feels like hours, though I know it's only moments. Suddenly I feel trapped inside my mind because what I've just heard is outrageous.

Absurd.

Laughable, really, though it's not funny at all.

I blink and my eyelids linger shut for beats longer than normal. When I open them again, I look down at Nikolai, my mouth open wide in misunderstanding and confusion.

When I speak, my words are measured, slow, so there is no possible way they can be misunderstood. "Did you *want* me to get pregnant with that monster's child? Is that what you *wanted*, Nikolai? Tell me. Tell me!" I shout.

"I wanted to punish you, *rabynya.*"

I slap him.

Then I slap him again.

I punch his shoulder, his chest, his stomach, and he groans in pain when I do.

"I'm sorry," he grunts. "I'm sorry, Anya. It was a mistake. I tried to make it right."

"Oh, you tried? Tried how?" I laugh. "Tell me, Nikolai, how did you try to make it right?"

"At the Leblancs'."

I tried to kill myself at their last quarterly meeting three months ago. I'd been caught by Vigo before I could do it and they went to the board to decide my punishment. Ezra and I had been locked together while our fate was decided. Ezra and I had made love there.

But then Nikolai took me for the night to serve my punishment by giving me pleasure that I didn't want. He fucked me over and over again that night.

That's how he tried to make it right?

I don't understand...

I don't....

Oh, God.

"I've been sick." I lift my head and meet Ezra's solemn green eyes. "I thought it was from malnourishment. I don't remember having a period... Oh, God. Ezra."

"Hey, it's okay," Ezra says to me. "It's all gonna be okay."

I feel composed and frantic all at once, my brain faltering and restarting again and again.

"Am I pregnant? I can't be pregnant. There's no way. With the stress my body's been through? No. *No.* It's not possible."

"Letter," Nikolai hardly gets the word out. "Lid."

"What?"

Ezra nods toward the lid of the box beside me on the floor and I reach for it, flipping it over. On the underside is a small envelope taped to the lid. I pull it free and tear it open. My hands shake as I look at the handwritten letter. The date at the top tells me it was written last week.

It's Nikolai's handwriting, all in Russian.

It's a letter he wrote to me.

> *Dear Anya,*
>
> *I don't know if I will ever give you this letter. But if you're reading it, then please know that I do feel regret— not for making you mine, but for selling you out of anger.*
>
> *I gave you everything you could have ever needed. But I'm starting to understand now that I never gave you what you wanted. I wanted you to have your pet. I would have let you love each other if only you had both loved me.*
>
> *Ezra was the perfect fit. The pet that would have given you the happiness you deserved while I was away. If only you had both obeyed. If only you had both recognized your true master. We all could have found our happiness*

together.

There's emptiness in this home without you. I know I hurt you. I wanted to hurt you. I've become obsessed with hurting you. But when you hurt me by bringing Ezra into your bed against my orders, I couldn't stand to look at you.

But I missed you only hours after you had gone.

It was a mistake to sell you to Vigo.

If the gods see fit to bless me with your child, I will take you back, claim you forever, and try to be better.

I suppose I never learned how to show it, but I do love you, Anya. Please forgive me.

Yours,
Nikolai

The paper crumples in my hand and it forms creases on my heart.

CHAPTER 4
NIKOLAI

I AM THE devil.

Destroyer of destinies.

Keeper of souls.

Lord of chaos and king of torment.

But if I'm to go down in my own hellfire—in the flames I willed to burn around me—then I'm glad that this is the way it had to happen. Ezra was the spark that ignited Anya in a white-hot blaze, and I was the one who poured the fuel that fed their fire.

I did this to them, and it ruined me.

There is no redemption for me.

I may have stolen Anya back from the Vittoris, but she's no longer mine. She gave her heart to Ezra, and I have no one to blame for that but myself. They don't know that they each hold half of my heart in their hands, and I feel them squeezing the life force out of me with their love for each other. They grow stronger together while I burn to ashes at their feet.

I'm tired of the ache, the longing, the inability to master them and make them honor me the way they were meant to. My whole life has been a carefully crafted series of lies and manipulations, and I'm sick of the fight, the fear, the loneliness.

I'm ready to burn for them.

I'm ready to burn *because* of them.

It's time for me to go down in a blaze and return to hell where I belong.

CHAPTER 5
Ezra

NIKOLAI'S PULSE IS fading. I could feel it pulsing when I gripped his hand, but now it's unrecognizable. With my free hand, I press two fingers to his wrist. I think I feel something there, but it's faint and slow.

I glance up at Anya, who is reading the letter, and though I don't know what it says, her emotions are precisely etched into her expression. One of her hands rises from the crumpled letter and she covers her mouth, fresh tears spilling from her wide blue eyes.

Nikolai gasps, stealing attention from both of us. His gray eyes widen for a moment, flicking to look at me, then at her. He holds her gaze and I watch her closely. More emotions than I can name dance across her glassy eyes. I can't look away from her. This hurt and pain and shock she's feeling sits like a heavy weight in my stomach. It's a weight that begs me to carry it so she doesn't have to. But whatever it is she's feeling in this moment...it belongs to her.

Her emotion, her burden, her weight.

Her hand falls heavily on his chest, almost as though she wants to hit him but stops herself at the last possible second. His head slowly rolls toward her and I look at him expectantly, waiting for his final words.

But they never come.

The light has gone from his eyes.

No breath or sound comes.

His pulse is gone.

I look at Anya and have the misfortune of having to watch as she comes to the realization that his heart is no longer beating

"Nikolai," she whispers, looking at him expectantly. She lifts her hand and lets it fall on his chest. "Nikolai?"

I shake my head, though she doesn't look at me. "I think he's—"

"Don't say it!" she shouts at me.

Her words hit me with such force that it pushes me backward as they echo through the studio. I sit on my heels, letting go of his hand and setting it on the floor by his side.

Anya bends over him, putting her hands on his cheeks. She smacks her right hand against his cheek, but he doesn't flinch.

He doesn't blink.

He doesn't breathe.

He doesn't move.

My blue-eyed girl's face is a dreadful mixture of all the worst emotions she could ever possibly express. I rub my palm over my chest, recognizing how my heart aches to see anything but happiness on her face.

This shouldn't be a sad moment…but it is.

She smacks his face again. "Don't you *dare*." Her voice is low, deep, full of fury and pain. "Look at me!" she screams and I watch helplessly as she slips into emotional overload, climbing on top of him, straddling his waist with her knees on either side. "*Look* at me!"

She lets go of his cheeks and his head falls limply to the side. She pounds a fist against his chest and waits.

She pounds again.

She slaps his cheek.

Then again.

She screams and beats on his chest with both fists, over and over. "I hate you! I detest you! You ruined me! You ruined my *life!*"

I rub my palms over my thighs, watching her with wide eyes. I don't really know what to do here; whether I should stop her or let her blaze in the fire of her emotions and wait for her to burn out on her own.

She grabs his face again and leans down over him, her voice shifting from anger to softness with one jarring beat.

"Nikolai. Nikolai, wake up. Look at me." Her entire body trembles. "If you really love me, you'll open your goddamn eyes and look at me…"

Anya presses her lips to his, lingering with a kiss, and I freeze. She has stunned me into silence, and I can't move.

What is she doing?

Why did she do that?

"Nikolai?" she says, her voice hardly a whisper as she stares at him, the tips of their noses practically touching. "Nikolai?"

Her voice catches and tears stream down her cheeks like waterfalls. She sobs, letting her cry echo through the open space of the dance studio, the sound of her sadness bouncing off the walls and slamming into my heart.

"It hurts. I hate him." Her sobs take over everything and nothing else is happening in the world right now. "I hate him so much. Why does this hurt? Why does it *hurt?*"

I latch my arms around her waist and drag her from Nikolai's dead body. She reaches for me as I pull her closer, her small limbs wrapping around me as I hold her tight. She squeezes me harder than ever before and sobs into the side of my neck, drenching me in her pain.

My own tears fall.

Not for Nikolai, but for my girl.

As far as I'm concerned, this is just one more awful thing that Nikolai has done to her. He tried to redeem himself at the final hour, only to go and die on her.

"Why does it hurt?" she repeats softly.

I rub my hands over her back, trying to comfort her when I have no idea how. I give her silence, letting her have her emotional purge. The longer we sit here with each other, the more she cries and hurts, the more my own pain washes over me. Before long I'm crying with her, and I can't even say why.

Nikolai stole us.

He enslaved us, he hurt us, he *brutalized* us.

He sold Anya to someone more sadistic than himself.

And then he helped us.

He helped us.

There are so many questions left unanswered and they're all rushing around in my head, scrambling my brain. But the questions tumble down our cheeks as tears because we will never get those answers.

The *whys,* the *what ifs,* the *how could he possibly…*

They all just died with Nikolai.

Anya's crying slows and her sobs fade into small hiccups of hurt. All her tears have been shed and she goes quiet and still in my arms. I reach up behind her, cradling the back of her head before stroking my hand down her long, dark hair. She pulls her head back so she can look at me and lets her forehead fall against mine.

"I'm sorry for being crazy again," she whispers.

"Nothing to apologize for."

"I kissed him." Her eyes glass over again with fresh tears as she looks at me. "I'm so sorry. I kissed him." She shakes her head. "I don't know why I kissed him."

"Hey. It's okay. It's okay, baby." I stroke her hair again. "It's all okay. I promise."

I take a deep breath, holding her gaze with hope that I can feed her strength from within me. It forces me to swallow my own pain—it *does* hurt that she willingly put her lips to his, but I don't feel justified judging her for that. I know my only choice is to get over it.

Somehow.

But that's not her concern.

This whole damn thing is the cluster fuck to end all cluster fucks.

I tuck her hair behind her ear. "The four families could be coming at any time."

She lifts her head from mine and nods. "I know."

"We're gonna have to drive out there to the helipad when they get here. We took the car. There's no way for them to get here once they land."

Anya's voice is quiet. "We could just leave them there to rot."

The corners of my lips curl up. "I would love nothing more. But we both know they would find a way to get to us."

She nods somberly. "I know."

I rub her back slowly before I speak, hoping my touch calms her. "Nikolai told me we should text a picture of the marriage certificate to Renata…to keep them from killing you on sight." Those words feel so vile as they break from my lips.

"It won't stop them from hurting you, Ezra." She looks at me so sadly, it feels like my heart is in a vice.

"I know that. But I stand a better chance if they know that you're…" I hesitate to say it, "Nikolai's wife.

She pinches her eyes shut. When she opens them again, she slides from my lap, crawling slowly around Nikolai's dead body to retrieve the box he left for her. She pulls out the marriage certificate and lays it on the floor beside her. I pull Nikolai's cell phone from my pocket.

And I realize it's locked.

"I'm gonna have to…use his fingerprint," I warn Anya—knowing the idea of lifting a dead man's hand to use his fingerprint to unlock his phone is morbid.

Her head bobs in something resembling a nod and she turns her attention away. I'd be lying to say I'm not bothered by her reaction to his death. This would all be so much easier if the death of her two sadistic masters brought her relief instead of agony. Vigo and Nikolai are both dead, and I don't entirely understand why she seems so upset by the loss. I just want to know what's going on inside her mind.

I get access to the phone and the first thing I do is change the fingerprint unlocking access so I don't have to use a dead man's finger ever again. Anya has smoothed the certificate out on the floor and I go to her, holding the phone above to take a clear picture of it—I do the same with the document showing the official name change. I find Renata's number and send her the pics, followed by a quick text message.

NIKOLAI Nikolai is dead, but not the last Mikhailov. Anya is his wife.

Anya comes up next to me as I press send. We watch the phone silently as we wait for a reply. Within minutes, the phone rings. Renata's name flashes across the screen with her call.

"Let me talk," she says, taking the phone from me and tapping to answer. "This is Anya."

"I want proof that Nikolai is dead." Renata's voice is smooth on the other end of the line.

"I will send you a video of his lifeless body if that would satisfy you," Anya says with an unusual edge to her voice.

"It would," Renata replies. "We'll be arriving in six hours. Have someone meet us at the helipad."

"Why? So you can kill us on sight? I want a guarantee that our fate will be considered judiciously."

"We consider all matters of the four families judiciously." There's a pause. "Though I wish to cut out your heart and keep it as a trophy for what you've done to my brother. You're lucky that I care more for my home and family than I care for your pathetic life. My family needs my leadership… now more than ever. And I'll be damned if I let my hatred for you get in the way of doing what must be done."

Anya's eyes show panic, fear, and a hint of curiosity, but she speaks with smoothness and determination. "I want confirmation from a Head of House. From Murphy O'Shea. If I'm not afforded the courtesy of the board to determine my fate fairly, then you can walk from the helipad to Mikhailov Manor for all I care. And knowing you, Renata, I imagine your current footwear is inappropriate for such a journey through the wilderness."

There's silence from Renata's end and fuck, I want to cheer for my girl. For all she's been through—all the pain, humiliation, for all the near-death experiences—she is still one brilliant, beautiful, powerhouse of a woman.

"Fine," Renata finally concedes. "I will have him call."

The phone beeps and the call ends from Renata's end of the line. We wait for a few minutes for Murphy to call, but I think we both realize they're going to make us wait for it. They want to keep the upper hand, as if Anya and I could ever hope to have a hand-up on them.

With a sigh, she holds out the phone for me to take and I put it in my back pocket for safe keeping. I hesitate in the quiet between us for a few moments before working up the nerve to ask the question that feels heavy in this space.

"Do you think we should find out if you're…" I trail off, wondering if I should even have brought it up right now.

She looks over at me, concern flashing off the sapphire blue of her eyes. She clears her throat and swallows nervously. "You're right. We should find a pregnancy test. I think Nikolai keeps them in his bathroom. He'd have me take one every so often…just to be sure." She shakes her head as if trying to shake away all of her worries.

I grab her cheeks and hold her face still, giving her the intensity of my stare. "Hey. It changes nothing between us if you're pregnant. Do you understand me? You didn't ask for any of this. You didn't choose this. Tell me you know that."

She hesitates. "I know. I do. It'll probably be negative anyway, right? What are the odds of a pregnancy surviving everything my body's been through…right?"

I don't have a fucking clue.

"Right," I agree, knowing that she's seeking assurance and that's all I can give her right now—even if it ends up being false assurance.

Fuck.

"Come on." I stand and hold out my hands for her, pulling her up when her palms land on mine.

We walk hand-in-hand out of the dance studio, though she pauses once at the door, turning to look back at Nikolai. He's a still, dead body in the middle of the room where we found each other—a lifeless corpse in the center of the space where my blue-eyed girl and I danced together and fell in love. I'm not sure if that's hauntingly poetic or morbidly gut-wrenching.

We follow the trail of blood Nikolai left as he bled out all the way from the dance studio back to the grand staircase. We ascend and Anya takes me to Nikolai's bedroom. She goes straight for his bathroom and I wait beside his bed, listening as she pulls open drawers and flings open cabinets. A minute or two later, she comes out with a small pink box in her hands.

"Found one," she says with a wry smile. "This one hasn't expired." She sucks in a harsh breath. "I don't want to do this here, though…not in his room."

I nod. "I know. Come on."

I take her by the hand and lead her back to her room…*my* room…*our* room. It's a part of Mikhailov Manor, but somehow, this room still feels like *our* space. She stops at the threshold.

"It…it looks the same as when I left it." She glances toward the bed. "My dress."

My gaze follows hers to the bright fuchsia gown she wore to the reception the night before she was sold to Vigo—the night of our performance.

"It never leaves the bed," I tell her. "I always sleep next to it."

She looks up at me with love and sadness in her eyes. I want to bend and kiss her, but then she sighs and turns away, looking down at the pink box hopelessly.

All the fucking boxes and secrets tonight.

"I just need to get this over with," she tells me, melancholy ripe in her tone.

She turns and wanders away without another word, her eyes glued to the box in her hands. I step after her, thinking I should hug her, kiss her, tell her again that everything will be okay. But before I can reach her, she closes the bathroom door behind her, transfixed on whatever words are printed on the back of the box.

I pace for a minute or so.

The toilet flushes.

The faucet runs.

The door clicks open.

She comes out empty-handed, arms crossed tightly over her chest. "It… it says to wait two minutes."

"Okay."

"Two pink lines is positive. One line is negative."

"Okay."

"I took both tests in the box. There were two. I left them on the sink."

"Okay."

Her eyebrows slant toward her nose. "Okay? Is that all you have to say? *Okay?*"

I toss up my hands. "I don't know what the fuck else to say, Anya. I'm at a loss here. Just a few hours ago, the only thing I had to worry about was saving your life. I never in a million fucking years would've thought pregnancy was even on the table."

Her jaw sets and ticks as she shakes her head. She's pissed and she's directing all that angry energy at me. I step closer, putting my hands on her biceps to comfort her. She tenses against my touch and I don't know what to do with that so I drop my arms and back away, lifting my palms as if I need to surrender.

Her forehead wrinkles, frustration with me peaking. "What are you doing? Don't back away from me, I just—" Her breath catches in her throat and she suddenly starts to cry. Her arms slip from their hold and slowly fall to her sides. "I don't know how to deal with all of this."

Fuck.

I feel like I'm handling everything wrong.

I dash to her, throwing my arms around her, pulling her close, impossibly close. I press one hand to the small of her back and hold her against me, the other traveling to the back of her head, guiding her to press her cheek to my chest.

"I'm sorry, Anya. I'm sorry. I know it's shit. It's all shit. I just…I don't know how to deal with this, either."

She cries into my chest and I hold her.

I just hold her.

I don't let go until her sobs have calmed and she pulls back. She lifts her head to look at me with those goddamn bewitching eyes of hers. "I think it's time."

I nod at her, give her a small smile, and place a kiss on the center of her forehead. "You want to look alone or together?"

"Together. Always together."

I release her from my hold and slip my hand down her arm. I catch her palm in mine and lock our fingers together. I let her lead us to the bathroom. Her fingers squeeze mine tighter and she puts her free hand over her heart, freezing in the doorway and pressing her eyes shut. She takes a deep breath, then another. I watch as she centers herself, finding her courage to face the truth, whatever it may be.

She steps past the threshold as she opens her eyes, going straight for the sink. I step with her but keep my eyes on her face. I don't want to see what the tests say—I don't *need* to. I just need to see her, know what she feels, and be ready to open my arms for her.

Standing squarely in front of the sink, she looks down to her right where two pregnancy tests lay side by side. Her eyes flicker, registering what she sees.

She stills.

She sucks in a sharp breath.

Her lips fall apart when she exhales and her forehead wrinkles as her eyebrows knit together.

Then her face falls.

The hand over her heart lifts to cover her mouth and her eyes catch her reflection in the mirror. She sways in my hold and her eyelids flutter, as if they want to force their way shut. She tilts away from me, her hand loosening from my grip.

"Anya!"

"I'm—" Her eyes roll back in her head and she starts to fall sideways, away from me.

I wrap my hand around her wrist and yank her upright, pulling her to fall into my arms instead. She's limp in my hold—she *fainted*. I bend and scoop my arms beneath her legs, lifting her and carrying her back to the bedroom. I carefully set her on her bed and check that she's breathing and that her heart is still beating.

She's alive, just exhausted, overwhelmed, and malnourished.

Fuck. I need to get her something to eat.

I leave her on the bed to dash back down to the kitchen. I grab juice from the fridge, some bread from the cabinet, and snatch a banana from the fruit bowl on the counter. I rush it all back to the bedroom, wondering on the way if we're completely alone in this mansion. I didn't see any signs of the chef or either of the people who clean the home. Of course, Nikolai probably dismissed them to return to their families while he was away for the quarterly meeting.

I get back to Anya just as she's opening her eyes. She pushes up to her elbows as I kick the door shut behind me. Rushing toward her, I set everything on the floor beside her bed and kneel.

"Take it easy," I murmur. "You passed out."

"Ezra, I'm…did you look at the tests?"

I shake my head. "No. You passed out. I set you down here and went to get you some food." I grab the single-serve juice bottle and open it before handing it to her. "Here, drink this."

She takes it from me and drinks slowly, taking several small sips before handing it back. I start to peel the banana for her. "I'll make you a proper meal as soon as I can, but I'm guessing your blood sugar is ridiculous right now. Eat this."

I hold out the fruit for her, but she doesn't take it. Instead, she gives me unflinching, soul-shattering eye contact.

"I'm pregnant."

No, she's not.

She can't be.

Fuck. She is.

I let out a heavy breath, sinking back to sit on my heels. "Well. Fuck."

"I'm so sorry."

My gaze jerks to hers. "What?"

"I'm sorry." She falls back to lay on her pillow, her hands coming up to cover her eyes.

"Hold on. What in the actual fuck are you *sorry* for? Anya," I take her wrists gently in my palms and pull her hands away from her face, "you didn't do this. You didn't *choose* this. You have nothing to apologize for."

My blue-eyed girl is pregnant.

My heart starts beating a quicker rhythm as reality starts to grip me. Anya is pregnant, and we don't know who the father is.

Anya is pregnant.

Pregnant.

"Ezra?" she says softly.

I shake my head, dragging myself out of this pit of worry I seem to have fallen into. I lean over her, pressing a soft kiss to her lips. "I love you. I love you forever. No matter what. We're gonna figure this out together."

Her blue irises flash from side to side as she looks deep into my eyes. "You promise you're mine? Still mine? Always mine?"

I lift her wrists and kiss her knuckles. "Still yours. *Always* yours."

"No matter what?"

"No matter what." I shove the banana into her hand and smile at her. "Now eat this so you can start getting your strength back. I have a feeling you're going to need it."

I think we're going to need all the strength in the universe to cope with this shit. I feel like I could break down over this. The woman I love is a Mikhailov by marriage and she's pregnant with *someone's* child—a child who very well could belong to either of the two sadist, slave-owning fathers…or a child who could belong to *me*.

It could be mine.

I could crumble under the weight of these unknowns.

I feel that weight settling on my shoulders and it's fucking heavy. But I have no choice other than to carry it. I have to carry my weight, and *hers*, because I can't stand the thought of her lifting a finger to shoulder this burden.

This is my time to step up.

PAS DE TROIS

This is my time to figure out how to be a fucking man—how to be *her* man. She needs me more than ever and I'm not going to fail her.

CHAPTER 6
Anya

EZRA HAS BEEN urging me to sleep since I regained consciousness. He's so worried about me and it shows. I don't want him to worry so much about me, but there's nothing I can do about it. Sometimes I think he loves me too much, so much that he would sacrifice his own well-being for mine. But I can't blame him for feeling that way.

Because I love him that much, too.

About an hour has gone by since I passed out from the devastation of the two pink lines. Nikolai's phone begins to ring in Ezra's back pocket. He reaches behind him, interrupting our prone embrace on my bed, and pulls out the phone. We both sit up slowly and he hands it over to me with a reassuring nod—his encouragement gives me confidence. He strokes my hair and somehow, that gives me strength.

I tap to answer the call. "This is Anya."

"Murphy O'Shea." His familiar Irish accent croons through the phone.

I open my mouth to speak again, but Murphy starts talking before I have the chance.

"Listen here, lass. You must have the luck of the Irish on your side. Fucking rainbows and four-leaf clovers. If that wanker old man of yours hadn't done his due diligence and made you a Mikhailov, we'd be busting arse to put a bullet between your eyes the moment we touch down. So, here's the good news for you. There are no other Mikhailov descendants, and *you* are the only person with his goddamn name. So, welcome to the fucking board. When we arrive, I expect you to be there to meet our helicopter. You and that slave boy bring two cars to accommodate all of us. We'll convene with you in the boardroom at Mikhailov Manor and decide what the fuck to do with the two of you *judiciously*, as you requested. We're all en route to you now. We'll be there in less than five hours. See you then."

The call ends.

I look at Ezra. "Five hours." I feel like ice is scraping over my bones as

I realize time is ticking.

He nods, then curls his hand around the side of my head and pulls me close. I rest my head on his shoulder as he strokes my hair.

"Let's sleep for three. Then we'll get ready and drive back to the helipad to meet them."

"Ezra, I'm scared. What will they do to you?"

"Don't worry about me. As long as they don't hurt you, I'll be okay. No matter what. As long as you're okay, then I'm okay. Now stop talking about it and let's worry about getting our heads in the game. We need to be sharp, clear-headed, prepared for anything, right?"

I nod against his shoulder, turning my head to press my face into the side of his neck. I inhale the sweetness of his scent before placing a kiss to his skin. He inhales and exhales sharply.

"How do you do that?" he whispers, his fingers snaking into my hair, his nails softly scratching my scalp.

I lift my head to look up at him. "Do what?"

"Make me forget about everything but the way you make me want you, even in the face of death?"

The green of his eyes appears to melt as the lighter vibrant color drains slowly, letting the darker shade of emerald wash over. It's a color that's urgent, greedy, hungry, and his hunger only sparks mine.

"I don't know," I say softly. "But I feel it with you, too."

His grip on my hair tightens, and though the possessiveness of it should alarm me, I find that it doesn't.

Not even a little bit.

Not at all.

Ezra's possession is wanted, *needed*. If I am his, then he is mine and I want nothing else.

"Ezra..." I say his name on a sigh and the spark in his eyes tells me he knows what I need.

How is this intense lust even possible from my abused, exhausted body?

He holds my head still and bends to kiss me recklessly. I moan against his lips as every bit of my body prickles to life with a hum of awareness. I part my lips for him, inviting him to taste me because I desperately need to taste him. He devours me with a fervor unlike anything I've felt from him before.

The way he claims his possession of me is desperate, needy, protective. This ferocity should scare me, but it doesn't because I'm as ferociously needy as he is. My fingers claw at his chest, madly trying to cling to his skin and hold him against me. Everything inside me collapses and clenches, coiling tightly, painfully, low in my belly. It transforms me into a body with lust so frantic that it demands to be released.

Now.

I climb onto his lap, straddling his hips. "Make me come," I beg between hectic kisses. "Make me come right now."

Something resembling a growl shudders his entire body and it shakes mine, too. His hands fall to my hips, gripping me tightly. Then he rolls me off him, slamming my back into the mattress, and lays down heavily on top of me.

There's hesitation in his eyes for the briefest moment. He doesn't want to be like them—like the monsters who raped me. But he could never be that. He can fuck me any way he wants to because he does it with such love for me. If I tell him to stop, he will…and because of that, I won't.

I want to see him lost in this, lost in me, lost in us.

I reach between us, working his buckle. I undo the button and zipper and slip my fingers beneath the elastic of his boxer briefs. I shove them down, unsheathing his hard cock. He groans, placing his forehead against mine as my fingers graze along his shaft.

I feel as possessive as he does as I run my fingers along the part of him that needs me so insistently. I wrap my hand around the base and tug gently.

"Mine?" I ask, sucking my bottom lip between my teeth.

"It's yours," he says and I melt, sinking deeper into the mattress, letting him smother me with his love. "Every part of me is yours."

"I want you inside me. *Please.*"

I'm still bare and exposed beneath Ezra's button-down shirt. His green eyes sparkle as he reaches down to position himself against my opening and his fingers find me already wet for him—it's true and honest arousal, and the slickness of it makes me feel powerful. I'm not dry and waiting to take the pain; I'm soaked and anxious for the pleasure.

He groans, letting his hand linger, his fingers playing with me—they slip along my folds, dip inside me, drag, and swirl and spread my wetness until I'm squirming beneath him.

I never thought I'd know such desire.

I never thought I'd want a man this way.

Ezra worships me with his touch and it makes me want to give him everything I have.

I gasp and moan as he circles my clit with his thumb, slowly pressing the tip of his cock inside me. "*Please,*" I beg, and he gives me what I need.

His hips thrust forward, and I feel every perfectly agonizing inch of him as he sinks inside me, stretching my pussy to accept his pulsing length. He rears back, sitting up on his knees as my legs encircle him.

He grabs my hips as he rises on his knees, dragging my body closer, burying his cock deep. He looks down at me as though he could consume my very soul with nothing more than a groan, a deep thrust, and a perfectly-timed kiss to devour me. I gasp at the feel of him, at the look on his face as he watches mine. When he starts to move, I feel as though I might die from this intensity.

He leans forward, his fists landing on the mattress, holding him up as he fucks me with a rocking motion that sets my insides on fire.

I can't speak.

I can hardly breathe.

My lungs beg for the release that will set them free from my panting and gasping need.

"You're pussy feels like heaven. Fuck. You feel incredible."

His words that worship me tighten in my chest. Not a painful tightening—it's more like a warm embrace around my heart. He watches me as his hips roll, his eyes flickering across my expression, and I know how he sees me.

He sees the way my face changes when he angles just right. He sees the tension in my jaw, the slant in my brow that forms with the creasing of my forehead. He sees my teeth tug on my bottom lip, then the way they part with a gasp in pleasure-filled surprise

"There," I gasp. "Right there. Oh, God. Make me come. Make me come, Ezra." I lift my head from the mattress, pressing up onto my elbows to look between us to see where we're joined.

Given all I've been through, the sight of a man thrusting inside me should be abhorrent. But with Ezra, it's anything but. Seeing the way we connect so perfectly, so beautifully at the end of his chiseled, sculpted, perfectly toned abs—beneath the patch of dirty blond hair that leads the trail to his cock—turns me on. He's so strong, so powerful with his lean muscle; a dream of a man brought to life that heaven sent to me.

Oh, God.

He looks so good.

I exhale harshly as the start of my climax tugs through my body, stretching from head to toe in a tight string of tingling tension. "*Oh. Ohh…*"

Ezra snatches my wrist, yanking my elbow out from beneath me, and I land flat on my back. He brings my hand down between us, encouraging my fingers to dance over my clit. I watch him while I rub, while his gaze falls down to observe carefully as I rapidly circle over my sensitive flesh.

It only takes moments like this and a groan from deep within his chest to ignite me. My heart stops as the string that pulls tension through my body stretches tighter and snaps in two, bursting all the tingling pressure right in my core. The soul-crushing climax bursts and ripples through my entire body.

I go limp on the mattress, but Ezra keeps fucking me. Thrust after thrust after thrust and…

Oh, God.

Oh, my fucking God.

His cock swells just before his orgasm spills inside me and the pressure only lifts me higher. Then I fall hard and fast into a second, unexpected orgasm.

That's never happened to me before.

Ezra could feel it. He could feel the way my walls clenched and pulsed around him, and I watch his face as a grin of pure satisfaction touches every feature. He brings such brightness to his face that you could fool me into thinking that the light haloing around him radiated from his soul, though I know it's only from the light fixture above him.

"Anya," he says with a sated chuckle. "*Fuck.*"

I lick my suddenly dry lips as I look up at him with half-hooded eyes. I feel so wet. The mess of him and me coming together drips from my sensitive pussy and the mere thought of it sends a tiny, clenching aftershock of pleasure—just a quick lightning bolt of bliss that strikes straight through to my clit.

He bends with a proud smile, kissing the corner of my lips sensually, kissing my cheek and along my jawline, nuzzling his nose over my earlobe. I reach for him, wrapping my arms around him and running my hands over his back.

"I've never felt so completely..." I struggle for words.

"Undone?" he offers.

"Fulfilled," I counter.

"Unhinged?"

"Satisfied."

"Content?" he asks.

I grab his face in both of my hands. "Complete. I feel so *complete* with you inside me."

He sighs, his brow slanting to form a V. "You're complete on your own without me."

What does he mean by that?

"No," I tell him. "I hate that. I feel complete with *you*."

"I know, baby." He brushes the sweat-stuck hair from my face. "I know what you mean. I feel it, too. But I don't ever want you to forget how perfect and amazing and complete you are as you. Just you."

"Stop that." My eyes narrow at him. "Just stop it. I don't want to be perfect and amazing and complete on my own. I want to be as complete as I feel with you. A part of me is missing without you." I feel strange, angry tears start to well up and I hate it. I hate it so much. "What are you even trying to say to me?"

"Hey, it's okay. I'm sorry. I'm not saying anything at all. I'm just saying that if...if something were to happen to me...you don't need me to—"

"Stop!" I shout, shoving at his chest and pushing him off me. I scoot to the edge of the bed and climb off as he rolls to sit up. "I hate what you're saying. You're saying I can live without you if they kill you. But I can't. I *can't*, Ezra. I can't live without you. I will die without you. I don't want to *exist* without you." My breaths turn shallow and rapid, and I find I'm pacing beside the bed. "I'm only complete when I'm with you. Don't tell me I'm complete on my own. Are *you* complete on your own?" I stop and turn to face where he sits at the edge of the bed. My voice lowers to a whisper. "*Are* you complete on your own? Without me? Is that what you're telling me?"

What is happening to me?

I've gone down a rabbit hole of insanity. Every thought and emotion buried within my soul is bursting to the surface and I can't seem to control it. I don't want to hear his response because I fear the worst. I fear he'll tell me that he *can* live without me. That he doesn't need me to be complete. I don't know how I'll survive if he tells me that.

I turn on my heel and storm off to the bathroom before he can respond, slamming the door shut. I stand still for a second and in moments, he's pounding on the door, begging to be let in.

"I have to pee. Leave me alone," I shout through the door before I realize I actually do have to pee.

"Fuck," he says through the door. "*Fine.*"

I wait a few seconds for quiet before heading to the toilet to handle my business. As I sit there, my eyes fall on the two pregnancy tests on the counter and I reach for one. I carefully pick it up, studying it as I sit.

Two pink lines.

Two pink lines that tell me my life has irrevocably changed.

"This is real," I whisper to myself. "This is really real."

I finish up and wash my hands before opening the door again, my cheeks flushing in embarrassment over my tirade. I bring the test out with me. Ezra is sitting on the edge of my bed—beautiful, naked, though sadness shines in his posture with his elbows on his knees and head in his hands.

I stand there in the doorway. "I'm sorry."

He looks up at me, pushing to stand and striding toward me as I speak.

"Just hours ago, I thought I was dead. I was under the water, trapped in that bathtub, and I was *dying.* I'd said goodbye to life, Ezra. I thought it was all over and then suddenly…it wasn't. And all of this? Nikolai dying, finding out that I'm his wife, that I'm pregnant with *someone's* baby…I feel like my mind is snapping and I'm sorry. I'm so sorry for fighting with you. I don't want to fight. I love you and I just need to hear that you love me, too."

His shoulders slump and he closes the space between us, slipping his arms around my waist and holding me tight. His body is warm against mine and it melts the iciness inside that makes me cold and hard.

"I love you, Anya. I love you forever. And I'm not complete without you.

I never was. Every minute we were apart was agony for me. I need you. And I'll remind you of that every minute of every day if that's what you need."

"That's insane." I chuckle through glassy eyes. "Every five minutes will be fine."

We both laugh, pulling apart just enough to look at each other, to watch each other, to love each other with silence and simple togetherness.

"Come on. We need to get some rest. I'll set the alarm on the phone. Come lay down with me and let me keep you safe while you sleep."

He takes my hand in his and leads me to the bed. I'm so grateful for him and the way he loves me.

Lying down side by side, comforted and protected in each other's arms, we somehow manage to fall into a quick, deep, dreamless slumber.

Nikolai once told me that I looked like a queen.

It was the night of my second annual performance in Nobility Hall. I wore a beautiful black evening gown that night. It had a boat neckline formed by sheer black fabric that stretched down to the smallest part of my waist—the sheerness was embroidered with decorative flowers and flourishes that hid my breasts and made the dress more modest.

I remember the way the gown cinched around my waist, flowing down to the floor in sweeping layers of black and gray tulle that dusted gracefully over the marble floor as I walked. I might've felt like a queen in that dress if I hadn't been in mourning.

After my performance, Nikolai had taken my second partner from me. His name was Erik, and though we were only just okay together as dancers, he was a friend.

And the loss of him hurt all the same.

With the four families' impending arrival, I do my best to steel myself, to harden myself, to freeze my soul in a protective layer of ice. I know I have to transform before they arrive. I can no longer remain the emotional, broken slave girl they'd seen me as before—that won't be tolerated as a Mikhailov and I won't be taken seriously.

I have to become like them.

I have to become regal, god-like.

I have to become a queen.

I need to make them see me as the bereaved wife, the strong and persevering goddess, the determined woman who would meet their force with force of her own as the sole surviving matriarch in the Mikhailov line.

It's what I have to become, without any time or preparation for such a role. But with Ezra by my side, I know I can do it. His presence emboldens me, empowers me, and inspires me to find the strength within myself to be who I need to be.

It's like any other performance—it's just playing a part. And to play a part successfully, I have to be convincing. I have to convince them, but more so, I must convince myself that I *am* who I pretend to be.

If I need to convince us all that I am a queen, then I must dress the part. I put on the same black gown that convinced Nikolai all those years ago that I could look like a ruler in his world.

Before I put on my costume, I use Renata as inspiration for my role, spending some time perfecting my appearance. I style my hair into perfect, long waves that softly curl over my shoulders and down to the middle of my back.

I paint my face with color, shading my eyes with a light shade of pink that makes the blue of my irises pop. I outline my lids with brushes of dark gray shadow and black eyeliner. I curl and plump my eyelashes, brushing them with black mascara to make them thick and sultry. I add a hint of bronze to my cheeks and draw dark pink gloss over my lips.

I put on my dress and stare at my reflection in the bathroom mirror. The small, ominous black box—the box that holds the diamond rings Nikolai purchased for me—sits on the counter, resting forebodingly beside the two positive pregnancy tests that I just can't seem to bring myself to throw away.

Not yet.

With a steeling breath, I reach over and pluck the box from the countertop, flipping open the lid. I'm met with a bright sparkle from the diamond rings within. It strikes an unresolved ache in my chest because I still don't know what to make of all this.

If Nikolai wanted to marry me, why did he treat me as his slave?

These rings symbolize how Nikolai has controlled my life, even now from beyond the grave. It's a symbol of my oppression, but it still stirs some strange feeling within me that I can't place. It's something I can only vaguely describe as gratitude, though I know that's not the right word.

I feel no gratitude toward that man.

Then why do my eyes well with tears at the reminder that he's gone?

I hear my bedroom door click open as Ezra returns to me. I sniffle back my sorrow and dab beneath my eyes to catch any tears that might ruin my makeup. I look at him as he crosses to me and the twinge of sadness fades away, and in its place, tremendous pride for the fact that I can call him mine.

He's so ridiculously handsome wearing a black suit. He's chosen a plain white shirt and a black necktie. He looks professional, in charge, prominent, and proud.

"You look perfect," I tell him as I set the jewelry box down on the marble counter.

Ezra moves behind me, his hands skimming down my sides as we both regard our reflection in the mirror. "You look spectacular. Stunning."

"Do I look like one of them?" I ask, hoping he'll say yes but also hoping he'll say no.

He nods before pressing his lips to my shoulder. "You look better than them. You *are* better than them. You look exactly as you should."

"Queen Mikhailov?" I say jokingly with a small, twisted smile.

"Just a queen. You don't have to be ruled by his name."

I spin to face him and trap him in my gaze for a beat. Any gratitude I might've felt toward Nikolai slips away entirely, because there's no room left for it when I'm filled to the brim with gratitude for Ezra.

He pulls away from my stare as his eyes draw to the sparkling diamonds on the countertop and he plucks the rings from the box. "I think you need to wear these." He swallows hard and pinches his eyes shut, then opens them again. "They need to see you wearing these rings."

I nod, though he doesn't see it. His eyes are transfixed on the diamonds between us and I wonder what he's thinking. I wait for him to tell me and eventually, he does, starting slowly.

"Nikolai owes me," he says. "He owes me a life for the life he's taken from me. He owes you a life, too. These rings…He wanted them to be a symbol of the life he took from you; a symbol that you belong to him. But I don't want them to mean you belong to him because you don't."

I sigh, closing my eyes. "I belong to *you*, Ezra." I open my eyes again just in time to see the corners of his lips curl up and I smile, too. He's just so relentlessly sexy, especially when he smiles at me like that.

"You only belong to me if you want to."

"You're the only man I ever want to belong to."

"If that's true, then…maybe these rings are mine. Maybe yours is the life he owes to me and mine is what he owes to you."

Oh, God.

That makes my heart beat wildly and my pulse thrums. "Ezra…"

"Maybe you can wear these and think of me. Maybe someday you can…marry me. And we can belong to each other forever. If we're ever lucky enough to get that chance."

I grab his face and kiss him. I kiss him with love and passion and gratitude. "You're my forever. I already know it…however long our forever might be."

He lets out a slow breath. "Then you'll wear these for me? Not for him."

"I'll wear them for you," I promise.

He takes my hand and slips both the wedding band and engagement ring onto my left ring finger. He doesn't know that in Russia, women wear their rings on the right hand. And I'm glad he doesn't know because wearing it on my right hand *would* feel like wearing them for Nikolai.

To wear them on the left makes it more special somehow.

It's for Ezra.

I wear them for *him*.

I reach up with one hand to caress his cheek, my thumb brushing over his skin.

"We can do this, Anya. You and me. We can face this."

"Mine?" I ask even though I already know the answer.

"Baby, I'm yours."

CHAPTER 7
Ezra

MY BLUE-EYED GIRL and I stand side-by-side on the gravel surrounding the helipad as an oversized helicopter gradually descends. My heart is thumping like crazy against my rib cage. I reach out and snatch Anya's tiny hand in mine, tangling my fingers with hers and locking us together.

I don't know what will happen and the uncertainty makes every muscle in my body seize with tension. I glance over at Anya as the chopper lands, the blades gradually slowing in their rotation.

She takes in a heavy breath and lifts her chin a little higher, pulling her shoulders back. I watch her face as she lets the coldness freeze her in determination—the same coldness she possessed when I first met her. She needs that now; she needs the fierceness that allows her to do what needs to be done.

I know all of that, but it still stings when her shields come up and she pulls her fingers free from mine. Still, she glances over at me appraisingly, asking me with her eyes if I understand and I nod in reassurance.

She needs to stand on her own as the regal, worthy queen of Mikhailov Manor.

The doors open and Murphy O'Shea is the first person out of the helicopter. He jumps out with intention, lands heavily on the asphalt, and pauses just long enough to straighten his waistcoat. His white shirt sleeves are already rolled up to his elbows, exposing his tattoo-covered forearms.

His eyes fall on us as Leo Leblanc climbs out behind him, looking svelte in comparison to Murphy's broad, muscular frame. Murphy charges toward us, long fast strides bringing him swiftly to where we stand. I start to move, to sidestep in front of Anya to protect her against his onrushing force, but she stops me, placing her hand on the crease of my arm.

She steps forward.

Fuck.

She steps forward and I've never been so terrified in my life. My pulse thrums, my fists clench, my muscles ache to fight for her, to protect her, to keep her safe. But her life depends on negotiation, not fists and blood and violence.

But then I realize she never needed me to stand in front of her for protection…because he's not going after her.

He's coming straight for *me*.

Murphy's jaw is set, eyes determined, and I'm overwhelmed by the surge of adrenaline inside me. But my instinct still pulls me toward Anya because I'd jump in front of a bullet for her without a second thought. I glance at her, and because my attention is on her, Murphy catches me off-guard with a sucker punch to my cheek.

The rings that he wears mar my face, adding an extra oomph to the shooting pain that bursts across my cheek. His other fist collides with my gut, doubling me over. When he hits me in the stomach a second time, I slump to my knees with a grunt and a groan.

The fucker packs a killer punch.

I lift my head just as he moves his attention to Anya, pointing a finger in her face. "You are proving to be far more trouble than your worth, lass."

She takes him on with a deadly stare. "I'm worth the entire fortune of the Mikhailov family," she says with the most convincing coldness.

Murphy chuckles, glancing back over his shoulder as Leo helps Renata off the aircraft, then his cousin Cordelia. "You sure have got a sizeable pair of balls, woman."

"Bigger than yours, I imagine," she returns with a lifted brow.

Murphy cocks his head to the side. "Get in the car. I'll drive."

Anya sets her jaw. "I have guests to greet first."

Murphy cracks his knuckles with another small laugh. "You're quite a proud little bitch for destroying two families, aren't you? If we didn't have to handle this as a board matter, I promise you, I'd have strangled you to death by now."

I plant one foot on the ground, ready to rise to my feet, practically trembling with rage, but Renata marches toward me with one long finger outstretched, pointed directly at me.

"Stay on your knees if you wish to live beyond this night, slave."

My jaw tenses. I open my mouth to retort, but Anya snaps at me, just like she used to in the beginning, "*Mal'chik.* Don't say a goddamn word."

Fuck, I want to fight.

I want to argue.

I want to shout.

I want to attack.

I force myself to dampen my natural urges because I know what has to happen here.

I'm not in control.

I don't have the power.

But Anya might just be able to take it for herself—for the *both* of us—if I just shut up and do as I'm told for once.

So, I keep my shit under control, and I do it for her.

I settle there on my knees, sitting back on my heels. I throw my hands up momentarily in surrender before I let them flop down onto my thighs when Renata appears satisfied with my concession. She rounds on Anya next, and it takes everything within me to remain where I am.

"You vile little slut!" Renata shouts at her, her words clipped and precise. "You killed my brother!"

I see a venomous smile touch Anya's cheek. "He deserved it."

Renata forces her way around Murphy, slapping Anya with a thwack that echoes through the clearing. She wraps her fist around Anya's hair, tugging her head sideways. Anya yelps and my muscles twitch.

"Stop it," Murphy says coolly. "She may have killed your brother, but she's a fucking *wife.* You can't behave this way, Renata."

Renata grits her teeth, hesitating with her grip on Anya, but after moments, she finally lets go. "Fine," she says, stepping back. "I'll be civilized."

Murphy laughs. "Right, you will."

Cordelia quickly finds her way to Renata's side, her face red and eyes glossy with tears. She links her arm with Renata's and pets her hair as if she's some broken creature who requires comfort. It's almost comical to watch these heathens pretend to be human, as if they have actual emotions and give a shit about human life.

When all the passengers have gathered and the whir of the helicopter's engine shuts off entirely, silence washes over the dark clearing. The wind whispers through the trees surrounding the circular space, encircling the stand-off between Anya and the board of the four families.

She stands alone, proud—as cold and hard as she needs to be—and utterly fucking strong. The sheer power of her will is a supernatural force that could bring them all to their knees…and I have no doubt that in time, she will.

"Is this everyone?" Anya asks without a hint of wavering in her tone, though I sense her anxiety rushing beneath the surface. "If you're all ready, I'm happy to take you to the manor and welcome you to my home."

Cordelia shouts, "That is *Nikolai's* home, not yours! You're a talent slave, no better."

Anya raises her chin. "I *am* better than a talent slave. I'm a Mikhailov. I'm Nikolai's bereaved bride. Surely, you would grant me some kindness in my time of *grief.*"

It's a total fuck-up on my part, but I just can't hold back my chuckle. Thankfully, they're all so high-strung that they don't seem to notice or care.

"Give me the keys and get in the backseat, lass. I'll drive that car," Murphy gestures to the car Anya drove here.

"Fine," she replies, holding out the keys for him.

She doesn't wait for anyone. She confidently strides away, turning her back on all of us, gliding away like a queen to her carriage.

I'm so fucking proud of her.

Head over fucking heels in love.

"Lorenzo, drive the other car," Murphy says to a man that must be a Vittori—he looks like a younger version of Vigo.

Lorenzo forces me into the backseat of the second car—separating me from my girl—and I'm forced to make the entire thirty-minute drive back to the manor with anxiety pricking pins and needles into my bones. I know she can handle her own, but I hate being apart from her.

I fear our separation, and not just for this relatively short car trip—it's deeper than that. I fear what will happen to her if they sell or kill me. I don't want to leave her behind to live this life alone.

We arrive at the manor and Anya is the first one out of the cars. She marches ahead to the main entryway, holding her long, layered skirt up with her hands near her hips. She moves with intent and grace. The rest of us get out and follow behind as she walks into Mikhailov Manor. She's leading this mission rather than falling in line and waiting for a command.

I love this side of her—this strong, take-no-shit, take-no-prisoners side of her. It's a part of her personality that's been repressed for far too long in captivity and it's shining now. She's playing a part, but she owns it, because it really is *her*.

No time is wasted as she heads straight for the staircase and the four families follow behind her. We cross the blood trail made by Nikolai and the throng pauses as Cordelia and Renata decide to trail off and follow it. Anya turns halfway up the grand staircase, her skirt twisting around and framing her as a worthy goddess, looming above them all. She's dignified and powerful, watching them as she waits for the two women to make their confirmation of Nikolai's passing.

They disappear inside the dance studio and I hear faint crying, as if either of these women might actually miss Nikolai. When they return, they look somber and it makes me fucking glad to see any form of hurt touch their features.

"It's true. He's dead." Renata confirms to the group in a solemn tone, then turns her head toward Anya. "She is the last Mikhailov."

A ripple of truth slithers through the air around us, coiling and wrapping around the board members. I can feel the buzz of awareness as they steal glances with one another, grappling to accept the new reality—two Heads of House murdered in one night, and only one member left of the Mikhailov family. Then, almost all at once, heads snap to Anya and I hold my breath as they look at her.

Silence descends and Anya stands taller.

"Well?" Renata asks.

"It's legitimate, all right. This marriage is legal. As is the name change," Murphy says.

I've been ordered to kneel in the far corner of the boardroom as this conversation carries on. My jacket is off and my wrists are zip-tied tightly in front of me. I sit back on my heels and struggle against my instinct to fight and shout and interject every other sentence with a sarcastic comment.

"This is unprecedented." Renata's eyebrows furrow.

"Oh?" Anya says from her spot at the head of the table. She took that spot the moment we walked in here, refusing to be told where to sit—and she looks fucking sexy as hell. "Didn't you just grant permission for Lorenzo to marry your talent slave?"

"Yes," Renata replies, "but Lorenzo is not a Vittori. He's a Fiore. Nor is he Head of House."

"But that has happened before, hasn't it? I recall Vigo saying something to that effect when Lorenzo first asked the family for permission to marry Olivia. I was there, Renata. We sat and listened to her practice her talent on the piano, and I remember *every* word of the exchange when they asked for permission to marry. I suppose you must have forgotten about me while I was a broken doll." Anya sits a little taller in her seat. "But I can assure you won't forget me now."

Renata smiles at her slowly, but there's no joy in it. "That's correct. But it doesn't matter in this scenario. You killed a Head of House, which in turn resulted in the fatal shooting of a second Head of House in the aftermath. Mikhailov or not, you will be punished severely. Blood taken requires blood given."

"I'm aware of your family's bloodlust, Renata." Anya speaks with a commanding voice. "But there is another item of information you'll want to be aware of before delivering any such punishment."

"And what is that?" Murphy asks.

I see the way Anya's throat contracts as she swallows. "I'm pregnant."

A stale silence falls over the room.

"Come again, lass?"

"I'm pregnant." Anya whips her head to meet Murphy's eyes. "I don't know how far along. But depending on the timing, it could belong to Nikolai or Vigo." She conveniently leaves out that it could also be mine. "If you recall, the board decided I should be given to Nikolai as punishment for my attempted suicide at the Leblancs' last quarter. We had unprotected sex several times that night."

"You're a damn, rotten liar," Cordelia sneers. "I went through your contract of sale with a fine-toothed comb that very night with Vigo. It plainly states that you are infertile…incapable of becoming pregnant."

"Nikolai *lied*," Anya replies. "I assure you, I am capable of becoming pregnant because I *am* pregnant. There are positive tests on my bathroom sink right now to prove it."

"I don't believe it. How could a pregnancy possibly survive all your body has been through?" Renata questions with a tilt of her head.

"I don't know," Anya replies. "I honestly don't know. What I *do* know is that this child is the descendant of Nikolai or Vigo."

Or me.

Cordelia fails at her attempt to hold back a sob, her hand coming up to cover her mouth as she pushes back from the table and practically runs from the room.

Murphy leans back from the table, running a hand over his beard. "Well, fuck all. If this is true, it changes everything."

"It changes *nothing*," Renata practically spits with fury. "She is responsible for the deaths of two Heads of House. She must be punished."

"And she will be, in due time. But we can't afford another change in family line if it can be avoided. The Leblancs' rise to take over the Campbells caused enough disruption in our distribution lines. We can't afford more this year. If the child is a boy, he can ascend to Head of House when he comes of age, whether he's a Mikhailov or a Vittori." Murphy pauses. "I propose Lorenzo take on temporary leadership of the Vittori family under Renata's advisement."

Renata's hands slaps the table as she leans forward. "*I* will lead our family.

Murphy leans forward on his elbows, raising an eyebrow at Renata. "We've been around and around this point of contention with you. You can't be Head of House. But you will bear some of the responsibility under Lorenzo. He's been part of the board long enough to know the ins and outs of the business. You're gonna need to focus your attention elsewhere."

"Oh?"

"I'm proposing Anya be sent to live at the Vittori home. Renata, you will provide her with the medical care she requires until she delivers."

Renata hisses, buzzing with fury. "You want me to take care of the woman who killed my brother?"

"Yes," Murphy replies, unaffected. "It will keep your grieving mind occupied with a more important task. She may very well be carrying your niece or nephew…remember that."

Anya struggles. I see the way her jaw ticks and her muscles flinch as she takes in the reality of that statement. The baby could be Vigo's and that's a hard fucking truth. But then, she adjusts her body and sits a little taller than before, her cold strength freezing her over again.

Renata turns her head slowly to look at Anya, scrutinizing her features with her narrowed eyes. Then, subtly, her face relaxes. Her eyes tell me that she's making the connection of her potential relation to the baby growing in Anya's belly.

I hang my head as the connection hits me all the same.

"I suppose that's true," Renata says. "But who will run the Mikhailov sector? Who will make decisions? Say the baby is a Mikhailov boy and can become Head of House when he comes of age, who will serve in his stead until that time comes?"

Murphy drums his fingers against the tabletop, considering a solution with squinted eyes. He jerks his head to look at Leo. "Any suggestions?"

"Kostya knows the sector well, doesn't he?" Leo suggests.

"Kostya?" Anya whips her head around to look at them. "Is he alive?"

"Yes," Murphy replies. "He's being treated and held prisoner at the Vittoris while his wound is tended to. He was shot in his right shoulder… nothing life-threatening." He sighs. "The problem with Kostya is that I don't know whether he can be trusted. I've always known him to be a loyal guard to the Mikhailov family…It could serve to reason that he was blindly following Nikolai's orders—like a good servant would—when he fired back during your escape. But, perhaps, he was more inclined to fire back because of his relationship with you and with Nikolai. How could I possibly know if he cares whether you live or die?"

"I can assure you," Anya begins and I can sense the lie coming, "Kostya was only following orders. He is fiercely loyal to the Mikhailov name. He followed Nikolai's orders blindly, even to his own detriment. You see where it got him…injured in gunfire."

"See, that's where I have a problem, lass. How am I to know if his loyalty now shifts to you? Perhaps he will blindly follow your orders now. I don't trust you as far as I can throw you."

"My only interest is in self-preservation," Anya says.

Murphy jabs his finger in her direction. "Don't test me, woman. I know better than that. You care about more than just self-preservation." He points his finger in my direction next. "*Him*, for one."

"So, what if I do?" she says, leaning forward on her elbows and folding her hands.

"It means we can leverage him against you when you start making stupid decisions. Notice my use of the word *when*, not *if*." Murphy grins sarcastically. "So, here's what's going to happen. I have a Vittori and I have a Mikhailov." He gestures to Renata and Anya, respectively. "I have two men aligned with each family, Lorenzo and Kostya, capable of making joint business decisions. If Leo agrees, let's say we create a temporary joint family board for overseeing the Vittori and Mikhailov sectors. Renata, Anya, Lorenzo, and Kostya will be the members of this joint board, and we'll require you to convene weekly to make any and all business decisions for either family sector. All decisions must be made with a three-fourths majority. Once we find out the gender and paternity of Anya's child, we'll re-evaluate how to proceed."

Anya's voice is quiet, but strong, "And what if the child is a girl?"

"We will re-evaluate your...value when the time comes." Murphy's tone is full of threats and warnings that make my stomach flip. He turns to Renata. "Until that time, Anya will be treated as a Mikhailov guest in your home. Do you understand?"

Begrudgingly, Renata replies, "Yes. I understand. But what is to become of the slave boy?" Her head nods toward me and I pull my shoulders back.

"He's still the Mikhailov talent slave, but I suppose the decision rests with your joint family board. We can kill him and require Anya to find another."

Shit.

"I don't think that will be necessary. I have an interest in him," Renata replies smoothly.

Murphy chuckles. "Of course, you do. But are you equipped to handle such an unruly slave in your home? One who pines for Anya? Can you manage him *and* your duty to provide care for her during her pregnancy?"

"Managing him will ensure I can provide for her care. You said it yourself, he's leverage. I can slowly take the blood she owes to my family from his veins. Drop by drop. I can use him against her when she thinks of doing something foolish. She can use him as her talent, but I want unilateral authority over him while he's in my home."

My fingers twitch with my sight set on wrapping them around her throat.

"Well," Murphy leans back, crossing his arms over his chest, "seems fair enough to me. Three-fourths of your family board is here now, so you can make that decision jointly. Kill him now and Anya finds new talent. Or let Renata take him on as her slave until his talent is needed. We know Renata's vote. Lorenzo?"

Lorenzo's eyes dart in my direction, then look to Anya. His expression twists as his eyes narrow in consideration. I watch as Anya lifts her chin and meets his gaze directly, waiting for his response. Her nostrils flare in fearful anticipation as she breathes deeply.

Lorenzo holds the power—right now in this moment—and his choice will determine whether I live or die. Obviously, Anya will vote for my life, even if it is to make me a slave to Renata Vittori. Lorenzo holds my fate in his hands.

His head tilts to the side and his expression softens as he states his vote, turning his eyes to Murphy. "Renata can keep him."

Anya's lips part as she tries to control the breath of relief that forces its way out. I clench my fists, wishing I could wrap my arms around her and hold her, wishing I could give her a safe space to break apart her icy shield and relax after this fucking awful meeting is done.

But I know I won't be given the opportunity to be there for her when she needs me most, and I fucking hate it.

"Do I even need to ask your vote?" Murphy says to Anya.

Anya clears her throat, turning her head toward him. "Renata may have him as her slave."

Hearing her say those words—in the cold, detached way that she has to—sucker punches me in the gut. I hate that she has to be this way…that she has to be like them to survive.

But she has no choice in the matter. Agree to let me be Renata's slave or see me die. It's no choice at all for her, just like it would be no choice for me.

How bad can Renata really be, anyway?

Murphy slaps his hands on the table, pushing himself up to stand roughly, his chair sliding away from the table. "Pack your bags, lass. We're all leaving here tonight. I don't have time to deal with this anymore. Everyone good?" He looks at each person pointedly, but quickly, as if he doesn't really care. "Good. I'll be downstairs dealing with the body in the dance studio."

CHAPTER 8
Anya

ANOTHER NIGHT HAS fallen upon us by the time we arrive at the Vittori mansion off the coast of Italy. It requires a feat of strength beyond measure for me to cross the threshold to enter the home we only just escaped from. I can no longer behave like a slave if I want to remain in the family's good graces—though to say the graces are good is an exaggeration.

I stay frozen behind my icy shield. I have to hide my panic, my fear, my absolute horror at coming back into this house, and it takes everything I've got to put on that brave face.

But I do it.

Somehow, I steel myself and walk inside, knowing that there is no other choice. To save my life—Ezra's life, my *baby's* life—I have to live here in this house like one of them.

I have to *be* one of them.

I can no longer be Anya Antonov, stolen and captive talent slave to the Mikhailov family. I have to be Anya Mikhailov, bereaved wife of the Mikhailov Head of House.

An entire houseful of Vittoris and extended relatives go from quiet chatter to utter silence as we enter. They stop and stare at us in the foyer. I didn't expect their quarterly meeting guests to be here when we arrived, but I suppose it makes sense. Family surrounds family when there's a loss, and I took away their most revered Head of House.

I killed Vigo.

And though I feel a brief rush of pride knowing that I ended the life of my vile abuser, I also know that these people regard me as his murderer.

I'm the killer of their brother, their cousin…their *family*.

I need Ezra's strength to bolster me as I face them, but I can't allow myself to connect with him. Though he's only steps behind me—his wrists bound in front of his body with a cable tie—there may as well be a mountain between us. I hate this emotional separation that I've had to force. I have to freeze him out, shield myself behind a glacial fortress to protect myself from feeling.

Because if I feel everything that's happened to me, my weakness and vulnerability will seep through the cracks—and these people will smell it on me.

I can't be weak here.

Renata stops in the open foyer, turning to face me, Ezra, and Lorenzo behind her, just as her loyal slave Luca comes through the throng of guests to be at her side. "Luca, would you be so kind as to show Ezra to his new quarters? Anya's box in the basement is vacant; he can stay there until he's trained."

My mouth automatically opens to protest, but I stop myself, sucking in a sharp breath through my nose. Somehow, I manage to force myself to swallow my rising panic as my heart hammers out of control. I'd rather go back into that box than think that Ezra might be put through the same tortures I suffered here at Vigo's hands.

Vigo is dead.

I killed him.

He can't hurt me anymore.

Renata tilts her head as she regards me with an undercurrent of fury and retribution on her mind. "Did you have some objection to that, Anya?"

She knows I care too much about Ezra. It's why she wants him to stay in the box in the basement. She wants him there to punish me. It's the only reason she wants him here at all, rather than dead...to torment me. I'm untouchable—for the time being—but Ezra is fair game.

I reason with myself that I need to appear detached and distant when it comes to matters involving Ezra and his treatment. If she thinks it doesn't bother me, perhaps she won't torture him in all the ways my abused mind imagines.

Wishful thinking?

I bolster my pride, forcing calm resignation into my expression, though I feel as though I could crumple in fear for the man I love. "Where will I be staying?" I ask.

Her face falls at my lack of reaction. She looks at Luca. His white button-down shirt is open in the front, baring his torso, and he's wearing his black leather collar as usual. I don't think he ever takes it off. Renata jerks her head in the direction of the kitchen, and he acts immediately. He grabs Ezra's arm, tugs him forward, and drags him toward the kitchen where the basement entrance hides behind a normal-looking wall.

Renata's nostrils flare in frustration as she returns her attention to me. "I'll show you to your room upstairs. Lorenzo, please tell our family that we'll join them for dinner tomorrow night to discuss Vigo's funeral and the new… structure of our business." Her eyes snap to mine. "Follow me."

She moves toward the staircase, expecting me to follow her, and there's a sort of snap inside my soul that tugs my attention to Ezra as he's dragged away, struggling against Luca. My skin prickles with goosebumps—knowing he's being taken to that god-awful box—and my heart demands that I let him in, just for a moment, so he can feel that I'm still here with him. My soul demands that he know I haven't abandoned him, that my spirit remains strong and true behind my shields.

Our eyes connect and mine tell him how much I love him, how much I want him, *need* him. How I'll do everything in my power to stay alive and to keep him alive, too. His fight against Luca stops and he nods, the slightest movement of acknowledgment and acceptance, and it unburdens my troubled mind…for now. His eyes tell me to do what I have to do, and he knows I will. Then, he disappears beyond the arched entryway to the kitchen.

His unwavering faith in me is disarming, nearly dismantling my protective walls altogether.

My pulse kicks into overdrive knowing where he's going, knowing that my love is going to suffer the same as I did being trapped in that transparent box in the basement. With my heart racing, I have to work twice as hard to build my walls back up, but I manage to do it somehow.

Renata snaps her fingers to get my attention—literally *snaps* her fingers. I jerk to look at her and I know my expression is filled with the indignation I feel toward her. Her expression nearly mirrors my own.

Malice reflecting malice.

"This way," she says, leading me up the staircase. "Leave your suitcase. It will be brought up shortly."

I wonder what happened to the silver hard-shell suitcase that was packed for me when Vigo first took me away from Nikolai. I never got to peek inside it to see what Nikolai had packed for me. Nearly all my belongings—at least my most treasured items—had remained in my room at Mikhailov Manor, and they're in the suitcase I brought with me today.

Maybe Nikolai hadn't packed me anything at all when he sold me.

Vigo had my silver suitcase discarded when I first arrived, so now I have Ezra's black suitcase full to the brim with everything I treasure and anything I thought might be important to Ezra. I have my box of photos of my sister, my most recent worn-in pair of ballet pointe shoes, and clothes for the both of us.

I have my underwear—such a simple thing that I never would've thought twice about before. Since that luxury had been stripped from me while I served as one of Vigo's broken dolls, it was comforting to know I had a way to cover myself now…to protect myself.

Vigo's dead.

He's gone.

I have to remind myself frequently that I killed him because it still feels like a dream, a nightmare. The ghost of him still haunts me.

As I carefully ascend the steps behind Renata, we pass Olivia—their former talent slave and now Lorenzo's fiancée—coming down the stairs. Her forehead wrinkles in confusion as she sees me with Renata who is, by all accounts, unnaturally calm for escorting the woman who murdered her brother.

I murdered him.

I'm a murderer.

We reach the balcony landing and we turn right—in the direction of Vigo's room, where I was tortured, humiliated, left to die a slow and horrible death, and down the hallway where I killed him.

My breath catches in my throat.

My steps slow as faint, distant voices from a memory leap to the surface of my mind.

Nikolai demanding that we leave.

Ezra urging me along.

Vigo threatening to come after us, to torture and kill Ezra and force me to watch.

The phantom pull of my hand as it covered Kostya's on the gun, my finger curling over his, aiming, and squeezing the trigger.

"Anya," Renata snaps at me again and my head jerks up to look at her.

I'm standing in the same spot, looking down at the dark stain on the carpet where Vigo's blood was spilled by my hand. When I look up, the voices in my mind fade and drift away, and I come back into reality. It takes me that long to realize we're standing in front of Vigo's bedroom door.

"You'll be staying here."

"No." I shake my head. "No, I'm not staying in Vigo's bedroom. Find me another room," I demand.

I feel uneasy being so bold. Nikolai spent years grooming it out of me, and taking it back is proving to be intensely challenging.

"There is no other room, Anya. You've seen our extended family is here and all the guest rooms are occupied. Unless, of course, you'd like a box in the basement."

Truthfully, I consider it. At least then I wouldn't be living in the space where I'd been tormented endlessly, forced to live with the ghost of the man who brought me to the brink of death so viciously. But I can only imagine what Ezra would have to say about that.

A twinge of pain pulls through my side. I place my palm over the ache and that motion alone reminds me that I'm pregnant.

I'm pregnant.

Oh, God. I'm pregnant.

I have to think about the baby. I don't even know how it survived everything I've been through—perhaps it won't survive much longer. It's a real-life miracle, though it's also a real-life nightmare. But its very existence offers me protection and want it or not, I have to take care of it, which also means taking care of myself.

It physically hurts me to consider having the child of a Vittori or Mikhailov. There's a small chance that it could be Ezra's because we'd had sex the same night Nikolai took me as punishment for trying to kill myself. But the most likely outcome is that it belongs to Vigo. He raped me more times than I care to count over the past six months.

Renata has already typed in the code on the keypad lock and the door clicks open. She sniffles, then clears her throat. "The code is 7-4-2-5. Both to get in and out." She pushes the door open and I follow her inside. "I'll send someone tomorrow morning to…to clear things out while our family doctor evaluates you."

A quick glance toward the bathroom shows that nothing has been touched since we escaped. The tiled floor is glossy with the water that spilled from the tub. The oversized mirror that trapped me inside still rests cockeyed on the tub. My heart pounds furiously and I take a step backward.

"Could you…could you close t-the bathroom door?" I stammer, nerves clawing at my confidence.

My eyes are fixed on the cold tiled floor as my panic is triggered. I think Renata's watching me discerningly, but I don't know for sure. All I can see is water—above me, around me, encapsulating me.

The noise she makes sounds pleased. "I'm not your servant, Anya. You may have risen in status on a technicality, but you're no better than I am. You and I, my dear, are on equal footing. Close the door yourself."

I only realize she's left when I hear the door click shut behind her. My head turns and I look at the doorknob with the keypad above it.

"Shit…shit."

Did it lock automatically?

What did she say the code was?

7-4-4-5…No.

7-4-5-…Shit, shit, shit.

I reach for the handle and pull down. It opens. The weight of my relief-filled sigh threatens to drag me down to my knees. My pulse sounds like an internal thunderstorm as it thrums behind my ears.

I should've known the door would open. Vigo always entered his code on the keypad once we were inside the room to lock me in.

I need to know that code.

I peek my head out into the hallway to see Renata walking away. I open my mouth to ask her, but I never even get a chance to. She must've heard the door click open. She halts, turns her head back toward me, and even from this far away, I think I can see a tear rolling slowly down her cheek.

"7-4-2-5," she says before I even ask.

Then, she disappears around the corner.

I can't bring myself to lie on the bed.

I won't sit on the small stool in front of the vanity.

I've been brutalized in every part of this room and I'm haunted by my memories. They cling to me like a virus for which there is no cure. But I'm exhausted—physically and emotionally—and I can hardly stand on my own two feet anymore. Without conscious thought, my body slumps and I sit on the carpet, right here where I'm standing in the middle of the room.

The sound of a running faucet ghosts across my mind and the phantom noise grips me, the sound gradually increasing until I find myself covering my ears to block it out.

It's not real.

The faucet is off.

Vigo is dead.

I'm safe for the moment.

Vigo is dead.

I close my eyes and all I can see is his face rippling above me as I look up at him from beneath water. My eyes snap open again immediately and I half expect to see him standing in front of me. I breathe in and out, in and out, willing my hammering heartbeat to settle, but it only beats faster. My lungs strain as my breaths quicken and shorten until I'm panting, desperate for a decent breath…as if I'm under water again.

I'm hyperventilating.

I'm panicking.

"Stop it," I say to myself. "Stop it, stop it, stop it."

I need Ezra.

I need to…to breathe.

I can't breathe.

I gasp with no success.

I topple sideways to the floor.

Consciousness slips away.

Crying.

I hear crying.

PAS DE TROIS

I open my eyes to see that I've fallen asleep in the rocking chair. I look down, though the baby isn't in my arms. I glance around the room until my eyes fall on the beautiful wooden crib in the corner. I'm humming an unfamiliar tune as I rise from my seat and slowly move toward it.

I look down over the side of it to see a tiny baby lying on his back, arms and legs stiffly pawing at the air as he reaches for his mother with uncoordinated movements.

He's brand-new to the world.

I want to keep him safe.

His eyes are closed as he cries out and I'm drawn to him. His one-piece pajamas have a pattern of tiny rainbows printed on them. At least, I think they're rainbows. I don't see any color. I blink, glancing around the room again and realize that nothing is in color.

Everything is black and white.

I'm still humming the tune I don't recognize.

The baby boy screams harder and I can't ignore the instinctual pull to lift him, to hold him, to comfort him in my arms. I reach over the edge of the crib and place my hand on his belly, rubbing a gentle, soft circle to comfort him with my touch.

That's when he opens his eyes.

That's when color returns to my world.

Bright green light sparkles in his familiar gaze and from it, color ripples throughout the room.

Green eyes.

Enchanting green eyes and sandy blond hair.

Ezra.

He looks like Ezra.

This is my baby...our baby.

I smile so wide it makes my cheeks ache and I lift the tiny squirming boy from his crib. I hold him closely to my chest, still humming that tune. Perhaps it's a lullaby I heard somewhere before.

My baby boy calms in my arms, his cries gently change to soft coos of happiness. He's where he belongs, right here in my arms.

"I'm so lucky to be yours." Ezra's voice comes from behind me and I turn to see him in the doorway to the nursery.

His eyes and our baby's look the same. Perfect, green, filled with light and goodness.

We smile at each other.

But then Ezra's eyebrows raise in shock and he gasps. He looks down and my eyes follow. Blood soaks his white T-shirt, circling outward, the spot growing larger as moments pass. And then he falls to the floor. I jump back, holding our baby tighter against my chest.

Ezra is dead and I didn't even see it coming.

Oh, God.

Why is he bleeding?

What caused the wound?

There was no gunshot, and I didn't see a knife. I don't understand how he's dead.

He's dead.

No. No!

I back away until my backside bumps into the edge of the crib. I don't know what to do. I want to help him, I want to save him, but I can't let go of our baby.

I have to protect our baby.

I'm still humming that song.

PAS DE TROIS

What song is this?

Where have I heard it before?

"Give me the child." Nikolai's voice booms from the doorway and my body goes rigid.

Nikolai is dead; he is death standing in my doorway. He still bleeds from his gunshot wound and it drips down to the carpet beneath his feet. His face is pale, expressionless, lifeless. He steps forward and I shout, but then he falls to his knees before dropping lifelessly onto the floor beside Ezra.

I'm humming the song.

I hum it louder as unseen voices swirl around me.

"Give me the baby."

"That baby is mine."

"He's a Mikhailov."

"He's a Vittori."

"He's mine."

"Kill him. Kill them both."

"Stop!" I scream and the voices fall silent.

But then the song comes again, only I'm no longer humming.

It's....it's Vigo.

His sound carries from the hallway outside the nursery. The humming becomes whistling, growing louder and louder until he finally appears in the doorway. Blood pours from him, from every part of his body, spilling like morbid waterfalls and pooling on the carpet. He bleeds so much and so fast that it cascades into the room like a flash flood. It spills and spills, filling the space.

And the pool rises.

Slowly, it rises.

The song.

The one he's whistling, the one that I was humming.

It's the tune he whistled when he left me to die in his bathtub, locked beneath the mirror and the running faucet.

The blood is to his knees when he stretches his arms out wide. He tilts his head back. As if he's willed it to happen, he explodes, bursting into crimson liquid that splatters the walls and drenches me and my baby in a thick coating.

I scream.

The baby cries and I look down, but he's no longer in my arms.

I dropped him.

He's sinking into the pool of blood that continues to rise.

I lunge after him, diving beneath the surface and reaching for him, but he's already gone. I can't find him. I don't know where he is. I rise to break the surface, to catch my breath, but my head hits something hard above me.

I open my eyes and immediately close them again.

I'm back in Vigo's bathtub, drowning beneath clear water, my reflection splintered in the cracked mirror that keeps me locked in my own watery grave.

Somewhere nearby, my baby cries again but I'm trapped. I can't get to him. But I have to get to him. I need to get to him. He needs me.

I hear....

Italian.

A woman's voice.

Renata.

Though I can't see her, I know she has my baby. He continues to cry and scream. He doesn't want her. He needs me.

"Sweet child. You were never meant for this world," she coos.

I try to scream for him but water fills my mouth.

"Your father is a slave. You never should have existed."

My baby screams louder and she only shushes him. His cries become muffled as if something smothers him.

"Go to sleep, baby. It'll all be over soon," she murmurs.

I scream as loud as I can, but the sound is swallowed by the water all around me. The air rushes out of me in bubbles as I scream and scream until I'm gasping for more air, but only taking in water. I'm drowning.

Drowning.

I hear the echo of Renata's voice somewhere above me.

My baby no longer cries.

I open my eyes beneath the water and see my reflection above me, but then it changes. With each ripple of water, it twists and morphs until it becomes Vigo above me.

He waves at me with a sadistic grin as I gulp in more water, my chest aching as it fills my lungs.

"It will be done soon," his reflection tells me. "Just a few more counts of eight. One. Two. Three. Four. Five. Six. Seven. Eight."

He counts.

He counts.

He counts.

And I fade away.

I awaken with a start, bolting upright as my eyes snap open. I look around me, quickly remembering that I'm in Vigo's room. I passed out on the floor in my panic-induced hyperventilation.

My hand falls to my stomach, a protective instinct to cover him and keep him safe.

Him.

The nightmare had been so vivid. I have to catch my breath because I feel like I truly had been drowning. Tears well, glassing over my vision before a sob forces them to fall down my cheeks.

My baby.

My baby was killed in my dream and it was the most horrifying thing I've ever experienced. More horrifying than anything Vigo or Nikolai had ever put me through. More horrifying than anything anyone could dream up to do to me. In my dream, my own life hardly mattered to me, but...

My baby.

My baby had to be protected at all costs.

Our baby.

It was just a dream, but I could feel it in my soul. The baby is a boy, and he belongs to Ezra.

This puts all our lives in grave danger. But oddly, this doesn't strike me with more fear. Instead, it injects me with more determination, with a fierce and powerful need to rise and become the queen that Nikolai granted me the ability to become with our marriage.

Our marriage is the only reason I'm not dead right now.

If it saves my life, Ezra's life, our baby's life, I will become ruthless, cold, and demanding. I will do what I have to do to save us.

CHAPTER 9
Anya

I SLEPT IN that same spot on the floor last night. It was uncomfortable… painful, actually. My back hurt, my neck hurt, my stomach felt stretched and achy. I know I was being stupid not to sleep on the bed, but I just couldn't.

The memories of what Vigo did to me on that bed when he had me drugged and paralyzed would flash across my mind each time I thought about going to lie down on it. So, the result was a painful night of unsatisfactory sleep on the floor.

Renata has just come to collect me for a visit with the family doctor this morning. She leads me downstairs to the first floor and I find myself constantly looking around me. My mind hasn't come to terms with the fact that Vigo is truly dead yet. I can just see him popping out from around a corner, grabbing me, dragging me into the nearest room, terrorizing me until night falls again. The thought of it appears like a crystal-clear vision in my mind, so clear that it makes me gasp and I stop dead in my tracks.

The vision of his torture won't let me go. It grips me like a rope coiling around my chest, squeezing my lungs, and crushing my heart. My heart explodes in a flurry of beats, pumping wildly as panic overtakes me again. One hand comes up to my chest as the other lands on the wall by my side to steady myself.

I feel like I can't catch a breath.

I feel like my lungs are being squeezed so tightly that they won't inflate, no matter how much I try.

I feel like I'm going to pass out again.

No, no.

Not here, not now.

I try to calm my mind and think of anything else, but the vision of Vigo in my mind keeps playing like a movie, an intrusion of a thought that I can't exorcise from within me, no matter what I do. So, I do the only thing my mind will let me do.

I count.

One. Two. Three. Four. Five. Six. Seven. Eight.

One. Two. Three. Four. Five. Six. Seven. Eight.

One. Two. Three. Four. Five. Six. Seven. Eight.

I count until the horror film plays out in my mind, until it fades away into non-existence and I can think of nothing but the numbers, the counts of eight, the basic structure of my dance steps, the dancing that makes me feel free.

Renata is at my side, as is another man. They speak in Italian with concern and their concern is directed at me. I realize that I'm on the floor, my back to the wall and my legs pulled up against my chest.

But I don't remember sitting.

The man puts a hand on my shoulder and I jolt at the sensation. He removes it as I turn my head to look up at him, as he crouches to his haunches beside me. I don't feel threatened by him—he doesn't give me the same creeping, prickling feeling down my arms that all the other Vittoris give me.

"I'm Doctor Lombardi," he says to me, his Italian accent thick but understandable. "I want to help you. Can you stand?"

I carefully study his face.

One. Two. Three. Four. Five. Six. Seven. Eight.

I believe he wants to help me. I nod and he holds out his hand to help me off the floor.

One. Two. Three. Four. Five. Six. Seven. Eight.

I take his hand and let him help me up. Renata says something in Italian, and though I don't know what she's saying, I do know what she's feeling. The anguish is written all over her face, and her rage and grief are all directed at me. Her feelings mix with mine in a tangled web of hopeless anxiety. There are dark circles beneath her eyes, the whites of which are tinged with red as if she's been crying.

Of course, she's been crying.

You killed her brother.

You're a murderer!

One. Two. Three. Four. Five. Six. Seven. Eight.

I can't let myself feel anything for her, for what I did to her brother. Because he wasn't just her brother; he was a demon spawned from hellfire—a monster in its truest form. He was a man who'd been born with the power, wealth, and privilege to do so much in this world, but he chose to burn it with his hate, his filth, his plague of darkness.

He deserved to die.

He deserved it and so did Nikolai.

Nikolai.

He's dead, too.

I look down at my hands to see myself unconsciously twist the diamond rings on my finger. The jewelry feels as heavy as the chain he used to clasp around my ankle. I hate Nikolai for these rings—these symbols of oppression and stolen freedom.

Yet, there's also a twinge of grief. It's an unwanted grief, like another fist squeezing my heart, though it doesn't hold on for too long. It lets go before I sink into another panic episode, as I recall that I made a promise to wear these rings for Ezra. The recognition of my choice to belong to Ezra calms my nerves.

Doctor Lombardi leads me into a nearby bedroom on the first floor. He stops at the door and turns to Renata. "Go eat, Renata. I will bring Anya directly to you after the exam."

Her eyes narrow at me, raking over my form as if I'm a dog who has pissed on her luxurious carpet. I don't feel badly about it—I feel the same way about her. She doesn't give me the benefit of speaking English in her response, but the way she jabs a finger in my direction as she talks to Doctor Lombardi gives me a good sense that she's told him to watch out for any bad behavior from me.

Good.

I want her to feel threatened by me.

The doctor closes the door behind her as she leaves. He turns to face me but stays where he stands, sensing my discomfort in being with an unknown person behind a closed door.

"I'm going to give you a physical. Is that okay, Anya?" His eyebrows lift in question and he waits for me to respond.

Wait…He's asking me?

Surprised, I nod, though I'm sure it's hardly perceptible, so I add, "Yes," with a quiet voice.

He holds his hand out toward the queen-sized bed behind me. "Please have a seat. I promise you, this will be very professional. I have no interest in harming you."

I swallow, skeptical by nature, though I still feel okay in his presence. Nothing is setting off any alarm bells in my mind, and I suppose I feel a bit calmer now that Renata is gone. I think I will always be skeptical of any man's intentions with me, except for Ezra. Ezra is my one great exception, my soul mate.

"Okay," I reply carefully, slowly lowering and perching on the very edge of the bed.

"Renata tells me you believe you're pregnant?"

"I *am* pregnant. I took two tests, and they were both positive."

He nods. "Good. Well, if you feel certain, then I'll give you an ultrasound so we can see how things are going."

"How will you do that? You have an ultrasound machine here?"

"Yes."

"Why?"

He clears his throat. "It's not my place to discuss. The equipment is here, so let us just feel fortunate for that."

He picks up a black laptop and pulls up an armchair from the corner to face me at a comfortable distance. He sits, then opens the laptop and starts typing as I sit in silence, waiting, twisting the rings around my finger.

"Just a few questions, Anya. When was your last period?"

My heads snaps toward him. "What?"

"Your last period."

My brow furrows and I glance down at the floor as I try to recall. But honestly, I don't know how he expects me to remember something like that. It's certainly been months, but I don't know how many. Vigo was practically starving me, so who knows if a skipped period was because of pregnancy or malnutrition. My body has gone through forced and brutal changes because of Vigo.

"I don't know," I tell him honestly. "Months."

He nods, though his eyes remain fixed on his computer screen and whatever it is he's typing. "Mm-hmm. Do you have any sense of when you conceived?"

I chuckle unintentionally. "I don't know. I've been raped with intense frequency over the past several years, doctor. My understanding is that my last owner stopped my birth control without my knowledge. I could've fallen pregnant anytime over the last six months."

"Mm-hmm. And do you think you are six months pregnant?" His eyes dip down over the laptop screen, scanning my relatively flat stomach.

Naturally, one of my hands float to rest over my belly button and I look down, too. I feel stupid now to think about it. I had noticed a slight difference in my shape before, but I wrote it off as being a result of my malnourishment and the fact that I couldn't care for myself properly.

"No," I finally respond to Doctor Lombardi's question.

"So, can you give me a guess as to when you might have become pregnant? It will help me to judge healthy development when we do your ultrasound."

I start to shake my head because I truthfully don't know when I conceived. But I know when I *hope* I conceived, so I tell him, "Three months."

We were at the Leblancs' three months ago. Three months ago, I had sex with Ezra and Nikolai on the same night. Three months is an estimate that gives me the hope that this baby might not belong to Vigo—even having Nikolai's baby feels somehow better than that.

I think I know the truth in my heart, or at least, I hope I do. I saw what I want to be the truth so vividly in my dream. That truth is that this baby belongs to Ezra by some absolute *miracle*, because the odds of that being true are poor at best.

Doctor Lombardi goes through an exhaustive list of health questions, only stopping when we both hear my stomach growl. I need to eat and I'm glad this man at least seems to have the understanding that we need to move this along.

He asks me to lay on the bed as he rolls a cart around with the ultrasound machine. I can't imagine that the Vittoris just happen to have an ultrasound machine sitting around. The doctor must have brought it here for some reason.

Perhaps she called him and he arrived with it last night. If not, someone else in this mansion must be pregnant, too.

Heaven forbid Renata should ever reproduce, though I wonder if that's even possible for her in her early forties. The only other women who live in this house are the elderly Vittori mother who I never did meet, children of Vittori cousins, and…the slaves.

I don't even want to think about what they would do if one of Vigo's broken dolls had become pregnant.

The same thing they would do to me if Nikolai hadn't made me a Mikhailov.

Oh, God.

Don't think about it.

Doctor Lombardi pulls me back to reality as he squirts a gel on my bare stomach—I hardly remember lifting my shirt. I watch the screen carefully, though I don't really understand what I'm seeing. I don't understand until…

I see the outline of the baby.

I see the outline of *my* baby.

"There it is," Doctor Lombardi says. "You see? Moving a lot."

I blink at the screen. It wasn't real until this moment. It was just two pink lines on a stick until just now. Now…now it's real…so, so real.

Doctor Lombardi tries to measure the baby, but the tiny squirming thing is moving around so much that he has to wait until he's still. Until then, it's just quiet, and we watch. Tiny limbs that look like arms wave and his legs kick as his body wriggles.

God, it looks like he's dancing.

My baby's dancing inside me.

Doctor Lombardi is clicking buttons on his machine with one hand as he performs the ultrasound with the other. "Heartbeat is strong. Good. Baby is measuring about twelve weeks and five days. You were right, just about three months. A few more days and it will be your second trimester."

"Is it a boy?" I'm eager as I ask.

"It is a little too early to say with imaging alone. But I will do a blood test to find out. *Signora* Vittori would like an early gender result, as well. I don't know whether she'll share that information with you."

"It's my baby."

"Yes," he nods, "I understand. But I am…limited." He gives a sympathetic smile.

I understand what he means by limited, and though it makes me feel indignant, I can't fault him for those limitations. What I know for now is enough—the baby growing inside me is healthy and strong.

And apparently, a dancer.

He finishes his exam and starts talking to me about nutrition and exercise during the pregnancy, but I don't hear a word of it. The image of my baby dancing keeps swirling through my thoughts and the feeling it gives me is indescribably perfect.

A perfect image to chase away all the bad ones.

But even that perfect image can't keep them away forever because I know there's so much bad yet to come.

I'm not safe.

Ezra's not safe.

Our baby is not safe.

Even if they kill us and keep him, he will never be safe with them. This is not the life I want for my baby.

I'll lay down my own to make him free.

CHAPTER 10
Ezra

I'M CAGED LIKE a fucking animal and all I want to do is claw the life out of my jailer.

I'm out of my mind with worry over Anya and whether she's okay. They said she'd be treated like a Mikhailov wife, which I guess sounds okay in theory, but these fuckers think in such warped ways that it's impossible to know for sure.

Luca—Renata's current boy toy—told me that this is the same cell they kept Anya in when she belonged to Vigo. It makes my insides boil with rage, heartache, and guilt.

So much goddamn guilt.

I can't help but blame myself for the fact that she was ever sold to that creep in the first place. I'd been the one to suggest we have sex for the first time in her room at Mikhailov Manor after our performance together as talent slaves—it was the reason we'd been caught by Nikolai.

We could've done it in any room in that mansion. Or at the least, I could have gone right back to my room after the first time we did it in her bed. But I'd been selfish, refusing to leave until we were both fully satisfied and beyond aching for rest. Because of that, we fell asleep and got caught.

That's my fault.

It's my fault she was sold and my fault she was kept in this stupid transparent box.

I'm agitated, exhausted, frustrated, driving myself insane with worry. Not to mention the way adrenaline pulses through my veins with a steady thrum, insistent that I keep moving, keep fighting, *fighting* to get out of this small space. I fight and pace and fight and before long, I'm fighting just to stay awake...just to stay upright.

Eventually, I let myself sit on the mattress that rests on the floor. I realize that Anya slept here, night after night, trapped in this cage, only to be taken out and tortured in ways I can't even let myself imagine.

I'd witnessed her last horrific torture with my own eyes, and I consider us lucky that I was able to pull her out of that tub in time. It was the most horrifying thing I'd ever experienced. Vigo had tied the mirror so tightly to the top of the tub that I honestly thought I might not get it off in time. There was a moment where I thought she would drown and I wouldn't be able to save her, a moment where I feared pulling her lifeless body from the water.

I'd been so overwhelmed with fear and the chemical rush to keep fighting that it hadn't even occurred to me to drain the fucking tub until the moment the mirror started to budge. If she'd died because of my stupidity, I would never have forgiven myself.

Fuck.

I would've killed myself because nothing matters without her.

Nikolai told me once that my impulsivity would destroy me. Well, if impulsivity made me that fucking stupid, then I guess he was right.

If anything happens to Anya, it will destroy me.

The girl in the box next to mine has fallen asleep and suddenly, I'm desperate to sleep, too. I let myself lay down, reasoning that it's okay for me to sleep, *good* for me to sleep. If I get the sleep I need and take care of myself, then I'll have the strength to keep fighting for her.

When I finally lay down, I swear I can smell her.

She always smells like fresh-cut roses.

Floral, fragrant, sweet, but heady.

Undeniably her.

The scent of my blue-eyed girl is all over this mattress and I revel in it.

It smells like home.

And because it smells like my home, I can feel her with me. We're apart, but at least we're in the same home…in the same *country*. At least I know she's not here, trapped in a box like me.

At least she's okay for now.

I close my eyes and fall asleep thinking about her blue eyes, her warm smile, and the electric touch of her skin.

"Ezra."

The sound of my name startles me awake and I bolt upright from the mattress on the floor. I glance around as I try to make sense of where I am. Reality comes crashing back into my mind as the dream I was pulled from swiftly fades, though I can still remember bits and pieces of it in flashes.

I dreamt that the four families took Anya from me, pinned her down, cut her stomach open, and took her baby as she screamed and bled. But the baby wasn't theirs to take. It didn't belong to them.

He belonged to us.

He was my baby boy.

My son.

Same green eyes and sandy blond hair.

He was undeniably, unquestionably mine.

But now, reality's back to bite me in the ass. Luca and Renata are opening the door to my cage.

"I have no intention to harm you right now, Ezra," Renata says as Luca pulls the transparent door all the way open, stepping back and allowing Renata to fill the space to stand in front of me. "But if you try to fight or run, you will regret it. There's simply no need for such incivility here."

I give Luca a once over as she speaks. He's shirtless, but he's wearing jeans and a black leather collar—a slave if I ever saw one. But he doesn't seem frightened of her. He doesn't even seem to show any hatred or disdain for simply being a captive and in her presence. My eyes narrow on him in my scrutiny because I don't understand what I'm seeing.

"I want to see Anya," I tell her.

She sighs. "You'll see her around. Although I don't have any reason to offer you assurance, I will tell you that she's fine if that troubles you. She's with our family doctor now."

"Where?" I climb to my feet, stepping toward her. "I *want* to see her."

She purses her lips. "You're in no place to make demands of me. If you cooperate and do as you're told, then you might get to see her this evening at dinner."

"What do you want from me?"

"You already know what I want from you," she says with a crooked smile. "Come with me. Don't keep me waiting." She turns on her heel and strides toward the staircase, high heels clicking along the cement floor.

Luca stands there, waiting for me to follow Renata, so I do. But not without glancing over my shoulder every few steps to keep an eye on him. I don't like having this guy behind me.

We arrive in the kitchen at the top of the basement steps. Renata closes the door behind Luca and types in a code on the keypad to lock it shut, hiding it behind the drywall.

A secret basement to keep women captive.

These people are fucking nuts, and Vigo was a straight up psychopath. But when I remember that *my* girl killed him, a slight smile twitches in the corner of my lips and I have to hide it. He tried to end her, but she won that battle and ended *him* instead. It reminds me that she's strong enough to win the whole damn war if we can just figure out how to do it.

"I assume you're hungry," Renata says.

Is she asking or telling me?

I shrug.

She reaches into a cabinet and pulls out a small plate. It's stark white, just like the rest of the kitchen.

"Did Luca introduce himself?" she asks, nodding toward her collared slave. She reaches into the fridge and pulls out a large bowl covered in plastic wrap. "You should get to know each other. You'll be serving me as he does."

"And how exactly will that be?" I ask slowly.

She looks over her shoulder at me and smiles. "Have patience. The fun is yet to come." She pulls the plastic wrap off the bowl and grabs a serving spoon, scooping fresh fruit onto the small plate. "Luca, come. Eat."

She lifts the plate from the counter and bends, setting it down on the floor beside her.

What the fuck?

Luca circles the short side of the oversized kitchen island, going around to the other side where Renata stands. Then, he lowers, disappearing behind the island. I must be misunderstanding because I think he's down on the floor, eating fruit off a plate like a dog.

What in the actual fuck?

My eyes remain fixed on the edge of the counter near where she stands, in the place where Luca disappeared behind it. When she tells him, "Good boy," and bends down to pat him—on the ass or the head, I don't know which—my eyes flicker up to look at her.

She's staring at me.

"Come, Ezra."

I can't help the chuckle that escapes me. "You've got to be kidding me."

"Ezra," she chides. "I won't ask you again. If I have to ask you again, then perhaps..." She places her hands on the island counter's edge, leaning forward with her arms apart and elbows locked. "Perhaps Anya finds herself accidentally falling down the staircase. Perhaps she bumps her head and slips away in her sleep from complications. Perhaps she finally succumbs to her depression and succeeds in ending her life. Should I go on? I can think of a thousand ways to kill her without drawing suspicion."

God fucking damnit.

I move, walking to her slowly. Luca eats from his plate on the floor, just like I thought—like a dog, bending over to pluck each bite from the plate with his teeth.

"I'm *not* eating like that," I tell her, pointing my finger in Luca's direction.

She moves toward me and I press back against the edge of the island, my ass hitting the counter's edge. She moves closer and closer until her body is flush with mine. She's at eye level with her heels on, but she may as well be seven feet tall by the way she makes me feel without saying a damn word.

My hands grip the counter on either side of my hips as I try to lean away from her. She turns away for a moment, only to reach into the bowl of fruit from the counter behind her. She plucks a strawberry from the bowl and moves impossibly closer to me. She presses in so close that her body holds me in place, and I feel more trapped here than I did in the cage.

She lifts the strawberry between us and taps the tip of it against my lips. I keep them pressed shut.

"Eat," she says.

"I'm not that hungry," I lie.

I'm fucking starving.

"You won't be given another opportunity to eat until lunchtime, so I suggest you take the opportunity now. I intend to keep you healthy. I expect you to take care of my needs and that simply won't be possible if I don't keep you," she pauses, her eyes skimming across my chest and down my torso, "strong and healthy."

My jaw sets and my muscles clench. "Might have been nice if your brother had adopted that same philosophy for his girls."

Her face drops and she shoves the strawberry hard where my lips meet until I'm forced to open. I take a quick bite and slam my lips shut again so she doesn't choke me with it. "Don't *ever* speak about my brother again. He was more man than you could ever hope to become, Ezra."

Movement off to the left steals our attention. A man clears his throat. "I've completed Mrs. Mikhailov's health screening and ultrasound."

Mrs. Mikhailov. Jesus.

Renata takes a step back, walking around Luca to approach the man on the opposite side of the kitchen island. He's an older gentleman. His jet-black hair has touches of gray, hinting at his age, and his presence doesn't immediately put me off, which seems unusual here in the Vittori home.

Then, there's that punch to the gut awareness as Anya slowly moves into the room, looking lost yet hopeful at the same time. I stare her down until she registers that I'm there and her eyes meet mine. Her eyebrows bend to frame her beautiful blue eyes before she grants me a small, secret smile.

My heart leaps out of control. I forget how to breathe when she puts her hand on her stomach and looks at me with love in her eyes. For a moment, I forget where I am, who I am, why I'm here. For a moment, it's just me looking at my girl, dreaming about a future we might never get to have.

Renata starts to say something to the man in Italian, but he lifts a hand.

"Please, *Signora* Vittori. I've told you before. I'm very happy to care for your family and…the others, but we must speak in the language the patient understands."

Her nostrils flare and her chest rises as she takes in a sharp breath, but then she concedes, which is shocking. This man must have a long-standing relationship with the family to be able to speak so boldly.

Renata forces herself to calmness, then she switches to English. "Anything notable I need to be aware of?"

"The baby is measuring around twelve weeks, five days, so she's just about into her second trimester. A miracle if you ask me. She's malnourished and weak. Frankly, I'm shocked the baby's heartbeat is as strong as it is. I'm going to recommend a nutritionist—"

"That won't be necessary," Renata says. "I'll ensure she receives a healthy diet moving forward. Her life circumstances have recently changed. When can a DNA test be performed?"

"A DNA test?"

"To determine paternity. The board would like this done as soon as possible."

"Oh, well, it's possible to do now with blood samples from both parents."

"Both of the potential fathers are recently deceased."

The doctor's eyebrows slant in toward his nose in consideration. "If you have access to the deceased remains, I think it can still be done. I may need to consult with a geneticist. I know of one who can be discreet in this matter."

"Fine," Renata replies. "Lorenzo can put you in contact with Murphy O'Shea before you leave. Murphy has graciously made the arrangements to handle both of the deceased in our time of grief."

My eyes practically roll out of my head.

He nods. "Good. I'll go speak with Lorenzo. And please ensure Anya gets the rest she needs. Her body is overtaxed and it's not good for her or the baby."

Renata dismisses the doctor and turns, glancing from me to Anya to Luca on the floor. "Luca, serve Anya breakfast. Eggs, toast, and fruit. Make sure she eats it all and clean up after her when she's done. Ezra, come with me."

She brushes past Anya with a conflicted look of disdain and moves toward the open archway that leads back to the foyer. Luca rises from the floor, moving about the kitchen as if everything happening here is perfectly normal.

I look at Anya. She tilts her head toward Renata's retreating form, mouthing the word, "Go," with pleading eyes.

How can she be so strong after everything she's been through?

How can she be strong enough to still be ordering me around and making sure I don't make things worse?

I've said it before and it's still true now—she's a goddamn beautiful powerhouse.

I walk toward her. She's standing in the path I need to take to follow Renata, and she stays intentionally, knowing I'll have to pass by her on my way through. Our eyes are locked as I come closer.

I choose to walk between her and the island, even though the space is narrow. I should walk around her on the other side, but I can't help myself. I squeeze into the narrow space, brushing against her body as I move past. I catch her palm in my hand for the briefest moment, just for a quick squeeze of reassurance.

Fuck, that was a bad idea.

The small touch is a lightning strike, a shockwave of connection that sears through my skin and burns through my soul. She gasps and I know she feels it, too.

I'm forced to let go as I stride past, Renata looking back impatiently from the bottom step of the staircase in the foyer. But I dare to steal one last glance over my shoulder at my glowing girl. She covers her smile with a cold expression, but her eyes hide nothing from me.

I'm the man she melts for.

I'm the man who knows what lies beneath the surface.

I'm the man she loves.

CHAPTER 11
Ezra

RENATA'S BEDROOM IS like a luxury hotel suite. It's smaller than I expected it would be, but certainly not lacking in extravagance. The room is all shades of gold, ivory, and cream, and I wonder how the fuck she keeps it all so clean looking.

Probably slaves.

Maybe me.

She gestures toward an armchair in the far corner of the room, angled toward the end of her sleek, modern-looking bed. "Sit."

I cautiously cross the space, turning and walking backward because I don't trust her behind me. She moves to her cream-colored dresser beside the door, and I watch her carefully as she pulls something out of the top drawer. I fight the warning tension in my muscles and slowly sit on the chair. I've learned the importance of obedience in this life, but I don't think I'll ever stop having the immediate urge for defiance. I'm wary while waiting to find out which particular brand of demon spawn Renata will prove to be.

"It's been a long time since I've had a second slave," she says, working on something in front of her, though her back is turned to me and I can't see what. "Luca has been with me for four years, since he turned twenty-one." Her head turns to look at me and her dark brown eyes catch mine. "He wasn't taken, you know. He's a willing slave."

I scoff, "Yeah, right."

I see half of her smile from her profile before she turns away again. "Is that so hard to believe? Luca enjoys being my slave. It's a lifestyle choice for him. There are places to find people like Luca. We met at an establishment that caters to the wealthy and their very particular wants and needs. He wanted to find a master and I wanted a willing slave. Immediately, Luca and I knew we'd make a good match…instant chemistry." She gives me a knowing look. "He asked to be mine and I brought him home. I provide well for him, and I could do the same for you, Ezra. He's happy here."

"I don't believe you."

"Believe what you like. It's the truth." She turns, crossing the room to stand in front of me with a square box in her hands. "I'm going to keep close tabs on you. I don't trust you in Anya's presence."

"I don't trust you in anyone's presence."

"I expect you to cooperate during your training. Luca has been given permission to provide you with guidance on serving me."

"Serving you?"

She drops the box in my lap and bends over me, grasping my chin tightly between her fingers and forcing me to look up at her. The red silk blouse she wears drapes open as she bends, leaving nothing to the imagination, and she doesn't seem to care.

"You will serve me or you will die. If that's not incentive enough for you, then I will remind you of all the ways I could make Anya's life end without drawing suspicion from anyone in the four families. And I will do just that if you deny me."

"What do you want from me? What do you need me for if you already have Luca? I thought I was here to service your bloodlust."

"Blood taken requires blood given, yes. Don't be mistaken, I *will* take from you, drops at a time." She releases my chin and turns, moving to sit on the edge of the bed across from me. She exhales slowly and captures me with her stare. "I find the fire behind your eyes alluring."

Okay.

Really, how do I respond to something like that?

She goes on as if she's having a casual conversation with a friend. "I was a married woman not so long ago. Giovanni was the perfect husband for a woman like me. He was strong, capable, dominant." A half-smile twists her lips. "He was dominant enough to handle me, if you can imagine. I was in love with him. Giovanni was my everything. We'd been seeing each other for years before we married, but I only spent a few days as his wife." She pauses and I sense she only does it for dramatic effect. "He was murdered… gone before I even had a chance to legally change my name. It's been two years since his death and I still grieve him daily." Her expression melts into vengeful honesty. "Trust me when I tell you that I understand pain. I know how to use the woman you love to hurt you, and I will if you deny me what

I need."

I swallow the raw truth I hear in her tone. "So, what do you what from me?"

She stands and moves slowly toward me. She pauses in front of me for a moment before she bends, placing her palms on my knees. I jerk backward, though my ass stays firmly planted in the seat. She pushes my knees apart, creating a V with my legs and she lowers until she's kneeling between them. I'm frozen in place, every muscle in my body hard and tense.

She tilts her head, giving me eye contact that I'd call uncomfortable at best. "Giovanni had eyes like yours…like a fire that refuses to stop burning. I miss that fire, that fervor, that all-consuming, reckless passion…the kind of passion you have for that awful girl." I clench my fists and pray I can keep myself from pounding them against her face. "Giovanni would share me with Luca, you know. We would play together. We'd command him and enjoy each other. It would be nice to have that again."

Ah, fuck.

Fucking heathens.

She grips my thighs and slowly slides her hands upward. I grab her wrists and forcefully remove them. "No," I say firmly.

"Yes." She yanks her arms from my grip and slaps her hands right back down on my thighs, digging her fingertips into my muscles.

I try to scoot back, but I'm already as far back as I can go. "Stop," I insist. Her fast fingers tug my shirt free from where it's still half tucked into my pants, and they quickly disappear beneath the hem. "Whoa. Fuck. *Stop* it." She starts undoing the button of my black slacks and I push through the armrests to stand. She leans back when I rise and sidestep free.

"Where do you think you're going?" she asks as I rush for the door.

I press down on the handle, but nothing clicks. It doesn't open. There's a keypad above it.

Fuck, I'm locked in.

I spin around just as she appears in front of me and I slam my back to the door. She comes in close, too close…*way* too fucking close.

"You seem uncomfortable, Ezra," she prods.

"I'm more than fucking uncomfortable. Knock it the fuck off."

She lets out a heavy sigh. "I don't want to do this the hard way, but I will."

I don't know if she's trying to sound threatening, but I'm not threatened by her. She makes me feel uneasy, not threatened. But then she turns and walks away, going to retrieve the box that fell from my lap when I got up, and she brings it over to me.

"Put this on," she says, lifting the lid of the box.

I laugh. It's a black leather collar, just like Luca's. "Fuck no."

"I didn't give you a choice. Put it on."

"Fucking *no.*" She's really pissing me off now.

She picks up the collar, sets the empty box onto the dresser beside me, and boldly crushes her body against mine. I draw back, but there's nowhere for me to go. So, I do what I have to. I grab her by both shoulders and physically shove her back, pushing and walking her until her legs hit the bed and she sits to avoid falling.

I step backward, pointing a finger at her. "Stay the fuck away from me."

She just smiles from where she sits, placing a palm on the mattress and leaning on it with a suggestive tilt. "I'm surprised at you. You're being very forward with me considering how submissive you were with Nikolai."

I take another backward step. "I was submissive because I had to be, for Anya's sake."

She pushes to stand and I turn again, jiggling the door handle uselessly. I feel her presence behind me before her hand lands on my shoulder, gentle fingers dragging down my arm. I jolt from her touch and the warning prickle that creeps over my skin.

"And you still have to be submissive, for Anya's sake." She hugs me from behind and it's fucking weird. She kisses between my shoulder blades and my shoulders shrug against what feels like an attack. "I hardly gave her a second thought when she was nothing but a slave. But since she killed my brother…" She pauses and I feel both her hands on my back, her cheek pressed there, freezing me in place. "Since she killed him, I've spent every waking moment imagining her blood on my hands. Consider your submission a way to quench my bloodlust for her. I'll take yours as her penance. I would enjoy slicing her open and playing with her insides. But perhaps your service to me will fulfill that need. Do you understand me?"

Fuck.

Shit fucking cock-sucking motherfucker.

There aren't enough curse words in existence to express my fury as my pulse hums and my insides heat to boiling. My fists ache from clenching and I punch one against the door, the sound and force of it slamming against the hard wood startles her enough that she backs up.

My forehead drops against the door as I will my quickening breaths to slow. I'm a raging bull and she's a matador who taunts me, dangling Anya's safety in front of me like a red cape—I'll keep charging for it as long as she teases me with it. I may be stronger—brute and determined—but she holds the real power in this bullfight.

My mind winds through loops in my fury that tug on the intensity of my anger, allowing me enough rationality to submit for Anya's safety. My shoulders slump and I force myself to give up the fight because I understand her threat crystal fucking clear. I would do anything to protect Anya, even if that means giving Renata goddamn Vittori my submission.

I turn around to find her holding out the collar she wants me to wear. I'm still wearing the white button-down I had on when we met with the families back at Mikhailov Manor, though I removed the jacket and necktie and left them in the basement. The top two buttons of my shirt are already open, leaving her enough room to place the collar on my bare skin. I turn when she moves to my side and dip down to let her latch it in place at the back of my neck. I let her do it without fighting because I have no choice.

Renata is dangerous in the worst kind of way. She's the kind of dangerous you don't feel threatened by until you're fucking dead on the floor.

Once the collar is securely latched, she moves in front of me again. She reaches out and begins to unbutton my shirt with nimble fingers. I push her hands away, but she just starts again.

"You belong to me now. If you behave, I'll ensure you enjoy being mine."

Mine?

Fuck no.

She's not allowed to call me hers. No one is—no one except Anya. The word triggers a new adrenaline rush that I can't ignore. I step forward, crowding Renata, forcing her backward.

"I will submit to you, but don't you dare think for a *second* that I'm yours. I'm *hers.* I belong to Anya, and she is the *only* reason I'll obey you."

Renata huffs and pulls something from the pocket of her sleek black pants. She shows me a small black rectangle in her hand—something that looks like a tiny remote. She lifts an eyebrow and it tugs the corner of her mouth up into a wicked smirk. I watch her thumb press down on the remote and a lightning bolt strikes through the side of my neck. The shock of it makes me seize, every muscle in my body jerking to a rigid stop at the jolt of it for just a moment before the pain stops.

She put a shock collar on me.

My hands shoot up to grip the leather, fingers scrambling to find the latch, and just as I do, another shock seizes my system. This one goes on for beat after beat before the searing pain stops.

I drop to my knees, and though it takes moments for my mind to shift back into focus, my fingers start moving again automatically, searching for the latch that will free me. But my hands are shaking and my fingers tremble as they clamber against the leather.

"Take this *off* me!"

"Be a good boy and I will help you. Come here," she says in such a deceptively cool way that I fully regret that I didn't just knock her on her ass when I had the chance.

Despite myself, I scoot on my knees to get to her because I need this *off*.

She looks down at me, pride on her face stolen from me. "Hold still."

She circles around behind me, dragging her hand from my shoulder, across my upper back until she reaches the latch at the base of my neck. I feel her pull on it, doing something I can't see, and in moments, I hear something metal *click*. My hands jump to touch it and I freeze. My fingers recognize the shape of a padlock at the back of my neck. It's hooked through the latch and locked in place.

The collar is padlocked around my neck.

A frenzy takes over and I'm desperate to get this thing off me. I pull and twist at the leather, somehow managing to spin it sideways, but it makes no difference. It's on and it's not coming off.

"You *bitch!*"

Her fingers slide into my hair, dig in, and grip the strands. She yanks my head back hard, stretching my throat until I'm looking up at her above me.

"You will call me *Signora* Vittori."

"*Bitch,*" I insist and hate the way the word sounds coming out of my mouth—it feels wrong to be so rude and disrespectful to a woman, but this one has earned it.

She clicks her tongue. "Ah-ah-ah. Think of Anya and try again."

She pulls my head back a little farther and bends down over me, running her tongue across my throat. I jerk sideways, yanking free from her hold. She circles around in front of me, crossing one arm over her torso, the other dangling the remote in her fingers.

She speaks slowly, as if I'm fucking stupid. "*Signora.* Vittori."

I breathe heavy through my nose, nostrils flaring in fury. "*Signora* Vittori,*" I repeat.

She bends again, touching her nose to mine. "Good boy. Now take off your clothes." She steps away, moving to occupy the armchair in front of me, crossing one long leg over the other.

My jaw sets, my teeth grinding together. My fists clench at my sides and I feel as rigid as a stone statue. At this point, I shouldn't be shocked by that command. I shouldn't be shocked by anything at all, really. But having the foresight to guess how she wants to use me fills me with an uncomfortable kind of anger I've never felt before. It's a rage that I have to control to keep my girl safe, a rage I've felt before, but it's still....different.

I feel like I'm no longer human. And to Renata, I'm not. I'm a physical object for her to control and use for her own purposes, and it makes my blood burn.

She lifts the small black remote, twisting it in her hand to remind me of what she will do when I don't obey. "Take off your clothes. I won't tell you again."

My lips pull back from the tension I hold in my face and I snarl. I feel nauseous. My fingers shake as I start to undo the buttons of my shirt. The way Renata ogles me as I do makes me feel small.

If my worth weren't already determined by the measure of Anya's love for me, Renata could make me feel like the most worthless piece of shit that ever existed. But I remind myself that I'm everything to Anya, so I'll be worthless to Renata if I have to be. I pull off my shirt and toss it aside as Renata drinks me in with her eyes.

"Kiss my feet," she says, running her tongue along her bottom lip.

"You're fucking ridiculous, you know that?" My eyes would literally roll out of my head if they weren't attached in there.

I can practically hear Anya in my head. *"Be quiet and do as you're told, mal'chik."* And I should have listened to that voice before my response because Renata sends a jolt of electricity through my neck. It goes on for longer this time, my muscles seizing, tightening beyond my control with the sharp pain of the shock burning my neck.

I immediately slump forward to the floor once the electricity finally stops. Luckily, I'm able to catch myself on my hands rather than face plant in front of her feet.

"I think I enjoy the look of you that way," she says as I balance on all fours, catching my breath. "Crawl to me and kiss my feet. Or disobey me, and I will find a way to destroy that girl. I promise you."

For her.

Do it for Anya.

Just do what you have to.

I crawl to her, fighting against every cell in my body that compels me to resist. I bend, resentfully placing a kiss on the top of her foot.

"Is that what you call a kiss?" she scoffs. "I'm certain you can do better than that. Wouldn't you do better than that for Anya?"

"Stop *fucking* saying her name." Renata isn't worthy enough to let a thought about my girl so much as cross her mind, let alone speak her name.

She kicks under my chin with the pointed toe of her bright red stiletto and my teeth slam together. "Shut your disrespectful mouth or I'll shut it for you." She wiggles her foot in front of me. "Now, do better."

Jesus fuck.

I press my lips to the top of Renata's delicate foot. I squeeze my eyes shut and because I'm thinking of her, my blue-eyed girl's perfect face steals space from all other conscious thought in my mind. I can see her so clearly when I let myself release all the tension of my fighting instinct.

It's only Anya behind my closed lids and she tells me to do what I have to for her. She tells me to imagine it's her that I kneel for and worship with my kiss. With her blue eyes sparkling in my mind, I can do just that.

Sitting back on my heels, I grip Renata's heel with one hand and slip the other behind her ankle. I cradle her foot as if it belongs to my girl, as if

Anya has asked me to revere her this way.

And I would.

I would do it for her if she asked.

If she asked, I would run my tongue from her toes to her ankle, just like this. I would squeeze her in my grip and run my hand up her calf. I would scatter wet kisses over every inch of skin atop her foot. I would nip at her skin with my teeth, then sooth the sharpness with a flick of my tongue.

Just like I do it now.

My hand is just behind her knee when she finally stops me. She snatches my wrist and holds my hand in place. I open my eyes and look up at her and the spell immediately breaks—I meet dark brown eyes instead of vibrant sapphire blue.

But because I was thinking of Anya, I'm panting. Because I was thinking of her, I'm half fucking hard. I don't want to be. I don't fucking *want* to be, but I am, and I hate myself for it.

A memory from soon after my kidnapping—when I first met Anya—dashes across my mind. We were in my room at Mikhailov Manor. Nikolai had his arms wrapped around Anya from behind, his fingers shoved inside her, stroking. She didn't want it from him, but he took from her anyway.

He always took from her.

But when her eyes met mine, she sparked, igniting into pure need. He stopped before she came, but she was wet, panting, needy when she crumpled to the floor beside me—panting and needy the way I feel now, and it's the worst fucking thing I've ever felt.

I feel sick.

I feel like a bastard.

I feel like I'm cheating on her, even though I know I have no choice.

I feel now what Anya felt when Nikolai abused her. I could only imagine the pain of it before, but now I *understand* it.

And hell, that woman is strong for surviving it all.

Stronger than me.

Stronger than any other person I've ever known.

Renata uncrosses her legs and puts my hand on the inside of her thigh. "I've put Anya in Vigo's bedroom."

"You did *what?*"

"She's staying in Vigo's bedroom. She slept on the floor last night. That's how I found her this morning…passed out on the rug. She must have been too traumatized by all the things my brother did to her to sleep in his bed. She wouldn't even use his bathroom. It's impossible for me to see what you see in her. I see nothing but a weak little girl." Her hand slips over my fingers on her thigh, gripping them, drawing my hand up farther. "But if you do me this service, I'll consider moving her to a new room. Perhaps then she can rest and recover."

A frustrated groan vibrates through my chest. "You're cruel."

If I thought I felt sick before, my gut churns now with the thought that Anya is enduring such torment in Vigo's room. It makes my heart hurt, as though Renata has reached inside and plucked it from my chest herself. It's all the worse because I already know I'll do what she wants to get Anya out of that room.

"You're interested." Renata smiles as her gaze flicks down over my crotch.

"I'm not interested in you."

"But you'll obey me," she says with all the confidence in the world—she knows she has me trapped in this.

I nod in response, but it's so slight I don't even know if she sees it until she drags my hand a little higher. She lets go and raises an eyebrow at me, a silent command to keep going.

I hate this.

I hate this so much.

My stomach clenches when my fingers slip up her hip and under the hem of her red blouse. My spine prickles with a warning to stop this madness when I reach for the button of her pants. I start shaking as I lower the zipper. And my heart leaps with relief when she shoves my hands away and suddenly stands. I look up at her as she looks down at me and she grins with sick satisfaction spread all over her face.

She reaches down and pats my head with her hand. "Good boy."

"I fucking hate you," I seethe.

"I know you do. I like that energy from you, though. Hang onto it." She crosses her arms. "The collar has sensors. As long as you remain in the house, you'll hardly notice you're wearing it before long. There's a minimal perimeter around the house. You can go as far as the fountain in the front and into the garden out back. If you breach that perimeter, I can assure you that you'll die. There will be enough electricity in the shock to stop your heart in moments and I will send no one to revive you. Otherwise, you'll be mostly free to move about as you like. Though you'll stay far away from Anya if you know what's good for you."

I smirk, narrowing my eyes at her. "You shouldn't trust me to roam freely in your home."

She bends, lifting my chin and holding my gaze. I can feel her warm breath as it dusts across my lips. "I trust that you will do anything to protect that whore you call your lover. This is not Mikhailov Manor. There are always people in my home who won't hesitate to kill you on the spot if you step out of line. Consider this collar your fraction of freedom here."

Her eyes dance as they flicker over my face and the light reflected there can't hide her emotion. This woman is grieving, hurt, lonely, desperate. I take stock of that and store it in my mind, knowing I can use that information to exploit her with affection, obedience, and care.

If I have to, I will charm her, seduce her, make her love me enough to let her guard down. And then I will use her to find a way to save Anya.

CHAPTER 12
Anya

ACCORDING TO RENATA, I lack the appropriate attire for tonight's family dinner. She's left me a small pile of clothes from Olivia's wardrobe on the bed in Vigo's room. Olivia's clothes are a size larger than what I normally wear, but Renata assured me she'll purchase me new clothing soon...maternity clothing.

I still can't wrap my mind around being pregnant. There's hardly a bulge in my belly at three months. Doctor Lombardi said I'll start to show more in the coming weeks—once I start eating regularly again and regaining the weight I'd lost in Vigo's care. Still, I can't imagine myself with a pregnant belly.

I sort through Olivia's clothes and decide that I want to look as much like Renata as possible for this first family dinner. She's the model for my performance—I want to mirror her so I can find a way to *become* her and destroy them all from within. I have no plan for how to do that, but I know the first thing I have to do is convince them that I *am* a Mikhailov, and a damn strong force to be reckoned with at that.

I select a smart, black pencil skirt and a cream-colored silk blouse that I tuck in at the waist. I should wear flat shoes, but I know I'll be too short to posture against Renata if I do. So, even though I'm still weak in my recovery from Vigo's torments, even though I'm pregnant and understand that I should avoid the possibility of a fall, I choose impractical high heels—burgundy, peep toe, with a strap around the ankle.

Luca is waiting outside the door when I come out of Vigo's bedroom. He waits for me to lead the way, recognizing my newfound rank. He's been with me all day, attending to my every need at Renata's orders. I haven't seen Ezra since this morning, but I know he's been with her.

It sends my heart racing to think of him alone with her, which is the exact reason why I've fought with myself all day not to think of him.

I have to focus. My mind must be clear, and I must act with intention.

Tonight is crucial for setting a tone on how I will behave with this newfound power.

Power.

It's something that's been beyond my reach for years, something I never dreamed I would have again. Now I have too much of it and it weighs on me. I'm terrified to make the wrong move.

Luca points me in the direction of the dining room on the first floor, a room I've never been in before. It's the size of a small ballroom, though there's only one large, wooden dining table at its center—it looks big enough to seat maybe fifteen people.

A flash of light draws my eyes down to my hand. Light bounces off the diamond rings on my finger from the crystalline chandelier above the table. I bring my hands in front of me and twist the shiny circles around my finger.

I'm a Mikhailov.

My breath catches. I could so easily slip into a panic with the reminder, but I know I can't. I can't do that here, not now. My diamond-decorated hand lands over my heart as I gasp in a sharp breath.

Just breathe and count.

One. Two. Three. Four. Five. Six. Seven. Eight.

One. Two. Three. Four—

"Sit here," Luca says, gesturing to a seat beside the head of the table. I'm thankful his instruction interrupted the anxiety building inside me.

Pull yourself together.

Lowering my hand to my side again, I look up at Luca and clear my throat. I know I must establish my place and I have to do it now. "No," I tell him bravely. "I'll sit here." I move toward the head of the table and pull out the chair with trembling hands.

"No, no." Luca reaches for the chair, but I sit before he can pull it away. "That is where *Signora* Vittori sits."

My heart stops, then starts again in a flurry. Sitting in a board member's seat would have gotten me killed when I was a slave. Though I know I'm one of them now and I can sit where I please, it doesn't stop me from feeling the fear of being disobedient to my master.

I wonder if I'll ever stop feeling like a slave.

Not until Ezra and I are free.

I feel like I can't breathe, but I will my body to stiffen, to straighten. I will myself to raise my chin and dismiss Luca as only a master would. "That will be all, Luca."

With my dismissal, he rushes from the room, probably running off to tell his mistress what I've done. I close my eyes, breathe in through my nose and out through my mouth.

One. Two. Three. Four. Five. Six. Seven. Eight.

My eyes snap open with a sudden flurry of noise. Lorenzo and Olivia enter the room, holding hands and chatting. Behind them is Bianca and my eyes widen. She's the girl who lived in the box next to mine in the basement—another of Vigo's broken dolls. I'm surprised that she's still alive, though I suppose I shouldn't be—no one would have had time to concern themselves with her life while chasing after me and Ezra.

Bianca's eyes catch mine and she stares at me with curiosity and something else in her expression, something resembling jealousy maybe. She and I never did get along, but I don't really feel anything toward her except for sadness. I feel sad for her because she's still a slave.

I was a slave a little more than a day ago.

There's a catch in my heartbeat that feels for her, for the fact that I'm only here and in this position because of sheer dumb luck—the same reason she's a slave. I wonder if they're going to take better care of her now that Vigo's gone. Perhaps they've brought her up to have dinner with the family.

My wondering is settled quickly as Lorenzo directs Bianca to the harp in the far corner of the room. She sits behind it and sighs as she stretches out her fingers.

"Play for us," Lorenzo tells her, "and don't fuck it up. Do well and you'll be our new talent slave."

Olivia was the talent slave before, a pianist. Olivia had the same turn of luck as I did. We each had a monster fall in love with us.

As Lorenzo turns toward the table to bring Olivia to sit, he sees me and I straighten in my seat. I feel my blood run cold with fear and I let it wash through my veins, an icy stream that slows my heartbeat and freezes over my soul. It helps me become the cold, hard, dominant bitch I have to be to protect myself.

I nod at him as he holds out a chair two seats away from me for Olivia.

Then he sits beside her, in the chair just to my left.

"That seat belongs to Renata," he says matter-of-factly.

"I guess it belongs to me now," I reply.

Lorenzo raises an eyebrow and smirks, amused. "If you say so."

He turns his body sideways toward Olivia, grabbing her face in his hands and catching her off-guard with a passionate kiss.

My iced-over heart thumps an extra beat in jealousy.

Will I see Ezra tonight?

Is he okay?

When will I kiss him again?

I don't have much time to let my mind wander as more people enter the room. There's an older man Lorenzo introduces to me as his father and he immediately questions who I am and why I'm sitting in Renata's chair. Lorenzo speaks to him in Italian, saying something that seems to calm him enough to sit without saying another word. Two others are introduced as cousins.

I'm taken by surprise when Kostya enters. He looks like he's been through hell. Obviously, he's recovering from the gunshot wound to his shoulder, and that's partly why I'm surprised to see him tonight. But he also has a black eye, stitches along a gash in his cheek, and he's limping. He looks as though he's been mauled.

I push to my feet, somehow feeling compelled to go and help him to the table, but his eyes widen and he practically shouts when I do. "Stay." The insistence in his tone is jarring and it freezes me in place. I give him a nod as he hobbles in my direction.

When he reaches me, he leans in close, whispering in Russian. He tells me to stay in my seat and refuse to give it up if asked. He tells me to be headstrong with Renata, to show the extended family my assertiveness and demonstrate my authority. He tells me to keep my head held high, and when he pulls back to look at me, he taps two fingers beneath his chin with a small smile.

Chin up.

I watch him as he moves to sit along the long edge of the table. Strangely, I feel comforted by his presence.

Soon after, the room begins to fill with family. Too many of them come in at once for introductions, one filing in after the other. In moments, the table is full—except for one seat directly opposite mine—but the deluge of people continues to flood the room.

Within minutes, the open space around the table is nearly filled as members of the family crowd into the room. They came here for the Vittori family's talent show and reception, but they stayed because of Vigo's death. I glance around the room and see faces filled with sadness, anger, and confusion. Their questions are about to be answered, and I don't think they'll be pleased to learn the truth.

I grow more uncomfortable as moments pass, as familiar family chatter continues, mostly in Italian. It's a fight to control my breathing, to keep from hyperventilating when I feel like a fish out of water.

I'm an impostor.
I don't belong here.
I can't pull this off.
Why did I sit here?

My racing pulse hisses through my veins and I feel my heart slam against my ribcage with every pounding beat. I twist the rings on my finger with my hands on my lap, hidden beneath the table. My fear climbs a mountain and reaches the peak.

But then the currents of anxiety that ripple from my chest come to a sudden, stomach grinding halt. My hands still and I press my palms against my thighs. My hissing pulse slows to a steady thrum. Awareness makes my heart skip a beat before forcing the insistent thrashing to dull into a calm, steady rhythm. A gentle prickle at the back of my neck sends a pleasant shiver down my spine.

Ezra.

I know he's near before he appears in the doorway beside Renata.

His eyes immediately land on mine without the need to glance around the crowded room for me. He felt the familiar tug and pull of our souls before he rounded the corner, just as I had.

Neither of us react; we just allow our eyes to connect, and in that connection, strength builds. He feeds me the power I need in his gaze, just like he always has. I want to touch him, kiss him, hold him more than anything else in the world right now, but I'll have to settle for this brief connection.

Our gaze is interrupted when Renata sees me. She puts her hand on the center of his chest—his bare chest—and crosses in front of him, charging toward me with a graceful but fierce walk. But my attention is still on Ezra, distracted by his naked chest and the black leather collar around his neck.

She really has made him her slave.

Oh, God.

My stomach flips with nausea, but then anger burns my skin. I know I should be grateful she hasn't killed him, but I feel sorely indignant that she thinks she can take what's mine and make it hers.

I don't care who she is, Ezra is *mine.*

She smiles at me as she comes closer and I turn my head, lifting my chin to look up at her from the seat I refuse to vacate. She slips her arm around my shoulders and bends, making it look as though she's merely greeting me as she bends to kiss my cheek. She lingers there, whispering into my ear so quietly, I have to strain to hear her. "You can have my seat. I have your lover."

My head ticks, jerking toward her as she straightens to look at me with a smug expression. I let a smile spread across my face. There are so many things I want to say to her in response, a million retorts scrambling across my mind.

But I breathe deeply and hold them all inside, deciding that my silence is more powerful than any words I could ever give her. I hold her stare, smiling up at her until her cheeks twitch from her faltering resolve and she walks away.

I try not to make it obvious when I blow out the breath I was holding.

Renata moves around the table and sits at the opposite end, facing me. Her family has gone quiet when she lowers regally into her seat and all eyes fall upon her. She snaps her fingers and Ezra moves to her side. I can see the tension rippling through every beautiful, bare muscle in his body, the familiar battle against himself to control his impulses to fight and run.

My mouth drops open when he lowers to his knees at Renata's side and bows his head, and I force myself to clamp it shut.

She knows.

She knows how much this hurts me.

She knows how much it hurts him.

PAS DE TROIS

But what did she tell him to make him bow so easily? It's not right…

My eyes are on Ezra, though his eyes fall to the floor. I want to kneel in front of him, lift his chin, kiss him like I've never kissed him before, and bring him back to life with me. But I can't do any of that.

Not here.

Not now.

The whole family looks at Renata expectantly. She looks directly at Lorenzo, says his name, and tells him something in Italian.

He nods and glances at me and Olivia on either side of him, then at Kostya across the table. "She's going to speak in Italian for the family. I will translate in English for you."

I give a single nod of understanding. Lorenzo may translate her words, but I'll be watching Renata—cataloging every twitch of her features, every flicker of her eyes, every movement of her body. She begins to speak slowly and clearly in her native language, and Lorenzo speaks quietly after her, translating in English.

"The events surrounding Vigo's death have been settled with the four families," Lorenzo begins. "There will be some changes to leadership." Renata pauses, as does Lorenzo, and quiet settles over the room for a few brief, tense moments. She begins again and Lorenzo's translations follow. "Lorenzo and I will serve together as Vittori Head of House to maintain our status and continue our business as one of the four families."

Someone I don't recognize shouts out something in Italian, and though I don't understand all the words, I clearly hear the name Nikolai Mikhailov.

I tense immediately.

Renata nods, then continues, as does Lorenzo. "Yes, it's true. Nikolai Mikhailov is dead. His former talent slave will be taking his place. As it turns out, she is his wife." The crowd breaks into a murmur of chatter.

Renata holds up a hand to silence the group, then gestures toward me. Lorenzo doesn't need to translate when she says my name. "Anya Mikhailov."

"Kostya Federov and Anya will serve together as Mikhailov Head of House. The Vittori and Mikhailov Heads of House will operate as a joint family board to make business decisions on behalf of both of our families. I know this is unexpected, but it has already been decided and it cannot be questioned. Anya is pregnant and the child may be of Vittori or Mikhailov blood."

More chatter comes with the thick tension in the room, all directed at me—as if I had any choice or say in what has happened to me in this life. I feel like shrinking, melting into the seat, dripping like liquid onto the floor and pooling safely beneath the table.

"Anya is to remain unharmed and treated with the same respect you would treat any Mikhailov with. I will hear no arguments to the contrary. Things will continue this way until we learn the paternity of the baby— the board will reconvene and evaluate the situation at our next quarterly meeting." Renata pauses, taking a beat too long to take in a steadying breath. "Funeral arrangements for Vigo are being made and I'll share that with you shortly. But first, I think some happy news is in order. Something our family can look forward to as we face these difficult challenges ahead."

Renata looks at Lorenzo and he nods, pushing to his feet. He speaks to the room in Italian, a genuine smile spreading across his face. Then, he gestures for Olivia to stand and she does.

What's happening?

Olivia smiles, looks at Lorenzo, then at Renata, who nods and smiles at her. Lorenzo snakes his arm around her waist and excitedly, Olivia announces, "We're having a baby!"

Lorenzo quickly translates to the room and there's an eruption of happiness—cheers and claps and overdramatic expressions of joy. I want to scream, puke, run from the room. My chest aches for the hypocrisy; the happiness over one former talent slave's pregnancy but not over another's.

Why should Olivia find happiness while I'm met with eternal dismay?

I recognize the jealousy and how it feeds my anger and I know I can't let it. I know it will only diminish my power.

Olivia glances at me with a sheepish grin and I force myself to grant her a small smile. I nod in acknowledgment of her…happy news. I don't care to interpret the pitying look she throws my way. I can't afford to give away any more of my power.

Lorenzo translates as Renata begins to share the details of the funeral arrangements being made for Vigo—a vigil and mass that will be held in his honor. I breathe deeply through it, struggling to swallow the bile that rises in my throat from the thought of him being honored.

PAS DE TROIS

Fuck Vigo Vittori and his fucking family.

I feel the way my lips pull into a hard line across my face, my cheeks pulling and tugging my features into a look of disgust as I listen. I know how my face is twisting and contorting in hatred and agony. But I also know I can't let my feelings show. Somehow, I manage to force calm indifference to my expression.

Before Lorenzo translates Renata's final sentence, people break into chatter and those not at the table filter out of the room.

Lorenzo leans in close so I can hear him over the noise. "She's sending them away to fill their plates in the kitchen. Only the immediate family is served here."

Quietly, I ask him, "Do they all know what the four families do?"

"They only know of the hierarchy. They know that our family's wealth is generated by the business. I think most of them have figured it out for themselves, but it's a precious secret. Our extended family would have nothing without the work of the four families. No one questions it."

"Won't the secret find its way to the authorities? These people don't all live here, do they?"

"No, most of them have their own homes. There's never a concern for the authorities, Anya. You should know that by now. The four families own everything that's important in the world. We're unstoppable." He says it with pride.

I glance at Olivia, who suddenly looks upset. She tucks a strand of golden-blond hair behind her ear as her gaze darts uncomfortably around the room.

She *should* feel uncomfortable. Her happiness is traitorous to all the other talent slaves who have served the four families, just like her. She got lucky, fucking *lucky* that Lorenzo fell for her—even luckier that the family accepted it, embraced it even, and are allowing her to become one of them. I shouldn't be angry at Olivia—it's not her fault—but I am angry.

Suddenly, Lorenzo's face falls and he pushes to his feet angrily. "Bianca!" he yells across the room at my former cell mate, who is still sitting behind the harp. "You should be playing right now. Why aren't you playing?" His anger switched on so quickly, it's jarring.

Bianca jumps, straightening her spine and nodding before reaching forward to tickle the strings of the instrument. She creates a beautiful melody that drifts around the room and a cloud of music covers us with her haunting tune.

Olivia bites her fingernail, her eyes flickering up to watch Lorenzo's anger-shrouded face before he finally settles back into his seat. She stiffens with tension, but then she smiles, relaxing a little when he returns his lavish attention to her, petting her, kissing her, holding her hand.

Calm to anger to calm with the flip of a switch.

Does Olivia worry that someday he'll treat her like a slave again?

She should.

Luca suddenly appears with a tray of salads. Renata bends to whisper something to Ezra, who is still kneeling beside her, and I shiver when he nods and stands. I watch as he meets Luca where he stands and the two of them begin to serve the family plates from the tray.

Ezra lays a plate and an empty wine glass in front of Renata first. She snatches his wrist and yanks him down before he can move to the next. She forces him to bend sideways as she presses her lips to his ear and whispers something I desperately wish I could hear. His cheeks redden with anger and his fingers clench to form a tight fist.

She releases his wrist.

I watch in horror as he places both his hands on her cheeks, bends deeper over her, and slams his lips to hers.

He's kissing her.

Ezra is kissing Renata.

And I can't do a goddamn thing about it.

CHAPTER 13
Ezra

RENATA TASTES LIKE sin and sadness and everything that I hate. She holds me captive to her kiss with her hand around the back of my head, her claw-like fingernails digging into my scalp. I only kiss her because she's threatened Anya again.

I hate the sharp pang of guilt I feel knowing that Anya is watching this. I can feel her eyes on me, and it burns. The moment Renata lets up on her grip, I jerk away and step back. I quickly grab another plate from the tray Luca carries and rush around the table to where Anya sits. She, Lorenzo, and Kostya get served after Renata and before everyone else.

I set a plate and empty wine glass in front of Lorenzo, then grab another and move to Anya. She sucks in a quick, subtle breath as I step up to her side, and I move in close, intentionally close. I slowly place her plate and glass in front of her and I feel the buzz of electricity before she moves.

Her voice is a soft whisper. "I'm so sorry if this gets you in trouble, but I have to." Her hands land on my cheeks, grabbing my face, and turning me toward her before slamming her lips roughly against mine.

Fuck.

One kiss from my girl makes the world fall away. Her boldness scares me, but fuck, does it excite me, too.

I have to open for her. My lips refuse to stay shut when her tongue runs along the seam, asking me to taste her. I let my tongue slip inside her mouth, and I lap at her eagerly, licking away the taste of Renata and letting Anya's sweetness replace it.

The kiss only lasts for a moment before she snaps her head away and sits up taller in her seat. I stand looking down at her with my chest heaving and I see the twitch of her lips as she hides a celebratory smile for feeding Renata her own medicine.

I swipe my lips with the back of my hand to hide my own smile as I steal a quick glance at Renata. Her eyes burn into Anya, but my blue-eyed girl is strong, holding Renata's gaze just as fiercely.

Somehow, I manage to move on, serving the rest of the table, then Luca opens a bottle of red wine. He pours for the table as I stand waiting by Renata's side.

"What happened to Kostya?" Anya asks as they all begin to eat. "How did he get the black eye and the cut on his cheek?"

Everyone at the table steals glances at Anya as they try to figure her out. Renata hesitates and Kostya looks over at her with quiet disdain. He really does look like shit.

"Your dead husband caused quite a bit of chaos when he took you," Renata finally replies. "Kostya had to be subdued, but as you can see, he's fine. He's recovering." She takes a sip from her glass of wine, then looks at Anya discerningly, cocking her head to the side. "Are you concerned that he's being mistreated?"

Anya scoffs, "Of course, I am."

"Despite your prior experiences here, I assure you that I'm a rather exceptional hostess for our guests…particularly those that serve the four families. I suggest you watch yourself and avoid insulting me at my own dinner table."

I'm bristling with the urge to knock Renata off her damn chair as I'm forced to listen to her.

But Anya lets it roll from her shoulders, lifting her fork and stabbing at her salad. "I'm not entirely certain that an exceptional hostess would make a Mikhailov wife sleep in the bedroom of her former tormentor."

Renata drops her fork and it clangs against her plate, the unexpected sound causing several guests' shoulders to jolt at the surprise. But not Anya. No, she's as cool as fucking ice.

"Your *tormentor* was my brother. And many would argue that I've given you the best room in our home. But I suppose if you're too weak-minded to handle the accommodation of a Head of House, I could find you another room. Perhaps something smaller, more befitting for your stature and general cowardice."

Anya's jaw sets. Her frame remains rigid and still. Her expression and body language give away nothing, but the flicker across her bright blue eyes is obvious—at least, it is to me. It's a flicker of fear, a look that only someone who's been through what she's been through could express in their eyes alone. I know she would've been happy to have a smaller room—anything to get her out of the room she almost died in. But now that Renata has challenged her strength and resiliency, I know she's gonna be stubborn as fuck about sticking it out there.

Anya swallows, lifting her chin a little higher. "I'm no coward, Renata. But you don't really know me all that well yet. You'll learn everything you need to know in time."

A flicker of a fake fucking smile tugs at the corners of Renata's lips, but falters just as quickly. She's pissed. She snaps her fingers at me again and I bend to take whatever order she's decided to give me.

As the table returns to side conversations and general chatter, Renata whispers to me, "Go remove the glass of wine from Anya's setting. She shouldn't be drinking in her condition. Take Olivia's glass, too."

Hmm. A request that's actually reasonable.

I stand to obey, but Renata latches her fingers around my wrist before I can straighten, yanking me closer to add a little something extra to her request.

"Spill both glasses down the front of Anya's blouse. That particular shade of ivory makes her look sallow, don't you think? Give her some red to bring out the pink of embarrassment in her cheeks."

"What? No."

"I'm not asking, Ezra. You know the consequences of your choices, so I suggest you do as I ask."

She is so fucking petty.

Spill red wine on her?

What the fuck is that supposed to accomplish?

Renata is acting like a petulant child and sure, I could give her leniency for the fact that she's just lost her brother at my girl's hand—which would make anyone want retribution—but this is just fucking dumb.

I shake my head as she releases my arm and I stand. I know I have to do it. I know I don't have a choice. Anya's life is reliant on my absolute obedience—Renata has made that crystal fucking clear.

I sigh, already feeling shitty about what I'm about to do as I move along the side of the table. I want to dump out both glasses on Renata's head and smash the glass into her face. I reach between Lorenzo and Olivia, removing her wine glass from the table. She's sweet, giving me a quick smile of gratitude for my service, and I can't help but feel sorry for her. This girl, marrying Lorenzo, would be like Anya marrying Nikolai—her captor, her tormentor, her master.

Fuck.

She did marry Nikolai.

My hands shake from the frustrated fury building inside me as I make my way to Anya's seat. She doesn't look up at me as I approach but continues eating silently. She looks restrained, like she wants to shovel the whole damn plate into her mouth but refuses for appearance's sake. She's stronger than I think she's ever been given credit for.

I admire her.

I adore her.

And that's why I feel like the biggest asshole in the world when I reach across the table in front of her and pick up her glass. I'm not able to catch her eyes before I do it, but I know I have her attention. I stand back up, one glass in each hand now.

Fuck, I hate this.

This is so childish and I fucking hate it.

"I have to, I'm sorry," I mutter quickly under my breath.

Anya turns her head to look up at me just at the moment I turn the half full wine glasses upside-down over her lap. I spill the liquid down the front of her shirt, and it pools onto her tight black skirt. She drops her fork and jerks backward in her chair, her hands raising in surprise as liquid tumbles from her lap, dripping down the chair and landing on the carpet beneath her.

I turn the empty glasses upright again. "I'm so sorry," I whisper before forcing myself to stride away while everything inside me screams to go back to my girl and help her get cleaned up.

I scowl at Renata's pleased grin as I return to her side.

Goddammit.

I fucking hate Renata Vittori.

Anya pushes her chair back and stands as silence falls in the room and everyone waits for something to happen. They're watching her, wanting to see her reaction—and I know how important it is that she reacts to this the right way in front of these fiends.

But who the fuck knows what way is the right way to act?

I took her completely off-guard by my malicious act, which was exactly why Renata asked *me* to do it. She could've had Luca do it, but the bitch wishes to torture me as much as she wants to torture Anya. But Anya is too strong to let it knock her down.

She brushes her hands down her front and shields her true feelings in her eyes behind a layer of icy blue. She pulls her shoulders back and steels herself. But as she opens her mouth to say something, Lorenzo slaps his palm on the table and leans forward, craning his neck around to look pointedly and severely at Renata.

"Will you *stop* it?" he practically shouts at her. "Is it really so much to ask for a peaceful family meal in Vigo's honor?"

Renata chuckles sourly. "In his honor with *her* at the table? His *murderer?*"

"There's nothing you can do about that!" Lorenzo says with anger edging his tone. "She's a Mikhailov, and she's one-quarter of our joint family board." He laughs a little, darkly. "This, *this* is why women aren't given the responsibility of being Heads of House. I suggest you keep yourself in check unless you want me to have a serious talk with Murphy and Leo about your emotional instability."

"Lorenzo…" Olivia carefully lays a hand on his on the table, but he jerks it back, pointing a finger at the poor girl as if he's going to start in on her now. But somehow, he softens when he looks at her, then settles back in his chair. He leans over to kiss Olivia on the cheek as he gradually calms, though the room still ripples with tension.

"Excuse me," Anya says quietly before she rushes with harsh strides from the room.

I'm itching to chase after her, grab her in the hallway, wrap my arms around her and tell her I'm sorry that I have to play Renata's wicked game with her.

I want to *be* there for her, and I can't be.

I have to be here at Renata's side.

I have to serve her to save Anya.

My blue-eyed girl comes striding back into the dining room about ten minutes later. She's always fierce and determined, but I don't think I've ever seen such cold hatred in her eyes. I hope all her hatred is directed toward Renata and not toward me, but I don't think I could blame her if it is.

Anya changed her clothes while she was gone and she looks so smoking hot, charging into the room with furious confidence, that I want to fall to my knees for her and worship her with my undying love. I don't know where she got these clothes I've never seen her in before, but she's come back daringly in a little red dress.

It's form-fitting, though it hangs a little loosely on her. Still, it has the same effect as if it were skintight. It stops just above her knees and the open neckline leaves little to the imagination. Her breasts are full and perky, and the low neckline gives her ample cleavage that makes me want to rip the dress right off her.

She struts across the room, heading right back to her chair—which Luca wiped clean—and she catches my eyes on her as she slowly sits. She blinks, giving me a brief glimpse of her understanding—a tiny, subtle smile— before she takes her position as the one and only Queen Mikhailov.

Anya takes her cloth napkin off the table, shaking it out and setting it on her lap just as Luca brings in a tray with the main course. "Thank you for the suggestion that I wear red, Renata. This dress does seem to better suit my small…What word did you use? Stature? It's more my style, wouldn't you agree?"

Renata's fingers are steepled in front of her chin as she waits for the next course to be served. "You look like a whore."

"Hmm. Your brother thought that, too. But let me remind you that this *whore* is now positioned to vote on business decisions for your family. It might be in your best interest to consider the way you treat me. Now, can't we just enjoy our family dinner? "

Anya is…She's just…She's fucking amazing.

I stare at her until she looks at me and she smiles before straightening her spine, leaning back casually in her seat, as if she owns the place.

She *could* own the place.

She has power now. She could rule and we could win.

For the first time I think we might actually have a shot at getting out of this alive.

CHAPTER 14

Anya

I COUNT THE nights by the number of times I pass Ezra in the hallway leaving Renata's room. After that first family dinner and the red wine incident, I was desperate to get to him, to find out how Renata was treating him, and most importantly, to tell him that I wasn't upset with him. He did what I'd helped him learn to do—keep his mouth shut and do as he's told to survive.

It was difficult to watch his movements during that first week leading up to Vigo's funeral weekend. The home was such chaos until that was over. I vomited during the eulogy Renata gave at his funeral mass. It was lucky that I was pregnant because I could blame my sickness on that. But really, it had only to do with the picture they painted of Vigo Vittori.

They said he was a strong and ferocious leader. A family man devoted to protecting and caring for his loved ones at all costs. A shrewd businessman whose savvy amassed a fortune that safeguarded the future of their entire extended family. An adoring cousin who loved playing with children.

That was the line that did me in.

But it was good to see for myself that he was well and truly dead. It brought me some semblance of peace and comfort, though it wasn't much. After the funeral weekend, the extended family began to depart in small groups. The mansion became less and less chaotic over the week that followed, and soon, I was able to see a routine develop.

I started to watch Ezra, tracking the routine Renata created for him. I made a point of cataloging when and where I ran into him, the times when he was with Renata, when he was with Luca, and when he was alone.

Renata had padlocked the collar to his neck, and I learned by asking Lorenzo that it kept him confined within the house. Every time I caught a glimpse of him—shirtless, wearing jeans that hugged his hips just right—I wanted two things more desperately than freedom. First, I wanted to find a strong pair of scissors and cut that fucking collar off him. Second, I wanted to...Well, there were actually a lot of things I wanted to do to him.

Initially, it had been only by sheer luck that I'd run into him, but I started to see the patterns in his days and nights. I kept quiet, watched, learned, waited until I knew with confidence when I could catch him alone without Renata noticing if he was gone for more than five minutes.

That time is now—just past midnight on our third Tuesday at the Vittori mansion.

I'm desperate for what we've both been denied for far too long—a touch, a breath, a kiss—just a moment of connection, if that's all that can be spared. I come out of my bedroom—Vigo's old bedroom that I stubbornly refused to leave after Renata's challenging remarks—and turn left, just as I always would to walk toward the staircase. But instead of descending, I keep walking to the opposite hallway. Renata's bedroom is at the far end.

I pause by the staircase, checking the watch I asked to have purchased for me. Ezra will exit Renata's room within the next five minutes or so. I'm going to walk down the hallway when he does, reach out for him, touch his hand, take what I can get for that brief moment.

Hardly a minute passes before I hear the sound of a door opening at the far end of the hall.

It's him.

I watch as he closes the door behind him. He pauses for a beat, looking down at the floor, his body riddled with tension that I wish I could release for him.

Oh, God.

I can't let my mind wander too far on such thoughts. I no longer feel sick all the time from these pregnancy hormones. Instead, they've turned me into a lust-filled, sex-starved woman who can't seem to keep her mind out of the gutter.

My mouth suddenly feels dry and I lick my lips as I watch Ezra rise to his full height and turn toward me. I step forward, directly in his path, only six doors separating us from meeting.

We see each other and there's a pause—a perfect pause of peaceful nothingness that I always get with him when we steal glances this way.

It's not that the pause is filled with nothing.

It's filled with everything.

But it's everything that's good and right and beautiful about the world—

even if it's a world we're not given the privilege of living in.

His chest rises heavy and falls the same and I see his cheek twitch, curling one side of his mouth into a smirk. I gasp noiselessly, the way he looks at me sending shameless need straight through my core.

I stride forward confidently, wearing the same form-fitting, knit black dress I've been wearing all day—I've been wearing it all day for *him*. My breasts are growing along with my stomach, not to say my pregnancy bump has grown all that much. In fact, if I weren't wearing such a tight dress, you would hardly notice I was pregnant at all, even at nearly four months.

Doctor Lombardi assures me it's nothing to worry about, often reminding me that pregnant bodies come in all different shapes and sizes. By all accounts it's true. Olivia is only three months along, though her stomach looks much bigger than mine.

Regardless, I feel confident in this dress, confident that Ezra will like to see me in it with the way the V-neck cuts down between my full-cup-size-larger breasts.

God, this feels so strange.

By all accounts, I should be ashamed of myself for wanting what I want from him.

How can I be so goddamn horny after all I've been through?

But the way he looks at me now as we walk toward each other in the empty hallway; he looks as needy as I feel. My heart flutters inside my chest, wings flapping desire through my body, making me feel lightheaded from lust. I feel like I can't catch my breath and I don't know what's come over me.

His eyes flick over my body and I see his chest rise and fall as his pace quickens. He needs me as much as I need him, and that makes me want him all the more.

I want more.

More than a touch.

I think we're going to collide as he aligns himself directly with the path I walk. He's not moving aside to brush past me. He's walking straight toward me. He moves with such determination to get to me, that I actually stop and take a step backward as he moves unexpectedly into my space.

We have to be careful that no one sees us—Renata would lose her mind.

"What are you—" I start, lifting my head to look up at him as he pushes me back.

"Come with me."

Ezra flashes me a perfect, white smile and I feel every organ inside my body liquefy. I'm a useless puddle for this man and I don't want it any other way. He drags me sideways, opening a bedroom door that's close to the staircase—the farthest from Renata's room. He pushes me inside.

I whirl around to face him as he slips in behind me, pushing the door shut and turning a deadbolt lock from the inside. I open my mouth to tell him I love him, but he swallows my words as he crashes into me, his lips landing on mine, bruising and desperate.

I'm stiff with shock for a moment, but when my brain catches up to what's happening, I sink into his hold. I grab his face as his arms curl around my waist, pulling me tight against him.

He doesn't kiss me so much as he devours me, tasting my tongue with hungry licks and groaning from his enjoyment. The way he kisses me makes me feel like a delicacy he's been starved from. He walks me backward until I hit a wall and he presses me to it, rough and demanding.

My breath catches as a brief jolt of unease threads through my mind. I pull back, breaking the kiss and resting my head against the wall behind me as I look up into his green eyes. With a single look, my unease at his roughness instantly fades.

He pants as he watches me, his body so close, I can feel him grow hard with need. His eyes study mine for a beat. "Too rough?"

"No," I say on a breath. "Only for a second. I just needed to see your eyes."

He smiles with such light that I swear the room brightens behind him. With a deep inhale, he presses his forehead to mine. "I've been watching you. I knew you'd be here tonight."

I bite my lip. "I've been watching you, too." My back arches off the wall, my body swelling with need and my breasts seeking his touch as I push against him. "Are we safe in here? How much time do we have?"

He nods, then rubs his nose against mine. "We're safe here. My absence won't be noticed for another forty-five minutes or so." He tilts his hips forward, grinding his ever-growing erection against me. "An hour if we feel like pushing our luck."

I can't help my smile as he moves his head to nuzzle against my neck, his perfect lips spotting kisses down to my chest. "I know I should be the voice of reason here," I say.

I feel his grin as his teeth playfully nip across my collarbone. "Nah. Don't do that, baby."

"I just..." I moan when he licks across the hollow of my throat. "God. I want to push my luck with you. I need you, Ezra."

When he lifts his head to look at me, his eyes filled with desire, I feel my body slip down the wall as need clenches low in my belly and wetness puddles between my legs.

He pulls me closer with one hand gripping my waist as the other comes up to catch my cheek. The touch of his hand on my face feels like I'm home. I let my head fall into it naturally as his fingers reach back to flick across my earlobe.

"Anya." He kisses my lips once. "I'm shaking with need for you."

I turn my head to kiss his palm and desire takes over, directing me to stick out my tongue and lick his hand. He groans, shrinks a little, and presses me harder against the wall as he grinds his cock against my belly. I watch the way his eyes change as his need grows, a shadow falling across the green that makes them look darker and lighter all at once, though I don't even know how that's possible.

I like the way he looks at me.

I like the way he makes me feel when he needs me this way.

I could only ever feel this way with Ezra.

"Are you still mine?" I whisper.

I turn my head, dragging my tongue across the back of his index finger, and suck it into my mouth. I don't think I've ever been this way with a man.

Raw and wanton.

Seductive.

Attempting to draw out his need to take me.

"Fuck," he mutters as I wrap my fingers around his wrist, pulling his hand back so I can release his finger from my mouth with a *pop* before sucking on his middle finger. "I'm always fucking yours. Jesus, what's gotten into you?" He grins.

I smile at him as I *pop* out his middle finger. "I'm pregnant and hormonal and sex-starved in a way I never thought possible."

He groans. "I wanna make you come."

I let go of his wrist and he drags his hand down my chest, wetness from where I sucked his fingers dragging along my exposed skin. He cups my breast over my dress, and I gasp as my suddenly filthy mind screams at him.

Touch me.

Don't tease me.

Oh, God, I already need to come.

"Put your mouth on me."

He leans in to kiss the corner of my lips, wet and languid. "Where, exactly, do you want me to put my mouth?"

I hook one finger through the metal loop at the front of his collar and yank his head down, holding his face close to mine. "Everywhere."

I kiss him, pushing off the wall, feeling an incessant need to mold my body to his. I reach between us, fumbling to grasp his cock through his jeans before I even make a conscious decision to do it. He shoves me back hard, forcing me against the wall again, pinning me in place as he squeezes my breast.

He only breaks the kiss to whisper against my ear, "Lift your skirt, slip off your panties, and spread your legs for me, blue-eyed girl."

I gasp at the command. I turn my head to meet his eyes, searching. I have to find my safety net there before I do what he asks. In truth, hearing him tell me what to do, knowing how much he wants me, makes my stomach clench and my clit throb with desire to be touched. Against reason, against all the life lessons I've learned in being a slave, I'm actually turned on by his command, by the fact that he has some plan to use my body and I'm not privy to it. This should have me running scared, even from Ezra. But when I look into his eyes, all I see is the way he wants to worship me. And if that weren't enough, he knows me enough to reassure me. That makes me want him even more.

"I just want to make you come, baby. You're in control. Always in control. Do you trust me?"

I don't say yes.

I just reach for the hem of my dress and shimmy it up over my hips. I slide my panties down next, and just as I let them go to drop to the floor, Ezra lowers to his knees. He takes my panties from around my ankles, guiding me to step out of them one foot at a time.

He looks up at me as he fists my underwear in one hand, rolling some of the fabric between his fingers.

"Jesus Christ. These are soaked," he says and I blush. "Fuck, I wish I could keep these."

Ezra brings the bunched-up underwear to his nose and inhales, long and deep. I shudder, my spine literally quaking at the sight of it. It's sinful the way he desires me—dirty, raw, completely, and utterly without shame—and I like it.

I want more like this.

I need this with him.

The confident, sexual woman I used to be before I met Nikolai claws her way to the surface to see Ezra like this. He makes me feel like the only woman in the world.

I spread my legs apart. "Don't make me wait. Please."

He pushes out a heavy breath that has a hint of a growl to it as he drops my panties on the floor, his hands splaying over my thighs. I slump against the wall with a whimper as he scoots in close and his hands wrap around to the backs of my legs. I feel another pulse of desire and a gush of wetness flow when his hands cup my ass cheeks, digging his fingers into my flesh, showing me how much he wants me.

He drags my hips forward and my body starts to come off the wall.

"Lean your back against the wall," he practically snarls at me, his eyes burning dark green with reckless lust. "I'll put your ass where I need it."

"Oh," I breathe out, "Ezra."

I need this.

I need this so much, I might die without it.

I lean back though he keeps my hips thrust forward toward him and my neck still cranes downward to look at him. Ezra wedges in between my open legs as he nudges my hem with his nose, pushing it higher so he can press his lips to my belly button. He licks his tongue over my lower stomach, the skin just above my dark curls, before kissing his way down.

I nearly cry out when his head dips and his lips and tongue attack my pussy—as if it's my mouth and he's kissing me for the last time. I clamp my hand over my mouth to keep quiet as he sweeps his tongue inside me, swirling, licking, curling all the way around my inner walls and leaving nothing untouched.

His hands shift, grasping my hips, holding me up as my knees tremble. I let my head fall back against the wall and my eyes fall shut as he moves his tongue along my folds, seeking and finding my clit.

I moan and his fingers clench me tighter.

I've never felt so *wet*.

Between my arousal and the saliva from his mouth as he consumes me, I'm a sloppy, wet mess and I actually love it. It's dirty and it feels so good that I don't ever want to feel clean again.

Ezra tastes me everywhere, leaving no part of my pussy untouched. I'm panting as his hand sneaks in behind his lips and I feel a jolt of naughty electricity when his fingers explore the area between my holes.

He plays with me, dipping his fingers inside with a teasing sort of touch. He gathers my wetness and spreads it back, almost all the way to my back entrance. It feels so good in such a bad way, but it also freezes me with tension. I want to give every part of myself to Ezra, but that part of me... It has been used as a punishment so many times before, and I don't think I can do it.

Not now.

I dig my fingers into his hair and pull his head back. When he looks up at me, it softens the tension immediately. His eyes are hooded and he pants. His face glistens from my slick arousal, and when he licks around his lips to taste it with a look of pure hunger on his face, I remember that he isn't one of them. I remember that he wants to please me, not punish me.

His chest heaves and I can see how his erection strains against his jeans. I see it in his eyes how he struggles to speak through his arousal, but the fact that he struggles and speaks anyway comforts me.

"Too much?" he finally asks between deep breaths

He let me stop him.

He asked if it was too much

He cares what I want.

I know for most normal women that's a minimum requirement, but for me, it means as much as if he were to give me the moon and stars.

"No," I tell him, holding him, not just with my hands, but with my gaze.

He grins up at me, rubbing his hands over my hips as he waits for me to release him. But as amazing as it feels to have his tongue between my legs—and it does feel unbelievably amazing—locking in on his stare like this is more erotic to me than any physical touch he could give me.

Gradually, I lower, sliding my back down the wall until I'm kneeling in front of him. I let my hands fall to his shoulders as I do, slowly drifting down to land on his bare chest.

His large hands reach out to grip my face, fingers reaching back and combing into my hair. His eyes flicker as they watch mine, seeing everything that I see reflected back at him. I lean in and press a soft kiss to his lips.

"I want you on top of me, inside me," I whisper. "I need to feel you come inside me."

One of his hands slips around to hold the back of my head, the other to my lower back, and as Ezra dips to kiss me, he takes me gently down to the floor. I uncurl my legs and spread my knees, waiting for him to settle between my legs before I squeeze them tight to his hips. I reach between us as he bends to kiss me. I taste myself on his tongue while I work his zipper, stretching my small arms down as far as they can reach to push off the barriers of his clothing and free his hard cock.

As soon as it's free, I find myself desperate for it, straddling the line drawn between sane lust and depraved lunacy. I buck my hips up, wiggling around with frenzied urgency to feel him inside me.

I nibble at his lower lip and he grins as he moves his mouth to my neck, lavishing my skin with his kisses and licks and nibbles.

"Now," I whisper. "Please. *Now.*"

He reaches down, grabs his shaft, and moves the tip to tease against my folds as he finds just the perfect angle to—

"*Oh...*"

"Fucking..." he trails off on whatever crass language he was beginning to speak.

I would mourn the loss of those dirty words if it weren't for the way he moves inside me, driving his hips forward to press all the way in. He holds me in that sweet, unmoving torture until I'm wriggling beneath him, practically writhing to get him to move.

"There are so many ways I want to fuck you, Anya." He licks a long line straight up the side of my neck, then his nose runs over the skin just behind my ear. He inhales deeply, taking in the scent of my hair. "A lifetime of ways to fuck you. I could make you come every hour of your life and it would never be enough."

"Just stay inside me forever."

He runs a hand over my hip, down to my knee, pressing and holding my leg against his side as he pulls out slowly, then pushes in again to the hilt. I moan at the delicious intrusion, the way his cock stretches my inner walls. He's so thick when he's hard, the perfect size to fill me completely.

"Forever, baby," he whispers into my ear. "You and me."

I smile as he sits up. He shuffles his knees in closer as he pumps in and out of me again. There's a little extra roughness at the end of his stroke and it shakes me from my core all the way through my skull. A sound escapes me—something like a moan, but more feral and raw. My eyes take in the sight of Ezra's sculpted body, his flexing ab muscles and strong shoulders, watching him fuck me slow but hard as he reaches for my left hand.

He pulls it to his lips, kissing the tops of my fingers, starting from the index, until he reaches my ring finger—the ring finger where I wear the diamonds Nikolai purchased for me. I shiver as he runs his tongue from the base of my palm, over the backs of the rings, all the way to the tip of that very finger.

"Mine?" he asks, taking the very question I always ask him and using it to claim me.

I refuse to belong to anyone else by force ever again. But I choose to belong to Ezra, *only* to Ezra, for the rest of my life. And it's okay for me to belong to him because he belongs to me, too.

Neither of us is slave to the other.

If anything, we serve together as slaves to our connection, our bond, our chemistry, our love. But neither of us will ever be less than to the other. We belong to each other and we belong together.

Always.

That's why it doesn't even give me pause when I tell him, "I'm yours. Always yours."

A low, guttural noise indicates his need to cement that vow from where our bodies join. He laces his fingers between mine, holding onto my left hand. His other hand pushes my knee down sideways to the floor, holding it down with his weight as he leans on it. And then, he fucks me, with rolling thrusts of his hips that drive his cock upward, forcing himself to rub against the perfect spot.

My eyes squeeze shut as that beautiful tension builds, twisting and dragging all the good feelings down low in my core. He thrusts and thrusts, bending to push our laced fingers to the floor just beside my head. He pushes down on my hand and my opposite knee so hard—bones-grinding-down-into-the-floor hard—that it causes the most incredible ache in my muscles. It doesn't hurt and it doesn't scare me, which surprises me.

It feels *good.*

I feel him everywhere.

I feel consumed by him.

I never want it to stop.

I'm shaking, literally trembling from the good feelings he gives me. He overwhelms my mind and takes control of my senses. I feel his eyes on me as he fucks me. I feel him pick up his pace when my muscles start to clench, when my fingers grip his harder, when I'm softly chanting, telling him of my frantic need for release with a single repeated syllable.

"Oh, oh, oh."

"Fuck. *Fuck.* Come for me, baby."

I feel his cock swelling, pulsing, nearing his own release. The extra tension as he grows inside me ignites a soul-searing fire—a flash fire that instantly consumes every part of my body.

It burns me, twists me, rumbles through me. I feel the explosion of it from deep within, bursting through my core. My pussy clenches and releases through a mind-numbing orgasm, tugging Ezra into coming hard inside me. His mouth drops open and somehow, I just know he won't be able to hold back a primal roar from his release.

I untangle my fingers from his as he pushes his cock inside me deep with his final thrust. I reach around, grabbing the back of his head with both of my hands. I yank him down to me and cover his mouth with mine, swallowing his groan, his shout of pleasure as he spills the last of his seed inside me.

As our orgasms fade into satiated calmness, we kiss. We kiss like it's the first time and the last time, like it's the *only* time. We kiss like we might never kiss again.

My heart thumps, and though I'm probably just being crazy, I swear I can feel Ezra's heart thump right along with mine, with the same rhythm and tempo.

This can't be the last.

"I can't live like this," I say bluntly, breaking our kiss.

He studies my expression, brushing the hair from my eyes with his hand and stroking down the side of my face. He doesn't say anything. He's just quiet, watching me, waiting for me to go on.

His silence reminds me of the first night we kissed in my bedroom at Mikhailov Manor—the night Nikolai raped me with Ezra's involvement. Ezra gave me silence when I needed it, allowing me quiet to process my thoughts before telling him what I was really thinking. He's doing the same now—one of the many things I love about him—giving me pause and letting me think. It makes me feel as though my thoughts are valued…wanted.

I press up onto my elbows and he moves as I do, sitting up and sitting back on his heels. "Ezra…we have to escape."

A neutral expression washes over his features and for the first time, I feel like I don't really know what he's thinking. He takes a breath, rises on his knees to pull his pants back up and buttons them, then lowers to sit back on his heels. "Do you mean it?"

I start to sit up, but it's a little challenging with my position; even with such a small bump, my movements have begun to feel awkward and clumsy. Ezra reaches down to help me, grabbing me easily from my armpits and practically lifting me off the floor toward him. He pulls me up onto his lap where he kneels, my knees spread on either side of him. Immediately, I look down between us as I feel the evidence of our encounter drip out from between my legs, right onto the crotch of his jeans.

"I'll leave a wet spot," I warn him.

But he only wraps his arms around me tightly, holding me close to him. "I don't give a fuck, Anya. Are you serious about escaping?"

I wrap one of my arms around his neck, but let the other fall between us, landing on my belly. "I've never thought it was possible. And I suppose I still believe that's true."

Hearing myself say that out loud makes me feel flutters in my belly like tiny butterfly wings that fan an anxious, urgent feeling through my body. It could be the baby moving for the first time—Doctor Lombardi said it would feel like tiny flutters at first, but likely not for several more weeks. More likely it's a feeling of instinct.

"This probably doesn't make any sense, but…I feel like I have to attempt the impossible. Like I'll regret it forever if I don't try. If *we* don't try." I lift my hand to join the other around his neck as I lean forward and place my forehead against his. "I know this baby is yours, Ezra. I just…I just know it. It has to be. I won't accept anything else. And even if he's not, the thought of him being raised among the four families?" I blow out a breath as the idea of it spikes anxiety and Ezra rubs my back. "It's unthinkable."

"It's absolutely unthinkable." He sighs. "Wait. You said *he?*"

I lift my head to look at him better. "I don't know for sure yet. But I had a dream. I have dreams all the time actually. Nightmares. But he's always a boy. Maybe it's just wishful thinking because I don't know what they'll do if the baby is a girl." They might kill her and probably me with her—not that I'd want to live if my baby died.

Ezra nods. "You know I've had dreams, too."

My cheeks twitch, tugging a smile from my lips. "Yeah?"

"Always a boy. A little blond-haired boy with my eyes."

My shoulders relax at that. "Always green eyes."

"I know it doesn't mean anything," Ezra says. "It's just a dream. But it feels real sometimes."

I kiss him, just a peck at first, but it turns into a slow burning fusion of my mouth with his. We stay that way for minutes, holding each other, kissing each other, loving each other to spite all the ways we've been denied that privilege.

"I do mean it," I tell him when we come to a stopping point. "I want to escape this life. I've been talking to Kostya."

"Yeah?"

"I think he's…Well, I feel like he's on our side. And with Nikolai gone, it almost feels like I'm the only family he has left. I think he might help us if I foster a friendship with him. I have to try. I *want* to try."

He seems relieved, as if he's been waiting for me to say something, as if it would be so easy to just up and leave.

It won't be anything resembling easy.

"Then I'll find a way for us, baby. I will."

"We'll do it together. Because we're better together?" For some reason, it comes out of me as a question.

His hands slide up from my back and he grabs hold of my face, leveling his eyes with mine. "Listen to me. You and me, together? We can do anything."

I nod and he kisses me. Then we wrap our arms around each other tight, and he hugs me in a way that warms my soul and positively melts me.

The icy cold exterior that's kept me shielded for all these years melts away, drop by drop, the permafrost threatening to fade away for good.

And I hope it does.

I want the tundra to become a desert.

I want to spark a fire in the dry heat, explode into flames, and burn down the four families with Ezra by my side.

CHAPTER 15
Ezra

"IT'S NOT TOO late to change your mind. You don't have to be punished this way." Renata runs her fingers down my bare chest.

The feel of her touch still makes my skin crawl, but sadly, I'm growing used to it. "Do your worst," I tell her through gritted teeth. "I'm not fucking you."

Her face slips from seductress to villainess as she takes a step back. "Have it your way, then. If I can't have your cum, then I'll take your blood."

"Drain me like the vampire you are. I'm. Not. Fucking. You."

She claims I have a choice, but it's no goddamn choice at all. Fuck her or let her hurt me. My blood is her retribution for her brother's death. I'd let her bleed me dry before ever letting her have my cock.

Her eyes narrow to slits and she snaps at Luca. The three of us are alone in her bedroom, as has often been the case over these past few weeks. He rushes to her side and begins to wrap the familiar coarse rope around my wrists. He's good at tying escape-proof knots, and I have a feeling Renata is the one who taught him how to do that.

I used to fight him, but that got me into trouble. It's not that I care if I get in trouble—it's just that I know if I'm causing problems, it comes down on Anya. Aside from the singular fact that I would do anything to keep them from hurting her, we need her to keep what little status and authority she's attained—which means keeping the inane dealings of an unruly slave far from her concern. Anya has to be a master in this realm as long as it takes for us to figure out how to escape together. So, while I do it with a sour attitude, I comply.

"Stand here, raise your arms." Renata guides me to the foot of the bed, positioning me to face it, and I lift my arms above my head.

She and Luca work to tie the ropes to the canopy, one knotted around each of my wrists. My arms stretch wide above my head, pulling apart into a V as they tie me. The wooden frame that forms the canopy is solid and I know the knots are, too. It doesn't stop me from giving a good yank to test them, though.

I'm locked down.

My heartbeat spikes.

I take in a slow breath and blow it out to steady myself.

"What'll it be tonight?" I ask. "More of the knife? Add a few more knicks and scars?" It's not pleasant when she punctures my skin and marks me with tiny scars, but it's not unbearable, either.

Somewhere behind me I hear a drawer open and shut, and I turn my head to look over my shoulder. It's not until Renata comes up to my side before I can see what she's holding in her hand.

"I think a good whipping is in order for you. Twenty lashes? Thirty? What do you think you deserve for denying me, Ezra?"

I laugh, though a ripple of anxious adrenaline pulses through my veins. "Make it fifty. I don't give a fuck."

"*Fifty?* Hmm. Have you ever been struck with a cat o' nine tails before?"

"No."

But I've been struck with a cane by my blue-eyed girl.

Anya struck me the first day I met her, when Nikolai brought me to her. She had me strung up in the dance studio and struck me eight times with the cane. That was when her only choice was to break me to save herself.

That was before we fell in love.

"I'll give you twenty lashes to start. If you're not begging for me to fuck you by then instead, then I'll give you thirty more and call it a night."

"Just get on with it. I'm tired of hearing you talk."

There's a sudden slicing through the air and then a crack before fire licks across my skin, just to the right of my spine. I groan as my body sways forward from the unexpected hit, my shoulders straining against the ropes.

"Fuck," I hiss.

"Oh, did that hurt?"

"Nah, I'm good," I lie.

Fire flashes again, only this time it's brighter, lashing in nearly the same spot as the first strike. I clench my hands into fists and swallow the shout that claws up my throat. I won't give her the satisfaction.

Renata's fingers trail from the base of my neck, slowly down my spine.

She intentionally strays from the path to trace over the line of flames—the way they flare against her touch tells me I'll have welts before this is over.

"Wouldn't it feel better to sink inside me?" she whispers.

I drop my head and my jaw ticks as I hold back my anger. "I can't think of anything that would feel worse."

"Fuck you!" she screams and strikes me again.

I grunt as I sway, but there's no time for me to take a breath, to calm myself, to prepare for the next lashing. I stripped her façade of control with my insult and I know I'm fucked now. She strikes, again and again, and fucking again.

She hits me with fury until my skin is ablaze.

She hits me until I shout for her to stop.

She hits me until my body slumps and the ropes hold my weight through my arms, until my head droops in surrender, and my heart is pounding.

She's given me fifty lashes, just as I asked for, and I already know this pain will last for days. I feel blood trickling down my back, and I can only imagine the scars this will leave on my body.

But those scars would be nothing compared to the emotional scars that would mar my heart if I had sex with anyone other than my girl.

I'm left to hang there in my physical pain—with my back bleeding and burning—as Renata and Luca move onto the bed. I close my eyes with my head hung as Luca removes her clothes and fucks her in front of me.

I hate it more than the pain when they do this. I'm ashamed of it, but I'm a fucking human man, and there's a porn movie playing out in front of me. It makes me hard—though I don't want it to—and being hard makes me think about my blue-eyed girl.

I'd prefer to keep her out of my mind when I'm here with Renata and her little fuck boy, but sex and Anya are permanently linked inside my mind. Especially, since we've been seeing each other in secret and making love in all the intense and passionate ways we were meant to. I can't keep her out of my mind, but I can protect the sanctity of our connection.

I don't let myself think about fucking Anya, touching her, making love to her. I let myself imagine her caring for me, nursing these burning wounds, showing me how much she loves me. It's what she's done with all the wounds Renata has given me over the past several weeks. Anya's love for me is stronger than Renata's hate.

I smile to myself.

Renata can hurt me, do whatever the fuck she wants to do to me, but she'll never break me down. I'll meet with Anya again in that secret room in two nights and she'll build me back up again.

Renata can't fucking win.

CHAPTER 16

Anya

EVERY OTHER TUESDAY night, Ezra and I meet for a secret rendezvous in that same bedroom on the east end of the second floor. Every other week, we kiss and touch and hold each other. I tend to his wounds inflicted by Renata, covering the would-be scars with ointment and showering him with attentive care. We survive the in-between times with stolen glances and our own daydreams.

But we won't get to sneak away together this week. Three months have passed since everything changed—since the night Ezra saved me, since I killed Vigo, since Nikolai died, and since I discovered I had become a Mikhailov.

This week we'll be attending the quarterly meeting of the four families at the O'Shea's mansion in Ireland. For the first time, I'm not here as a slave, I'm here as a member of the board.

Kostya has been helping me prepare for tonight's quarterly board meeting. He seems more human now that we've been spending more time together. My initial intent was to foster a relationship in the name of gaining trust, knowing he might be useful to me and Ezra in planning some sort of escape. But I've been surprised to find that Kostya's company has become a comforting presence—entirely different than when he followed me around as a slave to ensure I did what I was supposed to do.

He's nearby as I enter the O'Shea's recently refurbished theater-turned-opera house with my spine straight and my chin up, though I feel anything but regal or strong. My stomach is constantly growing and it's obvious that I'm six months pregnant.

Ezra loves how it looks.

Just thinking of the way he grins at me, rubs my belly, and tells me I'm a "cute little mama" every time he sees me makes my heart flutter and a smile threaten to undo my carefully crafted expression of stone-cold indifference.

I don't feel confident with this body, not in the way I used to be. I don't move the way I used to. And I certainly can't dress the way I used to. I was granted the privilege of selecting my own attire for this evening, but the options were scarce.

The gown I chose is a soft, blush pink with an empire waist. The top is made of lace that fits as closely as a second skin but has a low-cut V that dips between my newly ample breasts. It has long lacy sleeves that hug my arms. A metallic, rose gold belt without a buckle wraps around my waist, cinching me just beneath my breasts. The skirt flares out from there, all the way to my feet, with layers of fluffy chiffon that drape elegantly to the ground.

Though I tried as long as I could to wear high heels so I could at least match Renata's height, it simply isn't possible anymore. My feet are swollen—even after all the years of abuse my feet took dancing ballet, this particular ache is a torture I just can't stand. Doctor Lombardi has asked me to stop wearing heels anyway—he's afraid I might fall over and snap in two. According to him, I need to gain more weight, though I don't know where I'd put it. I feel bloated and swollen everywhere.

As I enter the new opera house, I feel the eyes of every member of the four families upon me. It's as though a thousand daggers are being shot from their eyes, stabbing me all at once, threatening to make me feel small, effectively cut down to size.

But I steel myself, remembering that tonight, I am one of them—a Mikhailov—and I have to demand to be treated as such. I glance over my shoulder to see Kostya somewhere behind me and he taps two fingers beneath his chin—a familiar, gentle nudge reminding me to display my strength and dignified grace.

Chin up.

I give him a grateful nod, then lift my chin a little higher, forcing myself to ignore the judgmental eyes and simply take in the beauty of my surroundings.

The opera house looks as though it belongs to kings, and in a way, I suppose it does. The O'Sheas are currently the only remaining family of the four who haven't been undone by all the upheaval from the past year. So, I suppose if anyone is king among these masters, it's Murphy O'Shea. Of course, he looks nothing like a king with his trimmed, but unruly-looking beard, and so many tattoos upon his arms that they creep out from beneath his suit jacket, tracing outward onto his hands.

Murphy stands in front of the first row of seats at the bottom of the house, looking outward and greeting those who feel compelled to say hello to the king of masters. I push out a breath, knowing I will have to greet him likewise.

I make my way down the aisle on the left, trudging down the dark-purple carpet that softens my steps along the lane. Rows of refinished wooden seats on either side of me are upholstered with a matching purple-and gold-embossed fabric. Everything in the theater is opulent, all shades of purple and gold and dark wood.

A massive crystal chandelier hangs from the center of the theater, casting light on the intricate wooden carvings along the rows of balcony seats on either side of the room. My heart thumps in a familiar rhythm as I approach the stage, feeling a tug from the performance space that calls to me still.

It's been nine months since Nikolai injured my ankle and sold me to Vigo. Nine months since I've really, truly danced, and the desire for it makes my entire body ache. Momentarily, I'm illogically jealous of the O'Shea talent slave because she will get to perform.

I glance behind me again, looking once more to Kostya for moral support, but he's stopped to greet someone nearby. I rub my sweaty palms on my skirt and move forward to greet Murphy on my own.

I plaster a fake smile to my face as I approach him and we greet each other with a kiss to the cheek, his hand landing on my elbow momentarily as he leans in. He's only doing what he's supposed to—I know he still considers me a lowly slave.

"You look well," he says with a tilt of his head. "How are things with the lady Vittori?"

"If you're asking me whether she's doing as she was told to do, then things are going as expected. My care has been managed."

He nods. "Good. I look forward to hearing from your joint family board at the meeting tonight. For your sake, I do hope profits are climbing."

I hate that I know anything about our profits from the sales of innocent human lives, but I am able to tell him with accuracy. "Yes. Unfortunately for the lives that were stolen, our profits are up."

I hear a snort of amusement behind me and turn to see a young woman sitting in the front row. "I like her," the girl says, pointing a finger from her crossed arms at me.

Her long, black hair dangles over her crossed arms and the scowl she wears indicates that she'd rather be anywhere but here. She might be my age, maybe a couple of years younger. I've never seen her before and wonder if she is their talent slave—though I can't imagine her getting away with speaking up like that if she is.

Murphy's lips purse together with a forced smile. "Anya, this is my new bride, Stella. She doesn't quite understand her place yet as an O'Shea wife. Perhaps I should develop a training program." He looks around me to raise his eyebrows threateningly at her and I turn my head to look back at her as she straightens in her seat.

"Maybe I'll develop a training program for *you* on the health risks associated with trying to mansplain your way through marriage." Her fingers come up to make air quotes on the word *marriage.*

I step aside because I fully expect Murphy to haul off, grab her from the chair, and take her from the room by force—I don't need to get knocked over in the midst. But Kostya appears at my side, stepping between Murphy and Stella, and greets the Head of House cordially, defusing their tension for a moment.

Once the social niceties have been observed, I take Kostya's arm and dismiss us away, allowing him to lead me back a few rows. I never thought I'd be thankful to have him around, especially since I distrusted him so much before Ezra came along and everything changed. But he's quickly become a true ally—it sets my hopes high that maybe one day soon, he'll help me and Ezra.

My nerves buzz with a prickling energy beneath my skin as we sit and wait. Movement from the aisle beside us catches my attention and I turn my head to see Renata striding forward along the aisleway toward Murphy. I see Ezra pass by our row, behind Luca, as Renata, Lorenzo, and Olivia greet our host.

Ezra's wearing a navy-blue suit, his white button-down shirt open at the neck to allow space for his collar to show. He turns his head and winks at me as he follows the others and my heart skips a beat. I fight every muscle in my face to hide my grin and surely flushing cheeks.

I will get to spend some time with him tonight. Renata is his keeper, but he's still my talent, and I'm allowed to have my talent as an escort at the reception. That's how it's always been, for no reason other than tradition—I don't mind the tradition when it grants me time with my love without fear or secrecy.

The Vittori/Fiore crew soon fill in half the row beside us, sitting next to Kostya and leaving me happily at the end. I lean forward, look down the row, and gaze in Ezra's direction, staring until he sees me. When he does, he gives me a secret grin, briefly putting his hand over his heart, as if he needs to hold it inside for the way it beats for me. I put a hand on my stomach, and though I can't smile at him right now, I tell him with my eyes how much I love him.

Murphy greets his audience and introduces their recently-acquired talent slave, a singer whose been with them just shy of a year. I feel a stab of pain in my gut and I know it's nothing to do with the baby—it's just a pang of knowing for this talent slave. Knowing what she is, what she is forced to do, how she was forced into captivity; it's an ache of compassion for her.

The lights in the house dim, chattering fades slowly into expectant silence, and the curtain begins to rise. The young talent slave appears on stage, her long, strawberry-blond hair sweeping in waves nearly to her waist, blending into her sparkling gold sequin gown. With her porcelain complexion and ginger-colored hair, she almost looks like she could be a younger version of Cordelia O'Shea.

The young woman entertains us by singing several beautiful melodies with impressive talent. She's a gorgeous young girl, a truly talented singer who had her whole life ahead of her. Her story is the same as my story. Funded by the O'Sheas' to develop her talent over the years, she's only recently been stolen away and made a slave. She'll likely serve them for years, possibly decades, missing out on every opportunity to live a full and happy life the way she wishes to. I wonder if Murphy and his family are as brutal with her as Nikolai and Vigo were with me.

Of course, they are.

Murphy is the ruthless king of masters.

We're all siphoned out of the theater following the performance. Renata and her clan exit fairly quickly, but Kostya stays behind with me as I sit and wait for the crowd to thin out a bit. My feet already hurt and I'm tired, so I don't feel in a major rush to wobble out of my seat and get to socializing with monsters any sooner than I have to. It's the same old routine at every quarterly meeting—talent show, reception, board meeting.

When Kostya and I finally exit the theater, I approach Renata where she stands with Luca and Ezra, waiting right by the door as was previously agreed upon. My eyes land on Ezra, inadvertently skimming down his body and taking in the absolutely perfect sight of him in a perfectly tailored suit.

My hormonal heart beats double time. "I'll take my escort off your hands now," I tell Renata.

My escort.

Just as I always was for Nikolai.

My left hand feels suddenly heavy at my side and I fight the urge to twirl my rings, averse to drawing attention to them.

Renata's scowl tells me how much she hates that I get to have Ezra on my arm for just a little while tonight. I have to fight my smile at that thought. This experience must be proving to be so eye-opening for her, to realize that it's these twisted traditions that oppress her so. If it weren't for tradition, she would be the sole leader of the Vittoris. But that's not the case and she'll just have to follow the damn rules like the rest of us.

Serves her right.

"There will be eyes on both of you this evening," she says as she nudges Ezra forward from the small of his back. "Don't try anything stupid."

"Stupid?" I say. "I wouldn't dream of it. I've always followed the rules." I tilt my head to the side. "Always."

"Come," she snaps at Luca and turns on her pointy heels.

I can't help but grin as Ezra holds out his arm for me and I take it. Kostya is in tow, following us into the reception space just outside the theater. I spare him a quick glance and a friendly smile over my shoulder.

Renata leads the way with Luca at her side and re-introduces me to practically every person at the reception. She does so begrudgingly, but it has to be someone's responsibility to do this—I thought it would be Murphy, as he's hosting, but he pawned off the task on Renata, much to her dismay. By the time I've been presented as Nikolai's bereaved wife to what feels like a thousand demons who I only vaguely remember, my feet and calves are aching and I'm desperate to get off my feet.

Olivia—a full month less pregnant than me—has already found a place to perch and put her feet up on Lorenzo's lap. He's taken off her shoes and is rubbing her feet.

They look happy.

I feel painfully jealous.

My mind flashes in envy and for a terrible moment, I see myself as Olivia—a happy girl with a smile on my face—and my feet on Nikolai's lap. It's a split-second vision and my heart drops into my stomach because that's not a vision I want.

I never wanted that…not with Nikolai.

Why doesn't my mind understand that my heart never wanted him?

Ezra taps my elbow and nods his head toward an ornate, traditional-looking loveseat in front of the fireplace—just big enough for two. I nod at him and we move to take the seat before someone else beats us to it. I plop down and Ezra tells me he'll be right back. I don't want him to leave me alone, but I'm not alone, really.

I'm surrounded by people.

I glance around the room as I wait and spot Kostya nearby, standing alone in the far corner, and I suddenly feel sad for him. He really has been all alone in his role, and I never stopped to think how lonely he might've been all these years. I smile at him and he nods at me graciously. His expression softens at my acknowledgment and that warms my heart.

Ezra returns with refreshments for me and I realize just how hungry I really am. "I can feed you if you want. I am your slave after all," he says with a joking smile as he sits beside me.

Our hips touch and I feel safe for the moment. We may be in a room full of trafficking, murderous criminals, but with Ezra by my side, I'm trapped in his sunshine, protected behind a thin layer of false normalcy. I give myself permission to enjoy it for the moment, because moments are all he and I have.

"I'll feed myself, thanks." I return his smile and take the small plate of hors d'oeuvres from him.

"I can't stop looking at you," Ezra tells me quietly as I eat.

I'm certain I'm blushing five different shades of pink. I wish he could crush my lips with a kiss right now. It's hard to breathe this close to him, knowing I can't touch him in a romantic way.

I glance around the room after popping another morsel into my mouth. I chew and swallow before speaking. "Do you notice how distracted they all are?"

"Who?"

"All of them. Renata, Murphy, Leo. They're all so busy socializing that they're not paying attention to us."

"Renata has eyes on us, though." Ezra turns his head and looks behind us, then jabs his thumb over his shoulder. "See? Luca's watching."

I follow where he indicates with my eyes and see that he's right. I also notice that Lorenzo isn't entirely distracted by Olivia. He glances over at us, and his brows lift when our eyes catch, giving me an expression that tells me he is, in fact, watching us. "Lorenzo, too," I tell him.

"Why do you mention it? What are you thinking?" he asks as I turn my attention back to him.

"I don't know. I guess I'm thinking that if there were ever a time to attempt escape, perhaps it would be during a reception. There's access to transportation—"

"Security is focused on guests more than perimeter guarding. We might be able to slip out unnoticed," Ezra finishes my train of thought.

I nod. "We know how to do it now. We got away from the Vittoris with Nikolai's help."

"Right," Ezra turns his body sideways to face me and lowers his voice. "And we could escape from Mikhailov Manor with Kostya's help. There's nothing stopping us now. No one's trailing Lidia and Emma. And Kostya promised Nikolai he'd keep your heart beating, right? He wanted to keep that promise to Nikolai, and even gave us those cell phones in hopes it would keep you from…" *Committing suicide* is what he means to say, but I know it's hard for him to say those words. "Even Nikolai didn't know about the cell phones. And Kostya put his life on the line when we fled the Vittoris. Got himself shot for us so we could escape."

"Three months," I start in a whisper, looking straight ahead rather than at Ezra. "The next quarterly meeting is supposed to be hosted by the Mikhailovs. Renata thinks we should host it jointly at the Vittori mansion, but if I can convince the board to let me host it at Mikhailov Manor—"

He sits up straighter with a burst of energy. "Yes. And if I perform, we'll have access to Nobility Hall. We could escape from there, even before the reception starts. They wouldn't notice we haven't shown up for thirty minutes, maybe as much as an hour if we're lucky."

I inhale a breath of hopeful longing. "You're right. They'll expect me to give you time to change before heading down to the reception…"

"Anya. It could work. We could escape from Mikhailov Manor with Kostya's help."

I put my hand over my heart, willing my racing pulse to slow. "It could work," I repeat and turn my head to give him a small smile.

He looks at my mouth and licks his lips, sending a pleasant shiver down my spine. "You look so fucking beautiful."

I melt, wishing I could kiss him, but I settle for briefly brushing my fingertips over his knee. He tenses at my touch and I know he wants more.

"What about your due date? Won't that be cutting it close? It's only a week before the next meeting, right? "

"It doesn't matter. It *can't* matter. It's our best chance. Maybe our only chance," I tell him with a confident tone, though a twinge of fear strikes within me about the timing.

The timing does cut it close, fearfully close. But I know that it doesn't matter to me. Whether I'm still pregnant, in labor, or have my baby in my arms, I'll take him with me in this fight to be free.

We could finally be free.

"We'll make a plan," I tell him. "We can do this. We can survive three more months of this…right?"

He nods, leaning in just a little. "Yes. We can and we will."

CHAPTER 17

Anya

AS THE RECEPTION hours pass us by and the time for the board meeting approaches, anxiety weighs heavily on my shoulders. I'm separated from Ezra for the night, and because I have no reason to return to my bedroom before the meeting, I don't. Instead, I use the restroom for the third time over the last hour—baby enjoys kicking my bladder—and I pace outside the boardroom.

I pace until my lower back starts to ache and my swollen feet demand to sit. Kostya is still with me and he suggests I return to the reception area to sit and wait until it's time. But thankfully—or perhaps, not so thankfully—Cordelia O'Shea makes her way toward us just then, moving past me to unlock the boardroom.

She forces herself to greet me with a simple, "Hello," though I see the way her hands shake in rage as she turns the key.

She's enraged because I killed Vigo—because, apparently, she had some sort of affection for the monster who almost killed me. I don't feel an ounce of remorse for the fact that I took her lover's life. I don't know much about Cordelia, but I do know that anyone who would willingly have a relationship with Vigo Vittori is either evil or a moron.

And she's probably both.

In any case, my nerves send a ripple of unease through my limbs as I cross the threshold of the boardroom. Kostya graciously shows me where to sit, leading me to the spot where Nikolai would sit.

Nikolai.

Fucking Nikolai.

Each reminder of him is like a wrecking ball of pain slamming into my chest, stealing my breath away at the reminder of everything he put me through and worse with the reminder that he's gone now. He chose my fate—*this* fate—before he died, and he left me to navigate this nightmare with the four families alone.

I'm happy that my seat isn't near either head of the long, rectangular table. In the middle, on the side, I can blend in and feel less like I'm on display. Still, I know I need to assert myself. Somehow, I think that will be easier from this position.

Board members file into the room and settle into their seats. Murphy enters last, moving around behind the chair at the head of the table and he begins to speak before he sits.

"Welcome. I think it's best that we avoid the pomp and circumstance and get right down to handling business, shall we? The changes we've seen in the organizational structure of the four families over the past year have been unprecedented and dramatic. We have some major decisions to make tonight and we're going to dive right in. The finalized agenda is in your folder." The others open the black leather folio placed in front of them, one at each spot around the table, and I follow suit to open mine. "Any changes, additions, or objections?" Murphy asks the room.

"I object to *all* of this." Every head in the room snaps to look at the sassy girl I met in the theater—Murphy's new wife, Stella.

She still looks surly with her arms wrapped tightly across her chest. She has an interesting appearance, though she doesn't quite look like she fits in with the four families. She wears a tight, deep burgundy dress that cuts low between her average-sized breasts, revealing a tattoo along her collarbone—a scribbling of words I can't make out—and more artwork appears on the side of her arm. Her nose is pierced and there's an unnaturally bright red streak of hair peeking out from behind her ear. Not to say there's anything wrong with her appearance—I like it on her—she just seems out of place here.

Murphy finally snaps, bending over the corner of the table and reaching out to wrap his hand around Stella's throat. "Be quiet, lass, or I'll make certain you won't speak again."

She looks up at him with surprise in her eyes, but I'm not exactly sure she looks as fearful as she should be. Honestly, I'm surprised with Murphy's restraint. He forces a strained smile as he removes his hand from her neck, one finger at a time. No one bats an eye at the fact that this poor girl was just publicly throttled by her husband.

Fucking monsters.

Murphy straightens, smooths his waistcoat, and continues, "Changes, additions, or objections?" His eyes fall on Stella beside him with an intent glare.

She meets his eyes with unwavering contact and there's an almost palpable crackle between them—a sizzle of heat and chemistry. It makes my pulse quicken and it sends my thoughts spiraling to Ezra.

No.

Pay attention.

I glance down at my agenda for the first time, only just realizing I should have looked at it before he called for changes or objections.

Focus.

Breathe and focus.

Item one is listed as:

Family M: *Gender & DNA Result*

My head snaps up more dramatically than it should, and I find myself glancing around the room—to look at what or whom, I really don't know.

Murphy's commanding voice demands my attention and I whip my head toward the sound, finding he's already lowered into his seat. "First item of business is the matter of Anya Mikhailov, the gender of her unborn child, and the DNA result which determines family placement."

"You know the gender and the father?" I ask with too much nervous energy.

I'd been given an ultrasound a month and a half ago where Doctor Lombardi was able to see the gender of the baby, but no one would tell me. Now I understand why—the four families are nothing if not dramatic. And revealing this information here and now—determining the fate of my baby and my future as a board decision—was about as dramatic as they could get.

Murphy flips through his folio and produces a single white sealed envelope. He places it on the table and gives it a push, sliding it across the smooth surface so it glides toward me. Kostya grabs it to spare me the embarrassment of attempting to reach over my protruding belly for it and hands it to me. My name is scribbled on the front.

Anya Mikhailov.

I swallow, looking at Murphy for direction.

"Open it," he urges. "Read it out loud for the board. This letter was sent to me directly by Doctor Lombardi. This first letter should contain the gender of your baby as determined via your twenty-week ultrasound. Depending on what this letter states, we may or may not need to open the second."

"Why?" I run my fingers along the edges of the envelope.

"If your baby is a girl, the paternity result doesn't really matter, now does it?"

My eyes immediately fall on Renata across the table from me. "Does she know?" I ask Murphy.

"No one knows. The result is in that envelope and in Doctor Lombardi's personal notes. We're all finding out together. For your sake, let's hope it's a boy. Now open it."

I open my mouth to ask what will happen if it's a girl, but I close it again, realizing I don't really want to know.

They might kill her.

They might let her live and kill me.

They might raise her as one of them.

They might sell her for profit.

My fingers tear open the envelope before I even make a conscious decision to do it. I can't bear not knowing. The baby *has* to be a boy and I need to prove it now. I need to know right now that he's a boy and that he'll be okay.

I need to know we'll be alive in three months to escape with Ezra.

I tug the single sheet of white paper free from the envelope and unfold it with trembling fingers. But before I can read what it says, I squeeze my eyes shut.

I can't bring myself to look.

I place it on the table and push it toward Kostya.

"What does it say?" I ask him.

I suck in a breath and hold it through a pause, a painful beat of not knowing. I hear the quiet rush of air as he sighs…a sound of relief.

"Boy," Kostya says, angling the paper toward me to see it before sliding it back across the table to Murphy.

I struggle to hold my cold, regal expression when I feel the rush of relief wash over my body.

I knew it.

I knew he was a boy.

My baby has always been precious to me, but because he's a boy, he's now precious to the four families as well—a direct heir of the Mikhailov or Vittori Head of House. Both my hands cover my belly as an instinctive urge to protect him takes hold of me.

They'll want him to become one of them. They'll raise him to be the next Head of House. They'll groom him for the role the same way they groomed Nikolai and Vigo. They'll prime him for violence and brutality. They'll strip him of his empathy and compassion.

Over my dead fucking body—and I will be dead if the results show he belongs to neither of them.

I inhale slowly and look at Murphy.

"Alright," he says, glancing over the paper before slapping it on the table in front of him. "Well done, lass. You've created the next Head of House." He flips through his pages and produces another white envelope, the sight of which makes my heart flip. "Now to find out if he's a Vittori or a Mikhailov."

Oh, God.

I feel sick.

He waves the envelope at me, but then he sets it on the table and pushes it to Renata on the opposite side. My mouth drops open in surprise that he's letting her open it. Those paternity results have *nothing* to do with her. I don't care if one of the fathers in question is her brother.

She tears into it and pulls the page out of the envelope, her eyes scanning it quickly to find the information she's seeking. Her face falls and my heart beats harder. I don't know which would upset her more—if my baby is her nephew or if he's not. I don't know if she's hopeful that he will be the last bit of Vigo she might find to hang onto now that he's gone, or if the idea of her nephew belonging to me makes her cry into her pillow at night.

She forces out a heavy breath and her nostrils flare as she pushes the paper back to Murphy. "He's not a Vittori."

He's not a Vittori.

I want to leap on the table and cheer.

The four most beautiful words I never thought I'd be so happy to hear.

He's not a Vittori.

But is he a Mikhailov?

"Hmm." Murphy's brow furrows as he looks over the page and I sit up a little higher. "Apparently, the DNA result from Nikolai was inconclusive."

Inconclusive?

Perhaps it was because they took his blood sample after he'd already been dead for hours. I don't know. I have no idea how DNA testing works or what would make it *inconclusive*. I'm not even sure I understand what *inconclusive* means.

But I don't feel upset.

In my heart, I know the truth. I know that this baby boy is Ezra's and I convince myself that's the reason why the results were inconclusive. Really, it's the best result I could've asked for. If they'd determined with certainty that the baby wasn't Nikolai's, then they might work out that it's Ezra's. But only Leo Leblanc knows that Ezra and I were left alone in his dungeon the night I would've fallen pregnant. And thank God, he hasn't said a word about it.

I look expectantly at Murphy. "So, what does this mean for me?"

His eyes narrow and his jaw sets as he runs a hand over his beard. "Leo?"

All eyes turn toward Leo at the other head of the table. He's the only other Head of House, but he's young and new. I remember thinking how out of place he seemed the first time I met him. But now he looks almost cold, like he's been hardened by the business in such a short time. His face holds an expression of indifference and apathy.

"So, we assume the child is a Mikhailov since we know it isn't a Vittori." His eyes dare a quick glance in my direction and my heart hammers an extra beat at his secretive look. "I say, let her remain in the care of the Vittoris. She seems to be doing well there now and it makes sense for her to stay given that the Mikhailovs and Vittoris are making joint business decisions. Let her stay for a year and if she proves herself trustworthy," Leo leans back in his chair crossing his arms over his chest, "then she and Kostya can move back to Mikhailov Manor to run the business."

Murphy leans forward on his elbows, his eyes narrowed in consideration as he nods.

I swallow. "What about the next quarterly meeting? It's the Mikhailovs—it's *our* turn to host." We *have* to host at Mikhailov Manor. We can only escape from there with Kostya's help, and I can't wait another year for that to happen. "I'd like to host it in my home."

"No," Murphy says plainly. "It's too close to your due date in January."

"But I'm due a week before the meeting—"

"And will be in no condition to travel to Russia with a newborn," he says with his eyebrows knitting together. "You'll host from the Vittoris' home. That's final."

I stare at him, willing him with my eyes to change his answer, but after several beats of stone-cold silence and his stubbornly powerful glare, I can see that he's not changing his mind. Not right now. But I know I have to host the next quarterly meeting at the manor, so I'll find a way to get a yes from Murphy. I just need to wait for the right time.

Cordelia suddenly leans forward. "Why do we need to give her any time with the baby at all?" she asks. "I would gladly take over care of the child after Anya gives birth. We won't need her after that. She can be decommissioned like the slave whore she's proven to be."

Decommissioned.

A nice way of saying she wants me dead.

Murphy snaps his head to glare at her. "She's a Mikhailov *wife*. We've been through this, Cordelia. We can't just off her."

"Can't we?" Renata asks with her arms crossed and her eyes burning into mine.

I shift uncomfortably in my seat.

Murphy bangs his fist on the table. "No. We *can't*. That's final. You can't just kill a wife because her husband is dead. If *I* died and you pulled this shit with Stella—"

His head turns a little to steal a glance at Stella beside him. She uncrosses her arms slowly as her expression melts from defiance and frustration to concern and sympathy. The sympathy isn't for me though, it's for Murphy.

His face transforms from angry king to indulgent husband. It's more than a little shocking the way that a single look from Stella has softened him so quickly. He takes a deep, controlled breath, then blows it out harshly. "The matter is *settled*," he says, gritting his teeth. "Renata will continue to coordinate Anya's care for another year. We'll reevaluate at the next O'Shea-hosted meeting."

Renata scoffs and it sparks a sudden fire in my belly. I'm already frustrated that I don't have approval to host the next meeting in Russia, and having her here to react like a child with her derisive noises only fuels that angry flame.

It angers me enough to clap back at her, even though I know it's stupid to bite the hand that feeds me. "Don't be such a bitch about it. Honestly, Renata, the way you behave is so childish. Sometimes I think you need a keeper. Really, Murphy," I say, catching his eyes, "that woman is emotionally unstable. She's lucky she has Lorenzo to help make her decisions because otherwise, she wouldn't know what side of the bed to get out of in the morning."

The men in the room snicker, enjoying my apt assessment of Renata. She and Cordelia are the only ones fuming at me. But Renata's fury is enough to make my spine tingle in warning.

A slow smile spreads across her face and she tilts her head slowly to one side. I feel a chill as she reminds me of the reason why I don't tell her every time I think she's acting like a whiny, entitled jackass.

"Darling girl, your lover still belongs to me," she says.

Ezra is still her slave when he's not my talent.

And she'll use him to hurt me.

CHAPTER 18

Ezra

I SHAKE MY head as I jolt awake—the side of my head that was perched on my fist slipped off when I drifted to sleep. My elbow was on the armrest propping me up, but now that I'm conscious again, I slam my arms down on the rests, pushing myself back in the seat and straightening my spine.

I'm determined to stay awake.

I want to be aware when Renata returns from the board meeting. I want to see her face, study her body language, get a sense for whether things went better for her than they did for Anya. If she comes back happy, then I'll know things didn't go well for my blue-eyed girl.

So, I hope she comes back angry as fuck.

I blink against the darkness. Renata had shut off the lights before she left me and Luca—chained to the floor by a cuff around the ankle—and locked us inside this bedroom. She told us to get some sleep, seeing that these board meetings are held late into the night.

But as tired as I am, I'm not going to sleep.

Luckily, I don't have to wait too long. I hear the click of the lock and in moments, it flings open wide, slamming back against the wall behind it with a thud that makes me jump.

The lights flash on and the door slams shut again. Renata starts spewing out a string of Italian words as she locks the door behind her. Luca springs up out of bed where he was sleeping and moves toward her. I have no idea what the fuck she's saying as he moves to her, putting his hands on her shoulders, stroking her arms in a comforting way.

Internally, I fucking cheer.

Everything about her demeanor screams that she's furious and I'm happy for it—it means my girl owned her shit in that meeting.

I push to my feet and cross my arms over my chest, waiting for Renata to start barking orders at me. If I have to watch her fuck Luca one more damn time, I swear I'm gonna claw my eyes out. As pissed off as she looks, I can't imagine she'll have the interest tonight, though I've been wrong before.

Luca rubs his hand down her hair, stroking the side of her face as she spits out rage-filled words that I don't understand. The poor kid is hopelessly in love with her, but Renata is so hateful, so prideful that she insists on drawing me into their twisted relationship instead of just focusing on the guy who actually gives a damn about her.

Her eyes catch mine during her tirade. She gives Luca an order and he's down on his knees in a second. But he sits back on his heels and bows his head instead of pushing her dress up over her hips and taking off her underwear.

Fuck.

She's coming after me.

She strides across the room and I drop my hands to my sides, fists clenched, skin buzzing with warning.

"Take off your clothes, Ezra."

My chest heaves with a heavy breath. Everything within me begs to resist her order, but I know I can't. She'll hurt me with the electric shock on my collar, but that's not what I fear. If I don't follow her orders, she'll hurt Anya and I will do *anything* to keep that from happening.

I took off my jacket, tie, and shirt from the reception before she left and I'm only left standing before her in my pants. I look down at the metal cuff around my ankle. "Am I supposed to do a magic trick or are you gonna remove the cuff?"

"Luca," she calls him over and he comes.

She pulls a key from her handbag and hands it to him. He bends to unlock the ankle cuff which is attached to a long chain that's bolted to the floor. Luca stands and gives the key back to her. It would never even occur to this sad sap to unlock his own damn cuff because he's so in love with this bitch that he wouldn't dare do something without asking her permission first.

I know the drill and I don't see any point in stalling, so I strip until I'm standing naked in front of her. It's happened often enough now that I've gotten used to being ogled by her.

Used to it, but not fucking happy about it.

Renata tilts her head, glancing down at my crotch. A nasty smirk lifts the side of her mouth and I can feel my nostrils flare with a slow-burning rage as I hold out my hands and narrow my eyes at her.

"What do you want from me tonight? Foot massage? Back rub? Tie you to the bed for fuck boy to use you? Maybe add another scar so you can play with my blood?"

"I'm taking your cock tonight, Ezra." Her hand lands on my chest and her fingers blaze a trail of fire until she reaches my belly button.

I dig my fingernails into my palms, fighting every raging instinct within me to slap her hand away. "Don't fucking touch my cock," I seethe through gritted teeth. "It doesn't belong to you." She steps into me and slaps her palm around my dick, gripping and tugging down to the tip. "Get your hands off me!" My jaw sets as every muscle in my body clenches in tension at her unwanted touch.

I take a step back, but my knees hit the armchair behind me and I fall to sit. She pulls the little black remote from her handbag. "No, don't—" She presses the button that sends a lightning strike of a shock right through me. "Fuck!" I manage to say before seizing from the pain that rips through my neck.

When the shock lets go of its searing hold on me, I slump heavily into my seat. My body goes limp and my chest heaves as I fight to catch my breath. Before I can move, before I can fight, Renata drops to her knees. She grips me around the base of my shaft, licks her tongue across the tip, then sucks me into her mouth.

Shit.

Fuck.

No!

Luca appears beside me and grabs my arm that's as limp as my dick. He wraps rope around my wrist, tying it tight before connecting it to my other wrist until my hands are bound together in front of me.

My limbs are weak from the electric shock, slowly prickling back into awareness. I will feeling to come back to me quicker and I stare at my fingers as I fight against my body for control. It's almost the exact moment that Luca finishes binding my wrists together that my fingers wiggle with intention.

My movements are floppy and gradual, but I manage to get my hands on top of Renata's head to try to push her away. But Luca grasps the rope from where it loops between my wrists and lifts my arms high, pulling them over my head as he moves to stand behind me.

My legs tingle and my muscles come back to life. I thrash in my seat, but fuck if that doesn't just slam my cock deeper into her warm, wet mouth. She moans and the vibration ripples through my shaft, sending an unwanted rush of pleasure through my spine.

Goddammit.

Do not get hard for this bitch.

Don't fucking do it!

Renata is insistent, stroking my base with her fingers, bobbing her head up and down with her warm lips and swirling tongue tugging me into tension that I don't want.

I try.

I really fucking try.

I fight it for as long as I can, but she's relentless.

My cock thickens against my will and I feel absolutely powerless— exactly the way she wants me to feel.

Her mouth finally comes off my cock with a crude popping sound and she looks up at me, her red lipstick smeared from her assault. I'm panting through fury and fear and depraved, forced lust. She smiles and though I want to thrust my knee up into her chin and break her damn jaw, I don't because I know what she's capable of doing to my girl.

She gives me her most serious look, the one that tells me she means business—the look that tells me she's deadly fucking serious and I'd be stupid to cross her. "You're going to fuck me tonight and you're going to come inside me. I've been patient enough with you, but I'm done being patient."

My molars grind together. "Good luck making me." My hands stay high above me, though I lean my head forward, my shoulders tugging backward as I attempt to get in her face. "I don't come for you."

"You only think that because I haven't fucked you yet. But you will come for me. You will come inside me." She pushes her hands up my thighs. "And you'll do it enthusiastically. Because if you don't, I'll hurt her. I'll make you bleed, and I'll make her suffer."

She pushes to stand and my breaths shorten and quicken, my chest heaving as my temper flares, and I fight to control it. She gathers the hem of her skirt, swaying her hips as if she could seduce me. Her fingers slip beneath the hem and she drops her underwear to the floor, stepping out and kicking it aside.

"You stay the *fuck* away from me!" I thrash, yanking my hands with all my might. But Luca is at least as strong as I am, pulling my arms farther behind me, higher above my head, and achingly stretching my shoulders back.

I slump in my seat, trying to sink away from Luca's grip, but I'm not quick enough. Renata climbs over me before I can get away, straddling my legs and squeezing my hips with her knees. She brushes the thin straps of her bright red gown off her shoulders, shoving at the neckline until her breasts are bare in front of my face.

"Shit. Fuck, *no,*" I push my ass back against the seat.

That was a bad move.

Her cunt drags across my swelling dick when I slide backward, and it makes blood rush to my groin.

It feels…good.

But it's only physical.

Emotionally, this is wrecking me.

"Ezra," she purrs, grasping my chin and lifting my head, "if you don't come inside me, things are going to go very badly for you. But if you let yourself enjoy me, then everything will be fine. We'll just keep this our… little…secret. Your precious Anya never has to know." She dips her head, kissing me as I purse my lips against it. "What will it be?" She licks her tongue across the crease of my lips, and I cringe.

"Do whatever the fuck you're gonna do. I don't believe for a second you won't tell her anyway. Your promises mean nothing to me."

"Hmm," she tilts her head, "you're probably right." A twitch forces a crooked smile to her face and she shifts her body, twisting her hips, brushing her cunt across my tip, and wiggling her way onto it. Once the tip is wedged inside her, she sits down hard on my cock and I lose my mind. I try to pull back, to get away, but moving my body only thrusts me within her, spurring her on.

"Get the *fuck* off me!" I scream at her, horrified. Completely unexpected tears well and glass over my vision. "I won't do this to her! Don't fucking do this—" My teeth grind and I tense up as she rocks back and forth with me deep inside her.

She moans as she uses me, nuzzling her cheek against mine. "All you have to do is enjoy it. That's all. Come while you're inside me and no one has to get hurt. No one needs to know."

I don't believe her.

I *can't* believe her.

She's full of shit, full of lies.

I want to throttle her. I want to choke the life out of her with my own two hands and break her in all the ways our lives have been broken by the four families.

This is a stupid plan on her part.

I can win this.

All I have to do is hate this. If I can just keep hating this, she'll get bored and she'll stop. I put all my attention and focus into thinking of things that are undeniably unsexy. It's not hard to do given everything we've been put through.

Renata raises and lowers, arching her back as she swirls her hips and plays the part of the seductress. She plays it well. She's a damn cougar— experienced and confident—and it makes me physically ill. It's like she's been trained to do this, to work unwilling men into a frenzy, turning them into begging, hopeless shells of their former selves. I don't want to be a begging, hopeless shell, but my balls feel tight and my cock is hard as a rock with the way she moves.

"Stop. Fucking. *Moving*," I hiss through gritted teeth as I try to yank my hands away from Luca—though the attempt is useless with the way my shoulders strain.

"No." Renata bends, pressing her lips to my throat and licking her tongue across the spot.

I groan, both from the unwanted feeling of pleasure it drives and from the strain of fighting pure physical, sexual need. It takes every ounce of my concentration to fight this. She injected my heart with black venom and it surges through my veins, infecting me with dark lust that poisons my senses. I squeeze my eyes shut, trying to imagine my heart pounding, reversing the venomous flow, the black liquid drawing back from the very ends of my veins and turning my heart black as night.

But Renata rises and falls. She moans and gasps and pants and makes sinful noises against my ear. She nibbles at my earlobe and tugs on it with her teeth and fuck, I see Anya in my mind doing the same fucking thing. It drives me crazy when she does that and now, she's in my head.

Get out of my head, Anya!

Shit, shit, shit.

The black poison gushes from my heart, pulsing through my veins, masking any color, and coating my blood in the pitch-black toxin of pure aching need. It's a lost cause from the moment Anya's face and her captivating blue eyes pop into my mind—the moment I see her, I'm lost, because the mere thought of her erases everything bad.

"You're gonna make me come, Ezra," Renata whispers and her words twist in my gut.

"Stop it…*Stop!*" I demand and then I groan.

Fuck. I can't stop this train wreck.

My voice turns to a hopeless, aching beg for her to stop. "Renata, please…"

But she only hears my begging and interprets it as me wanting her to do this. She becomes a rutting, desperate animal, a true fucking cougar in the wild taking down her prey—*me.*

And she really is taking me down because I feel all the blackened, poisoned blood in my body rush to my groin. I feel the familiar tightness coiling low and deep, tugging through the base of my cock, and I know it's going to happen in seconds. She's going to win. These few seconds of knowing are the most painful because I'm about to come inside a woman who isn't Anya.

Renata squeezes everything—my hips with her knees, my cock with her pussy, my heart in her fucking hands—and she gets exactly what she wanted from me.

I come inside her with a groan filled with heartache. My body feels incredible but my soul tears in two. As Renata comes from the pulsing waves of my swelling cock as I orgasm, nausea sets in and my body trembles.

I feel sick.

I feel disgusting.

I feel shame and guilt like I've never felt before.

I feel violated in a way I never thought possible.

Is this what Anya felt every time she was raped?

As soon as I think about it, tears creep down my cheeks and a broken sob escapes me. This is vulnerability in its rawest form, and though I despise the way it makes me feel, my breakdown is because of what I feel for my blue-eyed girl.

Renata climbs off me when she's done. She smooths down her gown and covers her naked chest as she pulls the straps back onto her shoulders. She bends and grabs my boxer briefs from the floor, tossing them at me carelessly as she slinks across the room to straighten her appearance in the mirror.

My heart empties of substance and collapses in on itself, sinking inside me like a black hole. It feels like a void that all the best parts of me circle around, constantly in threat of being sucked inside it and lost forever.

Did Anya's heart hollow out like this every time they raped her?

My girl is the strongest person on the face of this Earth. She's survived against insurmountable odds. She's stared death in the face, and though she's been tempted to chase it, she's found a way to stay strong and endure the shitshow that was forced upon her. She survived through this awful feeling of rawness, brokenness, hopelessness—and still found a way to love me.

She loves me.

But I don't deserve it.

Luca drops my bound hands after Renata gives him a quick nod. I grab my underwear in my lap and stand, pulling it on as quickly as I can because I urgently need that barrier of protection. I never would've thought that underwear could be this damn important to me.

"I suppose you were right," Renata says, turning around to face me again. "I think I will tell Anya about what we've done. I'm sure she'll enjoy knowing you came inside another woman."

She chuckles and a burning rage rinses away my own pain in favor of delivering it to her. Before I can think about the consequences of my actions, I charge for her. I hear Luca shout at me, but I'm faster than he is. I barrel into Renata's back, shoving her down to the floor. She manages to roll from her stomach to her back before I slam to my knees, straddling her tiny waist.

My hands are still bound at the wrists, but that doesn't stop me from wrapping my fingers around her throat. I want to snap it in two. I squeeze hard in my rage, my thumbs finding the hollow of her throat and pressing down hard. I hope I collapse her fucking windpipe. She gasps and writhes beneath me, her eyes popping wide as her slender fingers scratch at mine, trying to claw me away.

I throttle her until I can't anymore, until Luca rips me away from her and slams me to the floor instead. I kick and swing my arms. My bound fists collide with the side of his face, knocking him sideways to the floor. I scramble to get up, to get to Renata in my blind rage.

But then lightning strikes through my neck, the shock of my collar seizing control of my limbs as Renata presses the button on the remote she got to just in the nick of time. She holds it down, longer than she ever has before, ensuring that my body is nice and limp so she can control me.

I'm still on my back on the floor, watching her huff and puff to catch her breath as she stands above me. I don't know if my face muscles are responding yet, but internally, I smile seeing the red marks on her throat and the spots that will turn into bruises before long.

She clears her throat. "Lorenzo," she says to herself. "Luca, take him in the hallway."

Shit.

She storms to the door, flinging it open wide, marching out of the room, screaming, "Lorenzo!" before pounding on his door, which I know to be three doors down the hall.

Luca grabs beneath my arms, dragging me along the carpet as he spits out a string of words in Italian—I don't have to know the words to know that he's cursing at me.

My limbs start to tingle as feeling slowly comes back as I'm dragged out into the hallway to face Renata's wrath. The hallway quickly fills with people hearing the commotion and suddenly, I feel small.

Renata Vittori has stripped me of my pride, my self-worth, my confidence. And as my eyes lock on Anya's coming from the far end of the hallway with a look of shock and fear on her face, I feel utterly undeserving of her love.

CHAPTER 19
Ezra

"RENATA!" ANYA YELLS from down the hall as she charges forward with her hand on her stomach. She looks ethereal in that blush-colored gown which sweeps the floor as she comes toward us.

I can wiggle my fingers and toes now, and I'm slowly getting feeling back in my arms and legs.

Anya lifts her chin a little higher and pulls her shoulders back as she meets Renata in front of Lorenzo's closed door. "What are you doing with him?"

Renata's head whips to the side to look at her. "I don't answer to you, you self-righteous slut."

Adrenaline kicks up, urging my limbs to wake the fuck up so I can fight for my girl.

Anya's eyebrows draw together and she steps closer to Renata. "You have no right to talk to me like that. I am your equal now by name alone."

Renata turns toward Anya, stepping close enough to touch her baby bump. "My dear, you have never been anything but a slave and a whore. A warm body for Nikolai to fuck, one who happened to have a pretty face and a talent for dance."

It's a good thing I can't get up because I might beat the shit out of Renata if I could. But Anya doesn't need me to defend her. She's strong enough on her own, stronger than me.

"If that were true, then why did Nikolai go through the trouble of arranging a secret marriage with me? You're just angry you've met your match in me, that you've taken on a new slave boy who prefers me to you." Anya cocks her head to the side.

"Ezra *is* mine when he's not your talent," Renata insists. "He is a slave that Murphy put in my care. I make his rules and you know that."

"Yes, you're right. You don't have the power of a Head of House, so you take your orders from an Irish man a decade your junior." Anya smiles.

"Thank you for the reminder."

"Ezra's time here is over," Renata says with an eerie level of calm decisiveness.

My time here is over.

She pounds on Lorenzo's door again and he finally comes to answer, opening it wide. He and Renata argue in Italian as I start to move, slowly working to get myself up off the floor. Luca sees me moving and grabs beneath my arms again, hoisting me into position on my knees. He hisses in my ear, telling me to stay put. I do because I don't feel I have enough strength yet to get to my feet—it's not like I could do anything if I did as I'm quickly becoming outnumbered here.

Renata and Lorenzo's voices raise, and his girl Olivia appears beside him, asking in English about what's going on.

"Stay in the room," Lorenzo tells her as they both disappear from the doorway.

"Wait, what are you doing?" Olivia's voice sounds frantic out of sight and soon after, Lorenzo appears in the hallway with Renata.

Holding a *gun.*

"What are you doing?" Anya demands, rushing to stand in front of Lorenzo, bravely putting herself in his path toward me. "Stop! What are you doing?" She puts her hands on his chest to shove him back and my heart stops.

"He raped her," Lorenzo tells Anya, looking down at me with spitting fury. "He attacked them and *raped* her." Anya's mouth drops open in surprise.

"You lying, bitch," I utter under my breath, pissed but not surprised that Renata would pull a stunt like this to get me killed.

Lorenzo glances down with a furrowed brow at Anya's hands on his chest. "Get your hands off me."

"Give me the gun. I won't let you hurt him," Anya demands, shoving at his chest.

He whips his free hand around and snatches hold of her wrist, squeezing it tightly and holding it up between them. "I said, get your hands off me."

"Don't touch her!" I shout, my heart jumping into overdrive and fearful nausea rolling through my stomach.

Anya freezes in his grip and I know why—because I see what she sees.

Lorenzo's face has shifted and suddenly, he looks like Vigo. He holds the same unraveled expression that shadows the features of his face—the same vicious fire that would burn in Vigo's eyes. It's the same violence, the same brutality, the same disengagement from his humanity.

Vigo still haunts her through the rage of his family.

Lorenzo tosses her hand aside and slips past her, coming after me. I flinch when he starts to raise his gun, but terror grips me as I watch Anya step after him again. I shake my head at her furiously. "Anya, don't—" I start to say as she lunges for Lorenzo.

She reaches and latches her fingers around his wrist—the hand that holds the gun he was just starting to lift. She pulls back on his arm viciously, but is forced to let go and jump back when he whips around, shaking her grip from his wrist, and aiming the gun at her head.

She screams, throwing her hands up in front of her face as she sinks at the knees. The memory of Nikolai holding her at gunpoint just before he sold her to Vigo flashes across my mind and my body trembles with a pulse of adrenaline. "No!" I shout.

But then Lorenzo swings the gun around aiming at my head. My eyes widen as I watch it all happen in a blur.

He presses the barrel to the center of my forehead.

He cocks it…and pulls the trigger.

.

.

.

.

.

A click, then silence.

Silence from everyone except for Anya's piercing scream.

I gasp for a breath. If it weren't for the authenticity of my blue-eyed girl's scream, I'd believe I'd died and gone to hell—the same hell I've been living with the four families.

But I'm not in literal hell. I'm alive because the gun misfired. A violent sob bursts from Anya with her eyes squeezed shut. But then I see her features soften as she realizes she didn't hear the gunfire, either. I stare her down, willing her to open her eyes and look at me because I can't stand to see her this broken.

I can't die. I can't leave her here alone.

Lorenzo swears and Renata yells at him. He pops open the chamber to check for rounds and in a flash, Anya is in front of me—she jumps in front of me as a human shield for the next round and my heart disintegrates into ash.

"Anya, move," I plead, gripping her skirt with my bound hands, and tugging to get her attention. "Move, baby, *please.*"

She only shakes her head. "He can't harm me," she whispers. "I'm a Mikhailov." She lifts her chin. Even from behind her, I can see the tracks of tears streaming down the side of her cheek, streaking black streams from her make-up.

Lorenzo pushes the chamber back in and points the gun at her. I can't breathe.

I can't breathe.

"Move," he tells her.

Anya's voice is quiet power as she speaks through gritted teeth. "If Renata wants him dead, you'll have to kill us both." Her hands clench into shaking fists at her sides.

"I'll happily arrange that," Renata says, moving to stand beside Lorenzo.

Lorenzo steps forward, pushing the tip of the gun to Anya's belly, threatening her, threatening me, but more urgently, threatening the baby.

Anya stiffens. A strange sort of fear grips me, and I know she feels it, too—except, hers morphs into a protective fury. She doesn't scream and cower. She snarls, steels herself, straightens her spine, and pulls her shoulders back.

"I dare you," she practically growls at Lorenzo. "Pull the trigger. Kill a Mikhailov and her son and see if that will put you any closer to taking over the family bloodline. We all know that's what you want—for your Fiore name to be the one associated with the four families. We all know that's why you serve Renata the way you do."

His eyebrows raise and lower in surprise.

Olivia defies her order to stay in the bedroom and suddenly rushes out. "Stop!" she cries. "Why are you doing this?" Bravely, she wedges herself between Anya and the gun. She pushes Lorenzo's hand away from her stomach by grabbing his wrist and shoving back on his chest. "Why are you *doing* this? She's pregnant! They're in love, Lorenzo…in love like you and me! Renata's a liar. Why would he rape her? *Stop* this!"

Lorenzo looks at Olivia with a tilt of his head and drops his gun to the floor. The thud of it landing on the carpet makes us all flinch in fear that it might somehow go off. I watch in shock as he shoves Olivia back against the wall by her shoulders, shifting his anger to her instead of toward us. Olivia's eyes pop wide as tears pour down her cheeks and she opens her mouth to defend herself.

"I'm sorry," she says quietly. "I just…Lorenzo…d-don't hurt them." She puts her hands on his chest and grips the lapels of his jacket. "Please. This is insane. I was one of them. They're no different than we are."

There are a few tense moments where all I can hear is the pounding beat of my heart and Anya's rapid breaths in front of me. I think Lorenzo might hurt Olivia—the woman he claims to love.

But then, he sighs, softening for her, melting to her plea. He lifts a rigid finger between them, pointing it at her with intention. "Don't *ever* come between me and my gun like that again. Do you hear me, *amore*? I could've killed you."

"I won't. I won't," she says. "I promise."

He leans forward and kisses her and that's when I snap back to reality. I look at the gun on the ground. I glance at it and when I look back up, I see Renata lock her stare on Anya.

"Get the gun," I hurriedly whisper to my girl.

She doesn't take a moment to think, she just *moves*.

Anya and Renata both lunge for it at the same time. I hold my breath as Anya drops to her knees. Unable to bend at the waist to grab for it, she clambers on her hands and knees to get it. Anya reaches out, and just before Renata gets there, Anya grabs the gun. She raises it and cocks it, sitting back on her heels and aiming at Renata.

Her hands don't shake. She's as steady as steel. "I want Murphy O'Shea here. *Now*," she demands.

"Put the gun down, Anya," Renata says to her, backing away.

Anya's finger hovers over the trigger and I know she itches to pull it, to end Renata's life like she ended her brother's. I'd be proud of her if she did; I'd fucking cheer for her if she did. But I'm also terrified of the consequences if she does it. Her favor with the four families is—as it always has been—on razor-thin ice.

"Get. Him. Here. *Now.*" Anya's teeth grind together as she insists.

Lorenzo could knock the gun from her hand with ease, wrestle it from her without much struggle at all. And I think Olivia being so close is the only reason he doesn't.

Thank God for her presence.

Renata sighs heavily. "Luca, go get Murphy." He turns and runs down the hall.

I want to climb to my feet and barrel into someone, join this attack on Anya's side, but I don't dare move. She's got the gun and she's got *this.* I trust her, now more than ever, and I sense that she has a plan to get us out of this.

Shit.

I'm fucking lucky that gun misfired the first time.

I could be dead right now.

Soon we hear Murphy's voice echo from down the long hallway from somewhere behind me. "There'd better be a damn good reason this slave boy disturbed me and my wife."

I look at my blue-eyed girl on her knees a few feet in front of me in her lace and tulle gown, her gorgeous dark hair tumbling in soft waves down to the middle of her back, pointing a fucking gun at Renata Vittori. She's never looked more powerful as she does right now.

I can only imagine what this scene looks like to Murphy as he comes closer to us. A pregnant Mikhailov wife holding a Vittori hostage in front of a slave with his hands bound in rope, kneeling in his underwear. It must be intriguing, at the very least.

"Anya demands to speak with you, Murphy," Renata says as he approaches.

I turn my head to see him just a few feet away. He stops abruptly beside me. "Are you fucking—" He groans. "What the fuck is going on here?"

Anya speaks to him but doesn't dare turn to look at him, still aiming the gun at Renata. "Renata has attempted to kill the Mikhailov talent slave. She claimed he attacked and raped her, and I know she's lying. I will *not* have it, Murphy. There is no replacement for his talent, and we will *not* break the tradition of the four families just before my turn to host the quarterly meeting because of her false accusation. It's…" She nearly falters, but I think I'm the only one who notices it—she speaks in half-truths, trying to explain her motivations within a context that these vile creatures would understand. "This is my chance to prove myself worthy of my name, and I will not have her taking the life of our talent slave over a lie. It's unacceptable."

"You're quite the princess, aren't you?" Murphy says with a frustrated huff.

"He raped me, Murphy. He attacked me and Luca and then he raped me! I want him *dead*," Renata says it to Murphy, but her eyes never leave Anya. This whole thing is about Anya because Renata wants to hurt her.

"Oh, fuck off," Murphy says with a look of incredulity. "We both know that's not fucking true. This isn't the first time you've cried wolf to get a slave killed."

Renata looks insulted and I almost want to laugh. "I never—"

"Shut your mouth, Renata. Our family has been putting security cameras in Vittori family guest rooms for over a decade of meetings that we've hosted. Your family is always causing problems. Keep talking if you want me to go look at the footage from your room. Always fucking causing trouble, fucking Vittoris."

Her wide-open mouth clamps shut, and she turns her head away.

Murphy rubs his hand over his beard. "Well, fuck. This is going to end disastrously if I send you back home with her now."

I watch Anya's chest fall as she lets out a slow breath and though she tries to keep her tone even and her words steady, they come out hurried and insistently. "Let us stay here…under the care of the O'Sheas. I no longer feel safe with the Vittoris. If she puts Ezra's life at risk, the stress it causes me could be detrimental to the health of my baby. The four families can't afford to lose my child. Give me and Ezra shelter here and send the Vittoris home tonight. The safety of the Mikhailov heir has been threatened."

"I've made no such threat to your child's safety!" Renata charges forward, but Anya lifts her gun higher, with more confidence. "You're the one pointing a gun!"

"A gun you meant to have Ezra killed with! A gun Lorenzo nearly shot me in the stomach with because of your lies!"

"Ladies," Murphy interjects, pinching the bridge of his nose, "I'm not in the mood for this bullshit."

"*Please*, Murphy," Anya pleads gently. "I've been through enough. You wouldn't put Stella through what I've been through. Don't put me through more."

Murphy looks up, his eyes falling on the back of Anya's head. His face looks somehow kinder, but there's also a look of confusion, as if he's just figured something out that shouldn't make sense. "If I say yes, will you put the gun down?"

"If you say yes and arrange for Renata and Lorenzo to leave tonight, then I will put the gun down."

Renata points her finger in Murphy's direction. "I approved your bride as a favor, Murphy. Stella was never fit to be one of us, but I gave my approval because you asked me for it. You *owe* me." She turns her finger to me. "Kill Ezra and do it *now*."

I feel the shift in his energy from calm negotiator to all-powerful king. "I owe you *nothing*. We both know that giving you women first approval rights on brides is just a social nicety." He chuckles darkly. "Do you honestly believe I wouldn't have married her if you'd said no?"

Renata seethes, fury rippling from her in waves.

"This has gotten out of hand," Lorenzo finally says. "We'll leave now, but I want my gun back."

"Anya," Murphy starts, "give him his gun and go back to your room."

She shakes her head. "I'm not giving anyone this gun until my talent slave is away from here and his safety is assured."

"Christ." Murphy sighs. "Call your pilot to be ready for departure within the hour. I'll bring your gun when I have them settled." He shakes his head. "You Vittoris cause so much fucking drama."

Shock and rage clamber for control of Renata's features as I feel the burden of fear slowly lift from my shoulders.

Anya slowly, gradually lowers the gun, but she refuses to give it up.

CHAPTER 20
Anya

I HOLD MY position on my knees, gun in hand, aimed at Renata. At my insistence, she sends Luca to her room to get the key to remove the padlock and Ezra's collar. I wait until it falls free from his neck and lands heavily on the floor before I lower the gun. But I don't give it up. Not yet. I hold it tightly in my grip until Murphy has led Ezra and I back to my room and he shuts the door.

Murphy holds out his palm. "Hand it over, lass."

"Where will he be staying?" I'm not giving up this gun until I know Ezra will be behind a locked door that Renata and Lorenzo can't access before they leave.

Murphy sighs. "Am I going to regret it if he stays in your room?"

My pulse thrums with unexpected hope. "You would let him stay with me?"

"It's probably against my better judgment, but since my home is a fortress and there are extra security measures in place while my wife…adjusts to her new lot in life, I'll allow you to keep your talent slave for now. Do you have any plans to point a gun at my head?"

I swallow. "No." As a show of good faith, I hand him the gun.

He takes it with a sigh. "Fuck, I've gone soft. Listen," he points his finger in my face and I lean back from the intensity of it. "I'm only doing this for you because Renata is on my last fucking nerve. If you test me, you *will* regret it. If you behave yourselves, then we won't have a fucking problem. Understood? There is no escaping my home, so don't even think about trying."

I nod. "Understood."

Murphy turns and walks toward the door, then stops and spins back to us, looking at Ezra. "Do you understand what's at stake here, slave boy? You step out of line and try to cross me, and I will hurt you in ways you never imagined."

"Yeah, I get it," Ezra says.

Murphy gives him a once over. "I really hope you do." Then he looks at me pointedly. "Watch him. You're responsible for his behavior. He fucks up, *you've* fucked up. And you know I'll make you pay for it." He turns the knob and pulls the door open. "Lock this," he says before he slams the door shut behind him.

I practically run to the door, turning both the lock on the knob and the deadbolt above it. Then, I press my back to the door and take what feels like the first breath since I saw Ezra lying there on the floor, facing Renata's wrath in the hallway.

Our eyes meet and my heart aches at the look on his face, at the sight of him trembling and terrified.

Oh, God.

What did she do to him tonight?

He doesn't just seem frightened for me as he always has been—he looks tortured in his own right. We both move at the same time and meet in the middle of the space between us, nearly colliding. I reach for his bound wrists, my fingers instantly threading between the knots to free him.

"Are you okay?" I ask, my fingers working frantically to loosen the knots, but they're tied so tightly.

"No. No, I'm not fucking okay."

"I'm sorry," I tell him, though I don't know what I'm apologizing for.

"I didn't rape her."

"I know that, Ezra. I know. What did she do to you? God, what happened?"

"I need a fucking shower. Fuck. Are you okay?"

"I'm fine. I just..." my voice cracks, "he pulled the trigger on you and you would've died if it hadn't misfired." I manage to free one of the knots and focus my attention on pulling the long length of rope through the loop, rather than let the reality of that truth sink in.

A tense, terrified silence falls between us as I work quickly to undo the heavy knots. It feels like it takes me forever to pull them free. His wrists finally separate with the knot I've just undone, but the rope is still tied to his right wrist. As soon as he's able to pull his arms apart, he shoves my hands away and throws his arms around me. The dangling ends of rope whip around to lasso me to him.

"I thought I was dead," he whispers. "I thought I was dead, and I left you behind."

His words grip me and shake loose the tears I've been holding back. I press my face into his bare chest and let them fall free. "That was terrifying. I've never been more afraid in my life."

He half-sobs, half-chuckles as he kisses my hair. He pulls back to examine my face with his hands holding my cheeks. "Never? After all you've been through?"

I blink up at him and it's hard to see him clearly with the gloss of tears clouding my vision. "The thought of losing you, of living this life alone without you…it's the most frightening thing I can think of."

He bends and kisses my forehead before clutching me in his arms. I feel him shake. I feel the heaving of his chest as he cries, though he tries to hide it from me, muffling the sounds with his face nuzzled into the side of my neck. It threatens to shatter my aching heart, but I find my strength in his sadness, too. He's been strong for me so many times before and I want to give him this, give him my strength so he can fall apart here with me.

For the moment, we're safe.

Safe and together—a rare, precious moment for us to find in this world.

A minute or so passes before I quietly ask, "What happened with Renata?"

His body goes rigid. He pulls back and slips from my grasp. "I need a shower." He spins away, heading for the attached bathroom through the open door behind us.

I follow him but stop in the doorway. He marches straight toward the glass-enclosed shower, pulls open the door, and steps inside, still in his underwear. He closes the door shut behind him and my breath catches in my chest at the immediate separation he creates between us.

I move forward—stopping in front of the glass door—and watch as he rips off his boxer briefs, turns on the water, and dips his head under the flow. The rope still wrapped around his wrist looks heavy the way it hangs as he lifts his palms to press against the tile in front of him. He looks so troubled, so conflicted, but worst of all, distant.

I can't stand it.

I can't stand to have a barrier between us after what just happened.

When Lorenzo pulled the trigger on him, I thought I'd lost him forever. I don't even have words to describe the kind of primal, raw pain that tore through my soul as I stood by watching helplessly.

No.

No separation between us.

I kick off my shoes, tear open the glass door, and step inside the shower before he can protest.

I slip between him and the tiled wall where the waterfall spills down on me and soaks my dress. I flinch and tense up as the water rolls down my back—just as I always do anytime water touches me now—but I force my bravery for him because he needs me. I would jump into the ocean to save him if he were drowning.

"Don't shut me out," I tell him.

"Anya—"

"Don't. I don't know what she did to you. I don't know how she hurt you. But you can't avoid me. You *can't.* I need you to need me."

He stares down at me, his eyebrows slanting toward his nose as his eyes burn me with his mystical green flames. His voice is gruff and quiet and haunting. "She fucked me and made me come inside her and I've never felt so…"

Oh, God.

I don't know why that shocks me, but it does. I fall back, leaning against the wall behind me for support as I look up at him with the truest empathy.

I know what he feels.

I know there are no words fitting enough to describe it.

"Do you hate me?" he whispers with a tilt of his head.

"I *love* you." I can't get the words out fast enough. "Ezra, I love you, always. I'm so sorry."

He shakes his head, stepping in close, taking my face in his hands and pressing his forehead to mine. "I don't deserve you."

"Yes, you do. You *earned* me. You're mine. *Mine.* Not hers."

His hands slip down the sides of my neck, grazing my skin and landing on my shoulders. "Yours," he says, though it lacks conviction.

Does he feel unworthy?

"Say it again but mean it this time."

He sighs. "I want to be yours."

"You are mine. You *are*. Tell me you're mine, Ezra."

His eyes press shut, his face pulling tight, revealing the pain he feels from what Renata did to him. "Did you hear me, Anya? I came for her… *inside* her. How can you still call me yours? I wasn't strong enough for you. I couldn't fight it…I couldn't control myself."

I slam my hands against his chest and shove him back, pushing hard enough that he hits the wall behind him. His mouth drops open in surprise as my eyes narrow on him.

"For all the times Nikolai raped me and made me come for him when the *only* man I ever wanted to come for was you. Was I not worthy of you then? Did you disown me in your mind because he made my body do things my heart didn't want? Did that make me weak? Should I have fought my body harder when he demanded I come just to avoid painful punishment?" I shove him again. "How *dare* you say that to me?"

I turn away, flinching as the water splashes onto my face and I instinctively gasp for air. My body suddenly feels heavy, weighted down as if I were surrounded by water, drowning in it.

Take off the stupid dress.

I reach behind me for the zipper, but in my agitation, my fingers struggle to find it. I fumble and the fumbling quickly turns to urgency to remove the weight of the soaked layers of tulle and lace.

Just as my anxiety ticks up and my nerves spark, threatening a full-body blaze, Ezra's fingers find mine. He gently pushes them aside as he pulls the zipper down to my waist. I start to step forward, away from him, but he stops me with hands on my shoulders. He tenderly guides the long, lacy sleeves to slip down my arms, his fingers trailing behind the fabric across my skin. My breaths quicken at his tender touch and I'm frozen in time as he steps in close, bending to kiss my shoulder lovingly. His touch washes away my anger and pain.

"You're right," he says. "I'm sorry. You have to know how strong you are in my eyes. I never once thought you weren't. I never once thought you didn't fight enough. You fight every goddamn day—for you, for me, for the baby." His lips sweep in closer to my neck and he nudges the dress down, urging it to slip free from my hips and tumble onto the tile beneath our feet.

I'm left only in my strapless bra and panties. "When it was happening and I couldn't do anything to stop it…I felt defeated. I felt ashamed. Embarrassed. Broken. I felt things I couldn't even put words to. I'm in awe of you. You are the strongest woman alive."

"The courage it takes to let your body have control of you, to betray your own heart and soul because your master demands it of you. It's—"

"Fucking horrible."

"Tell me you're mine and *mean* it." I feel breathless waiting to hear it.

"Anya, let me prove it to you. I need…" He hesitates as his arms fold around me, hugging me closely from behind. "I can't stop thinking about it… about what she made me do. And the thought that I might've died tonight without one last chance to hold you, kiss you, make love to you—" his voice cracks and so does my heart. I can't bear to hear him in so much pain.

"Forget everything," I begin quietly, lifting my hands to grip his forearms draped across my breasts. "Forget where we are. Forget *who* we are. Forget about time and fear and death. Forget it all and just love me tonight…worship me. Show me how much you love me in all the ways you need to and replace everything that happened to you tonight with our love. Forget it all and make these memories with me."

I'm panting by the time I finish and he is, too. It's hard to be patient with this much wanting between us—it's hard to wait for him to touch me, to kiss me, to lead me into the physical connection we both so desperately need.

But I wait.

I wait with nothing more than the sounds of the waterfall and our uneven, heavy breaths surrounding us.

It's peaceful here and that's strange for me.

Showers are anything but peaceful anymore—the sound of the running faucet usually brings chaos and anxiety into my mind. But the sound of it now, here in this moment where I can breathe, alone with the man I love and safe for now…It's nothing but peace.

I lean into his embrace, resting my head back against his shoulder. The steady rise and fall of his chest sways me into a tranquil calm that I don't think I've really felt in years. We've never been told we could be alone together. We've never been given that permission, that time, that space. There's never been a moment of our love that wasn't rushed and urgent and dangerous.

He kisses the side of my head over and over again, softly, chastely. I cherish the sweetness of it and a true, happy, genuine smile spreads across my face.

How can he make me so happy amidst such despair?

I'm torn between enjoying the feeling of him holding me like this and wanting to turn around to see his face. But my decision to stay put is made for me as his hands move to my stomach, gently rubbing across my stretched skin. I sigh, loving the feel of his hands on my aching belly. He could almost make this moment feel normal.

But then I'm pulled back with him as he slumps against the wall behind him. When he sighs, I feel it deep within me. He's troubled and disconnected and that hurts my heart.

His lips brush against the shell of my ear. "I want to forget it all and just be here with you. I'm so stuck in my fucking head and I hate it."

I spin, breaking his hold on me and turning to face him. I look up at him and see a new sadness in his soul that I've never seen before. It shadows the brilliant green of his normally bright eyes. I thought maybe he needed more from me tonight, but I see the exhaustion draining his essence. He needs rest and comfort and a single peaceful night amidst the nightmare we've been living.

I grasp his arms just above his elbows and tug, encouraging him to spin around and change positions with me so he's under the flow of water. I want to tell him that I know what he's feeling, that I understand feeling trapped inside your own mind because reality is too much to bear.

But I don't say a word because that's not what he needs.

The O'Sheas have stocked their guest rooms with hotel-style amenities, so there's a small, travel-sized bottle of body wash on a ledge built into the tiled wall beside us. I reach for it and flip open the cap, pouring the silky, white soap onto my palm. I rub my hands together, working it into a lather, and I lift my fingertips to my nose, testing the scent. Satisfied with the clean, unscented freshness of it—knowing it won't mask the natural scent of him that I need for my own sanity—I press my palms to his chest.

I cleanse him diligently, spreading the soap over his pecs, up to his shoulders, and down his arms. When my fingers reach his, he snatches my hands in both of his. I lift my head to look up at him and he's staring down at me with love so intense, it could knock me backward—and it nearly does.

His voice is quiet and steady. "You're the best thing that's ever happened to me."

The air is sucked out of my lungs.

I see the rawness and truth in his gaze. My skin tingles at his honesty, knowing that loving me means being a part of this hell. For the years of abuse and pain and torment I've suffered, his pure, unconditional love for me still strikes me every single time. It's a lightning bolt straight through my heart that shocks my senses.

He drops my hands, grabs my face, and kisses me hard, so hard that his fingers curl around the back of my head and dig into my skin, holding me in place as his lips bruise mine with force.

He holds me there in that aching kiss for beat after beat, drawing in a long breath through his nose—drawing *me* in and taking me from the world around us. My hands find his skin without conscious thought, my fingers curving around the sides of his waist. His skin is slick from the soap as it rinses down his body and my hands slip over it.

My intention was to care for him—to help him cleanse the way he cleansed me the night of our first kiss. He carried me to my room, put me in the shower, and cared for me after the first time Nikolai raped me with his involvement.

I still intend to care for Ezra, but I feel him coming back to life with our kiss and I want him to get lost in this.

We both need this.

I let my hands drift down his stomach and his abs clench at my touch. His lips part, he groans, and our tongues lash. His nails dig into my scalp and I feel completely consumed by him.

My fingers draw lower, gliding down his front, and easily find the base of his cock. I don't care whether he gets hard. I don't care whether he fucks me. I just feel some instinctive primal need to reclaim him as mine. I know it should be wrong to feel that way considering…well, everything.

But I feel it.

So, I wrap my hand around his girth and slowly stroke down. He jerks in my hold, slamming his right palm on the wall behind me and I hear the slap of it loudly against my ear. I pull back, breaking our kiss just so I can look at him. His eyes are half-hooded as he looks at me and I can see the spark of something bringing the light back to his eyes. I stroke again, my hand striking the match to ignite that flame and fuel his fire. I stroke him slow and long, running my thumb over the tip of his cock at the end, making him shiver.

He grows hard and thick in my hand and his arousal triggers mine. I let out a moan on my exhale and his eyes widen in need. He crowds me against the wall, and I stroke him a little faster, grip him a little tighter. We stay this way for minutes, minutes that pass as quickly as seconds, minutes that I wish would stretch on for hours.

His eyes drift shut when I know he's getting close, when his cock is thrumming its own pulse in my grip and a groan rumbles deep in his chest.

"Ezra," I moan to get his attention and when his eyes meet mine, I ask for him to let me reclaim him fully. "Mine?"

His chest rises and falls heavily as I keep stroking, keep dragging him closer to the edge. He bends, his forehead touching mine, his nose nuzzling the tip of mine. I stroke faster.

Just on the edge, his hips jerk forward, thrusting himself harder into my hand. With a gruff voice, raw and stripped bare, he replies, "Yours"

I feel his sincerity. I feel it in my heart, in my soul, in the palm of my hand. His cock swells and throbs in my grip and I gasp at the feel of him, at the look of ecstasy on his face, at the pulse of his soul giving strength to mine.

He cries out when he comes, spilling and dripping over my stomach. I smile, moaning at the feeling of power he gives me. It's a power I can't take from him—it's something he gives me freely and it's something I treasure.

Finally, he smiles, big and bright and entirely disarming.

"Ezra, I love you. No matter what."

He slams me with a bewildering kiss and I'm lost in him.

CHAPTER 21
Ezra

"I WANT TO have the baby back home, at Mikhailov Manor," Anya says.

I drop my fork on my plate unintentionally and the metal clangs loudly against the porcelain dish. Murphy shoots daggers at me with his eyes, clenching his fork with a fierce grip before pointing a finger at me. His eyes narrow at me and he speaks through gritted teeth, "Be *careful*. Those were my grandmother's."

Well, shit.

Who knew monsters could be sentimental?

I raise my palms in mock surrender before making a show of how carefully I'm minding Grandma O'Shea's porcelain dishes. Murphy sniffs and his nostrils flare, and he cuts himself another bite of his rare steak.

I knew Anya was going to bring this up soon, but I didn't know it was going to happen tonight. Kostya's been here with us at the O'Sheas' estate for the past month, and he and Anya have been plotting. I shouldn't say plotting. Anya's been building a friendship with him. She's been successful in that, too, and just within the past week she's been putting a bug in his ear about escaping.

Kostya's come to our side—as fed up with the four families' bullshit as any of the rest of us—and though we can never really know for sure if he's lying, we have no choice but to hope and trust that he's with us…because there is no escape plan without him.

Kostya opened up to Anya, telling her that he really did care about his cousin Nikolai. He told her they'd been close friends, though the context of their relationship had them behaving like employer and employee— and that's because they were. Still, Kostya feels a sense of pride to keep his promises to Nikolai as a friend, and one of those was to keep Anya's heart beating.

He felt betrayed by the four families when he was injured in the escape from the Vittoris last quarter. He told Anya that he was tortured by the

Vittoris' extended family. It went on for hours when the board left to hunt us down at Mikhailov Manor after our escape with Nikolai. He said the board turned a blind eye to the torture because they thought he deserved it for helping Nikolai steal back Anya. But Kostya argued he should've been praised for doing his job and blindly following the orders of his leader, his family's Head of House—it's what he was trained to do, what he was *raised* to do.

But they didn't care, which is why he's now willing to help us escape to spite them, because he's ready to leave, too. At least, we have to trust that he is. I suppose we can't know for sure until we're gone from this nightmare. I have hope that he's truly on our side—with Nikolai and his family gone, he's got nothing and no one else except for the friendship Anya has so carefully curated with him.

And that makes us fucking lucky.

I glance furtively at Anya when I sense her eyes on me, her anxiety growing when Murphy doesn't respond to her. I tilt my head in his direction, urging her to speak up and try again.

"Murphy—"

"I heard you the first time, lass."

I feel the steeling breath she takes from where she sits beside me at the long rectangular table in the dining room. "Then I'd like to hear your response."

He sets his utensils down on his plate, folding his hands in front of him with his elbows on the table. It's unusually quiet in the dining room tonight. We're expected to be here for family dinners every Sunday and Wednesday night. But Murphy's parents are gone on an anniversary trip to their vacation home in Portugal and they took the O'Shea talent slave with them—and I honestly don't care to know why.

And today, it just so happened that his brothers needed to leave on important family business—a routine maintenance check at one of their factories. That sounds so innocent outside of context, but really, it means that they were popping in to do a surprise inspection of their *human assets* at one of the warehouses where they keep women they've kidnapped to sell. Kostya is off doing the same at one of the Mikhailov factories—factories that now belong to Anya. Thank fuck they don't expect her to do that. I'd surely have their blood on my hands if they tried to make her.

Murphy takes his time to chew and swallow. I see his wife Stella's annoyance with him tick as she leans back sullenly in her chair, crossing her arms over her chest. She sits on the far end so they each form bookends to the large dining table—they're as far apart as they can get. The dim lighting and crackling flames in the fireplace behind Murphy add to the uncomfortable ambience of this unusually quiet family dinner.

Murphy swallows and looks down the long expanse of table toward his wife and speaks slowly, almost strained. "Stella. Tell me your thoughts on this…as…a woman."

Stella's forehead wrinkles as she sits up taller in her seat, leaning forward on her elbows and clasping her hands, mimicking Murphy in every sense of the word. "You mean you'd like to hear my opinion as the only other child-bearing person in this room? Since that's all I'm good for?"

Christ, here we go again.

These two fight like fiends all the goddamn time. They're both temperamental as fuck. Anya thinks they both get off on the constant fighting. I think she's probably right.

"That horse is dead, *wife*. Put your damn stick down."

"Then it's a fucking zombie horse, Murphy, because it keeps getting up to rear its ugly fucking head."

"Watch your fucking foul-mouth. I'll wash it out with soap."

Stella tilts her head, a scowl spreading across her cheeks. "Promise?"

Murphy slams his fist on the table and both Anya and I jump but Stella doesn't. I guess she's had a little more time to get used to his temper. Her chest heaves as she takes in a breath and fire burns behind her eyes. It's her temper showing, but there's something else there, too. She feels something for Murphy. I wouldn't have recognized a look like that a year ago—not before I felt the inexplicable, bone-deep connection I found with Anya.

Then something unexpected happens.

Murphy laughs.

I stare at Anya because it's really fucking weird.

"Would you just speak your mind, woman?" he tells Stella.

But Stella's not giving up her fiery rage that easily. Her hands slam against the edge of the table and she pushes back hard, the chair legs squeaking as they scrape against the floor. She stands with ferocity and flips her middle finger with a flippant tilt of her head. "Go fuck yourself, you fucking misogynist pig." She side-steps and storms toward the door.

Murphy's on his feet in a flash, but she's quick, slipping through the exit before he can reach her. Still, he pursues, following her out, and the private dining room door swings shut behind them.

Anya and I look at each other in bewilderment. Then she smiles. "I love that girl."

My grin spreads wide. Anya's smile is like light from a star, burning hot and bright, always heating me and giving me life, even when I can't see it behind the torrential clouds of despair.

She stands and shuffles quickly to the door, standing beside it, leaning toward the frame as if she's straining to hear. She stands still, listening, and I watch her facial expressions shift as she does. She looks back at me, mouthing words I can't make out, but she looks so entertained that it keeps me amused.

I shake my head at her with a grin and she mouths something else, then jumps and rushes back to her seat beside me. She plants her ass in the chair at the exact moment Murphy comes back in through the door. He marches across the room and huffs as he takes his seat. Stella doesn't come back.

Murphy doesn't return to eating, but he looks at Anya pointedly. "I can't let the two of you and Kostya go back to Mikhailov Manor unchaperoned."

Anya perks up. "But you will let us go back? So, I can have my baby there?"

Murphy sighs, but he seems less agitated than before. "You're a lucky girl that I'm trying to win over my wife, who just so happens to think rather highly of you." He slaps his palm down on the table. "She does *not* make decisions on our behalf, let me be fucking clear about that." Anya nods and Murphy continues, "But she made a compelling argument in your favor. We'll leave in two weeks."

"*We?*"

"Stella and I will join you. Frankly, we could use a break from…family pressures. We'll consider it an extended vacation."

"In the middle of the forest?" Anya asks. "In Russia? In January? I'm not sure I'd call that a vacation."

Murphy's jaw ticks, but he maintains his composure. "I'm not explaining myself to you. And you should really think twice about passing judgment when I'm giving you exactly what you want."

Anya casts a furtive glance at me and I see humor in her eyes. "My apologies."

"As I was saying, you can have your baby at home, as you requested. If we leave in two weeks, that will allow you time to get settled in before the birth and give you additional time to prepare to host the quarterly meeting." Anya's due date is only a week before she's supposed to host, with me as her talent. "I think what I'm offering you is more than fair. It's more than I ever would've offered you if Stella didn't give a fuck. Understood?"

Anya glances at me, but I don't even look at her for fear I'll give something away. If our escape goes as planned, we'll be gone after I dance on the night of the quarterly meeting. We won't have to worry about what comes after that. We just need to get to Mikhailov Manor to ensure everything is in place. It's the only place Kostya can help us escape from.

"That's fair, Murphy," Anya tells him. "Thank you for your generosity."

Murphy O'Shea has been fair.

Fair and nearly reasonable in our time here with his family. It would be too easy for Anya and me to settle into our stay here, to become complacent in this new environment where violence has been minimal, and we've been granted the privilege of staying together as master and slave.

I'm a slave to that woman regardless of our place because she owns my heart and soul.

If it weren't for his wife, though, I think things would be different. I've seen how his parents treat the talent slave and obviously, Murphy is the product of their upbringing. But Murphy picked a firecracker of a bride, a woman who he's thankfully head over heels for because he bends to her wishes like a doting husband—even if he fights her every step of the way. Stella is smart, stubborn, and gives a shit about how other people are treated—a fucking lucky combination for us.

Miraculously lucky.

But for us to become content in this nearly safe environment would be stupid. Our fates are yet to be determined, and though the baby has bought us time, there will be another decision coming about Anya and what should be done with her.

We have to escape.

There is no complacent life here.

And our last opportunity is coming.

I'm not exactly thankful to be back at Mikhailov Manor, but I am thankful for this time in the dance studio. Not that I have any fondness for this space on its own. It's just that this studio is the place I first met Anya, the place where I first discovered a passionate hatred for her in her icy coldness, the place where I ultimately fell in love with the truth of her heart and the goodness of her soul.

The once pristinely clean floor now holds the faintest hint of staining that tells the tale of how I dragged Nikolai into this room to die—the brownish-red streaks pull across from the doorway into the center of the room. I didn't want to bring him in here—I wanted to let him die alone in the car at the time—but the human in me felt some tug toward fulfilling a dying man's last reasonable request, even if that dying man was a monster who destroyed our lives.

That was the difference between him and me. We may both have been reckless, impulsive men with flaring tempers, but I still had compassion, and I'd shown him that compassion in his final moments.

I'm struck still as the memory takes hold of me.

Everything changed that day.

Power and alliances had shifted. Anya had been thrust into a role she never wanted, but gratitude was due to Nikolai in some respect—in the fact that he had planned for her to have a future, even if it was without him. It didn't change that he was the fucking devil himself, but it was enough that it makes me feel compelled to spare a moment of reflection before I rehearse in this space where he bled and died.

It's strange, really.

It's strange to feel relief to be back here. After everything that we've been through and everything that's changed, this place is now granting us a small amount of peace. It's a reprieve from the fear and daily torment we suffered at Renata's hands and the uncertainty of continued harmony with the O'Sheas. But it's also comforting to be in a studio to dance again, to prepare a routine for the talent show at the next quarterly meeting, to have something other than overwhelming worry to focus my attention.

We're safe for the moment and a chance for us to escape is on the horizon.

Anya asked to select the music I'm going to perform to for the four families. I can sense some unease with her lately—aside from the constant battery of unease we experience being slaves to these families—and I think it has to do with how oddly the tables have turned.

For three years, she danced as the Mikhailov family's talent. Three different partners, all taken from her, until me. And now, she *is* a Mikhailov, pregnant, unable to dance, and instead, preparing for a dangerous, risky escape from this life that will surely keep us on the run for the rest of our lives.

She puts a song on the speaker, listens for a few counts of eight, then turns it off, scrolling through the playlist again.

"It doesn't have to be perfect," I tell her from where I stand in the center of the dance floor. "The stakes aren't as high as they were before."

She snaps her head around to look at me, the familiar, coldly professional look of our early times together twisting her face into an adorably serious look.

"It should always be perfect," she counters. "I want them to see you like I see you."

I smile, stretching with my fingers linked on top of my head. "Tell me how you see me."

The apples of her cheeks flush a perfect pink as she fights her smile as she looks back to her playlist. "Be quiet. No flirting. They'll hear you." She glances toward the doorway, knowing Murphy is wandering nearby and could pop in at any moment.

"I don't give a shit. Tell me anyway."

She hesitates, bringing her head back around slowly to look at me. "I see you always dancing. Vibrant, strong, *mine*." She smiles more broadly before turning back to the playlist, finally selecting a song.

I grin. "Yours, baby."

She turns back around and walks toward me as the music she selected begins to play. "Listen to this one. I think it's perfect for you."

I reach my hands out for her as she comes to stand in front of me. She's reluctant, but a quick glance over her shoulder gives her enough comfort to see that Murphy isn't standing in the doorway watching us. She's still so afraid of being caught in the act of intimacy, and I can't blame her for all that has cost us before. But I'm *her* talent slave and she can do what she wants with me. She steps closer to take my hands and immediately, I drag her against me, wrapping my arms around her before she can protest.

I sigh with contentment as soon as I have her safe in my hold. "Do you remember when we danced here together in the moonlight?" I ask, spinning her to face away from me and placing my hands on her hips. I kiss her shoulder softly, chastely.

"Do you think I could ever forget? That night was a precious gift to me. The first time Nikolai had allowed me to keep a partner. That night I was happy, full of hope." Anya sighs.

"Look how far we've come. Look at all we've survived. We're going to survive this, too." I lean in close and whisper into her ear, "We're going to be free again. We'll be free from this life. We'll have our own family." I let my hands roam to rub her baby bump.

She spins in my hold to face me again, holding up her palms. I place mine on hers, remembering the time I told her to do this, to listen to the music and feel her movement, to help her break free from her rigidity and perfection to find her soul's expression through dance. We sway together, walking through a few easy steps that we improvise in the moment. She can't do a whole lot right now, but she can do some, and she's all the more beautiful like this.

The corners of her mouth lift with her cheeks in pure joy, the kind of joy we only ever feel when we're dancing together. "It's our own little *pas de trois.*"

A dance performed by three—me, my blue-eyed girl, and our baby.

"Do you think he'll dance?" Anya asks, rubbing a hand over her belly.

"He'll have to if he wants to keep up with us."

I see Murphy come in behind her and I spin her out of a turn away from me. She sees him and comes to a stop.

"Murphy," she acknowledges him.

"I came to watch. I need a break from my wife." Murphy moves across the room and sits on the piano bench, then looks at us expectedly. "So? Are you going to dance or just stand there?"

Anya turns and gives me a final frustrated smile before moving away, going back to the stereo system behind where Murphy sits to restart the song.

I listen to the music and feel and dance as it tells me to. That's the way I've always created my routines. I've always choreographed them myself. But shit, do I miss dancing with Anya. I kind of hated dancing with partners before the mess of this life forced upon us by Nikolai.

Not that I didn't have great partners, but really, it never felt quite right when I danced with them. I was never able to pinpoint why I felt so off about it before. When I danced with Anya for the first time, I knew why. It was because she was the only partner I was ever meant to dance with. There was never a second when dancing with her felt wrong or unnatural or uncomfortable. We'd clicked from the very first count of eight.

I try a few things, some of them work with the music and some don't. Anya guides me, helps me with my transitions from one move to the next. She's the only person whose ever been able to see my failings and help me correct them. I've never known a dancer quite like Anya; one so spectacular with technique and teaching while also being so beautiful on the floor herself.

I wish I could dance with her now.

We'll dance together again one day.

"That was cool, you're a really good dancer," Stella says as she suddenly appears in the doorway, arms folded. "They force you to dance, don't they? Like their singer?" She nods toward Murphy, referring to the O'Shea family's talent slave.

"Yeah," I reply simply as Murphy shoots to his feet and marches across the room to Stella.

Anya leans back against the mirrored wall behind her, crossing her arms and glancing down and away. She knows better than to get involved in a conversation like this with Murphy and Stella, but it's clear it bothers her to stay out of it.

Stella lets her arms fall to her sides as Murphy approaches her. She looks up at him, raising her eyebrows in challenge and cocking her head to the side. "What? Am I not allowed to talk to people? Ask questions?"

Murphy grabs her elbow, turning her, trying to nudge her out of the room. "I expect you to talk to the *right* people, not to a fucking talent slave. You're my *wife*. You're above him."

Stella jerks her arm away from his grip. "I might as well be a slave. You don't let me leave. I get scolded for talking to anyone or asking questions. You leave me alone half the time and won't tell me what you're off doing."

I lock my fingers together on top of my head and spin away, pacing the floor while I wait for Murphy to blow. When I turn back around, I see Murphy grab her chin, yanking her head up to look at him.

My hands smack against my sides and I stomp toward them. Anya pushes off the mirror and shuffles in front of my path, holding up a hand to catch me on the chest before I haul off and knock Murphy on his ass for manhandling his woman like that. Anya gives me an admonishing look before whipping around to face them.

"Murphy," Anya pulls her shoulders back and puts on the Queen Mikhailov voice she's adopted to cope with her current position, "you're in my home and I ask that you find a way to use your words to convey your intent with your wife rather than your hands."

She's so fucking perfect.

I couldn't be more proud of her, though I know Murphy frightens her.

His shoulders stiffen and he stretches his neck from side to side before slowly loosening his grip on Stella's jaw, letting his hand slip down her shoulder, her arm, before releasing her all together. He slowly turns and faces Anya behind him. "Apologies, lass. She tests my patience."

"Something for you to work on, then? I don't imagine your wife desires to be treated like a slave."

Murphy smirks and something strange slips in Stella's expression. "She might," Murphy muses. "We'll let you two get back to it." Murphy spins to face Stella, twirling his finger. She spins to leave and he slaps her butt, making her jump before ushering her out of the dance studio.

What a fucking pair.

A moment later, Kostya appears and there's a long, still moment where we all just look at each other. Then Anya moves, jerking her head to indicate she wants us to follow her, and we do, to the stereo in the corner.

"Are you still in this with us, Kostya?" she asks him in a hushed tone.

"The quarterly meeting is right around the corner. I need to...*We* need to know. Do we really have a chance of escaping?"

Kostya glances behind him. "Yes, but it is risky."

Anya shrugs her shoulders. "It's riskier not to try. I can't risk my baby being raised as one of them, with or without me."

Kostya nods. "I know. I understand. I have a plan."

"You really think it will work?" I ask.

"No choice. It must work," Kostya says.

I reach out to grip his arm, making sure he has my attention. "Hey, your ass will be on the line if this fails. Are you sure about this?" I realize after I've said it that I'm giving him an out. I don't want to give him an out. We need him to make this work.

His eyes meet mine. "Yes. I made promise to Nikolai," he assures me in his broken English and thick Russian accent. "If you stay, they will kill her eventually. I hear things you don't. I owe Nikolai for our friendship."

Anya is a blur, lurching forward and throwing her arms around him. "Thank you. Thank you, thank you."

A tiny smile appears on Kostya's face, but it disappears just as quickly. He gently unwraps her and pushes her back. "There is a camera in here. This will look suspicious. I just came to tell you I have plan. We must leave after you dance, before the board meeting." He nods at me. "It is the only time we can leave without being followed."

Anya looks at me, then back to Kostya. "Then that's when we'll do it."

"You will have baby by then?" Kostya asks glancing at her ever-growing belly.

"I should. He's due the week before." Her eyes widen as she considers something. "Will they let me hold my baby while I'm hosting? Oh, God. Why didn't I think of that before? They wouldn't make me give him to someone else, would they? I couldn't. I won't. What if they want Renata or Cordelia to watch him?"

I press my palm to the small of her back as she rises to a panic.

"No worry," Kostya says in a hurry. His eyebrows furrow with concern and it's directed at her as he steps forward to touch her elbow softly. "They will let you keep him. Mother is important first year...they all know this. After that is what I worry about."

"What if he can't stay quiet when we try to leave?"

"It will be okay. It won't matter once we are off manor grounds."

She nods, his assurance seeming to calm her. Anya has come to trust Kostya, someone I never in a million years would've thought could be on our side. If Anya trusts him, then so do I. It's not like we have much choice.

Kostya quickly tells us his plan and then excuses himself, worried about what this looks like on the security cameras, though we don't really know if Murphy is keeping a watch on those. Regardless, it's not worth the risk of looking suspicious.

With a plan in motion, the only thing left for us to do is prepare for the performance. Everything must look as it normally would. I have to dance as I would if I were dancing for my life—the way that Anya had danced for Nikolai all these years. She'll never have to again, because she has me now and her turn to dance for them is over. Now it's my turn, and I will readily take that burden from her, now and forever more.

I'll dance for her.

I'll dance for the baby.

I'll dance for our future so that today's *pas de trois* with my girl and our boy won't be the last.

CHAPTER 22
Anya

IT'S HAPPENING TONIGHT.

Oh, God.

It's happening tonight.

The escape plan is simple, and I can't help but worry that it almost seems too simple to work.

Our plan is to sneak out of Nobility Hall after Ezra's performance as my talent slave, just after the four families have moved back over to the grand entrance of Mikhailov Manor through the connected hallway. The reception will start without us, as it usually does—that's always been the case with Heads of House and their talent slaves after a performance. The guests will socialize, drink, and eat and generally be too distracted to notice when too much time has passed beyond our reasonably late arrival.

We will already have met Kostya just outside Nobility Hall where he has a car waiting for us. We'll already be driving off the manor grounds, heading for the helipad. And if we're truly lucky, we'll be on the helicopter with the pilot that Kostya has paid handsomely to arrive at the pre-arranged time before the four families realize we've gone.

The helicopter will take us all to the nearest public airport and then we'll part ways with Kostya. We've all decided it's best that neither of us know the other's plans from there.

Ezra and I have cash, fake passports for the both of us and for the baby, and a credit card in Kostya's name. It will be traceable, but it's the only option we have—we can't book a flight without it. Our only hope is that we'll gain enough lead time on the four families to fly back to the States, maybe bribe someone into using their credit card to rent us a car in exchange for cash, and drive until we can't drive anymore.

A simple plan, but still so much room for error and complications. There has been one unforeseen complication that has us all on edge because nature is unforgivably unpredictable.

PAS DE TROIS

I'm still pregnant.

It's a full week past my due date—and I'm in denial. I deny the true nature of the cramps that started early this morning. I deny that they've been coming more frequently, increasing in their intensity, and quickly reaching a point where I can no longer ignore them.

Somehow, I've managed to greet my guests and welcome them. And now I sit in Nobility Hall waiting for Ezra's performance to begin.

Nikolai has cursed me.

I can't think differently when my labor comes a week past due and on the very night we've planned our escape.

Why is this happening now?

Maybe his secrets have cursed this seat, too.

Nikolai always sat right here during my annual performances—the same seat every damn time while I was his talent slave. I always thought it was strange for him to be so fond of this particular spot as it wasn't even the best seat in the house, though I'd never given it much thought before.

But it all made sense the night he died. He'd kept a box of secrets beneath this very seat, a box of secrets that brought me to be sitting here now as the woman who was not just his slave, but his unknowing wife.

Even though he's been dead and gone for months, I can still feel his presence here now. If there were such things as ghosts and Nikolai were one now, I believe he would haunt this place. There's an undeniable thickness in the air tonight and it's oppressive, overwhelming—just the way his living presence had been.

The four families have settled into their seats and it's time to begin. It's not just time to begin the performance, but time to begin our mental preparation for our risky escape from this life.

I wring my sweaty palms together, then place them on my huge belly as Ezra's music begins in Nobility Hall. My stomach feels stretched and tight and it makes me horribly uncomfortable to sit here.

I force my focus to Ezra as he comes out onto the stage, strong and masculine and the perfect specimen of a true performer. I could sit and watch him dance all day, every day, which I intend to make happen in our new reality.

This escape will work.

It has to.

Ezra's costume isn't really a costume at all. He's shirtless, which I'm not ashamed to admit is because of my encouragement, and he's wearing a pair of simple, black slacks that fit him loosely, like jogging pants.

Watching him perform feels like nothing short of a miracle. Ezra is power and grace, strength and agility, a mighty force that's perfectly balanced. My hand finds my heart as he dances, and I feel how it beats wildly beneath my palm. It beats for *him*, the same way he tells me his heart beats for me.

Shit.

Another one already.

I can't ignore the pain that creeps in from the lowest part of my stomach, radiating out across my taut skin, a pain that feels like stretching, pulling, kneading, punching. A muffled groan escapes me when it goes on for...

One. Two. Three. Four. Five. Six. Seven. Eight.

Seven full counts of eight.

No.

That contraction was longer and it came sooner than the last two. It was immeasurably more painful, and I don't know how no one around me seems to notice what's happening to me.

This can't be happening.

Not now, not now, not now!

I gasp for air when the pain recedes and grants me a break from the relentless ache and suddenly, Ezra's performance is over.

I didn't even see it because the pain was too great for me to focus. There's a standing ovation for him and I realize I'm the only one still sitting. I'm sure anyone could argue that it's because I'm so massively pregnant, but the last thing I want to do right now is draw attention to myself. Pushing through my hands on the armrests, I get to my feet and I feel a sudden trickle of fluid flow down the inside of my thigh.

What is that?

Am I bleeding?

What the fuck is happening?

Before the fluid reaches my knee, I side-step out of my end seat onto the red carpeted aisle, hoping that if I'm dripping blood—or whatever the hell this is—it will blend with the carpet and I can hide it with my long gown. I can't risk having the O'Sheas step in it and slip on the hardwood floor beneath the seats as they step out of the row after me.

No one can know.

No one can know what's happening right now.

I just have to wait for them all to leave, just like Nikolai always did to protect his secrets.

Everything will be okay.

One. Two. Three. Four. Five. Six. Seven. Eight.

I count as the four families move toward the exit. I hold my head up high, breathe intently through my nose, keep the coldly indifferent expression on my face, though inside I'm screaming and begging for help.

Only Ezra can help me.

Just wait.

Someone touches my elbow and I flinch, turning sideways as Renata moves to stand in front of me. "I look forward to catching up with you at the reception," she says coldly, dark shadows beneath her eyes and a sneer across her lips. She glances down at my stomach. "Olivia had her baby early…last week. Why do you think yours hasn't found his way out yet?"

Because I'm fucking cursed.

I force a condescending smile. "He'll come when he's ready. I don't think you and I need to do any catching up. I don't particularly care how your life has been since we saw each other last." My voice goes up on the last word as pain grips me again. I have to end this conversation quickly. "If you don't mind, I need some time alone with my talent slave. You can head back to the grand entrance with the others. Please, enjoy the reception."

"Don't think that you and Ezra have gotten away from me just because Murphy took pity on you. Your baby is one of us now, and I intend to make certain that's how he's raised."

I swallow hard as my face contorts in pain, though I mask it as barely controlled anger. It seems to work as she gives me a vile grin, satisfied that she thinks she's upset me. I let out a long breath when she finally turns and walks away, marching back up the aisle like she owns the goddamn place.

She can fucking have it.

As she walks away, my hand falls to my stomach as the contraction takes over and grips me entirely. I glance up to Ezra, who is still standing center stage, his chest heaving with his fists clenched at his sides. He's eager to get to me, but he has to wait until she's gone, too.

Somehow, I manage to hold on, to keep my posture, my expression, my composure, as an invisible boulder crushes my stomach. When the final person clears from the house, I reach down with one hand to grip the back of the chair in front of me, folding forward, breathing, and counting through the end of this god-awful fucking contraction. I hear Ezra's footsteps jogging after me as he rushes down from the stage and he sprints down a row of chairs to get to me.

"Shit," he says, "it can't be happening now."

"It is." Nearly a full minute goes by before the pain flows to a gradual stop and I'm able to stand upright. My fingers scramble to gather my layered tulle skirt, clawing it upward to peek beneath—it's the same blush-colored gown with long lacey sleeves that I wore to the O'Sheas' last quarter. "Something's happening. I'm leaking."

"Is it...Did your water break?"

"I don't know. I think it must have." Whatever is leaking from me is clear and I don't know what else it would be. It just keeps flowing in a continuous trickle down my legs.

"Okay." I sense the fear in Ezra's voice, and it makes me scared, too. "This is it, Anya. We have to go. Now. This is our only chance. All you have to do is get changed and get in the car, okay? Can you do that?"

"Yes," I rush out. "Yes, of course I can. I *will*. We have to leave tonight. There won't be another opportunity. I'll wait here. Go get the backpack."

Ezra takes off, jogging up the side steps onto the stage, then disappears behind the curtain. I wait, breathing through the pain, my eyes hyper-focused on the seat of Nikolai's chair beside me.

I'm cursed.

He's cursed me.

Will I ever be able to escape him?

Tears pool in the corners of my eyes as I wait.

All I can do is wait.

Wait for Ezra to return.

Wait for the next contraction.

Wait for success or failure.

Wait for life or death.

I'm terrified. There's no better word for it. It's all happening so fast and I have no control over any of it.

Ezra comes rushing back with a black backpack slung over one shoulder. We've packed our essentials in that single black bag—clothes to change into, cash and Kostya's credit card, our fake passports, some diapers and basics for the baby…just enough to get us through the airport.

That's all we're leaving with—that and hope.

"Hey." Ezra bends and meets my eyes, surely sensing my fear. "We're gonna make it, baby. We can do this together. I've got you."

I hold him there with my eyes for moments longer than we have to spare. But I need this—I need him connected with me. I need the power he always feeds me with his brilliant green gaze.

His cheeks lift as his signature disarming grin appears. "We've got this," he says.

With that and a deep, steadying breath, I find my courage. I nod and rise from my bent position. "Okay. Just leave my change of clothes in the bag," I tell him, "I might have to…The baby might come and I'll just have to take my jeans off again. The dress is easier."

His eyebrows slant toward his nose, erasing his smile as he pulls his clothes from the backpack. "Okay. Yeah, but I need you to put your sneakers on, okay?"

He helps me into my shoes, throwing on a T-shirt for himself and shoes of his own. We didn't have enough room in the bag for winter jackets to fight the bitter January cold, but it doesn't matter. We won't be outside long.

Ezra slings the backpack over one shoulder and takes my arm, guiding me up the red-carpeted aisleway. As I look ahead, to the doors leading out into the foyer, the truth hits me square in the chest.

We're leaving.

We're escaping.

This is really happening.

I'll never have to see this stage and all the horrific ghosts of my past partners again.

At the top of the aisle, Ezra tells me to wait while he pulls open the door to peek into the foyer for Kostya and the all-clear. I turn back for a moment, for one last look at the stage that was built for me, at the place where I danced for Nikolai. I feel the tug of something, a sharp yank on my heartstrings that draws my attention back to Nikolai's seat. When my eyes fall upon that spot, my heart drops into my stomach. I swear I can feel him there—Nikolai.

Cursed.

I want my last look upon this place to be a goodbye and a good riddance, but I still hold that faint sense of gratitude that Nikolai arranged for our legal marriage. Ultimately, it saved me and Ezra and somehow, it led us to this moment where we're finally able to attempt freedom with hope for a future.

"Goodbye, Nikolai," I murmur into the empty space.

I don't feel lighter or heavier for saying farewell to the vacant theater.

Suddenly, there's a crash and then the sound of a door slamming shut coming from the foyer. The sound makes me jump and immediately, I move, rushing after Ezra. If we're caught before we can escape I...I don't know what will happen to us.

I push through the door to the foyer and see Ezra in a defensive position to my left. I look to my right and see Stella, standing with her back to the interior door that leads back to the grand entrance of the manor—the door where all the guests filtered through to avoid going out into the bitter cold.

Stella?

Her eyes are wide and worried. "Where's Kostya?" she asks. "He's coming. Murphy's coming."

At that exact moment, Kostya opens the exterior door from the outside and all of us startle. He looks at Stella and I see the immediate sense of urgency wash over his features.

"Go," Stella says to Kostya. "I can stall him. But you have to hustle." Then, she looks at me and Ezra. "Get the fuck going!"

It hits me hard in the chest when I realize that Stella's helping us. She's putting herself on the line for us to help us escape. I don't know what Murphy will do or how he'll react when he finds out, and he *will* find out. Even when we're long gone, if she stalls him now, gives him the attention he wants from her, he'll make the connection later that she did that to help us.

I want to tell her to think twice. I want to make her understand that she can't put herself in that position. But more pain is sneaking in and I can't. I can't help her. I have to save my baby from this world.

"Come," Kostya says, pushing the exterior door open and motioning for us to follow. "Hurry."

We don't hesitate, we *move*.

The cold spreads around us as we step out into the night, cloaking us in a bitter chill that I somehow find comforting.

Coldness has saved me before, kept me alive, if only in the metaphorical sense. Freezing my heart, shielding it in a thick layer of ice has always given me the power to get through my worst moments, and now is no different. I let the real coldness that swirls around me seep in through my pores and strengthen the icy fortress of my soul to get me through the moments to come.

We use the darkness to hide us as we sweep around the corner of the manor outside to the car Kostya has parked nearby. He opens the back door of the sedan, waving us forward. "Lay down. Cover with the blanket."

Ezra steps forward. "I'll get on the floor. You lay across the seat. It's just until we get past the gate."

"We have to hurry," Kostya urges.

I nod at Ezra and climb in, practically falling across the bench seat, barely able to hold myself upright as that pain that was creeping in before punches low in my stomach. Ezra gets in after me, squeezing himself in on the floorboards. It's a tight fit for him, but he manages.

I moan as the full force of this contraction swells and spreads. My fists clench as I curl up on my left side, facing the front of the car. My eyes pinch shut and nothing exists but pain, pain, *pain*. I push out heavy, long breaths as Ezra reaches up to grab one of my clenched fists and I'm only vaguely aware of his attempt to comfort me.

The agony peaks as Kostya shifts above us, laying a large, black blanket over our bodies to conceal us. Ezra tugs at it, making sure we're sufficiently covered. If a guard wanted to look in the back seat, they would only need to turn a flashlight on us to know there are stowaways here.

But the only thing I can worry about is the pain.

I want to scream.

And I nearly do.

I gasp for breath as it ebbs and Kostya slams our door shut before he climbs into the driver's seat and starts the engine.

"Hang on, baby," Ezra whispers and I want to cry. I wish I could see his face in the dark beneath this blanket. I need to see him. "Hang on just a little longer."

Tears slip from the corner of my eye and I clamp my mouth shut to hide the sob that hiccups from my chest. The car moves forward and I'm scared. I'm scared for our escape and that it will be foiled before we've even had a chance. But more urgently, I'm scared of this pain. I'm scared of how much it hurts and how much more I know it will hurt before the end. I've endured horrifying things as a slave, but this is a fear I never could've prepared my mind to endure. I'm in pain like I've never been in pain before and it's all I can think about.

Time passes and it feels slow, though I know it's only been half a minute or so. We must be approaching the gate about now, but the car isn't slowing. Kostya is speeding up.

He speaks loud enough for us to hear him clearly. "No guard at the gate. It's open." He sounds as cautiously excited as that makes me feel. "It's clear."

It's clear?

No guard?

Why isn't there a guard at the gate?

My mind starts to question it, but my body shuts down my conscious thinking, forcing me to focus on the agony that's taking over. I start shaking, trembling out of control, and I can't stop it.

I feel the car turn. "We're out," Kostya says, and I hear the surprise in his tone. "We're on the road."

We're on the road.

We made it out.

We made it out?

No security stop?

Gate open?

Once I've finally caught my breath from the last contraction, another clutches me in devastating misery.

"No, no, no," I pant as it tightens and pulls and stretches across my belly, wrapping around my midsection and throbbing. It's like being crushed in a vice.

I can't speak through it.

I can't think through it.

The car speeds forward down the road, but our escape plan is lost to me now.

I don't exist.

My conscious thought disintegrates to the torture my body suffers.

Nothing exists now except for pain.

CHAPTER 23
Ezra

WE'VE BEEN ON the road toward the helipad for over twenty minutes and Anya is in agony. Despite the fact that we never expected her to be pregnant for this, let alone in labor, there's a feeling in my gut that I can't ignore—a nagging feeling that everything is wrong.

Fucking wrong.

Anya is trembling out of control and having what seems like contraction after contraction. I feel helpless and I can only imagine how much she's suffering. It makes me sick to my stomach.

We're sitting side by side on the bench seat with seatbelts on because the dirt path cutting through the woods is ice-covered—we've hit a few slick spots along the way, one that spun the car nearly all the way around. Anya's in the middle seat beside me, leaning sideways against me for support as she struggles through her pain.

It was easy getting through the gate at Mikhailov Manor.

Too easy.

There's a cadence of worry that's been continually running through my mind since we passed through and drove away from the manor grounds.

Too easy.

Though there's still the light of hope inside me, I can feel it slowly fade. It scares me because I can't make sense of this feeling, this unease. It's a heavy sense of foreboding weighing on my shoulders and I just can't seem to shake it.

Kostya follows a curve that opens into a straightaway. The car goes up an incline. Kostya reduces his speed as we crest over the peak of the hill, then lets the car roll down the long, gradual decline. I feel gravity tugging me forward in my seat and my grip around Anya's shoulders tightens.

I glance over at her to see her face contorted in absolute agony, her chin dropping toward her chest as she grits her teeth through another shattering contraction. A hiss and a moan escape her and morph into a piercing scream through the last seconds of her recurrent torture.

She gasps for a breath and I can see the sweat on her brow. "Hurry… *please*," she begs.

She *begs*, but there's nothing I can do. There's not a goddamn thing I can do for my blue-eyed girl.

The back tires screech as they catch and skid over ice, tugging the car toward the right. I tense, holding Anya tighter, probably only hurting her more, but I'm terrified to let go of her. I don't want her flung across the car. Kostya's able to correct and ease the car straight again and we continue down the never-ending decline.

Our path is lined with trees—rows and rows of them creating the dense forest surrounding us. The tree line begins only yards away from the car on either side. I look out of the window on my left and it's like looking out to see dark soldiers in the night, threatening to bring war upon us if we venture from our designated path.

The thick trunks are black in the night and they threaten to catch us, stop us dead in our tracks every time the car skids—and every time I'm certain we'll skid off the road and take a beating by one of the monstrous soldier trees. I turn to look at Anya on my right and I see that she's also looking out at them, at the rapidly falling snow that's intent on smothering us from above.

I catch her gaze and even in the dark, her blue eyes are bewitching.

Tell her you love her.

Tell her now.

Tell her fast.

The voice inside me is insistent and urgent, and the instinctual tug of it makes my heart drop into my stomach. I open my mouth to speak, but then Kostya shouts something in Russian, something urgent.

Anya's head snaps forward and her forehead wrinkles in confusion. "Spike strip?"

My chest feels hollow, my heart burning in acid where its sunk deep in my gut. This is it. That feeling that it's too easy, that everything is wrong. It's all going to hell and it's happening right fucking now.

It's unavoidable.

We feel the bump when the front tires roll over something in the road.

Spike strip?

There's a loud blast, quickly followed by another—the car teeters down in the front, then in the back, rocking us as the tires blow. We fishtail.

A fucking spike strip.

"Fuck!" I pull Anya hard into my side with one arm, my other grasping the handle at the ceiling.

We hit a patch of ice after the tire blowout and we spin. My body falls against Anya's, but I try to pull myself away with the handle, tugging her with me as the inertia threatens to throw her to the other side of the car. Her middle seat belt doesn't have a chest strap—only fitting across her lap under her belly—and I have instant regret for telling her to sit there where I could comfort her.

"Ezra!" she screams.

The blown-out tires snag on the edge of the road and the whole goddamn world shifts. Everything happens slowly and quickly all at once, and *fuck,* I think this might be the end of everything.

The car tilts.

It lifts.

It rolls.

It lands upside down and slides toward the dark warrior trees. One of their massive trunks is heading right for us—I can see it through the window on the opposite side of the car…like it's coming after Anya.

It slams into us, metal crumbling and crushing and closing in around us.

A sudden stop.

My head slams sideways against the doorframe.

And everything goes black.

I hear my name, but it's faraway.

A frantic voice is calling to me, but I'm struggling to wake from this darkness. I blink, hoping my eyes will open. It takes a few times, but when they finally do, I'm torn from this strange, dark slumber of nothingness. The voice is still calling to me, but my ears are ringing and it's not clear. I shake my head and though the ringing starts to fade, the movement makes me feel like I'm fucking falling.

I'm still in the car.

There was an accident.

Shit. Anya.

"Ezra! Ezra, *please!*" she says as I turn my head to look at her.

The world looks strange. Her hair stands up straight above her head and it takes me a minute to work out why. It's hard to make sense of things with the way my head throbs.

"We're…are we upside down?" I ask.

"Ezra," she cries. "Help me. I…I think the baby's coming…I feel like I need to push. Help me get out!"

She sounds frantic, unhinged, and desperate.

That wakes me right the fuck up.

My vision is fuzzy, but I act without thinking, ignoring how off-centered I feel. I fumble to find the latch of my belt buckle, but when my fingers find the button, I push and unhook myself without thought. I fall from my seat to the roof of the car and flinch from my landing. Thank God it didn't crush us when it rolled—a fucking miracle. Still, the space I have to work with is tight.

I maneuver myself around and realize right away that there's only one way out of the backseat. Anya's side of the car is curved around the trunk of a tree. The massive base is only a foot or so away from her and the sight of it spikes my adrenaline.

I've gotta get her out.

We have to go out the opposite side, through the door I sat beside. The window is blown out, and I know I can squeeze her out through it if I have to, though I'm hoping to God that the door will open. But first, I have to get her down.

"I've got you," I tell her, reaching up for the seat belt that comes across her lap.

I push the bright red button to unlatch it and she falls. I cradle her upper back and stretch out beneath her to guide her down, trying to ease her fall.

"Ahh," she whimpers, "mmm. I…need to push." I see the strain stretch her features as her body takes control of her.

She's pushing.

She's having the fucking baby.

"Fuck!"

I have to get her out of this car.

I shift her off me, turn, and crawl, reaching for the door latch. I lift it and push on the door, but it doesn't budge. "Shit." I find the lock mechanism and lift it up, praying there isn't some fucking child lock engaged, too. I lift the latch again and shove. It budges. I shove again, then again, and finally, the door slides open. "Thank fuck. Hang on, baby," I tell Anya, but she has no awareness of me or what I'm doing.

I crawl out through the small opening I've managed to create and scramble to my feet. I grab the outside edge of the door and pull back hard, dragging it open as far as it will go. I have to force it as it digs into the ground, hauling snow with it as it drags. I drop to my hands and knees and crawl back in just as Anya's head drops back and she screams.

"He's coming! Hurry, Ezra."

I have enough adrenaline rushing through me to flip the fucking car back over if I have to. I slip my arms beneath her back, grip her by the armpits, and fucking pull. I hear movement from the front of the car as I tug her out—Kostya groaning, the click of his buckle, and the rustle of him shifting from his seat. But I don't have time to worry about him.

Anya's backside runs over broken glass in the snow as I tug her free and I'm kicking myself for not brushing it out of the way first. Her soft pink gown snags on it, some of the tulle tearing away. As I pull her free, I see the left behind patches of fabric stuck to rough edges of the broken window in the snow. I move her to a small clearing between the overturned car and the dirt path we traveled, gently laying her on the fresh blanket of snow that covers the ground.

"Can…can you walk?" I ask, kneeling beside her. Unease rolls a wave of nausea through my stomach at the eerie silence of the forest around us. "We have to meet that helicopter, baby. We're *so* close."

She shakes her head furiously, sweat coating her forehead, though the temperature outside is below freezing. "No…no…I have to—" She presses up onto her elbows, bends her knees, and parts her legs. Her face strains and she drops her chin toward her chest as she squeezes her eyes shut.

She's pushing.

She's pushing and I'm…I'm frozen.

How does she even know what to do?

I'm literally shocked into stillness because I can't wrap my head around what the fuck is happening right now. She throws her head back and screams before gasping for a deep breath. She turns her head to look at me, just for a moment. Her eyes catch mine and she unknowingly feeds me her instinct, her strength, the depth of her courage. Suddenly, I know exactly what I need to do.

I dash back to the car and reach inside, pulling out the large black blanket we hid under to get past the gate. I rush back to Anya as I fold it in half, dropping to my knees at her feet. I wedge it between her legs and lay it on the ground, scooting in close and grasping the hem of her torn and tattered gown. I pull it up over her knees and tear her underwear down her legs, pulling them off and tossing them aside. That's when I get my first view of the nightmare that's happening to my blue-eyed girl.

I can see him.

I can see the baby's head.

How the fuck is she doing this?

"Oh, shit. Okay. Anya, I see his head. There's only one way out of this, baby, and you've just got to push, okay?"

"You can see him?" she pants.

I nod. "Yeah, he's…he's right there."

I watch as her face pinches tight and she groans with another contraction. She takes a deep breath and bears down with all her might.

She pushes for beat after beat, and then she *screams*.

It shakes through the trees and echoes in the dark forest and it completely stops my heart. There's nothing except for her scream and the darkness and the trees and the deafening silence. Large snowflakes drift to the ground all around us. The long beats of silence after her piercing scream reminds me just how alone we truly are. Kostya hasn't made an appearance and we're all alone in this now. All she has is me and all I have is her and the horror of this moment. We're stranded in this forest as she brings life into the world.

She takes another breath and pushes again, her strength and endurance bewildering. I beg my mind to switch away from the horror, to let adrenaline and instinct take over and help me help her—but fuck, this horror is so *real.* The baby's head is moving gradually, little by little, forcing his way out until she stops pushing to take another breath.

"Come on." I try to encourage her. "Come on, Anya. Don't stop. Push. It's almost done, he's coming."

Another breath.

Another push.

Then again.

And again.

His head slips out from the opening and I have no fucking clue how this is physically possible.

"Holy shit. Shit," I mutter, reaching for him, carefully wrapping my hands around his tiny head. "He's almost out. *Push.*"

I tug lightly and somehow, his shoulders slide free as Anya bears down one last time. With a final agony-filled scream, she's done what seems like the impossible. He's out. Her baby. Maybe *my* baby. Definitely *our* baby.

Beats pass in silence.

Silence, deafening stillness as Anya and I both hold our breath. But then a cry from our baby's quivering lips bursts into the night and I feel…I feel… fucking *everything*.

"Blanket," Anya pants out. "Cover him."

I set him down on the blanket between her legs and start to wrap him in it, shielding him from the frigid cold surrounding us. I lift him, wanting to show Anya, but the white snow that was hidden by the blanket instantly turns crimson. Blood rushes out of her, spilling fast and dark.

I look up at her just as her elbows slip out from beneath her and she falls onto her back, her knees slumping to the side as she instantly slips from consciousness.

"No!" I shout, shuffling to her side on my knees, still holding the baby in my arms. "Anya…"

She's still, silent, and I don't know what to do. The adrenaline in my veins spike again, but the frequent ebb and flow is draining me, making the chemical rush useless other than to agitate and cloud my senses.

I wait.

I watch.

I hope for something to happen.

Then she blinks and I gasp with relief.

Her eyes flutter and her head rolls lazily to the side, turning toward me. Her voice is unnervingly quiet. "I…I think something's…wrong." Her eyes roll back before jolting back into focus, but the focus is only there for a few moments at a time as she fights a terrifying sleep that threatens to steal her from me.

"Anya," my voice trembles, "you can't do this now. We're almost there. We've almost made it."

My breath catches in my lungs and my eyes threaten to shed tears that have no business being shed—we're *almost* there.

We were almost there.

"It's close," Anya whispers. She shuts her eyes and blinks out a lonely teardrop that rolls slowly down her cheek. She looks at me with a fierce determination when she opens her blue eyes again. "It's only another mile, maybe two," she gasps. "Cut the cord. Take him. And run."

Cut the cord.

Take him.

And run.

Take him and run.

"No, baby, no. I'm not leaving you here."

"I think you have to. Please. Go. If they catch you…they'll take him. They'll take him and…kill you…and they'll raise him as their own. Don't give them that. Don't let our baby have that fate. Please. *Go.* I can't go with you."

"You can't go with me? You have to. Anya, you *have* to." Agitation reaches my tone. "We're so *close,* so goddamn close!"

"I'm…losing a lot of blood, Ezra. Don't waste time."

"Baby, no, don't say that." My eyes are pulled away, trailing down her gown as I see the crimson life force pour from her, staining her gown, tainting it with gore, soaking the fabric, and spreading endlessly.

I meet her eyes again and her forehead wrinkles as her brow furrows. "I love you, Ezra. You did everything you could."

My face scrunches in anger and my heart thumps wildly. "Don't fucking tell me goodbye!"

She smiles at me, though I scream at her. "Mine?"

I shake my head furiously, emotion building pressure behind my eyes. "No. Don't."

Her eyes beg me. "Please…"

How can I deny her?

My head drops and I look at the tiny baby boy in my arms. Only his face is visible peeking out through the blanket, his skin streaked with blood. His screaming has slowed to squeaks and brief shouts of protest against the cold. Just as I look at him, he starts to blink his eyes open. I wish I could see the color of them, but we only have the residual lighting from the headlights of the overturned car and the bit of moonlight shining from up above. Still, it's as though I can see his entire life there in his tiny baby eyes.

Anya is bleeding.

She's not okay.

She can't run with me and I can't carry her.

Fuck. I can't carry her.

Overwhelming sadness shakes me from deep within my chest and I sob. I sob over Anya as she fades away from me.

"Yours," I choke out the word. "Always."

She gives me a sad smile and her tears fall with mine. "No regrets, Ezra."

I lose myself.

Bending over her, with the baby in my arms, I cry. I cry like I've never cried before.

I cry until Anya is quiet.

Until I feel the essence of her fade.

Until she shuts her eyes and turns her head away.

Until she's still.

A disturbing silence wraps around me like a snake, gripping me in its hold. The snow continues to fall in large, soft flakes that drift leisurely to the ground and it's calm, quiet…as if the whole world has stopped.

Because it has.

But then I hear it…the helicopter nearing.

There's a snap inside my chest, right over my heart, and it shocks me into action. I can't save Anya, but I can save her baby. *Our* baby. I can still end this. I can still come back and seek retribution against the four families for what they've done to us.

I set the baby on the ground beside Anya and run to the driver's side door of the car. Kostya is lying awkwardly on the roof, unmoving. I don't know whether he's dead or alive, but there's no time for me to wonder. I feel a stab of regret in my gut that I might be leaving him to die, knowing I'll never get the chance to thank him.

I reach around him to the center console where I remember seeing him put his gun, a knife, and a stun gun. I pop it open and the items I'm searching for fall out onto the roof beside Kostya. I grab the knife.

The sound of the helicopter is drawing nearer. I spot the black backpack we brought with cash and Kostya's credit card lodged in the passenger seat. I stretch, reaching farther across the console as the baby starts to cry, his protests echoing loudly into the night. I grab the strap of the bag and yank until it falls free.

I take the backpack and the knife and hurry back to Anya's side. I swallow hard, steeling myself before I use the knife to slice into the thick umbilical cord. I cut the tether and it's like slicing through my own fucking soul and leaving half of it behind.

I don't want to look at her.

I'm afraid that if I look it her, I won't be able to leave. I'll stay here and wait to be found and killed. They'll take the baby and he'll become the future Mikhailov Head of House.

I can't let that happen.

I toss the knife inside the backpack, sling it snugly over both shoulders, and slip my hands beneath the baby, repositioning the blanket to ensure he's covered well and protected from the cold.

I start to push to my feet, but I feel rooted to the spot.

How can I leave her?

How can I leave my blue-eyed girl behind?

She's asleep, unconscious…no awareness of whether I'm here or gone. Blood continues to spread across her gown, a slowly creeping darkness telling the tragedy of the life she was forced to live, reminding me that I'm powerless to help her. But I don't know if I can pull hard enough, fast enough, to yank myself free of the hold she has on me. My breath hitches and I let myself sob, let myself have one last look at her.

My blue-eyed girl.

I bend over her, pressing a kiss to her lips that are somehow still soft and warm.

They did this to her.

They did this to us.

There is no more time to waste and I won't fail her—I'll escape and I'll save our baby. I won't let them take him, too.

I cradle him in my arms and head toward the road. I look back the way we came as the clouds part and moonlight glints off the metal. I strain my eyes to see. There really was a spike strip laid across the dirt road, at the bottom of the long decline.

It was put there intentionally.

It's why there was no guard at the gate.

They knew this would foil any escape attempt.

Well, fuck them.

I can't take my girl with me, but her baby and I…we're getting the fuck out of here. Anger bolsters my intent, punches another rush of adrenaline, and fuels my determination.

I turn.

I take a deep breath.

And I run.

CHAPTER 24
Anya

ONE. TWO. THREE. *Four. Five. Six. Seven. Eight.*

One…Two…Three…Four…Five…Six…Seven…Eight.

One.

Two.

Three.

Four.

Five.

Six.

Seven.

Eight.

"Not now." I hear Kostya's frantic voice say to me in Russian. "You were almost there."

My chest hurts. Rhythmic pain pulses over and over on my ribcage. An engine rumbles in the distance, the sound drawing nearer and nearer.

"I promised him," Kostya utters in his native language. "I promised I would keep your heart beating. Come on, Anya!"

I want to scream at him to stop whatever it is he's doing to me because it hurts. Everything hurts. I've never been in this much pain. But I can't open my mouth to scream at him.

Suddenly, the pounding on my chest stops. The sound of the engine peaks in volume and then shuts off. Kostya's voice grows more distant and he begins to speak in English. "Murphy, I'm sorry. I did not—"

"Save it," Murphy says with an edge to his voice. "I'm not the one who put that fucking spike strip across the road."

"Please, don't—"

"My wife told me everything, Kostya. I know every detail of your involvement in this attempted escape."

"Then kill us now," Kostya says and I wish I could shout at him to stop talking. "Kill us before they come for us."

"She's alive?" It's Stella's voice this time, and when she speaks again, her voice is closer, as if she's right beside me. "Oh, my God. Murphy. Please. We have to help her."

"You've already gotten me into enough fucking trouble with your involvement, Stella. And where the fuck is Ezra?"

Kostya replies, "He's gone. With the baby. On the helicopter that left ten minutes ago."

"She's bleeding," Stella says, sadness touching her voice. "Did she give birth? Out here? Oh, my God. Murphy..." Her voice moves away. "Please. You told me you could change. You told me you could be a better man for me. You told me you had enough power now to make changes and be a better father

than your own. I'm fucking begging you. Don't let this poor girl die. Not like this."

Am I dying?

"You don't understand, Stella—"

"No, you don't understand, Murphy. You find a way to save her life or I go to the board and tell them everything. I'll tell them how I helped Kostya plan her escape and you know what will happen to me then. Are you willing to let me suffer those consequences? Or can you step the fuck up right fucking now?"

There's silence.

It stretches for too long.

Maybe I've died.

Maybe this dark awareness is what it's like to be dead.

But I still feel pain.

"Well, fuck. Let's get her outta here before the rest of the four families come looking."

"Where are we taking her?" Stella asks. "And what about Kostya?"

"I have a plan. Go get my phone from the car so I can call our pilot. I can stall the rest of them from coming out here for maybe a half hour. We need to move quickly. I can't afford any suspicion on my head. We'll tell them they all got away on the first chopper and you and I went after them in the second. Understood?"

Stella sounds relieved. "Thank you. Really, thank you, Murphy."

But I'm still not so sure I'm actually alive. Maybe this is all a dream. Perhaps death is simply this state of awareness where only darkness exists without a physical being. Maybe I'll be trapped inside my own rotting corpse forever.

Purgatory.

But then, I feel fresh cold along my back, the familiar damp cold of fresh, powdery snow, and I realize my body is being moved. I'm hoisted from the ground and I feel Murphy's shoulder jab into my stomach and it fucking hurts.

I scream and the movement stops.

"Anya? It's...You're gonna be okay, just hang on," Stella says.

Could she hear my scream?

Did I make a sound?

"Jesus, why would they do this?" she murmurs. "Why would they put a spike strip in the road?"

"Fucking Vittoris."

"It's...it's vile."

"We're all vile, sweetheart," Murphy says, and I realize he's carrying my limp body over his shoulder. "It's in our blood. It's our business."

"If you're so vile, then why are you helping her?"

"For you, lass. You wanted proof I could be a good man and stand up for you? Well, here it is, sweetheart. I'm saving her to show you that I've...that I'm capable of being better. This poor girl has been through enough. Maybe I'm a little tired of it, too."

I want to laugh.

I wish I could.

Murphy O'Shea, of all people, ruthless king of masters, has come to my rescue.

Unless he's too late to save me.

Unless I'm already dead.

CHAPTER 25

Ezra

1 Year Later

I PLACE MY silver laptop on the small table in front of me, lifting the screen and powering it on. I bring up my video chat app and wait for Lidia's call. She promised she'd check in with me at noon, New York time. I'm not exactly sure what time zone I'm in right now crossing the Atlantic Ocean.

The private jet we fly on was chartered by the agents that I've finally convinced to help me. The FBI and CIA were no use to me—they outright denied the existence of the four families and any such operations they ran in their trafficking factories. No doubt they were corrupted from within. I knew I had to take matters into my own hands when they were insistent in their naïve denial.

It hasn't been an easy journey getting where I am today. In fact, this past year has been arguably the second worst of my life—the first, of course, was being a captive of the four families.

When I left Anya—dying alone on the side of the road—I'd had enough adrenaline to fuel me, to keep me going to run the mile and a half to the helipad. I'd gotten there just before the pilot was about to take off again. My timing had been nothing other than pure fucking luck.

The pilot wasn't going to let me on at first without Kostya, but I pleaded with them, showing them my baby boy, fresh from the womb. I tried to get them to help me, to go back to get Anya somehow, but they refused. They had orders to pick-up and drop-off and nothing more.

I seriously thought about putting our son on the helicopter and running back to be with Anya. The pull of my soul to hers was still so strong, still urgent and desperate, and there was a purely selfish part of me that wanted to be by her side—even if she was dying, even if it meant leaving our child's life to chance, even if it meant I'd be with her for mere moments before losing her and facing the wrath of the four families on my own.

But there was no way I could turn back when I realized that Anya would never forgive me for abandoning her child, *our* child. I would never forgive myself for doing something like that. By then, the baby's tiny lips were turning blue from the cold, even while he was wrapped and bundled in the blanket.

The thought of losing the baby and Anya all in one fell swoop was horrifying. I knew I couldn't save her, and he was all I had left of her.

I couldn't lose him, too.

It was the hardest fucking thing in the world to leave her.

But somehow, I climbed on board the helicopter, knowing that my last act of love for her would be to ensure a long, happy, healthy life for her son.

Fuck, it hurts to think about that night.

Things got complicated when the pilot dropped me and the kid off at the nearest public airport. I had the credit card and cash Kostya had given us—if it had just been me and Anya, I could've booked us on the next flight home. But with a newborn baby in my arms that desperately needed to be fed and cared for, I had to make a decision that scared me.

I had to take him to the nearest hospital.

We were still in Russia, too close for comfort to wherever the fuck Mikhailov Manor was tucked away. I had no clever cover story. I walked into a hospital with signs I couldn't read and people who spoke a language I didn't understand. I showed them the baby and had to have faith that they wouldn't take us from each other.

I thought I knew fear before then, but I didn't.

The thought of them taking him from me—separating us—that was true fear.

But I guess we got lucky. A kind woman, a nurse, held out her arms and waited for me to hand him over and it took every ounce of strength I had to do it. She cradled him in her arms, smiled at him, looked up at me, and asked me something in Russian that I couldn't understand. It took a few tries and some gesturing for me to figure it out, but eventually, I worked out that she was asking for his name.

I didn't have a name for him.

Anya never told me what she wanted to call him.

I worried I would pick the wrong name, but I had to decide in a split-second. So, I did the only thing I could do and that was to rely on my gut. I said the first name that came to mind.

I told her to call him Brandon.

It was the plainest, most American name I could think of, because I thought Anya would want that. She was Russian born, but she loved the American life she'd been living since she was eleven. And after all she'd been through, I couldn't imagine her wanting him to have anything resembling a Russian name.

So, just like that, he was Brandon Bell.

The nurse waved me along with her as she took Brandon back to an area of stretchers divided by nothing other than a simple curtain between. The vinyl floor tiles were cheap and peeling, and the place was buzzing with noise, overcrowded with people and doctors and nurses. There was an overwhelming stench of bleach and cleaning chemicals that gave me an instant headache. The place was a hot mess compared to any hospital I've been to in the States.

The nurse gestured for me to sit on one of the stretchers at the very end of the long hallway, and she handed Brandon back to me as soon as I did. I felt such a massive amount of relief, knowing I was doing the right thing—if not for me then for my *son*. Because regardless of whether he was fathered by me or Nikolai, I knew right then that this child was *mine* because I'd claimed him as such.

The nurse cleaned him up, checked him over, and did everything that needed to be done to ensure he was okay. She stayed by our side when a surly-looking doctor came back to check Brandon, and she doted on him while he did.

She gave us bottles of formula, diapers, swaddling blankets, basic onesies, and wipes—things I think she had to sneak away to give us because this hospital didn't seem like it was made of money. She made sure we had everything we needed before we left the hospital and she walked us out a back entrance—I thought it was odd that no one asked for payment, but I think she knew, somehow, that we needed this off the record.

I tried to give her some cash from the pile in my backpack, but she absolutely refused to take it. I had no other way to thank her, but she seemed happy to have been able to help Brandon.

We left and I took the risk of getting a hotel room for the night, thankful they let me pay cash for it. Brandon and I were exhausted, and I couldn't wrap my head around getting on a plane just yet.

That first night was the hardest.

Brandon cried.

He cried a lot.

And so did I.

I cried over the loss of Anya. I cried angry tears at how close we'd been to having the life we deserved as our own family—me, Anya, and the baby. I cried that the three of us would never dance a *pas de trois*. All I'd ever wanted was a family of my own because I never really had one as a foster kid. And the closest I'd ever come to having a family was brutally taken from me by a spike strip across the road, placed by the vilest monsters on Earth.

I went to a local store the next morning and got some basic supplies, using cash as much as I could. We hurried off to the airport and booked the next flight out of Russia—two fucking layovers along the way, but then we'd land in New York and I would at least have the advantage of being on my home turf, even if they did come after me. I had to use the credit card to book the flight, so naturally, I was jumpy, anxious as hell waiting for our plane to board. Every stop along the way, I expected someone from the four families to show up, kill me, and kidnap Brandon.

Thank fuck no one ever tried.

When we finally got back to New York almost two full days later, I went straight to Emma's apartment, my ex-girlfriend. I went to her partly because I wanted to make sure they hadn't gotten to her, but also because I had no one else to help me.

And she did exactly that.

She let me sleep on her couch for four months with Brandon beside me in a portable crib. He was a fussy little fucker, had me up all hours of the night, too. She was an angel to put up with that for as long as she had, but each day that passed, I knew we were getting closer and closer to an eviction. Not because she wasn't happy to help, but because her relationship with her boyfriend had turned serious and I knew they'd want to be living together before long.

And it was probably for the best because seeing them together and happy hurt like fucking hell. They had everything I was supposed to have with Anya, and it twisted painfully in my gut every time they smiled, laughed, hugged, or said goodbye at the door with a kiss.

Emma tried to help me grieve the loss of Anya, but whenever she brought it up, something about it just didn't feel right. It didn't feel right inside me to think of her as being gone. It didn't feel like she *was* gone, absent from the Earth…and I don't think it ever really had felt that way.

Twice before that night in the forest, I'd been nearby when Anya almost died, and I'd felt the snap of it breaking my heart, followed by a hollowness in my gut. But that hollowness was quickly filled when her breath returned. It was once before when Nikolai drowned her in the pool and again when Vigo tried to drown her in the bathtub.

I remember thinking she seemed invincible for all that she'd been through, and that word was rolling around in my head more persistently.

Though I'd been sad, though I'd cried a billion tears, though I'd cursed the four families for causing the death of my blue-eyed girl, I didn't feel empty…I didn't feel hollow in my gut. At first, I thought it was just because I had Brandon to fill the empty spaces. But more and more, I was feeling her absence as something that needed to be corrected, as something that *could* be corrected.

My heart insisted that she was invincible.

Four months into my stay with Emma, four months of conversations with local police, the FBI, the CIA, I decided that I needed to find her, with or without the help of law enforcement.

But first, I had to find her sister. I'd already waited four months too long and my only excuse was that Brandon took up all my time and attention.

It was almost too easy to find her. Lidia Antonov was on several social media sites that she posted to regularly and that was shocking to me. It was shocking because the four families could've tracked her down and taken her out after our departure, even though Nikolai had called off his goons who took weekly pictures of her with a scope measurement from the rifle they aimed at her.

Initially, I thought that must mean that Anya was, without a doubt, dead. Because they would have no reason to go after Lidia if Anya were dead. After all, I had no ties to Lidia in their eyes. If Anya was somehow still alive and in their care, they might've killed Lidia as punishment. They might've taken Lidia and sold her. But that just didn't feel right to me.

And then I thought, *What if Anya is alive, but the four families don't know? And if she is alive, where the fuck is she?*

I'd gone to Lidia then and told her everything.

She believed me, thank fuck.

She believed me because Brandon looked like Anya, except for the eyes.

His eyes were a light gray with flecks of green and brown when he was a newborn. But gradually, the brown faded and so did the gray, leaving him with stunning green eyes and a quickly growing mop of thick, blond hair.

He and I share the same eyes and hair, but the rest of him is undoubtedly all the best parts of Anya.

Lidia took to Brandon instantly, and suddenly, I had a family. Unfortunately, I never got to meet Anya's mother. Lidia told me that she died of a heart attack a couple of years ago—undoubtedly, the stress of not knowing what happened to her oldest daughter took a toll on her health.

But right away, I bonded with Lidia and she stood by me as I lost my fucking mind deciding to pursue a potentially useless search for Anya. We both felt that if there were any possibility that she was still alive, that we would leave no stone unturned to bring her back.

We got a small place together because she insisted that I needed her help with Brandon. I did, but really, she wanted to be close to him because just like me, he was all she had left of Anya. It turned out that the 5,000,000 Rubles of Russian currency Kostya had given us was about 70,000 American dollars. It was enough to get by on while I went crazy in my overseas search. Lidia stepped up to take care of her nephew when I had to be gone to chase a new lead.

I talked to some unsavory people and I did some things that I'm not proud of, but if I hadn't, I never would've stumbled upon the underground group of rogue agents who had been trying to bring an end to the four families for two decades. It took me a couple of months to convince them of my story, to feed them the information I'd gathered about the four families so they could compare it to their own intel. Once I introduced them to Brandon and Lidia, that was it.

We partnered.

Their intel, military training and expertise, their insiders…they gave me access to everything they had to help me find Anya. They had a stake in finding her because undoubtedly, she could give them even better information than I had since she'd been temporarily the sole leader of the Mikhailov family.

Things were starting to fall apart for the four families. It had started with the Leblancs, formerly the Campbells. The insiders knew of the changeover in family leadership from the moment it happened—when the Campbells were punished for their role in killing Nikolai's family.

The agents had someone on the inside—a girl named Callista Campbell, the granddaughter of Charles Campbell, niece of the murdered Head of House Chandler Campbell. She wanted out when Chandler was killed, fearing for her life, but I guess they had convinced her to stay, took her away for some time and trained her in the art of becoming a trusted confidante to the new Head of House, Leo Leblanc.

Apparently, Callista was making waves. Though Leo was her first cousin once removed—the son of her great aunt and uncle—he had a thing for her. And Callista was using it to her advantage.

With the Leblanc family slowly unraveling and intel that Murphy and Stella O'Shea have started decommissioning some of their factories, the time for this group to act was now. And that meant they were willing to help me find Anya, which is exactly what they did.

It's why I'm flying across the Atlantic right now.

Lidia's name appears on my video chat and I click to bring her up.

"Hey," she says, a little out of breath, "sorry I'm a few minutes late. Brandon figured out how to get out of his diaper and took a shit behind the couch before I realized it."

We both laugh.

"Where is my precious little fucker?"

"Hang on," Lidia says, stepping away from the camera for a few seconds, returning with my boy, plopping him down on her lap. "Say hi to daddy."

I wave at my little buddy. "Hey, baby. I miss you."

Brandon babbles something incoherent at the screen and my grin makes my cheeks ache. Anya is the only other person I've loved as much as I love Brandon.

Lidia's face turns serious. "How long before you land in Oslo?"

"About twenty minutes."

"And how long before you reach the warehouse…the factory…whatever they call it?"

"It's a warehouse, but they call it a factory. It'll be at least another hour before we get there, but it'll be longer than that before we have her. If she's actually there."

"She *has* to be there. I know it, Ezra. She's my sister. I know she's not dead, I would *feel* it."

I nod a little. "I know. I promise you, the moment we know more, I'll call you."

The rogues have been watching Murphy O'Shea's movements for months. They noticed him spending a lot more time away from his factories and a lot more time at home with his wife. He's closed two factories over the course of the year. But they expected to have seen bodies moving—dead or alive—and being shipped to other factories. They hadn't seen any such movement. It was like the girls they kidnapped and kept just disappeared.

I think Stella had something to do with it all. I think Murphy fell hard for her, and because she's such a force to be reckoned with, something in him changed and shifted his perspective. I can only hope that's why. Falling in love with a good woman can take a weak man and make him stronger…can take a worse man and make him better.

Whatever the case, the agents spotted a girl who matched Anya's description living in the Oslo factory for the last six months or so, with no other signs of life there.

And we're on our way there now.

"Ezra, let's brief," one of the group members calls to me from the back of the private jet.

"I've gotta go," I tell Lidia.

"Call us the moment she's safe. Make sure she's safe, Ezra."

I smile and nod, too terrified to get my hopes up that it might be Anya living in that warehouse, too terrified to let Lidia down and remind her not to hold her breath.

I wave goodbye to my son and close the laptop, pushing to stand, buttoning my navy jacket, and brushing the wrinkles down from my lapels. I step out from my seat and straighten my tie as I move toward the back of the plane where the group of almost twenty men gather around a table with maps and plans.

"We've got five SUVs waiting for us at the airport in Oslo," the leader of the crew says. "The moment we land, we're piling in and heading out." He holds up a picture of my blue-eyed girl—she was younger in the photo, before she was stolen by Nikolai, but it looks like her all the same. "This is Anya Mikhailov. She is our lead mission today. She is a victim who needs to be recovered. Prioritize finding her. Take out any man who is armed. We don't really know what to expect at this factory. Others we've raided have been used as a prison for the women they kidnap. They keep these victims here while they break them, preparing them to sell off, sometimes by the hundreds. Any victims found, we will recover and transport via plane to Stockholm for treatment. Local authorities in Oslo cannot be trusted. The four families pay them for their silence."

"How do we transport them by the hundreds?" one of the men asks.

The leader clears his throat. "We've never actually recovered any of their human assets in the factories we've raided. Somehow, they always seem to get a tip and have them cleared out before we arrive. But our intel has shown us the deplorable conditions inside." He lays out a few photos on the table showing women packed in a row of prison-like cells. I shouldn't say women, because some of them are teenagers, *children.*

"What happens to these girls when the families clear out a factory on a tip?"

"They decommission them—their word, not ours. Normal people would call it murder. But that's why this mission is crucial. The four families are anything but normal." He holds up the picture of my girl again. "Anya Mikhailov is essential to our cause to end the four families once and for all. She has information that we need, and she needs to be recovered and protected. I want everyone clear-headed and focused on the mission. We land in fifteen, and I want silence on this flight until then. Take that time to focus, do what you need to do to switch from human to soldier, because that's all you are once we land. Understood?"

There's a murmur of agreement and the men disperse. I head back to my seat, drop my head, and press my eyes shut, wringing my sweaty palms together in front of me with my elbows on my knees. Behind my eyelids, there's a flash of sapphire blue and Anya's face comes brilliantly to the forefront of my mind.

I focus intently on her as my pulse kicks up and a steady rhythm of hope punches through my veins with each beat of my heart.

Hope. Hope. Hope.

If there is a God and he has any mercy at all, we'll find her, alive and well, and I'll have her safely in my arms before the sun sets on this day.

CHAPTER 26

Anya

JANUARY... NEW YEAR, new me.

It's been one year since I was left behind in the dark forest—one year since I danced across the line of death and somehow found my way back to the side of life.

It's taken me nearly the full year to get back to the level of health I maintained as Nikolai's slave while he owned me. Going through a pregnancy after the way Vigo ruined my body and my health had taken a toll on me.

By all accounts, I should be dead.

But there was one simple thing that kept me alive. It was the same thing that had kept me alive on three separate occasions since Ezra joined my captivity.

Hope.

Hope was something I'd long before lost, but Ezra brought it back to me. He brought hope back into my world and I fought for him because of it, fought for *us*.

Murphy and Stella had been the ones to find me that night in the forest with Kostya—unconscious, bleeding out, knocking on death's door. But instead of letting me die or taking us back to the four families, they had rescued us both.

They saved us.

They snuck us away into the night and flew us back to the four families' private airstrip via helicopter. Murphy pulled a cover-up for our escape out of thin air. He told the four families that we'd gotten away, that he and Stella were hunting us down, so they could carry on with business. He took off in one plane and headed straight for his Oslo factory that night. Stella and Kostya boarded a separate plane with me and took me to a local hospital in Moscow. I had a concussion, needed a blood transfusion, stitches where the baby tore me and for a gash in my side from the car accident.

The fact that I'm still standing is nothing short of miraculous.

Stella and Murphy stayed in close contact during my treatment. He insisted that they discharge me the moment I appeared even slightly stable because neither of us were safe there for long. When I found out he was arranging to take me to one of his factories, I was horrified. I thought I was about to enter a whole new nightmare, to become one of their human assets, to be sold as a slave to one of their clients.

But when we arrived in Oslo, Norway, the factory was inexplicably empty. Murphy had ordered it to be cleared out by his men in Oslo before we landed. I don't even know how they accomplished such a thing. Oslo wasn't their largest factory, but it was big enough to house dozens of girls in the basement.

It was horrifying to see the rows of cages in the wide-open rectangular space of the warehouse basement.

It was a prison.

The empty cages with metal bars, their doors now left open, reminded me of the box I lived in at Vigo's home. My cage held me in with plexiglass, but the women who'd been kept here were trapped by iron bars. I panicked when I saw them with Stella and Kostya, but Stella was surprisingly kind and gentle with me.

She made a promise to me that I didn't ask for and that I didn't believe she had any way of keeping. She promised she could end the O'Sheas' alliance with the four families. She promised that Murphy was a better man than even he knew. She told me that she intended to escape from him before, but seeing the realities of their sick work firsthand fueled her determination to change him.

It almost made me laugh when she said that, which was much needed at the time. I told her that men don't change and she either had to love him as a monster or leave him.

She wasn't convinced.

After a short visit from Murphy a week or so after that, Kostya and I were given burner cell phones, like the ones Kostya had given to me and Ezra when we were separated by Vigo and Nikolai. There were two contacts programmed in—one was Murphy and the other was one of his Oslo employees. That Oslo employee was ordered to ensure that Kostya and I didn't leave the city. But he was also to ensure that we had what we needed to survive comfortably in this warehouse until Murphy could figure a way around letting us go back to normal life.

Whatever *normal* is.

The first thing I asked Murphy's watchdog for was a laptop with internet access and new pointe shoes. Everything I asked for went through Murphy for approval. He approved the laptop, but he wouldn't allow internet access in the warehouse—he was afraid he could be tracked there. But there was a little coffee shop I was allowed to go to once a week with Kostya and the Oslo employee as our escort.

The first time I got on the internet, I did a Google search for Ezra Bell. I didn't know where he was, where my baby was, or whether they were okay. The first article that came up in the search was from over two years ago. It was a report that he was a dancer gone missing from a festival in Kyiv. I found his Instagram account, but nothing had been posted to it or updated since before he went missing.

I quickly realized that if he's alive and out there somewhere, he'd be in hiding, too. He couldn't have an online presence. The four families would find him and come after him, then they would kill him and take my son.

My heart split in two that day when I realized I had no way to find him. I was held hostage here in Oslo just as I was as a Mikhailov or Vittori slave. But what could I do? What choice did I have? I wouldn't give up on finding him. I just knew it in my gut that he was alive, out there in the world somewhere.

And that hope he gave me—hope that I used to think was terribly naïve—was burning bright inside me. I was incapable of freezing myself in an icy exterior of protection because Ezra's eternal sunshine still kept me warm.

So, I'd made Murphy a promise. I would stay there at the warehouse in Oslo. I wouldn't put up a fuss. I'd remain in hiding and I wouldn't try to run. I'd do all that if he promised me he would help me find Ezra. Murphy quickly realized that finding Ezra and giving me over to him would relinquish him of his and his wife's responsibility in this mess. If he gave me to Ezra, it would look as though we'd done just what Murphy had told the board had happened—that we had escaped on our own.

He agreed to search for Ezra and told me he would let me go with him, so long as I accepted that he couldn't keep me safe from the wrath of the four families if they found out we were alive and tracked us down.

I would happily choose to be on the run forever so long as I was running with Ezra. And so, I don't have much to complain about at the moment because I'm alive and there's *hope*.

Though I'm still captive in Oslo, I have Kostya to keep me company. I have an entire warehouse to myself. I've managed to make a nice little temporary home here. But the best part is that I have the space to dance—I was finally healthy enough to get back to it after a few months and it's how I spend most of my days.

I finish slipping on my broken-in, scuffed-up pointe shoes, wrapping and tying the ribbon securely around my ankle. I rise from the concrete floor of the main level of the warehouse and tug down a bit on my cotton shorts to adjust them.

It's late afternoon and the sun shines in from the row of square windows at the top of the high wall, near the ceiling. There are no ground-level windows, only the ones high up above, out of reach. The windows slice the orange sun glow so that it casts down across the concrete floor in stripes of alternating sunlight and gray stone.

I pull my long, dark hair up and away from the off-shoulder gray sweatshirt I have on, twisting and tying it into a messy bun on the top of my head. I place my wireless earbuds in my ears and bend down to my laptop on the floor, tapping play on the music I selected and turning the volume all the way up.

I only have one full-length mirror in the warehouse, which is to say that I don't have any mirrors to watch myself dance. But it doesn't matter to me now the way it used to. I don't care so much now about my movements being perfect and precise. I only want to dance what I feel, like Ezra taught me. I rise to my toes and bring my arms up high above my head, then bring them down the sides of my body, lowering them slowly as my feet begin to move.

I spin on the top of my toes in a pirouette, twirling around over and over before stepping out of the turn gracefully. I listen to the mood of the music and I follow it. The way I dance now is a fusion of ballet and contemporary style, the best of my world and the best of Ezra's. As I move, I find myself drifting, floating through movement with my eyes closed. Gradually, my movement morphs into the routine, *our* routine—the performance Ezra and I danced for Nikolai on stage in Nobility Hall.

As I move, I mark the leaps and lifts that required his hands on me. He would move me with such strength and effortless grace—each lift and spin that he would have been part of forces a bubble of sadness to rise in my chest. With the somber music playing through my earbuds, tears begin to fall.

But I don't stop dancing.

This is what Ezra taught me—how to move through the emotion, how to follow my feelings instead of the steps. My dancing becomes dramatic, wide sweeping arms and legs, erratic and desperate turning and falling and rising.

Thud.

The music crests and reaches a crescendo and I'm lost in it. I'm lost in the memory of his hands on me, his green eyes tracking my every move and feeding me fuel to live.

Thud.

Crash.

I spin and dip out of the turn, tumbling to the floor and rolling over, coming up on my knees—

I freeze.

Armed men burst through the front door while I was dancing and are coming toward me, guns raised. I rip my earbuds out and lift my hands, drawing back to sit on my heels as I look at the men dressed in all black with wide eyes.

"That's Anya," one of them shouts, and I hear the click of a man's dress shoes from behind the throng of at least a dozen men.

They've found me.

Oh, God…

The four families have found me, and they've come to kill me.

I'm a statue in my panic, dropping my terrified eyes to the floor.

"Clear the warehouse," someone says, and the crowd of men thins out as half of them sweep outward, away from the center of the clear open space where I kneel.

I focus on my breaths as terror grips me and I count.

One. Two. Three. Four. Five. Six. Seven. Eight.

One. Two. Three—

They lower their weapons.

The few men remaining part and my eyes lock onto a man's feet coming toward me from a distance, the click of his heels echoing in the warehouse. His footsteps stop in the center of the floor, but my eyes are glued to his feet.

Something in my soul pulses, causing my heart to skip a beat, and suddenly, I'm nervous. My hands tremble where I hold them above my bowed head, but it's not from fear, it's from…it's from a familiar, prickling awareness. My eyes draw a line up his pressed navy slacks, skimming across his tailored suit jacket, glancing over his white shirt and blue tie, his chin, his lips, his vibrant green eyes…

Oh, my God.

"Ezra?"

He sighs and then he brilliantly smiles and my heart beats wildly, beating furiously at the sight of him.

I rise from the floor and run to him.

He opens his arms for me and I leap. He catches me, pulling me close as I wrap my legs around his waist. I press my face into the crook of his neck and inhale the scent of him deeply.

Peaches and cream and sunshine.

He smells like him.

It's him.

Oh, God, it's really him!

I pull my head back to look at him, locking into his green gaze for only seconds before I let my mind truly believe that it's him, he's here, this is real.

This is real.

I kiss his face, his cheeks, his lips, his nose; every inch of skin, I cover with a kiss, tasting the salt of my own tears that drip from my eyes onto his skin.

I squeeze him tighter and press my face into his shoulder, sobbing into his nice, clean jacket. I say the only thing I can think to say. "Mine?"

I feel the tension in his body slump and fade and the sound of his voice as he responds sends a shiver down my spine. "Yours." He holds me tighter. "Forever, *forever* yours."

I kiss him.

I kiss him with my entire body because I can feel him everywhere. I don't ever, *ever* want to let him go.

"You found me," I say.

"I found you, baby. I found you and I'm taking you home."

Home.

Ezra found me and he's taking me home and all I can do is cry. But these tears aren't from sadness, or pain, or torment, or fear. These tears are an expression of pure joy that I welcome. These tears are cleansing my soul and for the first time in a long time, my soul is at peace.

I'm finally free and I'm going home.

CHAPTER 27

Anya

1 Week Later

"LIDIA?" I DROP my bag at the front door of the townhome Ezra rented just outside of Philadelphia. "Lidia!" I run to my little sister and throw my arms around her, knocking into her a little too hard.

We tumble to the floor in a fit of giggles and sobs as I hold her tight, stroking her hair as we lay on our sides. I pull my head back to look at her and fresh tears pool and fall.

"I've missed you *so* much," she tells me as she cries.

I press my forehead to hers. "I've missed you, too. So much."

"I'm just gonna—" Ezra literally steps over us to continue on past, and Kostya follows suit.

Lidia sits up, swiping beneath her eyes. "You're gonna make me mess up my mascara."

I sit up, reaching out to stroke her hair with a smile. "And you did such a nice job of putting it on, too. I remember the first time you did it when you were…maybe thirteen? You put on way too much and just when you finished—"

"I sneezed." She chuckles.

"Tiny little black lines all the way across your cheeks." I laugh. "You thought it was the end of the world."

"At the time, it was." Lidia laughs and the sound of it is so sweet. "I cried for an hour and all the black lines dripped down to my chin."

I smile at her. "And you're going to have them again if you don't stop crying now." I'm having a hard time seeing her as an adult. But it's been five years and she is one.

"Are you really okay?" she asks after a beat.

I nod. "Yes. I will be. Nothing's easy right now."

"I know. I just want you to be okay."

"I'm alive." I grin at her reassuringly. "And I'm here now. No one is ever going to take me away again. I won't let that happen."

A comfortable yet anticipatory silence falls.

"Do you want to…Are you ready to meet Brandon?" she finally asks.

I suck in a sharp breath as a bundle of nerves tugs tight in my gut. I got to see him on video chat every night this week while Ezra and I settled things and traveled back to the States. But this is my first time coming home.

Home.

Such a strange thought.

It's a happy one, but strange.

Ezra didn't want to live in New York anymore, not when he knew it would make us easier targets for the four families to track down, especially since we'd both lived there before we were taken. He'd lived in Philadelphia for a while with a foster family growing up and the foster father had a connection with a landlord here. He helped him rent a townhome for a steal, and Ezra created a life for us here.

Well, he created a life for him and Brandon and Lidia here. But he was clear with me before we came back that he wanted it to feel like my home, too.

I think it will just take time.

I climb to my feet and Lidia does the same. "I'm nervous," I admit as Ezra holds out his hand for me to take.

He grins at me and my heart melts. "Nothing to be nervous about."

"He won't know who I am," I remind him, looking nervously down at the space between us.

Ezra's fingers tickle beneath my chin with a spark of lightning that makes butterflies flap their wings in my stomach. "He'll learn who you are. You're his mom, the one and only."

My body sways toward him, the light in his eyes drawing me in like a moth to a flame. He releases my chin, catching me in his arms, pulling me closer. He's the same Ezra he always was, but somehow different. He's grown as a person, as a man. He's mature and responsible and so goddamn sexy it hurts.

"I love you," I tell him, pressing my cheek to his chest as he cradles me, rubbing a hand over my back.

"I love you, too." He pulls back and smiles. "Come on. I've been dreaming about seeing you with him and I can't wait anymore."

He takes my hand and pulls me along, leading me upstairs as Lidia shoos us away encouragingly. I realize I've completely forgotten about introducing Lidia and Kostya, and I turn my head back around to do it quickly.

Maybe it was stupid for us to let him come back with us. Maybe it makes us easier targets. But I've come to see him as my friend, and I couldn't leave him behind. It would've been hard for us to separate after the year we spent bonding in the Oslo factory.

Lidia surprises me with her confidence and maturity as she takes it upon herself to greet him without me. "You must be Kostya, it's good to meet you." She holds out her hand for him to shake and my heart thumps an extra beat—I've missed so much time with her and she's grown up so much.

Kostya smiles at her—a rare, happy, hopeful smile—and says hello.

Ezra tugs on my hand, drawing my attention back to him. "Come on," he says, grinning at me.

His townhouse—*our* townhouse—is humble, small but reasonably-sized for a family to live in comfortably. It's cozy and I feel immediately at ease, like I could actually relax and just exist here peacefully. There's a happy kind of energy in this space, like nothing I've ever felt before.

I stop again halfway up the staircase to look at the pictures hung neatly on the sky-blue wall.

Pictures of Brandon…of my son.

My son.

My heart skips a beat and I place my hand over my chest.

"Lidia put those up," Ezra tells me. "She decorated the nursery, too. Most of the place, really. She said it needed a woman's touch."

I give him a smile and squeeze his hand.

Did they seek comfort in each other when I was away, when they didn't know if I was dead or alive?

I swallow hard at the thought that came from nowhere.

It never even occurred to me to ask if he'd been involved with anyone in the year we were apart, least of all my sister. But realistically, they've been living together, raising Brandon together. He and Lidia are as close in age as Ezra and I are to each other.

A lump rises in my throat.

"What is it?" Ezra stops when we reach the landing, turning to face me, noticing my sudden introspection.

"I think I should ask you something, but not right now."

His eyebrows slant toward his nose. "Okay. Later tonight? After you spend some time with Brandon?"

I nod. I can feel the tension suddenly pulse out from my chest, poisoning the air between us. I don't like it. I don't like that this thought popped into my head. I don't like knowing that it could be true, though I hope it's not. I can see how my tension bothers him. He forces a half-smile and nods his head toward the end of the hallway before leading me forward.

We walk together to the second door on the left, at the end of the short hallway carpeted with brown shag. The hallway is dark and the door is shut. When we stop in front of it and he glances at me, I know this is the door to Brandon's nursery.

All conscious thought leaves me in a rush.

My heart stops and stutters, then thuds hard against my ribcage. I grip Ezra's hand tighter and he squeezes back.

"Ready?" he asks.

Am I?

I can't speak, so I just nod.

Slowly, he turns the knob. He steps forward as he cracks the door open gradually, blocking my view as he peeks in. I expect that we'll creep into the room and I'll see my baby for the first time, asleep in his crib.

But then Ezra speaks, and I feel nauseous. "Hey, bud, why aren't you sleeping?"

And then follows the sound I know I will treasure more than any other sound heard for the rest of my days…my baby, babbling back at Ezra.

Oh, God.

The sheer joyfulness of the sound is so intense that it sinks inside my gut and my body curls around my stomach. It's joy that grips me entirely, shooting like a burst of lightning from the pit of my stomach, like a starburst blasting its rays outward to the rest of my body. It forces tears to rise and spill and threatens to drop me to my knees.

But Ezra slips his arm around my waist and pulls me inside the room, shutting the door behind us. He lets me go with a quick rub over the small of my back and I slump against the wall behind me as I blink through the waterfall spilling from my eyes.

I have to concentrate. I have to focus to watch what's happening as my breath quickens toward hyperventilation. I don't want to miss a moment of this excruciating joy.

Brandon's standing in his crib, smiling a toothless grin that sets my world on fire. He reaches his tiny arms into the air, eagerly waiting for Ezra to pluck him from his bed, but he loses his balance when he lets go of the side, falling backward onto his butt. He pulls himself up again with his hands on the rail and his knees bounce with energy.

Ezra reaches for him, grips him beneath the armpits, and lifts him. He pulls Brandon close against his chest and that's when my knees buckle beneath me.

I fall to kneel on the floor.

Ezra crosses to me quickly, dropping to one knee, still holding Brandon tight to his side. "Are you okay?"

I nod through my tears. "I'm okay. It's just a lot."

His voice is soft and comforting. "I know. Just sit down there. Brandon will sit on your lap."

"He will?"

It feels so surreal.

"Yeah, of course." He looks at Brandon and smiles. "You'll sit with Mommy, won't you, buddy?"

Brandon coos.

Ezra sniffles and I see the sheen forming over his eyes.

If he cries, I don't stand a chance.

"This is your mommy," he says. "She's the best person you'll ever know." He moves to sit beside me as I sit with my back against the wall, both of us stretching our legs out.

I look over at Brandon and smile, quickly wiping away the tears from my cheeks with the backs of my hands. He looks at me with curiosity, blinking his bright green eyes. They're the same vibrant green as Ezra's and equally bewitching, actually more so. One look at him and I'm hopelessly in love. My smile for him brightens and after a few moments, he smiles back.

And then the most perfect thing happens.

Brandon reaches for me.

I gasp as the most unexplainable kind of happiness spreads warmth through my entire body. Ezra lifts him and shifts him over, sitting his bottom on my lap. I grip beneath his arms and hold him delicately with him facing me as his tiny legs spread across my thighs on either side.

"Hi, baby," I say quietly, afraid of my own voice. "I'm your mommy." My voice cracks and a joyful sob breaks through. I push a smile through my cheeks as Ezra's hand sneaks around my back and I lean into him.

Oh, God.

I've never felt this way before.

I feel like…

"I feel like I'm finally home."

Ezra turns his head and presses his lips to my cheek before a shallow sob hitches in his chest. He turns his head and nuzzles his face into the side of my neck.

"We're all finally home," he says.

CHAPTER 28
Ezra

I'VE NEVER BEEN happier in my life. Anya is alive and free and finally home with me where she belongs. It's probably silly to think this way, but it was almost like Brandon knew his mommy was coming home tonight. He's usually such a good sleeper, but tonight he was awake when I brought Anya in…like he was waiting up to see her.

Of course, it's an adjustment for everyone, and some things are going to take time and patience and care, but there was no sense of strangeness or discomfort between Anya and Brandon. There was intense and immediate love—the moment they met couldn't have been more perfect.

But as I shut the door to Brandon's room after we get him back down for the night and I lead Anya to my bedroom—*our* bedroom—I can tell something's weighing on her mind. She wanted to talk to me about something earlier, and I don't like the worry I feel pulsing from her as I show her our room.

Our master bedroom is a decent size with a connected bathroom. The carpet is an old, dark teal. There are hardwoods beneath that I want to restore someday, but for obvious reasons, that hasn't been a priority. We have a single dresser with an attached vanity mirror to the right of the queen-sized bed and there are two end tables on either side of that. There's a small closet, but that's pretty much it. It's nothing to write home about.

I close the door behind her after she enters and I stand there, watching her as she takes in her surroundings. She takes a few steps in, twirls around slowly and stills, her eyes falling on mine.

She grins. "So, this is it?"

I hold out my hands. "This is it."

She sighs, crossing her arms over her stomach. "Today has been a little overwhelming."

"Of course, it has. I can only imagine."

Anya lowers slowly to sit on the edge of the bed. Her ass only touches it for a moment before she pushes herself right back up to standing. "There's something I need to know, Ezra. I don't really know how to ask. And it's not really…I mean, I don't really have a reason to be upset if you did—"

"If I did what?" She crosses her arms again, looking down and away from me. She's nervous to ask, or maybe nervous for my answer, I don't know. But I don't like this. "Just ask me."

"It's been a year…" Words burst from her in a ramble. "And you were alone taking care of Brandon. You didn't know if I was dead or alive, and I can only imagine you had to go on living life as if I *had* actually died. My sister and I aren't all that dissimilar, and I know you've been living together for at least six months. I know I have no right to be upset if you and Lidia—" She shakes her head. "I just need to know. For my own peace of mind. Did you and Lidia…" She lets her unspoken, but crystal-clear question hang in the air.

My head tilts all the way to the side as I watch her squirm her way through her nervous words. Shit, it twists something painfully deep inside me to hear her ask me this. I get why she's asking; I get why she would think that Lidia and I had become something more than friends. I've wondered the same thing about her and Kostya having spent the past year together. But it kills me how it pains her to even think that could be true.

I charge across the room, rushing to stand in front of her, and I grip her face with both hands, turning her head to look at me. "No, we didn't. I never even thought about it, Anya. Lidia is as much a sister to me as she is to you. And you're not as similar as you think you are…you couldn't possibly be. There is no one, Anya, *no one* who could take your place in my heart, in my soul." I shuffle closer as her delicate hands land gently on my wrists and she blinks up at me with those perfect sapphire eyes. I lick my lips as I watch her mouth part to take in an uneven breath. "I have been achingly, *painfully* celibate since that last day I saw you in the forest. And I probably would've been forever if you hadn't survived. Something inside me knew I had to wait for you, knew that you were alive, knew that someday I would bring you back home."

I hardly get the last word out before Anya rises on her toes and slams her lips against mine with enough force that I have to take a step backward. She kisses me hard and pushes me back until my back hits the closed door behind me.

I drop my hands from her cheeks and grip her hips tightly, spinning her and pushing her against the door instead. I pull my head back to break our kiss, though my hips grind my cock against her lower stomach. "Are you sure you want this now?" We've only kissed since I've rescued her because she was struggling with something, struggling with herself, and she asked me to wait. "I'll wait for you. I'll wait years if that's what you want, but I need you so much right now. If we start this…"

Her shoulders relax as she drops her head back against the wall. "Everything feels right. Everything finally feels right. I want to start this, and I don't want to finish until the sun comes up."

I bring a hand up to stroke her cheek, tilting my head as I study the absolute beauty of her face. "This will never be finished."

She breathes out a sigh and as her lips part, I dive in. I kiss her and forget the world. Anya moans, her fingers tickling my skin as she slips them beneath the hem of my T-shirt. She lifts and tugs and our kiss breaks only for the time it takes to rip my shirt over my head and toss it to the floor.

I slam my hands to the wall on either side of her, bending to taste her again. This kiss is frantic, desperate, eager…it's fucking everything because I've been starving for this freedom with my blue-eyed girl since we met. I snake my hands around behind her, grip her ass tight, and lift her up along the door. She squeezes her legs around me and I groan, feeling her shift along my cock. I move one hand up to dig into her hair at the back of her head, tugging back on the strands ever so slightly to angle her face upward, just so I can bend over her and kiss her more deeply.

She is fucking everything.

I hold her close as I turn us and walk her to the dresser, setting her down on top of it, putting her ass level with my hips. She peels off her shirt, tossing it away as her eyes take me in, raking down my body and making me feel like the most desired man in the world. She reaches behind her and unhooks her black bra and my hips jut forward, pounding my cock against the edge of the dresser.

"Fuck," I groan.

Anya lets her bra fall from her shoulders and everything slows to the speed of the garment slipping so slowly down her arms. "Ezra…"

The way she breathes my name—as if I were the very air that filled her lungs—makes me fucking hard.

She reaches for me, her hands locking together around the back of my neck, and she pulls my head down to her, our foreheads touching. She pants and breathes as her knees squeeze my hips to hold me in place.

"I love you and I'll never stop," she says.

Christ.

That makes my whole goddamn body tingle for her.

"I need you *now*, baby." I'm panting, gasping for her like she's oxygen.

Her mouth drops open and her fingers find my buckle, working frantically to free me from my jeans. "I need you, too. Now."

I push her trembling hands away and take over, shoving my pants and boxer briefs down as soon as I get my jeans open. My dick is already hard and straining, springing free from my clothes and ready to be inside her.

I grab her leggings at her hips and tug, but the damn things are so tight that I pull her body down with them. Her covered pussy hits my stomach and she gasps. Holding her knees tight against my sides, she lifts her ass just enough for me to peel them off her and I toss them to the floor.

Then I stop.

I catch the reflection of her backside in the vanity mirror on the back of the dresser and I just have to pause to appreciate her perfectly imperfect figure. My eyes cast over her body, taking in the fullness of her curves—the stretch marks on her stomach where she carried our baby, the hint of extra weight she still carries there that reminds me she's a fucking warrior.

I revel at the contrast of her skin, smooth and supple in most places, but rough and weathered where she's been battered and abused and marked in her captivity. My thumb grazes over the scars at the top of her thigh, scars Nikolai put there with his switchblade.

She'll never be marked by them again.

This is the first time it's really hit me that it's true and relief washes over me. The literal weight of the world tumbles from my shoulders.

I *finally* feel free.

And it's because I'm with her.

I grab her face and kiss her hard, leaning her back against the mirror as her ass slips down to me at the edge of the dresser. I fist my cock, angle it against her pussy, and press inside her. I push in deep, probably too hard and too fast, but she's so goddamn warm and wet that it just slips right in.

"*Oh,*" she gasps as her heels dig into my ass, encouraging me to stay right there. "Oh, God."

She looks at me, her blue eyes sparkling, full of passion and life and love, more than I've *ever* seen before.

I pull out and shove back in and we both moan. Her eyes never leave mine; she never looks away, not for a second. I thrust again, starting to move in and out of her with long, hard thrusts. I fuck her recklessly while she makes love to me with her eyes.

When I start to feel her pussy clench around my cock, when she's shaking, tensing, trembling in my hold, gasping out those sweet little "*oh*" sounds that she makes for me, I put my thumb over her clit and press.

"Ezra!" Anya's arms whip around me and she squeezes me in her embrace, lifting her hips and changing our angle. "Yes…yes. Please, Ezra…I need you."

I need you.

"I'm yours, baby," I whisper against the shell of her ear, her hair tickling my face as I nip my teeth down the side of her neck.

When I lick behind her ear, it detonates her.

"Ezra!" She goes rigid and then she sinks, gasping through her orgasm, her arms losing their grip around me.

I grab onto her, hold her steady as I rut inside her, hard and fast. The edge of the dresser slams against the wall with a thud with each thrust.

Thud, thud, thud.

Her eyes drift shut while I fuck her and she smiles, looking sleepy, sated, happy. "Mine," she whispers and that's it for me.

I come inside her, hard and long, and I've never felt such a perfect release.

It feels like the first time.

It feels like the last time.

It feels like the only time.

And it's fucking *everything.*

It could be a dream, but I'm thankful it's not.

Anya and I are together in bed, in our cozy townhome in Philadelphia.

We lay on our sides, facing one another, only Anya has just pulled me from the only peaceful slumber I've had in months. I'm okay with it because reality is better than the dream of her.

We fell asleep naked, tangled in each other after an extended fuck session. It's still dark in the room and a quick glance at the bright red numbers on the digital clock behind her on the nightstand tells me its three o'clock in the morning.

I can't see her clearly in the dark, but I can see her well enough to make out the curved line of her smile. Her fingers softly trail up and down along my arm. Her coldness is gone. The icy exterior she used to shield herself as a slave has melted away, leaving her bare and exposed to me in her rawest, truest form.

I would move mountains for this woman.

She snuggles in close and presses her lips to mine, just a brush to test my interest. I'm tired, but I'm still fucking interested. I move a little closer and so does she, parting her lips and sliding her tongue along the seam of mine. I run my hand over her hip, slipping down to her knee, and I slowly lift her leg, encouraging her to wrap it over mine.

We kiss for minutes, slow and deep and relaxed. There's no rushing, no urgent need for release. Just the feel of us together without limits or fear. As my cock gradually thickens, I wedge it between her legs. I reach down between us to rub her clit, feeling how wet she already is for me. Without hurry, I angle and push my cock inside her, my hand on her lower back dragging her closer. She sighs into my mouth and I taste her love on my tongue.

We hold each other this way, kissing deeply, hips rocking slowly. I can't think of a better way to wake up. We rock and grind lazily, making love with our bodies connected deeply. The craziest thing is that I don't even need to come—and I don't think she needs it, either. This grinding is about our connection and the connection alone feels like heaven on Earth.

In fact, neither of us come this way.

We rock, we caress, we kiss, we moan.

And at some point along the way, we fall asleep like this, tangled up in

each other.
    Together.
    In love.
    Free and finally home.

EPILOGUE
Anya

3 Years Later

"ARE YOU READY for this?" Ezra grins as brightly as the sun.

My smile is no dimmer. I snatch his hand at my side and squeeze tight, the old, familiar bundle of nerves and excited energy pulsing from within me. I'm practically bouncing with excitement.

The smell of being in an open theater, a nearly full house in the audience, the thrill of the performance to come excites me in a way it never has before. Anxiety grips me, too, in a strange sort of way. I've been looking forward to this performance for months, but I never imagined I would be this nervous about it.

Ezra locks our fingers together and squeezes a little tighter. "Whatever happens on that stage, it's going to be perfect. You know it is."

I sigh, trying to blow out the anxiety. Ezra's touch helps to calm me, just as it always has.

The sounds of chattering fade into silence as the performance time nears, as they dim the lights and make the announcement to silence cell phones and enjoy the show. My heart kickstarts in a rush.

It's okay.

It's going to be okay.

It's going to be amazing.

When the curtains on the stage suddenly part down the middle, I gasp, my heart leaping into my throat and stifling my breath.

But it only lasts a moment.

Ezra shifts our two-year-old daughter, Faith, to a more comfortable position on his lap and she giggles in transit, reminding me that everything is okay as long as our family is together. I rub my hand over my pregnant belly, take a deep breath, and smile.

The music begins to play and Brandon's recital group walks onto the

713

stage in a straight line—well, as straight as a line can be with ten four-year-olds—and their tiny fists are on their hips as they march out.

"There he is!" I whisper excitedly, spotting him at the end of the line.

Brandon looks out at the audience and I wave at him excitedly, knowing that I shouldn't because he is the most distracted child in history. He spots us sitting there together in the third row and doesn't see the line stop. He keeps walking and bumps into the little girl in front of him, bouncing back a step. He giggles and the audience does, too. The children perform the steps of their synchronized routine and it's all lovely and good, but then it's time for Brandon's solo. He moves in front of the line of children, now with their hands on their knees, bobbing up and down to the beat of the music, and he starts his routine.

I never could have imagined that the product of Ezra and I—a contemporary dancer and a ballerina—would turn out to be a tiny breakdancing prodigy. Prodigy may be too strong a word, but that's what he is in my eyes.

Watching him spin and kick and dance and move in his own special way absolutely melts my heart. I remember when I first met Ezra, back when Nikolai wanted me to break him, and I'd mistakenly thought he might be a beat boy, a hip-hop dancer, judging by his clothing and the way he carried himself. But I'd been wrong. Looking at Brandon now, I almost have to wonder if that's what I had seen in Ezra at first—if I'd already seen the first hints of our future son that day when I looked into his bewitching green eyes.

Brandon and Ezra do look so much alike.

Brandon finishes his solo on the floor, lying on his side, elbow on the stage and his head propped in his hand. It's the most adorable, casually cool pose for this four-year-old charmer. He points a finger gun at the audience and winks and the house erupts into laughter and cheers. Ezra taught him that move, told him he'd have the audience in the palm of his hand if he did it.

And, of course, he was right.

Faith claps, her tiny little hands slamming together awkwardly as she sits on Ezra's lap.

This, right here, this moment…it's everything.

It's the life I thought I'd never have.

It's the life I'd been so sure was stolen from me forever.

But Ezra found me in my captivity and saved me. He kept his promise and now we have forever together.

I look at Kostya and Lidia to my right and it still amazes me how quickly and easily they connected—right from the start. He smiles at her, leaning over to whisper something into her ear, and she absolutely lights up. If someone had told me eight years ago that I'd someday be helping my little sister plan her wedding to the man who kept tabs on me for Nikolai, I would have laughed.

But I suppose stranger things have happened…and they have.

I became an advocate in my own case against the four families, working with the private team Ezra had hired to rescue me. It took years of diligent work and it took my open and honest bravery…it took coming out publicly and sharing what I knew. Going public was a huge risk, but Ezra and I knew we could face it together. We knew we would rather risk the danger of exposure for a chance at taking them down, rather than being on the run our entire lives.

But the risk was worth it.

It was worth it because we fucking took them down.

We found the Vittoris' island with the help of expert trackers, and Renata and Lorenzo were arrested. I don't know what happened to Olivia and their baby, but I hope they've found peace somewhere out there in the world.

Murphy disbanded his factories and worked with the authorities, earning himself some level of immunity from conviction. Part of me wanted him to spend the rest of his life in jail because he was one of them, too. But another part of me was okay with his immunity. He had saved my life and had given me a place to hide safely from the four families. I was grateful for that, and for Stella, too. They're still married, as far as I know.

Leo Leblanc disappeared, and no one knows if he's dead or alive.

According to the private team's intel, ninety percent of the factories they'd learned about had been swept and shut down by force. Hundreds of women and teenage girls were found alive and rescued, rehabilitated, and sent back home to their families.

There was still much work to be done. There are still extended family members out there in the world, some still running factories that the private team hasn't tracked locations for just yet. And furthermore, the four families certainly aren't the only traffickers that exist in the world. There are still victims being taken and sold.

If I hadn't gone public, the four families would've remained strong. As an international conglomerate that's been in successful operation for generations, I'm proud that the risk I took effectively disabled them.

I still dance daily for myself, but my career desires changed dramatically after my captivity. With Ezra's help, I started a non-profit group that seeks to support and rehabilitate trafficked survivors through dance therapy—the Encore Center for Survivors.

I didn't have a college degree or really any knowledge of my own at first, but going public about what I'd endured earned me both monetary and expert support—I heard from dozens of psychologists, sociologists, social workers, counselors, and dance and music therapists after our news special aired. I didn't have the therapy knowledge or the business knowledge when I started, but I learned. I learned a lot and I worked constantly, and I'm proud of the work I'm doing now.

I get to dance.

I get to teach.

I get to help survivors find their way back to a happy and healthy life.

But most important of all, I get to be with my family....a family Ezra and I created from the nothing we had when we were slaves. Brandon's life saved us in so many ways. If he hadn't existed, the events that led to our eventual escape would never have come to be, and Ezra and I both would likely be dead.

The fact that I'm able to watch him now, performing happily on stage, makes everything I've endured worth it.

He's a miracle.

After the show, we collect our little ray of sunshine from backstage and I hold his hand as he bounces through the parking lot. I look over at Ezra, carrying Faith on his hip, and I smile with nothing but pure joy glowing from within.

Ezra turns his attention away from our beautiful baby girl in his arms to return my smile with a dazzling white grin of his own. "Whoever would've thought I'd have two beautiful blue-eyed girls?"

I catch Faith's eyes in my gaze and make a silly face at her, making her giggle. Looking into her eyes is like seeing my own reflected back at me. They're big and blue and bright and happy. If I could only do one thing for the rest of my life, it would be to fight for her to have a life that keeps the sparkle in her eyes, to fight to keep her blue eyes vibrant, innocent, and wondering.

I will fight to find and destroy the bad men and women in this world who seek to steal, abuse, and destroy human lives. I will fight for the rest of my life to ensure that my babies will know nothing but happiness and freedom.

We reach the car that we'll soon have to trade in for something larger when the third little Bell baby comes along. Ezra and I split on either side of the car and I buckle in Brandon while he does the same with Faith. We shut their doors at the same time and though I reach for the handle of the passenger seat to climb in, he walks around the back of the car and reaches out for me, pulling me into his arms.

"I'm so in love with you, you know that?" He kisses the corner of my lips on one side, then the other.

"I know." I smile at him, holding up my left hand to display the engagement ring and wedding band he bought for me soon after he brought me home to Philadelphia—we were married and had my name changed from Mikhailov to Bell as soon as we were able to make it legal. "You did promise me forever, so…"

His hips push against my protruding belly as he leans me back against the car. "I'd like to spend forever between your legs once we get these two adorable little shits down for the night."

"Oh, you would?" I tilt my head, biting my lip. "I think I'd be okay with that."

"I thought so." He kisses me once and heads back around the car and we both climb in.

He starts up the engine and we both look behind us before he backs out of the space—I've made a bad habit of double-checking when he drives because heaven forbid we should hit something with my babies in the car.

Brandon catches my eyes and gives me the biggest grin. He holds out his little arms like he wants a hug, and I'll give him a damn big one when we get home. "Mine?" he says in the sweetest little voice.

And at the same time, Ezra and I recognize our truth, declaring our loyalty to both our children—and the baby to come—that our hearts will always belong to them. We speak a single syllable in unison that expresses our absolute devotion to our family, to each other, now and forever.

"Yours."

THE END

PAS DE TROIS
PLAYLIST

STREAM ON SPOTIFY
bit.ly/spotify-brynnford

Shallow by Lady Gaga & Bradley Cooper
Good Years by ZAYN
Take Me to Church by Hozier
Easy Way Out by Low Roar
Lost Without You by Freya Ridings
Dark Side by Bishop Briggs
Smile by Maisie Peters
War of Hearts by Ruelle
Dangerous Woman by Ariana Grande
Rewrite the Stars by Jess and Gabriel
Run For Your Life by K. Flay
Nothing's Gonna Stop Us Now by Chase Holfelder
Salvation by Gabrielle Aplin
There You Are by ZAYN
Dance Inside by The All-American Rejects

FINAL NOTE FROM THE AUTHOR

Anya and Ezra's story is a work of fiction—intended only for the purpose of entertainment—but human trafficking is a very real issue that demands our collective attention. While all aspects of the Four Families series is fictitious, it's important for us to acknowledge the experiences of real-life victims and bring attention to this serious issue.

If you or someone you know is a victim of human trafficking, there are resources that can help. One such resource in the United States is the National Human Trafficking Hotline.

National Human Trafficking Hotline
1 (888) 373-7888
SMS: 233733 (Text "HELP" or "INFO")
Website: humantraffickinghotline.org

Everyone deserves a happy ending to their story.

ACKNOWLEDGMENTS

I cannot believe that the *Four Families* trilogy is complete! I spent a little over a year lost in writing Anya and Ezra's story and I can't explain how hard it has been to say goodbye to these characters. But I could not have done what I needed to do to tell their story if it weren't for the help of some truly amazing people.

First and foremost, I have to thank my best friend, Sara. Though she's physically gone, her spirit has been with me throughout this entire series and I wouldn't have had the bravery to tell this story without her. I owe my boldness to her, and without that, this series would never have made it into your hands, readers. And to my ride or die crew that exist because of her, you have to know that I couldn't do this without your support. Rachel, Carrie, Kaylan—you girls are everything.

To my editor, Silvia. You are a godsend! I'm so happy I found you. My writing has improved so much as a result of your magnificent work and I'm so grateful for the time you've put into making this series shine!

Rachel, Danielle, Ashlee, Mary, and Maria—I'm so lucky to have you on my beta read team! You all give me confidence and inspire me to have faith in my work, especially when I'm struggling through rough rewrites and wondering if I should scrap the whole thing and start over. I can't think you enough for that. For all the promo you do for my books…I just have no words. You're all amazing and I love you!

Najla and Nada Qamber and their team over at Najla Qamber Designs have done such fabulous things to make my work sparkle and shine with gorgeous design work. You all are truly wonderful to work with and I'm so grateful I found you!

To my husband and children, thank you for letting me have my time with my stories! I wouldn't be able to do this without your support and willingness to give me the time and space I need to write.

Anya and Ezra…you may just be characters on a page, but to me you are real, and I'm humbled to have been the one to tell your story. Thank you for letting me put you through hell and I wish you a happily ever after as you continue on in the minds of my readers!

And you, daring reader…I am beyond thankful that you picked up this series. To know that you've connected to this story or these characters in some way, however big or small, means more to me than you could ever possibly know. Thank you for reading this story. Your love and support mean everything to me.

CONNECT WITH BRYNN FORD

WEBSITE

www.brynnford.com

Click "Newsletter" to subscribe
to my author newsletter!

GOODREADS

goodreads.com/brynnfordauthor

AMAZON

amazon.com/author/brynnford

BOOKBUB

bookbub.com/profile/brynn-ford

INSTAGRAM

@brynnfordauthor
instagram.com/brynnfordauthor

TIKTOK

@brynnfordauthor
tiktok.com/@brynnfordauthor

FACEBOOK

facebook.com/brynnfordauthor

FACEBOOK GROUP

Brynn's Daring Darlings
bit.ly/brynnsdarlings

ABOUT THE AUTHOR

Brynn Ford is a USA Today Bestselling Author of dark romance for daring readers. She writes emotionally heavy love stories that will twist your soul and shatter your heart before pulling you back together with a hopeful happily-ever-after.

Brynn's books are dark, sometimes disturbing, and often overwhelming. But they're always brightened by an insistent, spicy romance that will live rent-free in your head long after you've turned the final page.

When Brynn isn't obsessively writing, you may find her binge-watching favorite shows while eating far too much junk food or fanatically reading, always seeking to lose herself in the emotional roller coaster of a damn good story. She's a firm believer that her characters continue to live outside the pages in the minds of her readers. Stories don't end just because there aren't any more pages to turn.